# African Adventures: 4

# African Adventures: 4

The Ghost Kings

★

The Yellow Idol

## H. Rider Haggard

*African Adventures: 4—The Ghost Kings & The Yellow Idol*
by H. Rider Haggard

Leonaur is an imprint of Oakpast Ltd



ISBN: 978-1-84677-800-10 (hardcover)
ISBN: 978-1-84677-799-8 (softcover)

**http://www.leonaur.com**

**Publisher's Notes**

The views expressed in this book are not necessarily those of the publisher.

# Contents

# The Ghost Kings

## Extract from letter headed—
## The King's Kraal, Zululand, 12th May, 1855

*The Zulus about here have a strange story of a white girl who in Dingaan's day was supposed to 'hold the spirit' of some legendary goddess of theirs who is also white. This girl, they say, was very beautiful and brave, and had great power in the land before the battle of the Blood River, which they fought with the emigrant Boers. Her title was Lady of the Zulus, or more shortly, Zoola, which means Heaven.*

*She seems to have been the daughter of a wandering, pioneer missionary, but the king, I mean Dingaan, murdered her parents, of whom he was jealous, after which she went mad and cursed the nation, and it is to this curse that they still attribute the death of Dingaan, and their defeats and other misfortunes of that time.*

*Ultimately, it appears, in order to be rid of this girl and her evil eye, they sold her to the doctors of a dwarf people, who lived far away in a forest and worshipped trees, since when nothing more has been heard of her. But according to them the curse stopped behind.*

*If I can find out anything more of this curious story I will let you know, but I doubt if I shall be able to do so. Although fifteen years or so have passed since Dingaan's death in 1840 the Kaffirs are very shy of talking about this poor lady, and, I think, only did so to me because I am neither an official nor a missionary, but one whom they look upon as a friend because I have doctored so many of them. When I asked the Indunas about her at first they pretended total ignorance, but on my pressing the question, one of them said that 'all that tale was unlucky and "went beyond" with Mopo.' Now Mopo, as I think I wrote to you, was the man who stabbed King Chaka, Dingaan's brother. He is supposed to have been mixed up in the death of Dingaan also, and to be dead himself. At any rate he vanished away after Panda came to the throne.*

## CHAPTER 1

# The Girl

The afternoon was intensely, terribly hot. Looked at from the high ground where they were encamped above the river, the sea, a mile or two to her right—for this was the coast of Pondoland—to little Rachel Dove staring at it with sad eyes, seemed an illimitable sheet of stagnant oil. Yet there was no sun, for a grey haze hung like a veil beneath the arch of the sky, so dense and thick that its rays were cut off from the earth which lay below silent and stifled. Tom, the Kaffir driver, had told her that a storm was coming, a father of storms, which would end the great drought. Therefore he had gone to a *kloof* in the mountains where the oxen were in charge of the other two native boys—since on this upland there was no pasturage to drive them back to the wagon. For, as he explained to her, in such tempests cattle are apt to take fright and rush away for miles, and without cattle their plight would be even worse than it was at present.

At least this was what Tom said, but Rachel, who had been brought up among natives and understood their mind, knew that his real reason was that he wished to be out of the way when the baby was buried. Kaffirs do not like death, unless it comes by the *assegai* in war, and Tom, a good creature, had been fond of that baby during its short little life. Well, it was buried now; he had finished digging its resting-place in the hard soil before he went. Rachel, poor child, for she was but fifteen, had borne it to its last bed, and her father had unpacked his surplice from a box, put it on and read the Burial Service over the grave. Afterwards together they had filled in that dry, red earth, and rolled stones on to it, and as there were few flowers at this season of the year, placed a shrivelled branch or two of mimosa upon the stones—the best offering they had to make.

Rachel and her father were the sole mourners at this funeral, if we may omit two rock rabbits that sat upon a shelf of stone in a neighbouring cliff, and an old baboon which peered at these strange proceedings from its crest, and finally pushed down a boulder before it departed, barking indignantly. Her mother could not come because she was ill with grief and fever in a little tent by the wagon. When it was all over they returned to her, and there had been a painful scene.

Mrs. Dove was lying on a bed made of the cartel, or frame strung with strips of green hide, which had been removed from the wagon, a pretty, pale-faced woman with a profusion of fair hair. Rachel always remembered that scene. The hot tent with its flaps turned up to let in whatever air there might be. Her mother in a blue dressing-gown, dingy with wear and travel, from which one of the ribbon bows hung by a thread, her face turned to the canvas and weeping silently. The gaunt form of her father with his fanatical, saint-like face, pale beneath its tan, his high forehead over which fell one grizzled lock, his thin, set lips and far-away grey eyes, taking off his surplice and folding it up with quick movements of his nervous hands, and herself, a scared, wondering child, watching them both and longing to slip away to indulge her grief in solitude. It seemed an age before that surplice was folded, pushed into a linen bag which in their old home used to hold dirty clothes, and finally stowed away in a deal box with a broken hinge. At length it was done, and her father straightened himself with a sigh, and said in a voice that tried to be cheerful:

"Do not weep, Janey. Remember this is all for the best. The Lord hath taken away, blessed be the name of the Lord."

Her mother sat up looking at him reproachfully with her blue eyes, and answered in her soft Scotch accent:

"You said that to me before, John, when the other one went, down at Grahamstown, and I am tired of hearing it. Don't ask me to bless the Lord when He takes my babes, no, nor any mother, He Who could spare them if He chose. Why should the Lord give me fever so that I could not nurse it, and make a snake bite the cow so that it died? If the Lord's ways are such, then those of the savages are more merciful."

"Janey, Janey, do not blaspheme," her father had exclaimed. "You should rejoice that the child is in Heaven."

"Then do you rejoice and leave me to grieve. From today I only make one prayer, that I may never have another. John," she added with a sudden outburst, "it is your fault. You know well I told you how it would be. I told you that if you would come this mad journey the babe would die, aye, and I tell you"—here her voice sank to a kind of wailing whisper—"before the tale is ended others will die too, all of us, except Rachel there, who was born to live her life. Well, for my part, the sooner the better, for I wish to go to sleep with my children."

"This is evil," broke in her husband, "evil and rebellious—"

"Then evil and rebellious let it be, John. But why am I evil if I have the second sight like my mother before me? Oh! she warned me what must come if I married you, and I would not listen; now I warn you, and you will not listen. Well, so be it, we must *dree* our own weird, everyone of us, a short one; all save Rachel, who was born to live her life. Man, I tell you, that the Spirit drives you on to convert the heathen just for one thing, that the heathen may make a martyr of you."

"So let them," her father answered proudly. "I seek no better end."

"Aye," she moaned, sinking back upon the cartel, "so let them, but my babe, my poor babe! Why should my babe die because too much religion has made you mad to win a martyr's crown? Martyrs should not marry and have children, John."

Then, unable to bear any more of it, Rachel had fled from the tent, and sat herself down at a distance to watch the oily sea.

It has been said that Rachel was only fifteen, but in Southern Africa girls grow quickly to womanhood; also her experiences had been of a nature to ripen her intelligence. Thus she was quite able to form a judgment of her parents, their virtues and their weaknesses. Rachel was English born, but had no recollection of England since she came to South Africa when she was four years old. It was shortly after her birth that this missionary-fury seized upon her father as a result of some meetings which he had attended in London. He was then a clergyman with a good living in a quiet Hertfordshire parish, and possessed of some private means, but nothing would suit him short of abandoning all his prospects and sailing for South Africa, in obedience to his "call." Rachel knew all this because her mother had often told her, adding that she and her people, who were of a good Scotch family, had struggled against this South African scheme even to the verge of open quarrel.

At length, indeed, it came to a choice between submission and separation. Mr. Dove had declared that not even for her sake would he be guilty of "sin against the Spirit" which had chosen him to bring light to those who sat in darkness—that is, the Kaffirs, and especially to that section of them who were in bondage to the Boers. For at this time an agitation was in progress in England which led ultimately to the freeing of the slaves of the Cape Dutch, and afterwards to the exodus of the latter into the wilderness and most of those wars with which our generation is familiar. So, as she was devoted to her husband, who, apart from his religious enthusiasm, or rather possession, was in truth a very lovable man, she gave way and came. Before they sailed, however, the general gloom was darkened by Mrs. Dove announcing that something in her heart told her that neither of them would ever see home again, as they were doomed to die at the hands of savages.

Now whatever the reason or explanation, scientifically impossible as the fact might be, it remained a fact that Janey Dove, like her mother and several of her Scottish ancestors, was foresighted, or at least so her kith and kin believed. Therefore, when she communicated to them her conviction as though it were a piece of everyday intelligence, they never doubted its accuracy for a minute, but only redoubled their efforts to prevent her from going to Africa. Even her husband did not doubt it, but remarked irritably that it seemed a pity she could not sometimes be foresighted as to agreeable future events, since for his part he was quite willing to wait for disagreeable ones until they happened. Not that he quailed personally from the prospect of martyrdom; this he could contemplate with complacency and even enthusiasm, but, zealot though he was, he did shrink from the thought that his beautiful and delicate wife might be called upon to share the glory of that crown. Indeed, as his own purpose was unalterable, he now himself suggested that he should go forth to seek it alone.

Then it was that his wife showed an unsuspected strength of character. She said that she had married him for better or for worse against the wishes of her family; that she loved and respected him, and that she would rather be murdered by Kaffirs in due season than endure a separation which might be lifelong. So in the end the pair of them with their little daughter Rachel departed in a sailing ship, and their friends and relations knew them no more.

Their subsequent history up to the date of the opening of this story may be told in very few words. As a missionary the Reverend John Dove was not a success. The Boers in the eastern part of the Cape Colony where he laboured, did not appreciate his efforts to Christianise their slaves. The slaves did not appreciate them either, inasmuch as, saint though he might be, he quite lacked the sympathetic insight which would enable him to understand that a native with thousands of generations of savagery behind him is a different being from a highly educated Christian, and one who should be judged by another law. Their sins, amongst which he included all their most cherished inherited customs, appalled him, as he continually proclaimed from the housetops. Moreover, when occasionally he did snatch a brand from the burning, and the said brand subsequently proved that it was still alight, or worse still, replaced its original failings by those of the white man, such as drink, theft and lying, whereof before it had been innocent, he would openly condemn it to eternal punishment. Further, he was too insubordinate, or, as he called it, too honest, to submit to the authority of his local superiors in the Church, and therefore would only work for his own hand. Finally he caused his "cup to overflow," as he described it, or, in plain English, made the country too hot to hold him, by becoming involved in a bitter quarrel with the Boers. Of these, on the whole, worthy folk, he formed the worst; and in the main a very unjust opinion, which he sent to England to be reprinted in Church papers, or to the Home Government to be published in Blue-books. In due course these documents reached South Africa again, where they were translated into Dutch and became incidentally one of the causes of the Great Trek.

The Boers were furious and threatened to shoot him as a slanderer. The English authorities were also furious, and requested him to cease from controversy or to leave the country. At last, stubborn as he might be, circumstances proved too much for him, and as his conscience would not allow him to be silent, Mr. Dove chose the latter alternative. The only question was whither he should go. As he was well off, having inherited a moderate fortune in addition to what he had before he left England, his poor wife pleaded with him to return home, pointing out that there he would be able to lay his case before the British public. This course had attractions for him, but after a night's reflection and prayer, he rejected it as a specious temptation sent by Satan.

What, he argued, should he return to live in luxury in England not only unmartyred but a palpable failure, his mission quite unfulfilled? His wife might go if she liked, and take their surviving children, Rachel and the new-born baby boy, with her (they had buried two other little girls), but he would stick to his post and his duty. He had seen some Englishmen who had visited the country called Natal where white people were beginning to settle. In that land it seemed there were no slave-driving Boers, and the natives, according to all accounts, much needed the guidance of the Gospel, especially a certain king of the people called Zulus, who was named Chaka or Dingaan, he was not sure which. This ferocious person he particularly desired to encounter, having little doubt that in the absence of the contaminating Boer, he would be able to induce him to see the error of his ways and change the national customs, especially those of fighting and, worse still, of polygamy.

His unhappy wife listened and wept, for now the martyr's crown which she had always foreseen, seemed uncomfortably near, indeed as it were, it glowed blood red within reach of her hand. Moreover, in her heart she did not believe that Kaffirs could be converted, at any rate at present. They were fighting men, as her Highland forefathers had been, and her Scottish blood could understand the weakness, while, as for this polygamy, she had long ago secretly concluded that the practice was one which suited them very well, as it had suited David and Solomon, and even Abraham. But for all this, although she was sure in her uncanny fashion that her baby's death would come of her staying, she refused to leave her husband as she had refused eleven years before.

Doubtless affection was at the bottom of it, for Janey Dove was a very faithful woman; also there were other things—her fatalism, and stronger still, her weariness. She believed that they were doomed. Well, let the doom fall; she had no fear of the Beyond. At the best it might be happy, and at the worst deep, everlasting rest and peace, and she felt as though she needed thousands of years of rest and peace. Moreover, she was sure no harm would come to Rachel, the very apple of her eye; that she was marked to live and to find happiness even in this wild land. So it came about that she refused her husband's offer to allow her to return home where she had no longer any ties, and for perhaps the twentieth time prepared herself to journey she knew not whither.

Rachel, seated there in the sunless, sweltering heat, reflected on these things. Of course she did not know all the story, but most of it had come under her observation in one way or other, and being shrewd by nature, she could guess the rest, for she who was companionless had much time for reflection and for guessing. She sympathised with her father in his ideas, understanding vaguely that there was something large and noble about them, but in the main, body and mind, she was her mother's child. Already she showed her mother's dreamy beauty, to which were added her father's straight features and clear grey eyes, together with a promise of his height. But of his character she had little, that is outside of a courage and fixity of purpose which marked them both.

For the rest she was far, or fore-seeing, like her mother, apprehending the end of things by some strange instinct; also very faithful in character.

Rachel was unhappy. She did not mind the hardship and the heat, for she was accustomed to both, and her health was so perfect that it would have needed much worse things to affect her. But she loved the baby that was gone, and wondered whether she would ever see it again.

On the whole she thought so, for here that intuition of hers came in, but at the best she was sure that there would be long to wait. She loved her mother also, and grieved more for her than for herself, especially now when she was so ill. Moreover, she knew and shared her mind. This journey, she felt, was foolishness; her father was a man "led by a star" as the natives say, and would follow it over the edge of the world and be no nearer. He was not fit to have charge of her mother.

Of herself she did not think so much. Still, at Grahamstown, for a year or so there had been other children for companions, Dutch most of them, it is true, and all rough in mind and manner. Yet they were white and human. While she played with them she could forget she knew so much more than they did; that, for instance, she could read the Gospels in Greek—which her father had taught her ever since she was a little child—while they could scarcely spell them out in the Taal, or Boer dialect, and that they had never heard even of William the Conqueror. She did not care particularly about Greek and William the Conqueror, but she did care for friends, and now they were all gone from her, gone like the baby, as far off as William the Conqueror. And she, she was alone in the wilderness with a father who talked and thought of Heaven all day long, and a mother who lived in memories and walked in the shadow of doom, and oh! she was unhappy.

Her grey eyes filled with tears so that she could no longer see that everlasting ocean, which she did not regret as it wearied her. She wiped them with the back of her hand that was burnt quite brown by the sun, and turning impatiently, fell to watching two of those strange insects known as the Praying Mantis, or often in South Africa as Hottentot gods, which after a series of genuflections, were now fighting desperately among the dead stalks of grass at her feet. Men could not be more savage, she reflected, for really their ferocity was hideous. Then a great tear fell upon the head of one of them, and astonished by this phenomenon, or thinking perhaps that it had begun to rain, it ran away and hid itself, while its adversary sat up and looked about it triumphantly, taking to itself all the credit of conquest.

She heard a step behind her, and having again furtively wiped her eyes with her hand, the only handkerchief available, looked round to see her father stalking towards her.

"Why are you crying, Rachel?" he asked in an irritable voice. "It is wrong to cry because your little brother has been taken to glory."

"Jesus cried over Lazarus, and He wasn't even His brother," she answered in a reflective voice, then by way of defending herself added inconsequently: "I was watching two Hottentot gods fight."

As Mr. Dove could think of no reply to her very final Scriptural example, he attacked her on the latter point.

"A cruel amusement," he said, "especially as I have heard that boys, yes, and men, too, pit these poor insects against each other, and make bets upon them."

"Nature, is cruel, not I father. Nature is always cruel," and she glanced towards the little grave under the rock. Then, while for the second time her father hesitated, not knowing what to answer, she added quickly, "Is mother better now?"

"No," he said, "worse, I think, very hysterical and quite unable to see things in the true light."

She rose and faced him, for she was a courageous child, then asked:

"Father, why don't you take her back? She isn't fit to go on. It is wrong to drag her into this wilderness."

At this question he grew very angry, and began to scold and to talk of the wickedness of abandoning his "call."

"But mother has not got a 'call,'" she broke in.

Then, as for the third time he could find no answer, he declared vehemently that they were both in league against him, instruments used by the Evil One to tempt him from his duty by working on his natural fears and affections, and so forth.

The child watched him with her clear grey eyes, saying nothing further, till at last he grew calm and paused.

"We are all much upset," he went on, rubbing his high forehead with his thin hand. "I suppose it is the heat and this—this—trial of our faith. What did I come to speak to you about? Oh! I remember; your mother will eat nothing, and keeps asking for fruit. Do you know where there is any fruit?"

"It doesn't grow here, father." Then her face brightened, and she added: "Yes, it does, though. The day that we outspanned in this camp mother and I went down to the river and walked to that kind of island beyond the dry *donga* to get some flowers that grow on the wet ground. I saw lots of Cape gooseberries there, all quite ripe."

"Then go and get some, dear. You will have plenty of time before dark."

She started up as though to obey, then checked herself and said:

"Mother told me that I was not to go to the river alone, because we saw the spoor of lions and crocodiles in the mud."

"God will guard you from the lions and the crocodiles, if there are any," he answered doggedly, for was not this an opportunity to show his faith? "You are not afraid, are you?"

"No, father. I am afraid of nothing, perhaps because I don't care what happens. I will get the basket and go at once."

In another minute she was walking quickly towards the river, a lonely little figure in that great place. Mr. Dove watched her uneasily till she was hidden in the haze, for his reason told him that this was a foolish journey.

"The Lord will send His angels to protect her," he muttered to himself. "Oh! if only I could have more faith, all these troubles come upon me from a lack of faith, and through that I am continually tempted. I think I will run after her and go, too. No, there is Janey calling me, I cannot leave her alone. The Lord will protect her, but I need not mention to Janey that she has gone, unless she asks me outright. She will be quite safe, the storm will not break tonight."

## CHAPTER 2
# The Boy

The river towards which Rachel headed, one of the mouths of the Umtavuna, was much further off than it looked; it was, indeed, not less than a mile and a half away. She had said that she feared nothing, and it was true, for extraordinary courage was one of this child's characteristics. She could scarcely ever remember having felt afraid—for herself, except sometimes of her father when he grew angry—or was it mad that he grew?—and raged at her, threatening her with punishment in another world in reward for her childish sins. Even then the sensation did not last long, because she could not believe in that punishment which he so vividly imagined. So it came about that now she had no fear when there was so much cause.

For this place was lonely; not a living creature could be seen. Moreover, a dreadful hush brooded on the face of earth, and in the sky above; only far away over the mountains the lightning flickered incessantly, as though a monster in the skies were licking their precipices and pinnacles with a thousand tongues of fire. Nothing stirred, not even an insect; every creature that drew breath had hidden itself away until the coming terror was over-past.

The atmosphere was full of electricity struggling to be free. Although she knew not what it was, Rachel felt it in her blood and brain. In some strange way it affected her mind, opening windows there through which the eyes of her soul looked out. She became aware of some new influence drawing near to her life; of a sudden her budding womanhood burst into flower in her breast, shone on by an unseen sun; she was no more a child. Her being quickened and acknowledged the kinship of all things that are. That brooding, flame-threaded sky—she was a part of it, the earth she trod, it was a part of her; the Mind that caused the stars to roll and her to live, dwelt in her bosom, and like a babe she nestled within the arm of its almighty will.

Now, as in a dream, Rachel descended the steep, rock-strewn banks of the dry branch of the river-bed, wending her way between the boulders and noting that rotten weeds and peeled brushwood rested against the stems of the mimosa thorns which grew—there, tokens which told her that here in times of flood the water flowed. Well, there was little enough of it now, only a pool or two to form a mirror for the lightning. In front of her lay the island where grew the Cape gooseberries, or winter cherries as they are sometimes called, which she came to seek. It was a low piece of ground, a quarter of a mile long, perhaps, but in the centre of it were some great rocks and growing among the rocks, trees, one of them higher than the rest. Beyond it ran the true river, even now at the end of the dry season three or four hundred yards in breadth, though so shallow that it could be forded by an ox-drawn wagon.

It was raining on the mountains yonder, raining in torrents poured from those inky clouds, as it had done off and on for the past twenty-four hours, and above their fire-laced bosom floated glorious-coloured masses of misty vapour, enflamed in a thousand hues by the arrows of the sinking sun. Above her, however, there was no sun, nothing but the curtain of cloud which grew gradually from grey to black and minute by minute sank nearer to the earth.

Walking through the dry river-bed, Rachel reached the island which was the last and highest of a line of similar islands that, separated from each other by narrow breadths of water, lay like a chain, between the dry *donga* and the river. Here she began to gather her gooseberries, picking the silvery, octagonal pods from the green stems on which they grew. At first she opened these pods, removing from each the yellow, sub-acid berry, thinking that thus her basket would hold more, but presently abandoned that plan as it took too much time. Also although the plants were plentiful enough, in that low and curious light it was not easy to see them among the dense growth of reedy vegetation.

While she was thus engaged she became aware of a low moaning noise and a stirring of the air about her which caused the leaves and grasses to quiver without bending. Then followed an ice-cold wind that grew in strength until it blew keen and hard, ruffling the surface of the marshy pools. Still Rachel went on with her task, for her basket was not more than half full, till presently the heavens above her began to mutter and to groan, and drops of rain as large as shillings fell upon her back and hands. Now she understood that it was time for her to be going, and started to walk across the island—for at the moment she was near its farther side—to reach the deep, rocky river-bed or *donga*.

Before ever she came there, with awful suddenness and inconceivable fury, the tempest burst. A hurricane of wind tore down the valley to the sea, and for a few minutes the darkness became so dense that she could scarcely stumble forward. Then there was light, a dreadful light; all the heavens seemed to take fire, yes, and the earth, too; it was as though its last dread catastrophe had fallen on the world.

Buffeted, breathless, Rachel at length reached the edge of the deep river-bed that may have been fifty yards in width, and was about to step into it when she became aware of two things. The first was a seething, roaring noise so loud that it seemed to still even the bellowing of the thunder, and the next, now seen, now lost, as the lightning pulsed and darkened, the figure of a youth, a white youth, who had dismounted from a horse that remained near to but above him, and stood, a gun in his hand, upon a rock at the farther side of the *donga*.

He had seen her also and was shouting to her, of this she was sure, for although the sound of his voice was lost in the tumult, she could perceive his gesticulations when the lightning flared, and even the movement of his lips.

Wondering vaguely what a white boy could be doing in such a place and very glad at the prospect of his company, Rachel began to advance towards him in short rushes whenever the lightning showed her where to set her feet. She had made two of these rushes when from the violence and character of his movements at length she understood that he was trying to prevent her from coming further, and paused confused.

Another instant and she knew why. Some hundreds of yards above her the river bed took a turn, and suddenly round this turn, crested with foam, appeared a wall of water in which trees and the carcases of animals were whirled along like straws. The flood had come down from the mountains, and was advancing on her more swiftly than a horse could gallop. Rachel ran forward a little way, then understanding that she had no time to cross, stood bewildered, for the fearful tumult of the elements and the dreadful roaring of that advancing wall of foam overwhelmed her senses. The lightnings went out for a moment, then began to play again with tenfold frequency and force. They struck upon, the nearing torrent, they struck in the dry bed before it, and leapt upwards from the earth as though Titans and gods were hurling spears at one another.

In the lurid sheen of them she saw the lad leap from his rock and rush towards her. A flash fell and split a boulder not thirty paces from him, causing him to stagger, but he recovered himself and ran on.

Now he was quite close, but the water was closer still. It was coming in tiers or ledges, a thin sheet of foam in front, then other layers laid upon it, each of them a few yards behind its fellow. On the top ledge, in its very crest, was a bull buffalo, dead, but held head on and down as though it were charging, and Rachel thought vaguely that from the direction in which it came in a few moments its horns would strike her. Another second and an arm was about her waist—she noted how white it was where the sleeve was rolled up, dead white in the lightning—and she was being dragged towards the shore that she had left. The first film of water struck her and nearly washed her from her feet, but she was strong and active, and the touch of that arm seemed to have given her back her wit, so she regained them and splashed forward. Now the next tier took them both above the knees, but for a moment shallowed so that they did not fall. The high bank was scarce five yards away, and the wall of waters perhaps a score.

"Together for life or death!" said an English voice in her ear, and the shout of it only reached her in a whisper.

The boy and the girl leapt forward like bucks. They reached the bank and struggled up it. The hungry waters sprang at them like a living thing, grasping their feet and legs as though with hands; a stick as it whirled by them struck the lad upon the shoulder, and where it struck the clothes were rent away and red blood appeared. Almost he fell, but this time it was Rachel who supported him. Then one more struggle and they rolled exhausted on the ground just clear of the lip of the racing flood.

Thus through tempest, threatened by the waters of death from which he snatched her, and companioned by heaven's lightnings, did Richard Darrien come into the life of Rachel Dove.

Presently, having recovered their breath, they sat up and looked at each other by lightning light, which was all there was. He was a handsome lad of about seventeen, though short for his years; sturdy in build, very fair-skinned and curiously enough with a singular resemblance to Rachel, except that his hair was a few shades darker than hers. They had the same clear grey eyes, and the same well-cut features; indeed seen together, most people would have thought them brother and sister, and remarked upon their family likeness. Rachel spoke the first.

"Who are you?" she shouted into his ear in one of the intervals of darkness, "and why did you come here?"

"My name is Richard Darrien," he answered at the top of his voice, "and I don't know why I came. I suppose something sent me to save you."

"Yes," she replied with conviction, "something sent you. If you had not come I should be dead, shouldn't I? In glory, as my father says."

"I don't know about glory, or what it is," he remarked, after thinking this saying over, "but you would have been rolling out to sea in the flood water, like that buffalo, with not a whole bone in you, which isn't my idea of glory."

"That's because your father isn't a missionary," said Rachel.

"No, he is an officer, naval officer, or at least he was, now he trades and hunts. We are coming down from Natal. But what's your name?"

"Rachel Dove."

"Well, Rachel Dove—that's very pretty, Rachel Dove, as you would be if you were cleaner—it is going to rain presently. Is there any place where we can shelter here?"

"I am as clean as you are," she answered indignantly. "The river muddied me, that's all. You can go and shelter, I will stop and let the rain wash me."

"And die of the cold or be struck by lightning. Of course I knew you weren't dirty really. Is there any, place?"

She nodded, mollified.

"I think I know one. Come," and she stretched out her hand.

He took it, and thus hand in hand they made their way to the highest point of the island where the trees grew, for here the rocks piled up together made a kind of cave in which Rachel and her mother had sat for a little while when they visited the place. As they groped their way towards it the lightning blazed out and they saw a great jagged flash strike the tallest tree and shatter it, causing some wild beast that had sheltered there to rush past them snorting.

"That doesn't look very safe," said Richard halting, "but come on, it isn't likely to hit the same spot twice."

"Hadn't you better leave your gun?" she suggested, for all this while that weapon had been slung to his back and she knew that lightning has an affinity for iron.

"Certainly not," he answered, "it is a new one which my father gave me, and I won't be parted from it."

Then they went on and reached the little cave just as the rain broke over them in earnest. As it chanced the place was dry, being so situated that all water ran away from it. They crouched in it shivering, trying to cover themselves with dead sticks and brushwood that had lodged here in the wet season when the whole island was under water.

"It would be nice enough if only we had a fire," said Rachel, her teeth chattering as she spoke.

The lad Richard thought a while. Then he opened a leather case that hung on his rifle sling and took from it a powder flask and flint and steel and some tinder. Pouring a little powder on the damp tinder, he struck the flint until at length a spark caught and fired the powder. The tinder caught also, though reluctantly, and while Rachel blew on it, he felt round for dead leaves and little sticks, some of which were coaxed into flame.

After this things were easy since fuel lay about in abundance, so that soon they had a splendid fire burning in the mouth of the cave whence the smoke escaped. Now they were able to warm and dry themselves, and as the heat entered into their chilled bodies, their spirits rose. Indeed the contrast between this snug hiding place and blazing fire of drift wood and the roaring tempest without, conduced to cheerfulness in young people who had just narrowly escaped from drowning.

"I am so hungry," said Rachel, presently.

Again Richard began to search, and this time produced from the pocket of his coat a long and thick strip of sun-dried meat.

"Can you eat biltong?" he asked.

"Of course," she answered eagerly.

"Then you must cut it up," he said, giving her the meat and his knife. "My arm hurts me, I can't."

"Oh!" she exclaimed, "how selfish I am. I forgot about that stick striking you. Let me see the place."

He took off his coat and knelt down while she stood over him and examined his wound by the light of the fire, to find that the left upper arm was bruised, torn and bleeding. As it will be remembered that Rachel had no handkerchief, she asked Richard for his, which she soaked in a pool of rain water just outside the cave. Then, having washed the hurt thoroughly, she bandaged his arm with the handkerchief and bade him put on his coat again, saying confidently that he would be well in a few days.

"You are clever," he remarked with admiration. "Who taught you to bandage wounds?"

"My father always doctors the Kaffirs and I help him," Rachel answered, as, having stretched out her hands for the pouring rain to wash them, she took the biltong and began to cut it in thin slices.

These she made him eat before she touched any herself, for she saw that the loss of blood had weakened him. Indeed her own meal was a light one, since half the strip of meat must, she declared, be put aside in case they should not be able to get off the island. Then he saw why she had made him eat first and was very angry with himself and her, but she only laughed at him and answered that she had learned from the Kaffirs that men must be fed before women as they were more important in the world.

"You mean more selfish," he answered, contemplating this wise little maid and her tiny portion of biltong, which she swallowed very slowly, perhaps to pretend that her appetite was already satisfied with its superabundance. Then he fell to imploring her to take the rest, saying that he would be able to shoot some game in the morning, but she only shook her little head and set her lips obstinately.

"Are you a hunter?" she asked to change the subject.

"Yes," he answered with pride, "that is, almost. At any rate I have shot eland, and an elephant, but no lions yet. I was following the spoor of a lion just now, but it got up between the rocks and bolted away before I could shoot. I think that it must have been after you."

"Perhaps," said Rachel. "There are some about here; I have heard them roaring at night."

"Then," he went on, "while I was staring at you running across this island, I heard the sound of the water and saw it rushing down the *donga*, and saw too that you must be drowned, and—you know the rest."

"Yes, I know the rest," she said, looking at him with shining eyes. "You risked your life to save mine, and therefore," she added with quiet conviction, "it belongs to you."

He stared at her and remarked simply:

"I wish it did. This morning I wished to kill a lion with my new *roer*," and he pointed to the heavy gun at his side, "above everything else, but tonight I wish that your life belonged to me—above anything else."

Their eyes met, and child though she was, Rachel saw something in those of Richard that caused her to turn her head.

"Where are you going?" she asked quickly.

"Back to my father's farm in Graaf-Reinet, to sell the ivory. There are three others besides my father, two Boers and one Englishman."

"And I am going to Natal where you come from," she answered, "so I suppose that after tonight we shall never see each other again, although my life does belong to you—that is if we escape."

Just then the tempest which had lulled a little, came on again in fury, accompanied by a hurricane of wind and deluge of rain, through which the lightning blazed incessantly. The thunderclaps too were so loud and constant that the sound of them, which shook the earth, made it impossible for Richard and Rachel to hear each other speak. So they were silent perforce. Only Richard rose and looked out of the cave, then turned and beckoned to his companion. She came to him and watched, till suddenly a blinding sheet of flame lit up the whole landscape. Then she saw what he was looking at, for now nearly all the island, except that high part of it on which they stood, was under water, hidden by a brown, seething torrent, that tore past them to the sea.

"If it rises much more, we shall be drowned," he shouted in her ear.

She nodded, then cried back:

"Let us say our prayers and get ready," for it seemed to Rachel that the "glory" of which her father spoke so often was nearer to them than ever.

Then she drew him back into the cave and motioned to him to kneel beside her, which he did bashfully enough, and for a while the two children, for they were little more, remained thus with clasped hands and moving lips. Presently the thunder lessened a little so that once more they could hear each other speak.

"What did you pray about?" he asked when they had risen from their knees.

"I prayed that you might escape, and that my mother might not grieve for me too much," she answered simply. "And you?"

"I? Oh! the same—that you might escape. I did not pray for my mother as she is dead, and I forgot about father."

"Look, look!" exclaimed Rachel, pointing to the mouth of the cave.

He stared out at the darkness, and there, through the thin flames of the fire, saw two great yellow shapes which appeared to be walking up and down and glaring into the cave.

"Lions," he gasped, snatching at his gun.

"Don't shoot," she cried, "you might make them angry. Perhaps they only want to take refuge like ourselves. The fire will keep them away."

He nodded, then remembering that the charge and priming, of his flint-lock *roer* must be damp, hurriedly set to work by the help of Rachel to draw it with the screw on the end of his ramrod, and this done, to reload with some powder that he had already placed to dry on a flat stone near the fire. This operation took five minutes or more. When at length it was finished, and the lock re-primed with the dry powder, the two of them, Richard holding the *roer*, crept to the mouth of the cave and looked out again.

The great storm was passing now, and the rain grew thinner, but from time to time the lightning, no longer forked or chain-shaped, flared in wide sheets. By its ghastly illumination they saw a strange sight. There on the island top the two lions marched backwards and forwards as though they were in a cage, making a kind of whimpering noise as they went, and staring round them uneasily. Moreover, these were not alone, for gathered there were various other animals, driven down by the flood from the islands above them, reed and water bucks, and a great eland. Among these the lions walked without making the slightest effort to attack them, nor did the antelopes, which stood sniffing and staring at the torrent, take any notice of the lions, or attempt to escape.

"You are right," said Richard, "they are all frightened, and will not harm us, unless the water rises more, and they rush into the cave. Come, make up the fire."

They did so, and sat down on its further side, watching till, as nothing happened, their dread of the lions passed away, and they began to talk again, telling to each other the stories of their lives.

Richard Darrien, it seemed, had been in Africa about five years, his father having emigrated there on the death of his mother, as he had nothing but the half-pay of a retired naval captain, and he hoped to better his fortunes in a new land. He had been granted a farm in the Graaf-Reinet district, but like many other of the early settlers, met with misfortunes. Now, to make money, he had taken to elephant-hunting, and with his partners was just returning from a very successful expedition in the coast lands of Natal, at that time an almost unexplored territory. His father had allowed Richard to accompany the party, but when they got back, added the boy with sorrow, he was to be sent for two or three years to the college at Capetown, since until then his father had not been able to afford him the luxury of an education. Afterwards he wished him to adopt a profession, but on this point he—Richard—had made up his mind, although at present he said little about that. He would be a hunter, and nothing else, until he grew too old to hunt, when he intended to take to farming.

His story done, Rachel told him hers, to which he listened eagerly.

"Is your father mad?" he asked when she had finished.

"No," she answered. "How dare you suggest it? He is only very good; much better than anybody else."

"Well, it seems to come to much the same thing, doesn't it?" said Richard, "for otherwise he would not have sent you to gather gooseberries here with such a storm coming on."

"Then why did your father send you to hunt lions with such a storm coming on?" she asked.

"He didn't send me. I came of myself; I said that I wanted to shoot a buck, and finding the spoor of a lion I followed it. The wagons must be a long way ahead now, for when I left them I returned to that *kloof* where I had seen the buck. I don't know how I shall overtake them again, and certainly nobody will ever think of looking for me here, as after this rain they can't spoor the horse."

"Supposing you don't find it—I mean your horse—tomorrow, what shall you do?" asked Rachel. "We haven't got any to lend you."

"Walk and try to catch them up," he replied.

"And if you can't catch them up?"

"Come back to you, as the wild Kaffirs ahead would kill me if I went on alone."

"Oh! But what would your father think?"

"He would think there was one boy the less, that's all, and be sorry for a while. People often vanish in Africa where there are so many lions and savages."

Rachel reflected a while, then finding the subject difficult, suggested that he should find out what their own particular lions were doing. So Richard went to look, and reported that the storm had ceased, and that by the moonlight he could see no lions or any other animals, so he thought that they must have gone away somewhere. The flood waters also appeared to be running down. Comforted by this intelligence Rachel piled on the fire nearly all the wood that remained to them. Then they sat down again side by side, and tried to continue their conversation. By degrees it drooped, however, and the end of it was that presently this pair were fast asleep in each other's arms.

## CHAPTER 3
# Goodbye

Rachel was the first to wake, which she did, feeling cold, for the fire had burnt almost out. She rose and walked from the cave. The dawn was breaking quietly, for now no wind stirred, and no rain fell. So dense was the mist which rose from the river and sodden land, however, that she could not see two yards in front of her, and fearing lest she should stumble on the lions or some other animals, she did not dare to wander far from the mouth of the cave. Near to it was a large, hollow-surfaced rock, filled now with water like a bath. From this she drank, then washed and tidied herself as well as she could without the aid of soap, comb or towels, which done, she returned to the cave.

As Richard was still sleeping, very quietly she laid a little more wood on the embers to keep him warm, then sat down by his side and watched him, for now the grey light of the dawning crept into their place of refuge. To her this slumbering lad looked beautiful, and as she studied him her childish heart was filled with a strange, new tenderness, such as she had never felt before. Somehow he had grown dear to her, and Rachel knew that she would never forget him while she lived. Then following this wave of affection came a sharp and sudden pain, for she remembered that presently they must part, and never see each other any more. At least this seemed certain, for how could they when he was travelling to the Cape and she to Natal?

And yet, and yet a strange conviction told her otherwise. The power of prescience which came to her from her mother and her Highland forefathers awoke in her breast, and she knew that her life and this lad's life were interwoven. Perhaps she dozed off again, sitting there by the fire. At any rate it appeared to her that she dreamed and saw things in her dream. Wild tumultuous scenes opened themselves before her in a vision; scenes of blood and terror, sounds, too, of voices crying war. It appeared to her as if she were mad, and yet ruled a queen, death came near to her a score of times, but always fled away at her command. Now Richard Darrien was with her, and how she had lost him and sought—ah! how she sought through dark places of doom and unnatural night. It was as though he were dead, and she yet living, searched for him among the habitations of the dead. She found him also, and drew him towards her. How, she did not know.

Then there was a scene, a last scene, which remained fixed in her mind after everything else had faded away. She saw the huge trunks of forest trees, enormous, towering trees, gloomy trees beneath which the darkness could be felt. Down their avenues shot the level arrows of the dawn. They fell on her, Rachel, dressed in robes of white skin, turning her long, outspread hair to gold. They fell upon little people with faces of a dusky pallor, one of them crouched against the bole of a tree, a wizened monkey of a man who in all that vastness looked small. They fell upon another man, white-skinned, half-naked, with a yellow beard, who was lashed by hide ropes to a second tree. It was Richard Darrien grown older, and at his feet lay a broad-bladed spear!

The vision left her, or she was awakened from her sleep, whichever it might be, by the pleasant voice of this same Richard, who stood yawning before her, and said:

"It is time to get up. I say, why do you look so queer? Are you ill?"

"I have been up, long ago," she answered, struggling to her feet. "What do you mean?"

"Nothing, except that you seemed a ghost a minute ago. Now you are a girl again, it must have been the light."

"Did I? Well, I dreamed of ghosts, or something of the sort," and she told him of the vision of the trees, though of the rest she could remember little.

"That's a queer story," he said when she had finished. "I wish you had got to the end of it, I should like to know what happened."

"We shall find out one day," she answered solemnly.

"Do you mean to say that you believe it is true, Rachel?"

"Yes, Richard, one day I shall see you tied to that tree."

"Then I hope you will cut me loose, that is all. What a funny girl you are," he added doubtfully. "I know what it is, you want something to eat. Have the rest of that biltong."

"No," she answered. "I could not touch it. There is a pool of water out there, go and bathe your arm, and I will bind it up again."

He went, still wondering, and a few minutes later returned, his face and head dripping, and whispered:

"Give me the gun. There is a reed buck standing close by. I saw it through the mist; we'll have a jolly breakfast off him."

She handed him the *roer*, and crept after him out of the cave. About thirty yards away to the right, looming very large through the dense fog, stood the fat reed buck. Richard wriggled towards it, for he wanted to make sure of his shot, while Rachel crouched behind a stone. The buck becoming alarmed, turned its head, and began to sniff at the air, whereon he lifted the gun and just as it was about to spring away, aimed and fired. Down it went dead, whereon, rejoicing in his triumph like any other young hunter who thinks not of the wonderful and happy life that he has destroyed, Richard sprang upon it exultantly, drawing his knife as he came, while Rachel, who always shrank from such sights, retreated to the cave. Half an hour later, however, being healthy and hungry, she had no objection to eating venison toasted upon sticks in the red embers of their fire.

Their meal finished at length, they reloaded the gun, and although the mist was still very dense, set out upon a journey of exploration, as by now the sun was shining brightly above the curtain of low-lying vapour. Stumbling on through the rocks, they discovered that the water had fallen almost as quickly as it rose on the previous night. The island was strewn, however, with the trunks of trees and other debris that it had brought down, amongst which lay the carcases of bucks and smaller creatures, and with them a number of drowned snakes. The two lions, however, appeared to have escaped by swimming, at least they saw nothing of them. Walking cautiously, they came to the edge of the *donga*, and sat down upon a stone, since as yet they could not see how wide and deep the water ran.

Whilst they remained thus, suddenly through the mist they heard a voice shouting from the other side of the *donga*.

"Missie," cried the voice in Dutch, "are you there missie?"

"That is Tom, our driver," she said, "come to look for me. Answer for me, Richard."

So the lad, who had very good lungs, roared in reply:

"Yes, I'm here, safe, waiting for the mist to lift, and the water to run down."

"God be thanked," yelled the distant Tom. "We thought that you were surely drowned. But, then, why is your voice changed?"

"Because an English *heer* is with me," cried Rachel. "Go and look for his horse and bring a rope, then wait till the mist rises. Also send to tell the pastor and my mother that I am safe."

"I am here, Rachel," shouted another voice, her father's. "I have been looking for you all night, and we have got the Englishman's horse. Don't come into the water yet. Wait till we can see."

"That's good news, any way," said Richard, "though I shall have to ride hard to catch up the wagons."

Rachel's face fell.

"Yes," she said; "very good news."

"Are you glad that I am going, then?" he asked in an offended tone.

"It was you who said the news was good," she replied gently.

"I meant I was glad that they had caught my horse, not that I had to ride away on it. Are you sorry, then?" and he glanced at her anxiously.

"Yes, I am sorry, for we have made friends, haven't we? It won't matter to you who will find plenty of people down there at the Cape, but you see when you are gone I shall have no friend left in this wilderness, shall I?"

Again Richard looked at her, and saw that her sweet grey eyes were full of tears. Then there rose within the breast of this lad who, be it remembered, was verging upon manhood, a sensation strangely similar, had he but known it, to that which had been experienced an hour or two before by the child at his side when she watched him sleeping in the cave. He felt as though these tear-laden grey eyes were drawing his heart as a magnet draws iron. Of love he knew nothing, it was but a name to him, but this feeling was certainly very new and queer.

"What have you done to me?" he asked brusquely. "I don't want to go away from you at all, which is odd, as I never liked girls much. I tell you," he went on with gathering vehemence, "that if it wasn't that it would be mean to play such a trick upon my father, I wouldn't go. I'd come with you, or follow after—all my life. Answer me—what have you done?"

"Nothing, nothing at all," said Rachel with a little sob, "except tie up your arm."

"That can't be it," he replied. "Anyone could tie up my arm. Oh! I know it is wrong, but I hope I shan't be able to overtake the wagons, for if I can't I will come back."

"You mustn't come back; you must go away, quite away, as soon as you can. Yes, as soon as you can. Your father will be very anxious," and she began to cry outright.

"Stop it," said Richard. "Do you hear me, stop it. I am not going to be made to snivel too, just because I shan't see a little girl any more whom I never met—till yesterday."

These last words came out with a gulp, and what is more, two tears came with them and trickled down his nose.

For a moment they sat thus looking at each other pitifully, and—the truth must be told—weeping, both of them. Then something got the better of Richard, let us call it primeval instinct, so that he put his arms about Rachel and kissed her, after which they continued to weep, their heads resting upon each other's shoulders. At length he let her go and stood up, saying argumentatively:

"You see now we are really friends."

"Yes," she answered, again rubbing her eyes with the back of her hand for lack of a pocket handkerchief in the fashion that on the previous day had so irritated her father, "but I don't know why you should kiss me like that, just because you are my friend, or" she added with an outburst of truthfulness, "why I should kiss you."

Richard stood over her frowning and reflecting. Then he gave up the problem as beyond his powers of interpretation, and said:

"You remember that rubbish you dreamt just now, about my being tied to a tree and the rest of it? Well, it wasn't nice, and it gives me the creeps to think of it, like the lions outside the cave. But I want to tell you that I hope it is true, for then we shall meet again, if it is only to say good-night."

"Yes, Richard," she answered, placing her slim fingers into his big brown hand, "we shall meet again, I am sure—I am quite sure. And I think that it will be to say, not good-night," and she looked up at him and smiled, "but good-morning."

As Rachel spoke a puff of wind blew down the *donga*, rolling up the mist before it, and of a sudden shining above them they saw the glorious sun. As though by magic butterflies appeared basking upon the rain-shattered lily blooms; bright birds flitted from tree to tree, ringdoves began to coo. The terror of the tempest and the darkness of night were over-past; the world awoke again to life and love and joy. Instantly this change reflected itself in their young hearts. They whose natures had as it were ripened prematurely in the stress of danger and the shadow of death, became children once again. The very real emotions that they had experienced were forgotten, or at any rate sank into abeyance. Now they thought, not of separation or of the dim, mysterious future that stretched before them, but only of how they should ford the stream and gain its further side, where Rachel saw her father, Tom, the driver, and the other Kaffirs, and Richard saw his horse which he had feared was lost.

They ran down to the brink of the water and examined it, but here it was still too deep for them to attempt its crossing. Then, directed by the shouts and motions of the Kaffir Tom and Mr. Dove, they proceeded up stream for several hundred yards, till they came to a rapid where the lessening flood ran thinly over a ridge of rock, and after investigation, proceeded to try its passage hand in hand. It proved difficult but not dangerous, for when they came near to the further side where the current was swift and the water rather deep, Tom threw them a wagon rope, clinging on to which they were dragged—wet, but laughing—in safety to the further bank.

*"Ow!"* exclaimed the Kaffirs, clapping their hands. "She is alive, the lightnings have turned away from her, she rules the waters, and the lightnings!" and then and there, after the native fashion, they gave Rachel a name which was destined to play a great part in her future. That name was "Lady of the Lightnings," or, to translate it more accurately, "of the Heavens."

"I never thought to see you again," said her father, looking at Rachel with a face that was still white and scared. "It was very wrong of me to send you so far with that storm coming on, and I have had a terrible night—yes, a terrible night; and so has your poor mother. However, she knows that you are safe by now, thank God, thank God!" and he took her in his arms and kissed her.

"Well, father, you said that He would look after me, didn't you? And so He did, for He sent Richard here If it hadn't been for Richard I should have been drowned," she added inconsequently.

"Yes, yes," said Mr. Dove. "Providence manifests itself in many ways. But who is your young friend whom you call Richard? I suppose he has some other name."

"Of course," answered that youth himself, "everybody has except Kaffirs. Mine is Darrien."

"Darrien?" said Mr. Dove. "I had a friend called Darrien at school. I never saw him after I left, but I believe that he went into the Navy."

"Then he must be my father, sir, for I have heard him say that there had been no other Darrien in the service for a hundred years."

"I think so," answered Mr. Dove, "for now that I look at you, I can see a likeness. We slept side by side in the same dormitory once five-and-thirty years ago, so I remember. And now you have saved my daughter; it is very strange. But tell me the story."

So between them they told it, although to one scene of it—the last—neither of them thought it necessary to allude; or perhaps it was forgotten.

"Truly the Almighty has had you both in His keeping," exclaimed Mr. Dove, when their tale was done. "And now, Richard, my boy, what are you going to do? You see, we caught your horse—it was grazing about a mile away with the saddle twisted under its stomach—and wondered what white man could possibly have been riding it in this desolate place. Afterwards, however, one of my *voorloopers* reported that he had seen two wagons yesterday afternoon trekking through the *poort* about five miles to the north there. The white men with them said that they were travelling towards the Cape, and pushing on to get out of the hills before the storm broke. They bade him, if he met you, to bid you follow after them as quickly as you could, and to say that they would wait for you, if you did not arrive before, at the Three Sluit outspan on this side of the Pondo country, at which you stopped some months ago."

"Yes," answered Richard, "I remember, but that outspan is thirty miles away, so I must be getting on, or they will come back to hunt for me."

"First you will stop and eat with us, will you not?" said Mr. Dove.

"No, no, I have eaten. Also I have saved some meat in my pouch. I must go, I must indeed, for otherwise my father will be angry with me. You see," he added, "I went out shooting without his leave."

"Ah! my boy," remarked Mr. Dove, who seldom neglected an opportunity for a word in season, "now you know what comes of disobedience."

"Yes, I know, sir," he answered looking at Rachel. "I was just in time to save your daughter's life here; as you said just now, Providence sent me. Well, goodbye, and don't think me wicked if I am very glad that I was disobedient, as I believe you are, too."

"Yes, I am. Good comes out of evil sometimes, though that is no reason why we should do evil," the missionary added, not knowing what else to say. Richard did not attempt to argue the point, for at the moment he was engaged in bidding farewell to Rachel. It was a very silent farewell; neither of them spoke a word, they only shook each other's hand and looked into each other's eyes. Then muttering something which it was as well that Mr. Dove did not hear, Richard swung himself into the saddle, for his horse stood at hand, and, without even looking back, cantered away towards the mountains.

"Oh!" exclaimed Rachel presently, "call him, father."

"What for?" asked Mr. Dove.

"I want to give him our address, and to get his."

"We have no address, Rachel. Also he is too far off, and why should you want the address of a chance acquaintance?"

"Because he saved my life and I do," replied the child, setting her face. Then, without another word, she turned and began to walk towards their camp—a very heavy journey it was to Rachel.

When Rachel reached the wagon she found that her mother was more or less recovered. At any rate the attack of fever had left her so that she felt able to rise from her bed. Now, although still weak, she was engaged in packing away the garments of her dead baby in a travelling chest, weeping in a silent, piteous manner as she worked. It was a very sad sight. When she saw Rachel she opened her arms without a word, and embraced her.

"You were not frightened about me, mother?" asked the child.

"No, my love," she answered, "because I knew that no harm would come to you. I have always known that. It was a mad thing of your father to send you to such a place at such a time, but no folly of his or of anyone else can hurt you who are destined to live. Never be afraid of anything, Rachel, for remember always you will only die in old age."

"I am not sure that I am glad of that," answered the girl, as she pulled off her wet clothes. "Life isn't a very happy thing, is it, mother, at least for those who live as we do?"

"There is good and bad in it, dear; we can't have one without the other—most of us. At any rate, we must take it as it comes, who have to walk a path that we did not make, and stop walking when our path comes to an end, not a step before or after. But, Rachel, you are changed since yesterday. I see it in your face. What has happened to you?"

"Lots of things, mother. I will tell you the story, all of it, every word. Would you like to hear it?"

Her mother nodded, and, the baby-clothes being at last packed away, shut the lid of-the box with a sigh, sat down upon it and listened.

Rachel told her of her meeting with Richard Darrien, and of how he saved her from the flood. She told of the strange night that they had spent together in the little cave while the lions marched up and down without. She told of her vigil over the sleeping Richard at the daybreak, and of the dream that she had dreamed when she seemed to see him grown to manhood, and herself grown to womanhood, and clad in white skins, watching him lashed to the trunk of a gigantic tree as the first arrows of sunrise struck down the lanes of some mysterious forest. She told of how her heart had been stirred, and of how afterwards in the mist by the water's brink his heart had been stirred also, and of how they had kissed each other and wept because they must part.

Then she stopped, expecting that her mother would be angry with her and scold her for her thoughts and conduct, as she knew well her father would have done. But she was not angry, and she did not scold. She only stretched out her thin hands and stroked the child's fair hair, saying:

"Don't be frightened, Rachel, and don't be sad. You think that you have lost him, but soon or late he will come back to you, perhaps as you dreamed—perhaps otherwise."

"If I were sure of that, mother, I would not mind anything," said the girl, "though really I don't know why I should care," she added defiantly.

"No, you don't know now, but you will one day, and when you do, remember that, however long it seems to wait, you may be quite sure, because I who have the gift of knowing, told you so. Now tell me again what Richard Darrien was like while you remember, for perhaps I may never live to see his face, and I wish to get it into my mind."

So Rachel told her, and when she had described every detail, asked suddenly:

"Must we really go on, mother, into this awful wilderness? Would not father turn back if you asked him?"

"Perhaps," she answered. "But I shall not ask. He would never forgive me for preventing him from doing what he thinks his duty. It is a madness when we might be happy in the Cape or in England, but that cannot be helped, for it is also his destiny and ours. Don't judge hardly of your father, Rachel, because he is a saint, and this world is a bad place for saints and their families, especially their families. You think that he does not feel; that he is heartless about me and the poor babe, and sacrifices us all, but I tell you he feels more than either you or I can do. At night when I pretend to go to sleep I watch him groaning over his loss and for me, and praying for strength to bear it, and for help to enable him to do his duty. Last night he was nearly crazed about you, and in all that awful storm, when the Kaffirs would not stir from the wagon, went alone down to the river guided by the lightnings, but of course returned half dead, having found nothing. By dawn he was back there again, for love and fear would not let him rest a minute. Yet he will never tell you anything of that, lest you should think that his faith in Providence was shaken. I know that he is strange—it is no use hiding it, but if I were to thwart him he would go quite mad, and then I should never forgive myself, who took him for better and for worse, just as he is, and not as I should like him to be. So, Rachel, be as happy as you can, and make the best of things, as I try to do, for your life is all before you, whereas mine lies behind me, and yonder," and she pointed towards the place where the infant was buried. "Hush! here he comes. Now, help me with the packing, for we are to trek to the ford this afternoon."

## Chapter 4
# Ishmael

It may he doubted whether any well-born young English lady ever had a stranger bringing-up than that which fell to the lot of Rachel Dove. To begin with, she had absolutely no associates, male or female, of her own age and station, for at that period in its history such people did not exist in the country where she dwelt. Practically her only companions were her father, a religious enthusiast, and her mother, a half broken-hearted woman, who never for a single hour could forget the children she had lost, and whose constitutional mysticism increased upon her continually until at times it seemed as though she had added some new quality to her normal human nature.

Then there were the natives, amongst whom from the beginning Rachel was a sort of queen. In those first days of settlement they had never seen anybody in the least like her, no one so beautiful—for she grew up beautiful—so fearless, or so kind. The tale of that adventure of hers as a child upon the island in the midst of the flooded torrent spread all through the country with many fabulous additions. Thus the Kaffirs said that she was a "Heaven-herd," that is, a magical person who can ward off or direct the lightnings, which she was supposed to have done upon this night; also that she could walk upon the waters, for otherwise how did she escape the flood? And, lastly, that the wild beasts were her servants, for had not the driver Tom and the natives seen the spoor of great lions right at the mouth of the cave where she and her companion sheltered, and had they not heard that she called these lions into the cave to protect her and him from the other creatures? Therefore, as has been said, they gave her a name, a very long name that meant Chieftainess, or Lady of Heaven, *Inkosazana-y-Zoola*; for Zulu or Zoola, which we know as the title of that people, means Heaven, and *Udade-y-Silwana*, or Sister of wild beasts. As these appellations proved too lengthy for general use, even among the Bantu races, who have plenty of time for talking, ultimately it was shortened to Zoola alone, so that throughout that part of South-Eastern Africa Rachel came to enjoy the lofty title of "Heaven," the first girl, probably, who was ever so called.

With all natives from her childhood up, Rachel was on the best of terms. She was never familiar with them indeed, for that is not the way for a white person to win the affection, or even the respect of a Kaffir. But she was intimate in the sense that she could enter into their thoughts and nature, a very rare gift. We whites are apt to consider ourselves the superior of such folk, whereas we are only different. In fact, taken altogether, it is quite a question whether the higher sections of the Bantu peoples are not our equals. Of course, we have learned more things, and our best men are their betters. But, on the other hand, among them there is nothing so low as the inhabitants of our slums, nor have they any vices which can surpass our vices. Is an *assegai* so much more savage than a shell? Is there any great gulf fixed between a Chaka and a Napoleon? At least they are not hypocrites, and they are not vulgar; that is the privilege of civilised nations.

Well, with these folk Rachel was intimate. She could talk to the warrior of his wars, to the woman of her garden and her children to the children of that wonder world which surrounds childhood throughout the universe. And yet there was never a one of these but lifted the hand to her in salute when her shadow fell upon them. To them all she was the *Inkosazana*, the Great Lady. They would laugh at her father and mimic him behind his back, but Rachel they never laughed at or mimicked. Of her mother also, although she kept herself apart from them, much the same may be said. For her they had a curious name which they would not, or were unable to explain. They called her "Flower-that-grows-on-a-grave." For Mr. Dove their appellation was less poetical. It was "Shouter-about-Things-he-does-not-understand," or, more briefly, "The Shouter," a name that he had acquired from his habit of raising his voice when he grew moved in speaking to them. The things that he did not understand, it may be explained, were not to their minds his religious views, which, although they considered them remarkable, were evidently his own affair, but their private customs. Especially their family customs that he was never weary of denouncing to the bewilderment of these poor heathens, who for their part were not greatly impressed by those of the few white people with whom they came in contact. Therefore, with native politeness, they concluded that he spoke thus rudely because he did not understand. Hence his name.

But Rachel had other friends. In truth she was Nature's child, if in a better and a purer sense than Byron uses that description. The sea, the *veld*, the sky, the forest and the river, these were her companions, for among them she dwelt solitary. Their denizens, too, knew her well, for unless she were driven to it, never would she lift her hand against anything that drew the breath of life. The buck would let her pass quite close to them, nor at her coming did the birds stir from off their trees. Often she stood and watched the great elephants feeding or at rest, and even dared to wander among the herds of savage buffalo. Of only two living things was she afraid—the snake and the crocodile, that are cursed above all cattle, and above every beast of the field, because being cursed they have no sympathy or gentleness. She feared nothing else, she who was always fearless, nor brute or bird, did they fear her.

After Rachel's adventure in the flooded river she and her parents pursued their journey by slow and tedious marches, and at length, though in those days this was strange enough, reached Natal unharmed. At first they went to live where the city of Durban now stands, which at that time had but just received its name. It was inhabited by a few rough men, who made a living by trading and hunting, and surrounded themselves with natives, refugees for the most part from the Zulu country. Amongst these people and their servants Mr. Dove commenced his labours, but ere long a bitter quarrel grew up between him and them.

These dwellers in the midst of barbarism led strange lives, and Mr. Dove, who rightly held it to be his duty to denounce wrong-doing of every sort, attacked them and their vices in no measured terms, and upon all occasions. For long years he kept up the fight, until at length he found himself ostracised. If they could avoid it, no white men would speak to him, nor would they allow him to instruct their Kaffirs. Thus his work came to an end in Durban as it had done in other places. Now, again, his wife and daughter hoped that he would leave South Africa for good, and return home. But it was not to be, for once more he announced that it was laid upon him to follow the example of his divine Master, and that the Spirit drove him into the wilderness. So, with a few attendants, they trekked away from Durban.

On this occasion it was his wild design to settle in Zululand—where Chaka, the great king, being dead, Dingaan, his brother and murderer, ruled in his place—and there devote himself to the conversion of the Zulus. Indeed, it is probable that he would have carried out this plan had he not been prevented by an accident. One night when they were about forty miles from Durban they camped on a stream, a tributary of the Tugela River, which ran close by, and formed the boundary of the Zulu country. It was a singularly beautiful spot, for to the east of them, about a mile away, stretched the placid Indian Ocean, while to the west, overshadowing them almost, rose a towering cliff, over which the stream poured itself, looking like a line of smoke against its rocky face. They had outspanned upon a rising hillock at the foot of which this little river wound away like a silver snake till it joined the great Tugela. In its general aspect the country was like an English park, dotted here and there with timber, around which grazed or rested great elands and other buck, and amongst them a huge rhinoceros.

When the wagon had creaked to the top of the rise, for, of course, there was no road, and the Kaffirs were beginning to unyoke the hungry oxen, Rachel, who was riding with her father, sprang from her horse and ran to it to help her mother to descend. She was now a tall young woman, full of health and vigour, strong and straightly shaped. Mrs. Dove, frail, delicate, grey-haired, placed her foot upon the *disselboom* and hesitated, for to her the ground seemed far off, and the heels of the cattle very near.

"Jump," said Rachel in her clear, laughing voice, as she smacked the near after-ox to make it turn round, which it did obediently, for all the team knew her. "I'll catch you."

But her mother still hesitated, so thrusting her way between the ox and the front wheel Rachel stretched out her arms and lifted her bodily to the ground.

"How strong you are, my love!" said her mother, with a sort of wondering admiration and a sad little smile; "it seems strange to think that I ever carried you."

"One had need to be in this country, dear," replied Rachel cheerfully. "Come and walk a little way, you must be stiff with sitting in that horrid wagon," and she led her quite to the top of the knoll. "There," she added, "isn't the view lovely? I never saw such a pretty place in all Africa. And oh! look at those buck, and yes—that is a rhinoceros. I hope it won't charge us."

Mrs. Dove obeyed, gazing first at the glorious sea, then at the plain and the trees, and lastly behind her at the towering cliff steeped in shadow—for the sun was westering—down the face of which the waterfall seemed to hang like a silver rope.

As her eyes fell upon this cliff Mrs. Dove's face changed.

"I know this spot," she said in a hurried voice. "I have seen it before."

"Nonsense, mother," answered Rachel. "We have never trekked here, so how could you?"

"I can't say, love, but I have. I remember that cliff and the waterfall; yes, and those three trees, and the buck standing under them."

"One often feels like that, about having seen places, I mean, mother, but of course it is all nonsense, because it is impossible, unless one dreams of them first."

"Yes, love, unless one dreams. Well, I think that I must have dreamt. What was the dream now? Rachel weeping—Rachel weeping—my love, I think that we are going to live here, and I think—I think——"

"All right," broke in her daughter quickly, with a shade of anxiety in her voice as though she did not wish to learn what her mother thought. "I don't mind, I am sure. I don't want to go to Zululand, and see this horrid Dingaan, who is always killing people, and I am quite sure that father would never convert him, the wicked monster. It is like the Garden of Eden, isn't it, with the sea thrown in. There are all the animals, and that green tree with the fruit on it might be the Tree of Life, and—oh, my goodness, there is Adam!"

Mrs. Dove followed the line of her daughter's outstretched hand, and perceived three or four hundred yards away, as in that sparkling atmosphere it was easy to do, a white man apparently clad in skins. He was engaged in crawling up a little rise of ground with the obvious intention of shooting at some blesbuck which stood in a hollow beyond with quaggas and other animals, while behind him was a mounted Kaffir who held his master's horse.

"I see," said Mrs. Dove, mildly interested. "But he looks more like Robinson Crusoe without his umbrella. Adam did not kill the animals in the Garden, my dear."

"He must have lived on something besides forbidden apples," remarked Rachel, "unless perhaps he was a vegetarian as father wants to be. There—he has fired!"

As she spoke a cloud of smoke arose above the man, and presently the loud report of a *roer* reached their ears. One of the buck rolled over and lay struggling on the ground, while the rest, together with many others at a distance, turned and galloped off this way and that, frightened by this new and terrible noise. The old rhinoceros under the tree rose snorting, sniffed the air, then thundered away up wind towards the man, its pig-like tail held straight above its back.

"Adam has spoilt our Eden; I hope the rhinoceros will catch him," said Rachel viciously. "Look, he has seen it and is running to his horse."

Rachel was right. Adam—or whatever his name might be—was

running with remarkable swiftness. Reaching the horse just as the rhinoceros appeared within forty yards of him, he bounded to the saddle, and with his servant galloped off to the right. The rhinoceros came to a standstill for a few moments as though it were wondering whether it dared attack these strange creatures, then making up its mind in the negative, rushed on and vanished. When it was gone, the white man and the Kaffir, who had pulled up their horses at a distance, returned to the fallen buck, cut its throat, and lifted it on to the Kaffir's horse, then rode slowly towards the wagon.

"They are coming to call," said Rachel. "How should one receive a gentleman in skins?"

Apparently some misgivings as to the effect that might be produced by his appearance occurred to the hunter. At any rate, he looked first at the two white women standing on the brow, and next at his own peculiar attire, which appeared to consist chiefly of the pelt of a lion, plus a very striking pair of trousers manufactured from the hide of a zebra, and halted about sixty yards away, staring at them. Rachel, whose sight was exceedingly keen, could see his face well, for the light of the setting sun fell on it, and he wore no head covering. It was a dark, handsome face of a man about thirty-five years of age, with strongly-marked features, black eyes and beard, and long black hair that fell down on to his shoulders. They gazed at each other for a while, then the man turned to his after-rider, gave him an order in a clear, strong voice, and rode away inland. The after-rider, on the contrary, directed his horse up the rise until he was within a few yards of them, then sprang to the ground and saluted.

"What is it?" asked Rachel in Zulu, a language which she now spoke perfectly.

*"Inkosikaas"* (that is—Lady), answered the man, "my master thinks that you may be hungry and sends you a present of this buck," and, as he spoke, he loosed the *riem* or hide rope by which it was fastened behind his saddle, and let the animal fall to the ground.

Rachel turned her eyes from it, for it was covered with blood, and unpleasant to look at, then replied:

"My father and my mother thank your master. How is he named, and where does he dwell?"

"Lady, among us black people he is named Ibubesi (lion), but his white name is Hishmel."

"Hishmel, Hishmel?" said Rachel. "Oh! I know, he means Ishmael. There, mother, I told you he was something biblical, and of course Ishmael dwelt in the wilderness, didn't he, after his father had behaved so badly to poor Hagar, and was a wild man whose hand was against every man's."

"Rachel, Rachel," said her mother suppressing a little smile. "Your father would be very angry if he heard you. You should not speak lightly of holy persons."

"Well, mother, Abraham may have been a holy person, but we should think him a mean old thing nowadays, almost as mean as Sarah. You know they were most of them mean, so what is the use of pretending they were not?"

Then without waiting for an answer she asked the Kaffir again: "Where does the *Inkoos* Ishmael dwell?"

"In the wilderness," answered the man appropriately. "Now his *kraal* is yonder, two hours' ride away. It is called Mafooti," and he pointed over the top of the precipice, adding: "he is a hunter and trades with the Zulus."

"Is he Dutch?" asked Rachel, whose curiosity was excited.

The Kaffir shook his head. "No, he hates the Dutch; he is of the people of George."

"The people of George? Why, he must mean a subject of King George—an Englishman."

"Yes, yes, Lady, an Englishman, like you," and he grinned at her. "Have you any message for the *Inkoos* Hishmel?"

"Yes. Say to the *Inkoos* Ishmael or Lion-who-dwells-in-the-wilderness, hates the Dutch and wears zebra-skin trousers, that my father and my mother thank him very much for his present, and hope that his health is good. Go. That is all."

The man grinned again, suspecting a joke, for the Zulus have a sense of humour, then repeated the message word for word, trying to pronounce Ishmael as Rachel did, saluted, mounted his horse, and galloped off after his master.

"Perhaps you should have kept that Kaffir until your father came," suggested Mrs. Dove doubtfully.

"What was the good?" said Rachel. "He would only have asked Mr. Ishmael to call in order that he might find out his religious opinions, and I don't want to see any more of the man."

"Why not, Rachel?"

"Because I don't like him, mother. I think he is worse than any of the rest down there, too bad to stop among them probably, and—" she added with conviction, "I think we shall have more of his company than we want before all is done. Oh! it is no good to say that I am prejudiced—I do, and what is more, he came into our Garden of Eden and shot the buck. I hope he will meet that rhinoceros on the way home. There!"

Although she disapproved, or tried to think that she did, of such strong opinions so strongly expressed, Mrs. Dove offered no further opposition to them. The fact was that her daughter's bodily and mental vigour overshadowed her, as they did her husband also. Indeed, it seemed curious that this girl, so powerful in body and in mind, should have sprung from such a pair, a wrong-headed, narrow-viewed saint whose right place in the world would have been in a cell in the monastery or one of the stricter orders, and a gentle, uncomplaining, high-bred woman with a mind distinguished by its affectionate and mystical nature, a mind so unusual and refined that it seemed to be, and in truth was, open to influences whereof, mercifully enough, the majority of us never feel the subtle, secret power.

Of her father there was absolutely no trace in Rachel, except a certain physical resemblance—so far as he was concerned she must have thrown back to some earlier progenitor. Even their intellects and moral outlook were quite different. She had, it is true, something of his scholarly power; thus, notwithstanding her wild upbringing, as has been said, she could read the Greek Testament almost as well as he could, or even Homer, which she liked because the old, bloodthirsty heroes reminded her of the Zulus. He had taught her this and other knowledge, and she was an apt pupil. But there the resemblance stopped. Whereas his intelligence was narrow and enslaved by the priestly tradition, hers was wide and human. She searched and she criticised; she believed in God as he did, but she saw His purpose working in the evil as in the good. In her own thought she often compared these forces to the Day and Night, and believed both of them to be necessary to the human world. For her, savagery had virtues as well as civilisation, although it is true of the latter she knew but little.

From her mother Rachel had inherited more, for instance her grace of speech and bearing, and her intuition, or foresight. Only in her case this curious gift did not dominate her, her other forces held it in check. She felt and she knew, but feeling and knowledge did not frighten or make her weak, any more than the strength of her frame or of her spirit made her unwomanly. She accepted these things as part of her mental equipment, that was all, being aware that to her a door was opened which is shut firmly enough in the faces of most folk, but not on that account in the least afraid of looking through it as her mother was.

Thus when she saw the man called Ishmael, she knew well enough that he was destined to bring great evil upon her and hers, as when as a child she met the boy Richard Darrien, she had known other things. But she did not, therefore, fear the man and his attendant evil. She only shrank from the first and looked through the second, onward and outward to the ultimate good which she was convinced lay at the end of everything, and meanwhile, being young and merry, she found his zebra-skin trousers very ridiculous.

Just as Rachel and her mother finished their conversation about Mr. Ishmael, Mr. Dove arrived from a little *kloof*, where he had been engaged with the Kaffirs in cutting bushes to make a thorn fence round their camp as a protection against lions and hyenas. He looked older than when we last met him, and save for a fringe of white hair, which increased his monkish appearance, was quite bald. His face, too, was even thinner and more eager, and his grey eyes were more far-away than formerly; also he had grown a long white beard.

"Where did that buck come from?" he asked, looking at the dead creature.

Rachel told him the story with the result that, as her mother had expected, he was very indignant with her. It was most unkind, and indeed, un-Christian, he said, not to have asked this very courteous gentleman into the camp, as he would much have liked to converse with him. He had often reproved her habit of judging by external, and in the *veld*, lion and zebra skins furnish a very suitable covering. She should remember that such were given to our first parents.

"Oh! I know, father," broke in Rachel, "when the climate grew too cold for leaf petticoats and the rest. Now don't begin to scold me, because I must go to cook the dinner. I didn't like the look of the man; besides, he rode off. Then it wasn't my business to ask him here, but mother's, who stood staring at him and never said a single word. If you want to see him so much, you can go to call upon him tomorrow, only don't take me, please. And now will you send Tom to skin the buck?"

Mr. Dove answered that Tom was busy with the fence, and, ceasing from argument which he felt to be useless with Rachel, suggested doubtfully that he had better be his own butcher.

"No, no," she replied, "you know you hate that sort of thing, as I do. Let it be till the Kaffirs have time. We have the cold meat left for supper, and I will boil some mealies. Go and help with the fence, father while I light the fire."

Usually Rachel was the best of sleepers. So soon as she laid her head upon whatever happened to serve her for a pillow, generally a saddle, her eyes shut to open no more till daylight came. On this night, however, it was not so. She had her bed in a little flap tent which hooked on to the side of the wagon that was occupied by her parents. Here she lay wide awake for a long while, listening to the Kaffirs who, having partaken heartily of the buck, were now making themselves drunk by smoking *dakka*, or Indian hemp, a habit of which Mr. Dove had tried in vain to break them. At length the fire around which they sat near the thorn fence on the further side of the wagon, grew low, and their incoherent talk ended in silence, punctuated by snores. Rachel began to dose but was awakened by the laughing cries of the hyenas quite close to her. The brutes had scented the dead buck and were wandering round the fence in hope of a midnight meal. Rachel rose, and taking the gun that lay at her side, threw a cloak over her shoulders and left the tent.

The moon was shining brightly and by its light she saw the hyenas, two of them, wolves as they are called in South Africa, long grey creatures that prowled round the thorn fence hungrily, causing the oxen that were tied to the trek tow and the horses picketed on the other side of the wagon, to low and whinny in an uneasy fashion. The hyenas saw her also, for her head rose above the rough fence, and being cowardly beasts, slunk away. She could have shot them had she chose, but did not, first because she hated killing anything unnecessarily, even a wolf, and secondly because it would have aroused the camp. So she contented herself by throwing more dry wood on to the fire, stepping over the Kaffirs, who slept like logs, in order to do so. Then, resting upon her gun like some Amazon on guard, she gazed a while at the lovely moonlit sea, and the long line of game trekking silently to their drinking place, until seeing no more of the wolves or other dangerous beasts, she turned and sought her bed again.

She was thinking of Mr. Ishmael and his zebra-skin trousers; wondering why the man should have filled her with such an unreasoning dislike. If she had disliked him at a distance of fifty paces, how she would hate him when he was near! And yet he was probably only one of those broken soldiers of fortune of whom she had met several, who took to the wilderness as a last resource, and by degrees sank to the level of the savages among whom they lived, a person who was not worth a second thought. So she tried to put him from her mind, and by way of an antidote, since still she could not sleep, filled it with her recollections of Richard Darrien. Some years had gone by since they had met, and from that time to this she had never heard a word of him in which she could put the slightest faith. She did not even know whether he were alive or dead, only she believed that if he were dead she would be aware of it. No, she had never heard of him, and it seemed probable that she never would hear of him again. Yet she did not believe that either. Had she done so her happiness—for on the whole Rachel was a happy girl—would have departed from her, since this once seen lad never left her heart, nor had she forgotten their farewell kiss.

Reflecting thus, at length Rachel fell off to sleep and began to dream, still of Richard Darrien. It was a long dream whereof afterwards she could remember but little, but in it there were shoutings, and black faces, and the flashing of spears; also the white man Ishmael was present there. One part, however, she did remember; Richard Darrien, grown taller, changed and yet the same, leaning over her, warning her of danger to come, warning her against this man Ishmael.

She awoke suddenly to see that the light of dawn was creeping into her tent, that low, soft light which is so beautiful in Southern Africa. Rachel was disturbed, she felt the need of action, of anything that would change the current of her thoughts. No one was about yet. What should she do? She knew; the sea was not more than a mile away, she would go down to it and bathe, and be back before the rest of them were awake.

## Chapter 5
# Noie

That a girl should set out alone to bathe through a country inhabited chiefly by wild beasts and a few wandering savages, sounds a somewhat dangerous form of amusement. So it was indeed, but Rachel cared nothing for such dangers, in fact she never even thought of them. Long ago she had discovered that the animals would not harm her if she did not harm them, except perhaps the rhinoceros, which is given to charging on sight, and that was large and could generally be discovered at a distance. As for elephants and lions, or even buffalo, her experience was that they ran away, except on rare occasions when they stood still, and stared at her. Nor was she afraid of the savages, who always treated her with the utmost respect, even if they had never seen her before. Still, in case of accidents she took her double-barrelled gun, loaded in one barrel with ball, and in the other with *loopers* or slugs, and awakened Tom, the driver, to tell him where she was going. The man stared at her sleepily, and murmured a remonstrance, but taking no heed of him she pulled out some thorns from the fence to make a passage, and in another minute was lost to sight in the morning mist.

Following a game path through the dew-drenched grass which grew upon the swells and valleys of the *veld*, and passing many small buck upon her way, in about twenty minutes, just as the light was really beginning to grow, Rachel reached the sea. It was dead calm, and the tide chancing to be out, soon she found the very place she sought—a large, rock-bound pool where there would be no fear of sharks that never stay in such a spot, fearing lest they should be stranded. Slipping off her clothes she plunged into the cool and crystal water and began to swim round and across the pool, for at this art she was expert, diving and playing like a sea-nymph. Her bath done she dried herself with a towel she had brought, all except her long, fair hair, which she let loose for the wind to blow on, and having dressed, stood a while waiting to see the glory of the sun rising from the ocean.

Whilst she remained thus, suddenly she heard the sound of horses galloping towards her, two of them she could tell that from the hoof beats, although the low-lying mist made them invisible. A few more seconds and they emerged out of the fog. The first thing that she saw were stripes which caused her to laugh, thinking that she had mistaken zebras for horses. Then the laugh died on her lips as she recognised that the stripes were those of Mr. Ishmael's trousers. Yes, there was no doubt about it, Mr. Ishmael, wearing a rough coat instead of his lion-skin, but with the rest of his attire unchanged, was galloping down upon her furiously, leading a riderless horse. Remembering her wet and dishevelled hair, Rachel threw the towel over it, whence it hung like an old Egyptian head-dress, setting her beautiful face in a most becoming frame. Next she picked up the double-barrelled gun and cocked it, for she misdoubted her of this man's intentions. Not many modern books came her way, but she had read stories of young women who were carried off by force.

For an instance she was frightened, but as she lifted the hammer of the second barrel her constitutional courage returned.

"Let him try it," she thought to herself. "If he had come ten minutes ago it would have been awful, but now I don't care."

By this time Mr. Ishmael had arrived, and was dragging his horse to its haunches; also she saw that evidently he was much more frightened than she had been. The man's handsome face was quite white, and his lips were trembling. "Perhaps that rhinoceros is after him again, thought Rachel, then added aloud quietly:

"What is the matter?"

"Forgive me," he answered in a rich, and to Rachel's astonishment, perfectly educated voice, "forgive me for disturbing you. I am ashamed, but it is necessary. The Zulus—" and he paused.

"Well, sir," asked Rachel, "what about the Zulus?"

"A regiment of them are coming down here on the warpath. They are hunting fugitives. The fugitives, about fifty of them, passed my camp over an hour ago, and I saw the *Impi* following them. I rode to warn you all. They told me you were down by the sea. I came to bring you back to your wagon lest you should be cut off."

"Thank you very much," said Rachel. "But I am not afraid of the Zulus. I do not think that they will hurt me."

"Not hurt you! Not hurt you! White and beautiful as you are. Why not?"

"Oh! I don't know," she replied with a laugh, "but you see I am called *Inkosazana-y-Zoola*. They won't touch one with that name."

"*Inkosazana-y-Zoola*," he repeated astonished. "Why she is their Spirit, yes, and I remember—white like you, so they say. How did you get that name? But mount, mount! They will kill you first, and ask how you were called afterwards. Your father is much afraid."

"My mother would not be afraid; she knows," muttered Rachel to herself, as she sprang to the saddle of the led-horse.

Then, without more words, they began to gallop back towards the camp. Before they reached the crest of the second rise the sun shone out in earnest, thinning the seaward mist, although between them and the camp it still hung thick. Then suddenly in the fog-edge Rachel saw this sight: Towards them ran a delicately shaped and beautiful native girl, naked except for her *moocha*, and of a very light, copper-colour, whilst after her, brandishing an *assegai*, came a Zulu warrior. Evidently the girl was in the last stage of exhaustion; indeed she reeled over the ground, her tongue protruded from her lips and her eyes seemed to be starting from her head.

"Come on," shouted the man called Ishmael. "It is only one of the fugitives whom they are killing."

But Rachel did nothing of the sort; she pulled up her horse and waited. The girl caught sight of her and with a wild hoarse scream, redoubled her efforts, so that her pursuer, who had been quite close, was left behind. She reached Rachel and flung her arms about her legs gasping:

"Save me, white lady, save me!"

"Shoot her if she won't leave go," shouted Ishmael, "and come on."

But Rachel only sprang from the horse and stood face to face with the advancing Zulu.

"Stand," she said, and the man stopped.

"Now," she asked, "what do you want with this woman?"

"To take her or to kill her," gasped the soldier.

"By whose order?"

"By order of Dingaan the King,"

"For what crime?"

"Witchcraft; but who are you who question me, white woman?"

"One whom you must obey," answered Rachel proudly. "Go back and leave the girl. She is mine."

The man stared at her, then laughed aloud and began to advance again.

"Go back," repeated Rachel.

He took no heed but still came on.

"Go back or die," she said for the third time.

"I shall certainly die if I go back to Dingaan without the girl," replied the soldier who was a bold-looking savage. "Now you, Noie, will you return with me or shall I kill you? Say, witch," and he lifted his *assegai*.

The girl sank in a heap upon the *veld*. "Kill," she murmured faintly, "I will not go back. I did not bewitch him to make him dream of me, and I will be Death's wife, not his; a ghost in his *kraal*, not a woman."

"Good," said the man, "I will carry your word to the king. Farewell, Noie," and he raised the *assegai* still higher, adding: "Stand aside, white woman, for I have no order to kill you also."

By way of answer Rachel put the gun to her shoulder and pointed it at him.

"Are you mad?" shouted Ishmael. "If you touch him they will murder every one of us. Are you mad?"

"Are you a coward?" she asked quietly, without taking her eyes off the soldier. Then she said in Zulu, "Listen. The land on this side of the Tugela has been given by Dingaan to the English. Here he has no right to kill. This girl is mine, not his. Come one step nearer and you die."

"We shall soon see who will die," answered the warrior with a laugh, and he sprang forward.

They were his last words. Rachel aimed and pressed the trigger, the gun exploded heavily in the mist; the Zulu leapt into the air and fell upon his back, dead. The white man, Ishmael, rode to them, pulled up his horse and sat still, staring. It was a strange picture in that lonely, silent spot. The soldier so very still and dead, his face hidden by the shield that had fallen across it; the tall, white girl, rigid as a statue, in whose hand the gun still smoked, the delicate, fragile Kaffir maiden kneeling on the *veld*, and looking at her wildly as though she were a spirit, and the two horses, one with its ears pricked in curiosity, and the other already cropping grass.

"My God! What have you done?" exclaimed Ishmael.

"Justice," answered Rachel.

"Then your blood be on your own head. I am not going to stop here to have my throat cut."

"Don't," answered Rachel. "I have a better guardian than you, and will look after my own blood."

To this speech the white man seemed to be able to find no answer. Turning his horse he galloped off swearing, but not towards the camp, whereon the other horse galloped after him, and presently they all vanished in the mist, leaving the two women alone.

At this moment from the direction of the wagon they heard the sound of shouting and of screams, which appeared to come from the valley between them and it.

"The king's men are killing my people," muttered the girl Noie. "Go, or they will kill you too."

Rachel thought a moment. Evidently it was impossible to get through to the camp; indeed, even had they tried to do so on the horses they would have been cut off. An idea came to her. They stood upon the edge of a steep, bush-clothed *kloof*, where in the wet season a stream ran down to the sea. This stream was now represented by a chain of deep and muddy pools, one of which pools lay directly underneath them.

"Help me to throw him into the water," said Rachel.

The girl understood, and with desperate energy they seized the dead soldier, dragged him to the edge of the little cliff and thrust him over. He fell with a heavy splash into the pool and vanished.

"Crocodiles live there," said Rachel, "I saw one as I passed. Now take the shield and spear and follow me."

She obeyed, for with hope her strength seemed, to have returned to her, and the two of them scrambled down the cliffs into the *kloof*. As they reached the edge of the pool they saw great snouts and a disturbance in the water. Rachel was right, crocodiles lived there.

"Now," she said, "throw your *moocha* on that rock. They will find it and think——"

Noie nodded and did so, rending its fastening and wetting it in the water. Then quite naked she took Rachel's hand and swiftly, swiftly, the two of them leapt from stone to stone, so as to leave no footprints, heading for the sea. Only the fugitive stopped once to drink of the fresh water, for she was perishing with thirst. Now when Rachel was bathing she had observed upon the farther side of her pool and opening out of it, as it were, a little pocket in the rock, where the water was not more than three feet deep and covered by a dense growth of beautiful seaweed, some black and some ribbon-like and yellow. The pool was long, perhaps two hundred paces in all, and to go round it they would be obliged to expose themselves upon the sand, and thus become visible from a long way off.

"Can you swim?" said Rachel to Noie.

Again she nodded, and the two of them slipped into the water and swam across the pool till they reached the pocket-like place, on the edge of which they sat down, covering themselves with the seaweed.

They had not been there five minutes when they heard the sound of voices drawing near down the *kloof*, and at once slid into the water, covering themselves in it in such fashion that only their heads remained above the surface, mixed with the black and yellow seaweed, so that without close search none could have said which was hair and which was weed.

"The Zulus," said Noie, shivering so that the water shook about her, "they seek me."

"Lie still, then," answered Rachel. "I can't shoot now, the gun is wet."

The voices died away, and the two girls thought that the speakers had gone, but rendered cautious, still remained hidden in the water. It was well for them that they did so for presently they heard the voices again and much nearer. The Zulus were walking round the pool. Two of them came quite close to their little hiding-place, and sat down on some rocks to rest, and talk. Peeping through her covering of seaweed Rachel could see them, great men who held red spears in their hands.

"You are a fool," said one of them to the other, "and have given us this walk for nothing, as though our feet were not sore enough already. The crocodiles have that Noie, her witchcraft could not save her from them; it was a baboon's spoor you saw in the mud, not a woman's."

"It would seem so, brother," answered the other, "as we found the *moocha*. Still, if so, where is Bomba who was running her down? And what made that blood-mark on the grass?"

"Doubtless," replied the first man, "Bomba came up with her there and wounded her, whereon being a woman and a coward, she ran from him and jumped into the pool in which the crocodiles finished her. As for Bomba, I expect that he has gone back to Zululand, or is asleep somewhere resting. The other spoor we saw was that of a white woman, who puts skins upon her feet. There is a camp of them up yonder, but you remember, our orders were not to touch any of the people of George, so we need not trouble about them."

"Well, brother, if you are sure, we had better be starting back, lest there should be trouble with the white people. Dingaan will be satisfied when we show him the *moocha*, and sleep in peace henceforth. She must really have been *tagati* (uncanny), that little Noie, for otherwise, although it is true she was pretty, why should Dingaan who has all Zululand to choose from, have fallen in love with her, and why should she have refused to enter his house, and persuaded all her *kraal* to run away? For my part, I don't believe that she is dead now, notwithstanding the *moocha*. I think that she is a witch, and has changed into something else—a bird or a snake, perhaps. Well, the rest of them will never change into anything, except black mould. Let us see. We have killed every one; all the common people, the mother of Noie, the dwarf-wizard Seyapi her father, and her other mothers, four of them, and her brothers and sisters, twelve in all."

At these words Noie again trembled beneath her seaweed, so that the water shook all about her.

"There is a fish there," said the first Kaffir, "I saw it rise. It is a small pool, shall we try to catch it?"

"No, brother," answered the other, "only coast people eat fish. I am hungry, but I will wait for man's food. Take that, fish!" and he threw a stone into the pool which struck Rachel on the side, and caused her fair hair to float about among the yellow seaweed.

Then the two of them got up and went away, walking arm-in-arm like friends and amiable men, as they were in their own fashion.

For a long time the girls remained beneath their seaweed, fearing lest the men or others should return, until at length they could bear the cold of the water no longer, and crept out of it to the brink of the little pool, where, still wreathed in seaweed, they sat and warmed themselves in the hot sunlight. Now Noie seemed to be half dead; indeed Rachel thought that she would die.

"Awake," she said, "life is still before you."

"Would that it were behind me, Lady," moaned the poor girl. "You understand our tongue—did you not hear? My father, my own mother, my other mothers, my brothers and sisters, all killed, all killed for my sake, and I left living. Oh! you meant kindly, but why did you not let Bomba pass his spear through me? It would have been quickly over, and now I should sleep with the rest."

Rachel made no answer, for she saw that talking was useless in such a case. Only she took Noie's hand and pressed it in silent sympathy, until at length the poor girl, utterly outworn with agony and the fatigue of her long flight, fell asleep, there in the sunshine. Rachel let her sleep, knowing that she would take no harm in that warmth. Quietly she sat at her side for hour after hour while the fierce sun, from which she protected her head with seaweed, dried her garments. At length the shadows told her that midday was past, and the sea water which began to trickle over the surrounding rocks that the tide was approaching its full. They could stop there no longer unless they wished to be drowned.

"Come," she said to Noie, "the Zulus have gone, and the sea is here. We must swim to the shore and go back to my father's camp."

"What place have I in your *kraal*, Lady?" asked the girl when her senses had returned to her.

"I will find you a place," Rachel answered; "you are mine now."

"Yes, Lady, that is true," said Noie heavily, "I am yours and no one else's," and taking Rachel's hand she pressed it to her forehead.

Then together once more they swam the pool, and not too soon, for the tide was pouring into it. Reaching the shore in safety, no easy task for Rachel, who must hold the heavy gun above her head, Noie tied Rachel's towel about her middle to take the place of her *moocha*, and very cautiously they crept up the *kloof*, fearing lest some of the Zulus might still be lurking in the neighbourhood.

At length they came to the pool into which they had thrown the soldier Bomba, and saw two crocodiles doubtless those that had eaten him, lying asleep in the sun upon flat rocks at its edge. Here they were obliged to leave the *kloof* both because they feared to pass the crocodiles, and for the reason that their road to the camp ran another way. So they climbed up the cliff and looked about, but could see only a pair of oribe bucks, one lying down under a tree, and one eating grass quite close to its mate.

"The Zulus have gone or there would be no buck here," said Rachel. "Come, now, hold the shield before you and the spear in your hand, to hide that you are a woman, and let us go on boldly."

So they went till they reached the crest of the next rise, and then sprang back behind it, for lying here and there they saw people who seemed to be asleep.

"The Zulus resting!" exclaimed Rachel.

"Nay," answered the girl with a sigh. "My people, dead! See the vultures gathered round them."

Rachel looked again, and saw that it was so. Without a word they walked forward, and as they passed each body Noie gave it its name. Here lay a brother, there a sister, yonder four folk of her father's *kraal*. They came to a tall and handsome woman of middle age, and she shivered as she had done in the pool and said in an icy voice:

"The mother who bore me!"

A few more steps and in a patch of high grass that grew round an ant-heap, they found two Zulu soldiers, each pierced through with a spear. Seated against the ant-heap also, as though he were but resting, was a light-coloured man, a dwarf in stature, spare of frame, and with sharp features. His dress, if he wore any, seemed to have been removed from him, for he was almost naked, and Rachel noticed that no wound could be seen on him.

"Behold my father!" said Noie in the same icy voice.

"But," whispered Rachel, "he only sleeps. No spear has touched him."

"Not so, he is dead, dead by the White Death after the fashion of his people."

Now Rachel wondered what this White Death might be, and of which people the man was one. That he was not a Zulu who had been stunted in his growth she could see for herself, nor had she ever met a native who at all resembled him. Still she could ask no questions at that time; the thing was too awful. Moreover Noie had knelt down before the body, and with her arms thrown around its neck, was whispering into its ear. For a full minute she whispered thus, then set her own ear to the cold stirless lips, and for another minute or more, seemed to listen intently, nodding her head from time to time. Never before had Rachel witnessed anything so uncanny, and oddly enough, the fact that this scene was enacted in the bright sunlight added to its terrors. She stood paralysed, forgetting the Zulus, forgetting everything except that to all appearance the living was holding converse with the dead.

At length Noie rose, and turning to her companion said:

"My Spirit has been good to me; I thank my Spirit, which brought me here before it was too late for us to talk together. Now I have the message."

"The message! Oh! what message?" gasped Rachel.

An inscrutable look gathered on the face of the beautiful native girl.

"It is to me alone," she answered, "but this I may say, much of it was of you, *Inkosazana-y-Zoola*."

"Who told you that was my native name?" asked Rachel, springing back.

"It was in the message, O thou before whom kings shall bow."

"Nonsense," exclaimed Rachel, "you have heard it from our people."

"So be it, Lady; I have heard it from your people whom I have never seen. Now let us go, your father is troubled for you."

Again Rachel looked at her sideways, and Noie went on:

"Lady, from henceforth I am your servant, am I not? and that service will not be light."

"She thinks I shall make her dig," thought Rachel to herself, as the girl continued in her low, soft voice:

"Now I ask you one thing—when I tell you my story, let it be for your breast alone. Say only that I am a common girl whom you saved from the soldier."

"Why not?" answered Rachel. "That is all I have to tell."

Then once more they went on, Rachel wondering if she dreamed, the girl Noie walking at her side, stern and cold-faced as a statue.

## CHAPTER 6

# The Casting of the Lots

They reached the crest of the last rise, and there, facing them on the slope of the opposite wave of land, stood the wagon, surrounded by the thorn fence, within which the cattle and horses were still enclosed, doubtless for fear of the Zulus. Nothing could be more peaceful than the aspect of that camp. To look at it no one would have believed that within a few hundred yards a hideous massacre had just taken place. Presently, however, voices began to shout, and heads to bob up over the fence. Then it occurred to Rachel that they must think she was a prisoner in the charge of a Zulu, and she told Noie to lower the shield which she still held in front of her. The next instant some thorns were torn out, and her father, a gun in his hand, appeared striding towards them.

"Thank God that you are safe," he said as they met. "I have suffered great anxiety, although I hoped that the white man Israel—no, Ishmael—had rescued you. He came here to warn us," he added in explanation, "very early this morning, then galloped off to find you. Indeed his after-rider, whose horse he took, is still here. Where on earth have you been, Rachel, and"—suddenly becoming aware of Noie, who, arrayed only in a towel, a shield, and a stabbing spear, presented a curious if an impressive spectacle—"who is this young person?"

"She is a native girl I saved from the massacre," replied Rachel, answering the last question first. "It is a long story, but I shot the man who was going to kill her, and we hid in a pool. Are you all safe, and where is mother?"

"Shot the man! Shed human blood! Hid in a pool!" ejaculated Mr. Dove, overcome. "Really, Rachel, you are a most trying daughter. Why should you go out before daybreak and do such things?"

"I don't know, I am sure, father; predestination, I suppose—to save her life, you know."

Again he contemplated the beautiful Noie, then, murmuring something about a blanket, ran back to the camp. By this time Mrs. Dove had climbed out of the wagon, and arrived with the Kaffirs.

"I knew you would be safe, Rachel," she said in her gentle voice, "because nothing can hurt you. Still you do upset your poor father dreadfully, and—what are you going to do with that naked young woman?"

"Give her something to eat, dear," answered Rachel. "Don't ask me any more questions now. We have been sitting up to our necks in water for hours, and are starved and frozen, to say nothing of worse things."

At this moment Mr. Dove arrived with a blanket, which he offered to Noie, who took it from him and threw it round her body. Then they went into the camp, where Rachel changed her damp clothes, whilst Noie sat by her in a corner of the tent. Presently, too, food was brought, and Rachel ate hungrily, forcing Noie to do the same. Then she went out, leaving the girl to rest in the tent, and with certain omissions, such as the conduct of Noie when she found her dead father, told all the story which, wild as were the times and strange as were the things that happened in them, they found wonderful enough.

When she had done Mr. Dove knelt down and offered up thanks for his daughter's preservation through great danger, and with them prayers that she might be forgiven for having shot the Zulu, a deed that, except for the physical horror of it, did not weigh upon Rachel's mind.

"You know, father, you would have done the same yourself," she explained, "and so would mother there, if she could hold a gun, so what is the good of pretending that it is a sin? Also no one saw it except that white man and the crocodiles which buried the body, so the less we say about the matter the better it will be for all of us."

"I admit," answered Mr. Dove, "that the circumstances justified the deed, though I fear that the truth will out, since blood calls for blood. But what are we to do with the girl? They will come to seek her and kill us all."

"They will not seek, father, because they think that she is dead, and will never know otherwise unless that white man tells them, which he will scarcely do, as the Zulus would think that he shot the soldier, not I. She has been sent to us, and it is our duty to keep her."

"I suppose so," said her father doubtfully. "Poor thing! Truly she has cause for gratitude to Providence: all her relations killed by those bloodthirsty savages, and she saved!"

"If all of you were killed and I were saved, I do not know that I should feel particularly grateful," answered Rachel. "But it is no use arguing about such things, so let us be thankful that we are not killed too. Now I am tired out, and going to lie down, for of course we can't leave this place at present, unless we trek back to Durban."

Such was the finding of Noie.

********

When Rachel awoke from the sleep into which she had fallen, sunset was near at hand. She left the tent where Noie still lay slumbering or lost in stupor, to find that only her mother and Ishmael's after-rider remained in the camp, her father having gone out with the Kaffirs, in order to bury as many of the dead as possible before night came, and with it the jackals and hyenas. Rachel made up the fire and set to work with her mother's help to cook their evening meal. Whilst they were thus engaged her quick ears caught the sound of horses' hoofs, and she looked up to perceive the white man, Ishmael, still leading the spare horse on which she had ridden that morning. He had halted on the crest of ground where she had first seen him upon the previous day, and was peering at the camp, with the object apparently of ascertaining whether its occupants were still alive.

"I will go and ask him in," said Rachel, who, for reasons of her own, wished to have a word or two with the man.

Presently she came up to him, and saw at once that he seemed to be very much ashamed of himself.

"Well," she said cheerfully, "you see here I am, safe enough, and I am glad that you are the same."

"You are a wonderful woman," he replied, letting his eyes sink before her clear gaze, "as wonderful as you are beautiful."

"No compliments, please," said Rachel, "they are out of place in this savage land."

"I beg your pardon, I could not help speaking the truth. Did they kill the girl and let you go?"

"No, I managed to hide up with her; she is here now."

"That is very dangerous, Miss Dove. I know all about it; it is she whom Dingaan was after. When he hears that you have sheltered her he will send and kill you all. Take my advice and turn her out at once. I say it is most dangerous."

"Perhaps," answered Rachel calmly, "but all the same I shall do nothing of the sort unless she wishes to go, nor do I think that my father will either. Now please listen a minute. If this story comes to the ears of the Zulus—and I do not see why it should, as the crocodiles have eaten that soldier—who will they think shot him, I or the white man who was with me? Do you understand?"

"I understand and shall hold my tongue, for your sake."

"No, for your own. Well, by way of making the bargain fair, for my part I shall say as little as possible of how we separated this morning. Not that I blame you for riding off and leaving an obstinate young woman whom you did not know to take her chance. Still, other people might think differently."

"Yes," he answered, "they might, and I admit that I am ashamed of myself. But you don't know the Zulus as I do, and I thought that they would be all on us in a moment; also I was mad with you and lost my nerve. Really I am very sorry."

"Please don't apologise. It was quite natural, and what is more, all for the best. If we had gone on we should have ridden right into them, and perhaps never ridden out again. Now here comes my father; we have agreed that you will not say too much about this girl, have we not?"

He nodded and advanced with her, leading the horses, for he had dismounted, to meet Mr. Dove at the opening in the fence.

"Good evening," said the clergyman, who seemed depressed after his sad task, as he motioned to one of the Kaffirs to put down his mattock and take the horses. "I don't quite know what happened this morning, but I have to thank you for trying to save my daughter from those cruel men. I have been burying their victims in a little cleft that we found, or rather some of them. The vultures you know——" and he paused.

"I didn't save her, sir," answered the stranger humbly. "It seemed hopeless, as she would not leave the Kaffir girl."

Mr. Dove looked at him searchingly, and there was a suspicion of contempt in his voice as he replied:

"You would not have had her abandon the poor thing, would you? For the rest, God saved them both, so it does not much matter exactly how, as everything has turned out for the best. Won't you come in and have some supper, Mr.—Ishmael—I am afraid I do not know the rest of your name."

"There is no more to know, Mr. Dove," he replied doggedly, then added: "Look here, sir, as I daresay you have found out, this is a rough country, and people come to it, some of them, whose luck has been rough elsewhere. Now, perhaps I am as well born as you are, and perhaps *my* luck was rough in other lands, so that I chose to come and live in a place where there are no laws or civilisation. Perhaps, too, I took the name of another man who was driven into the wilderness—you will remember all about him—also that it does not seem to have been his fault. Any way, if we should be thrown up together I'll ask you to take me as I am, that is, a hunter and a trader 'in the Zulu,' and not to bother about what I have been. Whatever I was christened, my name is Ishmael now, or among the Kaffirs Ibubesi, and if you want another, let us call it Smith."

"Quite so, Mr. Ishmael. It is no affair of mine," replied Mr. Dove with a smile, for he had met people of this sort before in Africa.

But within himself already he determined that this white and perchance fallen wanderer was one whom, perhaps, it would be his duty to lead back into the paths of Christian propriety and peace.

These matters settled, they went into the little camp, and a sentry having been set, for now the night was falling fast, Ishmael was introduced to Mrs. Dove, who looked him up and down and said little, after which they began their supper. When their simple meal was finished, Ishmael lit his pipe and sat himself upon the *disselboom* of the wagon, looking extremely handsome and picturesque in the flare of the firelight which fell upon his dark face, long black hair and curious garments, for although he had replaced his lion-skin by an old coat, his zebra-hide trousers and waistcoat made of an otter's pelt still remained. Contemplating him, Rachel felt sure that whatever his present and past might be, he had spoken the truth when he hinted that he was well-born. Indeed, this might be gathered from his voice and method of expressing himself when he grew more at ease, although it was true that sometimes he substituted a Zulu for an English word, and employed its idioms in his sentences, doubtless because for years he had been accustomed to speak and even to think in that language.

Now he was explaining to Mr. Dove the political and social position among that people, whose cruel laws and customs led to constant fights on the part of tribes or families, who knew that they were doomed, and their consequent massacre if caught, as had happened that day. Of course, the clergyman, who had lived for some years at Durban, knew that this was true, although, never having actually witnessed one of these dreadful events till now, he did not realise all their horror.

"I fear that my task will be even harder than I thought," he said with a sigh.

"What task?" asked Ishmael.

"That of converting the Zulus. I am trekking to the king's *kraal* now, and propose to settle there."

Ishmael knocked out his pipe and filled it again before he answered. Apparently he could find no words in which to express his thoughts, but when at length these came they were vigorous enough.

"Why not trek to hell and settle *there* at once?" he asked, "I beg pardon, I meant heaven, for you and your likes. Man," he went on excitedly, "have you any heart? Do you care about your wife and daughter?"

"I have always imagined that I did, Mr. Ishmael," replied the missionary in a cold voice.

"Then do you wish to see their throats cut before your eyes, or," and he looked at Rachel, "worse?"

"How can you ask such questions?" said Mr. Dove, indignantly. "Of course I know that there are risks among all wild peoples, but I trust to Providence to protect us."

Mr. Ishmael puffed at his pipe and swore to himself in Zulu.

"Yes," he said, when he had recovered a little, "so I suppose did Seyapi and his people, but you have been burying them this afternoon—haven't you?—all except the girl, Noie, whom you have sheltered, for which deed Dingaan will bury you all if you go into Zululand, or rather throw you to the vultures. Don't think that your being an *umfundusi*, I mean a teacher, will save you. The Almighty Himself can't save you there. You will be dead and forgotten in a month. What's more, you will have to drive your own wagon in, for your Kaffirs won't, they know better. A Bible won't turn the blade of an *assegai*."

"Please, Mr. Ishmael, please do not speak so—so irreligiously," said Mr. Dove in an irritated but nervous voice. "You do not seem to understand that I have a mission to perform, and if that should involve martyrdom——"

"Oh! bother martyrdom, which is what you are after, no doubt, 'casting down your golden crown upon a crystal sea,' and the rest of it—I remember the stuff. The question is, do you wish to murder your wife and daughter, for that's the plain English of it?"

"Of course not. How can you suggest such a thing?"

"Then you had better not cross the Tugela. Go back to Durban, or stop where you are at least, for, unless he finds out anything, Dingaan is not likely to interfere with a white man on this side of the river."

"That would involve abandoning my most cherished ambition, and impulses that—but I will not speak to you of things which perhaps you might not understand."

"I dare say I shouldn't, but I do understand what it feels like to have your neck twisted out of joint. Look here, sir, if you want to go into Zululand, you should go alone; it is no place for white ladies."

"That is for them to judge, sir," answered Mr. Dove. "I believe that their faith will be equal to this trial," and he looked at his wife almost imploringly.

For once, however, she failed him.

"My dear John," she said, "if you want my opinion, I think that this gentleman is quite right. For myself I don't care much, but it can never have been intended that we should absolutely throw away our lives. I have always given way to you, and followed you to many strange places without grumbling, although, as you know, we might be quite comfortable at home, or at any rate in some civilised town. Now I say that I think you ought not to go to Zululand, especially as there is Rachel to think of."

"Oh! don't trouble about me," interrupted that young lady, with a shrug of her shoulders. "I can take my chance as I have often done before—today, for instance."

"But I do trouble about you, my dear, although it is true I don't believe that you will be killed; you know I have always said so. Still I do trouble, and John—John," she added in a kind of pitiful cry, "can't you see that you have worn me out? Can't you understand that I am getting old and weak? Is there nobody to whom you have a duty as well as to the heathen? Are there not enough heathen here?" she went on with gathering passion. "If you must mix with them, do what this gentleman says, and stop here, that is, if you won't go back. Build a house and let us have a little peace before we die, for death will come soon enough, and terribly enough, I am sure," and she burst into a fit of weeping.

"My dear," said Mr. Dove, "you are upset; the unhappy occurrences of today, which—did we but know it—are doubtless all for the best, and your anxiety for Rachel have been too much for you. I think that you had better go to bed, and you too, Rachel. I will talk the matter over further with Mr. Ishmael, who, perhaps, has been sent to guide me. I am not unreasonable, as you think, and if he can convince me that there is any risk to your lives—for my own I care nothing—I will consider the suggestion of building a mission-station outside Zululand, at any rate for a few years. It may be that it is not intended that we should enter that country at present."

So Mrs. Dove and her daughter went, but for two hours or more Rachel heard her father and the hunter talking earnestly, and wondered in a sleepy fashion to what conclusion he had come. Personally she did not mind much on which side of the Tugela they were to live, if they must bide at all in the region of that river. Still, for her mother's sake she determined that if she could bring it about, they should stay where they were. Indeed there was no choice between this and returning to England, as her father had quarrelled too bitterly with the white men at Durban to allow of his taking up his residence among them again.

When Rachel woke on the following morning the first thing she saw in the growing light was the orphaned native Noie, seated on the further side of the little tent, her head resting upon her hand, and gazing at her vacantly. Rachel watched her a while, pretending to be still asleep, and for the first time understood how beautiful this girl was in her own fashion. Although small, that is in comparison with most Kaffir women, she was perfectly shaped and developed. Her soft skin in that light looked almost white, although it had about it nothing of the muddy colour of the half-breed; her hair was long, black and curly, and worn naturally, not forced into artificial shapes as is common among the Kaffirs. Her features were finely cut and intellectual, and her eyes, shaded by long lashes, somewhat oblong in shape, of a brown colour, and soft as those of a buck. Certainly for a native she was lovely, and what is more, quite unlike any Bantu that Rachel had ever seen, except indeed that dead man whom she said was her father, and who, although he was so small, had managed to kill two great Zulu warriors before, mysteriously enough, he died himself.

"Noie," said Rachel, when she had completed her observations, whereon with a quick and agile movement the girl rose, sank again on her knees beside her, took the hand that hung from the bed between her own, and pressed it to her lips, saying in the soft Zulu tongue,

"*Inkosazana*, I am here."

"Is that white man still asleep, Noie?"

"Nay, he has gone. He and his servant rode away before the light, fearing lest there might still be Zulus between him and his *kraal*."

"Do you know anything about him, Noie?"

"Yes, Lady, I have seen him in Zululand. He is a bad man. They call him there 'Lion,' not because he is brave, but because he hunts and springs by night."

"Just what I should have thought of him," answered Rachel, "and we know that he is not brave," she added with a smile. "But never mind this jackal in a lion's hide; tell me your story, Noie, if you will, only speak low, for this tent is thin."

"Lady," said the girl, "you who were born white in body and in spirit, hear me. I am but half a Zulu. My father who died yesterday in the flesh, departing back to the world of ghosts, was of another people who live far to the north, a small people but a strong. They live among the trees, they worship trees; they die when their tree dies; they are dealers in dreams; they are the companions of ghosts, little men before whom the tribes tremble; who hate the sun, and dwell in the deep of the forest. Myself I do not know them; I have never seen them, but my father told me these things, and others that I may not repeat. When he was a young man my father fled from his people."

"Why?" asked Rachel, for the girl paused.

"Lady, I do not know; I think it was because he would have been their priest, or one of their priests, and he feared I think that he had seen a woman, a slave to them, whom therefore he might not marry. I think that woman was my mother. So he fled from them—with her, and came to live among the Zulus. He was a great doctor there in Chaka's time, not one of the *Abangomas*, not one of the 'Smellers-out-of-witches,' not a 'Bringer-down-to-death,' for like all his race he hated bloodshed. No, none of these things, but a doctor of medicines, a master of magic, an interpreter of dreams, a lord of wisdom; yes, it was his wisdom that made Chaka great, and when he withdrew it from him because of his cruelties, then Chaka died.

"Lady, Dingaan rules in Chaka's place, Dingaan who slew him, but although he had been Chaka's doctor, my father was spared because they feared him. I was the only child of my mother, but he took other wives after the Zulu fashion, not because he loved them, I think, but that he might not seem different to other men. So he grew great and rich, and lived in peace because they feared him. Lady, my father loved me, and to me alone he taught his language and his wisdom. I helped him with his medicines; I interpreted the dreams which he could not interpret, his blanket fell upon me. Often I was sought in marriage, but I did not wish to marry, Wisdom is my husband.

"There came an evil day; we knew that it must come, my father and I, and I wished to fly the land, but he could not do so because of his other wives and children. The maidens of my district were marshalled for the king to see. His eye fell upon me, and he thought me fair because I am different from Zulu women, and—you can guess. Yet I was saved, for the other doctors and the head wives of the king said that it was not wise that I should be taken into his house, I who knew too many secrets and could bewitch him if I willed, or prison him with drugs that leave no trace. So I escaped a while and was thankful. Now it came about that because he might not take me Dingaan began to think much of me, and to dream of me at nights. At last he asked me of my father, as a gift, not as a right, for so he thought that no ill would come with me. But I prayed my father to keep me from Dingaan, for I hated Dingaan, and told him that if I were sent to the king, I would poison him. My father listened to me because he loved me and could not bear to part with me, and said Dingaan nay. Now Dingaan grew very angry and asked counsel of his other doctors, but they would give him none because they feared my father. Then he asked counsel of that white man, Hishmel, who is called the Lion, and who is much at the *kraal* of Umgungundhlovu."

"Ah!" said Rachel, "now I understand why he wished you to be killed."

"The white man, Hishmel, the jackal in a lion's skin, as you named him, laughed at Dingaan's fears. He said to him, 'It is of the father, Seyapi, you should be afraid. He has the magic, not the girl. Kill the father, and his house, and take the daughter whom your heart desires, and be happy.'

"So spoke Hishmel, and Dingaan thought his counsel good, and paid him for it with the teeth of elephants, and certain women for whom he asked. Now my father foreboded ill, and I also, for both of us had dreamed a dream. Still we did not fly until the slayers were almost at the gates, because of his other wives and his children. Nor, save for them would he have fled then, or I either, but would have died after the fashion of his people, as he did at last."

"The White Death?" queried Rachel.

"Yes, Lady, the White Death. Still in the end we fled, thinking to gain the protection of the white men down yonder. I went first to escape the king's men who had orders to take me alive and bring me to him, that is why we were not together at the end. Lady, you know the rest. Hishmel doubtless had seen you, and thinking that the *Impi* would kill you, came to warn you. Then we met just as I was about to die, though perhaps not by that soldier's spear, as you thought. I have spoken."

"What message came to you when you knelt down before your dead father?" asked Rachel for the second time, since on this point she was intensely curious.

Again that inscrutable look gathered on the girl's face, and she answered.

"Did I not tell you it was for my ear alone, O *Inkosazana-y-Zoola*? I dare not say it, be satisfied. But this I may say. Your fate and mine are intertwined; yours and mine and another's, for our spirits are sisters which have dwelt together in past days."

"Indeed," said Rachel smiling, for she who had mixed with them from her childhood knew something of the mysticism of the natives, also that it was often nonsense. "Well, Noie, I love you, I know not why. Perhaps, for all you have suffered. Yet I say to you that if you wish to remain my sister in the spirit, you had better separate from me in the flesh. That jackal man knows your secret, girl, and soon or late will loose the *assegai* on you."

"Doubtless," she answered, "doubtless many things will come about. But they are doomed to come about. Whether I go or whether I stay they will happen. Say you therefore, Lady, and I will obey. Shall I go or shall I stay, or shall I die before your eyes?"

"It is on your own head," answered Rachel shrugging her shoulders.

"Nay, nay, Lady, you forget, it is on yours also, seeing that if I stay I may bring peril on you and your house. Have you then no order for me?"

"Noie, I have answered—one. Judge you."

"I will not judge. Let Heaven-above judge. Lady, give me a hair from your head."

Rachel plucked out the hair and handed it, a shining thread of gold, to Noie who drew one from her own dark tresses, and laid them side by side.

"See," she said, "they are of the same length. Now, without the wind blows gently; come then to the door of the tent, and I will throw these two hairs into the wind. If that which is black floats first to the ground, then I stay, if that which is golden, then I go to seek my hair. Is it agreed?"

"It is agreed."

So the two girls went to the entrance of the tent, and Noie with a swift motion tossed up the hairs. As it happened one of those little eddies of wind which are common in South Africa, caught them, causing them to rise almost perpendicularly into the air. At a certain height, about forty feet, the supporting wind seemed to fail, that is so far as the hair from Noie's head was concerned, for there it floated high above them like a black thread in the sunlight, and gently by slow degrees came to the earth just at their feet. But the hair from Rachel's head, being caught by the fringe of the whirlwind, was borne upwards and onwards very swiftly, until at length it vanished from their sight.

"It seems that I stay," said Noie.

"Yes," answered Rachel. "I am very glad; also if any evil comes of it we are not to blame, the wind is to blame."

"Yes, Lady, but what makes the wind to blow?"

Again Rachel shrugged her shoulders, and asked a question in her turn.

"Whither has that hair of mine been borne, Noie?"

"I do not know, Lady. Perhaps my father's spirit took it for his own ends. I think so. I think it went northwards. At any rate when mine fell, it was snatched away, was it not? And yet they both floated up together. I think that one day you will follow that hair of yours, Lady, follow it to the land where great trees whisper secrets to the night."

## Chapter 7

# The Message of the King

So it chanced that Noie became a member of the Dove household. For obvious reasons she changed her name, and thenceforward was called Nonha. Also it happened that Mr. Dove abandoned his idea of settling as a missionary in Zululand, and instead, took up his residence at this beautiful spot. He called it Ramah because it was a place of weeping, for here all the family and dependents of Seyapi had been destroyed by the spear. Mrs. Dove thought it an ill-omened name enough, but after her manner gave way to her husband in the matter.

"I think there will be more weeping here before everything is done," she said.

Rachel answered, however, that it was as good as any other, since names could alter nothing. Here, then, at Ramah, Mr. Dove built him a house on that knoll where first he had pitched his camp. It was a very good house after its fashion, for, as has been said, he did not lack for means, and was, moreover, clever in such matters. He hired a mason who had drifted to Natal to cut stone, of which a plenty lay at hand, and two half-breed carpenters to execute the wood-work, whilst the Kaffirs thatched the whole as only they can do. Then he set to work upon a church, which was placed on the crest of the opposite knoll where the white man, Ishmael, had appeared on the evening of their arrival. Like the house, it was excellent of its sort, and when at length it was finished after more than a year of labour, Mr. Dove felt a proud man.

Indeed at Ramah he was happier than he had ever been since he landed upon the shores of Africa, for now at length his dream seemed to be in the way of realisation. Very soon a considerable native village sprang up around him, peopled almost entirely by remnants of the Natal tribes whom Chaka had destroyed and who were but too glad to settle under the aegis of the white man, especially when they discovered how good he was. Of the doctrines which he preached to them day and night, most of them, it is true, did not understand much. Still they accepted them as the price of being allowed "to live in his shadow," but in the vast majority of cases they sturdily refused to put away all wives but one, as he earnestly exhorted them to do.

At first he wished to eject them from the settlement in punishment of this sin, but when it came to the point they absolutely refused to go, demonstrating to him that they had as much right to live there as he had, an argument that he was unable to controvert. So he was obliged to submit to the presence of this abomination, which he did in the hope that in time their hard hearts would be softened.

"Continue to preach to us, O Shouter," they said, "and we will listen. Mayhap in years to come we shall learn to think as you do. Meanwhile give us space to consider the point."

So he continued to preach, and contented himself with baptising the children and very old people who took no more wives. Except on this one point, however, they got on excellently together. Indeed, never since Chaka broke upon them like a destroying demon had these poor folk been so happy. The missionary imported ploughs and taught them to improve their agriculture, so that ere long this rich, virgin soil brought forth abundantly. Their few cattle multiplied also in an amazing fashion, as did their families, and soon they were as prosperous as they had been in the good old days before they knew the Zulu *assegai*, especially as, to their amazement, the Shouter never took from them even a calf or a bundle of corn by way of tax. Only the shadow of that Zulu *assegai* still lay upon them, for if Chaka was dead Dingaan ruled a few miles away across the Tugela. Moreover, hearing of the rise of this new town, and of certain strange matters connected with it, he sent spies to inspect and enquire. The spies returned and reported that there dwelt in it only a white medicine-man with his wife, and a number of Natal Kaffirs. Also they reported in great detail many wonderful stories concerning the beautiful maiden with a high name who passed as the white teacher's daughter, and who had already become the subject of so much native talk and rumour. On learning all these things Dingaan despatched an embassy, who delivered this message:

"I, Dingaan, king of the Zulus, have heard that you, O White Shouter, have built a town upon my borders, and peopled it with the puppies of the jackals whom Chaka hunted. I send to you now to say that you and your jackals shall have peace from me so long as you harbour none of my runaways, but if I find but one of them there, then an *Impi* shall wipe you out. I hear also that there dwells with you a beautiful white maiden said to be your daughter, who is known, throughout the land as *Inkosazana-y-Zoola*. Now that is the name of our Spirit who, the doctors say, is also white, and it is strange to us that this maiden should bear that great name. Some of the *Isanusis*, the prophetesses, declare that she is our Spirit in the flesh, but that meat sticks in my throat, I cannot swallow it. Still, I invite this maiden to visit me that I may see her and judge of her, and I swear to you, and to her, by the ghosts of my ancestors, that no harm shall come to her then or at any time. He who so much as lays a finger upon her shall die, he and all his house. Because of her name, which I am told she has borne from a child, all the territories of the Zulus are her *kraal* and all the thousands of the Zulus are her servants. Yea, because of her high name I give to her power of life and death wherever men obey my word, and for an offering I send to her twelve of my royal white cattle and a bull, also an ox trained to riding. When she visits me let her ride upon the white ox that she may be known, but let no man come with her, for among the people of the Zulus she must be attended by Zulus only. I have spoken. I pray that she who is named Princess of the Zulus will appear before my messengers and acknowledge the gift of the King of the Zulus, that they may see her in the flesh and make report of her to me."

Now when Mr. Dove had received this message, one evening at sundown, he went into the house and repeated it to Rachel, for it puzzled him much, and he knew not what to answer.

Rachel in her turn took counsel with Noie who was hidden, away lest some of the embassy should see and recognise her.

"Speak with the messengers," said Noie, "it is well to have power among the Zulus. I, who have some knowledge of this business, say, speak with them alone, and speak softly, saying that one day you will come."

So having explained the matter to her father, and obtained his consent, Rachel, who desired to impress these savages, threw a white shawl about her, as Noie instructed her to do. Then, letting her long, golden hair hang down, she went out alone carrying a light *assegai* in her hand, to the place where the messengers, six of them, and those who had driven the cattle from Zululand, were encamped in the guest *kraal*, at the gate of which, as it chanced, lay a great boulder of rock. On this boulder she took her stand, unobserved, waiting there till the full moon shone out from behind a dark cloud, turning her white robe to silver. Now of a sudden the messengers who were seated together, talking and taking snuff, looked up and saw her.

"*Inkosazana-y-Zoola*!" exclaimed one of them, rising, whereon they all sprang to their feet and perceiving this beautiful and mysterious figure, by a common impulse lifted their right arms and gave to her what no woman had ever received before—the royal salute.

*"Bayète!"* they cried, *"Bayète!"* then stood silent.

"I hear you," said Rachel, who spoke their tongue as well as she did her own. "It has been reported to me that you wished to see me, O Mouths of the King. Behold I am pleased to appear before you. What would you of *Inkosazana-y-Zoola,* O Mouths of the King?"

Then their spokesman, an old man of high rank, with a withered hand, stepped forward from the line of his companions, stared at her for a while, and saluted again.

"Lady," he said humbly, "Lady or Spirit, we would know how thou earnest by that great name of thine."

"It was given me as a child far away from here," she answered, "because in a mighty tempest the lightnings turned aside and smote me not; because the waters raged yet drowned me not; because the lions slept with me yet harmed me not. It came to me from the high Heaven that was my friend. I do not know how it came."

"We have heard the story," answered the old man (which indeed they had with many additions), "and we believe. We believe that the Heavens above gave thee their own name which is the name of the Spirit of our people. That Spirit I have seen in a dream, and she was like to thee, O *Inkosazana-y-Zoola.*"

"It may be so, Mouth of the King, still I am woman, not spirit."

"Yet in every woman there dwells a spirit, or so we believe, and in thee a great one, or so we have heard and believe, O Lady of the Heavens. To thee, then, again we repeat the words of Dingaan and of his council which today we have said in the ears of him who thinks himself thy father. To thee the roads are open; thine are the cattle and the *kraal*s; here is an earnest of them. Thine are the lives of men. Command now, if thou wilt, that one of us be slain before thee, and whilst thou watchest, he shall look his last upon the moon."

"I hear you," said Rachel, quietly, "but I seek the life of none who are good. I thank the King for his gift; I wish the King well. I remember that life and death lie in my hands. Say these words to the King."

"We will say them, but wilt thou not come, O Lady, as the King desires? A regiment shall meet thee on the river bank and lead thee to his house. Unharmed shalt thou come, unharmed shalt thou return, and what thou askest that shall be given thee."

"One day, perchance, I will come, but not now. Go in peace, O Mouths of the King."

As she spoke another dark cloud floated across the moon, and when it had passed away she stood no more upon the rock. Then, seeing that she was gone, those messengers gathered up their spears and mats, and returned swiftly to Zululand.

When she readied the house again Rachel told her father and mother all that had passed, laughing as she spoke.

"It seems scarcely right, my dear," said Mr. Dove, when she had done. "Those benighted heathens will really believe that you are something unearthly."

"Then let them," she answered. "It can do no one any harm, and the power of life and death with the rest of it, unless it was all talk as I suspect, might be very useful one day. Who knows? And now the Princess of the Heavens will go and set the supper, as Noie—I beg pardon, Nonha—is off duty for the present."

Afterwards she asked Noie who was the old man with a withered hand who had spoken as the "King's Mouth."

"Mopo[1] is his name, Mopo or Umbopo, none other, O Zoola," she answered. "It was he who stabbed T'Chaka, the Black One. It is said also that alone among men living, he has seen the White Spirit: the *Inkosazana*. Thrice he has seen her, or so goes the tale that my father, who knew everything, told to me. That is why Dingaan sent him here to make report of you." And she told her all the wonderful story of Mopo and of the death of T'Chaka, which Rachel treasured in her mind.

Such was Rachel's first introduction to the Zulus, an occasion on which her undoubted histrionic abilities stood her in good stead.

This matter of the embassy happened and in due course was almost forgotten, that is until a certain event occurred which brought it into mind. For some time, however, Rachel thought of it a good deal, wondering how it came about that her native name and the strange significance which they appeared to give to it had taken such a hold of the imagination of the Zulus. Ultimately she discovered that the white man, Ishmael, was the chief cause of these things. He had lived so long among savages that he had caught something of their mind and dark superstitions. To him, as to them, it seemed a marvellous thing that she should have acquired the title of the legendary Spirit of the Zulu people. The calm courage, too, so unusual in a woman, which she showed when she shot the warrior, and at the risk of her own life saved that of the girl, Noie, impressed him as something almost ultra-human, especially when he remembered his

1. For the history of Mopo, see *Nada the Lily*.

own conduct on that occasion. All of this story, of course, he did not tell to the Zulus for he feared lest they should take vengeance for his share in it. But of Rachel he discoursed to the King and his *indunas*, or great men, as a white witch-doctoress of super-natural power, whose name showed that she was mixed up with the fortunes of the race. Therefore, in the end, Dingaan sent Mopo, "he who knew the Spirit," to make report of her.

When he was not absent upon his hunting or trading expeditions, Ishmael visited Ramah a great deal and, as Rachel soon discovered, not without an object. Indeed, almost from the first, her feminine instincts led her to suspect that this man who, notwithstanding his good looks, repelled her so intensely, was falling in love with her, which in truth he had done once and for all at their first meeting. In the beginning he did not, it is true, say much that could be so interpreted, but his whole attitude towards her suggested it, as did other things. For instance, when he came to visit the Doves, he discarded his garments of hide, including the picturesque zebra-skin trousers, and appeared dressed in smart European clothes which he had contrived to obtain from Durban, and a large hat with a white ostrich feather, that struck Rachel as even more ludicrous than the famous trousers. Also he was continuously sending presents of game and of skins, or of rare *karosses*, that is, fur rugs, which he ordered to be delivered to her personally—tokens, all of them, that she could not misunderstand. Her father, however, misunderstood them persistently, although her mother saw something of the truth, and did her best to shield her from attentions which she knew to be unwelcome. Mr. Dove believed that it was his company which Ishmael sought. Indeed in this matter the man was very clever, contriving to give the clergyman the impression that he required spiritual instruction and comfort, which, of course, he found forthcoming in an abundant supply. When Mrs. Dove remonstrated, saying that she misdoubted her of him and his character, her husband answered obstinately, that it was his duty to turn a sinner from his way, and declined to pursue the conversation. So Ishmael continued to come.

For her part Rachel did her best to avoid him, instructing Noie to keep a constant look-out both with her eyes and through the Kaffirs, and to warn her of his advent. Then she would slip away into the bush or down to the seashore, and remain there till he was gone, or if he came when she could not do so, in the evening for instance, would keep Noie at her side, and on the first opportunity retire to her own room.

Now the result of this method of self-protection was to cause

Ishmael to hate Noie as bitterly as she hated him. He guessed that the girl knew the dreadful truth about him; that it was he, and no other, who had counselled Dingaan to kill her father and all his family, and take her by force into his house, and although she said nothing of it, he suspected that she had told everything to Rachel. Moreover, it was she who always thwarted him, who prevented him time upon time from having a single word alone with her mistress. Therefore he determined to be revenged upon Noie whenever an opportunity occurred.

But as yet he could find none, since if he were to tell the Zulus that she still lived, and cause her to be killed or taken away, he was sure that it would mean a final breach with the Dove family, all of whom had learned to love this beautiful orphan maid. So he nursed his rage in secret.

Meanwhile his passion increased daily, burning ever more fiercely for its continued repression, until at length the chance for which he had waited so long came to him.

Having become aware of Rachel's habit of slipping away whenever he appeared, he showed himself on horseback at a little distance, then waited a while and, instead of going up to the mission station, rode round it, and hid in some bush whence he could command a view of the surrounding country. Presently he saw Rachel, who was alone, for she had not waited to call Noie, hurrying towards the seashore, along the edge of that *kloof* down which ran the stream where the crocodiles lived. Presently, when she had gone too far to return to the house if she caught sight of him, he followed after her, and, leaving his horse, at last came up with her seated on a rock by the pool in which she had bathed on the morning of the massacre.

Walking softly in his *veldschoens*, or shoes made of raw hide, on the sand, Rachel knew nothing of his coming until his shadow fell upon her. Then she sprang up and saw him, smiling and bowing, the ostrich-plume hat in his hand. Her first impulse was to run away, but recovering herself she nodded in a friendly fashion, and bade him "Good day," adding:

"What are you doing here, Mr. Ishmael, hunting?"

"Yes," he answered, "that's it. Hunting you. It has been a long chase, but I have caught you at last."

"Really, I am not a wild creature, Mr. Ishmael," she said indignantly.

"No," he answered, "you are more beautiful and more dangerous than any wild creature."

Rachel looked at him. Then she made, as though she would pass him, saying that she was going home. Now Ishmael stood between two rocks filling the only egress from this place.

He stretched out his arms so that his fingers touched the rocks on either side, and said:

"You can't. You must listen to me first. I came here to say what I have wanted to tell you for a long time. I love you, and I ask you to marry me."

"Indeed," she replied, setting her face. "How can that be? I understood that you were already married—several times over."

"Who told you that?" he asked, angrily. "I know—that accursed little witch, Noie."

"Don't speak any ill of Noie, please; she is my friend."

"Then you have a liar for your friend. Those women are only my servants."

"It doesn't matter to me what they are, Mr. Ishmael. I have no wish to know your private affairs. Shall we stop this talk, which is not pleasant?"

"No," he answered. "I tell you that I love you and I mean to marry you, with your will or without it. Let it be with your will, Rachel," he added, pleadingly, "for I will make you a good husband. Also I am well-born, much better than you think, and I am rich, rich enough to take you out of this country, if you like. I have thousands of cattle, and a great deal of money put by, good English gold that I have got from the sale of ivory. You shall come with me from among all these savage people back to England, and live as you like."

"Thank you, but I prefer the savages, as you seem to have done until now. No, do not try to touch me; you know that I can defend myself if I choose," and she glanced at the pistol which she always carried in that wild land, "I am not afraid of you, Mr. Ishmael; it is you who are afraid of me."

"Perhaps I am," he exclaimed, "because those Zulus are right, you are *tagati*, an enchantress, not like other women, white or black. If it were not so, would you have driven me mad as you have done? I tell you I can't sleep for thinking of you. Oh! Rachel, Rachel, don't be angry with me. Have pity on me. Give me some hope. I know that my life has been rough in the past, but I will become good again for your sake and live like a Christian. But if you refuse me, if you send me back to hell—then you shall learn what I can be."

"I know what you are, Mr. Ishmael, and that is quite enough. I do not wish to be unkind, or to say anything that will pain you, but please go away, and never try to speak to me again like this, as it is quite useless. You must understand that I will never marry you, never."

"Are you in love with somebody else?" he asked hoarsely, and at the question, do what she would to prevent it, Rachel coloured a little.

"How can I be in love here, unless it were with a dream?"

"A dream, a dream of a man you mean. Well, don't let him cross my path, or it will soon be the dream of a ghost. I tell you I'd kill him. If I can't have you, no one else shall. Do you understand?"

"I understand that I am tired of this. Let me go home, please."

"Home! Soon you will have no home to go to except mine—that is, if you don't change your mind about me. I have power here—don't you understand? I have power."

As he spoke these words the man looked so evil that Rachel shivered a little. But she answered boldly enough:

"I understand that you have no power at all against me; no one has. It is I who have the power."

"Yes, because as I said, you are *tagati*, but there are others——"

As these words passed his lips someone slipped by him. Starting back, he saw that it was Noie, draped in her usual white robe, for nothing would induce her to wear European clothes. Passing him as though she saw him not, she went to Rachel and said:

"*Inkosazana*, I was at my work in the house yonder and I thought that I heard you calling me down here by the seashore, so I came. Is it your pleasure that I should accompany you home?"

"For instance," he went on furiously, "there is that black slut whom you are fond of. Well, if I can't hurt you, I can hurt her. Daughter of Seyapi, you know how runaways die in Zululand, or if you don't you shall soon learn. I will pay you back for all your tricks," and he stopped, choking with rage.

Noie looked him up and down with her soft, dreamy brown eyes.

"Do you think so, Night-prowler?" she asked. "Do you think that what you did to the father and his house, you will do to the daughter also? Well, it is strange, but last night, just before the cock crew, I sat by Seyapi's grave, and he spoke to me of you, White Man. Listen, now, and I will tell you what he said," and stepping forward she whispered in his ear.

Rachel, watching, saw the man's swarthy face turn pale as he hearkened, then he lifted his hand as though to strike her, let it fall again, and muttering curses in English and in Zulu, turned and walked, or rather staggered away.

"What did you tell him, Noie?" asked Rachel.

"Never mind, Zoola," she answered. "Perhaps the truth; perhaps what came into my mind. At any rate I frightened him away. He was making love to you, was he not, the low *silwana* (wild beast)? Ah! I thought so, for that he has wished to do for long. And he threatened, did he not? Well, you are right; he cannot hurt you at all, and me only a little, I think. But he is very dangerous and very strong, and can hurt others. If your father is wise he will leave this place, Zoola."

"I think so too," answered Rachel. "Let us go home and tell him so."

## Chapter 8

# Mr. Dove Visits Ishmael

When Rachel and Noie reached the house, which they did not do for some time, as they waited to make sure that Ishmael had really gone, it was to see the man himself riding away from its gate.

"Be prepared," said Noie; "I think that he has been here before us to pour poison into your father's ears."

So it proved to be, indeed, for on the *stoep* or veranda they found Mr. Dove walking up and down evidently much disturbed in mind.

"What is all this trouble, Rachel?" he asked. "What have you done to Mr. Smith"—for Mr. Dove in pursuance of the suggestion made by the man, had adopted that name for him which he considered less peculiar than Ishmael. "He has been here much upset, declaring that you have used him cruelly, and that Nonha threatened him with terrible things in the future, of which, of course, she can know nothing."

"Well, father, if you wish to hear," answered Rachel, "Mr. Ishmael, or Mr. Smith as you call him, has been asking me to marry him, and when I refused, as of course I did, behaved very unpleasantly."

"Indeed, Rachel. I gathered from him that something of the sort had happened, only his story is that it was you who behaved unpleasantly, speaking to him as though he were dirt. Now, Rachel, of course I do not want you to marry this person, in fact, I should dislike it, although I have seen a great change for the better in him lately—I mean spiritually, of course—and an earnest repentance for the errors of his past life. All I mean is that the proffered affection of an honest man should not be met with scorn and sharp words."

Up to this point Rachel endured the lecture in silence, but now she could bear no more.

"Honest man!" she exclaimed. "Father, are you deaf and blind, or only so good yourself that you cannot see evil in others? Do you know that it was this 'honest man' who brought about the murder of all Noie's people in order that he might curry favour with the Zulus?"

Mr. Dove started, and turning, asked:

"Is that so, Nonha?"

"It is so, Teacher," answered Noie, "although I have never spoken of it to you. Afterwards I will tell you the story, if you wish."

"And do you know," went on Rachel, "why he will never let you visit his *kraal* among the hills yonder? Well, I will tell you. It is because this 'honest man,' who wishes me to marry him, keeps his Kaffir wives and children there!"

"Rachel!" replied her father, in much distress, "I will never believe it; you are only repeating native scandal. Why, he has often spoken to me with horror of such things."

"I daresay he has, father. Well, now, I ask you to judge for yourself. Take a guide and start two hours before daybreak tomorrow morning to visit that *kraal*, and see if what I say is not true."

"I will, indeed," exclaimed Mr. Dove, who was now thoroughly aroused, for it was conduct of this sort that had caused his bitter quarrel with the first settlers in Natal. "I cannot believe the story, Rachel, I really cannot; but I promise you that if I should find cause to do so, the man shall never put foot in my house again."

"Then I think that I am rid of him," said Rachel, with a sigh of relief, "only be careful, dear, that he does not do you a mischief, for such men do not like to be found out." Then she left the *stoep*, and went to tell her mother all that had happened.

When she had heard the story, Mrs. Dove, who detested Ishmael as much as her daughter did, tried to persuade her husband not to visit his *kraal*, saying that it would only breed a feud, and that under the circumstances, it would be easy to forbid him the house upon other grounds. But Mr. Dove, obstinate as usual, refused to listen to her, saying that he would not judge the man without evidence, and that of the natives could not be relied on. Also, if the tale were true, it was his duty as his spiritual adviser to remonstrate with him.

So his poor wife gave up arguing, as she always did, and long before dawn on the following morning, Mr. Dove, accompanied by two guides, departed upon his errand.

After he had ridden some twelve miles across the plain which lay behind Ramah, just at daybreak, he reached a pass or *nek* between two swelling hills, beyond which the guides said lay the *kraal* that was called Mafooti. Presently he saw it, a place situated in a cup-like valley, chosen evidently because the approaches to it were easy to defend. On a knoll in the centre of this rich valley stood the *kraal*, a small native town surrounded by walls, and stone enclosures full of cattle. As they approached the *kraal*, from its main entrance issued four or five good-looking native women, one of them accompanied by a boy, and all carrying hoes in their hands, for they were going out at sunrise to work in the mealie fields. When they saw Mr. Dove they stood still, staring at him, till he called to them not to be afraid, and riding up, asked them who they were.

"We are of the number of the wives of Ibubesi, the Lion," answered their spokeswoman, who held the little boy by the hand.

"Do you mean the *Umlungu* (that is, the white man), Ishmael?" he asked again.

"Whom else should we mean?" she answered. "I am his head wife, now that he has put away old Mami, and this is his son. If the light were stronger you would see that he is almost white," she added, with pride.

Mr. Dove knew not what to answer; this intelligence overwhelmed him, and he sat silent on his horse. The wives of Ishmael prepared to pass on to the mealie fields, then stopped, and began to whisper together. At length the mother of the boy turned and addressed him, while the others crowded behind her to listen.

"We desire to ask you a question, Teacher," she said, somewhat shyly, for evidently they knew well enough who he was. "Is it true that we are to have a new sister?"

"A new sister! What do you mean?" asked Mr. Dove.

"We mean, Teacher," she replied smiling, "that we have heard that Ibubesi is courting the beautiful Zoola, the daughter of your head wife, and we thought that perhaps you had come to arrange about the cattle that he must pay for her. Doubtless if she is so fair, it will be a whole herd."

This was too much, even for Mr. Dove.

"How dare you talk so, you heathen hussies?" he gasped. "Where is the white man?"

"Teacher," she replied with indignation, and drawing herself up, "why do you call us bad names? We are respectable women, the wives of one husband, as respectable as your own, although not so numerous, or so we hear from Ibubesi. If you desire to see him, he is in the big hut, yonder, with our youngest sister, she whom he married last month. We wish you good day, as we go to hoe our lord's fields, and we hope that when she comes, the *Inkosazana*, your daughter, will not be as rude as you are, for if so, how shall we love her as we wish to do?" Then wrapping her blanket round her with a dignified air, the offended lady stalked off, followed by her various "sisters."

As for Mr. Dove, who for once in his life was in a towering rage, he cut his horse viciously with the *sjambok*, or hippopotamus-hide whip, which he carried, and followed by his guides, galloped forward to a big hut in the centre of the *kraal*.

Apparently Ishmael heard the sound of his horse's hoofs, for as the missionary was dismounting he crawled out of the bee-hole of the hut upon his hands and knees, as a Kaffir does, followed by a young woman in the lightest of attire, who was yawning as though she had just been aroused from sleep. What is more, except for the colour of his skin, he *was* a Kaffir and nothing else, for his costume consisted of a skin *moocha* such as the natives wear, and a fur *kaross* thrown over his shoulders. Straightening himself, Ishmael saw for the first time who was his visitor. His jaw dropped, and he uttered an ejaculation that need not be recorded, then stood silent. Mr. Dove was silent also; for his wrath would not allow him to speak.

"How do you do, sir?" Ishmael jerked out at last. "You are an early visitor, and find me somewhat unprepared. If I had known that you were coming I would"—then suddenly he remembered his attire, or the lack of it, also his companion who was leaning on his shoulder, and peeping at the white man over it. Drawing the *kaross* tightly about him, he gave the poor girl a backward kick, and with a Kaffir oath bade her begone, then went on hurriedly: "I am afraid my dress is not quite what you are accustomed to, but among these poor heathens I find it necessary to conform more or less to their ways in order to gain their confidence and—um—affection. Will you come into the hut? My servant there will get you some *tywala* (Kaffir beer)—I mean some *amasi* (curdled milk) at once, and I will have a calf killed for breakfast."

Mr. Dove could bear it no longer.

"Ishmael, or Smith, or Ibubesi—whichever name you may prefer," he broke out, "do not lie to me about your servant, for now I know all the truth, which I refused to believe when my daughter and Nonha told it me. You are a black-hearted villain. But yesterday you dared to come and ask Rachel to marry you, and now I find that you are living—oh! I cannot say it, it makes me ashamed of my race. Listen to me, sir. If ever you dare to set foot in Ramah again, or to speak to my wife and daughter, the Kaffirs shall whip you off the place. Indeed," he added, shaking his *sjambok* in Ishmael's face, "although I am an older man than you are, were it not for my office I would give you the thrashing you deserve."

At first Ishmael had shrunk beneath this torrent of invective, but the threat of violence roused his fierce nature. His face grew evil, and his long black hair and beard bristled with wrath.

"You had best get out of this, you prayer-snuffling old humbug," he said savagely, "for if you stop much longer I will make you sing another tune. We have sea-cow whips here, too, and you shall learn what a hiding means, such a hiding that your own family won't know you, if you live to get back to them. Look here, I offered to marry your daughter on the square, and I meant what I said. I'd have got rid of all this black baggage, and she should have been the only one. Well, I'll marry her yet, only now she'll just take her place with the others. We are all one flesh and blood, black and white, ain't we? I have often heard you preach it. So what will she have to complain of?" he sneered. "She can go and hoe mealies like the rest."

As this brutal talk fell upon his ears Mr. Dove's reason departed from him entirely. After all, he was an English gentleman first, and a clergyman afterwards; also he loved his daughter, and to hear her spoken of like this was intolerable to him, as it would have been to any father. Lifting the *sjambok* he cut Ishmael across the mouth so sharply that the blood came from his lips, then suddenly remembering that this deed would probably mean his death, stood still awaiting the issue. As it chanced it did not, for the man, like most brutes and bullies, was a coward, as Rachel had already found out. Obeying his first impulse he sprang at the clergyman with an oath, then seeing that his two guides, who carried *assegai*s, had ranged themselves beside him, checked himself, for he feared lest those spears should pierce his heart.

"You are in my house," he said, wiping the blood from his beard, "and an old man, so I can't kill you as I would anyone else. But you have made me your enemy now, you fool, and others can. I have protected you so far for your daughter's sake, but I won't do it any longer. You think of that when your time comes."

"My time, like yours, will come when God wills," answered Mr. Dove unflinchingly, "not when you or anyone else wills. I do not fear you in the least. Still, I am sorry that I struck you, it was a sin of which I repent as I pray that you may repent."

Then he mounted his horse and rode away from the *kraal* Mafooti.

********

When Mr. Dove reached Ramah he only said to Rachel that what she had heard was quite true, and that he had forbidden Ishmael the house. Of course, however, Noie soon learnt the whole story from the Kaffir guides, and repeated it to her mistress. To his wife, on the other hand, he told everything, with the result that she was very much disturbed. She pointed out to him that this white outcast was a most dangerous man, who would certainly be revenged upon them in one way or another. Again she implored him, as she had often done before, to leave these savage countries wherein he had laboured for all the best years of his life, saying that it was not right that he should expose their daughter to the risks of them.

"But," answered her husband, "you have often told me that you were sure no harm would come to Rachel, and I think that, too."

"Yes, dear, I am sure; still, for many reasons it does not seem right to keep her here." She did not add, poor, unselfish woman, that there was another who should be considered as well as Rachel.

"How can I go away," he went on excitedly, "just when all the seed that I have sown is ripening to harvest? If I did so, my work would be utterly lost, and my people relapse into barbarism again. I am not afraid of this man, or of anything that he can do to my body, but if I ran away from him it would be injuring my soul, and what account should I give of my cowardice when my time comes? Do you go, my love, and take Rachel with you if you wish, leaving me to finish my work alone."

But now, as before, Mrs. Dove would not go, and Rachel, when she was asked, shrugged her shoulders and answered laughing that she was not afraid of anybody or anything, and, except for her mother's sake, did not care whether she went or stayed. Certainly she would not leave her, nor, she added, did she wish to say goodbye to Africa.

When she was asked why, she replied vaguely that she had grown up there, and it was her home. But her mother, watching her, knew well enough that she had another reason, although no word of it every passed her lips. In Africa she had met Richard Darrien as a child, and in Africa and nowhere else she believed she would meet him again as a woman.

The weeks and months went by, bringing to the Ramah household no sight or tidings of the white man, Ishmael. They heard through the Kaffirs, indeed, that although he still kept his *kraal* at Mafooti, he himself had gone away on some trading journey far to the north, and did not expect to return for a year, news at which everyone rejoiced, except Noie, who shook her wise little head and said nothing.

So all fear of the man gradually died away, and things were very peaceful and prosperous at Ramah.

In fact this quiet proved to be but the lull before the storm.

One day, about eight months after Mr. Dove had visited the *kraal* Mafooti, another embassy came to Rachel from the Zulu king, Dingaan, bringing with it a present of more white cattle. She received them as she had done before, at night and alone, for they refused to speak to her in the presence of other people.

In substance their petition was the same that it had been before, namely, that she would visit Zululand, as the king and his *indunas* desired her counsel upon an important matter. When asked what this matter was they either were, or pretended to be, ignorant, saying that it had not been confided to them. Thereon she said that if Dingaan chose to submit the question to her by messenger, she would give him her opinion on it, but that she could not come to his *kraal*. They asked why, seeing that the whole nation would guard her, and no hair of her head be harmed.

"Because I am a child in the house of my people, and they will not allow me to leave even for a day," she answered, thinking that this reply would appeal to a race who believe absolutely in obedience to parents and every established authority.

"Is it so?" remarked the old *induna* who spoke as Dingaan's Mouth—not Mopo, but another. "Now, how can the *Inkosazana-y-Zoola*, before whom a whole nation will bow, be in bonds to a white *Umfundusi*, a mere sky-doctor? Shall the wide heavens obey a cloud?"

"If they are bred of that cloud," retorted Rachel.

"The heavens breed the cloud, not the cloud the heavens," answered the *induna* aptly.

Now it occurred to Rachel that this thing was going further than it should. To be set up as a kind of guardian spirit to the Zulus had seemed a very good joke, and naturally appealed to the love of power which is common to women. But when it involved, at any rate in the eyes of that people, dominion over her own parents, the joke was, she felt, becoming serious. So she determined suddenly to bring it to an end.

"What mean you, Messenger of the King?" she asked. "I am but the child of my parents, and the parents are greater than the child, and must be obeyed of her."

"*Inkosazana*," answered the old man with a deprecatory smile, "if it pleases you to tell us such tales, our ears must listen, as if it pleased you to order us to be killed, we must be killed. But learn that we know the truth. We know how as a child you came down from above in the lightning, and how these white people with whom you dwell found you lying in the mist on the mountain top, and took you to their home in place of a babe whom they had buried."

"Who told you that story?" asked Rachel amazed.

"It was revealed to the council of the doctors, Lady."

"Then that was revealed which is not true. I was born as other women are, and my name of 'Lady of the Heavens' came to me by chance, as by chance I resemble the Spirit of your people."

"We hear you," answered the "Mouth" politely. "You were born as other women are, by chance you had your high name, by chance you are tall and fair and golden-haired like the Spirit of our people. We hear you."

Then Rachel gave it up.

"Bear my words to the King," she said, and they rose, saluted her with a *Bayète*, that royal salute which never before had been given to woman, and departed.

When they had gone Rachel went into supper and told her parents all the story. Mr. Dove, now that she seemed to take a serious view of the matter, affected to treat it as absurd, although when she had laughed, his attitude, it may be remembered, was different. He talked of the silly Zulu superstitions, showed how they had twisted up the story of the death of her baby brother, and her escape from the flood in the Umtavuna river, into that which they had narrated to her. He even suggested that the whole thing was nonsense, part of some political move to enable the King, or a party in the state, to declare that they had with them the word of their traditional spirit and oracle.

Mrs. Dove, however, who that night was strangely depressed and uneasy, thought far otherwise. She pointed out that they were playing with vast and cruel forces, and that whatever these people exactly believed about Rachel, it was a dreadful thing for a girl to be put in a position in which the lives of hundreds might hang upon her nod.

"Yes, and," she added hysterically, "perhaps our own lives also—perhaps our own lives also!"

To change the conversation, which was growing painful, Rachel asked if anyone had seen Noie. Her father answered that two hours ago, just before the embassy arrived, he had met her going down to the banks of the stream, as he supposed, to gather flowers for the table. Then he began to talk about the girl, saying what a sweet creature she was, and how strange it seemed to him that although she appeared to accept all the doctrines of the Christian faith, as yet she had never consented to be baptised.

It was while he was speaking thus that Rachel suddenly observed her mother fall forward, so that her body rested on the table, as though a kind of fit had seized her. Rachel sprang towards her, but before she reached her she appeared to have quite recovered, only her face looked very white.

"What on earth is the matter, mother?"

"Oh! don't ask me," she answered, "a terrible thing, a sort of fancy that came to me from talking about those Zulus. I thought I saw this place all red with blood and tongues of fire licking it up. It went as quickly as it came, and of course I know that it is nonsense."

## Chapter 9

# The Taking of Noie

Presently Mrs. Dove, who seemed to have quite recovered from, her curious seizure, went to bed.

"I don't like it, father," said Rachel when the door had closed behind her. "Of course it is contrary to experience and all that, but I believe that mother is fore-sighted."

"Nonsense, dear, nonsense," said her father. "It is her Scotch superstition, that is all. We have been married for five-and-twenty years now, and I have heard this sort of thing again and again, but although we have lived in wild places where anything might happen to us, nothing out of the way ever has happened; in fact, we have always been most mercifully preserved."

"That's true, father, still I am not sure; perhaps because I am rather that way myself, sometimes. Thus I *know* that she is right about me; no harm will happen to me, at least no permanent harm. I feel that I shall live out my life, as I feel something else."

"What else, Rachel?"

"Do you remember the lad, Richard Darrien?" she asked, colouring a little.

"What? The boy who was with you that night on the island? Yes, I remember him, although I have not thought of him for years."

"Well, I feel that I shall see him again."

Mr. Dove laughed. "Is that all?" he said. "If he is still alive and in Africa, it wouldn't be very wonderful if you did, would it? And at any rate, of course, you will one day when we all cease to be alive. Really," he added with irritation, "there are enough bothers in life without rubbish of this kind, which comes from living among savages and absorbing their ideas. I am beginning to think that I shall have to give way and leave Africa, though it will break my heart just when, after all the striving, my efforts are being crowned with success."

"I have always told you, father, that I don't want to leave Africa, still, there is mother to be considered. Her health is not what it was."

"Well," he said impatiently, "I will talk to her and weigh the thing. Perhaps I shall receive guidance, though for my part I cannot see what it matters. We've got to die some time, and if necessary I prefer that it should be while doing my duty. 'Take no thought for the morrow, sufficient unto the day is the evil thereof,' has always been my motto, who am content with what it pleases Providence to send me."

Then Rachel, seeing no use in continuing the conversation, bade him good-night, and went to look for Noie, only to discover that she was not in the house. This disturbed her very much, although it occurred to her that she might possibly be with friends in the village, hiding till she was sure the Zulu embassy had gone. So she went to bed without troubling her father.

At daybreak next morning she rose, not having slept very well, and went out to look for the girl, without success, for no one had heard or seen anything of her. As she was returning to the house, however, she met a solitary Zulu, a dignified middle-aged man, whom she thought she recognised as one of the embassy, although of this she could not be sure, as she had only seen these people in the moonlight. The man, who was quite unarmed, except for a *kerry* which he carried, crouched down on catching sight of heir in token of respect. As she approached he rose, and gave her the royal salute. Then she was sure. "Speak," she said.

"*Inkosazana*," he answered humbly, "be not angry with me, I am Tamboosa, one of the King's *indunas*. You saw me with the others last night."

"I saw you."

"*Inkosazana*, there has been dwelling with you one Noie, the daughter of Seyapi the wizard, who with all his house was slain at this place by order of the King. She also should have been slain, but we have learned that you called down lightning from Heaven, and that with it you slew the soldier who had run her down, slew him and burned him up, as you had the right to do, and took the girl to be your slave, as you had the right to do."

"Speak on," said Rachel, showing none of the surprise which she felt.

"*Inkosazana*, we know that you have come to love this girl. Therefore, yesterday before we spoke with you we seized her as we were commanded, and hid her away, awaiting your answer to our message. Had you consented to visit the King at his Great Place, we would have let her go. But as you did not consent my companions have taken her to the King."

"An ill deed. What more, Tamboosa?"

"This; the King says by my mouth—Let the *Inkosazana* come and command, and her servant Noie shall go free and unharmed, for is she not a dog in her hut? But if she comes not and at once, then the girl dies."

"How know I that this tale is true, Tamboosa?" asked Rachel, controlling herself with an effort, for she loved Noie dearly.

The man turned towards some bushes that grew at a distance of about twenty paces, and cried: "Come hither."

Thereon from among the bushes where she lay hidden, rose a little maid of about fourteen, whom Rachel knew well as a girl that Noie often took with her to carry baskets and other things.

"Tell now the tale of the taking of Noie and deliver the message that she gave to you," commanded Tamboosa.

Thereon the trembling child began, and after the native fashion, suppressing no detail or circumstance, however small, narrated how the Zulus had surprised her and Noie while they were gathering flowers, and having bound their arms, had caused them to be hurried away unseen to some dense bush about four miles off. Here they had been kept hidden till in the night the embassy returned. Then they had spoken with Noie, who in the end called her and gave her a message. This was the message: "Say to the *Inkosazana* that the Zulus have caught me, and are taking me to Dingaan the King. Say that they declare that if she is pleased to come and speak the word, I shall be set free unharmed, that is, if she comes at once. But if she does not come, then I shall be killed. Say to her that I do not ask that she should come who am ready to die, and that though I believe that no harm will happen to her in Zululand, I think that she had better not come. Say that, living or dead, I love her."

Then the maid described how the embassy went on with Noie, leaving her in the charge of the man Tamboosa, who at the first break of dawn brought her back to Ramah, and made her hide in the bush.

Now Rachel had no more doubts. Clearly the tale was true, and the question was—what must be done? She thought a while, then bade Tamboosa and the child to follow her to the mission-house. On the *stoep* she found her father and mother sitting in the sun and drinking coffee, after the South African fashion.

"What is it?" asked Mr. Dove, looking at the man anxiously.

Rachel ordered him to repeat his story, and this he did, addressing Rachel alone, for of her father and mother he would take no notice. When he had done the child told her tale also.

"Go now, and wait without," said Rachel, when it was finished.

"*Inkosazana*, I go," answered the man, "but if it pleases you to save your servant, know that you must come swiftly. If you are not across the Tugela by sunset this night, word will be passed to the King, and she dies at once. Know also that you must come alone with me, for if any, white or black, accompany you, they will be killed."

"Now," said Rachel when the three of them were left alone, "now what is to be done?"

Mrs. Dove shook her head helplessly, and looked at her husband, who broke into a tirade against the Zulus, their superstitions, cruelties, customs, and everything that was theirs, and ended by declaring that it was of course utterly impossible that Rachel should go upon such a mad errand, and thus place herself in the power of savages.

"But, father," she said when he had done, "do you understand that you are pronouncing Noie's death sentence? If you were in my place, would you not go?"

"Of course I would. In fact I propose to do so as it is. No doubt Dingaan will listen to me."

"You mean that Dingaan will kill you. Did you not hear what that man Tamboosa said? Father, you must not go."

"No, John," broke in Mrs. Dove, "Rachel is right, you must not go, for you would never come back again. Also, how can you be so cruel as to think of leaving me here alone?"

"Then I suppose that we must abandon that poor girl to her fate," exclaimed Mr. Dove.

"How can you suppose anything so merciless, father, when it is in my power to save her?" asked Rachel. "If I let those horrible Zulus kill her I shall never be happy again all my life."

"And what if the horrible Zulus kill you?"

"They will not kill me, father; mother knows they will not, and so do I. But as they have got this madness into their heads, I am sure that if I do not go they will send an *impi* here to kill everybody else, and take me prisoner. The kidnapping of Noie is only a first move. It is one of two things: either I must visit Zululand, save Noie, and play my part there as best I can, or we must desert Noie, and all leave this place at once, tomorrow if possible. But then, as I told you, I shall never forgive myself, especially as I am not in the least afraid of the Zulus."

"It is true that God can protect you as much in Zululand as He can here," replied Mr. Dove, beginning to weaken in face of this desperate alternative.

"Of course, father, but if I go to Zululand I want you and mother to trek to Durban, and remain there till I return."

"Why, Rachel? It is absurd."

"Because I do not think that you are safe here, and it is not at all absurd," she answered stubbornly. "These people choose to believe that I am in some way in bondage to you; you remember all their talk about the heavens and the cloud. Of course it may mean nothing, but you will be much better in Durban for a while, where you can take to the water if necessary."

Now Mr. Dove's obstinacy asserted itself. He refused to entertain any such idea, giving reason after reason why he should not do so. Thus for another half hour the argument raged till at length a compromise was arrived at, as usual in such cases, not of too satisfactory an order. Rachel was to be allowed to undertake her mission on behalf of Noie, and her parents were to remain at Ramah. On her return, which they hoped would be within a week or eight days, the question of the abandonment of the mission was to be settled by the help of the experience she had gained. To this arrangement, then, they agreed, reluctantly enough all of them, in order, to save Noie's life, and for no other reason.

The momentous decision once taken, in half an hour Rachel was ready for her journey, which she determined she would make upon her own horse, a grey mare that she had ridden for a long while, and could rely on in every way. The white riding-ox that Dingaan had sent as a present was also to accompany her, to carry her spare garments and other articles packed in skin bags, such as coffee, sugar and a few medicines, and to serve as a remount in case anything should happen to the horse. When it was laden Rachel sent for the Zulu, Tamboosa, and, pointing to the ox, said:

"I come to visit Dingaan the king, and to claim my servant. Lead the beast on, I will overtake you presently."

The man saluted and began to *bonga*, that is, to give her titles of praise, but she cut him short with a wave of her hand, and he departed leading the ox.

Now while Mr. Dove saw to the saddling of the horses, for he was to ride with her as far as the Tugela, Rachel went to bid farewell to her mother. She found her by herself in the sitting-room, seated at an open window, and looking out sadly towards the sea.

"I am quite ready, dear," she said in a cheerful voice. "Don't look so sad, I shall be back again in a week with Noie."

"Yes," answered Mrs. Dove, "I think that you and Noie will come back safely, but—" and she paused.

"But what, mother?"

"Oh! I don't know. I am very much oppressed, my heart is heavy in me. I hate parting with you, Rachel. Remember we have never been separated since you were born."

Her daughter looked at her, and was filled with grief and compunction.

"Mother," she said, "if you feel like that—well, I love Noie, but after all you are more to me than Noie, and if you wish I will give up this business and stop with you. It is very terrible, but it can't be helped; Noie will understand, poor thing," and her eyes filled with tears at the thought of the girl's dreadful fate.

"No, Rachel, somehow I think it best that you should go, not only for Noie's sake, but for your own. If your father would leave here today or tomorrow, as you suggested, it might be otherwise, but he won't do that, so it is no use talking of it. Let us hope for the best."

"As you wish, mother."

"Now, dear kiss me and go. I hear your father calling you; and, Rachel, if we should not meet again in this world, I know you won't forget me, or that there is another where we shall. I did not want to frighten you with my fancies, which come from my not being well. Goodbye, my love, goodbye. God be with you, and make you happy, always—always."

Then Rachel kissed her in silence, for she could not trust herself to speak, and turning, left the room whence her mother watched her go, also in silence. In another minute she was mounted, and, accompanied by her father, riding on the road along which Tamboosa had led the white ox.

Presently they overtook him, whereon he stopped, and looking at Mr. Dove, said:

"*Inkosazana*, the King's orders are that none should accompany you into Zululand."

"Be silent," answered Rachel, proudly. "He rides with me as far as the river bank."

Then they went on, and Rachel was relieved to find that whatever might have been her mother's mood, that of her father was fairly cheerful. Indeed, his mind was so occupied with the details and object of her journey that he quite forgot its dangers.

Two hours' steady riding brought them to the ford of the Tugela river, across which lay Zululand. On the hills beyond it they could see a number of Kaffirs watching, who on catching sight of Rachel, ran down to the river and entered it, shouting and beating the water with their sticks, as she guessed, to scare away any crocodiles that might be lurking there.

Now that the moment of separation had come, Mr. Dove grew loth to part with his daughter, and again suggested to Tamboosa that he should accompany her to Dingaan's Great Place.

"If you set a foot across that river, Praying Man," answered the *induna* grimly, "you shall die; look, there are the spears that will kill you."

As he spoke he pointed to the crest of the opposing hill over which, running swiftly in ordered companies, now appeared a Zulu regiment who carried large white shields and wore white plumes rising from their head rings.

"It is the escort of the *Inkosazana*," he added. "Do you think that she can take hurt among so many? And do you think, if you dare to disobey the words of Dingaan, that you can escape so many? Go back new, lest they should come over and kill you where you are."

Then, seeing that both argument and resistance were useless, and that Tamboosa would brook no delay, Mr. Dove hurriedly embraced his daughter in farewell. Indeed, Rachel was glad that there was no time for words, for this parting was more terrible to her than she cared to own, and she feared lest she should break down before the Zulu who was watching her, and thereby be lowered in his eyes and in those of his people.

It was over and done. She had entered the water, riding her grey mare while Tamboosa led the white ox at her side. Presently she looked, back, and saw her father kneeling in prayer upon the bank.

"What does the man?" asked Tamboosa, uneasily. "Is he bewitching us?"

"Nay," she answered, "he prays to the Heavens for us."

On they went between the two lines of natives, who ceased their beating of the water, and were silent as she passed. The river was shallow, and they crossed it with ease. By now the regiment was gathered on its further bank, two thousand men or more, brought hither to do honour to this white girl in whom they chose to consider that the guardian spirit of their people was incarnate. Contemplating them, Rachel wondered how it came about that they should be thus prepared for her advent. The answer rose in her mind. If she had refused to visit Zululand, it was their mission to fetch her. It was wise, therefore, that she had come of her own will.

Forward she rode, a striking figure in her long white cloak, down which her bright hair hung, sitting very proud and upright on her horse, without a sign of doubt or fear. As she approached, the captains of the regiment ran forward to meet her with lifted shield and crouching bodies.

"Hail!" cried their leader. "In the name of the Great Elephant, of Dingaan the King, hail to thee, Princess of the Heavens, Holder of the Spirit of Nomkubulwana."

Rachel rode on, taking no notice, marvelling who Nomkubulwana, whose spirit she was supposed to enshrine, might be. Afterwards she discovered that it was only another name for the *Inkosazana-y-Zoola*, that mysterious white ghost believed by this people to control their destinies, with whom it had pleased them to identify her. As her horse left the wide river and set foot upon dry land, every man of the two thousand soldiers, who were watching, as it seemed to her, with wonder and awe, began to beat his ox-hide shield with the handle of his spear. They beat very softly at first, producing a sound like the distant murmur of the sea, then harder and harder till its volume grew to a mighty roar, impossible to describe, a sound like the sound of thunder that echoed along the water and from hill to hill. The mighty noise sank and died away as it had begun, and for a moment there was silence. Then at some signal every spear flashed aloft in the sunlight, and from every throat came the royal salute—*Bayète*. It was a tremendous and most imposing welcome, so tremendous that Rachel could no longer doubt that this people regarded her as a being apart, and above the other white folk whom they knew.

At the time, however, she had little space for such thoughts, since the mare she rode, terrified by the tumult, bucked and shied so violently that she could scarcely keep her seat. She was a good rider, which was fortunate for her, since, had she been ignominiously thrown upon such an occasion, her prestige must have suffered, if indeed it were not destroyed. As it proved, it was greatly enhanced by this accident. Many of the Zulus of that day had never even seen a horse, which was considered by all of them to be a dangerous if not a magical beast. That a woman could remain seated on such a wild animal when it sprang into the air, and swerved from side to side, struck them, therefore, as something marvellous and out of experience, a proof indeed that she was not as others are.

She quieted the mare, and rode on between the white-shielded ranks, who, their greeting finished, remained absolutely still like bronze statues watching her with wondering eyes. When at length they were passed, the captains and a guard of about fifty men ran ahead of her.

Then she came, and after her Tamboosa, leading the white ox, followed by another guard, which in turn was followed by the entire regiment. Thus royally escorted, asking no questions, and speaking no word, did Rachel make her entry into Zululand. Only in her heart she wondered whither she was going, and how that strange journey would end, wondered, too, how it would fare with her father and her mother till she returned to them.

Well might she wonder.

When she had ridden thus for about two hours an incident occurred which showed her how great, and indeed how dreadful was the eminence on which she had been set among these people. Suddenly some cattle, frightened by the approach of the *impi*, rushed through it towards their *kraal*, and a bull that was with them, seeing this unaccustomed apparition of a white woman mounted on a strange animal, put down its head and charged her furiously. She saw it coming, and by pulling the mare on to its haunches, avoided its rush. Now at the time she was riding on a path which ran along the edge of a little rock-strewn *donga* not more than eight or ten feet deep, but steep-sided. Into this *donga* the bull, which had shut its eyes to charge after the fashion of its kind, plunged headlong, and as it chanced struck its horns against a stone, twisting and dislocating the neck, so that it lay there still and dead.

When the Zulus saw what had happened they uttered a long-drawn *Ow-w* of amazement, for had not the beast dared to attack the White Spirit, and had not the Spirit rewarded it with instant death? Then a captain made a motion with his hand and instantly men sprang upon the remaining cattle, four or five of them that were following the bull, and despatched them with *assegai*s. Before Rachel could interfere they were pierced with a hundred wounds. Now there was a little pause, while the carcases of the beasts were dragged out of her path, and the bloodstains covered from her eyes with fresh earth. Just as this task was finished there appeared, scrambling up the *denga*, and followed, by some men, a fat and hideous-looking woman, with fish bladders in her hair, and snake-skins tied about her, who, from her costume, Rachel knew at once must be an *Isanuzi* or witch-doctoress. Evidently she was in a fury, as might be seen by the workings of her face, and the extraordinary swiftness with which she moved notwithstanding her years and bulk.

"Who has dared to kill my cattle?" she screamed. "Is it thou whom men name Nomkubulwana?"

"Woman," answered Rachel quietly, "the Heavens killed the bull which would have hurt me. For the rest, ask of the captains of the King."

The witch-doctoress glanced at the dead bull which lay in the *donga*, its head twisted up in an unnatural fashion at right angles to the body, and for a moment seemed afraid. Then her rage at the loss of her herd broke out afresh, for she was a person in authority, one accustomed to be feared because of her black arts and her office.

"When the *Inkosazana* is seen in Zululand," she gasped, "death walks with her. There is the token of it," and she pointed to the dead cattle. "So it has ever been and so shall it ever be. Red is thy road through life, White One. Go back, go back now to thine own *kraal*, and see whether or no my words are true," and springing at the horse she seized it by the bridle as though she would drag it round.

Now in her hand Rachel held a little rod of white rhinoceros horn which she used as a riding whip, and with this rod she pointed at the woman, meaning that some of those with her should cause her to loose the bridle. Too late she remembered that in this savage land such a motion when made by the King or one in supreme command, had another dreadful interpretation—death without pity or reprieve.

In an instant, before she could interfere, before she could speak, the witch-doctoress lay dead upon the carcase of the dead bull.

"What of the others, Queen, what of the others?" asked the chief of the slayers, bending low before her, and pointing with his spear to the attendants of the witch-doctoress, who fled aghast. "Do they join this evil-doer who dared to lift her hand against thee?"

"Nay," she answered in a low voice, for horror had made her almost dumb. "I give them life. Forward."

"She gives them life!" shouted the praisers about her. "The Bearer of life and death gives life to the children of the evil-doer," and as the great cavalcade marched forward, company after company took up these words and sang them as a song.

## Chapter 10

# The Omen of the Star

As it chanced and can easily be understood, Rachel could not have made a more effective entry into Zululand, or one more calculated to confirm her supernatural reputation. When the "wild beast" she rode plunged about she had remained seated on it as though she grew there, whereas every warrior knew that he would have fallen off. When the bull charged her that bull had died, slain by the Heavens. When the *Isanuzi*, a witch of repute, had lifted voice and hand against her she had commanded her death, showing that she feared no rival magic. True the woman would have been killed in any case, for such was the order of the King as to all who should dare to affront the *Inkosazana*, yet the captains had waited to see what Rachel would do that they might judge her accordingly. If she had shown fear, if she had even neglected to avenge, they might have marvelled whether after all she were more than a beautiful white maiden filled with the wisdom of the whites.

Now they knew better; she was a Spirit having the power of a Spirit over beast and man, who smote as a Spirit should. The fame of it went throughout the land, and little chance thence forward had Rachel of escaping from the shadow of her own fearful renown.

Towards sundown they came to a *kraal* set upon a hill, and it was asked of her if she were pleased to spend the night there. She bowed her head in assent, and they entered the *kraal*. It was quite empty save for certain maidens dressed in bead petticoats, who waited there to serve her. All the other inhabitants had gone. They took her to a large and beautifully clean hut. Kneeling on their knees, the maidens presented her with food—meat and curdled milk, and roasted cobs of corn. She ate of the corn and the milk, but the meat she sent away as a gift to the captains. Then alone in that *kraal*, in which after they had served her even the girls seemed to fear to stay, Rachel slept as best she might in such solitude, while without the fence two thousand armed savages watched over her safety.

It was a troubled sleep, for she dreamed always of that dreadful-looking *Isanuzi* with the fish-bladders in her hair, yelling to her that her path through life was watered with blood, and bidding her go back to her own *kraal* and see whether the words were true, an ominous saying of which she could not read the riddle. She dreamed also of the woman's coarse, furious face turned suddenly to one of abject terror, and then of the dreadful end the red death without mercy and without appeal which she had let loose by a motion of her hand. Another dream she had was of her father and her mother, who seemed to be lying side by side staring towards her with wide-open eyes, and that when she spoke to them they would not answer.

So the long night wore away, till at length Rachel woke with a start thinking that a hand had been laid upon her face, to see by the faint light of dawn which struggled into the hut through the cracks of the door-boards that the hand was only a great rat that had crawled over her and now nibbled at her hair. She sat up, frightening it and its companions away, then rose and washed herself with water that stood by in great gourds while without she heard the women singing some kind of song or hymn of which she could not catch the words.

Scarcely was she ready than they entered the hut, saluting her and bringing more food. Rachel ate, then bade one of them say to the captain of the *impi* that she was ready to start. Presently the girl returned with the message that all was prepared. She walked from the *kraal* to find her mare, which had been well fed and groomed by Tamboosa, who had seen horses in Natal, and knew how they should be treated, saddled and waiting, whilst before and behind it, arranged as on the previous day, stood the warriors, who received her in dead, respectful silence.

She mounted, and the procession went forward. With a two hours' halt at midday they marched on over hill and dale, passing many villages of beehive-shaped huts. As they came the inhabitants of these places deserted them and fled, crying *"Nomkubulwana! Nomkubulwana!"* It was evident to Rachel that the tale of the death of the *Isanuzi* had preceded her, and they feared lest, should they cross her path, her fate would be their fate. Indeed, one of the strangest circumstances of this strange adventure was the complete loneliness in which she lived. Except those who were actually ordered to wait upon her, none dared come near to Rachel; she was holy, a Spirit, to approach whom unbidden might mean death.

At nightfall they reached another empty *kraal*, where again she slept alone. When they left it in the morning she called Tamboosa to her and asked him at what hour they would come to Dingaan's great town, Umgugundhlovo, which means the Place of the trumpeting of the Elephant. He answered, at sunset.

So she rode on all that day also till as the sun began to sink, from a hill whereon grew large euphorbia trees, on a plain backed by mountains, she saw the town surrounded by a fence, inside of which were thousands of huts, that in their turn surrounded a great open space. Now they pushed forward quickly, and as darkness fell approached the main gate of the place, where, as usual, there was no one to be seen. But here they did not enter, marching on till they came to another gate, that of the *Intunkulu*, the King's house, where, their escort done, the regiment turned and went away, leaving Rachel alone with the envoy, Tamboosa, who still led the white ox. They entered this gate, and presently came to a second. It was that of the *Emposeni*, the Dwelling of the King's wives, out of which appeared women crawling on the ground before Rachel, and holding in their left hands torches of grass. These undid the baggage from the ox, and at their signals, for they did not seem to dare to speak to her, Rachel dismounted. Thereon Tamboosa saluted her, and taking the horse by the bridle, led it away with the ox.

Then Rachel felt that she was indeed alone, for Tamboosa at any rate had seen her home, which now was so far away. Still proudly enough she followed the women, who, bent double as before, led her to a great hut lit by a rude lamp filled with melted hippopotamus fat, where they set down her bags, and departed, to return presently with food and water.

Having washed off the dust of her long journey, and combed out her hair, Rachel ate all she could, for she was hungry, and guessed that she might need her strength that night. Then she lay down upon a pile of beautiful *karosses* that had been placed ready for her, and rested. An hour or more went by, and just as she was beginning to fall asleep the door-board of the hut was thrust aside, and a tall woman entered, who knelt to her and said:

"Hail, *Inkosazana*! The King asks whether it be thy pleasure to appear before him this night."

"It is my pleasure," answered Rachel; "for that purpose have I travelled here. Lead me to the King."

So the woman went out of the hut, Rachel following her to find that the moon shone brightly in a clear sky. The woman conducted her through tortuous reed fences, until presently they came to an open court where, in the shadow of a hut, sat a number of men wrapped about with fur *karosses*. Guessing that she was in the presence of Dingaan, Rachel drew her white cloak round her tall form and walked forward slowly, till she reached the centre of the space, where she stopped and stood quite still, looking like a ghost in the moonlight. Then all the men to right and left rose and saluted her silently by the uplifting of one arm; only he who was in the midst of them remained seated and did not salute. Still she stayed motionless, uttering no word for a long while, six or seven minutes, perhaps. Her silence fought against theirs, and she knew that the one who spoke first would own to inferiority.

At length, in answering salutation, she lifted the little wand of white horn that she carried and turned slowly as though to leave the place, so that now the moonlight glistened on her lovely hair. Then, fearing perhaps lest she should depart or vanish away, the man seated in the centre said in a low half-awed voice:

"I am Dingaan, King of the Amazulu. Say, White One, who art thou?"

"By what name am I known here, O Dingaan the King?" she replied, answering the question with a question.

"By a high name, White One, a name that is seldom spoken, the name of *Inkosazana-y-Zoola*, the title of Nomkubulwana, the Spirit of our people. How camest thou by that name?"

"My name is my name," she said.

"We know, White One; the wind has borne all that story through the land, it whispers it from the leaves of the forest and the reeds of the water and the grass of the plains. We know that the Heavens gave thee their own name, O Child of Heaven, O Holder of the Spirit of Nomkubulwana."

"Thou sayest it, King. I do not say it, thou sayest it."

"I say it, and having seen thee I know that it is true, for thy beauty, White One, is not the beauty of woman alone, although still thou beest woman. Now I confirm to thee the words my messengers bore thee in past days. Here, with me, thou rulest. The land is thine, my *impis* wait thy word. Death and life are in thy hands; command, and they go forth to slay; command, and they return again. Only thou rulest alone with me, and the black folk, not the white, shall be thy servants."

"I hear thee, King. Now, as a first fruit, give to me Noie, daughter of Seyapi, my slave whom the soldiers stole away from Ramah beyond the river where I dwell."

"She is dead, White One, she is dead for her crimes," answered Dingaan, looking at her.

Now Rachel's heart sank in her, for it might well be that a trick had been played on her, and that this was true. Or perhaps this tale of Noie's death was but a trap to test her powers; moreover, it was not likely that the King, who had promised that she should live, would dare to break his word to one whom he believed or half-believed to be a spirit.

For a moment she thought; then, after her nature, determined to be bold and hazard all upon a throw. Therefore she did not argue or reproach, but said:

"She is not dead. I have questioned every spear in Zululand, and none of them is red with her blood."

"Thou art right," he answered; "the spears are clean. She died in the river."

Now Rachel was sure, and answered in her clear voice:

"I have questioned the waters, and I have questioned the crocodiles, and they answer that Noie has passed them safely."

"Thou art right, White One. She died by a rope in yonder huts."

Now Rachel looked at the huts and cried:

"Noie, I hear thee, I see thee, I smell thee out. Come forth, Noie."

The King and his councillors stared at her, whispering to one another, and before ever they had done their whisperings out from among the gloom of the huts crept Noie.

To Rachel she crept, taking no heed even of the King, and crouching down in the faint shadow of her that the moonlight threw, she flung her arms about her knees and pressed her forehead on her feet. Now Rachel's heart bounded with joy at the sight of her, and she longed to bend down and kiss her, but did not, lest her great dignity should be lessened in the eyes of the King; only she said:

"I greet you, Noie; be seated in my shadow, where you are safe, and tell me, have these men dealt well by you?"

"Not so ill, *Inkosazana*, that is since I reached the Great *Kraal*. But one of them, he who sits yonder," and she pointed to a certain *induna*, "struck me on the journey, and took away my food."

Now Rachel looked at the man angrily, playing with the little wand in her hand, whereon this *induna* shivered with terror, fearing lest she should point it at him. Rising, he came to Rachel and flung himself down before her.

"What have you to say," asked Rachel, "you who have dared to strike my servant?"

"*Inkosazana*," he mumbled, "the maid was obstinate, and tried to run away, and our orders were to bring her to the King. Spare my life, I pray thee."

"King," said Rachel, "I have power over this man, have I not?"

"It is so," answered Dingaan. "Kill him if thou wilt."

Rachel seemed to consider while the poor wretch, with chattering teeth, implored her to forgive. Then she turned to Noie, saying:

"He struck you, not me. I give him to you to do by as you will. Shall he sleep tonight with the living or the dead?"

Noie looked at him, and next at a mark on her arm, and the *induna*, ceasing from his prayers to Rachel, clutched Noie by the ankle, and begged her mercy.

"Your life has been given to you," he said, "give mine to me, lest ill-fortune follow you."

"Do you remember," asked Noie contemptuously, "how, when you had beaten me, yonder by the Tugela, you said you hoped that it would be your luck to put a spear through this heart of mine? And do you remember that I answered you that the spear would be over your own heart first, and that thereon you called me 'Daughter of Wizards' and struck me again—me, the child of Seyapi, upon whom the mantle of the *Inkosazana* lies, me who have drunk of her wisdom and of his—you struck *me*, you dog," and lifting her foot she spurned him in the face.

Now the King and his company, concluding that the thing was finished, glanced at Rachel to see her point with the rod and thus give the man to death. But Rachel waited, sure that Noie had not done. Moreover, whatever Noie might say, she had determined to save him.

Meanwhile, the girl, after a pause, said:

"Were you a man you would be too proud to ask your life of me, but you are a dog; and, Dog, I remember that you have children, among them a daughter of my own age, whom, I saw come out to greet you. For her sake, then, take your life, and with it this new name that I give you—'Soldier-who-strikes-girls.'"

So the man rose, and weak with shame and the agony of suspense, crept swiftly from the place, fearing lest the *Inkosazana* or her servant might change her mind and kill him after all. But Noie's name clung to him so closely that at length, unable to bear the ridicule of it, he and his family fled from Zululand.

So this matter ended.

Now the King spoke, saying:

"White One, thy magic is great, and thine eyes could pierce the darkness and see thy servant hidden, and call her forth to thee. Yet know, she is mine, not thine, for when she fled I had already chosen her to be my wife, and afterwards I sent and killed the wizard Seyapi, and all his House."

"But this girl thou didst not kill, O King, for I saved her."

"It is so, White One. I have heard lately how thou didst call down the lightning and burn up my soldier who followed after her, so that nothing of him remained."

"Yes," said Rachel quietly, "as, were it to please me, I could burn thee up also, O King," a saying at which. Dingaan looked afraid.

"Yet," he went on, waving his hand as though to put aside this unpleasant suggestion, "the maid is mine, not thine, and therefore I took her."

"How didst thou learn that she dwelt at my *kraal*?" asked Rachel.

The King hesitated.

"The white man, Ishmael, he whom thou callest Ibubesi, told thee, did he not?"

Dingaan bowed his head.

"And he told thee that thou couldst make what promises thou wouldst to me as to the girl's life, but that afterwards when thou hadst called me here to claim it, thou mightest kill her or keep her as a wife, as it pleased thee."

"I can hide nought from thee; it is so," said Dingaan.

"Is that still in thy mind, O King?" asked Rachel again, beginning to play with the little wand.

"Not so, not so," he answered hurriedly. "Hadst thou not come the girl would have died, as she deserved to do according to our law. But thou hast come and claimed her, O Holder of the Spirit of Nomkubulwana, and she sits in thy shadow and is clothed with thy garment. Take her then, for henceforth she is holy, as thou art holy."

Rachel heard, and without any change of countenance waved her hand to show that this question was finished. Then she asked suddenly:

"What is this great matter whereof thou wouldst speak with me, O King?"

"Surely thy wisdom has told thee, White One," he answered uneasily.

"Perchance, yet I would have it from thy lips, and now."

Now Dingaan consulted a little with his council.

"White One," he said presently, "the thing is grave, and we need guidance. Therefore, as the circle of the witch-doctors have declared must be done, we ask it of thee who art named with the name of the Spirit of our people and hast of her wisdom. Thou knowest, White

One, of the fights in past years between the white people of Natal and the Zulus, in which many were slain on either side. But now, when we are at peace with the English, we hear of another white people, the Amaboona" (*i.e.* the Dutch Boers), "who are marching towards us from the Cape, and have already fought with Moselikatze—the traitor who was once my captain—and killed thousands of his men. These Amaboona threaten us also, and say aloud that they will eat us up, for they are brave and armed with the white man's weapons that spit out lightning. Now, White One, what shall we do? Shall I send out my *impis* and fall on them while they are unprepared, and make an end of them, as seems wisest, and is the wish of my *indunas*? Or, shall I sit at home and watch, trying to be at peace with them, and only strike back if they strike at me? Answer not lightly, O Zoola, for much may hang upon thy words. Remember also that he whose name may not be spoken, the Lion who ruled before me and is gone, with his last breath uttered a certain prophecy concerning the white people and this land."

"Let me hear that prophecy, O King."

"Come forth," said Dingaan pointing to a councillor who sat in the circle, "come forth, thou who knowest, and tell the tale in the ears of this White One."

A figure rose, a draped figure whose face was hidden in a hood of blanket. It came forward, and as it came it drew the blanket tighter about it. Rachel, watching all things, saw, or thought she saw, that one of its hands was white as though it had been burned with fire. Surely she had seen such a hand before.

"Speak," she said.

"Name me by my name and tell me who I am and I will obey thee," answered the man.

Then she was sure, for she remembered the voice. She looked at him indifferently and asked:

"By what name shall I name you, O Slayer of a King? Will you be called Mopo or Umbopa, who have borne them both?"

Now Dingaan stared, and the shrouded form before her started as though in surprise.

"Why do you seek to mock me?" she went on. "Can a blanket of bark hide that face of yours from these eyes of mine which saw it a while ago at Ramah, when you came thither to judge of me, O Mouth of the King?"

Now the man let the blanket slip from his head and looked at her.

"It seems that it cannot," he answered. "Then I told thee that I had dreamed of the Spirit of our people, and that thou, White One, wast like to her of whom I had dreamed. Canst thou tell me what was the fashion of that dream of mine?"

Now Rachel understood that notwithstanding his words at Ramah, this man still doubted her, and was set up to prove her, and all that Noie had told her about him and the secret history of the Zulus came back into her mind.

"Surely Mopo or Umbopa," she replied, "you dreamed three dreams, not one. Is it of the last you speak?—that dream at the *kraal* Duguza, when the *Inkosazana* rode past you on a storm clothed in lightning, and shaking in her hand a spear of fire?"

"Yes, I speak of it," he replied in an awed voice, "but if thou art but a woman as thou hast said, how knowest thou these things?"

"Perchance I am both woman and spirit, and perchance the past tells them to me," Rachel answered; "but the past has many voices, and now that I dwell in the flesh I cannot hear them all. Let me search you out. Let me read your heart," and she bent forward and fixed her eyes upon him, holding him with her eyes.

"Ah! now I see and I hear," she said presently. "Had you not a sister, Mopo, a certain Baleka, who afterwards entered the house of the Black One and bore a son and died in the Tatiyana Cleft? Shall I tell you how she died?"

"Tell it not! Tell it not!" exclaimed the old man quaveringly.

"So be it. There is no need. Yet ere she died you made a promise to this Baleka, and that promise you kept at the *kraal* Duguza, you and the prince Umhlangana, and another prince whose name I forget," and she looked at Dingaan, who put his hand before his face. "You kept that promise with an *assegai*—let me look, let me look into your heart—yes, with a little *assegai* handled with the royal red wood, an *assegai* that had drunk much blood."

Now a low moan broke from the lips of Dingaan, and those who sat with them, while Umbopa shivered as though with cold.

"Have mercy, I pray thee," he gasped. "Forgive me if at times since we met at Ramah I thought thee but a white maiden, beautiful and bold, as thou didst declare thyself to be. Now I see thou hast the spirit, or else how didst thou know these things?"

Noie heard and smiled in the shadow, but Rachel stood silent.

"I was bidden to tell thee of the last words of the Black One," went on Umbopa hurriedly; "but what need is there to tell thee anything who knowest all? They were that he heard the sound of the running of the feet of a great white people which shall stamp out the children of the Zulus."

"Nay," answered Rachel, "I think they were; *'Where-fore wouldst thou kill me, Mopo?'*"

Again Dingaan moaned, for he had heard these very words spoken. Umbopa turned and stared at him, and he stared at Umbopa.

"Come hither," said Rachel, beckoning to the old man.

He obeyed, and she threw the corner of her cloak over his head, and whispered into his ear. He listened to her whisperings, then with a cry broke from her and fled away out of the council of the King.

When he had gone there was silence, though Dingaan looked a question with his eyes.

"Ask it not," she said, "ask it not of me, or of him. I think this Mopo here had his secrets in the past. I think that once he sat in a hut at night and bargained with certain Great Ones, a prince who lives, and a prince who died. Come hither, come hither, thou son of Senzangacona, come from the fields of Death and tell me what was that bargain which thou madest with Mopo, thou and another?" and once again Rachel beckoned, this time upwards in the air.

Now the face of Dingaan went grey, even in the moonlight it went grey beneath the blackness of his skin, for there rose before his mind a vision of a hut and of Mopo and of Umhlangana, the prince his brother whom he had slain, and of himself, seated in the darkness, their heads together beneath a blanket whispering of the murder of a king.

"Thou knowest all," he gasped, "thou art Nomkubulwana and no other. Spare us, Spirit who canst summon our dead sins from the grave of time, and make them walk alive before us."

"Nay, nay," she answered, mockingly, "surely I am but a woman, daughter of a Teacher who lives yonder over the Tugela, a white maiden who eats and sleeps and drinks as other maidens do. Take notice, King, and you his captains, that I am no spirit, nothing but a woman who chances to bear a high name, and to have some wisdom. Only," she added with meaning, "if any harm should come to me, if I should die, then I think that I should become a spirit, a terrible spirit, and that ill would it go with that people against whom my blood was laid."

"Oh!" said the King, who still shook with fear, "we know, we know. Mock us not, I pray. Thou art the Spirit who hast chosen to wear the robe of woman, as flame hides itself in flint, and woe be to the hand that strikes the fire from this stone. White One, give us now that wisdom whereof thou speakest. Shall I fall upon the Boers or shall I let them be?"

Rachel looked upwards, studying the stars.

"She takes counsel with the Heavens, she who is their daughter," muttered one of the *indunas* in a low voice.

As he spoke it chanced that a bright meteor travelling from the south-west swept across the sky to burst and vanish over the *kraal* of Umgugundhlovo.

"It is a messenger to her," said one. "I saw the fire shine upon her hair and vanish in her breast."

"Nay," answered another, "it is the *Ehlose*, the guardian ghost of the Amazulu that appears and dies."

"Not so," broke in a third, "that light shows the Amaboona travelling from the south-west to be eaten up in the blackness of our *impis*."

"Such a star runs ever before the death of king. It fell the night ere the Black One died," murmured a fourth as though he spoke to himself.

Only Dingaan, taking no heed of them, said, addressing Rachel:

"Read thou the omen."

"Nay," she replied upon the swift impulse of the moment, "I read it not. Interpret it as ye will. Here is my answer to thy question, King. *Those who lift the spear shall perish by the spear.*"

At this saying the captains murmured a little, for they, who desired war, understood that she counselled peace between them and the Boers, though others thought that she meant that the Boers would perish. Dingaan also looked downcast. Watching their faces, Rachel was sure that not even her hand could hold them back from their desire. That war must come. Again she spoke:

"The star travels whither it is thrown by the hand of the *Umkulunkulu*, the Master of men; the spear finds the heart to which it is appointed. Read you the omen as you will. I have spoken, but ye will not understand. That which shall be, shall be."

She bent her head, and turned her ear towards the ground as though to hearken.

"What was that tale of the last words of the Great Lion who is gone?" she went on. "Ask it of Mopo, ask it of Dingaan the King. It seems to me that I also hear the feet of a people travelling over plain and mountain, and the rivers behind them run red with blood. Are they black feet or white feet? Read ye the omen as ye will. I have spoken for the first time and the last; trouble me no more with this matter of the white men and your war," and turning, Rachel glided from the court, followed by Noie with bowed head.

## Chapter 11

# Ishmael Visits the Inkosazana

When at last they were in the hut and the door-board had been safely closed, Rachel took Noie in her arms and kissed her. But Noie did not kiss her back; she only pressed her hand against her forehead.

"Why do you not kiss me, Noie?" asked Rachel.

"How can I kiss you, *Inkosazana*," replied the girl humbly, "I who am but the dog at your feet, the dog whom twice it has pleased you to save from death."

"*Inkosazana*!" exclaimed Rachel. "I weary of that name. I am but a woman like yourself, and I hate this part which I must play."

"Yet it is a high part, and you play it very well. While I listened to you tonight, Zoola, twice and thrice I wondered if you are not something more than you deem yourself to be. That beautiful body of yours is but a cup like those of other women, but say, who fills the cup with the wine of wisdom? Why do kings and councillors fear you, and why do you fear nothing? Why did dead Seyapi talk to me of you in dreams? What strange chance gave you that name of yours and made you holy in these men's eyes? What power teaches you the truth and gives you wit and strength to speak it? Why are you different from the rest of maidens, white or black?"

"I do not know, Noie. Something tells me what to do and say. Also, I understand these Zulus, and you have taught me much. You told me all the hidden tale of yonder Mopo a year gone by, or more, as you have told me many of the darkest secrets of this people that you had from your father, who knew them all. At the pinch I remembered it, no more, and played upon them by my knowledge."

"What was it you said to Mopo under your cloak, Lady?"

Rachel smiled as she answered:

"I only asked him if it were not in his mind, having killed one king, to kill another also, and that spear went home."

"Ah!" exclaimed Noie in admiration, "at least I never told you that."

"No; I read it in his eyes; for a moment all his heart was open to me—yes, and the heart of Dingaan also. He fears Mopo, and Mopo hates him, and one day hate and fear will come together."

"Ah!" said Noie again, "you know much."

"Yes," answered Rachel with sudden passion, "more than I wish to know. Noie, you are right, I am not altogether as others are; there is a power in my blood. I see and hear what should not be seen and heard; at times fears fill me, or joys lift me up, and I think that I draw near to another world than ours. No; it is folly. I am over-wrought. Who would not be that must endure so much and be set upon this throne, a goddess among barbarians with life and death upon my lips? Oh! when the King asked me his riddle I knew not what to answer, who feared lest ten thousand lives might pay the price of a girl's incautious words. Then that meteor broke; there have been several this night, but none noted them till I looked upwards, and you know the rest. Let them guess its meaning, which they cannot, for it has none."

"Why did you not speak more plainly, Zoola?"

"Oh! because I dared not. Who am I to meddle with such matters, who came here but to save you? I warned them not to make war upon the Boers; what more could I do? Moreover, it is useless, for fight they must and will and pay the price. Of that I am sure. I feel it here," and she pressed her hand upon her heart. "Yes, and other nearer things! Oh! Noie, I would that I were back at home. Say, can we start tomorrow at the dawn?"

Noie shook her head.

"I do not think that they will let you go; they will keep you to be their great doctoress. You should not have come. I sent you word—what did my life matter?"

"Keep me," answered Rachel, stamping her foot. "They dare not; here at least I am the *Inkosazana*, and I will be obeyed."

Noie made no answer; only she said:

"Ishmael is here. I have seen him. He wished to have me killed at once because he is afraid of me. But when he was sure that you were coming, Dingaan would not break his word which he had sent to you."

Rachel's face fell.

"Ishmael!" she exclaimed in dismay, then recovered herself and added: "Well, I am not afraid of Ishmael, for here his life is in my hand. Oh! I am worn out; I cannot talk of the man tonight. I must sleep, Noie, I must sleep. Come, lie at my side and let us sleep."

"Nay," answered the girl; "my place is at the door. But drink this milk and lay you down without fear, for I will watch."

Rachel obeyed, and Noie sat by her, holding her hand, till presently her eyes shut and she slept. But Noie did not sleep. All that night she sat there watching and listening, till at length the dawn came and she lay down also by the door and rested.

The sun was high in the heavens when Rachel woke.

"Good morrow to you, Zoola," said the sweet voice of Noie. "You have slept well. Now you must rise, bathe yourself and eat, for already messengers from the King have been to the outer gate, saying that they wait to escort you to a better house that has been made ready for you."

"I hoped that they waited to escort me out of Zululand," answered Rachel.

"I asked them of that, Zoola, but they declared it must not be, as the council of the doctors had been summoned to consider your sayings, and two days will pass before it can meet. Also they declare that your horse is sick and not fit to travel, meaning that they will not let you go."

"But I have the right to go, Noie."

"The bird has the right to fly, but what if it is in a cage, Zoola?"

"I am queen here, Noie; the bars will burst at my word."

"It may be so, Zoola, but what if the bird should find that it has no nest to fly to?"

"What do you mean?" asked Rachel, paling.

"Only that it seems best that you should not anger these Zulus, Lady, lest it should come into their minds to destroy your nest, thinking that so you might come to love this cage. No, no, I have heard nothing, but I guess their thoughts. You need rest; bide here, where you are safe, a day or two, and let us see what happens."

"Speak plainly, Noie. I do not understand your parable of birds and cages."

"Zoola, I obey. I think that if you say you will go, none, not the King himself, would dare to stay you, though you would have to go on foot, for then that horse would die. But an *impi* would go with you, or before you, and woe betide those who held you from returning to Zululand! Do you understand me now?"

"Yes," answered Rachel. "You mean!—oh! I cannot speak it. I will remain here a few days."

So she rose and bathed herself and was dressed by Noie, and ate of the food that had been brought to the door of the hut. Then she went out, and in the little courtyard found a litter waiting that was hung round with grass mats.

"The King's word is that you should enter the litter," said Noie.

She did so, whereon Noie clapped her hands and girls in bead dresses ran in, and having prostrated themselves before the litter, lifted it up and carried it away, Noie walking at its side.

Rachel, peeping between the mats, saw that she was borne out of the town, surrounded, but at a distance, by a guard of hundreds of armed men. Presently they began to ascend a hill, whereon grew many trees, and after climbing it for a while, reached a large *kraal* with huts between the outer and inner fence, and in its centre a great space of park-like land through which ran a stream.

Here, by the banks of the stream, stood a large new hut, and behind at a little distance two or three other huts. In front of this great hut the litter was set down by, the bearers, who at once went away. Then at Noie's bidding Rachel came out of it and looked at the place which had been given her in which to dwell.

It was a beautiful spot, away from the dust and the noises of the Great *Kraal*, and so placed upon a shoulder of the hillside that the soldiers who guarded this House of the *Inkosazana*, as it was called, could not be seen or heard. Yet Rachel looked at it with distaste, feeling that it was that cage of which Noie had spoken,

A cage it proved indeed, a solitary cage, for here Rachel abode in regal seclusion and in state that could only be called awful. No man might approach her house unbidden, and the maidens who waited upon her did so with downcast eyes, never speaking, and falling on to their knees if addressed. On the first day of her imprisonment, for it was nothing less, an unhappy Zulu, through ignorance or folly, slipped through the outer guard and came near to the inner fence. Rachel, who was seated above, heard some shouts of rage and horror, and saw soldiers running towards him, and in another minute a body being carried away upon a shield. He had died for his sacrilege.

Once a day ambassadors came to her from the King to ask of her health, and if she had orders to give, but now even these, men were not allowed to look upon her. They were led in by the women, each of them with a piece of bark cloth over his head, and from beneath this cloth they addressed her as though she were in truth divine. On the first day she bade them tell the King that her mission being ended, it was her desire to depart to her own home beyond the river. They heard her words in silence, then asked if she had anything to add. She replied—yes, it was her will that they should cease to wear veils in her presence, also that no more men should be killed upon her account as had happened that morning. They said that they would convey the order at once, as several were under sentence of death who had argued as to whether she were really the *Inkosazana*, So she sent them away instantly, fearing lest they should be too late, and they were led off backwards bowing and giving the royal salute. Afterwards she rejoiced to hear that her commands had arrived just in time, and that the blood of these poor people was not upon her head.

Next day the messengers returned at the same hour, unveiled as she desired, bearing the answer of the King and his council. It was to the effect that the *Inkosazana* had no need to ask permission to come or to go. Her Spirit, they knew, was mighty and could wander where it willed; all the *impis* of the Zulus could not hold her Sprint. But—and here came the sting of this clever answer—it was necessary, until her sayings had been considered, that the body in which that Spirit abode should remain with them a while. Therefore the King and his counsellors and the whole nation of the Zulus prayed her to be satisfied with the sending of her Spirit across the Tugela, leaving her body to dwell a space in the House of the *Inkosazana*.

Rachel looked at them in despair, for what was she to reply to such reasoning as this? Before she could make up her mind, their spokesman said that a white man, Ibubesi, who said that he had often spoken with her, asked leave to visit her in her house.

Now Rachel thought a while. Ishmael was the last person in the whole world whom she wished to see. After the interview when they parted, and all that had happened since, it could not be otherwise. She remembered the threats he had uttered then, and to her father afterwards, the brutal and revolting threats. Some of these had been directed against Noie, and subsequently Noie was kidnapped by the Zulus. That those directed at herself had not been fulfilled was, she felt sure, due to a lack of opportunity alone.

Little wonder, then, that she feared and hated the man. Still he was of white blood, and perhaps for this reason had authority among the Zulus, who, as she knew, often consulted him. Moreover, notwithstanding his vapourings, like the Zulus whose superstitions he had contracted, he looked upon herself with something akin to fear. If she saw him she had no cause to dread anything that he could do to her, at any rate in this country where she was supreme, whereas on the other hand she might obtain information from him which would be very useful, or make use of him to enable her to escape from Zululand. On the whole, then, it seemed wisest to grant him an interview, especially as she gathered from the fact that the question was raised by Dingaan's *indunas*, that for some reason of his own, the King hoped that she would do so.

Still she hesitated, loathing and despising him as she did.

"You have heard," she said in English to Noie, who stood behind her. "Now what shall I say?"

"Say—come," answered Noie in the same tongue.

"Read his black heart and find out truth; he no can keep it from you. Say—come with soldiers. If he behave bad, tell them kill him. They obey you. No mind me. I not afraid of that wild beast now."

Then Rachel said to the *indunas*:

"I hear the King's word, and understand that he wishes me to receive this Ibubesi. Yet I know that man, as I know all men, white and black. He is an evil man, and it is not my pleasure to speak with him alone. Let him come with a guard of six captains, and let the captains be armed with spears, so that if I give the word there may be an end of this Ibubesi."

Then the messengers saluted and departed as before.

On the morrow at about the same hour a praiser, or herald, arrived outside the inner fence of the *kraal*, and after he had shouted out Rachel's titles, attributes, beauties and supernatural powers for at least ten minutes, never repeating himself, announced that the *indunas* of the King were without accompanied by the white man, Ibubesi, awaiting her permission to enter. She gave it through Noie; and, the horn wand in her hand, seated herself upon a carved stool in front of the great hut. Presently an altercation arose upon the further side of the reed fence in which she recognised Ishmael's strident voice, mingled with the deeper tones of the Zulus, who seemed to be insisting upon something.

"They command him to take off his headdress," said Noie, "and threaten to beat him if he will not."

"Go, tell them to admit him as he is, that I may see his face, and learn if he be the white man whom I knew, or another," answered Rachel, and she went.

Then the gate was opened and the messengers were led in by women. After these came six captains, carrying broad spears, as she had commanded, and last of all Ishmael himself. Rachel's whole nature shrank at the sight of his dark, handsome features. She loathed the man now as always; her instinct warned her of danger at his hands. Also she remembered his threats when last they met and she rejected him, and what had passed between him and her father on the following day. But of all this she showed nothing, remaining seated in silence with calm, set face.

Ishmael was advancing with a somewhat defiant air. Except for a *kaross* upon his shoulders he wore European dress, and the ridiculous hat with the white ostrich feather in it, both of them now much the worse for wear, which she remembered so well. Also he had a lighted pipe in his mouth. Presently one of the captains appeared to become suddenly aware of this pipe, for, stretching out his hand, he snatched it away, and the hat with it, throwing them upon the ground. Ishmael, whose teeth and lips were hurt, turned on the man with an oath and struck him, whereon instantly he was seized, and would perhaps have been killed before Rachel could interfere had it not been unlawful to shed blood in her presence. As it was, with a motion of her wand, she signified that he was to be loosed, a command that Noie interpreted to them. At any rate, they let him go, though a captain placed his feet on the hat and pipe. Then Ishmael came forward and said awkwardly:

"How do you do? I did not expect to see you here," and he devoured her beauty with his bold, greedy eyes, though not without doubt and dread, or so thought Rachel.

Taking no notice of his greeting, she said in a cold voice:

"I have sent for you here to ask if you have any reason as to why I should not order you to be killed for your crime against my servant, Noie, and therefore against me?"

Now Ishmael paled, for he had not expected such a welcome, and began to deny the thing.

"Spare your falsehoods," went on Rachel. "I have it from the King's lips, and from my own knowledge. Remember only that here I am the *Inkosazana*, with power of life and death. If I speak the word, or point at you with this wand, in a minute you will have gone to your account."

"*Inkosazana* or not," he answered in a cowed voice, "you know too much. Well, then, she was taken that you might follow her to Zululand to ask her life, and you see that the plan was good, for you came; and," he added, recovering some of his insolence and familiarity: "we are here together, two white people among all these silly niggers."

Rachel looked him up and down; then she looked at the *indunas* seated in silence before her, at the great limbed captains with their broad spears beyond, reminding her in their plumes and attitudes of some picture that she had seen of Roman gladiators about to die. Lastly she looked at the delicately shaped Noie by her side, with her sweet, inscrutable face, the woman whose parents and kin this outcast had brought to a bloody death, the woman whom to forward his base ends he had vilely striven to murder. Slowly she looked at them all and at him, and said:

"Shall I explain to these nobles and captains what you call them, and what you are called among your own people? Shall I tell them something of your story, Mr. Ishmael?"

"You can do what you like," he answered sullenly. "You know why I got you here—because I love you: I told you that many months ago. While you were down at Ramah I had no chance with you, because of that old hypocrite of a father of yours, and this black girl," and he looked at Noie viciously. "Here I thought that it would be different—that you would be glad of my company, but you have turned yourself into a kind of goddess and hold me off," and he paused.

"Go on," said Rachel.

"All right, I will. You may think yourself a goddess, as I do myself sometimes. But I know that you are a woman too, and that soon you will get tired of this business. You want to go home to your father and mother, don't you? Well, you can't. You are a prisoner here, for these fools have got it into their heads that you are their Spirit, and that it would be unlucky to let you out of the country. So here you must stop, for years perhaps, or till they are sick of you and kill you. Just understand, Rachel, that nobody can help you to escape except me, and that I shan't do so for nothing."

Rachel straightened herself upon her seat, gripping the edge of it with her hands, for her temper was rising, while Noie bent forward and said something in her ear.

"What is that black devil whispering to you?" he asked. "Telling you to have me killed, I expect. Well, you daren't, for what would your holy parents say? It would be murder, wouldn't it, and you would go to hell, where I daresay you come from, for otherwise how could you be such a witch? Look here," he went on, changing his tone, "don't let's squabble. Make it up with me. I'll get you clear of this and marry you afterwards on the square. If you won't, it will be the worse for you—and everybody else, yes, everybody else."

"Mr. Ishmael," answered Rachel calmly, "you are making a very great mistake, about my scruples as to taking life I mean, amongst other things. Once when it was necessary you saw me kill a man. Well, if I am forced to it, what I did then I will do again, only not with my own hand. Mr. Ishmael, you said just now that you could get me out of Zululand. I take you at your word, not for my own sake, for I am comfortable enough here, but for that of my father and mother, who will be anxious," and her voice weakened a little as she spoke of them.

"Do you? Well, I won't. I am comfortable here also, and shall be more so as the husband of the *Inkosazana*. This is a very pretty *kraal*, and it is quite big enough for two," he added with an amorous sneer.

Now for a minute at least Rachel sat still and rigid. When she spoke again it was in a kind of gasp:

"Never," she said, "have you gone nearer to your death, you wanderer without name or shame. Listen now. I give you one week to arrange my escape home. If it is not done within that time, I will pay you back for those words. Be silent, I will hear no more."

Then she called out:

"Rise, men, and bear the message of the *Inkosazana* to Dingaan, King of the Zulus. Say to Dingaan that this wandering white dog whom he has sent into my house has done me insult. Say that he has asked me, the *Inkosazana-y-Zoola*, to be one of his wives."

At these words the counsellors and captains uttered a shout of rage, and two of the latter seized Ishmael by the arm, lifting their spears to plunge them into him. Rachel waved her wand and they let them fall again.

"Not yet," she said. "Take him to the King, and if my word comes to the King, then he dies, and not till then. I would not have his vile blood on my hands. Unless I speak, I, Queen of the Heavens, leave him to the vengeance of the Heavens. My mantle is over him, lead him back to the King and let me see his face no more."

"We hear and it shall be so," they answered with one voice, then forgetting their ceremony hustled Ishmael from the *kraal*.

"Have I done well?" asked Rachel of Noie, when they were alone.

"No, Zoola," she answered, "you should have killed the snake while you were hot against him, since when your blood grows cold you can never do it, and he will live to bite you."

"I have no right to kill a man, Noie, just because he makes love to me, and I hate him. Also, if I did so he could not help me to escape from Zululand, which he will do now because he is afraid of me."

"Will he be afraid of you when you are both across the Tugela?" asked Noie. "*Inkosazana*, give me power and ask no questions. Ibubesi killed my father and mother and brethren, and has tried to kill me. Therefore my heart would not be sore if, after the fashion of this land, I paid him spears for battle-axes, for he deserves to die."

"Perhaps, Noie, but not by my word."

"Perhaps by your hand, then," said Noie, looking at her curiously. "Well, soon or late he will die a red death—the reddest of deaths, I learned that from the spirit of my father."

"The spirit of your father?" said Rachel, looking at her.

"Certainly, it speaks to me often and tells me many things, though I may not repeat them to you till they are accomplished. Thus I was not afraid in the hands of Dingaan, for it told me that you would save me."

"I wish it would speak to me and tell me when I can go home," said Rachel with a sigh.

"It would if it could, Zoola, but it cannot because the curtain is too thick. Had all you loved been slain before your eyes, then the veil would be worn thin as mine is, and through it, you who are akin to them, would hear the talk of the ghosts, and dimly see them wandering beneath their trees."

"Beneath their trees——!"

"Yes, the trees of their life, of which all the boughs are deeds and all the leaves are words, under the shadow of which they must abide for ever. My people could tell you of those trees, and perhaps they will one day when we visit them together. Nay, pay no heed, I was wandering in my talk. It is the sight of that wild beast, Ibubesi. You will not let me kill him! Well, doubtless it is fated so. I think one day you will be sorry—but too late."

## Chapter 12
# Rachel Sees a Vision

That evening Ishmael was brought before the King. He was in evil case, for the captains, some of whom had grudges against him, when he tried to break away from them outside the gate, had beaten him with their spear shafts nearly all the way from the *kraal* to the Great Place, remarking that he fought and remonstrated, that the *Inkosazana* had forbidden them to kill him, but had said nothing as to giving him the flogging which he deserved. His clothes were torn, his hat and pipe were lost—indeed hours before Noie had thrown both of them into the fire—his eyes were black from the blow of a heavy stick and he was bruised all over.

Such was his appearance when he was thrust before Dingaan, seething with rage which he could scarcely suppress, even in that presence.

"Did you visit the *Inkosazana* today, White Man?" asked the King blandly, while the *indunas* stared at him with grim amusement.

Then Ishmael broke out into a recital of his wrongs, demanding that the captains who had beaten him, a white man, and a great person, should be killed.

"Silence," said Dingaan at length. "The question, Night-prowler, is whether you should not be killed, you dog who dared to insult the *Inkosazana* by offering yourself to her as a husband. Had she commanded you to be speared, she would have done well, and if you trouble me with your shoutings, I will send you to sleep with the jackals tonight without waiting for her word."

Now, seeing his danger, Ishmael was silent, and the King went on:

"Did you discover, as I bade you, why it is that the *Inkosazana* desires to leave us?"

"Yes, King. It is because she would return to her own people, the old prayer-doctor and his wife."

"They are not her people!" exclaimed Dingaan. "We know that she came to them out of the storm, and that they are but the foster-parents chosen for her by the Heavens. You were the first to tell us that story, and how she caused the lightning to burn up my soldier yonder at Ramah. We are her people and no others. Can the *Inkosazana* have a father and a mother?"

"I don't know," answered Ishmael, "but she is a woman and I never knew a woman who was without them. At least I am sure that she looks upon them as her father and mother, obeying them in all things, and that she will never leave them while they live, unless they command her to do so."

Dingaan stared at him with his pig-like eyes, repeating after him—"while they live, unless they command her to do so." Then he asked:

"If the *Inkosazana* desires to go, who is there that dares to stay her, and if she puts out her magic, who is there that has the power? If a hand is lifted against her, will she not lay a curse on us and bring destruction upon us?"

"I don't know," answered Ishmael again, "but if she goes back among the white folk and is angry, I think that she will bring the Boers upon you."

Now Dingaan's face grew very troubled, and bidding Ishmael stand back awhile, he consulted with his council. Then he said:

"Listen to me, White Man. It would be a very evil thing if the *Inkosazana* were to leave us, for with her would go the Spirit of our people, and their good luck, so say the witch-doctors with one voice, and I believe them. Further, it is our desire that she should remain with us a while. This day the Council of the Diviners has spoken, saying that the words of the *Inkosazana* which she uttered here are too hard for them, and that other doctors of a people who live far away, must be sent for and brought face to face with her. Therefore here at Umgugundhlovo she should abide until they come."

"Indeed," answered Ishmael indifferently.

In the doctors who dwell far away, and the council of the Diviners he had no belief. But understanding the natives as he did he guessed correctly enough that the latter found themselves in a cleft stick. Worked on by their superstitions, which he had first awakened for his own ends, they had accepted Rachel as something more than human, as the incarnation of the Spirit of their people. This Mopo, who was said to have killed Chaka by command of that Spirit, had acknowledged her to be, and therefore they did not dare to declare that her words spoken as an oracle were empty words. But neither did they dare to interpret the saying that she meant that no attack must be made upon the Boers and should be obeyed.

To do this would be to fly in the face of the martial aspirations of the nation and the secret wishes of the King, and perhaps if war ultimately broke out, would cost them their lives. So it came about that they announced that they could not understand her sayings, and had decided to thrust off the responsibility on to the shoulders of some other diviners, though who these men might be Ishmael neither knew nor took the trouble to ask.

"But," went on the King, "who can force the dove to build in a tree that does not please it, seeing that it has wings and can fly away? Yet if its own tree, that in which it was reared from the nest, could be brought to it, it might be pleased to abide there. Do you understand, White Man?"

"No," answered Ishmael, though in fact he understood well enough that the King was playing upon Rachel's English name of Dove, and that he meant that her home might be moved into Zululand. "No, the *Inkosazana* is not a bird, and who can carry trees about?"

"Have the spear-shafts knocked the wit out of you, Ibubesi," asked Dingaan, impatiently, "or are you drunk with beer? Learn then my meaning. The *Inkosazana* will not stay because her home is yonder, therefore it must be brought here and she will stay. At first I gave orders that if this old white teacher and his wife tried to accompany her, they should be killed. Now I eat up those words. They must come to Zululand."

"How will you persuade them to be such fools?" asked Ishmael.

"How did I persuade the *Inkosazana* herself to come? Was it not to seek one whom she loved?"

"They will think that you have killed her, and wish to kill them also."

"No, because you will go in command of an *impi* and show them otherwise."

"I cannot go; your brutes of captains have hurt my head, and lamed me; I cannot walk or ride."

"Then you can be carried in a litter, or," he added threateningly, "you can abide here with the vultures. The *Inkosazana* is merciful, but why should I not avenge her wrongs upon you, white dog, who have dared to scratch at the *kraal* gate of the *Inkosazana-y-Zoola*?"

Now Ishmael saw that he had no choice; also a dark thought rose dimly in his mind. He desired to win Rachel above everything on earth, he was mad with love—or what he understood as love—of her, and this business might be worked to his advantage. Moreover, to stay was death. So he fell to bargaining for a reward for his services, a large reward in cattle and ivory; half of it to be paid down at once, and it was promised to him. Then he took his instructions. These were that he was to travel to the mission station of Ramah in command of a small *impi* of three hundred men, whose only orders would be that they were to obey him in all things! That he was to tell the *Umfundusi* who was called Shouter, that if they wished to see her any more, he and his wife must come to dwell with the *Inkosazana*, in Zululand: that if they refused he was to bring them by force. If, perchance, the *Inkosazana*, choosing to exercise her authority, crossed the Tugela and reached Ramah before he could do this, he was still to bring them, for then she would follow. In the same way, if the Shouter and his wife met her on the road, they were to travel on, for then she would turn and, accompany them. He was to go at once and execute these orders.

"I hear," said Ishmael, "and will start as soon as the cattle have been delivered and sent on with the ivory to my *kraal*, Mafooti."

There was something in the man's voice, or in the look of low cunning which spread itself over his face, that attracted Dingaan's attention.

"The cattle and the ivory shall be sent," he said, sternly, "but ill shall it be for you, Ibubesi, if you seek to trick me in this matter. You have grown rich on my bounty, and yonder at your place, Mafooti, you have many cows, many wives, many children—my spies have given me count of all of them. Now, if you play me false, or if you dare to lift a finger against the White One, know that I will burn that *kraal* and slay the inhabitants with the spear and take the cattle, and when I catch you, Ibubesi, I will kill you, slowly, slowly. I have spoken, go.

"I go, Great Elephant, Calf of the Black Cow, and I will obey in all things," answered Ishmael in a humble voice, for he was frightened. "The white people shall be brought, only I trust to you to protect me from the anger of the *Inkosazana* for all that I may do."

"You must make your own peace with the *Inkosazana*," answered Dingaan, and turning, he crept into his hut.

An hour later the great *induna*, Tamboosa, appeared at Rachel's *kraal*, and craved leave to speak with her.

"What is it?" asked Rachel when he had been admitted. "Have you come to lead me out of Zululand, Tamboosa?"

"Nay, White One," he answered, "the land needs you yet awhile. I have come to tell you that Dingaan would speak with your servant Noie, if it be your good pleasure to let her visit him. Fear not. No harm shall come to her, if it does you may order me to be put to death. You, yourself, could not be safer than she shall be."

"Are you afraid to go?" asked Rachel of Noie.

"Not I," answered the girl, with a laugh. "I trust to the King's word and to your might."

"Depart then," said Rachel, "and come back as swiftly as you may. Tamboosa shall lead you."

So Noie went.

Two hours after sundown, while Rachel was eating her evening meal in her Great Hut, attended by the maidens, the door-board was drawn aside, and Noie entered, saluted, and sat down. Rachel signed to the women to clear away the food and depart. When they had gone she asked what the King's business was, eagerly enough, for she hoped that it had to do with her leaving Zululand.

"It is a long story, Zoola," answered Noie, "but here is the heart of it. I told you when first we met that I am not of this people, although my mother was a Zulu. I told you that I am of the Dream-people, the Ghost-people, the little Grey-people, who live away to the north beneath their trees, and worship their trees."

"Yes," answered Rachel, "and that is why you care nothing for men as other women do, but dream dreams and talk with spirits. But what of it?"

"That is why I dream dreams and talk with spirits, as one day I hope that I shall teach you to do, you whose soul is sister to my soul," replied Noie, her large eyes shining strangely in her delicate face. "And this of it—the Ghost-people are diviners, they can read the future and see the hearts of men; there are no diviners like them. Therefore chiefs and peoples who dwell far away send to them with great gifts, and pray them come read their fate, but they will seldom listen or obey. Now Dingaan and his councillors are troubled about this matter of the Boers, and the meaning of the words you spoke as to their waging war on them, and of the omen of the falling star. The council of the doctors can interpret none of these things, nor dare they ask you to do so, since you bade them speak no more to you of that matter, and they know, that if they did, either you would not answer, or, worse still, say words that would displease them."

"They are right there," said Rachel. "To have to play the dark oracle once is enough for me. If I speak again, it shall be plainly."

"Therefore they have bethought them of the Dealers in Dreams and desire to bring you face to face with their prophets, the Ghost-Kings, that these may see your greatness and tell them the meaning of your words, and of the omen that you caused to travel through the skies."

"Do you mean that they wish me to visit these Ghost-Kings, Noie?"

"Not so, Zoola, for then they must part with your presence. They wish that the priests of the Ghost-Kings should visit you, bearing with them the word of the Mother of the Trees."

"Visit me! How can they? Who will bring them here?"

"They wish that I should bring them, for as they know, I am of their blood, and I alone can talk their language, which my father taught me from a child."

"But, Noie, that would moan that we must be separated," said Rachel, in alarm.

"Yes, it would mean that, still I think it best that you should humour them and let me go, for otherwise I do not know how you will ever escape from Zululand. Now I told the King that I thought you would permit it on one condition only—that after you had been brought face to face with the priests of the Ghost-Kings, and they had interpreted your riddle, you should be escorted whence you came, and he answered that it should be so, and that meanwhile you could abide here in honour, peace and safety. Moreover, he promised that a messenger should be sent to Ramah to explain the reason of your delay."

"But how long will you be on the journey, Noie, and what if these prophets of yours refuse to visit Dingaan?"

"I cannot tell you who have never travelled that road. But I will march fast, and if I tire, swift runners shall bear me in a litter. To those who have the secret of its gate that country is not so very far away. Also, the Old Mother of the Trees is my father's aunt, and I think that the prophets will come at my prayer, or at the least send the answer to the question. Indeed, I am sure of it—ask me not why."

Still for a long while Rachel reasoned against this separation, which she dreaded, while Noie reasoned for it. She pointed out that here at least none could harm her, as they had seen in the treatment meted out to Ishmael a white man whom the Zulus looked upon as their friend. Also she said with conviction that these mysterious Ghost-Kings were very powerful, and could free her from the clutches of the Zulus, and protect her from them afterwards, as they would do when they came to know her case.

The end of it was that Rachel gave way, not because Noie's arguments convinced her, but because she was sure that she had other reasons she did not choose to advance.

From that day when each of them tossed up a hair from her head at Ramah, notwithstanding the difference of their race and circumstances, these two had been as sisters. Rachel believed in Noie more, perhaps, than in any other living being, and thus also did Noie believe in Rachel. They knew that their destinies were intertwined, and were sure that not rivers or mountains or the will and violence of men, could keep them separate.

"I see," said Rachel, at length, "that you believe that my fate hangs upon this embassy of yours,"

"I do believe it," answered Noie, confidently.

"Then go, but come back as swiftly as you may, for, my sister, I know not how without you I shall live on in this lonely greatness," and she took her in her arms and kissed her lips.

Afterwards, as they were laying themselves down to sleep, Rachel asked her if she had heard anything about Ishmael. She answered that she learned at the Great *Kraal* that he had been brought before the King that afternoon, and then taken back to his hut, where he was under guard. One of her escort told her, too, that since he saw the King, Ibubesi had fallen very sick, it was thought from a blow that he had received at the house of *Inkosazana*, and that now he was out of his mind and being attended by the doctors. "I wish," added Noie viciously, "that he were out of his body also, for then much sorrow would be spared. But that cannot be before the time."

On the next day before noon, Noie departed upon her journey. Rachel sent for the captains of her escort and the *Isanusis*, or doctors, who were to accompany her, and in a few stern words gave her into their charge, saying that they should answer for her safety with their lives, to which they replied that they knew it, and would do so. If any harm came to the daughter of Seyapi through their fault, they were prepared to die. Then she talked for a long while with Noie, telling her all she knew of the Boers and the purpose of their wanderings, that she might be able to repeat it to her people, and show them how dreadful would be a war between this white folk and the Zulus.

Noie answered that she would give her message, but that it was needless, since the Ghost-Kings could see all that passed "in the bowls of water beneath their trees, and doubtless knew already of her coming and of the cause of it," a reply of which Rachel had not time to inquire the meaning. After this they embraced and parted, not without some tears.

When the gate shut behind Noie, Rachel walked to the high ground at the back of her hut, whence she could see over the fence of the *kraal*, and watched her departure. She had an escort of a hundred picked soldiers, with whom went fifty or sixty strong bearers, who carried food, *karosses*, and a litter. Also there were three doctors of magic and medicine, and two women, widows of high rank who were to attend upon her. At the head of this procession, save for two guides, walked Noie herself, with sandals on her feet, a white robe about her shoulders, and in her hand a little bough on which grew shining leaves, whereof Rachel did not know the meaning. She watched them until they passed over the brow of the hill, on the crest of which Noie turned and waved the bough towards her. Then Rachel went back to her hut, and sat there alone and wept.

This was the beginning of many dreadful days, most of which she passed wandering about within the circuit of the *kraal* fence, a space of some three or four acres, or seated under the shadow of certain beautiful trees, which overhung a deep, clear pool of the stream that ran through the *kraal*, a reed-fringed pool whereon floated blooming lilies. That quiet water, the happy birds that nested in the trees and the flowering lilies seemed to be her only friends. Of the last, indeed, she would count the buds, watching them open in the morning and close again for their sleep at night, until a day came when their loveliness turned to decay, and others appeared in their place.

On the morrow of Noie's departure, Tamboosa and other *indunas* visited her, and asked her if she would not descend to the *kraal* of the King, and help him and his council to try cases, since while she was in the land she was its first judge. She answered, "No, that place smelt too much of blood." If they had cases for her to try, let them be brought before her in her own house. This she said idly, thinking no more of it, but next day was astonished to learn that the plaintiff and defendant in a great suit, with their respective advocates, and from thirty to forty witnesses, were waiting without to know when it was her pleasure to attend to their business.

With characteristic courage Rachel answered, "Now." Her knowledge of law was, it is true, limited to what, for lack of anything more exciting, she had read in some handbooks belonging to her father, who had been a justice of the peace in the Cape Colony, and to a few cases which she had seen tried in a rough-and-ready fashion at Durban, to which must be added an intimate acquaintance with Kaffir customs. Still, being possessed with a sincere desire to discover the truth and execute justice, she did very well. The matter in dispute was a large one, that of the ownership of a great herd of cattle which was claimed as an inheritance by each of the parties. Rachel soon discovered that both these men were very powerful chiefs, and that the reason of their cause being remitted to her was that the King knew that if he decided in favour of either of them he would mortally offend the other.

For a long while Rachel, seated on her stool, listened silently to the impassioned pleadings of the plaintiff's lawyers. Presently this plaintiff was called as a witness, and in the course of his evidence said something which convinced her that he was lying. Then breaking her silence for the first time, she asked him how he dared to give false witness before the *Inkosazana-y-Zoola*, to whom the truth was always open, and who was acquainted with every circumstance connected with the cattle in dispute. The man, seeing her eyes fixed upon him, and being convinced of her supernatural powers, grew afraid, broke down, and publicly confessed his attempted fraud, into which he said he had been led by envy of his cousin, the defendant's, riches.

Rachel gave judgment accordingly, commanding that he should pay the costs in cattle and a fine to the King, and warned him to be more upright in future. The result was that her fame as a judge spread throughout the land, and every day her gates were beset with suitors whose causes she dealt with to the best of her ability, and to their entire satisfaction. Criminal prosecutions that involved the death-sentence or matters connected with witchcraft, however, she steadily refused to try, saying that the *Inkosazana* should not cause blood to flow. These things she left to the King and his Council, confining herself to such actions as in England would come before the Court of Chancery. Thus to her reputation as a spiritual queen, Rachel added that of an upright judge who could not be influenced by fear or bribes, the first, perhaps, that had ever been known in Zululand.

But she could not try such cases all day, the strain was too great, although in the end most of them partook of the nature of arbitrations, since the parties involved, having come to the conclusion that it was not possible to deceive one so wise, grew truthful and submitted their differences to the decision of her wisdom.

After they were dismissed, which was always at noon, for she opened her court at seven and would not sit more than five hours, Rachel was left in her solitary state until the next morning, and oh! the hours hung heavily upon her hands. A messenger was despatched to Ramah, but after ten days he returned saying that the Tugela was in flood, and he could not cross it. She sent him out again, and a week later was told that he had been killed by a lion on his journey. Then another messenger was chosen, but what became of him she never knew.

It was about this time that Rachel learned that Ishmael, having recovered from his sickness, had escaped from Umgugundhlovo by night, whither none seemed to know. From that moment fears gathered thick upon the poor girl. She dreaded Ishmael and guessed that his departure without communicating with her boded her no good. Indeed, once or twice she almost wished that she had taken Noie's counsel and given him over to the justice of the King. Meanwhile of Noie herself nothing had been heard. She had vanished into the wilderness.

Living this strange and most unnatural life, Rachel's nerves began to give way. While she tried her cases she seemed stern and calm. But when the crowd of humble suitors had dispersed from the outer court in which she sat as a judge, and the shouts of the praisers rushing up and down beyond the fence and roaring out her titles had died away, and having dismissed the obsequious maidens who waited upon her, she retired to the solitude of her hut to rest—ah! then it was different. Then she lay down upon her bed of rich furs and at times burst into tears because she who seemed to be a supernatural queen, was really but a white girl deserted by God and man.

Now it was the season of thunderstorms, and almost every afternoon these dreadful tempests broke over her *kraal*, which shook in the roll and crash of the meeting clouds, while beyond the fence the jagged lightning struck and struck again upon the ironstone of the hillside.

She had never feared such storms before, but now they terrified her. She dreaded their advent, and the worst of it was that she must not show her dread, she who was supposed to rule and direct the lightning. Indeed, the bounteous rains which fell ensuring a full harvest after several years of drought, were universally attributed to the good influence of her presence in the land. In the same way when a thunderbolt struck the hut of a doctor who but a day or two before had openly declared his disbelief in her powers, killing him and his principal wife, and destroying his *kraal* by fire, the accident was attributed to her vengeance, or to that of the Heavens, who were angry at this lack of faith. After this remarkable exhibition of supernatural strength, needless to say, the voice of adverse criticism was stayed; Rachel became supreme.

But the storms passed, and when they had rolled away at length, doing her no hurt, and the sun shone out again, she would go and sit beneath the trees at the edge of the beautiful pool until the closing lilies and the chill of the air told her that night drew on.

Oh! those long nights—how endless they seemed to Rachel in her loneliness. Now she who used to sleep so well, could not sleep, or when she slept she dreamed. She dreamed of her mother, always of her mother, that she was ill, and calling her, until she came to believe that in truth this was so. So much did this conviction work upon her mind, that she determined not to wait for the return of Noie, but at all costs to try to leave Zululand, and through Tamboosa declared her will to the King.

Next morning the answer cams back that of course none could control her movements, but if she would go, she must fly, as all the rivers were in flood, as she might see if she would walk to the top of the mountain behind her *kraal.* Tamboosa added that a company of men who had been sent to recapture Ishmael, were kept for a week upon the banks of the first of them, and at length, being unable to cross, had returned, as her messenger had done. Knowing from other sources that this was true, Rachel made no answer. What she did not know, however, was that Ishmael had crossed the smaller rivers before the flood came down, and gone on to meet the soldiers, who were ordered to await him on the banks of the Tugela.

Escape was evidently impossible at present, and if it had been otherwise, clearly the Zulus did not mean to let her go. She must abide here in the company of her terrors and her dreams.

At length, happily for her, these distressing dreams of Rachel's began to be varied by others of a pleasanter complexion, of which, although they were vivid enough, she could only remember upon waking that they had to do with Richard Darrien, the companion of her adventure in the river, of whom she had heard nothing for so many years. For aught she knew he might have died long ago, and yet she did not think that he was dead. Well, if he lived he might have forgotten her, and yet she did not believe that he had forgotten her, he who as a boy had wished to follow her all his life, and whom she had thought of day by day from that hour to this. Yes, she had thought of him, but not thus. Why, at such a time, did he arise in strength before her, seeming to occupy all her soul? Why was her mind never free of him? Could it be that they were about to meet again? She shivered as the hope took hold of her, shivered with joy, and remembered that her mother had always said that they would meet. Could it be that he of all men on the earth, for if he lived he was a man now, was coming to rescue her? Oh! then she would fear nothing. Then in every peril she would feel safe as a child in its mother's arms. No, the thing was too happy to come about; her imagination played tricks with her, no more. And yet, and yet, why did he haunt her sleep?

The dreary days went on; a month had passed since Noie vanished over yonder ridge, and worst of all, for three nights the dreams of Richard had departed, while those of her mother remained.

Rachel was worn out; she was in despair. All that morning she had spent in trying a long and heavy case, which occupied but wearied her mind, one of those eternal cases about the inheritance of cattle which were claimed by three brothers, descendants of different wives of a grandfather who had owned the herd. Finally she had effected a compromise between the parties, and amidst their salutes and acclamations, retired to her hut. But she could not eat; the sameness of the food disgusted her. Neither could she rest, for the daily tempest was coming up, and the heavy atmosphere, or the electricity with which it was charged, and the overpowering heat, exasperated her nervous system and made sleep impossible. At length came the usual rush of icy wind and the bursting of the great storm. The thunder crashed and bellowed; the lightning flickered and flared; the rain fell in a torrent. It passed as it always did, and the sun shone out again. Gasping with relief, Rachel went out of the oven-like hut into the cool, sweet air, and sat down upon a tanned bull's hide which she had ordered her servants to spread for her by the pool of water upon the bank beneath the trees. It was very pleasant here, and the raindrops shaken from the wet leaves fell upon her fevered face and hands and refreshed her.

She tried to forget her troubles for a little while, and began to think of Richard Darrien, her boy-lover of a long-past hour, wondering what he looked like now that he was grown to be a man.

"If only you would come to help me! Oh! Richard, if only you would come to help me," the poor, worn-out girl murmured to herself, and so murmuring fell asleep.

Suddenly it seemed to her that she was wide awake, and staring into a part of the pool beneath her where the bottom was of granite and the water clear. In this water she saw a picture. She saw a great laager of wagons, and outside of one of them a group of bearded, jovial-looking men smoking and talking. Presently another man of sturdy build and resolute carriage, who was followed by a weary Kaffir, walked up to them. His back was towards her so that she could not see his face, but now she was able to hear all that was said, although the voices seemed thin and far away.

"What is it, Nephew?" asked the oldest of the bearded men, speaking in Dutch. "Why are you in such a hurry?"

"This, Uncle," he answered, in the same language, and in a pleasant voice that sounded familiar to Rachel's ears. "That spy, Quabi, whom we sent out a long time ago and who was reported dead, reached Dingaan's *kraal*, and has come back with a strange story."

"Almighty!" grunted the old man, "all these spies have strange stories, but let him tell it. Speak on, *swartzel*."[2]

Then the tired spy began to talk, telling a long tale. He described how he had got into Zululand, and reached Umgugundhlovo and

2. Black-fellow.

lodged there with a relative of his, and done his best to collect information as to the attitude of the King and *indunas* towards the Boers. While he was there the news came that the white Spirit, who was called *Inkosazana-y-Zoola*, was approaching the *kraal* from Natal, where she dwelt with her parents, who were teachers.

"Almighty!" interrupted the old man again, "What rubbish is this? How can a Spirit, white or black, have parents who are teachers?"

The weary-looking spy answered that he did not know, it was not for him to answer riddles, all he knew was that there was great excitement about the coming of this Queen of the Heavens, and he, being desirous of obtaining first-hand information, slipped out of the town with his relative, and walked more than a day's journey on the path that ran to the Tugela, till they came to a place where they hid themselves to see her pass. This place he described with minuteness, so minutely, indeed, that in her dream, Rachel recognised it well. It was the spot where the witch-doctoress had died. He went on with his story; he told of her appearance riding on the white horse and surrounded by an *impi*. He described her beauty, her white cloak, her hair hanging down her back, the rod of horn she carried in her hand, the colour of her eyes, the shape of her features, everything about her, as only a native can. Then he told of the incident of the cattle rushing across her path, of the death of the bull that charged her, of the appearance of the furious witch-doctoress who seized the rein of the horse, of the pointing of the wand, and the instant execution of the woman.

He told of how he had followed the *impi* to the Great Place, of the story of Noie as he had heard it, and the reports that had reached him concerning the interview between the King and this white *Inkosazana*, who, it was said, advised him not to fight the Boers.

"And where is she now?" asked the old Dutchman.

"There; at Umgugundhlovo," he answered, "ruling the land as its head *Isanuzi*, though it is said that she desires to escape, only the Zulus will not let her go."

"I think that we should find out more about this woman, especially as she seems to be a friend to our people," said the old Boer. "Now, who dares to go and learn the truth?"

"I will go," said the young man who had brought in the spy, and as he spoke he turned, and lo! *his face was the face of Richard Darrien*, bearded and grown to manhood, but without doubt Richard Darrien and none other.

"Why do you offer to undertake so dangerous a mission?" asked the Boer, looking at the young man kindly. "Is it because you wish to see this beautiful white witch of whom yonder Quabi tells us such lies, Nephew?"

The shadow of Richard nodded, and his face reddened, for the Boers around him were laughing at him.

"That is right, Uncle," he answered boldly. "You think me a fool, but I am not. Many years ago I knew a little maid who was the daughter of a teacher, and who, if she lives, must have grown into such a woman as Quabi describes. Well, I joined you Boers last year in order to look for that maid, and I am going to begin to look for her across the river yonder."

As the words reached whatever sense of Rachel's it was that heard them, of a sudden, in an instant, laager, Boers, and Richard vanished. In her sleep she tried to recreate them, at first without avail, then the curtain of darkness appeared to lift, and in the still water of the pool she saw another picture, that of Richard Darrien mounted on a black horse with one white foot, riding along a native path through a bush-clad country, while by his side trotted the spy whose name was Quabi.

They were talking together, and she heard, or, at any rate, knew their words.

"How far is it now to Umgugundhlovo?" asked Richard.

"Three days' journey, *Inkosi*, if we are not stopped by flooded rivers," answered Quabi.

For one second only Rachel saw and heard these things, then they, too, passed away, and she awoke to see in front of her the pool empty save for its lilies, and above to hear the whispering of the evening wind among the trees.

## CHAPTER 13

# Richard Comes

As the sun set Rachel rose and walked to her hut. She was utterly dazed, she could not understand. Was this but a fiction of an overwrought and disordered mind, or had she seen a vision of things passing, or that had passed, far away? If it were a dream, then this was but another drop in her cup of bitterness. If a true vision—oh! then what did it mean to her? It meant that Richard Darrien lived, Richard, of whom her heart had been full for years. It meant that his heart was full of her also, for had she not seemed to hear him say that he had travelled from the Cape with the Boers to look for her, and was he not journeying alone through a hostile land to pursue his search? Who would do such a thing for the sake of a girl unless—unless? It meant that he would protect her, would rescue her from her terrible plight, would take her from among these savages to her home again—oh! and perhaps much more that she did not dare to picture to herself.

Yet how could such things be? They were contrary to experience, at any rate, to the experience of white folk, though natives would believe in them easily enough. Yet in Nature things might be possible which were generally held to be impossible. Her mother had certain gifts—had she, perhaps, inherited them? Had her helplessness appealed to the pity of some higher power? Had her ceaseless prayers been heard? Yet, why should the universal laws be stretched for her? Why should she be allowed to lift a corner of the black veil of ignorance that hems us in, and see a glimpse of what lies beyond? If Richard were really coming, in a day or two she would have learned of his arrival naturally; there was no need that these mysterious influences should be set to work to inform her of his approach.

How selfish she was. The warning might concern him, not her. It was probable enough that the Zulus would kill a solitary white man, especially if they discovered that he proposed to visit their *Inkosazana.*

Well, she had the power to protect him. If she "threw her mantle" over him, no man in all the land would dare to do him violence. Surely it was for this reason that she had been allowed to learn these things, if she had learned them, not for her own sake, but his. *If* she had learned them! Well, she would take the risk, would run the chance of failure and of mockery, yes, and of the loss of her power among these people. It should be done at once.

Rachel clapped her hands, and a maiden appeared whom she bade summon the captain of the guard without the gate. Presently he came, surrounded by a band of her women, since no man might visit the *Inkosazana* alone. Bidding him to cease from his salutations, she commanded him to go swiftly to the Great Place and pray of Dingaan that he would send her an escort and a litter, as she must see him that night on a matter which would not brook delay.

In an hour, just after she had finished her food, which she ate with more appetite than she had known for days, it was reported that they were there. Throwing on her white cloak, and taking her horn wand, she entered the litter and, guarded by a hundred men, was borne swiftly to the House of Dingaan. At its gate she descended, and once more entered that court by the moonlight.

As before, there sat the King and his *indunas* without the Great Hut, and while she walked towards them every man rose crying "Hail! *Inkosazana*." Yes, even Dingaan, mountain of flesh though he was, struggled from his stool and saluted her. Rachel acknowledged the salutation by raising her wand, motioned to them to be seated, and waited.

"Art thou come, White One," asked Dingaan, "to make clear those dark words thou spokest to us a moon ago?"

"Nay, King," she answered, "what I said then, I said once and for all. Read thou the saying as thou wilt, or let the Ghost-people interpret it to thee. Hear me, King and Councillors. Ye have kept me here when I would be gone, my business being ended, that I might be a judge among this people. Ye have told me that the rivers were in flood, that the beast I rode was sick, that evil would befall the land if I deserted you. Now I know, and ye know, that if it pleased me I could have departed when and whither I would, but it was not fitting that the *Inkosazana* should creep out of Zululand like a thief in the night, so I abode on in my house yonder. Yet my heart grew wrath with you, and I, to whom the white people listen also, was half minded to bring hither the thousands of the Amaboona who are encamped beyond the Buffalo River, that they might escort me to my home."

Now at these bold words the King looked uneasy, and one of the councillors whispered to another,

"How knows she that the white men are camped beyond the Buffalo?"

"Yet," went on Rachel, "I did not do so, for then there must have been much fighting and bloodshed, and blood I hate. But I have done this. With these Amaboona travels an English chief, a young man, one Darrien, whom I knew from long years ago, and who does me reverence. Him, then, I have commanded to journey hither, and to lead me to my own place across the Tugela. Tonight I am told he sleeps a short three days' journey from this town, and I am come here to bid you send out swift messengers to guide him hither."

She ceased, and they stared at her awhile. Then the King asked,

"What messenger is it, *Inkosazana*, that thou hast sent to this white chief, Dario? We have seen none pass from thy house."

"Dost thou think, then, King, that thou canst see my messengers? My thoughts flew from me to him, and called in his ear in the night, and I saw his coming in the still pool that lies near my huts."

"*Ow!*" exclaimed one of the Council, "she sent her thoughts to him like birds, and she saw his coming in the water of the pool. Great is the magic of the *Inkosazana*."

"The chief, Darrien," went on Rachel, without heeding the interruption, although she noted that it was Mopo of the withered hand who had spoken from beneath the blanket wrapped about his head, "may be known thus. He is fair of face, with eyes like my eyes, and beard and hair of the colour of gold. If I saw right, he rides upon a black horse with one white foot and his only companion is a Kaffir named Quabi who, I think," and she passed her hand across her forehead, "yes, who was surely visiting a relation of his, at this, the Great Place, when I crossed the Tugela."

Now the King asked if any knew of this Quabi, and an *induna* answered in an awed voice, that it was true that a man so called had been in the town at the time given by the *Inkosazana*, staying with a soldier whose name he mentioned, but who was now away on service. He had, however, departed before the *Inkosazana* arrived, or so he believed, whither he knew not.

"I thought it was so," went on Rachel. "As I saw him in the pool he is a thin man whose shoulders stoop, and whose beard is white, although his hair is black. He wears no ring upon his head."

"That is the man," said the *induna*, "being a stranger I noted him well, as it was my business to do."

"Summon the messengers swiftly, King," went on Rachel, "and let them depart at once, for know that this white chief and his servant are under the protection of the Heavens, and if harm comes to them, then I lay my curse upon the land, and it shall break up in blood and ruin. Bid them say to Darrien, that the *Inkosazana-y-Zoola*, she who stood with him once on the rock in the river while the lightnings fell and the lions roared about them, sends him greetings and awaits him."

Now Dingaan turned to an *induna* and said,

"Go, do the bidding of the *Inkosazana*. Bid swift runners search out this white chief, and lead him to her house, and remember that if aught of ill befalls him, those men die, and thou diest also."

The *induna* leapt up and departed, and Rachel also made ready to go. A moment later the captain of the gate entered, fell upon his knees before Dingaan, and said,

"O King, tidings."

"What are they, man?" he asked.

"King, the watchmen report that it has been called from hilltop to hilltop that a white man who rides a black horse, has crossed the Buffalo, and travels towards the Great Place. What is thy pleasure? Shall he be killed or driven back?"

"When did that news come?" asked the King in the silence which followed this announcement.

"Not a minute gone," he answered. "The inner watchman ran with it, and is without the gates. There has been no other tidings from the West for days."

"Thy watchmen call but slowly, King, the water in the pool speaks swifter," said Rachel, then still in the midst of a heavy silence, for this thing was fearful to them, she turned and departed.

"So it is true, so it is true!" Rachel kept repeating to herself, the words suiting themselves to the time of the footfall of her bearers. She was spent with all the labour and emotions of that long day, culminating in the last scene, when she must play her dangerous, superhuman part before these keen-witted savages. She could think no more; scarcely could she undress and throw herself upon her bed in the hut. Yet that night she slept soundly, better than she had done since Noie went away. No dreams came to trouble her and in the morning she woke refreshed.

But now doubts did come. Might she not be mistaken after all? She knew the marvellous powers of the natives in the matter of the transmission of news, powers so strange that many, even among white people, attributed them to witchcraft. She had no doubt, therefore, as to the fact of some Englishman or Boer having entered Zululand. Doubtless the news of his arrival had been conveyed over scores of miles of country by the calling of it as the captain said, from hill to hill, or in some other fashion. But might not this arrival and the circumstance of her dream or vision be a mere coincidence? What was there to show that the stranger who was riding a black horse was really Richard Darrien? Perhaps it was all a mistake, and he was only one of those white wanderers of the stamp of the outcast Ishmael who, even at that date, made their way into savage countries for the purposes of gain or to enjoy a life of licence. And yet, and yet Quabi, of whom she also dreamed, had visited the Great Place—as she dreamed.

The next two days were terrible to Rachel. She endured them as she had endured all those that went before, trying the cases that were brought to her, keeping up her appearance of distant dignity and utter indifference. She asked no questions, since to do so would be to show doubt and weakness, although she was aware that the tale of her vision had spread through the land, and that the issue of the matter was of intense interest to thousands. From some talk which she overheard while she pretended to be listening to evidence, she learned even that two men going to execution had discussed it, saying that they regretted they would not live to know the truth. On the second day she did hear one piece of news, for although she sat by her pool and again tried to sleep by its waters, these remained blind and dumb.

The *induna*, Tamboosa, on one of his ceremonial visits, after speaking of the health of her mare, which, it seemed was improving, mentioned incidentally that the messengers running night and day had met the white man and "called back" that he was safe and well. He added that had it not been for her vision this said white man would certainly have been killed as a spy.

"Yes, I knew that," answered Rachel, indifferently, although her heart thumped within her bosom. "I forget if I said that the *Inkosi* was to be brought straight here when he arrives. If not, let it be known that such is my command. The King can receive him afterwards if it pleases him to do so, as probably we shall not depart until the next day."

Then she yawned, and as though by an afterthought asked if any news had been "called back" from Noie.

Tamboosa answered, No; no system of intelligence had been organised in the direction in which she had gone, for that country was empty of enemies, and indeed of population. However, this would not distress the *Inkosazana*, who had only to consult her Spirit to see all that happened to her servant.

Rachel replied that of course this was so, but as a matter of fact she had not troubled about the matter, then waved her hand to show that the interview was at an end.

It was the morning of the third day, and while Rachel was delivering judgment in a case, a messenger entered and whispered something to the *induna* on duty, who rose and saluted her.

"What is it?" she asked.

"Only this, *Inkosazana*; the white *Inkoos* from the Buffalo River has arrived, and is without."

"Good," said Rachel, "let him wait there." Then she went on with her judgment. Yes, she went on, although her eyes were blind, and the blood beating in her ears sounded like the roll of drums. She finished it, and after a decent interval, bowed her head in acknowledgement of the customary salutes, and made the sign which intimated that the Court was to be cleared.

Slowly, slowly, all the crowd melted away, leaving her alone with her women.

"Go," she said to one of them, "and bid the captain admit this white chief. Say that he is to come unarmed and alone. Then depart, all of you. If I should need you I will call."

The girl went on her errand while her companions filed away through the back gate of the inner fence. Rachel glanced round to make sure of her solitude. It was complete, no one was left. There she sat in state upon her carved stool, her wand in her hand, her white cloak upon her shoulders, and the sunlight that passed over the round of the hut behind her glinting on her hair till it shone like a crown of gold, but leaving her face in shadow; sat quite still like some lovely tinted statue.

The gate of the inner fence opened and closed again after a man who entered. He walked forward a few paces, then stood still, for the flood of light that revealed him so clearly at first prevented him from seeing her seated in the shadow. Oh! there could be no further doubt—before her was Richard Darrien, the lad grown to manhood, from, whom she had parted so many years ago. Now, as then, he was not tall, though very strongly built, and for the rest, save for his short beard, the change in him seemed little. The same clear, thoughtful, grey eyes, the same pleasant, open face, the same determined mouth. She was not disappointed in him, she knew this at once. She liked him as well as she had done at the first.

Now he caught sight of her and stayed there, staring. She tried to speak, to welcome him, but could not, no words would come. He also seemed to be smitten with dumbness, and thus the two of them remained a while. At last he took off his hat almost mechanically, as though from instinct, and said vaguely,

"You are the *Inkosazana-y-Zoola*, are you not?"

"I am so called," she answered softly, and with effort.

The moment that he heard her voice, with a movement so swift that it was almost a spring, he advanced to her, saying,

"Now I am sure; you are Rachel Dove, the little girl who—Oh, Rachel, how lovely you have grown!"

"I am glad you think so, Richard," she answered again in the same low, deep voice, a voice laden with the love within her, and reddening to her eyes. Then she let fall her wand, and rising, stretched out both her hands to him.

They were face to face, now, but he did not take those hands; he passed his arms about her, drew her to him unresisting, and kissed her on the lips. She slipped from his embrace down on to her stool, white now as she had been red. Then while he stood over her, trembling and confused, Rachel looked up, her beautiful eyes filled with tears, and whispered, "Why should I be ashamed? It is Fate."

"Yes," he answered, "Fate."

For so both, of them knew it to be. Though they had seen each other but once before, their love was so great, the bond between their natures so perfect and complete, that this outward expression of it would not be denied. Here was a mighty truth which burst through all wrappings of convention and proclaimed itself in its pure strength and beauty. That kiss of theirs was the declaration of an existent unity which circumstances did not create, nor their will control, and thus they confessed it to each other.

"How long?" she asked, looking up at him.

"Eight years today," he answered, "since I rode away after those wagons."

"Eight years," she repeated, "and no word from you all that time. You have behaved badly to me, Richard."

"No, no, I could not find out. I wrote three times, but always the letters were returned, except one that went to the wrong people, who were angry about it. Then two years ago, I heard that your father and mother had been in Natal, but had gone to England, and that you were dead. Yes, a man told me that you were dead," he added with a gulp. "I suppose he was speaking of somebody else, as he could not remember whether the name was Dove or Cove, or perhaps he was just lying. At any rate, I did not believe, him. I always felt that you were alive."

"Why did you not come to see, Richard?"

"Why? Because it was impossible. For years my father was an invalid, paralysed; and I was his only child, and could not leave him."

She looked a question at him.

"Yes," he answered with a nod, "dead, ten months ago, and for a few weeks I had to remain to arrange about the property, of which he left a good deal, for we did well of late years. Just then I heard a rumour of an English missionary and his wife and daughter who were said to be living somewhere beyond the boundaries of Natal, in a savage place on the Transvaal side of the Drakensberg, and as some Boers I knew were trekking into that country I came with them on the chance—a pretty poor one, as the story was vague enough."

"You came—you came to seek the girl, Rachel Dove?"

"Of course. Otherwise why should I have left my farms down in the Cape to risk my neck among these savages?"

"And then," went on Rachel, "you or somebody else sent in the spy, Quabi, who returned to the Boer camp with his story about the *Inkosazana-y-Zoola*. You remember you brought him in limping to that old fellow with a grey beard and a large pipe, and the others who laughed at the tale. I mean when you said that this *Inkosazana* seemed very like an English maid, 'the daughter of a teacher,' whom you were looking for, and that you would go to find out the truth of the business."

"Yes, that's all right; but Rachel," he added with a start, "how do you know anything about it—*Oom* Piet and the rest, and the words I used? Your spies must be very good and quick, for you can't have seen Quabi."

"My spies are good and quick. Did you get my message sent by the King's men? It was that she who stood with you on the rock in the river, greeted you and awaited you?"

"Yes, I could not understand. I do not understand now. Just before that they were going to kill me as a Boer spy. Who told you everything?"

"My heart," she answered smiling. "I dreamed it all. I suppose that I was allowed to save your life that I might bring you here to save me. Listen now, Richard, while I tell you the strangest story that you ever heard; and if you don't believe it, go and ask the King and his *indunas*."

Then she told him of her vision by the pool and all that happened after it. When she had finished Richard could only shake his head and say:

"Still I don't understand; but no wonder these Zulus have made a goddess of you. Well, Rachel, what is to happen now? If you are to stop here they mayn't care for me as a high priest."

"I am not; I am going home, and you must take me. I told them that you were coming to do so. You have your horse, have you not, the black horse with the white forefoot? Well, we will start at once—no, you must eat first, and there are things to arrange. Now stand at a distance from me and look as respectful as you can, for I fill a strange position here."

Then Rachel clapped her hands and the women came running in.

"Bring food for the *Inkosi* Darrien," she said, "and send hither the captain of the gate."

Presently the man arrived crouched up in token of respect, and shouting her titles.

"Go to the King," said Rachel, "and tell him the *Inkosazana* commands that the horse on which she came be brought to her at once, as she leaves Zululand for a while; also that an *impi* be assembled within an hour to escort her and this white chief, her servant, to the Tugela. Say that the *Inkosi* Darrien has brought her tidings which make it needful that she should travel hence speedily if the Zulus, her people, are to be saved from great misfortune, and say, too, that he goes with her. If the King or his *indunas* would see the *Inkosazana*, or the chief Darrien, let him or the *indunas* meet them on their road, since they have no time to visit the Great Place. Let Tamboosa be in command of the *impi*, and say also that if it is not here at once, the *Inkosazana* will be angry and summon an *impi* of her own. Go now, for the lives of many hang upon your speed; yes, the lives of the greatest in the land."

The man saluted and shot away like an arrow.

"Will they obey you?" asked Richard.

"I think so, because they are afraid of me, especially since I saw you coming. At any rate we must act at once, it is our best chance—before they have time to think. Here is some food—eat. Woman, go, tell the guard that the *Inkosi*'s horse must be fed at the gate, for he will need it presently, and his servant also."

"I have no servant, *Inkosazana*," broke in Richard. "I left Quabi at a *kraal* fifty miles away, laid up with a cut foot. As soon as he is better he will slip back across the Buffalo River."

Then while Richard ate, which he did heartily enough, for joy had made him very hungry, they talked, who had much to tell. He asked her why she thought it necessary to leave Zululand at once. She answered, for two reasons, first because of her desperate anxiety about her father and mother, as to whom her heart foreboded ill, and secondly for his own sake. She explained that the Zulus who had set her up as an image or a token of the guiding Spirit of their nation, were madly jealous concerning her, so jealous that if he remained here long she was by no means certain that even her power could protect him when they came to understand that he was much to her. It was impossible that she could see him often, and much more so that he could remain in her *kraal.* Therefore if they were detained he would be obliged to live at some distance from her where an *assegai* might find him at night or poison be put in his food. At present they were impressed by her foreknowledge of his arrival, and that was why he had been admitted to her at once. But this would wear off—and then who could say, especially if Ishmael returned?

He asked who Ishmael was and what he had to do with her. Rachel told him briefly, and though she suppressed much, he looked very grave at that story.

While she was finishing it a woman called without for leave to enter, and, as before, Rachel bade him stand in a respectful attitude, and at a distance from her. Richard obeyed, and the woman came in to say that certain of the King's *indunas* craved audience with her. They were admitted and saluted her in their usual humble fashion, but of Richard, beyond eyeing him curiously and, as she thought, hostilely, they took not the slightest heed.

"Are all things ready for my journey, as I commanded?" asked Rachel at once.

"*Inkosazana*," answered their spokesman, "they are ready, for how canst thou be disobeyed? Tamboosa and the *impi* wait without. Yet, *Inkosazana*, the heart of the Black One and the hearts of his councillors, and of all the Zulu people are cut in two because thou wouldst go and leave them mourning. Their hearts are sore also with this white man Dario, who has come to lead thee hence, so sore, that were he not thy servant," the *induna* added grimly, "he at least should stay in Zululand."

"He is my servant," answered Rachel haughtily, "whom I sent for. Let that suffice. Remember my words, all of you, and let them be told again in the ears of the King, that if any harm comes to this white chief who is my guest and yours, then there will be blood between me and the people of the Zulus that shall be terribly avenged in blood."

The *indunas* seemed to cower at this declaration, but made no answer. Only the chief of them said:

"The King would know if the *Inkosi*, thy servant, brings thee any tidings of the Amaboona, the white folk with whom he has been journeying."

"He brings tidings that they seek peace with the Zulus, to whom they will do no hurt if no hurt is done to them. Shall I tell them that the Zulus also seek peace?"

"The King gave us no message on that matter, *Inkosazana*," replied the *induna*. "He awaits the coming of the prophets of the Ghost-folk to interpret the meaning of thy words, and of the omen of the falling star."

"So be it," said Rachel. "When my servant, Noie, returns, let her be sent on to me at once, that I may hear and consider the words of her people," and she began to rise from her seat to intimate that the interview was finished.

"*Inkosazana*," said the *induna* hurriedly, "one question from the King—when dost thou return to Zululand?"

"I return when it is needful. Fear not, I think that I shall return, but I say to the King and to all of you: Be careful when I come that there is no blood between me and you, lest great evil fall upon your heads from Heaven. I have spoken. Good fortune go with you till we meet again."

The *indunas* looked at each other, then rose and departed humbly as they had entered.

********

An hour later, surrounded by the *impi*, and followed by Richard, Rachel was on the Tugela road. At the crest of a hill she pulled rein and looked back at the great *kraal*, Umgugundhlovu. Then she beckoned Richard to her side and said:

"I think that before long I shall see that hateful place again."

"Why?" he asked.

"Because of the way in which those *indunas* looked at each other just now. There was some evil secret in their eyes. Richard, I am afraid."

## Chapter 14

# What Chanced at Ramah

The news which reached Rachel that Ishmael had been ill after the rough handling of the captains in her presence, was true enough. For many days he was far too ill to travel, and when he recovered sufficiently to start he could only journey slowly to the Tugela.

It will be remembered that she was told that he had escaped, as indeed he seemed to do, slipping off at night, but this escape of his was carefully arranged beforehand, nor did any attempt to re-capture him upon his way. When at length he came to the river he found the small *impi* awaiting him, not knowing whither they were to go or what they were to do, their only orders being that they must obey him in all things. He found also that the Tugela was in furious flood, so that to ford it proved quite impossible. Here, then, he was obliged to remain for ten full days while the water ran down.

Ishmael was not idle during those ten days, which be spent in recovering his health, and incidentally in reflection. Thus he thought a great deal of his past life, and did not find the record satisfactory. With his exact history we need not trouble ourselves. He was well-born, as he had told Rachel, but had been badly brought up. His strong passions had led him into trouble while young, and instead of trying to reform him his belongings had cast him off. Then he had enlisted in the army, and so reached South Africa. There he committed a crime—as a matter of fact it was murder or something like it—and fled from justice far into the wilderness, where a touch of imagination prompted him to take the name of Ishmael.

For a while this new existence suited him well enough. Thus he had wives in plenty of a sort, and he grew rich, becoming just such a person as might be expected from his environment and unchecked natural tendencies. At length it happened that he met Rachel, who awoke in him certain forgotten associations. She was an English lady, and he remembered that once he had been an English gentleman, years and years ago. Also she was beautiful, which appealed to his strong animal nature, and spiritual, which appealed to a materialist soaked in Kaffir superstition. So he fell in love with her, really in love; that is to say, he came to desire to make her his wife more than he desired anything else on earth. For her sake he grew to dislike his black consorts, however handsome; even the heaping up of herds of cattle after the native fashion ceased to appeal to him. He wanted to live as his forbears had lived, quietly, respectably, with a woman of his own class.

So he made advances to her, with the results we know. For fifteen years or more he had been a savage, and he could not hide his savagery from her eyes any more than he could break off the ties and entanglements that had grown up about him. Had she happened to care for him, it is very possible, however, that in this he would have succeeded in time. He might even have reformed himself completely, and died in old age a much-respected colonial gentleman; perhaps a member of the local Legislature. But she did not; she detested him; she knew him for what he was, a cowardly outcast whose good looks did not appeal to her. So the spark of his new aspirations was trampled out beneath her merciless heel, and there remained only the acquired savagery and superstition mixed with the inborn instincts of a blackguard.

It was this superstition of his that had, brought all her troubles upon Rachel, for however it came about, he had conceived the idea that she was something more than an ordinary woman and, with many tales of her mysterious origin and powers, imparted it to the Zulus, in whose minds it was fostered by the accident of the coincidence of her native name and personal loveliness with those of the traditional white Spirit of their race, and by Mopo's identification of her with that Spirit. Thus she became their goddess and his; at any rate for a time. But while they desired to worship her only, and use her rumoured wisdom as an oracle, he sought to make her his wife; the more impossible it became, the more he sought it. She refused him with contumely, and he laid plots to decoy her to Zululand, thinking that there she would be in his power. In the end he succeeded, basely enough, only to find that he was in her power, and that the contumely, and more, were still his share.

But all this did not in the least deter him from his aim, and as it chanced, fortune had put other cards into his hand. He knew that Rachel would not stay among the Zulus, as they knew it. Therefore they had commissioned him to bring her people to her. If her people were not brought he was sure that she would come to seek them, and *if she found no one*, then where could she go, or at least who would be at hand to help her? Surely his opportunity had come at last, and marriage by capture did not occur to him, who had spent so many years among savages, as a crime from which to shrink. Only he feared that the prospective captive, the *Inkosazana-y-Zoola*, was not one with whom it was safe to trifle. But his love was stronger than his fear. He thought that he would take the risk.

Such were the reflections of Ishmael upon the banks of the flooded Tugela, and when at length the waters went down sufficiently to enable him and the soldiers under his command to cross into Natal, he was fully determined to put them into practice, if the chance came his way. How this might best be done he left to luck, for if it could be avoided he did not wish to have more blood upon his hands. Only Rachel must be rendered homeless and friendless, for then who could protect her from him? An answer came into his mind—she might protect herself, or that Power which seemed to go with her might protect her. Something warned him that this evil enterprise was very dangerous. Yet the fire that burnt within him drove him on to face the danger.

Ishmael was still on the Zululand bank of the river when one day about noon an urgent message reached him from Dingaan. It said that the King was angry as a wounded buffalo to learn, as he had just done, that he, Ibubesi, still lingered on his road, and had not carried out his mission. The *Inkosazana*, accompanied by a white man, was travelling to Ramah, and unless he went forward at once, would overtake him. Therefore he must march instantly and bring back the old Teacher and his wife as he had been bidden. Should he meet the *Inkosazana* and her companion as he returned with the white prisoners she must not be touched or insulted in any way, only his ears and those of the soldiers with him were to be deaf to her orders or entreaties to release them, for then she would surely turn and follow of her own accord back to the Great Place. If the white man with her made trouble or resisted, he was to be bound, but on no account must his blood be made to flow, for if this happened it would bring a curse upon the land, and he, Dingaan, swore by the head of the Black One who was gone (that is Chaka) that he would kill him, Ibubesi, in payment. Yes, he would smear him with honey and bind him over an ant-heap in the sun till he died, if he hunted Africa from end to end to catch him. Moreover, should he fail in the business, he would send a regiment and destroy his town at Mafooti, and, put his wives and people to the spear, and seize his cattle. All this also he swore by the head of the Black One.

Now when Ishmael received this message he was much frightened, for he knew that these were not idle threats. Indeed, the exhausted messenger told him that never had any living man seen Dingaan so mad with rage as he was when he learned that he, Ibubesi, was still lingering on the banks of the Tugela, adding that he had foamed at the mouth with fury and uttered terrible threats. Ishmael sent him back with a humble answer, pointing out that it had been impossible to cross the river, which was "in wrath," but that now he would do all things as he was commanded, and especially that not a hair of the white man's head should be harmed.

"Then you must do them quickly," said the messenger with a grim smile as he rose and prepared to go, "for know that the *Inkosazana* is not more than half a day's march behind you, accompanied by the white *Inkoos* Dario."

"What is this Dario like?" asked Ishmael.

"Oh! he is young and very handsome, with hair and beard of gold, and eyes that are such as those of the *Inkosazana* herself. Some say that he is her brother, another child of the Heavens, and some that he is her husband. Who am I that I should speak of such high things? But it is evident that she loves him very much, for by her magic she told the King of his coming, and even when he is behind her she is always trying to turn her head to look at him."

"Oh! she loves him very much, does she?" said Ishmael, setting his white teeth. Then he turned, and calling the captain of the *impi*, gave orders that the river must be crossed at once, for so the King commanded, and it was better to die with honour by water than with shame by the spear.

So they waded and swam the river with great difficulty, but, as it chanced, without loss of life, Ishmael being borne over it upon the shoulders of the strongest men. Upon its further bank he summoned the captains and delivered to them the orders of the King. Then they set out for Ramah, Ishmael carried in a litter made of boughs.

Whilst the soldiers were constructing this litter, he called two men of the Swamp-dwellers, who had their homes upon the banks of the Tugela, and promising them a reward, bade them run to his town, Mafooti, and tell his head man there to come at once with thirty of the best soldiers, and to hide them in the bush of the *kloof* above Ramah, where he would join them that night. The men, who knew Ibubesi, and what happened to those who failed upon his business, went swiftly, and a little while afterwards, the litter being finished, Ishmael entered it, and the *impi* started for Ramah.

Before sundown they appeared upon a ridge overlooking the settlement, just as the herds were driving the cattle into their *kraals*. Seeing the Zulus while as yet they were some way off, these herds shouted an alarm, whereon the people of the place, thinking that Dingaan had sent a regiment to wipe them out, fled to the bush, the herds driving the cattle after them. Man, woman, and child, deserting their pastor, who knew nothing of all this, being occupied with a sad business, they fled, incontinently, so that when Ishmael and the *impi* entered Ramah, no one was left in it save a few aged and sick people, who could not walk.

At the outskirts of the town Ishmael descended from his litter and commanded the soldiers to surround it, with orders that they were to hurt no one, but if the white *Umfundusi*, who was called Shouter, or his wife attempted to escape, they were to be seized and brought to him. Then taking with him some of the captains and a guard of ten men, he advanced to the mission-house.

The door was open, and, followed by the Zulus, he entered to search the place, for he feared that its inhabitants might have seen them, and have gone with the others. Looking into the first room that they reached, of which, as it chanced, the door was also open, Ishmael saw that this was not so, for there upon the bed lay Mrs. Dove, apparently very ill, while by the side of the bed knelt her husband, praying. For a few moments Ishmael and the savages behind him stood still, staring at the pair, till suddenly Mrs. Dove turned her head and saw them. Lifting herself in the bed she pointed with her finger, and Ishmael noticed that her lips were quite blue, and that she did not seem to be able to speak. Then Mr. Dove, observing her outstretched hand, looked round. He had not seen Ishmael since that day when he struck him after their stormy interview at Mafooti, but recognising the man at once, he asked sternly:

"What are you doing, sir, with these savages in my house? Cannot you see that my wife is sick, and must not be disturbed?"

"I am sorry," Ishmael answered shamefacedly, for in his heart he was afraid of Mr. Dove, "but I am sent to you with a message from Dingaan the King, and," he added as an afterthought, "from your daughter."

"From my daughter!" exclaimed Mr. Dove eagerly. "What of her? Is she well? We cannot get any certain news of her, only rumours."

"I saw her but once." replied Ishmael, "and she was well enough, then. You know the Zulus have made her their *Inkosazana*, and keep her guarded."

"Does she live quite alone then with these savages?"

"She did, but I am sorry I must tell you that she seems to have a companion now, some scoundrel of a white man with whom she has taken up," he sneered.

"My daughter take up with a scoundrel of a white man! It is false. What is this man's name?"

"I don't know, but the natives call him Dario, and say that he is young, and has fair hair, and that she is in love with him. That's all I can tell you about the man."

Mr. Dove shook his head, but his wife sat up suddenly in bed, and plucked him by the sleeve, for she had been listening intently to everything that passed.

"Dario! Young, fair hair, in love with him—" she repeated in a thick whisper, then added, "John, it is Richard Darrien grown up—the boy who saved her in the Umtooma River, years ago, and whom she has never forgotten. Oh! thank God! Thank God! With him she will be safe. I always knew that he would find her, for they belong to each other," and she sank back exhausted.

"That's what the Zulus say, that they belong to each other," replied Ishmael, with another sneer. "Perhaps they are married native fashion."

"Stop insulting my daughter, sir," said Mr. Dove angrily. "She would not take a husband as you take your wives, nor if this man is Richard Darrien, as I pray, would he be a party to such a thing. Tell me, are they coming here?"

"Not they, they are far too comfortable where they are. Also the Zulus would prevent them. But don't be sad about it, for I am sent to take you both to join her at the Great Place where you are to live."

"To join her! It is impossible," ejaculated Mr. Dove, glancing at his sick wife.

"Impossible or not, you've got to come at once, both of you. That is the King's order and the *Inkosazana*'s wish, and what is more there is an *impi* outside to see that you obey. Now I give you five minutes to get ready, and then we start."

"Man, are you mad? How can my wife travel to Zululand in her state? She cannot walk a step."

"Then she can be carried," answered Ishmael callously. "Come, don't waste time in talking. Those are my orders, and I am not going to have my throat cut for either of you. If Mrs. Dove won't dress wrap her up in blankets."

"You go, John, you go," whispered his wife, "or they will kill you. Never mind about me; my time has come, and I die happy, for Richard Darrien is with Rachel."

The mention of Richard's name seemed to infuriate Ishmael. At any rate he said brutally:

"Are you coming, or must I use force?"

"Coming, you wicked villain! How can I come?" shouted Mr. Dove, for he was mad with grief and rage. "Be off with your savages. I will shoot the first man who lays a finger on my wife," and as he spoke he snatched a double-barrelled pistol which hung upon the wall and cocked it.

Ishmael turned to the Zulus who stood behind him watching this scene with curiosity.

"Seize the Shouter," he said, "and bind him. Lift the old woman on her mattress, and carry her. If she dies on the road we cannot help it."

The captains hesitated, not from fear, but because Mrs. Dove's condition moved even their savage hearts to pity.

"Why do you not obey?" roared Ishmael. "Dogs and cowards, it is the King's word. Take her up or you shall die, every man of you, you know how. Knock down the old Evildoer with your sticks if he gives trouble."

Now the men hesitated no longer. Springing forward, several of them seized the mattress and began to lift it bodily. Mrs. Dove rose and tried to struggle from the bed, then uttered a low moaning cry, fell back, and lay still.

"You devils, you have killed her!" gasped Mr. Dove, as lifting the pistol he fired at the Zulu nearest to him, shooting him through the body so that he sank upon the floor dying. Then, fearing lest he should shoot again, the captains fell upon the poor old man, striking him with *kerries* and the handles of their spears, for they sought to disable him and make him drop the pistol.

As it chanced, though this was not their intention, in the confusion a heavy blow from a knob-stick struck him on the temple. The second barrel of the pistol went off, and the bullet from it but just missed Ishmael who was standing to one side. When the smoke cleared away it was seen that Mr. Dove had fallen backwards on to the bed. The martyrdom he always sought and expected had overtaken him. He was quite dead. They were both dead!

The head *induna* in command of the *impi* stepped forward and looked at them, then felt their hearts.

"*Wow!*" he said, "these white people have 'gone beyond.' They have gone to join the spirits, both of them. What now, Ibubesi?"

Ishmael, who stood in the corner, very white-faced, and staring with round eyes, for the tragedy had taken a turn that he did not intend or expect, shook himself and rubbed his forehead with his hand, answering:

"Carry them into the Great Place, I suppose. The King ordered that they should be brought there. Why did you kill that old Shouter, you fools?" he added with irritation. "You have brought his blood and the curse of the *Inkosazana* on our heads."

"*Wow!*" answered the *induna* again, "you bade us strike him with sticks, and our orders were to obey you. Who would have guessed that the old man's skull was so thin from thinking? You or I would never have felt a tap like that. But they are 'gone beyond,' and we will not defile ourselves by touching them. Dead bones are of no use to anyone, and their ghosts might haunt us. Come, brethren, let us go back to the King and make report. The order was Ibubesi's, and we are not to blame."

"Yes," they answered, "let us go back and make report. Are you coming, Ibubesi?"

"Not I," he answered. "Do I want to have my neck twisted because of your clumsiness? Go you and win your own peace if you can, but if you see the *Inkosazana*, my advice is that you avoid her lest she learn the truth, and bring your deaths upon you, for, know, she travels hither, and she called these folk father and mother."

"Without doubt we will avoid her," said the captain, "who fear her terrible curse. But, Ibubesi, it is on you that it will fall, not on us who did but obey you as we were bidden; yes, on you she will bring down death before this moon dies. Make your peace with the Heavens, if you can, Ibubesi, as we go to try to make ours with the King."

"Would you bewitch me, you ill-omened dog?" shouted Ishmael, wiping the sweat of fear off his brow, "May you soon be stiff!"

"Nay, nay, Ibubesi, it is you who shall be stiff. The *Inkosazana* will see to that, and were I not sure of it I would make you so myself, who am a noble who will not be called names by a white *umfagozan*, a low-born fellow who plots for blood, but leaves its shedding to brave men. Farewell, Ibubesi; if the jackals leave anything of you after the *Inkosazana* has spoken, we will return to bury your bones," and he turned to go.

"Stay," cried the dying man on the floor, "would you leave me here in pain, my brothers?"

The *induna* stepped to him and examined him.

"It is mortal," he said, shaking his head, "right through the liver. Why did not the white man's thunder smite Ibubesi instead of you, and save the *Inkosazana* some trouble? Well, your arms are still strong and here is a spear; you know where to strike. Be quick with your messages. Yes, yes, I will see that they are delivered. Good-night, my brother. Do you remember how we stood side by side in that big fight twenty years ago, when the Pondo giant got me down and you fell on the top of me and thrust upwards and killed him? It was a very good fight, was it not? We will talk it over again in the World of Spirits. Good-night, my brother. Yes, yes, I will deliver the message to your little girl, and tell her where the necklace is to be found, and that you wish her to name her firstborn son after you. Good-night. Use that *assegai* at once, for your wound must be painful, or perhaps as you are down upon the ground Ibubesi will do it for you. Good-night, my brother, and Ibubesi, goodnight to you also. We cross the Tugela by another drift, wait you here for the *Inkosazana*, and tell her how the Shouter died."

Then they turned and went. The wounded man watched them pass the door, and when the last of them had gone he used the *assegai* upon himself, and with his failing hand flung it feebly at Ishmael.

The dying Zulu's spear struck Ishmael, who had turned his head away, upon the cheek, just pricking it and causing the blood to flow, no more. Ishmael was still also, paralysed almost, or so he seemed, for even the pain of the cut did not make him move. He stared at the bodies of Mr. and Mrs. Dove; he stared at the dead Zulu, and in his heart a voice cried: "You have murdered them. By now they are pleading to God for vengeance on you, Ishmael, the outcast. You will never dare to be alone again, for they will haunt you."

As he thought it the relaxed hand of the old clergyman who had fallen in a sitting posture on the bed, slipped from his wounded head which he had clasped just before he died, and for a moment seemed to point at him. He shivered, but still he could not stir. How dreadful and solemn was that face! And those eyes, how they searched out the black record of his heart! The quiet rays of the afternoon sun suddenly flowed in through the window place and illumined the awful, accusing face till it shone like that of a saint in glory. A drop of blood from the cut upon his cheek splashed on to the floor, and the noise of it struck on his strained nerves loud as a pistol-shot. Blood, his own blood wherewith he must pay for that which he had shed. The sight and the thought seemed to break the spell. With an oath he bounded out of the room like a frightened wolf, those dead staring at him as he went, and rushed from the house that held them.

Beyond its walls Ishmael paused. The Zulus had fled in one direction, and the inhabitants of Ramah in another; there was no one to be seen. His eye fell upon the dense mass of bush above the station, and he remembered the message that he had sent to his own people to meet him there. Perhaps they had already arrived. He would go to see, he who was in such sore need of human company. As he went his numbed faculties returned to him, and in the open light of day some of his terror passed. He began to think again. What was done was done; he could not bring the dead back to life. He was not really to blame, and after all, things had worked out well for him. Save for this white man, Dario, Rachel was now alone in the world, and dead people did not speak, there was no one to tell her of his share in the tragedy. Why should she not turn to him who had no one else to whom she could go? The white man, if he were still with her, could be got rid of somehow; very likely he would run away, and they two would be left quite alone. At any rate it was for her sake that be had entered on this black road of sin, and what did one step more matter, the step that led him to his reward? Of course it might lead him somewhere else. Rachel was a woman to be feared, and the Zulus were to be feared, and other things to which he could give no shape or name, but that he felt pressing round him, were still more to be feared. Perhaps he would do best to fly, far into the interior, or by ship to some other land where none would know him and his black story. What! Fly companioned by those ghosts, and leave Rachel, the woman for whom he burned, with this Dario, whom the Zulus said she loved, and with whom her mother, just before her end, had declared that she would be safe? Never. She was his; he had bought her with blood, and he would have the due the devil owed him.

He was in the bush now, and a voice called him, that of his head man.

"Come out, you dog," he said, searching the dense foliage with his eyes, and the man appeared, saluting him humbly.

"We received your message and we have come, *Inkoos*. We are but just arrived. What has chanced here that the town is so still?"

"The Zulus have been and gone. They have killed the white Teacher and his wife, though I thought to save them—look at my wound. Also the people are fled."

"Ah!" replied the head man, "that was an ill deed, for he was holy, and a great prophet, and doubtless his spirit is strong to revenge. Well for you is it, Master, that you had no hand in the deed, as at first I feared might be the case, for know that last night a strange dog climbed on to your hut and howled there and would not be driven away, nor could we kill it with spears, so we think it was a ghost. All your wives thought that evil had drawn near to you."

Ishmael struck him across the mouth, exclaiming.

"Be silent, you accursed wizard, or you shall howl louder than your ghost-dog."

"I meant no harm," answered the man humbly, but with a curious gleam in his eye. "What are your commands, Chief?"

"That we watch here. I think that the daughter of the Shouter, she who is called *Inkosazana-y-Zoola*, is coming, and she may need help. Have you brought thirty men with you as I bade you through my messengers?"

"Aye, Ibubesi, they are all hidden in the bush. I go to summon them, though I think that the mighty *Inkosazana*, who can command all the Zulu *impis* and all the spirits of the dead, will need little help from us."

Chapter 15

# Rachel Comes Home

As Rachel had travelled up from the Tugela to the Great Place, so she travelled back from the Great Place to the Tugela in state and dignity such as became a thing divine, perhaps the first white woman, moreover, who had ever entered Zululand. All day she rode alone, Tamboosa leading the white ox before her and Richard following behind, while in front and to the rear marched the serried ranks of the *impi*, her escort. At night, as before, she slept alone in the empty *kraal*s provided for her, attended by the best-born maidens, Richard being lodged in some hut without the fence.

So at length, about noon one day, they reached the banks of the Tugela, not many hours after Ishmael had crossed it, and camped there. Now, after she had eaten, Rachel sent for Richard, with whom she had found but few opportunities to talk during that journey. He came and stood before her, as all must do, and she addressed him in English while the spies and captains watched him sullenly, for they were angry at this use of a foreign tongue which they could not understand. Preserving a cold and distant air, she asked him of his health, and how he had fared.

"Well enough," he answered. "And now, what are your plans? The river is in flood, you will find it difficult to cross. Still it can be done, for I hear that the white man, Ishmael, of whom you told me, forded it this morning with a company of armed men."

Aware of the eyes that watched her, with an effort Rachel showed no surprise.

"How is that?" she asked. "I thought the man fled from Zululand many days ago. Why then does he leave the country with soldiers?"

"I can't tell you, Rachel. There is something queer about the business. When I inquire, everyone shrugs his shoulders. They say that the King knows his own business. If I were you I would ask no questions, for you will learn nothing, and if you do not ask they will think that you know all."

"I understand," she said. "But, Richard, I must cross the river today. You and I must cross it alone and reach Ramah tonight. Richard, something weighs upon my heart; I am terribly afraid."

"How will you manage it?" he asked, ignoring the rest.

"I can't tell you yet, Richard, but keep my horse and yours saddled there where you are encamped," and she nodded towards a hut about fifty yards away. "I think that I shall come to you presently. Now go."

So he saluted her and went.

Presently Rachel sent for Tamboosa and the captains, and asked the state of the river which was out of sight about half a mile from them. They replied that it was "very angry"; none could think of attempting its passage, as much water was coming down.

"Is it so?" she said indifferently. "Well, I must look," and with slow steps she walked towards the hut where she knew the horses were, followed by Tamboosa and the captains.

Reaching it, she saw them standing saddled on its further side, and by them Richard, seated on the ground smoking. As she came he rose and saluted her, but, taking no heed of him, she went to her grey mare, and, placing her foot in the stirrup, sprang to the saddle, motioning to him to do likewise.

"Whither goest thou, *Inkosazana*?" asked Tamboosa anxiously.

"To throw a charm on the waters," she answered, "so that they may run down and I can cross them to morrow. Come, Dario, and come Tamboosa, but let the rest stay behind, since common eyes must not look upon my magic, and he who dares to look shall be struck with blindness."

The captains hesitated, and turning on them fiercely she commanded them to obey her word lest some evil should befall them.

Then they fell back and she rode towards the Tugela, followed by Richard on horseback and Tamboosa on foot. Arrived at that spot on the bank where she had received the salutation of the regiment when she entered Zululand, Rachel saw at once that although the great river was full it could easily be forded on horseback. Calling Richard to her, she said:

"We must go, and now, while there is no one to stop us but Tamboosa. Do not hurt him unless he tries to spear you, for he has been kind to me."

Then she addressed Tamboosa, saying:

"I have spoken to the waters and they will not harm me. The hour has come when I must leave my people for a while, and go forward alone with my white servant, Dario. These are my commands, that none should dare to follow me save only yourself, Tamboosa, who can bring on the white ox with its load so soon as the water has run down and deliver them to me at Ramah. Do you hear me?"

"I hear, *Inkosazana*," answered the old *induna*, "and thy words split my heart."

"Yet you will obey them, Tamboosa."

"Yes, I will obey them who know what would befall me otherwise, and that it is the King's will that none should dare to thwart thee, even if they could. Yet I think that very soon thou wilt return to thy children. Therefore, why not abide with us until tomorrow, when the waters will be low?"

"Tamboosa," said Rachel, leaning forward and looking him in the eyes, "why did Ibubesi cross this river with soldiers but a few hours ago—Ibubesi, who fled from the Great Place when the moon was young that now is full? Look, there goes their spoor in the mud."

"I know not," he answered, looking down. "*Inkosazana*, tomorrow I will bring on the white ox to Ramah, and I will bring it alone."

"So be it, Tamboosa, but if by chance you should not find me, ask where Ibubesi is, and if need be, seek for me with an *impi*, Tamboosa—for me and for this white man, Dario," and again she bent forward and looked at him.

"I know not what thou meanest, *Inkosazana*," he replied. "But of this be sure, that if I cannot find thee, then I will seek for thee, if need be with every spear in Zululand at my back."

"Farewell, then, Tamboosa, and to the regiment farewell also. Say to the captains that it is my will that they should return to the Great Place, bearing my greetings to the King and those of the white lord, Dario. Look for me tomorrow at Ramah."

Then, followed by Richard, she rode her horse past him into the lip of the water. As she went Tamboosa drew himself up and gave her the *Bayète*, the royal salute.

Although it was red with earth and flecked with foam and the roar of it was loud as it sped towards the sea, the river did not prove very difficult to ford. But once, indeed, were the horses swept off their feet and forced to swim, and then but for a few paces, after which they regained them, and plunged to the farther bank without accident.

"Free at last, Rachel, with our lives before us and nothing more to fear," called Richard in his cheery voice, as he forced his horse alongside of hers. Then suddenly he caught sight of her face and saw that it was white and drawn as though with pain; also that she leaned forward on her saddle, clasping its pommel as though she were about to faint.

"What is it?" he exclaimed in alarm. "Did the flood frighten you, Rachel—are you ill?"

For a few moments she made no answer, then straightened herself with a sigh and said in a low voice:

"Richard, I have been so long among those Zulus playing the part of a spirit that I begin to think I am one, or that their magic has got hold of me. I tell you that in the roar of the water I heard voices—the voices of my father and mother calling me and speaking of you—and, Richard, they seemed to be in great fear and pain, for a minute or more I heard them, then a dreadful cold wind blew on me not this wind, it seemed to come from above—and everything passed away, leaving my mind numb and empty so that I do not remember how we came out of the river. Don't laugh at me, Richard; it is so. The Kaffirs are right; I have some power of the sort. Remember how I saw you travelling towards me in the pool."

"Why should I laugh at you, dearest?" he asked anxiously, for something of this uncanny fear passed from her mind into his, with which it was in tune. "Indeed, I don't laugh who know that you are not quite like other women. But, Rachel, the strain of those two months has worn you out, and now the reaction is too much. Perhaps it is nothing.".

"Perhaps," she answered sadly, "I hope so. Richard, what is the time?"

"About a quarter to six, to judge by the sun," he answered,

"Then we shall not be able to reach Ramah before dark."

"No, Rachel, but there is a good moon."

"Yes, there is a good moon; I wonder what it will show us," and she shivered.

Then they pressed their horses to a canter and rode on, speaking little, for the fount of words seemed to be frozen in them, although Richard recollected, with a curious sense of wonder how he had looked forward to this opportunity of long, unfettered talk with Rachel and how much he had to tell her. Over hill and valley, through bush and stream they rode, till at last with the short twilight they reached the plain that ran to Ramah. Then came the dark in which they must ride slowly, till presently the round edge of the moon pushed itself up above the shoulder of a hill and there was light again—pure, peaceful light that turned the *veld* to silver and shone whitely on the pale face of Rachel.

Ramah was before them. They had met no living thing save some wild game trekking to the water, and heard no sound save the distant roar of some beast of prey. Ramah was before them. The moon shone on the roofs of the Mission-house and the little church and the clusters of Kaffir huts beyond. But, oh! it was silent: no cattle lowed, no child cried, nor did the bell of the church ring for evening prayer as at this hour it should have done. Also no lamp showed in the windows of the Mission-house and no smoke rose from the cooking fires of the *kraals*.

"Where are all the people, Richard?" whispered Rachel. "There is the place unharmed, but where are the people?"

But Richard could only shake his head: the terror of something dreadful had got hold of him also, and he knew not what to say.

Now they had come to the wall of the Mission-house and sprang from their horses which they left loose. As they advanced side by side towards the open gate, something leapt the *stoep* and rushed through it. It was a striped hyena; they could see the hair bristle on its back as it passed them with a whining growl. Hand in hand they ran to the house across the little garden patch—Rachel, led by some instinct, guiding her companion straight to her parents' room whereof the windows, that opened like doors, stood wide as the gate had done.

One more moment and they were there; another, and the moonlight showed them all.

For a long while—to Richard it seemed hours—Rachel said nothing; only stood still like the statue of a woman, staring at those cold faces that looked back at her through the unearthly moonlight. Indeed, it was Richard who spoke first, feeling that if he did not this dreadful silence would choke him or cause him to faint.

"The Zulus have murdered them," he said hoarsely, glancing at the dead Kaffir on the floor.

"No," she answered in a cold, small voice; "Ishmael, Ishmael!" and she pointed to something that lay at his feet.

Richard stooped and picked it up. It was a fly wisp of rhinoceros horn which the man had let fall when the Zulu's spear struck him.

"I know it," she went on; "he always carried it. He is the real murderer. The Zulus would not have dared," and she choked and was silent.

"Let me think," said Richard confusedly. "There is something in my mind. What is it? Oh! I know. If you are right that devil has not done this for nothing. He is somewhere near; he wants to take you"; and he ground his teeth at the thought, then added: "Rachel, we must get out of this and ride for Durban, at once—at once; the white people will protect you there."

"Who will bury my father and mother?" she asked in the same cold voice.

"I do not know, it does not matter, the living are more than the dead. I can return and see to it afterwards."

"You are right," she answered. Then she knelt down by the bed and lifting her beautiful, agonised face, put up some silent prayer. Next she rose and kissed first her father, then her mother, kissed their dead brows in a last farewell and turned to go. As she went her eyes fell upon the *assegai* that lay near to the dead Zulu. Stooping down, she took it and with it in her hand passed on to the *stoep*. Here her strength seemed to fail her, for she reeled against the wall, then with an effort flung herself into Richard's arms, moaning:

"Only you left, Richard, only you. Oh! if you were taken from me also, what would become of me?"

A moment later she became aware that the *stoep* was swarming with men who seemed to arise out of the shadows. A voice said in the Kaffir tongue:

"Seize that fellow and bind him."

Instantly, before he could do anything, before he could even turn, Richard was torn from her, struggling furiously, and thrown to the ground. Rachel sprang to the wall and stood with her back to it, raising the spear she held. It flashed into her mind that these were Zulus, and of Zulus she was not afraid.

"What dogs are these," she cried, "that dare to lift a hand against the *Inkosazana* and her servant?"

The black men about her swayed and murmured, then made way for a man who walked up the steps of the *stoep*. The moonlight fell upon him and she saw that it was Ishmael.

"Rachel," he said, taking off his hat politely, "these are my people. We saw that white scoundrel assault you, and of course seized him at once. As you know a dreadful thing has happened here. This afternoon the Zulus killed your father and mother, or rather they killed your father, and your mother, who was ill, died with the shock, because they refused to go to Zululand whither Dingaan had ordered that they should be taken. So seeing that you were travelling here I came to rescue you, lest you should fall into their hands, and," he added lamely, "you know the rest."

Ishmael had spoken in English, but Rachel answered him in Zulu.

"I know all, Night-prowler," she cried aloud. "I know that my father and mother were killed by your order, and in your presence; their spirits told me so but now, and for that crime I sentence you to death!" and she pointed at him with the spear. "Heaven above and earth beneath," she went on, "bear witness that I sentence this man to death.

People of the Zulus, hear me in your *kraals* far away. Hear me, Dingaan, sitting in your Great Place. Hear me, every captain and *induna*, hear the voice of your *Inkosazana*: I sentence this man to death, since because of him there is blood between me and my people, the blood of my father and my mother. Now, Night-prowler, do your worst before you die, but know this, you his servants, that if I am harmed, or if this white man, the chief Dario, is harmed, then you shall die also, every one of you. What is your will, Night-prowler?"

"I will tell you that at Mafooti," answered Ishmael, trying to look bold. "I am not afraid of you like those Zulu savages, and Dingaan is a long way off. Will you come quietly? I hope so, for I don't want to hurt you or put you to shame, but you've got to come, and this Dario, too. If you make any trouble, I will have him killed at once. Understand, Rachel, that if you don't come, he shall be killed at once. My people may be afraid of you, but they won't mind cutting his throat," he added significantly.

"Never mind about me," said Richard in a choked voice from the ground where he was pinned down by the Kaffirs. "Do what you think best for yourself, Rachel."

Now Rachel, whose wits were made keen by doubt and anguish, looked at the faces of the natives about her, and even in that dim moonlight read them like a book, as she could always do. She saw that they were afraid of her, and that if she commanded them, they would let her go free, whatever their master might say or do. But she saw also that Ishmael spoke truth when he declared that they had no such dread of Richard, and might even believe that he was doing her some violence. If she escaped therefore it would be at the cost of Richard's life. Instantly in her bold fashion she made up her mind. It was borne in upon her that she had declared the truth; that Ishmael was doomed, that he had no power to work her any hurt, however sore her case might seem. Since Richard's life hung on it she would go with him.

"Servants of Ibubesi," she said, "lift the white chief Dario to his feet, and listen to my words."

They obeyed her at once, without even waiting for their master to speak, only holding Richard by the arms.

Now the most of the men went into the garden followed by Ishmael, and taking Richard with them, but a few remained to watch her. From this garden presently arose a sound of great quarrelling. Rachel was too far off to understand what was said, but from the sounds she judged that Ishmael was giving orders to his people which they refused to obey, for she could hear him cursing them furiously. Presently she heard something else—the loud report of a gun followed by groans. Then a Kaffir ran up to them and whispered something to those who surrounded her; it was that head man whom Ishmael had struck on the mouth in the bush when he told him that a dog had howled upon his hut, and his face was very frightened.

Rachel leaned against the wall and looked at him, for she could not speak, she who thought that Richard had been murdered.

"Have no fear, *Inkosazana*," said the man, answering the question in her eyes. "Ibubesi has killed one of us because we do not like this business and would clean it off our hands, that is all. The chief Dario is safe, and I swear to thee that no harm shall come to him from us. We will care for him and protect him to the death, and if we lead him away a prisoner it is because we must, since otherwise Ibubesi will kill us all. Therefore be merciful to us when the spear of thy power is lifted."

Before Rachel could answer Ishmael's voice was heard asking why they did not bring the *Inkosazana* as the horses were ready.

"I pray thee come, Zoola," said the man hurriedly "or he will shoot more of us."

So Rachel walked down the steps of the *stoep* in front of them, holding her head high, leaving behind her the house of Ramah and its dead. At the gate of the garden stood the horses, on one of which, his own, Richard was already mounted, his arms bound, his feet made fast beneath it with a hide rope. Her path lay past him, and as she went by he said in a voice that was choking with rage:

"I am helpless, I cannot save you, but our hour will come."

"Yes, Richard," she answered quietly, "our hour will come when his has gone," and with the spear in her hand once more she pointed at Ishmael, who stood by watching them sullenly. Then she mounted her horse—how she could never remember—and they were separated.

After this she seemed to hear Ishmael talking to her, arguing, explaining, but she made no answer to his words. Her mind was a blank, and all she knew was that they were riding on for hours. Her tired horse stumbled up a pass and down its further side. Then she heard dogs bark and saw lights. The horse stopped and she slid from it, and as she was too exhausted to walk, was supported or carried into a hut, as she thought by women who seemed very much afraid of touching her, after which she seemed to sink into blackness.

Rachel woke from her stupor to find herself lying on a bed in a great Kaffir hut that was furnished like a European room, for in it were chairs and a table, also rough window places closed with reed mats that took the place of glass. Through the smoke-hole at the top of the hut struck a straight ray of sunlight, by which she judged that it must be about midday. She began to think, till by degrees everything came back to her, and in that hour she nearly died of horror and of grief. Indeed she was minded to die. There at her side lay a means of death—the *assegai* which she had found by the body of the Zulu in Ramah, and none had taken from her. She lifted it and felt its edge, then laid it down again. Into the darkness of her despair some comfort seemed to creep. She was sure that Richard lived, and if she died, he would die also. While he lived, why should she die? Moreover, it would be a crime which she should only dare when all hope had gone and she stood face to face with shame.

Thrusting aside these thoughts she rose. On the table stood curdled milk and other food of which she forced herself to eat, that her strength might return to her, for she knew that she would need it all. Then she washed and dressed herself, for in a corner of the hut was water in wooden bowls, and even a comb and other things, that apparently had been set there for her to use. This done, she went to the door, which was made like that of a house, and finding that it was not secured, opened it and looked out. Beyond was a piece of ground floored with the soil taken from ant-heaps, and polished black after the native fashion. This space was surrounded by a high stone wall, and had at the end of it another very strong door. In its centre grew a large, shady tree under which was placed a bench. Taking the *assegai* with her she went to the door in the high wall and found that it was barred on the further side. Then she returned and sat down on the bench under the tree.

It seemed that she had been observed, for a little while afterwards bolts were shot back, the door in the wall opened, and Ishmael entered, closing it behind him. She looked at the man, and at the sight of his handsome, furtive face, his dark, guilt-laden eyes, her gorge rose. She was alone in this secret place with the murderer of her father and her mother, who sought her love. Yet, strangely enough, her heart was filled not with tears, but with contempt and icy anger. She did not shrink away from him as he came towards her in his gaudy clothes, with an assumed air of insolent confidence, but sat pale and proud, as she had sat at Umgugundhlovu, when the Zulus brought their causes before her for judgment.

He advanced into the shadow of the tree, took off his hat with a flourish and bowed. Then as she made no answer to these salutations, but only searched him with her grey eyes, he began to speak in jerky sentences.

"I hope you have slept well, Rachel; I am, glad to see you looking so fresh. I was afraid that you would be over-tired after your long day. You rode many miles. Of course what you found at Ramah must have been a great shock to you. I want to explain to you quietly that I am not in the least to blame about that terrible business. It was those accursed Zulus who exceeded their orders."

So he went on, pausing between each remark for an answer, but no answer came. At length he stopped, confused, and Rachel, lifting the *assegai*, examined its blade, and asked him suddenly:

"Whose blood is on this spear? Yours?"

"A little of it, perhaps," he answered. "That fool of a Kaffir flourished it about after your father shot him and cut me with it accidentally," and he pointed to the wound on his face.

Rachel bent down and began to rub the blade against the foot of the bench as though to clean it. He did not know what she meant by this act, yet it frightened him.

"What are you doing?" he asked.

She paused in her task and said, looking up at him:

"I do not wish that your blood should defile mine even in death," and went on with her cleansing of the spear.

He watched her for a little while, then broke out:

"Curse it all! I don't understand you. What do you mean?"

"Ask the Zulus," she answered. "They understand me, and they will tell you. Or if there is no time, ask my father and mother—afterwards."

Ishmael paled visibly, then recovered himself with an effort and said: "Let us finish with all this witch-doctor nonsense, and come to business. I had nothing to do with the death of your parents, indeed, I was wounded in trying to protect them——"

"Then why do I see both of them behind you with such accusing eyes?" she asked quietly.

He stalled, turned his head and stared about him.

"You won't frighten me like that," he went on. "I am not a silly Kaffir, so give it up. Look here, Rachel, you know I have loved you for a long while, and though you treat me so badly I love you more than ever now. Will you marry me?"

"I told you last night that you would be dead in a few days. Do not waste your time in talking of marriage. Sit in the dust and repent your sins before you go down into the dust."

"All right, Rachel, I know you are a good prophet——"

"Noie, too, is a good prophet," she broke in reflectively. "You used the

Zulus to kill *her* father and mother also, did you not? Do you remember a message that she gave you from Seyapi one evening, down by the sea, before you kidnapped her to be a bait to trap me in Zululand?"

"Remember!" he answered, scowling. "Am I likely to forget her devilries? If you are the witch, she is the familiar, the black *ehlosé* (spirit) who whispers in your ears. Had she not gone I should never have caught you."

"But she will come back—although I fear not in time to bid you farewell."

"You tell me that I shall soon be dead," he exclaimed, ignoring this talk of Noie. "Well, I am not frightened. I don't believe you know anything about it, but if you are right the more reason I should live while I can. According to you, Rachel, we have no time to waste in a long engagement. When is it to be?"

"Never!" she answered contemptuously, "in this or any other world. Never! Why, you are hateful to me; when I see you, I shiver as though a snake crawled across my foot, and when I look at your hands they are red with blood, the blood of my parents and of Noie's parents, and of many others. That is my answer."

He looked at her a while, then said:

"You seem to forget that I am only asking for what I can take. No one can see you or hear you here, except my women. You are in my power at last, Rachel Dove."

These words which Ishmael intended should frighten her, as they might well have done, produced, as it chanced, a quite different effect. Rachel broke into a scornful laugh.

"Look," she said, pointing to an eagle that circled so high in the blue heavens above them that it seemed no larger than a hawk, "that bird is more in your power, and nearer to you than I am. Before you laid a finger on me I would find a dozen means of death, but that, I tell you again, you will never live to do."

For a while Ishmael was silent, weighing her words in his mind. Apparently he could find no answer to them, for when he spoke again it was of another matter.

"You say that you hate me, Rachel. If so, it is because of that accursed fellow, Darrien—whom you don't hate. Well, he, at any rate, is in my power. Now look here. You've got to make your choice. Either you stop all this nonsense and become my wife, or—your friend Darrien dies. Do you hear me?"

Rachel made no answer. Now for the first time she was really frightened, and feared lest her speech should show it.

"You have been through a lot," he went on, slowly; "you are tired out, and don't know what you say, and you believe that I killed the old people, which I didn't, and, of course, that has set you against me. Now, I don't want to be rough, or to hurry you, especially as I have plenty of things to see about before we are married. So I give you three days. If you don't change your mind at the end of them, the young man dies, that's all, and afterwards we will see whether or no you are in my power. Oh! you needn't stare. I've gone too far to turn back, and I don't mind a few extra risks. Meanwhile make yourself easy, dear Richard shall be well looked after, and I won't bother you with any more love-making. That can wait."

Rachel rose from her seat and pointed with the spear to the door in the wall.

"Go," she said.

"All right, I am going, Rachel. Goodbye till this time three days. I hope my women will make you as comfortable as possible in this rough place. Ask them for anything you want. Goodbye, Rachel," and he went, bolting the wall door behind him.

## Chapter 16
# The Three Days

He was gone, his presence had ceased to poison the air, and, the long strain over, Rachel gave a gasp of relief. Then she sat down upon the bench and began to think. Her position, and that of Richard, was desperate; it seemed scarcely possible that they could escape with their lives, for if he died, she would die also—as to that she was quite determined. But at least they had three days, and who could say what would happen in three days? For instance, they might escape somehow, the Providence in which she believed might intervene, or the Zulus might come to seek her, if they only knew where she was gone. Oh! why had she not brought a guard of them with her to Ramah? At least they would never have insulted her, and Ishmael's shrift would have been short.

She wondered why he had given her three days. A reason suggested itself to her mind. Perhaps he believed what she had told him—that she was as safe from him as the eagle in the air—and was sure that the only way to snare her was by using Richard as a lure, in other words, by threatening to murder him. It is true that he could have brought the matter to a head at once, but then, if she remained obdurate, he must carry out his threat, and this, she believed, he was afraid to do unless it was absolutely forced upon him. Doubtless he had reflected that in three days she might weaken and give way.

Whilst Rachel brooded thus the door in the wall opened, and through it came three women, who saluted her respectfully, and announced that they were sent to clean the hut, and attend upon her. Rachel took stock of them carefully. Two of them were young, ordinary, good-looking Kaffirs, but the third was between thirty and forty, and no longer attractive, having become old early, as natives do. Moreover, her face was sad and sympathetic. Rachel asked her her name. She answered that it was Mami, and that they were all the wives of Ibubesi.

The women went about their duties in the hut in silence, and a while afterwards announced that all was made clean, and that they would return presently with food. Rachel answered that it was not necessary that three of them should be put to so much trouble. It would be enough if Mami came. She desired to be waited on by Mami alone, her sisters need not come any more.

They all three saluted again, and said that she should be obeyed; the two younger ones with alacrity. To Rachel it was evident that these women were much afraid of her. Her reputation had reached them, and they shrank from this task of attending on the mighty *Inkosazana* of the Zulus in her cage, not knowing what evil it might bring upon them.

An hour later the door was unbolted, and Mami reappeared with the food that had been very carefully cooked. Rachel ate of it, for she was determined to grow strong again, she who might need all her strength, and while she ate talked to Mami, who squatted on the ground before her. Soon she drew her story from her. The woman was Ishmael's first Kaffir wife, but he had never cared for her, and against all law and custom she was discarded, and made a slave. Even some of her cattle had been taken from her and given to other wives. So her heart was bitter against Ishmael, and she said that although once she was proud to be the wife of a white man, now she wished that she had never seen his face.

Here, then, was material ready to Rachel's hand, but she did not press the matter too far at this time. Only she said that she wished Mami to stay with her after the evening meal, and to sleep in her hut, as she was not accustomed to be alone at night. Mami replied that she would do so gladly if Ibubesi allowed it, although she was not worthy of such honour.

As it happened, Ishmael did allow it, for he thought that he could trust this old drudge, and told her to act as a spy upon Rachel, and report to him all that she said or did. Very soon Rachel found this out and warned her against obeying him, since if she did so it would come to her knowledge, and then great evil would fall on one who betrayed the words of the *Inkosazana.*

Mami answered that she knew it, and that Rachel need not be afraid. Any tale would do for Ishmael, whom she hated. Then, saying little herself, Rachel encouraged her to talk, which Mami did freely. So she heard some news. She learned, for instance, that the whole town of Mafooti, whereof Ibubesi was chief, which counted some sixty or seventy heads of families, was much disturbed by the events of the last few days. They did not like the *Inkosazana* being brought there, thinking that where she went the Zulus would follow, and as they were of Zulu blood themselves, they knew what that meant. They were alarmed at the deaths of the white sky-doctor, who was called Shouter, and his wife, with which Ibubesi had something to do, for they feared lest they should be held responsible for their blood. They objected to the imprisonment of the white chief, Dario, among them, because "he had hurt no one, and was under the mantle of the *Inkosazana*, who was a spirit, not a woman," and who had warned them that if any harm came to her or to him, death would be their reward. They were angry, also, because Ibubesi had killed one of them in some quarrel about the chief Dario at Ramah. Still, they were so much afraid of Ibubesi, who was a great tyrant, that they did not dare to interfere with him and his plans, lest they should lose their cattle, or, perhaps, their lives. So they did not know what to do. As for Ibubesi himself, he was actively engaged in strengthening the fortifications of the place; even the old people and the children were being forced to carry stones to the walls, from which it was evident that he feared some attack.

When Rachel had gathered this and much other information concerning Ishmael's past and habits, she asked Mami if she could convey a message from her to Richard. The woman answered that she would try on the following morning. So Rachel told her to say that she was safe and well, but that he must watch his footsteps, as both of them were in great danger. More she did not dare to say, fearing lest Mami should betray her, or be beaten till she confessed everything. Then, as there was nothing more to be done, Rachel lay down and slept as best she could.

The next day passed in much the same fashion as the first had done. For the most of it Rachel sat under the tree in the walled yard, companioned only by her terrible thoughts and fears. Nobody came near her, and nothing happened. In the morning Mami went out, and returning at the dinner hour, told Rachel that she had seen Ishmael, who had questioned her closely as to what the *Inkosazana* had done and said, to which she replied that she had only eaten and slept, and invoked the spirits on her knees. As for words, none had passed her lips. She had not been able to get near the huts where Dario was in prison, as Ishmael was watching her. For the rest, the work of fortification went on without cease, even Ishmael's own wives being employed thereon.

In the afternoon Mami went out again and did not return till night, when she had much to tell. To begin with, while the sentry was dozing, being wearied with carrying stones to the wall, she had managed to approach the fence of the hut where Richard was confined. She said that he was walking up and down inside the fence with his hands tied, and she had spoken to him through a crack in the reeds, and given him Rachel's message. He listened eagerly, and bade her tell the *Inkosazana* that he thanked her for her words; that he, too, was strong and well, though much troubled in mind, but the future was in the hands of the Heavens, and that she must keep a high heart. Just then the sentry woke up, so Mami could not wait to hear any more.

That evening, however, a lad who had been sent out of the town to drive in some cattle, had returned with the tidings which she, Mami, heard him deliver to Ibubesi with her own ears.

He said that whilst he was collecting the oxen, a ringed Zulu came upon him, who from his manner and bearing he took to be a great chief, although he was alone, and seemed to be tired with walking. The Zulu has asked him if it were true that the *Inkosazana* and the white chief Dario were in prison at Mafooti, and when he hesitated about replying, threatened him with his *assegai*, saying that he would cut out his heart unless he told the truth. The Zulu replied that he knew it, as he had just come from Ramah, where he had seen strange things, and spoken with a man of Ibubesi's, whom he found dying in the garden of the house. Then he had given him this message:

"Say to Ibubesi that I know all his wickedness, and that if the *Inkosazana* is harmed, or if drop of the blood of the white chief, Dario, is shed, I will destroy him and everything that lives in his town down to the rats. Say to him also that he cannot escape, as already he is ringed in by the children of the Shouter, who have come back, and are watching him."

The lad had asked who it was that sent such a message, whereon he answered, "I am the Horn of the Black Bull; I am the Trunk of the Elephant; I am the Mouth of Dingaan."

Then straightway he turned and departed at a run towards Zululand. Moreover, Mami described the man in the words of the lad, and Rachel thought that he could be none other than Tamboosa, whom she had commanded to follow her with the white ox. Mami added that when he received this message Ibubesi seemed much disturbed, though to his people he declared that it was all nonsense, as Dingaan's Mouth would not come alone, or deliver the King's word to a boy. But the people thought otherwise, and murmured among themselves, fearing the terrible vengeance of Dingaan.

On the next day Mami went out again. At nightfall, when she returned, she told Rachel that she had not found it possible to approach the huts where Dario was, as the hole she made in the fence to speak with him had been discovered, and a stricter watch was kept over him. Ibubesi, she said, was in an ill humour, and working furiously to finish his fortifications, as he was now sure that the town was being watched, either by the Kaffirs of Ramah, or others. As for the people of Mafooti, they were grumbling very much, both on account of the heavy-labour of working at the walls, and because they were in terror of being attacked and killed in payment for the evil deeds of their chief. Mami declared, indeed, that so great was their fear and discontent, that she thought they would desert the town in a body, were it not that they dreaded lest they should fall into the hands of the Kaffirs who were watching it. Rachel asked her whether they would not then take her and Dario and deliver them up to the Zulus, or to the white people on the coast. Mami answered she thought they would be afraid to do this, as Ibubesi alone had guns, and would shoot plenty of them; also if the Zulus found them with their *Inkosazana* they would kill them. She added that she had seen Ibubesi, who bade her tell the *Inkosazana* that he was coming for her answer on the morrow.

Rachel slept ill that night. The space of her reprieve had gone by, and next morning she must face the issue. For herself she did not so greatly care, for at the worst she had a refuge whither Ishmael could not follow her—the grave. After all she had endured it seemed to her that this must be a peaceful place; moreover, in her case what Power could blame her? But there was Richard to be thought of. If she refused Ishmael he swore that he would kill Richard. And yet how could she pay that price even to save her lover's life? Perhaps he would not kill him after all; perhaps he would be afraid of the vengeance of the Zulus, and was only trying to frighten her. Ah! if only the Zulus would come—before it was too late! It was scarcely to be hoped for. Tamboosa, if it were he who had spoken with the lad, would not have had time to return to Zululand and collect an *impi*, and when they did come, the deed might be done. If only these servants of Ibubesi would rise against him and kill him, or carry off Richard and herself! Alas! they feared the man too much, and she could not get at them to persuade them. There was nothing that she could do except pray. Richard and she must take their chance. Things must go as they were decreed.

If she could have seen Ishmael at this hour and read his thoughts, that sight and knowledge might have brought some comfort to her tortured heart. The man was seated in his hut alone, staring at the floor and pulling his long black beard with hands rough from toiling at the walls. He was drinking also, stiff tots of rum and water, but the fiery liquor seemed to bring him no comfort. As he drank, he thought. He was determined to get possession of Rachel; that desire had become a madness with him. He could never abandon it while he lived. But *she* might not live. She had sworn that she would rather die than become his wife, and she was not a woman who broke her word. Also she hated him bitterly, and with good cause. There was only one way to work on her—through her love for this man, Richard Darrien; for that she did love him, he had little doubt. If it were choice between yielding and the death of Darrien, then perhaps she might give way. But there came the rub.

Dingaan had sworn to him that if he made Darrien's blood to flow, then he should be killed, and, like Rachel, Dingaan kept his oaths. Moreover, that Zulu who met the cattle herd had sworn it again in almost the same words. Therefore it would seem that if he wished to continue to breathe, Darrien's blood must not be made to flow. All the rest might be explained when the *impi* came, as it would do sooner or later, especially if he could show to them that the *Inkosazana* was his willing wife, but the murder of Darrien could never be explained. Well, the man might die, or seem to die, and then who could hold him responsible? Or if they did, if any of his people remained faithful to him, an attack might be beaten off. Brave as they were, the Zulus could not storm those walls on which he had spent so much labour, though now he almost wished that he had left the walls alone and settled the affair of Rachel and of Darrien first.

Ishmael poured out more rum and drank it, neat this time, as though to nerve himself for some undertaking. Then he went to the door of the hut and called, whereon presently a hideous old woman crept in and squatted down in the circle of light thrown by the lamp. She was wrinkled and deformed, and her snake-skin *moocha*, with the inflated fish-bladder in her hair, showed that she was a witch-doctoress.

"Well, Mother," he said, "have you made the poison?"

"Yes, Ibubesi, yes. I have made it as I alone can do. Oh! it is a wonderful drug, worth many cows. How many did you say you would give me? Six?"

"No, three; but if it does what is wanted you shall have the other three as well. Tell me again, how does it work?"

"Thus, Ibubesi. Whoever drinks this medicine becomes like one dead—none can tell the difference, no, not a doctor even—and remains so for a long while—perhaps one day, perhaps two, perhaps even three. Then life returns, and by degrees strength, but not memory; for whole moons the memory is gone, and he who has drunk remains like a child that has everything to learn."

"You lie, Mother. I never heard of such a medicine."

"You never heard of it because none can make it save me, and I had its secret from my grandmother; also few can afford to pay me for it. Still, it has been used, and were I not afraid I could give you cases. Stay, I will show you. Call that beast," and she pointed to a dog that was asleep at the side of the hut. "Here is milk; I will show you."

Ishmael hesitated, for he was fond of this dog; then as he wished to test the stuff he called it. It came and sat down beside him, looking up in his face with faithful eyes. Then the old witch poured milk into a bowl, and in the milk mixed some white powder which she took out of a folded leaf, and offered it to the animal. The dog sniffed the milk, growled slightly, and refused it.

"The evil beast does not like me; he bit me the other day," said the old doctoress. "Do you give it to him, Ibubesi; he will trust you."

So Ishmael patted the dog on the head, then, offered it the milk, which it lapped up to the last drop.

"There, evil beast," said the woman, with a chuckle, "you won't bite me any more; you'll forget all about me for a long time. Look at him, Ibubesi, look at him."

As she spoke, the poor dog's eyes began to stare; then it uttered a low howl, ran to Ishmael, tried to lick his hand, and rolled over, to all appearance quite dead.

"You have killed my dog, which I love, you hag!" he said angrily.

"Then why did you give medicine to what you love, Ibubesi? But have no fear, the evil beast has only taken a small dose; tomorrow morning it will awake, but it will not know you or anyone. Who is the medicine for, Ibubesi? The Lady Zoola? If so, it may not work on her, for she is mighty, and cannot be harmed."

"Fool! Do you think that I would play tricks with the *Inkosazana*?"

"No, you want to marry her, don't you? but it seems to me that she has no mind that way. Then it is for the man for whom she has a mind for? Well, Ibubesi, you have promised the six cows, and you saved me once from being killed for witchcraft, so I will say something. Don't give it to the chief Dario."

"Why not, you old fool; will it kill him after all?"

"No, no; it will do what I said, no less and no more, in this quantity," and she handed him another powder wrapped in dry leaves; "but I have had bad dreams about you, Ibubesi, and they were mixed up with the *Inkosazana* and this white man Dario. I dreamed they brought your death upon you—a dreadful death. Ibubesi, be wise, set Dario free, and change your mind as to marrying the *Inkosazana*, who is not for you."

"How can I change my mind, Descendant of Wizards?" broke out Ishmael. "Can a river penned between rocks change its course? Can it run backwards from the sea to the hill? This woman draws me as the sea draws the river; because of her my blood is afire. I had rather win her and die, than live rich and safe without her to old age. The more she hates and scorns me, the more I love her."

"I understand," said the doctoress, nodding her head till the bladder in her hair bobbed about like a float at which a fish is pulling. "I understand. I have seen people like this before—men and women too—when a bad spirit enters into them because of some crime they have committed. The *Inkosazana*, or those who guard her, have sent you this bad spirit, and, Ibubesi, you must run the road upon which it is appointed that you should travel; for joy or sorrow you must run that road. But when we meet in the world of ghosts, which I think will be soon, do not blame me, do not say that I did not warn you. Now it is all right about those cows, is it not? although I dare say the Zulus will milk them and not I, for tonight I seem to smell Zulus in the air," and she lifted her broad nose and sniffed like a hound. "I wish you could have left the *Inkosazana* alone, and that Dario too, for he is a part of her; in my dreams they seemed to be one. But you won't, you will walk your own path; so good night, Ibubesi. The dog will wake again in the morning, but he will not know you. Good night, Ibubesi—of course I understand that the cows will be young ones that have not had more than two calves. Mix the powder in milk, or water, or anything; it is without taste or colour. Good night, Ibubesi," and without waiting for an answer the old wretch crept out of the hut.

When she was gone Ishmael cursed her aloud, then drank some more rum, which he seemed to need. The place was very lonely, and the sight of his dog, lying to all appearance dead at his side, oppressed him. He patted its head and it did not move; he lifted its paw and it fell down flabbily. The brute was as dead as anything could be. It occurred to him that before night came again he might look like that dog. His story might be told; he might have left the earth in company of all the deeds that he had done thereon. He had imagination enough to know his sins, and they were an evil host to face. Old Dove and his wife, for instance—holy people who believed in

God and Vengeance, and had never done any wrong, only striven for years and years to benefit others; it would not be pleasant to meet them. Rachel had said that she saw them standing behind him, and he felt as though they were there at that moment. Look, one of them crossed between him and the lamp—there was the mark of the *kerry* on his head—and the woman followed; he could see her blue lips as she bent down to look at the dog. It was unbearable. He would go and talk to Rachel, and ask her if she had made up her mind. No, for if he broke in on her thus at night, he was sure that she would kill either herself or him with that spear she had taken from the dead Zulu, reddened with his own blood. He would keep faith with her and wait till the morrow. He would send for one of his wives. No, the thought of those women made him sick. He would go round the fortifications and beat any sentries whom he found asleep, or receive the reports of the spies. To stop in that hut in the company of a dog which seemed to be dead, and of imaginations that no rum could drown, was impossible.

********

Once more the morning came, and Rachel sat in the walled yard awaiting the dreadful hour of her trial, for it was the day and time that Ishmael had appointed for her answer. Until now Rachel had cherished hopes that something might happen: that the people of Mafooti might intervene to save her and Richard; that the Zulus might appear, even that Ishmael might relent and let them go. But Mami had been out that morning and brought back tidings which dispelled these hopes. She had ventured to sound some of the leading men, and said that, like all the people, they were very sullen and alarmed, but declared, as she had expected, that they dare do nothing, for Ibubesi would kill them, and if they escape him the Zulus would kill them because the *Inkosazana* was found in their possession. Of the Zulus themselves, scouts who had been out for miles, reported that they had seen no sign. It was clear also that Ishmael was as determined as ever, for he had sent her a message by Mami that he would wait upon her as he had promised, and bring the white man with him.

Then what should she say and what should she do? Rachel could think of no plan; she could only sit still and pray while the shadow of that awful hour crept ever nearer.

It had come; she heard voices without the wall, among them Ishmael's. Her heart stopped, then bounded like a live thing in her breast. He was commanding someone to "catch that dog and tie it up, for it was bewitched, and did not know him or anyone," then the sound of a dog being dragged away, whining feebly, and then the door opened. First Ishmael came in with an affectation of swaggering boldness, but looking like a man suffering from the effects of a long debauch. About his eyes were great black rings, and in them was a stare of sleeplessness. He carried a double-barrelled gun under his arm, but the hand with which he supported it shook visibly, and at every unusual sound he started. After him came Richard, his wrists bound together behind him, and on his legs hide shackles which only just allowed him to shuffle forward slowly. Moreover he was guarded by four men who carried spears. Rachel glanced quickly at his face, and saw that it was pale and resolute; quite untouched by fear.

"Are you well?" she asked quietly, taking no note of Ishmael.

"Yes," he answered, "and you, Rachel?"

"Quite well bodily, Richard, but oh! my soul is sick."

Before he could reply Ishmael turned on him savagely, and bade him be silent, or it would be the worse for him. Then he took off his hat with his shaking hand, and bowed to Rachel.

"Rachel," he said, "I have kept my promise, and left you alone for three days, but time is up and now this gentleman and I have come to hear your decision, which is so important to both of us."

"What am I to decide?" she asked in a low voice, looking straight before her.

"Have you forgotten? Your memory must be very bad. Well, it is best to have no mistake, and no doubt our friend here would like to know exactly how things stand. You have to decide whether you will take me as your husband today of your own free will, or whether Mr. Richard Darrien shall suffer the punishment of death, for having tried to kill his sentry and escape, a crime of which he has been guilty, and afterwards I should take you as my wife with, or without, your consent."

When Richard heard these words the veins in his forehead swelled with rage and horror till it seemed as though they would burst.

"You unutterable villain," he gasped, "you cowardly hound! Oh! if only my hands were free."

"Well, they ain't, Mr. Darrien, and it's no use your tugging at that buffalo hide, so hold your tongue, and let us hear the lady's answer," sneered Ishmael.

"Richard, Richard," said Rachel in a kind of wail, "you have heard. It is a matter of your life. What am I to do?"

"Do?" he answered, in loud, firm tones, "do? How can you ask me such a question? The matter is not one of my life, but of your—of your—oh! I cannot say it. Let this foul beast kill me, of course, and then, if you care enough, follow the same road. A few years sooner or later make little difference, and so we shall soon be together again."

She thought a moment, then said quietly:

"Yes, I care enough, and a hundred times more than that. Yes, that is the only way out. Listen, you Ishmael:—Richard Darrien, the man to whom I am sworn, and I, give you this answer. Murder him if you will, and bring God's everlasting vengeance on your head. He will not buy his life on such terms, and if I consented to them I should be false to him. Murder him as you murdered my father and mother, and when I know that he is dead I will go to join him and them."

"All right, Rachel," said Ishmael, whose face was white with fury, "I think I will take you at your word, and you can go to look for him down below, if you like, for if I am not to get you here, he shan't. Now then, say your prayers, Mr. Darrien," and stepping forward slowly he cocked the double-barrelled gun.

"Men of Mafooti," exclaimed Rachel in Zulu, "Ibubesi is about to do murder on one who like myself is under the mantle of Dingaan. If his blood should flow today or tomorrow, yours shall flow in payment, yours, and that of your wives and children, for the crime of the chief is the crime of the people."

At her words the four natives who had been watching this scene uneasily, although they could not understand the English talk, called out to Ishmael in remonstrance. His only answer was to lift the gun, and for an instant that seemed infinite Rachel waited to hear its explosion, and to see the grey-eyed, open-faced man she loved, who stood there like a rock, fall a shattered corpse. Then one of the Kaffirs, bolder than the rest, struck up the barrels with his arm, and not too soon, for whether or no he had meant to pull the trigger, the rifle went off.

"Try the other barrel," said Richard sarcastically, as the smoke cleared away, "that shot was too high."

Perhaps Ishmael might have done so, for the man was beside himself, but the Kaffirs would have no more of it. They rushed between them, lifting their spears threateningly, and shouting that they would not allow the blood of the white lord and the curse of the *Inkosazana* to be brought upon their heads and those of their families. Rather than that they would bind him, Ibubesi, and give him over to the Zulus. Then, whether or not he had really meant to kill Richard, Ishmael thought it politic to give way.

"So be it," he said to Rachel, "I am merciful, and both of you shall have another chance. I am going with this fellow, but the woman, Mami, shall come to you. If within three hours you send her to me with a message to say that you have changed your mind, he shall be spared. If not, before nightfall you shall see his body, and afterwards we will settle matters."

"Rachel, Rachel," cried Richard, "swear that you will send no such message."

Now the brute, Ishmael, rushed at him to strike him in the face. But Richard saw him coming, and bound though he was, put down his head and butted at him so fiercely, that being much the stronger man, he knocked him to the ground, where he lay breathless.

"Swear, Rachel, swear," he repeated, "or dead or living, I will never forgive you."

"I swear," she said, faintly.

Then he shuffled towards her. Bending down he kissed her on the face, and she kissed him back; no more words passed between them; this was their farewell. Two of the Kaffirs lifted Ishmael, and helped him from the yard, whilst the other two led away Richard, who made no resistance. At the gate he turned, and their eyes met for a moment. Then it closed behind him, and she was left alone again.

## Chapter 17

# Rachel Loses Her Spirit

A little while later Mami entered, and said that she had been sent by Ibubesi to serve the *Inkosazana* as a messenger, should she need one. Rachel, seated on the bench, motioned to her to go into the hut and bide there, and she obeyed.

Minute by minute the time ebbed away, and still Rachel sat motionless on the bench. Towards the end of the third hour someone unbolted and knocked at the door. Mami opened it and reported that Ibubesi stood without, and desired to know whether she had any word for him.

"None," answered Rachel, remembering her oath, and the door was barred again.

After this a great silence seemed to fall upon the place. The sky was grey with distant rain, and the air heavy, and whatever may have been the cause, no sound came from man or beast without. To Rachel's strained nerves it seemed as though the Angel of Death had spread his wings above the town. There she sat paralysed, wondering what evil thing was being worked upon her lover; wondering if she had done right to give him as a sacrifice to this savage in order to save herself from dreadful wrong—wondering, wondering till the powers of her mind seemed to die within her, leaving it grey and empty as the grey and empty sky above.

Night drew on and the setting sun, bursting through the envelope of cloud, filled earth and sky with fire, and it came into Rachel's heart, she knew not whence, that fire was near, that soon it would swallow up all this place.

Look! the door was opening; it swung wide, and through it advanced eight Kaffirs, carrying something on a litter made of shields, something that was covered with a blanket of bark. They drew near to her with bent heads, and set down their burden at her feet. Then one of them lifted the blanket, revealing the body of Richard Darrien, and saying in an awed voice, "*Inkosazana*, Ibubesi sends you this to look or to show you that he keeps his word. Later he will visit you himself."

Rachel knelt down by the litter of shields and looked at Richard's face. The stamp of death was on it. She felt his hand, it was turning cold; she felt his heart, it did not beat.

"Show me this dead lord's wounds," she said in an awful whisper, "that presently mine may be like to them."

"*Inkosazana*," said the spokesman, "he has no wound."

"How, then, did he die? Strange that he should die, and I not feel his spirit pass."

"*Inkosazana*, he was thirsty, and drank, then he died."

"So, so! he was slain by poison, and I have no poison. Mami, come forth and look on the white lord whom Ibubesi has murdered by poison."

The woman Mami, who had been sleeping in the hut, awoke and obeyed. She saw, and wailed aloud.

"Woe to Mafooti!" she cried, like one inspired, "and woe, woe to those that dwell therein, for now vengeance, red vengeance, shall fall on them from Heaven. The blood of the innocent is upon them, the curse of the *Inkosazana* is upon them, the spears of the Zulus are upon them. Slay the *silwana*, the wild beast—Ibubesi, and fly, people of Mafooti, fly, fly with that dead thing. Leave it not here to bear witness against you. Carry it far away, and heap a mountain on it. Bury it in a valley that no man can find; bury it in the black water, lest it should arise and bear witness against you. Leave it not here, but let the darkness cover it, and fly with it into the darkness, as I do," and turning she sped to the door and through it.

The light from the sunk sun went out smothered in the gathering thunder-clouds. Through the gloom the terrified bearers muttered to each other.

"Throw it down and away!" said one.

"Nay," answered another, "wisdom has come to Mami, her *ehlosé* has spoken to her. Take it with you, lest it should remain to bear witness against us."

"Remember what the Zulu swore," said a third, "that if harm came to this lord they would kill all, down to the rats. Take it away so that it may not be found. If you meet Ibubesi, spear him. If not, leave him the vengeance for his share."

Now, moved as though by a common impulse, the bearers cast

back the blanket over the corpse, and lifting the litter, departed at a run. The door was shut and bolted behind them, and darkness fell upon the earth.

For a while Rachel stood still in the darkness.

"Now I am alone," she said in a quiet voice, yet to her ears the words seemed to be uttered with a roar of thunder that echoed through the firmament, and pierced upwards to the feet of God.

Then suddenly something snapped in her brain and she was changed. The horror left her, the terror left her, she felt very well and strong, so well that she laughed aloud, and again that laugh filled earth and heaven. Oh! she was hungry, and food stood on a table near by. She sprang to it and ate, ate heartily. Then she drank, muttering to herself, "Richard drank before he died. Let me drink also and cease to be alone."

Her meal finished, she walked up and down the place singing a song that seemed to be caught up triumphantly by a million voices, the voices of all who had ever lived and died. Their awful music stunned her and she ceased. Look! Wild beasts wearing the face of Ibubesi were licking the clouds with their tongues of fire. It was curious, but in that high-walled place she could not see it well. Now from the top of the hut the view would be better. Yes, and Ishmael was coming to visit her. Well, they would meet for the last time on the top of the hut. She was not afraid of him, not at all; but it would be strange to see him scrambling up the hut, and they would talk there for a little while with their faces close together, till—ah!—till what—? Till something strange happened, something unhappy for Ishmael. Oh! no, no, she would not kill herself, she would wait to see what it was that happened to Ishmael, that strange thing which she knew so well, and yet could not remember.

How easy this hut was to climb, a cat could not have run up with less trouble. Now she stood on the top of it, her spear in one hand, and holding with the other to the pole that was set there to scare away the lightning; stood for a long time watching the wild beasts licking the clouds with their red tongues.

The beasts grew weary of lapping up clouds. Their appetites were satisfied for a while, at any rate she saw their tongues no more. The air was very hot and heavy, and the darkness very dense, it seemed to press about her as though she were plunged in cream. Yet Rachel thought that she heard sounds through it, a sound of feet to the west and a sound of feet to the east.

Then she heard another sound, that of the door in the wall opening, and of a soft, tentative footfall, like to the footfall of a questing wolf. She knew it at once, for now her senses were sharper than those of any savage; it was the step of Ibubesi, the Night-prowler. She felt inclined to laugh; it was so funny to think of herself standing there on the top of a hut while the Night-prowler slunk about below looking for her. But she refrained, remembering the dreadful noise when all the Heavens began to laugh in answer. So she was silent, for the Heavens do not reverberate silence, although she could hear her own thoughts passing through them, passing up one by one on their infinite journey.

Listen! He was walking round and round the yard. He went to the bench beneath the tree and felt along it with his fingers to see if she were there. Now he was entering the hut and groping at the bedstead, and now he had kindled a light, for the rays of it shone faintly up through the smoke-hole. Discovering nothing he came out again, leaving the lamp burning within, and called her softly.

"Rachel," he said, "Rachel, where are you?"

There was no answer, and he began to talk to himself.

"Has she got away?" he muttered. "Some of them have gone, I know, the accursed, cowardly fools. No, it is not possible, the watch was too good, unless she is really a spirit, and has melted, as spirits do. I hope not, for if so she will haunt me, and I want her company in the flesh, not in the spirit. I ought to have it too, for it has cost me pretty dear. She must have bewitched me, or why should I risk everything for her, just one white woman who hates the sight of me? The devil is at the back of it. This was his road from the first."

So he went on until Rachel could bear it no more, the thing was too absurd.

"Yes, yes," she said from the top of the hut, "his road from the first, and it ends not far away, at the red gates of Hell, Night-prowler."

The man below gasped, and fell against the fence.

"Whose voice is that? Where are you?" he asked of the air.

Then as there was no answer, he added: "It sounded like Rachel, but it spoke above me. I suppose that she has killed herself. I thought she might, but better that she should be dead than belong to that fellow. Only then why does she speak?"

He started to feel his way towards the hut, perhaps to fetch the lamp, when suddenly the skies behind were illumined in a blaze of light, a broad slow blaze that endured for several seconds. By it the eyes of Rachel, made quick with madness, saw many things. From her perch on the top of the hut she saw the town of Mafooti. On the plain to the west she saw a number of black dots, which she took to be people and cattle travelling away from the town. In the *nek* to the east she saw more dots, each of them crested with white, and carrying something white. Surely it was a Zulu *impi* marching! Some of these dots had come to the wall of the town; yes, and some of them were on the crest of it, while yet others were creeping down its main street not a hundred yards away.

Also these caught sight of something, for they paused and seemed to fall together as though in fear. Lastly, just before the light went out, she perceived Ishmael in the yard below, glaring up at her, for he, too, had seen her. Seen her standing above him in the air, the spear in her hand, and in her eyes fire. But of the dots to the east and of the dots to the west he had seen nothing. He appeared to fall to his knees and remain there muttering. Then the Heavens blazed again, for the storm was coming up, and by the flare of them he read the truth. This was no ghost, but the living woman.

"Oh!" he said, recovering himself, "that's where you've got to, is it? Come down, Rachel, and let us talk."

She made no answer, none at all, she who was so curious to see what he would do. For quite a long while he harangued her from below, walking round and round the hut. Then at length in despair he began to climb it. But in that darkness which now and again turned to dazzling light, unlike Rachel, he found the task difficult, and once, missing his hold, he fell to the ground heavily. Finding his feet he rushed at the hut with an oath, and clutching the straw and the grass strings that bound it, struggled almost to the top, to be met by the point of Rachel's spear held in his face. There then he hung, looking like a toad on the slope of a rock, unable to advance because of that spear, and unwilling to go down, lest his labour must be begun again.

"Rachel," he said, "come down, Rachel. Whatever I have done has been for your sake, come down and tell me that you forgive me."

She laughed out loud, a wild, screaming laugh, for really he looked most ridiculous, sprawling there on the bend of the hut, and the lightning showed her all sorts of pictures in his eyes.

"Did Richard Darrien forgive you?" she asked. "And what did you mix that poison with? Milk? The milk of human kindness! It was a very good poison, Toad, so good that I think you must have drawn it from your own blood. When you are dead all the Bushmen should come and dip their arrows in you, for then even crocodiles and the big snakes would die at a scratch."

He made no answer, so she went on.

"Have your people forgiven you? If so, why do they flee away, carrying that white thing which was a man? Have my father and mother forgiven you? Do you hear what they are saying to me—that judgment is the Lord's? Have the Zulus forgiven you, the Zulus who believe that judgment is the King's—and the *Inkosazana*'s? Turn now, and ask them, for here they are," and she pointed over his head with her spear. "Turn, Toad, and set out your case and I will stand above and try it, the case of Dingaan against Ibubesi, and one by one I will call up all those who died through you, and they shall give their evidence, and I, the Judge, will sum it up to a jury of sharp spears. See, here come the spears. Look at the wall, Toad, *look at the wall!*"

As she raved on and pointed with her *assegai*, the lightning blazed out, and Ishmael, who had looked round at her bidding, saw Zulu warriors leaping down from the crest of the wall, and Zulu captains rushing in by the opened door. At this terrible sight he slid to the ground purposing to reach his gun which he had left there, and defend or kill himself, who knows which? But before ever he could lay a hand upon it, those fierce men had pounced upon him like leopards on a goat. Now they held him fast, and a voice—it was that of Tamboosa, called through the darkness,

"Hail to thee! *Inkosazana*. Come down now and pass judgment on this wild beast who would have harmed thee."

"Tamboosa," she cried, "the *Inkosazana* has fled away, only the white woman in whom she dwelt remains; her spirit hangs in wrath over the people of the Zulus, as an eagle hangs above a hare. Tamboosa, there is blood between the *Inkosazana* and the people of the Zulus, the blood of those who gave her the body that she wore, who lie slain by them upon the bed at Kamah. Tamboosa, there is blood between her and Ibubesi, the blood of the white man who loved the body that she wore, and whom she loved, the white lord whom Ibubesi did to death this day because she who was the *Inkosazana* would not give herself to him. Tamboosa, the *Inkosazana* has suffered much from this Ibubesi, many an insult, many a shame, and when she called upon the Zulus, out of all their thousand thousands there was not a single spear to help her, because they were too busy killing those holy ones whom she called her father and her mother. And so, Tamboosa, the spirit of the *Inkosazana* departed like a bird from the egg, leaving but this shell behind, that is full or sorrows and of dreams. Yet, Tamboosa, she still speaks through these lips of mine, and she says that from the seed of blood that they have sown, her people, the Zulus, must harvest woe upon woe, as while she dwelt among them, she warned them that it would be if ill came to those she loved. Tamboosa, this is her command—that ye shield the breast in which she hid from the wild beast, Ibubesi and all evil men, and that ye lead this shape to Noie, the daughter of Seyapi, whom Ibubesi brought to death, for with Noie it would dwell."

Thus she wailed through the deep darkness, while the soldiers who packed the space below groaned in their grief and terror because the soul of the *Inkosazana* had been made a wanderer by their sins, and the curse of the *Inkosazana* had fallen on their land.

Again the lightning flared, and in it they saw her standing on the crest of the hut. She had let drop the spear as though she needed it no more, and her arms were outstretched to the Heavens, and her beautiful face was upturned, and her long hair floated in the wind. Seen thus by that quick, white light, which shone in the madness of her eyes, she seemed no woman but what they had fabled her to be, a queen of Spirits, and at the vision of her they groaned again, while some of them fell to the earth and hid their faces with their hands.

The darkness fell once more, and a man went into the hut to bring out the lamp that burned there. When he returned Rachel stood among them; they had not seen or heard her descend. Ishmael saw her also, and feeling his doom in the fierce eyes that glowered at him, stretched out his hand and caught her by the robe, praying for pity.

At his touch she uttered a wild scream, which pierced like a knife through the hearts of all that heard it.

"Suffer it not," she cried, "oh! my people, suffer not that I be thus defiled."

They rent him from her with blows and execrations, looking up to their chief for his word to tear him to pieces.

"No," said Tamboosa, grimly, "he shall to the King to tell this story ere he die."

"Save me, Rachel, save me," he moaned. "You don't know what they mean. I was mad with love for you, do not judge me harshly and send me to be tortured."

This appeal of his seemed to pierce the darkness of her brain, and for a little while her face grew human.

"I judge not," she answered in Zulu; "pray to the Great One above who judges. Oh! man, man," she went on in a kind of eerie whisper, "what have I done to you that you should treat me thus? Why did you command the soldiers to kill my father and my mother? Why did you poison my lover? Why did you drive away my soul, and fill me with this madness? Take me away from this accursed town, Tamboosa, before Heaven's vengeance falls on it, and let me see that face no more."

Then some of them made a guard about her and led her thence, along the central street, and through the barricaded gates, that they broke down for her passage. They led her to a little cave in the slope of the opposing hill, for although no rain fell, the gathered storm was breaking; the lightning flashed thick and fast, the thunder groaned and bellowed, and a wild wind beat the screeching trees.

Here in the mouth of this cave Rachel sat herself down and looked at the *kraal*, Mafooti, awaiting she knew not what, while the *impi* pillaged the town, and Ishmael, already half dead with fear, remained bound to the roof-tree of the hut that had been her prison.

Whilst she waited thus, and watched, of a sudden one of the outer huts began to burn, though whether the lightning or some soldier had fired it none could tell. Then, in an instant, as it seemed, driven by the raging wind, the flame leapt from roof to roof till Mafooti was but a sheet of fire. The soldiers at their work of pillage saw, and rushed hither and thither, confusedly, for they did not know the paths, and were tangled in the fences.

A figure appeared running down the central street, a figure of flame, for his clothes burned on him, and those by Rachel said,

"See, see, *Ibubesi!*"

He could not reach the gate, for a blazing hut fell across his path. Turning he sped to the edge of a cliff that rose near by, where, because of its steepness, there was no wall. Here for a while he ran up and down till the wind-driven fire from new-lit huts at its brink leapt out upon him like thin, scarlet tongues. He threw himself to the ground, he rose again, beating his head with his hand, for his long hair was ablaze. Then in his torment and despair, of a sudden he threw himself backwards into the dark gulf beneath. Fifty feet and more he fell to the rocks below, and where he fell there he lay till he died, and on the morrow the Zulus found and buried him.

Thus did Ishmael depart out of the life of Rachel to the end which he had earned.

Nor did he go alone, for of the Zulus in the town many were caught by the fire, and perished, so many that when the regiment mustered at dawn, that same regiment which had escorted the *Inkosazana* to the banks of the Tugela, fifty and one men were missing, whilst numbers of others appeared burned and blistered.

"Ah!" said Tamboosa as he surveyed the injured and counted the dead, "the curse is quickly at work among us, and I think that this is but the beginning of evil. Well, I expected it, no less."

As for the town of Mafooti it was utterly destroyed. To this day the place is a wilderness where the grass grows rank between the crumbling, fire-blackened walls. For the people of Ibubesi who had fled, returned thither no more, nor would others build where it had been, since still they swear that the spot is haunted by the figure of a white man who, in times of thunder, rushes across it wrapped in fire, and plunges blazing into the gulf upon its northern side.

After the storm came the rain which poured all night long, a steady sheet of water reaching from earth to heaven. Rachel watched it vacantly for a while, then went to the head of the little cave and lay down wrapped in *karosses* that they had made ready for her. Moreover, she slept as a child sleeps until the sun shone bright on the morrow, then she woke and asked for food.

But the *impi* did not sleep. All night long the soldiers stood in huddled groups beneath such shelter as the trees and rocks would give to them, while the water poured on them pitilessly till their teeth chattered and their limbs were frozen. Some died of the cold that night, and afterwards many others fell sick of agues and fevers of the lungs which killed a number of them.

In the morning when the storm was past and the sun shone hotly Tamboosa called the Council of the captains together, and consulted with them as to whether they should follow after the people of Mafooti who had fled, and destroy them, or return straight to Zululand. Most of the captains answered that of Mafooti and its people they had seen enough. Ibubesi was dead, slain by the vengeance of Heaven; the *Inkosazana* they had rescued, alive, though filled with madness; the white lord, Dario, had been murdered by Ibubesi, it was said with poison, and doubtless his body was burned in the fire. As for the people of Mafooti themselves, it would seem that most of them were innocent as they had fled the place, deserting their chief. To these arguments other captains answered that the people of Mafooti were not innocent inasmuch as they had helped Ibubesi to carry off the *Inkosazana* and the white lord, Dario, from Ramah, and consented to their imprisonment and to the death of one of them, only flying when they had tidings that the *impi* was on the way. Moreover the command was that every one of these dogs should be killed, whereas they had killed none of them, but only taken those cattle which were left behind in their flight. At length the dispute growing fierce, the captains being unable to come to an agreement, decided that they would lay the matter before the *Inkosazana*, and be guided by the words that fell from her, if they could understand them.

So Tamboosa went into the cave with one other man, and talked to Rachel, who sat staring at him with stony eyes as though she understood nothing. When at length he ceased, however, she cried: "Lead me to Noie at the Great Place. Lead me to Noie," nor would she say any more.

So, as the people of Mafooti had fled they knew not where, and they had secured some of the cattle, and as many of the soldiers were sick from the cold and burns received in the fire, Tamboosa told the regiment that it was the will of the *Inkosazana* that they should return to Zululand.

A while later they started, those of them who were so badly burned that they could not travel, being carried on shields. But Rachel would not be carried, choosing to walk alone surrounded at a distance by a ring of soldiers who guarded her. For hours she walked thus, showing no sign of weariness, but now and again bursting out into shrill laughter, as though she saw things that moved her to merriment. Only the regiment that listened was not merry, for it had heard the words that the *Inkosazana* spoke in the town of Mafooti, foretelling evil to the Zulus because of the blood that was between them and her. They thought that she laughed over the misfortunes that were to come, and over those that had already befallen them in the fire and in the rain.

About midday they halted to eat, and as before Rachel took food in plenty, for now that her mind was wandering her body seemed to call for sustenance. When their meal was finished they moved down to the banks of the Buffalo River, which ran near by, to find that it was in great flood after the heavy rain and that it was not safe to try the ford. So they determined to camp there on the banks, murmuring among themselves that all went ill with them upon this journey, as was to be expected, and that they would have done better if they had spent the time in hunting down the people of Mafooti, instead of sitting idle like tired storks upon the banks of a river. Yet bad as things might seem, they were destined to be worse, for while some of them were cutting boughs and grass to make a hut for the *Inkosazana*, Rachel, who stood watching them with empty eyes, of a sudden laughed in her mad fashion, and sped like a swallow to the lip of the foaming ford. Here, before they could come up with her, she threw off the outer cloak she wore and rushed into the water till the current bore her from her feet. Then while the whole regiment shouted in dismay, she began to swim, striking out for the further bank, and being swept downwards by the stream. Now Tamboosa, who was almost crazed with fear lest she should drown, called out that where the *Inkosazana* went, they must follow, even to their deaths.

"It is so!" answered the soldiers, as each man locking his arms round the middle of him who stood in front, company by company, they plunged into the water in a fourfold chain, hoping thus to bridge it from bank to bank.

Meanwhile Rachel swam on in the strength of her madness as a woman has seldom swum before. Again and again the muddy waters broke over her head and the soldiers groaned, thinking that she was drowned. But always that golden hair reappeared above them. A great tree swept down upon her but she dived beneath it. She was dashed against a tall rock, but she warded herself away from it with her hands and still swam on, till at length with a shout of joy the Zulus saw her find her feet and struggle slowly to the further bank. Yes, and up it till she reached its crest where she stood and watched them idly as though unconscious of the danger she had passed, and of the water that ran from her hair and breast.

"Where a woman can go, we can follow," said some, but others answered:

"She is not a woman, but a spirit. Death himself cannot kill her."

Now the fourfold chain was near the centre of the ford, when suddenly those at the tip of it were lifted from their feet as Rachel had been, nor could those behind hold on to them. They were torn from their grasp and swept away, the most of them never to be seen again, for of these men but few could swim. Thrice this happened until strong swimmers were sent to the front, and at length these men won across as Rachel had done, and caught hold of the stones on the further side, thus forming a living chain from bank to bank, whereof the centre floated and was bent outwards by the weight of the water as the back of a bow bends when the string is drawn.

By the help of this human rope thus formed the companies began to come over, supporting themselves against it, till presently the strain and the push of them and of the angry river overcame its strength, and the chain burst in the middle so that many were borne down the stream and drowned. Yet with risk and toil and loss it joined itself together again and held fast until every man was over, save the sick and some lads who were left to tend them and the cattle on the further bank. Then that cable of brave warriors began to struggle forward like a great snake dragging its tail after it, and, so by degrees drew itself to safety and gasping out foam and water saluted the *Inkosazana* where she stood.

Many were drowned, and others were bruised by rocks, but of this they thought little since she was safe and they had found her again, to have lost whom would have been a shame from generation to generation. She watched the captains reckoning up the number of the dead, and when Tamboosa and some of them came to make report of it to her, a shadow as of pity floated across her stony eyes.

"Not on my head," she cried, "not on my head! There is blood between the *Inkosazana* and her people of the Zulus, and that blood avenges itself in blood," and she laughed her eerie laugh.

"It is true, it is just, O Queen," answered Tamboosa solemnly; "the nation must pay for the sin of its children as the wild beast, Ibubesi, has paid for his sins."

Then as they could travel no further that day, they built a hut, and lit a great fire by which Rachel sat and dried herself, nor did she take any harm from the water, for as the Zulus had said, it seemed as though nothing could harm her now.

The soldiers also lit fires and despatched messengers to neighbouring *kraals* commanding them to bring food, and to send maidens to attend on the *Inkosazana*, while others went to a mountain to call all this ill-tidings from hill to hill till it came to the Great Place of the King.

## Chapter 18
# The Curse of the Inkosazana

That night the regiment and Rachel slept upon the bank of the river, and nothing happened save that lions carried off two soldiers, while two more who had been injured against the rocks, died. Also others fell sick. On the following morning food arrived in plenty from the neighbouring *kraal*s, and with it some girls of high birth to attend upon the *Inkosazana.*

But with these Rachel would have nothing to do, and when they came near to her only said:

"Where is Noie, daughter of Seyapi? Lead me to Noie."

So they began their march again, Rachel walking as before in the centre of a ring of soldiers, and that night slept at a *kraal* upon a hill. Here messengers from the King met them charged with many fine words, to which Rachel listened without understanding them, and then scared them away with her laughter. Also they brought a beautiful cloak made of the skins of a rare white monkey, and this she took and wrapped herself in it, for she seemed to understand that her clothes were ragged.

That day they passed through fertile country, where much corn was grown. Here they saw a strange sight, for as they went clouds seemed to arise in the sky from behind them, which presently were seen to be not clouds, but tens of millions of great winged grasshoppers that lit upon the corn, devouring it and every other green thing. Within a few hours nothing was left except the roots and bare branches, while the women of that land ran to and fro wailing, knowing that next winter they and their children must starve, and the cattle lowed about them hungrily, for the locusts had devoured all the grass. Moreover, having eaten everything, these insects themselves began to die in myriads so that soon the air was poisoned. The waters were also poisoned with their dead bodies, and at once sickness came which presently grew into a pestilence.

Now the men of the country sent a deputation to the *Inkosazana*, praying her to remove the curse, but when they had spoken she only repeated the words she had used upon the banks of the Buffalo River.

"Not on my head, not on my head! There is blood between the *Inkosazana* and her people of the Zulus. Famine and war and death upon the people of the Zulus because they have shed the holy blood!"

Then the men grew afraid and went away, and the regiment marched on accompanied by the myriads of the locusts that wasted all the land through which they passed.

At length, followed by a wail of misery, they came to the Great Place and entered it, preceded by the locusts which already were heaped up in the streets like winter leaves, and for lack of other provender gnawed at the straw of the huts, and the shields and *moochas* of the soldiers. It was a strange sight to see the men trying to stamp them to death, and the women and children rushing to and fro shrieking and brushing them from their hair.

Amid such scenes as these they passed through the town of Umgugundhlovu into which Rachel had been brought in order that the people might see that their *Inkosazana* had returned, and on to that *kraal* upon the hill, where she had spent all those weary weeks until Richard came. She reached it as the sun was setting, and although she did not seem to know any of them was received with joy and adoration by the women who had been her attendants. Here she slept that night, for they thought that she must be too weary to see the King at once; moreover, he desired first to receive the reports of Tamboosa and the captains, and to learn all that had happened in this strange business.

Next morning, whilst Rachel sat by the pool in which, once she had seen the vision of Richard, Tamboosa and an escort came to bring her to Dingaan. When they told her this, she said neither yea nor nay, but, refusing to enter a litter they had brought, walked at the head of them, back to the Great Place, and, watched by thousands, through the locust-strewn streets to the *Intunkulu*, the House of the King. Here, in front of his hut, and surrounded by his Council, sat Dingaan and the *indunas* who rose to greet her with the royal salute. She advanced towards them slowly, looking more beautiful than ever she had done, but with wild, wandering eyes. They set a stool for her, and she sat down on the stool, staring at the ground. Then as she said nothing, Dingaan, who seemed very sad and full of fear, commanded Tamboosa to report all that had happened in the ears of the Council, and he took up his tale.

He told of the journey to the Tugela, and of how the *Inkosazana* and the white lord, Dario, had crossed the river alone but a few hours after Ibubesi, ordering him to follow next day, also alone, with the white ox that bore her baggage. He told how he had done so, and on reaching Ramah had found the white *Umfundusi* and his wife lying dead in their room, and on the floor of it a Zulu of the men who had been sent with Ibubesi, also dead, and in the garden of the house a man of the people of Ibubesi, dying, who, with his last breath narrated to him the story of the taking of the *Inkosazana* and the white lord, by Ibubesi. He told of how he had run to the town of Mafooti, to find out the truth, and of the message that he had sent by the herd boy to Ibubesi and his people. Lastly he told all the rest of that story, of how he had come back to Zululand "as though he had wings," and finding the regiment that had escorted the *Inkosazana* still in camp near the river, had returned with them to attack Mafooti, which they discovered to be deserted by its people.

While he described how by the flare of the lightning they saw the *Inkosazana* standing on the roof of a hut, how they captured the wild beast, Ibubesi, how they learned that the Spirit of the *Inkosazana* was "wandering," and the dreadful words she said, the burning of Mafooti, and the fearful death of Ibubesi by fire, all the Council listened in utter silence. Thus they listened also whilst he showed how evil after evil had fallen upon the regiment, evil by fire and water and sickness, as evil had fallen upon the land also by the plague of locusts.

At length Tamboosa's story was finished, and certain men were brought forward bound, who had been the captains of the band that went with Ishmael, among them those who had killed, or caused to die, the white teacher and his wife.

Upon the stern command of the King these men also told their story, saying that they had not meant to kill the white man and that what they did was done at the word of Ibubesi, whom they were ordered to obey in all things, but who, as they now understood, had dared to lay a plot to capture the *Inkosazana* for himself. When they had finished the King rose and poured out his wrath on them, because through their deeds the Spirit of the *Inkosazana* had been driven away, and her curse laid upon the land, where already it was at work. Then he commanded that they should be led thence, all of them, and put to a terrible death, and with them those captains of the regiment who had spoken against the following of the people of Mafooti, who should, he said, have been destroyed, every one.

At his words executioners rushed in to seize these wretched men, and then it was that Rachel, who all this while had sat as though she heard nothing, lifted her head and spoke, for the first time.

"Set them free, set them, free!" she commanded. "Vengeance is from Heaven, and Heaven will pour it out in plenty. Not on my hands, not on my hands shall be the blood of those who sent the Spirit of the *Inkosazana* to wander in the skies. Who was it that bade an *impi* run to Ramah, and what did they there in the house of those who gave me birth? When the Master calls, the dogs must search and kill. Set them free, lest there be more blood between the *Inkosazana* and her people of the Zulus."

When he heard these words, spoken in a strange, wailing voice, Dingaan trembled, for he knew that it was he who had bidden his dogs to run.

"Let them go," he said, "and let the land see them no more for ever."

So those men went thankfully enough, and the land saw them no more. As they passed the gate other men entered, starved and hungry-looking men, whose bones almost pierced their skins, and who carried in their hands remnants of shields that looked as though they had been gnawed by rats. They saluted the King with feeble voices, and squatted down upon the ground.

"Who are those skeletons," he asked angrily, "who dare to break in upon my Council?"

"King," answered their spokesman, "we are captains of the Nobambe, the Nodwenge, and the Isangu regiments whom thou didst send to destroy the chief, Madaku and his people, who dwell far away in the swamp land to the north near where the Great River runs into the sea. King, we could not come at this chief because he fled away on rafts and in boats, he and his people, and we lost our path among the reeds where again and again we were ambushed, and many of us sank in the swamps and were drowned. Also, we found no food, and were forced to live upon our shields," and he held up a gnawed fragment in his hand. "So we perished by hundreds, and of all who went forth but twenty-one times ten remain alive."

When Dingaan heard this he groaned, for his arms had been defeated and three of his best regiments destroyed. But Rachel laughed aloud, the terrible laugh at which all who heard it shivered.

"Did I not say," she asked, "that Heaven would pour out its vengeance in plenty because of the blood that runs between the Spirit of the *Inkosazana* and her people of the Zulus?"

"Truly this curse works fast and well," exclaimed Dingaan. Then, turning to the men, he shouted: "Be gone, you starved rats, you cowards who do not know how to fight, and be thankful that the Great Elephant (Chaka) is dead, for surely he would have fed you upon shields until you perished."

So these captains crept away also.

Ere they were well gone a man appeared craving audience, a fat man who wore a woeful countenance, for tears ran down his bloated cheeks. Dingaan knew him well, for every week he saw him, and sometimes oftener.

"What is it, Movo, keeper of the kine," he asked anxiously, "that you break in on me thus at my Council?"

"O King," answered the fat man, "pardon me, but, O King, my tidings are so sad that I availed myself of my privilege, and pushed past the guards at the gate."

"Those who bear ill news ever run quickly," grunted the King. "Stop that weeping and out with it, Movo."

"Shaker of the Earth! Eater up of Enemies!" said Movo, "thou thyself art eaten up, or at least thy cattle are, the cattle that I love. A sore sickness has fallen on the great herd, the royal herd, the white herd with the twisted horns, and," here he paused to sob, "a thousand of them are dead, and many more are sick. Soon there will be no herd left," and he wept outright.

Now Dingaan leapt up in his wrath and struck the man so sharply with the shaft of the spear he held that it broke upon his head.

"Fat fool that you are," he exclaimed. "What have you done to my cattle? Speak, or you shall be slain for an evil-doer who has bewitched them."

"Is it a crime to be fat, O King," answered the indignant Movo, rubbing his skull, "when others are so much fatter?" and he looked reproachfully at Dingaan's enormous person. "Can I help it if a thousand of thy oxen are now but hides for shields?"

"Will you answer, or will you taste the other end of the spear?" asked Dingaan, grasping the broken shaft just above the blade. "What have you done to my cattle?"

"O King, I have done nothing to them. Can I help it if those accursed beasts choose to eat dead locusts instead of grass, and foam at the mouth and choke? Can the cattle help it if all the grass has become locusts so that there is nothing else for them to eat? I am not to blame, and the cattle are not to blame. Blame the Heavens above, to whom thou, or rather," he added hastily, "some wicked wizard must have given offence, for no such thing as this has been known before in Zululand."

Again Rachel broke in with her wild laughter, and said:

"Did I not tell thee that vengeance would be poured down in plenty, poured down like the rain, O Dingaan? Vengeance on the

King, vengeance on the people, vengeance on the soldiers, vengeance on the corn, vengeance on the kine, vengeance on the whole land, because blood runs between the Spirit of the *Inkosazana* and the race of the Amazulu, whom once she loved!"

"It is true, it is true, White One, but why dost thou say it so often?" groaned the maddened Dingaan. "Why show the whip to those who must feel the blow? Now, you Movo, have you done?"

"Not quite, O King," answered the melancholy Movo, still rubbing his head. "The cattle of all the *kraal*s around are dying of this same sickness, and the crops are quite eaten, so that next winter everyone must perish of famine."

"Is that all, O Movo?"

"Not quite, O King, since messengers have come to me, as head keeper of the kine, to say that all the other royal herds within two days' journey are also stricken, although if I understand them right, of some other pest. Also, which I forgot to add—"

"Hunt out this bearer of ill-tidings," roared Dingaan, "hunt him out, and send orders that his own cattle be taken to fill up the holes in my blanket."

Now some attendants sprang on the luckless Movo and began to beat him with their sticks. Still, before he reached the gates he succeeded in turning round weeping in good earnest and shouted:

"It is quite useless, O King, all my cattle are dead, too. They will find nothing but the horns and the hoofs, for I have sold the hides to the shield-makers."

Then they thrust him forth.

He was gone, and for a while there was silence, for despair filled the hearts of the King and his Councillors, as they gazed at Rachel dismayed, wondering within themselves how they might be rid of her and of the evils which she had brought upon them because of the blood of her people which lay at her doors.

Whilst they still stared thus in silence yet another messenger came running through the gate like one in great haste.

"Now I am minded to order this fellow to be killed before he opens his mouth," said Dingaan, "for of a surety he also is a bearer of ill-tidings."

"Nay, O King," cried out the man in alarm, "my news is only that an embassy awaits without."

"From whom?" asked Dingaan anxiously. "The white Amaboona?"

"Nay, O King, from the queen of the Ghost-people to whom thou didst dispatch Noie, daughter of Seyapi, a while ago."

Hearing the name Noie, Rachel lifted her head, and for the first time her face grew human.

"I remember," said Dingaan. "Admit the embassy."

Then followed a long pause. At length the gate opened and through it appeared Noie herself, clad in a garb of spotless white, and somewhat travel-worn, but beautiful as ever. She was escorted by four gigantic men who were naked except for their *moochas*, but wore copper ornaments on their wrists and ankles, and great rings of copper in their ears. After her came three litters whereof the grass curtains were tightly drawn, carried by bearers of the same size and race, and after these a bodyguard of fifty soldiers of a like stature. This strange and barbarous-looking company advanced slowly, whilst the Council stared at them wondering, for never before had they seen people so huge, and arriving in front of the King set down the litters, staring back in answer with their great round eyes.

As they came Rachel rose from her stool and turned slowly so that she and Noie, who walked in front of the embassy, stood face to face. For a moment they gazed at each other, then Noie, running forward, knelt before Rachel and kissed the hem of her robe, but Rachel bent down and lifted her up in her strong arms, embracing her as a mother embraces a child.

"Where hast thou been, Sister?" she asked. "I have sought thee long."

"Surely on thy business, Zoola," answered Noie, scanning her curiously. "Dost thou not remember?"

"Nay, I remember naught, Noie, save that I have sought thee long. My Spirit wanders, Noie."

"Lady," she said, "my people told me that it was so. They told me many terrible things, they who can see afar, they for whom distance has no gates, but I did not believe them. Now I see with my own eyes. Be at peace, Lady, my people will give thee back thy Spirit, though perchance thou must travel to find it, for in their land all spirits dwell. Be at peace and listen."

"With thee, Noie, I am at peace," replied Rachel, and still holding her hand, she reseated herself upon the stool.

"Where are the messengers?" asked Dingaan. "I see none."

"King," answered Noie, "they shall appear."

Then she made signs to the escort of giants, some of whom came forward and drew the curtains of the litters, whilst others opened huge umbrellas of split cane which they carried in their hands.

"Now what weapons are these?" asked Dingaan. "Daughter of Seyapi, you know that none may appear before the King armed."

"Weapons against the sun, O King, which my people hate."

"And who are the wizards that hate the sun?" queried Dingaan again in an astonished voice. Then he was silent, for out of the first litter came a little man, pale as the shoot from a bulb that has grown in darkness, with large, soft eyes like the eyes of an owl, that blinked in the light, and long hair out of which all the colour seemed to have faded.

As the man, who, like Noie, was dressed in a white robe, and in size measured no more than a twelve-year-old child, set his sandaled feet upon the ground, one of the huge guards sprang forward to shield him with the umbrella, but being awkward, struck his leg against the pole of the litter and stumbled against him, nearly knocking him to the ground, and in his efforts to save himself, letting fall the umbrella. The little man turned on him furiously, and holding one hand above his head as though to shield himself from the sun, with the other pointed at him, speaking in a low sibilant voice that sounded like the hiss of a snake. Thereon the guard fell to his knees, and bending down with outstretched arms, beat his forehead on the earth as though in prayer for mercy. The sight of this giant making supplication to one whom he could have killed with a blow, was so strange that Dingaan, unable to restrain his curiosity, asked Noie if the dwarf was ordering the other to be killed.

"Nay, King," answered Noie, "for blood is hateful to these people. He is saying that the soldier has offended many times. Therefore he curses him and tells him that he shall wither like a plucked leaf and die without seeing his home again."

"And will he die?" asked Dingaan.

"Certainly, King; those upon whom the Ghost-people lay their curse must obey the curse. Moreover, this man deserves his doom, for on the journey he killed another to take his food."

"Of a truth a terrible people!" said Dingaan uneasily. "Bid them lay no curse on me lest they should see more blood than they wish for."

"It is foolish to threaten the Great Ones of the Ghost-folk, King, for they hear even what they seem not to understand," answered Noie quietly.

"Wow!" exclaimed the King; "let my words be forgotten. I am sorry that I troubled them to come so far to visit me."

Meanwhile the offender had crept back upon his hands and knees, looking like a great beaten dog, whilst another soldier, taking his umbrella, held it over the angry dwarf. Also from the other litters two more dwarfs had descended, so like to the first that it was difficult to tell them apart, and were in the same fashion sheltered by guards with umbrellas. Mats were brought for them also, and on these they sat themselves down at right angles to Dingaan, and to Rachel, whose stool was set in front of the King, whilst behind them stood three of their escort, each holding an umbrella over the head of one of them with the left hand, while with the right they fanned them with small branches upon which the leaves, although they were dead, remained green and shining.

With Dingaan and his Council the three dwarfs did not seem to trouble themselves, but at Rachel they peered earnestly. Then one of them made a sign and muttered something, whereon a soldier of the escort stepped forward with a fourth umbrella, which he opened over the heads of Rachel, and of Noie who stood at her side.

"Why does he do that?" asked Dingaan. "The *Inkosazana* is not a bat that she fears the sun."

"He does it," answered Noie, "that the *Inkosazana* may sit in the shade of the wisdom of the Ghost-people, and that her heart which is hot with many wrongs, may grow cool in the shade."

"What does he know about the *Inkosazana* and her wrongs?" asked Dingaan again, but Noie only shrugged her shoulders and made no answer.

Now one of the dwarfs made another sign, whereon more guards advanced, carrying small bowls of polished wood. These bowls they set upon the ground before the three dwarfs, one before each of them, filling them to the brim with water from a gourd.

"If your people are thirsty, Noie," exclaimed the King, "I have beer for them to drink, for at least the locusts have left me that. Bid them throw away the water, and I will give them beer."

"It is not water, King," she answered, "but dew gathered from certain trees before sunrise, and it is their spirits that are thirsty for knowledge, not their bodies, for in this dew they read the truth."

"Then the *Inkosazana* must be of their family, Noie, for she read of the coming of the white chief Dario in water, or so they say."

"Perhaps, O King, if it is so these prophets will know it and acknowledge her."

Now for a long while there was silence, so long a while indeed that Dingaan and his Councillors began to move uneasily, for they felt as though the dwarf men were fingering their heart-strings. At length the three dwarfs lifted their wrinkled faces that were bleached to the colour of half-ripe corn, and gazed at each other with their round, owl-like eyes; then as though with one accord they said to each other:

"What seest thou, Priest?" and at same sign from them Noie translated the words into Zulu.

Now the first of them, he who had cursed the soldier, spoke in his low hissing voice, a voice like to the whisper of leaves in the wind, Noie rendering his words.

"I see two maidens standing by a house that moves when cattle draw it. One of them is dark-skinned, it is she," and he pointed to Noie, "the other is fair-skinned, it is she," and he pointed to Rachel. "They cast, each of them, a hair from her head into the air. The black hair falls to the ground, but a spirit catches the hair of gold and bears it northward. It is the spirit of Seyapi whom the Zulus slew. Northwards he bears it, and lays it in the hand of the Mother of the Trees, and with it a message."

"Yes, with it a message," repeated the other two nodding their heads.

Then one of them drew a little package wrapped in leaves from his robe, and motioned to Noie that she should give it to Rachel. Noie obeyed, and the man said:

"Let us see if she has vision. Tell us, thou White One, what lies within the leaves."

Rachel, who had been sitting like a person in a dream, took the packet, and, without looking at it, answered:

"Many other leaves, and within the last of them a hair from this head of mine. I see it, but three knots have been tied therein. They are three great troubles."

"Open," said the dwarf to Noie, who cut the fibre binding the packet, and unfolded many layers of leaves. Within the last leaf was a golden hair, and in it were tied three knots.

Noie laid the hair upon the head of Rachel—it was hers. Then she showed it to the King and his Council, who stared at the knots not knowing what to say, and after they had looked at it, refolded it in the leaves and returned the packet to the dwarf.

Now the dwarf who had read the picture in his bowl turned to him who sat nearest and asked:

"What seest thou, Priest?"

The man stared at the limpid water and answered:

"I see this place at night. I see yonder King and his Councillors talking to a white man with evil eyes and the face of a hawk, who has been wounded on the head and foot. I read their lips. They bargain together; it is of the bringing of an old prophet and his wife hither by force. I see the prophet and his wife in a house, and with them Zulus. By the command of the white man with the evil eyes the Zulus kill the prophet whose head is bald, and his wife dies upon the bed. Before they kill the prophet he slays one of the Zulus with smoke that comes from an iron tube."

When he heard all this Dingaan groaned, but the dwarf who had spoken, taking no heed of him, said to the third dwarf:

"What seest thou, Priest?" to which that dwarf answered:

"I see the White One yonder standing on a hut, but her Spirit has fled from her, it has fled from her to haunt the Trees. In her hand is a spear, and below is the white man with, the evil eyes, held by Zulus. I read her words: she says that there is blood," and he shivered as he said the word, "yes, blood between her Spirit and the people of the Zulus. She prophesies evil to them. I see the ill; I see many burnt in a great fire. I see many drowned in an angry river. I see the demons of sickness lay hold of many. I see her Spirit call up the locusts from the coast land. I see it bring disaster on their arms; I see it scatter plague among their cattle; I see a dim shape that it summons striding towards this land. It travels fast over a winter *veld*, and the head of it is the head of a skull, and the name of it is Famine."

As he ended his words the three dwarfs bent forward, and with one movement seized their bowls and emptied them on to the ground, saying: "Earth, Earth, drink, drink and bear record of these visions!"

Now the Council was much disturbed, for, although there were great witch doctors among them, none had known magic like to this. Only Dingaan stared down brooding. Then he looked up, and his fat body shook with hoarse laughter.

"You play pretty tricks, little men," he said, "with your giants and your boughs and your huts that open, and your bowls of water. But for all that they are only tricks, since Noie, or others have told you of these things that happened in the past. Now if you are wizards indeed, read me the riddle of the words of the *Inkosazana* that she spoke before her Spirit left her because of the evil acts of the wolf, Ibubesi. Show me the answer to them in your bowls of water, little men, or be driven hence as cheats and liars. Also tell us your names by which we may know you."

When Noie had translated this speech the three dwarfs gathered themselves under one umbrella, and spoke to each other; then they slid back to their places, and the first of them, he who had cursed the soldier, said:

"King of the Zulus, I am Eddo, this on my right is Pani, and that on my left is Hana. We are children of the Mother of the Trees; we are high-priests of the Grey-people, the Dream-people, who rule by dreams and wisdom, not by spears as thou dost, O King. We are the Ghost-kings whom the ghosts obey, we are the masters of the dead, and the readers of hearts. Those are our names and titles, O King. We have travelled hither because thou sentest a messenger of our own blood who whispered a strange tale in the ear of the Mother of the Trees, a tale of one of whom we knew already but desired to see," and all three of them nodded towards Rachel seated on her stool. "We will read thy riddle, O King, but first thou must fix the fee."

"What do you demand, Ghost-people?" asked Dingaan. "Cattle are somewhat scarce here just now, and wives, I think, would be of little use to you. What is there, then, that you desire, and I can give?"

They looked at each other, then Eddo said, pointing with his thin hand upon which the nails grew long:

"We ask for the White One who sits there. We think that her Spirit dwells with us already, and we ask her body that we may join it to the Spirit again."

Now the Council murmured, but Dingaan replied:

"Once we sought to keep her in whom dwelt the *Inkosazana* of the Zulus. But things have gone amiss, and she brings curses on us. If shape and spirit were joined together again, mayhap the curses would be taken off our heads. Yet we dare not give her to you, unless she gives herself of her own will. Moreover, first the divination, then the pay. Is that enough?"

"It is enough," they answered, speaking all together. "Set out the matter, King of the Zulus, and we will see what we can do."

Then Dingaan beckoned to a man with a withered hand who sat close to him, listening and noting all things, but saying nothing, and said:

"Stand forth, thou Mopo, and tell the tale."

So Mopo rose and began his story. He told how he alone among the people of the Zulus had thrice seen the spirit of the *Inkosazana* in the days of the "Black-One-who-was-gone." He told how many moons ago the white man, Ibubesi, had come to the Great Place speaking of a beautiful white maiden who was known by the name of the *Inkosazana-y-Zoola*, a maiden who ruled the lightning, and was not as other maidens are, and how he had been sent to see her, and found that as was the Spirit of the *Inkosazana* which he knew, so was this maiden.

"*Wow!*" he added, "save that the one walked on air and the other on earth, they are the same."

Moreover, as a spirit she seemed wise. He told of the trapping of Noie, and of the decoying of Rachel into Zululand, and of the interview between her and the King by moonlight when she smelt out

Noie. Now he was going on to speak of the question put by Dingaan to the *Inkosazana*, and the answer that she gave to him, when one of the little men who all this while sat as though they were asleep, blinking their eyes in the light—it was Eddo—said:

"Surely thou forgettest something. Tongue of the King, thou who are named Mopo, or Umbopa, Son of Makedama; thou forgettest certain words which the *Inkosazana* whispered to thee when she threw her cloak about thy head ere thou fleddest away from the Council of the King. Of course, we do not know the words, but why dost thou not repeat them, Tongue of the King?"

Mopo stared at them, and his teeth chattered, then he answered:

"Because they have nothing to do with the story, Ghost-men; because they were of my own death, which is a little matter."

The three dwarfs turned their heads towards each other and said, each to the other:

"Hearest thou, Priest, and hearest thou, Priest, and hearest thou, Priest? He says that the words were of his own death and have nothing to do with the story," and they smiled and nodded, and appeared to go to sleep again.

Now Mopo went on with his tale. He told of the question of the King, how he had asked the *Inkosazana* whether he should fall upon the Boers or let them be; of how she had searched the Heavens with her eyes; of how the meteor had travelled before them, and burst over the *kraal*, Umgugundhlovu, that star which she said was thrown by the hand of the Great-Great, the *Umkulunkulu*, and of how she had sworn that she also heard the feet of a people travelling over plain and mountain, and saw the rivers behind them running red with blood. Lastly, he told of how she had refused to add to or take from her words, or to set out their meaning.

Then Mopo sat himself down again in the circle of the Councillors, and watched and hearkened like a hungry wolf.

"Ye have heard, Ghost-men," said the King. "Now, if ye are really wise, interpret to us the meaning of this saying of the *Inkosazana*, and of the running star which none can read."

The priests awoke and consulted with each other, then Eddo said:

"This matter is too high for us, King of the Zulus."

Dingaan heard, and laughed angrily.

"I thought it, I thought it!" he cried. "Ye are but cheats after all who, like any common doctor, repeat the gossip that ye have heard, and pretend that it is a message from Heaven. Now why should I not whip you from my town with rods till ye see that red blood which ye so greatly fear?"

At the mention of the word blood, the little men seemed to curl up like cut grass before fire; then Eddo smiled, a sickly smile, and answered:

"Be gentle, King, walk softly, King. We are but poor cheats, yet we will do our best, we, or another for us. A new bowl, a big bowl, a red bowl for the red King, and fill it to the brink with dew."

As he piped out the words a man from among their company appeared with a vessel much larger than those into which they had gazed, and made of beautiful, polished, blood-hued wood that gleamed in the sunlight. Eddo took it in his hand and another slave filled it with water from the gourd; the last drop of the water filled it to the brim. Then the three of them muttered invocations over it, and Eddo, beckoning to Noie, bade her bear it to the *Inkosazana* that she might gaze therein.

Rachel received it and looked; as she looked all the emptiness left her eyes which grew quick and active and full of horror.

"Thou seest something, Maiden?" queried Eddo.

"Aye," answered Rachel, "I see much. Must I speak?"

"Nay, nay! Breathe on the water thrice and fix the visions. Now bear the bowl to yonder King and let him look. Perchance he also will see something."

Rachel breathed on the water thrice, rose like one in a trance, and advancing to Dingaan placed the brimming bowl upon his knees.

"Look, King, look," cried Eddo, "and tell us if in what thou seest lies an answer to the oracle of the *Inkosazana*."

Dingaan stared at the water, angrily at first, as one who smells a trick. Then his face changed.

"By the head of the Black One," he said, "I see people fighting in this *kraal*, white men and Zulus, and the white men are mastered and the Zulus drag them out to death. The Zulus conquer, O my people. It is as I thought that it would be—that is the meaning of the riddle of the *Inkosazana*."

"Good, good," said the Council. "Doubtless it shall come to pass."

But the dwarf Eddo only smiled again and waved his hand.

"Look once more, King," he said in his low, hissing voice, and Dingaan looked.

Now his face darkened. "I see fire," he said. "Yes, in this *kraal*. Umgugundhlovu burns, my royal House burns, and yonder come the white men riding upon horses. Oh! they are gone."

Eddo waved his hand, saying:

"Look again and tell us what thou seest, King."

Unwillingly enough, but as though he could not resist, Dingaan looked and said:

"I see a mountain whereof the top is like the shape of a woman, and between her knees is the mouth of a cave. Beneath the floor of that cave I see bodies, the body of a great man and the body of a girl; she must have been fair, that girl."

Now when he heard this the Councillor who was named Mopo, he with the withered hand, started up, then sat down again, but all were so intent upon listening to Dingaan that none noticed his movements save Noie and the priests of the ghosts.

"I see a man, a fat man come out of the cave," went on Dingaan. "He seems to be wounded and weary, also his stomach is sunken as though with hunger. Two other men seize him, a tall warrior with muscles that stand out on his legs, and another that is thin and short. They drag him up the mountain to a great cleft that is between the breasts of her who sits thereon. They speak with him, but I cannot see their faces, for they are wrapped in mist, or the face of the fat man, for that also is wrapped in mist. They hale him to the edge of the cleft, they hurl him over, he falls headlong, and the mist is swept from his face. Ah! *it is my own face!*"[3]

"Priest," whispered each of the little men to his fellow in the dead silence that followed, "Priest, this King says that he sees his own face. Priest, tell me now, has not the spirit of the *Inkosazana* interpreted the oracle of the *Inkosazana*? Will not yonder King be hurled down this cleft? Is *he* not the star that falls?"

And they nodded and smiled at each other.

But Dingaan leapt up in his rage and terror, and with him leapt up the Councillors and witch doctors, all save he who was named Mopo, son of Makedama, who sat still gazing at the ground. Dingaan leapt up, and seizing the bowl hurled it from him so that the water in it fell over Rachel like rain from the clouds. He leapt up, and he cursed the Ghost-priests as evil wizards, bidding them begone from his land. He raved at them, he threatened them, he cursed them again and again. The little men sat still and smiled till he grew weary and ceased. Then they spoke to each other, saying:

"He has sprinkled the White One with the dew of out Trees, and henceforth she belongs to the Trees. Is it not so, Priest?"

They nodded in assent, and Eddo rose and addressed the King in a new voice, a shrill commanding voice, saying:

"O man, thou that art called a King and causest much blood to flow, thou are but a bubble on a river of blood, thou slayer that shalt be slain, thou thrower of spears upon whom the spear shall fall, thou who

3. See *Nada the Lily*, chapter 35.

shalt look upon the Face of Stone that knows not pity, thou whom the earth shall swallow, thou who shalt perish at the hands of—"

"The faces of the slayers were veiled, Priest," broke in the other two dwarfs, peeping up at him from beneath the shadow of their umbrellas; "surely the faces of those slayers were veiled, O Priest."

"Thou who shalt perish at the hands of avengers whose faces are veiled, thy riddle is read for thee as the Mother of the Trees decreed that it should be read. It is well read, it is truly read, it shall befall in its season. Now give to thy servants their reward and let them depart in peace. Give to them, that White One whose lost Spirit spoke to thee from the water."

"Take her," roared Dingaan, "take her and begone, for to the Zulus she and Noie, the witch, bring naught but ill."

But one of the Council cried:

"The *Inkosazana* cannot be sent away with these magicians unless it is her will to go."

Then the little men nodded to Noie, and Noie whispered in the ear of Rachel.

Rachel listened and answered: "Whither thou goest, Noie, thither I go with thee, I who seek my Spirit."

So Noïe took Rachel by the hand and led her from the Council-place of the King, and as she went, followed by the Ghost-priests and their escort, for the last time all the Councillors rose up and gave to her the royal salute. Only Dingaan sat upon the ground and beat it with his fists in fury.

Thus did the *Inkosazana-y-Zoola* depart from the Great Place of the King of the Zulus, and Mopo, the son of Makedama, shading his eyes with his hand, watched her go from between his withered fingers.

## CHAPTER 19

# Rachel Finds Her Spirit

Northward, ever northward, journeyed Rachel with the Ghost-priests; for days and weeks they journeyed, slowly, and for the most part at night, since these people dreaded the glare of the sun. Sometimes she was borne along in a litter with Noie upon the shoulders of the huge slaves, but more often she walked between the litters in the midst of a guard of soldiers, for now she was so strong that she never seemed to weary, nor even in the fever swamps where many fell ill, did any sickness touch her. Also this labour of the body seemed to soothe her wandering and tormented mind, as did the touch of Noie's hand and the sound of Noie's voice. At times, however, her madness got hold of her and she broke out into those bursts of wild laughter which had scared the Zulus. Then Eddo would descend from his litter and lay his long fingers on her forehead and look into her eyes in such a fashion that she went to sleep and was at peace. But if Noie spoke to her in these sleeps, she answered her questions, and even talked reasonably as she had done before the people of Mafooti laid the body of Richard at her feet, and she stood upon the roof of the hut which Ishmael strove to climb.

Thus it was that Noie came to learn all that had happened to her since they parted, for though she had gathered much from them, the Zulus could not, or would not tell her everything. In past days she had heard from Rachel of the lad, Richard Darrien, who had been her companion years before through that night of storm on the island in the river, and now she understood that her lady loved this Richard, and that it was because of his murder by the wild brute, Ibubesi, that she had become mad.

Yes, she was mad, and for that reason Noie rejoiced that the dwarf people were taking her to their home, since if she could be cured at all, they were able to heal her, they the great doctors. Moreover, if these priests and the Zulus would have let her go, whither else could she have gone whose parents and lover were dead, except to the white people on the coast, who did not reverence the insane, as do all black folk, but would have locked her up in a house with others like her until she died. No although she knew that there were dangers before them, many and great dangers, Noie rejoiced that things had befallen thus.

Also in her tender care already Rachel improved much, and Noie believed that one day she would be herself again. Only she wished that she and her lady were alone together; that there were no priests with them, and above all no Eddo. For Eddo as she knew well was jealous of her authority over Rachel; jealous too of the love that they bore one to the other. He wished to use this crazed white chieftainess who had been accepted as their *Inkosazana* by the great Zulu people, for his own purposes. This had been clear from the beginning, and that was why when he first heard of her he had consented to go on the embassy to Dingaan, since by his magic he could foresee much of the future that was dark to Noie, whose blood was mixed and who had not all the gifts of the Ghost-kings.

Moreover, the Mother of the Trees was Noie's great aunt, being the sister of her grandfather, or of his father, Noie was not sure which, for she had dwelt among them but a few days, and never thought to inquire of the matter. But of one thing she was sure, that Eddo the first priest, hated this Mother of the Trees, who was named Nya, and desired that "when her tree fell" the next mother should be his servant, which Nya was not. Perhaps, reflected Noie, it was in his mind that her lady would fill this part, and being mad, obey him in all things.

Still she kept a watch upon her words, and even on her thoughts, for Eddo and his fellow-priests, Pani and Hana, were able to peer into human hearts, and read their secrets. Also she protected Rachel from him as much as she was able, never leaving her side for a moment, however weary she might be, for she feared lest he should become the master of her will. Only when the fits of madness fell upon her mistress, she was forced to allow Eddo to quell them with his touch and eye, since herself she lacked this power, nor dared she call the others to her help, for they were under the hand of Eddo.

Northward, ever northward. First they passed through the Zulus and their subject tribes who knew of them and of the *Inkosazana*. All of these were suffering from the curse that lay upon the land because, as they believed, there was blood between the *Inkosazana* and her people. The locusts devoured their crops and the plague ravaged their cattle, so that they were terrified of her, and of the little Grey-folk with whom she travelled, the wizards who had shown fearful things to Dingaan and left him sick with dread. They fled at their approach, only leaving a few of their old people to prostrate themselves before this *Inkosazana* who wandered in search of her own Spirit, and the Dream-men who dwelt with the ghosts in the heart of a forest, and to pray her and them to lift this cloud of evil from the land, bringing gifts of such things as were left to them.

At length all the Zulus were passed, and they entered into the territories of other tribes, wild, wandering tribes.

But even these knew of the Ghost-kings, and attempted nothing against them, as they had attempted nothing against Noie and her escort when she travelled through this land on her embassy to the People of the Trees. Indeed, some of their doctors would visit them at their camps and ask an oracle, or an interpretation of dreams, or a charm against their enemies, or a deadly poison, offering great gifts in return. At times Eddo and his fellow-priests would listen, and the giants would bring a tiny bowl filled with dew into which they gazed, telling them the pictures they saw there, though this they did but seldom, as the supply of dew which they had brought with them from their own country ran low, and since it could not be used twice they kept it for their own purposes.

Next they came to a country of vast swamps, where dwelt few men and many wild beasts, a country full of fevers and reeds and pools, in which lived snakes and crocodiles. Yet no harm came to them from these things, for the Ghost-priests had medicines that warded off sickness, and charms that protected them from all evil creatures, and in their bowls they read what road to take and how dangers could be avoided. So they passed the swamps safely; only here that slave whom Eddo had cursed at the *kraal* of Dingaan, and who from that day onward had wasted till he seemed to be nothing but a great skeleton, sickened and died.

"Did I not tell you that it should be so?" said Eddo to the other slaves, who trembled before him as reeds tremble in the wind. "Be warned, ye fools, who think that the strength of men lies in their bodies and their spears." Then he kicked the corpse of the dead giant gently with his sandaled foot, and bade his brothers throw him into a pool for the crocodiles to eat.

Having passed the swamps and many rivers, at length they turned westward, travelling for days over grassy uplands like to those of Natal, among which wandered pastoral tribes with their herds of cattle. On these plains were multitudes of game and many lions, especially in the bush-clad slopes of great isolated mountains that rose up here and there. These lions roared round them at night, but the priests did not seem to be afraid, for when the brutes became overbold they placed deadly poison in the carcases of buck that the nomad tribes brought them as offerings, of which the lions ate and died in numbers. Also they sold some of the poison to the tribe for a great price in cattle, as to the delivery of which cattle they gave minute directions, for they knew that none dared to cheat the Mother of the Trees and her prophets.

After the plains were left behind, they reached a vast, fertile and low-lying country that sloped upwards for miles and miles, which, as Noie explained to Rachel, when she would listen, was the outer territory of the Ghost-people, for here dwelt the race of the Umkulus, or Great Ones, who were their slaves, that folk to which the soldiers of their escort belonged. Of these there were thousands and tens of thousands who earned their living by agriculture, since although they were so huge and fierce-looking, they did not fight unless they were attacked. The chiefs of this people had their dwellings in vast caves in the sides of cliffs which, if need be, could be turned into impregnable fortresses, but their real ruler was the Mother of the Trees, and their office was to protect the country of the Trees and furnish it with food, since the Tree-people were dreamers who did little work.

While they travelled through this land all the headmen of the Umkulus accompanied them, and every morning a council was held at which these made report to the priests of all that had chanced of late, and laid their causes before them for judgment. These causes Eddo and his fellow-priests heard and settled as seemed best to them, nor did any dare to dispute their rulings. Indeed, even when they deposed a high chief and set another in his place, the man who had lost all knelt before them and thanked them for their goodness. Also they tried criminals who had stolen women or committed murder, but they never ordered such men to be slain outright. Sometimes Eddo would look at them dreamily and curse them in his slow, hissing voice, bidding them waste in body and in mind, as he had done to the soldier at Umgugundhlovu, and die within one year, or two, or three, as the case might be. Or sometimes, if the crime was very bad, he would command that they should be sent to "travel in the desert," that is, wander to and fro without food or water until death found them. Now and again miserable-looking men, mere skeletons, with hollow cheeks, and eyes that seemed to start from their heads, would appear at their camps weeping and imploring that the curse which had been laid upon them in past days should be taken off their heads. At such people Eddo and his brother-priests, Pani and Hana, would laugh softly, asking them how they throve upon the wrath of the Mother of the Trees, and whether they thought that others who saw them would be encouraged to sin as they had done. But when the poor wretches prayed that they might be killed outright with the spear, the priests shrank up in horror beneath their umbrellas, and asked if they were mad that they should wish them to "sprinkle their trees with blood."

One morning a number of these bewitched Umkulus, men, women and children, appeared, and when the three priests mocked them, as was their wont, and the guards, some of whom were their own relatives, sought to beat them away with sticks, threw themselves upon the ground and burst into weeping. Rachel, who was camped at a little distance with Noie, in a reed tent that the guard had made for her, which they folded up and carried as they did the umbrellas, heard the sound of this lamentation, and came out followed by Noie. For a space she stood contemplating their misery with a troubled air, then asked Noie why these people seemed so starved and why they wept. Noie told her that when she was on her embassy the head of their *kraal*, an enormous man of middle age, whom she pointed out to Rachel, had sought to detain her because she was beautiful, and he wished to make her his wife, although he knew well that she was on an embassy to the Mother of the Trees. She had escaped, but it was for this reason that the curse of which they were perishing had been laid upon him and his folk.

Now Rachel went on to where the three priests sat beneath their umbrellas dozing away the hours of sunlight, beckoning to the doomed family to follow her.

"Wake, priests," she cried in a loud voice, and they looked up astonished, rubbing their eyes, and asked what was the matter.

"This," said Rachel. "I command you to lift the weight of your malediction off the head of these people who have suffered enough."

"Thou commandest us!" exclaimed Eddo astonished. "And if we will not, Beautiful One, what then?"

"Then," answered Rachel, "*I* will lift it and set it on to your heads, and you shall perish as they are perishing. Oh! you think me mad, you priests, who kill more cruelly than did the Zulus, and mad I am whose Spirit wanders. Yet I tell you that new powers grow within me, though whence they come I know not, and what I say I can perform."

Now they stared at her muttering together, and sending for a wooden bowl, peeped into it. Whatever it was they saw there did not please them, for at length Eddo addressed the crowd of suppliants, saying:

"The Mother of the Trees forgives; the knot she tied she looses; the tree she planted she digs up. You are forgiven. Bones, put on strength; mouths, receive food; eyes, forget your blindness, and feet, your wanderings. Grow fat and laugh; increase and multiply; for the curse we give you a blessing, such is the will of the Mother of the Trees."

"Nay, nay," cried Rachel, when she understood their words, "believe him not, ye starvelings. Such is the will of the *Inkosazana* of the Zulus, she who has lost her Spirit and another's, and travels all this weary way to find them."

Then her madness seemed to come upon her again, for she tossed her arms on high and burst into one of her wild fits of laughter. But those whom she had redeemed heeded it not, for they ran to her, and since they dared not touch her, or even her robe, kissed the ground on which she had stood and blessed her. Moreover from that moment they began to mend, and within a few days were changed folk. This Noie knew, for they followed up Rachel to the confines of the desert, and she saw it with her eyes. Also the fame of the deed spread among the Umkulu people who groaned under the cruel rule of the Ghost-kings, and mad or sane, from that day forward they adored Rachel even more than the Zulus had done, and like the Zulus believed her to be a Spirit. No mere human being, they declared, could have lifted off the curse of the Mother of the Trees from those upon whom it had fallen.

Thenceforward Eddo, Pani, and Hana hid their judgments from Rachel, and would not suffer such suppliants to approach the camp. Also when they seized a number of men because these had conspired together to rebel against the Ghost-people, and brought them on towards their own country for a certain purpose, they forced them to act as bearers like the others, so that Rachel might not guess their doom. For now, with all their power, they also were afraid of this white *Inkosazana*, as Dingaan had been afraid.

So they travelled up this endless slope of fertile land, leaving all the *kraal*s of the giant Umkulus behind them, and one morning at the dawn camped upon the edge of a terrible desert; a place of dry sands and sun-blasted rocks, that looked like the bottom of a drained ocean, where nothing lived save the fire lizards and certain venomous snakes that buried themselves in the sand, all except their heads, and only crawled out at night. After the people of the Umkulus this horrible waste was the great defence of the Ghost-kings, whose country it ringed about, since none could pass it without guides and water. Indeed, Noie had been forced to stay here for days with her escort, until the Mother of the Trees, learning of her coming in some strange fashion, had sent priests and guards to bring her to her land. But the

Zulus who were with her they did not bring, except one witch-doctor to bear witness to her words. These they left among the Umkulus till she should return, nor were those Zulus sorry who had already heard enough of the magic of the Ghost-kings, and feared to come face to face with them.

But it is true that they also feared the Umkulus, whom, because of their great size and the fierceness of their air, the Zulus took to be evil spirits, though if this were so, they could not understand why they should obey a handful of grey dwarfs who lived far from them beyond the desert. Still these Umkulus did them no harm, for on her return Noie found them all safe and well.

That afternoon Rachel and the dwarfs plunged into the dreadful wilderness, heading straight for the ball of the sinking sun. Here, although she wished to do so, she was not allowed to walk, for fear lest the serpents should bite her, said Eddo, but must journey in the litter with Noie. So they entered it, and were borne forward at a great pace, the bearers travelling at a run, and being often changed. Also many other bearers came with them, and on the shoulders of each of them was strapped a hide bag of water. Of this they soon discovered the reason, for the sand of that wilderness was white with salt; the air also seemed to be full of salt, so that the thirst of those who travelled there was sharp and constant, and if it could not be satisfied they died.

It was a very strange journey, and although she did not seem to take much note of them at the time, its details and surroundings burned themselves deeply into Rachel's mind. The hush of the infinite desert, the white moonlight gleaming upon the salt, white sand; the tall rocks which stood up here and there like unfinished obelisks and colossal statues, the snowy clouds of dust that rose beneath the feet of the company; the hoarse shouts of the guides, the close heat, the halts for water which was greedily swallowed in great gulps; the occasional cry and confusion when a man fell out exhausted, or because he had been bitten by one of the serpents—all these things, amongst others, were very strange.

Once Rachel asked vaguely what became of these outworn and snake-poisoned men, and Noie only shook her head in answer, for she did not think fit to tell her that they were left to find their way back, or to perish, as might chance.

All that night and for the first hours of the day that followed, they went forward swiftly, camping at last to eat and sleep in the shadow of a mass of rock that looked like a gigantic castle with walls and towers. Here they remained in the burning heat until the sun began to sink once more, and then went on again, leaving some of the bearers behind them, because there was no longer water for so many. There the great men sat in patient resignation and watched them go, they who knew that having little or no water, few of them could hope to see their homes again. Still, so great was their dread of the Ghost-priests, that they never dared to murmur, or to ask that any of the store of water should be given to them, they who were but cattle to be used until they died.

The second night's journey was like the first, for this desert never changed, its aspect, and on the following morning they halted beneath another pile of fantastic, sand-burnished rocks, from some of which hung salt like icicles. Here one of the bearers who had been denied water as a punishment for laziness, although in truth he was sick, began to suck the salt-icicles. Suddenly he went raving mad, and rushing with a knife at Eddo, Pani, and Hana where they sat under their cane umbrellas that, for the sake of coolness, were damped with this precious water, he tried to kill them.

Then as they saw the knife gleaming, all their imperturbable calm departed from these dwarfs. They squeaked in terror with thin voices as rats speak; they rolled upon the ground yelling to the slaves to save them from a "red death." The man was seized and, though he fought with all his giant strength, held down and choked in the sand. Once, however, he twisted his head free, howling a curse at them. Also he managed to hurl his knife at Eddo, and the point of it scratched him on the hand, causing the pale blood to flow, a sight at which Eddo and the other priests broke into tears and lamentations, that continued long after the Umkulu was dead.

"Why are they such cowards?" asked Rachel, dreamily, for she had not seen the murder of the slave, and thought that Eddo had only scratched himself.

"Because they fear the sight of blood, Zoola," answered Noie, "which is a very evil omen to them. Death they do not fear who are already among ghosts, but if it is a red death, their souls are spilt with their life, or so they believe."

Towards noon that day the sky banked up with lurid-coloured clouds; the sun which should have shone so hotly, went out, and a hush that was almost fearful in its heat and intensity, fell upon the desert. The Umkulu bearers became disturbed, and gathered together into knots, talking in low tones. Eddo and his brother priests who, either because of the adventure of the morning or the oppressive air, could not sleep, as was usual with them, were also disturbed. They crept from beneath their umbrellas which, as the sun had vanished, were of no use to them, and stood together staring at the salty plain, which under that leaden and lowering sky looked white as snow, and at the brooding clouds above. They even sent for their bowls to read in them pictures of what was about to happen, but there was no dew left, so these could not be used.

Then they consulted with the captains of the bearers, who told then what no magic was needed to guess that a mighty storm was gathering, and that if it overtook them in the desert, they would be buried beneath the drifting sand. Now this was a "white death" which the dwarfs did not seem to desire, so they ordered an instant departure, instead of delaying the start until sunset, as they had intended, for then, if all went well, they would have arrived at their homes by dawn, and not in the middle of the night. So that litters were made ready, and they went forward through the overpowering heat, that caused the bearers to hang out their tongues and reel as they walked.

Towards evening the storm began to stir. Little wandering puffs of wind blew upon them and died away, and lightnings flickered intermittently. Then a hot breeze sprang up that gradually increased in strength until the sand rolled and rippled before it, now one way and now another, for this breeze seemed to blow in turn from every quarter of the heavens. Suddenly, however, after trying them all, it settled in the west, and drove straight into their faces with ever increasing force. Now Eddo thrust out his head between the curtains of his litter and called to the bearers to hurry, as they had but a little distance of desert left to pass, after which came the grass country where there would be no danger from the sand. They heard and obeyed, changing the pole gangs frequently, as those who carried the litters became exhausted.

But the storm was quicker than they; it burst upon them while they were still in the waste, though not in its full strength. Then the darkness came, utter darkness, for no moon or stars could be seen, and salt and sand drove down on them like hail. Through it all, the bearers fought on, though how they found their way Noie, who was watching them, could not guess, since no landmarks were left to guide them. They fought on, blinded, choked with the salt sand that drove into their eyes and lungs, till man after man, they fell down and perished. Others took their places, and yet they fought on.

It must have been near to midnight when the company, or those who were left of them, staggered to the edge of that dreadful wilderness which was but a vast plain of stone and sand, bordered on the west as on the east by slopes of fertile soil. For a while the fierce tempest lifted a little, and the light of the stars which struggled through breaks in the clouds showed that they were marching down a steep descent of grassland. Thus they went on for several more hours, till at length the bearers of the litter in which were Rachel and Noie, who for a long time had been staggering to and fro like drunken men, came to a halt, and litter and all, sank to the ground, utterly exhausted.

Rachel and Noie disentangled themselves from the litter, for they were unhurt, and stood by it, not knowing where to go, till presently two other litters containing the priests came up, for the third had been abandoned, and its occupant crowded in with Eddo. Now a great clamour arose in the darkness, the priests hissing commands to the surviving bearers to take up the litter and proceed. But great as was their strength, this the poor men could not do. There they lay upon the ground answering that Eddo might curse them if he wished, or even kill them as their brothers had been killed, but they were unable to stir another step until they had rested and drunk. Where they were, there they must lie until rain fell. Then the priests wished Rachel to enter one of their litters, leaving Noie to walk, which they were afraid to do themselves. But when she understood, Rachel cut the matter short by answering,

"Not so, I will walk," and picking up the spear of one of the fallen Umkulu to serve as a staff, she took Noie by the hand and started forward down the hill.

One of the priests clasped her robe to draw her back, but she turned on him with the spear, whereon he shrank back into his litter like a snail into his shell and left her alone. So following the steep path they marched on, and after them came the two litters with the priests, carried by all the bearers who could still stand, for these old men weighed no more than children. From far below them rose a mighty sound as of an angry sea.

"What is that noise?" called Rachel into the ear of Noie, for the gale was rising again.

"The sound of wind in the forest where the Tree-folk dwell," she answered.

Then the dawn broke, an awful, blood-red dawn, and by degrees they saw. Beneath them ran a shallow river, and beyond it, stretching for league upon league farther than the eye could see, lay the mighty forest whereof the trees soared two hundred feet or more into the air; the dark illimitable forest that rolled as the sea rolls beneath the pressure of the gale, and indeed, seen from above, looked like a green and tossing ocean. At the sight of the water Rachel and Noie began to run towards it hand in hand, for they were parched with thirst whose mouths were full of the salt dust of the desert. The bearers of the litters in which were the three priests ran also, paying no heed to the cries of the dwarfs within. At length it was reached, and throwing themselves down they drank until that raging thirst of theirs was satisfied; even Eddo and his companions crawled out of their litters and drank. Then having washed their hands and faces in the cool water, they forded the fleet stream, and, filled with a new life, followed the road that ran beyond towards the forest. Scarcely had they set foot upon the farther bank when the heart of the tempest, which had been eddying round them all night long, burst over them in its fury. The lightnings blazed, the thunder rolled, and the wild wind grew to a hurricane, so fierce that the litters in which were Eddo, Pani, and Hana were torn from the grasp of the bearers and rolled upon the ground. From the wreck of them, for they were but frail things, the little grey priests emerged trembling, or rather were dragged by the hands of their giant bearers, to whom they clung as a frightened infant clings to its mother. Rachel saw them and, laughed.

"Look at the Masters of Magic!" she cried to Noie, "those who kill with a curse, those who rule the Ghosts," and she pointed to the tiny, contemptible figures with fluttering robes being dragged along by those giants whom but a little while before they had threatened with death.

"I see them," answered Noie into her ear. "Their spirits are strong when they are at peace, but in trouble they fear doom more than others. Now, if I were those Umkulu, I would make an end of them while they can."

But these great, patient men did otherwise; indeed, when the dwarfs, worn out and bewildered by the hurricane, could walk no more, they took them up and carried them as a woman carries a babe.

Now they were passing a belt of open land between the river and the forest in which terrified mobs of cattle rushed to and fro, while their herds, slave-men of large size like the Umkulu, tried to drive them to some place where they would be safe from the tempest In this belt also grew broad fields of grain, which furnished food for the Tree-folk. At last they came to the confines of the forest, and Rachel, looking round her with wondering eyes, saw at the foot of each great tree a tiny hut shaped like a tent, and in front of the hut a dwarf seated on the ground staring into a bowl of water, and beating his breast with his hands.

"What do they?" she asked of Noie.

"They strive to read their fates, Lady, and weep because the wind ripples the dew in their bowls, so that they can see nothing, and cannot be sure whether their tree will stand or fall. Follow me, follow me; I know the way, here we are not safe."

The hurricane was at its height; the huge trees about them rocked and bent like reeds, great boughs came crashing down; one of them fell upon a praying dwarf and crushed him to a pulp. Those around him saw it and uttered a wild shrill scream; Eddo, Pani, and Hana saw it and screamed also, in the arms of their bearers, for this sight of blood was terrible to them. The forest was alive with the voices of the storm, it seemed to howl and groan, and the lightnings illumined its gloomy aisles. The grandeur and the fearfulness of the scene excited Rachel; she waved the spear she carried, and began to laugh in the wild fashion of her madness, so that even the grey dwarfs, seated each at the foot of his tree, ceased from his prayers to glance at her askance.

On they went, expecting death at every step, but always escaping it, until they reached a wide clearing in the forest. In the centre of this clearing grew a tree more huge than any that Rachel had ever dreamed of, the bole of it, that sprang a hundred feet without a branch, was thicker than Dingaan's Great Hut, and its topmost boughs were lost in the scudding clouds. In front of this tree was gathered a multitude of people, men, women, and children, all dwarfs, and all of them on their knees engaged in prayer. At its bole, by a tent-shaped house, stood a little figure, a woman whose long grey hair streamed upon the wind.

"The Mother of the Trees," cried Noie through the screaming gale. "Come to her, she will shelter us," and she gripped Rachel's arm to lead her forward.

Scarcely had they gone a step when the lightning blazed above them fearfully, and with it came an awful rush of wind. Perhaps that flash fell upon the tree, or perhaps the wind snapped its roots. At least its mighty trunk burst in twain, and with a crash that for a moment seemed to master even the roar of the volleying thunder, down it came to earth. Two huge limbs fell on either side of Rachel and Noie, but they were not touched. A bough struck the Umkulu slave who was carrying Eddo, and swept off his head, leaving the dwarf unharmed. Another bough fell upon Pani and his bearer, and buried them in the earth beneath its bulk, so that they were never seen again. As it chanced the most of the worshippers were beyond the reach of the falling branches, but some of these that were torn loose in the fall, or shattered by the lightning, the wind caught and hurled among them, slaying several and wounding others.

In ten seconds the catastrophe had come and gone, the Queen-Tree that had ruled the forest for a thousand years was down, a stack of green leaves, through which the shattered branches showed like bones, and a prostrate, splintered trunk. The shock threw Noie and Rachel to the ground, but Rachel, rising swiftly, pulled Noie to her feet after her; then, acting upon some impulse, leapt forward, and climbing on to the trunk where it forked, ran down it till she almost reached its base, and stood there against the great shield of earth that had been torn up with the roots. After that last fearful outburst a stillness fell, the storm seemed to have exhausted itself, at any rate for a while. Rachel was able to get her breath and look about her.

All around were lines of enormous trees, solemn aisles that seemed to lead up to the Queen of the Trees, and down these aisles, piercing the shadows cast by the interlacing branches overhead, shone the lights of that lurid morning. Rachel saw, and something struggled in the darkness of her brain, as the light struggled in the darkness of the forest aisles. She remembered—oh! what was it she remembered? Now she knew. It was the dream she had dreamed upon the island in the river, years and years ago, a dream of such trees as these, and of little grey people like to these, and of the boy, Richard, grown to manhood, lashed to the trunk of one of the trees. What had happened to her? She could recall nothing since she saw the body of Richard upon its bier in the *kraal* Mafooti.

But this was not the *kraal* Mafooti, nor had Noie, who stood at her side, been with her there, Noie, who had gone on an embassy to her father's folk, the dwarf people. Ah! these people were dwarfs. Look at them running to and fro screaming like little monkeys. She must have been dreaming a long, bad dream, whereof the pictures had escaped her. Doubtless she was still dreaming and presently would awake. Well, the torment had gone out of it, and the fear, only the wonder remained. She would stand still and see what happened. Something was happening now. A little thin hand appeared, gripping the rough bark at the side of the fallen tree.

She peeped over the swell of it and saw an old dwarf woman with long white hair, whose feet were set in a cleft of the shattered bole, and who hung to it as an ape hangs. Beneath her to the ground was a fall of full thirty feet, for the base of the bole was held high up by the roots, so that the little woman's hair hung down straight towards the ground, whither she must presently fall and be killed. Rachel wondered how she had come there, if she had clung to the trunk when it fell, or been thrown up by the shock, or lifted by a bough.

Next she wondered how long it would be before she was obliged to leave go, and whether her white head or her back would first strike the earth all that depth beneath. Then it occurred to her that she might be saved.

"Hold my feet," she said to Noie, who had followed her along the trunk, speaking in her own natural voice, at the sound of which Noie looked at her in joyful wonder. "Hold my feet; I think I can reach that old woman," and without waiting for an answer she laid herself down upon the bole, her body hanging over the curve of it.

Now Noie saw her purpose, and seating herself with her heels set against the roughness of the bark, grasped her by the ankles. Supporting some of her weight on one hand, with the other Rachel reached downwards all the length of her long arm, and just as the grasp of the old woman below was slackening, contrived to grip her by the wrist. The dwarf swung loose, hanging in the air, but she was very light, of the weight of a five-year-old child, perhaps, no more, and Rachel was very strong. With an effort she lifted her up till the monkey-like fingers gripped the rough bark again. Another effort and the little body was resting on the round of the tree, one more and she was beside her.

Now Rachel rose to her feet again and laughed, but it was not the mad laughter that had scared Ishmael and the Zulus; it was her own laughter, that of a healthy, cultured woman.

The little creature, crouching on hands and knees at Rachel's feet, lifted her head and stared with her round eyes. At that moment, too, the sun broke out, and its rays, shining where they had never shone for ages, fell upon Rachel, upon her bright hair, and the white robes in which the dwarfs had clothed her, and the gleaming spear in her hand, causing her to look like some ancient statue of a goddess upon a temple roof.

"Who art thou," said the dwarf woman in the hissing voice of her race, "thou Beautiful One? I know! I know! Thou art that *Inkosazana* of the Zulus of whom we have had many visions, she for whom I sent. But the *Inkosazana* was mad, she had lost her Spirit; it has been seen here. Beautiful One, *thou* art not mad."

"What does she say, Noie?" asked Rachel. "I can only understand some words."

Noie told her, and Rachel hid her eyes in her hand. Presently she let it fall, saying:

"She is right. I lost my Spirit for a while; it went away with another Spirit. But I think that I have found it again. Tell her, Noie, that I have travelled far to seek my Spirit, and that I have found it again."

Noie, who could scarcely take her eyes from Rachel's face, obeyed, but the old woman hardly seemed to heed her words; a grief had got hold of her. She rocked herself to and fro like a monkey that has lost its young, and cried out:

"My tree has fallen, the tree of my House, which stood from the beginning of the world, has fallen, but that of Eddo still stands," and she pointed to another giant of the forest that soared up, unharmed, at a little distance. "Nya's tree has fallen—Eddo's tree still stands. His magic has prevailed against me, his magic has prevailed against me!"

As she spoke a man appeared scrambling along the bole towards them; it was Eddo himself. His round eyes shone, on his pale face there was a look of triumph, for whoever might be lost, the danger had passed him by.

"Nya," he piped, tapping her on the shoulder, "thy Ghost has deserted thee, old woman, thy tree is down. See, I spit upon it," and he did so. "Thou art no longer Mother of the Trees; thou art only the old woman Nya. The Ghost people, the Dream people, the little Grey people, have a new queen, and I am her minister, for I rule her Spirit. Yonder she stands," and he pointed at the tall and glittering Rachel. "Now, thou new-born Mother of the Trees, who wast the *Inkosazana* of the Zulus, obey me. Give death to this old woman, the Red Death, that her spirit may be spilt with her blood, and lost for ever. Give it to her with that spear in thy hand, while I hide my eyes, and reign thou in her place through me," and he bowed his head and waited.

"Not the Red Death, not the Red Death," wailed Nya. "Give me the White Death and save my soul, Beautiful One, and in return I will give thee something that thou desirest, who am still the wisest of them all, although my Tree is down."

Noie whispered for a while in Rachel's ear. Then while all the dwarf people gathered beneath them, watching, Rachel bent forward, and putting her arms about the trembling creature, lifted her up as though she were a child, and held her to her bosom.

"Mother," she said, "I give thee no death, red or white; I give thee love. Thy tree is down; sit thou in my shadow and be safer On him who harms thee"—and she looked at Eddo—"on him shall the Red Death fall."

## CHAPTER 20

# The Mother of the Trees

When Eddo understood these words he lifted his head and stared at Rachel amazed.

"This is thy doing, Bastard," he said savagely, addressing Noie, who had translated them. "I have felt thee fighting against me for long, and now thou causest this *Inkosazana* to defy me. It was thou who didst work upon that old woman, thine aunt, to command that the white witch should be brought hither, and because as yet I dared not disobey, I made a terrible journey to bring her. Yes, and I did this gladly, for when my eyes fell upon her, there in the town of Dingaan, I saw that she was great and beautiful, but that her Spirit had gone, and I knew that I could make her mouth to speak my words, and her pure eyes to see things that are denied to mine, even the future as, when I bade her, she saw it yonder in the court of Dingaan. But now it seems that her Spirit has returned to her, so that there is no room for mine in her heart, and she speaks her own words, not my words. And thou hast done this thing, O Bastard."

"Perhaps," answered Noie unconcernedly.

"Thou thinkest," went on Eddo, in his fury beating the bole on which he sat, "thou thinkest to protect that old hag, Nya, because her blood runs in thee. But, fool, it is in vain, for her tree is down, her tree is down, and as its leaves wither, and its sap dries up, so must she wither and her blood dry up until she dies, she who thought to live on for many years."

"What does that matter?" asked Noie, "seeing that then she will only join the great company of the ghosts with whom she longs to be, and return with them to torment thee, Eddo, until thou, too, art one of them, and lookest on the face of Judgment."

"Thou thinkest," screamed the dwarf, ignoring this ominous suggestion, "thou thinkest, when she is gone, to be queen in her place, or to rule as high priestess through this White One."

"If I do, that will be a bad hour for thee, Eddo," replied Noie.

"It shall not be, woman. No bastard shall reign here as Mother of the Trees while the nations round cringe before her feet. I have spells; I have poisons; I have slaves who can shoot with arrows."

"Then use them if thou canst, thou evil-doer," said "Noie contemptuously.

"Aye, I will use them all, and not on thee only, but on that white witch whom thou lovest. She shall never pass living from this land that is ringed in by the desert and the forest. She shall choose me to reign through her as her high priest, or she shall die—die miserably. For a little while that old hag, Nya, may protect her with her wisdom, but when she passes, as she must, and quickly, for I will light fires beneath this fallen tree of hers, then I tell thee the Beautiful One shall choose between my rule and doom."

Now Noie would hear no more. "Dog," she cried, "filthy night-bird, darest thou speak thus of the *Inkosazana*? Another word and I will offer that heart of thine to the sun thou hatest," and snatching the spear from Rachel's hand, she charged at him, holding it aloft.

Eddo saw her come. With a scream of fear he leapt to his feet, and ran swiftly along the bole till he reached the mass of the fallen branches. Into these he sprang, swinging himself from bough to bough like an ape until he vanished amongst the dark green foliage. Then, having quite lost sight of him, Noie returned laughing to Rachel, by whom stood the old Mother of the Trees who had slid from her arms, and gave her back the spear, saying in the dwarf language:

"This Eddo speaks great words, but he is also a great coward."

"Yes, yes," answered the old woman, "he is a great coward, because like all our folk he fears the Red Death; but, child, I tell thee he is terrible. He hates me because I rule through the white art, not the black, but while my tree stood he must obey me, and I was safe. Now it is down, and he may kill me if he can, according to the custom of my land, and set up another to be queen, she at whose feet my tree bowed itself and fell by the will of the Heavens, and whom, therefore, the people will accept. Through her he will wield all the power of the Ghost-kings, over whom no man may rule, but a woman only. Come, Child, and thou, White One, come also. I know where we may hide. Lady, the power that was mine is thine; protect me till I die, and in payment I will give thee whatever thy heart desires."

"I ask no payment," Rachel answered wearily, when she understood the words; "and I think that it is I who need protection from that wicked dwarf."

Then, guided by Nya, who clung to Rachel's hand, they walked down the bole of the tree and along a great branch, till at length they reached a place whence they could climb to the ground. Before they were clear of the boughs the dethroned Mother, from whose round eyes the tears fell, turned and kissed the bark of one of them, wailing aloud.

"Farewell, thou mighty one, under whose shade I, and the queens of my race before me, have dreamed for centuries. Thou art fallen beneath the stroke of Heaven, and great was thy fall, and I am fallen with thee. Save me from the Red Death, O Spirit of my tree, that in the land of ghosts I still may sleep beneath thy shade for ever."

Then she ran to the very point of the tree and broke off its topmost twig, which was covered with narrow and shining green leaves, and holding it in her hand, returned to Rachel.

"I will plant it," she said, "and perchance it will grow to be the house of queens unborn. Come, now, come," and she turned her face towards the forest.

The thunder had rolled away, and from time to time the sun shone fiercely, so fiercely that, unable to bear its rays, all the dwarfs who were gathered about the fallen tree had retreated into the shadow of the other trees around the open space. There they stood and sat watching the three of them go by. Men, women and children, they all watched, and Rachel they saluted with their raised hands; but to her who had been their mother for unknown years they did no reverence. Only one hideous little man ran up to her and called out:

"Thou didst punish me once, old woman, now why should I not kill thee in payment? Thy tree is down at last."

Nya looked at him sadly, and answered:

"I remember. Thou shouldst have died, for thy sin was great, but I laid a lesser burden on thee. Man, thou canst not kill me yet; my tree is down, but it is not dead."

She held up the green bough in her hand and looked at him from beneath it, then went on slowly: "Man, my wisdom remains within me, and I tell thee that before I die thou shalt die, and not as thou desirest. Remember my words, people of the Ghosts."

Then she walked on with the others, leaving the dwarf staring after her with a face wherein hate struggled with fear.

"Thou liest," he screamed; "thy power is gone with thy tree."

Scarcely were the words out of his mouth when they heard a crash which caused them to look round. A bough, broken by the storm, had fallen from on high. It had fallen on to the head of the dwarf, and there he lay crushed and dead.

"Ah!" piped the other dwarfs, pointing towards the corpse with their fingers, and closing their eyes to shut out the sight of blood, "ah! Nya is right; she still has power. Those who would kill her must wait till her tree dies."

Taking no heed of what had happened, Nya walked on into the forest. For a while Rachel noted the little huts built, each of them, at the foot of a tree. There were hundreds of these huts that they could see, showing that the people were many, but by degrees they grew fewer, only one was visible here and there, set beneath some particularly vigorous and handsome timber. At last they ceased altogether; they had passed through that city, the strangest city in the world.

Trees—everywhere trees, hundreds of trees, tens of thousands of trees soaring up to heaven, making a canopy of their interlacing boughs, shutting out the light so that beneath them was a deep oppressive gloom. There was silence also, for if any beasts or birds dwelt there the hurricane had scared them away, silence only broken from time to time by the crash of some giant of the forest that, its length of days fulfilled at last, sank suddenly to ruin, to be buried in a tomb of brushwood whence in due course its successor would arise.

"Another life gone," said the old woman, Nya, flitting before them like a little grey ghost, every time that this weird sound struck upon their ears; "whose was it, I wonder? I will look in my bowl, I will look in my bowl."

For, as Rachel discovered afterwards, these people believed that the spirit of each tree of the forest is attached to the spirit of a human being, although that being may dwell in other lands, far away, which dies when the tree dies, sometimes slowly by disease, and sometimes in swift collapse, so that they pass together into the world of ghosts.

On they flitted through the gloom, on for mile after mile. Although the leaf-strewn ground showed no traces of it, evidently they were following some kind of path, for no fallen trunks barred their progress, nor were there any creepers or brushwood, although to right and left of them all these could be seen in plenty. At last, quite of a sudden, for the bole of a tree at the end of the path had hidden it from them, they came upon a clearing in the forest. It seemed to be a natural, or, at any rate, a very ancient clearing, since in it no stumps were visible, nor any scrub, or creepers, only tall grass and flowering plants. In the centre of this place, covering a quarter of it, perhaps, was a vast circular wall, fifty feet or more in height, and clothed with ferns. This wall, they noted, was built of huge blocks of stone, so huge indeed that it seemed wonderful that they could have been moved by human beings. At the sight of that marvellous wall Rachel and Noie halted involuntarily, and Noie asked:

"Who made it, Mother?"

"The giants who lived when the world was young. Can our hands lift such stones?" Nya answered, as, bending down, she thrust the top shoot from her fallen tree deep into the humid soil, then added: "On, child; there is danger here."

As she spoke something hissed through the air just above her head, and stuck fast in the bark of a sapling. Noie sprang forward and plucked it out. It was a little reed, feathered with grasses, and having a sharp ivory point, smeared with some green substance.

"Touch it not," cried Nya, "it is deadly poison. Eddo's work, Eddo's work! but my hour is not yet. Into the open before another comes."

So they ran forward, all three of them, seeing and bearing nothing of the shooter of the arrow. As they approached the titanic wall they saw that it enclosed a mound, on the top of which mound grew a cedar-like tree with branches so wide that they seemed to overshadow half of the enclosure. There were no gates to this wall, but while they wondered how it could be entered, Nya led them to a kind of cleft in its stones, not more than two feet in width, across which cleft were stretched strings of plaited grass. She pressed herself against them, breaking them, and walked forward, followed by Rachel and Noie. Suddenly they heard a noise above them, and, looking up, saw white-robed dwarfs perched upon the stones of the cleft, holding bent bows in their hands, whereof the arrows were pointed at their breasts. Nya halted, beckoning to them, whereon, recognising her, they dropped the arrows into the little quivers which they wore, and scrambled off, whither Rachel could not see.

"These are the guardians of the Temple that cannot either speak or hear, who were summoned by the breaking of the thread," said Nya, and went forward again.

Now to the right, and now to the left, ran the narrow path that wound its way in the thickness of the mighty wall, which towered so high above them that they walked almost in darkness, and at each turn of it were recesses; and above these projecting stones, where archers could stand for its defence. At length this path ended in a *cul-de-sac*, for in front of them was nothing but blank masonry. Whilst Rachel and Noie stared at it wondering whither they should go now, a large stone in this wall turned, leaving a narrow doorway through which they passed, whereon it shut again behind them, though by what machinery they could not see.

Thus they passed through the wall, emerging, however, at a different point in its circumference to that at which they had entered. In the centre of the enclosure rose the hill of earth that they had seen from without, which evidently was kept free from weeds and swept, and on its crest grew the huge cedar-like tree, the Tree of the Tribe. Between the base of this hill and the foot of the wall was a wide ring of level ground, also swept and weeded, and on this space, neatly arranged in lines, were hundreds of little hillocks that resembled ant-heaps.

"The burying-place of the Ghost-priests, Lady," said Nya, nodding at the hillocks. "Soon my bones will be added to them."

Walking across this strange cemetery, they came to the foot of the mound that was entirely overshadowed by the cedar above, from the outspread limbs of which hung long grey moss, that swayed ceaselessly in the wind. Here dwarfs appeared from right and left, the same whom they had seen within the thickness of the wall, or others like to them, some male and some female; melancholy-eyed little creatures who bowed to Nya, and looked with fear and wonder at the tall while Rachel. Evidently they were all of them deaf mutes, for they made signs to Nya, who answered them with other signs, the purport of which seemed to sadden and disturb them greatly.

"They have seen the fall of my tree in their bowls," explained Nya to Noie, "and ask me if it is a true vision. I tell them that I am come here to die and that is why they are sad. This is the place of dying of all the Ghost-priests, whence they pass into the world of spirits, and here no blood may be shed, no, not that of the most wicked evil-doer. If any one of the family of the priests reaches this place living, the glory of the White Death is won. Follow and see."

So they followed her up the mound, past what looked like the entrance to a cave, until they reached a low fence of reeds whereof the gate stood open.

"The gate is open, but enter not there," whispered the old Mother of the Trees, "for those who enter there live not long. Look, Lady, look."

Rachel peered through the gate, but so dense was the gloom in that holy spot that at first she could only see the enormous red bole of the cedar, and the ghostly, moss-clad branches which sprang from it at no great height above the ground. Presently, however, her eyes, grown accustomed to the light, distinguished several little white-robed figures seated upon the earth at some distance from the trunk staring into vessels of wood which were placed before them. These figures appeared to be those of both men and women, while one was that of a child. Even as they watched, the figure nearest to them fell forward over its bowl and lay quite still, whereon those around it set up a feeble, piping cry, that yet had in it a note of gladness. The dwarf-mutes who had accompanied them, and who alone seemed to have a right of entry into this sad place, ran forward and looked. Then very gently they lifted up the fallen figure and bore it out. As it was carried past them Rachel noted that it was the body of quite a young woman, whose little face, wasted to nothing, still looked sweet and gentle.

"Was she ill?" asked Rachel in an awed voice.

"Perhaps," answered the Mother, shaking her grey head, "or perhaps she was very unhappy, and came here to die. What does it matter? She is happy now."

"Ask her, Noie, if all must die who sit beneath that tree," said Rachel.

"Aye," answered Nya, "all save these dumb people who have been priests of the Tree from generation to generation. To touch its stem is to perish soon or late, for it is the Tree of Life and Death, and in it dwells the Spirit of the whole race."

"What then would happen if it fell down, or was destroyed like your tree, Mother?"

"Then the race would perish also," answered Nya, "since their Spirit would lack a home and depart to the world of Ghosts, whither they must follow. When it dies of old age, if it should ever die, then the race will die with it."

"And if someone should cut it down, Mother, what then?"

Now when Noie translated these words to her, the face of the old queen was filled with horror, and as her face was, so was Noie's face.

"White Maiden," she gasped, "speak not such wickedness lest the very thought of it should bring the curse upon us all. He who destroyed that tree would bring ruin upon this people. They would fly away, every one of them, far into the heart of the forest, and be seen no more by man. Moreover, he who did this evil thing would perish and pass down to vengeance among the ghosts, such vengeance as may not be spoken. Put that thought from thy mind, I pray thee, and let it never pass thy lips again."

"Do you believe all this, Noie?" asked Rachel in English with a smile.

"Yes, Zoola," answered Noie, shuddering, "for it is true. My father told me of it, and of what happened once to some wild men who broke into the sanctuary, and shot arrows at the Tree. No, no, I will not tell the story; it is dreadful."

"Yet it must be foolishness, Noie, for how can a tree have power over the lives of men?"

"I do not know, but it has, it has! If I were but to cast a stone at it, I should be dead in a day, and so would you—yes, even you—nothing could save you. Oh!" she went on earnestly, "swear to me, Sister, that you will never so much as touch that tree; I pray you, swear."

So Rachel swore, to please her, for she was tired of this tree and its powers. Then they went down the hill again, till they came to the mouth of the cave.

"Enter, Lady," Nya said, "for this must be thy home a while until thou goest to rule as Mother of the Trees after me, or, if it pleases thee better, up yonder to die."

They went into the cave, having no choice. It was a great place lit dimly by the outer light, and farther down its length with lamps. Looking round her, Rachel saw that its roof was supported by white columns which she knew to be stalactites, for as a child she had seen their like. At the end of it, where the lamps burned and a fountain bubbled from the ground, rose a very large column shaped like the trunk of a tree, with branches at the top that looked like the boughs of a tree. Gazing at it Rachel understood why these dwarfs, or some ancient people before them, had chosen this cave as their temple.

"The ghost Tree of my race," said old Nya, pointing to it, "the only tree that never falls, the Tree that lives and grows for ever. Yes, it grows, for it is larger now than when my mother was a child."

As they drew near to this wondrous and ghostly looking object Rachel saw piled around and beyond it many precious things. There was gold in dust and heaps, and rings and nuggets; there were shining stones, red and green and white, that she knew were jewels; there were tusks of ivory and carvings in ivory; there were *karosses* and furs mouldering to decay; there were grotesque gods, fetishes of wood and stone.

"Offerings," said Nya, "which all the nations that live in darkness bring to the Mother of the Trees, and the priests of the Cave. Costly things which they value, but we value them not, who prize power and wisdom only. Yes, yes, costly things which they give to the Mother of the Trees, the fools without a spirit, when they come here to ask her oracle. Look, there are some of the gifts which were sent by Dingaan of the Zulus in payment for the oracle of his death. Thou broughtest them, Noie, my child."

"Yes," answered Noie, "I brought them, and the *Inkosazana* here, she delivered the oracle. Eddo gave her the bowl, and she saw pictures in the bowl and showed them to Dingaan."

"Nay, nay," said the old woman testily, "it was I who saw the pictures, and I showed them to Eddo and to this white virgin. You cannot understand, but it was so, it was so. Eddo's gift of vision is small, mine is great. None have ever had it as I have it, and that is why Eddo and the others have suffered my tree to live so long, because the light of my wisdom has shone about their heads and spoken through their tongues, and when I am gone they will seek and find it not. In thee they might have found it, Maiden, had thy heart remained empty, but now, it is full again and what room is there for wisdom such as ours?—the wisdom of the ghosts, not the wisdom of life and love and beating hearts."

Noie translated the words, but Rachel seemed to take no heed of them.

"Dingaan?" she asked. "Is Dingaan dead? He was well enough when—when Richard came to Zululand, and since then I have seen nothing of him. How did he die?"

"He did not die, Zoola," answered Noie, "though I think that ere long he will die, for you told him so. It was you who died for a while, not Dingaan. By-and-bye you shall learn all that story. Now you are very weary and must rest."

"Yes," said Rachel with a sob, "I think I died when Richard died, but now I seem to have come to life again—that is the worst of it. Oh!! Noie, Noie, why did you not let me remain dead, instead of bringing me to life again in this dreadful place?"

"Because it was otherwise fated, Sister," replied Noie. "No, do not begin to laugh and cry; it was otherwise fated," and bending down she whispered something into Nya's ear.

The old dwarf nodded, then, taking Rachel by the hand, led her to where some skins were spread upon the floor.

"Lie down," she said, "and rest. Rest, beautiful White One, and wake up to eat and be strong again," and she gazed into Rachel's eyes as Eddo had done when the fits of wild laughter were on her, singing something as she gazed.

While she sang the madness that was gathering there again went out of Rachel's eyes, the lids closed over them, and presently they were fast shut in sleep, nor did she open them again for many hours.

Rachel awoke and sat up looking round her wonderingly. Then by the dim light of the lamps she saw Noie seated at her side, and the old dwarf-woman, who was called Mother of the Trees, squatted at a little distance watching them both—and remembered.

"Thou hast had happy dreams, Lady, and thou art well again, is it not so?" queried Nya.

"Aye, Mother," she answered, "too happy, for they make my waking the more sad. And I am well, I who desire to die."

"Then go up through the open gate which thou sawest not so long ago, and satisfy thy desire, as it is easy to do," replied Nya grimly. "Nay," she added in a changed voice, "go not up, thou art too young and fair, the blood runs too red in those blue veins of thine. What hast thou to do with ghosts and death, and the darkness of the trees, thou child of the air and sunshine? Death for the dwarf-folk, death for the dealers in dreams, death for the death-lovers, but for thee life—life."

"Tell her, Noie," said Rachel, "that my mother, who was fore-sighted, always said that I should live out my days, and I fear that it is true, who must live them out alone."

"Yes, yes, she was right, that mother of thine," answered Nya, "and for the rest, who knows? But thou art hungry, eat; afterwards we will talk," and she pointed to a stool upon which was food.

Rachel tasted and found it very good, a kind of porridge, made of she knew not what, and with it forest fruits, but no flesh. So she ate heartily, and Noie ate with her. Nya ate also, but only a very little.

"Why should I trouble to eat?" she said, "I to whom death draws near?"

When they had finished eating, at some signal which Rachel did not perceive, mutes came in who bore away the fragments of the meal. After they had gone the three women washed themselves in the water of the fountain. Then Noie combed out Rachel's golden hair, and clothed her again in her robe of silken fur that she had cleansed, throwing over it a mantle of snowy white fibre, such as the dwarfs wove into cloth, which she and Nya had made ready while Rachel slept.

As Noie put it about her mistress and stepped back to see how it became her beauty, two of the dwarf-mutes appeared creeping up the cave, and squatting down before Nya began to make signs to her.

"What is it?" asked Rachel nervously.

"Eddo is without," answered the Mother, "and would speak with us."

"I fear Eddo and will not go," exclaimed Rachel.

"Nay, have no fear, Maiden, for here he can not harm thee or any of us; it is the place of sanctuary. Come, let us see this priest; perhaps we may learn something from him."

## Chapter 21
# The City of the Dead

Nya led the way down the cave, followed by Rachel and Noie. Squatted in its entrance, so as to be out of reach of the rays of the sun, sat Eddo, looking like a malevolent toad, and with him were Hana and some other priests. As Rachel approached they all rose and saluted, but to Nya and Noie they gave no salute. Only to Nya Eddo said:

"Why art thou not within the Fence, old woman?" and he pointed with his chin towards the place of death above. "Thy tree is down, and all last night we were hacking off its branches that it may dry up the sooner. It is time for thee to die."

"I die when my tree dies, not before, Priest," answered Nya. "I have still some work to do before I die, also I have planted my tree again in good soil, and it may grow."

"I saw," said Eddo; "it is without the wall there, but many a generation must go by before a new Mother sits beneath its shade. Well, die when it pleases you, it does not matter when, since thou art no more our Mother. Moreover, learn that all have deserted thee, save a very few, most of whom have just now passed within the Fence above that they may attend thee amongst the ghosts."

"I thank them," said Nya simply, "and in that world we will rule together."

"The rest," went on Eddo, "have turned against thee, having heard how thou didst bring one of us to the Red Death yesterday by thy evil magic, him upon whom the bough fell."

"Who was it that strove to bring me to the Red Death before I reached the sanctuary? Who shot the poisoned arrow, Priest?"

"I do not know," answered Eddo, "but it seems that he shot badly for thou art still here. Now enough of thee, old woman. For many years we bore thy rule, which was always foolish, and sometimes bad, because we could not help it, for the tree of her who went before thee fell at thy feet, as thy tree has fallen at the feet of the White Virgin there. For long thou and I have struggled for the mastery, and now thou art dead and I have won, so be silent, old woman, and since that arrow missed thee, go hence in peace, for none need thee any more, who hast neither youth, nor comeliness, nor power."

"Aye," answered Nya, stung to fury by these insults, "I shall go hence in peace, but thou shalt not abide in peace, thou traitor, nor those who follow thee. When youth and comeliness fade then wisdom grows, and wisdom is power, Eddo, true power. I tell thee that last night I looked in my bowl and saw things concerning thee—aye, and all of our people, that are hid from thy eyes, terrible things, things that have not befallen since the Tree of the Tribe was a seed, and the Spirit of the Tribe came to dwell within it."

"Speak them, then," said Eddo, striving to hide the fear which showed through his round eyes.

"Nay, Priest, I speak them not. Live on and thou shalt discover them, thou and thy traitors. Well have I served you all for many years, mercy have I given to all, white magic have I practised and not black, none have died that I could save, none have suffered whom I could protect, no, not even the slave-peoples beneath our rule. All this have I done, knowing that ye plotted against me, knowing that ye strove to kill my tree by spells, knowing what the end must be. It has come at last, as come it must, and I do not grieve. Fool, I knew that it would come, and I knew the manner of its coming. It was I who sent for this virgin queen whom ye would set up to rule over you, foreseeing that at her feet my tree would fall. The ghost of Seyapi, who is of my blood, Seyapi whom years ago ye drove away for no offence, to dwell in a strange land, told me of her and of this Noie, his daughter, and of the end of it all. So she came; thou didst not bring her as thou thoughtest, *I* brought her, and my tree fell at her feet as it was doomed to fall, and she saved me from the Red Death as she was doomed to do, giving me love, not hate, as I gave her love not hate. For the rest ye shall see—all of you. I am finished—I am dead—but I live on elsewhere, and ye shall see."

Now Eddo would have answered, but the priest Hana, who appeared to be much frightened by Nya's words, plucked at his sleeve, whispering in his ear, and he was silent. Presently he spoke again, but to Rachel, bidding Noie translate:

"Thou White Maid," he said, "who wast called Princess of the Zulus, pay no heed to this old dotard, but listen to me. When thy Spirit wandered yonder, even then I saw the seeds of greatness in thee, and begged thee from the savage Dingaan. Also I and Pani, who is dead, and Hana, who lives, read by our magic that at thy feet the tree of Nya would fall, and that after her thou wast appointed to rule over us. All the Ghost-people read it also, and now they have named thee their Mother, and chosen thee a tree, a great tree, but young and strong, that shall stand for ages. Come forth, then, and take thy seat beneath that tree, and be our queen."

"Why should I come?" asked Rachel. "It seems that you dwarfs bring your queens to ill ends. Choose you another Mother."

"*Inkosazana*, we cannot if we would," answered Eddo, "for these matters are not in our hands, but in those of our Spirit. Hearken, we will deal well with thee; we will make thee great, and grow in thy greatness, for thou shall give us of thy wisdom, that although thou knowest it not, thou hast above all other women. We weary of little things, we would rule the world. All the nations from sea to sea shall bow down before thee, and seek thine oracle. Thou shall take their wealth, thou shalt drive them hither and thither as the wind drives clouds. Thou shalt make war, thou shalt ordain peace. At thy pleasure they shall rise up in life and lie down in death. Their kings shall cower before thee, their princes shall bring thee tribute, thou shalt reign a god."

"Until it shall please Eddo to bring thee to thine end, Lady, as it pleases him to bring me to mine," muttered Nya behind her. "Be not beguiled, Maiden; remain a woman and uncrowned, for so thou shalt find most joy."

"Thou meanest, Eddo," said Rachel, "that thou wilt rule and I do thy bidding. Noie, tell him that I will have none of it. When I came here a great sorrow had made me mad, and I knew nothing. Now I have found my Spirit again, and presently I go hence."

At this answer Eddo grew very angry.

"One thing I promise thee, Zoola," he said; "in the name of all the Ghost-people I promise it, that thou shalt not go hence alive. In this sanctuary thou art safe indeed, seated in the shadow of the Death-tree that is the Tree of Life, but soon or late a way will be found to draw thee hence, and then thou shalt learn who is the stronger—thou or Eddo—as the old woman behind thee has learned. Fare thee well for a while. I will tell the people that thou art weary and restest, and meanwhile I rule in thy name. Fare thee well, *Inkosazana*, till we meet without the wall," and he rose and went, accompanied by Hana and the other priests.

When he had gone a little way he turned, and pointing up the hill, screamed back to Nya:

"Go and look within the Fence, old hag. There thou wilt see the best of those that clung to thee, seeking for peace. Art thou a coward that thou lingerest behind them?"

"Nay, Eddo," she answered, "thou art the coward that hast driven them to death, because they are good and thou art evil. When my hour is ripe I join them, not before. Nor shalt thou abide here long behind me. One short day of triumph for thee, Eddo, and then night, black night for ever."

Eddo heard, and his yellow face grew white with rage, or fear. He stamped upon the ground, he shook his small fat fists, and spat out curses as a toad spits venom. Nya did not stay to listen to them, but walked up the cave and sat herself down upon her mat.

"Why does he hate thee so, Mother?" asked Rachel.

"Because those that are bad hate those that are good, Maiden. For many a year Eddo has sought to rule through me, and to work evil in the world, but I have not suffered it. He would abandon our secret, ancient faith, and reign a king, as Dingaan the Zulu reigns. He would send the slave-tribes out to war and conquer the nations, and build him a great house, and have many wives. But I held him fast, so that he could do few of these things. Therefore he plotted against me, but my magic was greater than his, and while my tree stood he could not prevail. At length it fell at thy feet, as he knew that it was doomed to fall, for all these things are fore-ordained, and at once he would have slain me by the Red Death, but thou didst protect me, and for that blessed be thou for ever."

"And why does he wish to make me Mother in thy place, Nya?"

"Because my tree fell at thy feet, and all the people demand it. Because he thinks that once the bond of the priesthood is tied between you, and his blood runs in thee, thy pure spirit will protect his spirit from its sins, and that thy wisdom, which he sees in thee, will make him greater than any of the Ghost-people that ever lived. Yet consent not, for afterwards if thou dost thwart him, he will find a way to bring down thy tree, and with it thy life, and set another to rule in thy place. Consent not, for know that here thou art safe from him."

"It may be so, Mother, but how can I dwell on in this dismal place? Already my heart is broken with its sorrows, and soon, like those poor folk, I should seek peace within the Fence."

"Tell me of those sorrows," said Nya gently. "Perhaps I do not know them all, and perhaps I could help thee."

So Rachel sat herself down also, and Noie, interpreting for her, told all her tale up to that point when she saw the body of Richard borne away, for after this she remembered nothing until she found herself standing upon the fallen tree in the land of the Ghost Kings. It was a long tale, and before ever she finished it night fell, but throughout its telling the old dwarf-woman said never a word, only watched Rachel's face with her kind, soft eyes. At last it was done, and she said:

"A sad story. Truly there is much evil in the world beyond the country of the Trees, for here at least we shed little blood. Now, Maiden, what is thy desire?"

"This is my desire," said Rachel, "to be joined again to him I love, whom Ishmael slew; yes, and to my father and mother also, whom the Zulus slew at the command of Ishmael."

"If they are all dead, how can that be, Maiden, unless thou seekest them in death? Pass within the Fence yonder, and let the poison of the Tree of the Tribe fall upon thee, and soon thou wilt find them."

"Nay, Mother, I may not, for it would be self-murder, and my faith knows few greater crimes."

"Then thou must wait till death finds thee, and that road may be very long."

"Already it is long, Mother, so long that I know not how to travel it, who am alone in the world without a friend save Noie here," and she began to weep.

"Not so. Thou hast another friend," and she laid her hand upon Rachel's heart, "though it is true that I may bide with thee but a little while."

After this they were all silent for a space, until Nya looked up at Rachel and asked suddenly:

"Art thou brave?"

"The Zulus and others thought so, Mother; but what can courage avail me now?"

"Courage of the body, nothing, Maiden; courage of the spirit much, perhaps. If thou sawest this lover of thine, and knew for certain that he lives on beneath the world awaiting thee, would it bring thee comfort?"

Rachel's breast heaved and her eyes sparkled with joy, as she answered: "Comfort! What is there that could bring so much? But how can it be, Mother, seeing that the last gulf divides us, a gulf which mortals may not pass and live?"

"Thou sayest it; still I have great power, and thy spirit is white and clean. Perhaps I could despatch it across that gulf and call it back to earth again. Yet there are dangers, dangers to me of which I reck little, and dangers to thee. Whither I sent thee, there thou mightest bide."

"I care not if I bide there, Mother, if only it be with him! Oh! send me on this journey to his side, and living or dead I will bless thee."

Now Nya thought a while and answered:

"For thy sake I will try what I would try for none other who has breathed, or breathes, for thou didst save me from the Red Death at the hands of Eddo. Yes, I will try, but not yet—first thou must eat and rest. Obey, or I do nothing."

So Rachel ate, and afterwards, feeling drowsy, even slept a while, perhaps because she was still weary with her journeying and her new-found mind needed repose, or perhaps because some drug had been mingled with her drink. When she awoke Nya led her to the mouth of the cave. There they stood awhile studying the stars. No breath of air stirred, and the silence was intense, only from time to time the sound of trees falling in the forest reached their ears. Sometimes it was quite soft, as though a fleece of wool had been dropped to the earth, that was when the tree that died had grown miles and miles away from them; and sometimes the crash was as that of sudden thunder, that was when the tree which died had grown near to them.

A sense of the mystery and wonder of the place and hour sank into Rachel's heart. The stars above, the mighty entombing forest, in which the trees fell unceasingly after their long centuries of life, the encircling wall, built perhaps by hands that had ceased from their labours hundreds of thousands of years before those trees began to grow; the huge moss-clad cedar upon the mound beneath the shadow of whose branches day by day its worshippers gave up their breath, that immemorial cedar whereof, as they believed, the life was the life of the nation; the wizened little witch-woman at her side with the seal of doom already set upon her brow and the stare of farewell in her eyes; the sad, spiritual face of Noie, who held her hand, the loving, faithful Noie, who in that light seemed half a thing of air; the grey little dwarf-mutes who squatted on their mats staring at the ground, or now and again passed down the hill from the Fence of Death above, bearing between them a body to its burial; all were mysterious, all were wonderful.

As she looked and listened, a new strength stirred in Rachel's heart. At first she had felt afraid, but now courage flowed into her, and it seemed to come from the old, old woman at her side, the mistress of mysteries, the mother of magic, in whom was gathered the wisdom of a hundred generations of this half human race.

"Look at the stars, and the night," she was saying in her soft voice, "for soon thou shalt be beyond them all, and perchance thou shall never see them more. Art thou fearful? If so, speak, and we will not try this journey in search of one whom we may not find."

"No," answered Rachel; "but, Mother, whither go we?"

"We go to the Land, of Death. Come, then, the moment is at hand. It is hard on midnight. See, yonder star stands above the holy Tree," and she pointed to a bright orb that hung almost over the topmost bough of the cedar, "it marks thy road, and if thou wouldst pass it, now is the hour."

"Mother," asked Noie, "may I come with her? I also have my dead, and where my Sister goes I follow."

"Aye, if thou wilt, daughter of Seyapi, the path is wide enough for three, and if I stay on high, perchance thou that art of my blood mayest find strength to guide her earthwards through the wandering worlds."

Then Nya walked up the cave and sat herself down within the circle of the lamps with her back to the stalactite that was shaped like a tree, bidding Rachel and Noie be seated in front of her. Two of the dwarf-mutes appeared, women both of them, and squatted to right and left, each gazing into a bowl of limpid dew. Nya made a sign, and still gazing into their bowls, these dwarfs began to beat upon little drums that gave out a curious, rolling noise, while Nya sang to the sound of the drums a wild, low song. With her thin little hands she grasped the right hand of Rachel and of Noie and gazed into their eyes.

Things changed to Rachel. The dwarfs to right and left vanished away, but the low murmuring of their drums grew to a mighty music, and the stars danced to it. The song of Nya swelled and swelled till it filled all the space between earth and heaven; it was the rush of the gale among the forests, it was the beating of the sea upon an illimitable coast, it was the shout of all the armies of the world, it was the weeping of all the women of the world. It lessened again, she seemed to be passing away from it, she heard it far beneath her, it grew tiny in its volume—tiny as if it were an infinite speck or point of sound which she could still discern for millions and millions of miles, till at length distance and vastness overcame it, and it ceased. It ceased, this song of the earth, but a new song began, the song of the rushing worlds. Far away she could hear it, that ineffable music, far in the utter depths of space. Nearer it would come and nearer, a ringing, glorious sound, a sound and yet a voice, one mighty voice that sang and was answered by other voices as sun crossed the path of sun, and caught up and re-echoed by the innumerable choir of the constellations.

They were falling past her, those vast, glowing suns, those rounded planets that were now vivid with light, and now steeped in gloom, those infinite showers of distant stars. They were gone, they and their music together; she was far beyond them in a region where all life was forgotten, beyond the rush of the uttermost comet, beyond the last glimmer of the spies and outposts of the universe. One shape of light she sped into the black bosom of fathomless space, and its solitude shrivelled up her soul. She could not endure, she longed for some shore on which to set her mortal feet.

Behold! far away a shore appeared, a towering, cliff-bound shore, upon whose iron coasts all the black waves of space beat vainly and were eternally rolled back. Here there was light, but no such light as she had ever known; it did not fall from sun or star, but, changeful and radiant, welled upward from that land in a thousand hues, as light might well from a world of opal. In its dazzling, beautiful rays she saw fantastic palaces and pyramids, she saw seas and pure white mountains, she saw plains and new-hued flowers, she saw gulfs and precipices, and pale lakes pregnant with wavering flame. All that she had ever conceived of as lovely or as fearful, she beheld, far lovelier or a thousandfold more fearful.

Like a great rose of glory that world bloomed and changed beneath her. Petal by petal its splendours fell away and were swallowed in the sea of space, whilst from the deep heart of the immortal rose new splendours took their birth, and fresh-fashioned, mysterious, wonderful, reappeared the measureless city with its columns, its towers, and its glittering gates. It endured a moment, or a million years, she knew not which, and lo! where it had been, stood another city, different, utterly different, only a hundred times more glorious. Out of the prodigal heart of the world-rose were they created, into the black bosom of nothingness were they gathered; whilst others, ever more perfect, pressed into their place. So, too, changed the mountains, and so the trees, while the gulfs became a garden and the fiery lakes a pleasant stream, and from the seed of the strange flowers grew immemorial forests wreathed about with rosy mists and bedecked in glimmering dew. With music they were born, on the wings of music they fled away, and after them that sweet music wailed like memories.

A hand took hers and drew her downwards, and up to meet her leapt myriads of points of light, in every point a tiny face. They gazed at her with their golden eyes; they whispered together concerning her, and the sound of their whispering was the sound of a sea at peace. They accompanied her to the very heart of the opal rose of life whence all these wonders welled, they set her in a great grey hall roofed in with leaning cliffs, and there they left her desolate.

Fear came upon her, the loneliness choked her, it held her by the throat like a thing alive. She seemed about to die of it, when she became aware that once more she was companioned. Shapes stood about her. She could not see the shapes, save dimly now and again as they moved, but their eyes she could see, their great calm, pitiful eyes, which looked down on her, as the eye of a giant might look down upon a babe. They were terrible, but she did not fear them so much as the loneliness, for at least they lived.

One of the shapes bent over her, for its holy eyes drew near to her, and she heard a voice in her heart asking her for what great cause she had dared to journey hither before the time. She answered, in her heart, not with her lips, that she was bereaved of all she loved and came to seek them. Then; still in her heart, she heard that voice command:

"Let all this Rachel's dead be brought before her."

Instantly doors swung open at the end of that grey hall, and through them with noiseless steps, with shadowy wings, floated a being that bore in its arms a child. Before her it stayed, and the light of its starry head illumined the face of the child. She knew it at once—it was that baby brother whose bones lay by the shore of the African sea. It awoke from its sleep, it opened its eyes, it stretched out its arms and smiled at her. Then it was gone.

Other Shapes appeared, each of them bearing its burden—a companion who had died at school, friends of her youth and childhood whom she had thought yet living, a young man who once had wished to marry her and who was drowned, the soldier whom she had killed to save the life of Noie. At the sight of him she shrank, for his blood was on her hands, but he only smiled like the rest, and was borne away, to be followed by that witch-doctoress whom the Zulus had slain because of her, who neither smiled nor frowned but passed like one who wonders.

Then another shadow swept down the hall, and in its arms her mother—her mother with joyful eyes, who held thin hands above her as though in blessing, and to whom she strove to speak but strove in vain. She was borne on still blessing her, and where she had been was her father, who blessed her also, and whose presence seemed to shed peace upon her soul. He pointed upwards and was gone, gazing at her earnestly, and lo! a form of darkness cast something at her feet. It was Ishmael who knelt before her, Ishmael whose tormented face gazed up at her as though imploring pardon.

A struggle rent her heart. Could she forgive? Oh! could she forgive him who had slain them all? Now she was aware that the place was filled with the points of light that were Spirits, and that every one of them looked at her awaiting the free verdict of her heart. Rank upon rank, also, the mighty Shapes gathered about her, and in their arms her dead, and all of them looked and looked, awaiting the free verdict of her heart. Then it arose within her, drawn how she knew not from every fibre of her infinite being, it arose within her, that spirit of pity and of pardon. As the dead had stretched out their arms above her, so she stretched out her arms over the head of that tortured soul, and for the first time her lips were given power to speak.

"As I hope for pardon, so I pardon," she said. "Go in peace!"

Voices and trumpets caught up the words, and through the grey hall they rang and echoed, proclaimed for ever and as they died away he too was gone, and with him went the myriad points of flame, in each of which gleamed a tiny face. She looked about her seeking another Spirit, that Spirit she had, travelled so far and dared so much to find. But there came only a little dwarf that shambled alone down the great hall. She knew him at once for Pani, the priest, he who had been crushed in the tempest, Pani, the brother of Eddo. No Shape bore him, for he who on earth had been half a ghost, could walk this ghost-world on his mortal feet, or so her mind conceived. Past her he shuffled shamefaced, and was gone.

Now the great doors at the end of the hall closed; from far away she could see them roll together like lightning-severed clouds, and once more that awful loneliness overcame her. Her knees gave way beneath her, she sank down upon the floor, one little spot of white in its expanse, wishing that the roof of rock would fall and hide her. She covered her face with her golden hair, and wept behind its veil. She looked up and saw two great eyes gazing at her—no face, only two great, steady eyes. Then a voice speaking in her heart asked her why she wept, whose desire had been fulfilled, and she answered that it was because she could not find him whom she sought, Richard Darrien. Instantly the tongues and trumpets took up the name.

"Richard Darrien!" they cried, "Richard Darrien!"

But no Shape swept in bearing the spirit of Richard in its arms.

"He is not here," said the voice in her heart. "Go, seek him in some other world."

She grew angry.

"Thou mockest me," she answered, "He is dead, and this is the home of the dead; therefore he must be here. Shadow, thou mockest me."

"I mock not," came the swift answer. "Mortal, look now and learn."

Again the doors burst open, and through them poured the infinite rout of the dead. That hall would not hold them all, therefore it grew and grew till her sight could scarcely reach from wall to wall. Shapes headed and marshalled them by races and by generations, perhaps because thus only could her human heart imagine them, but now none were borne in their arms. They came in myriads and in millions, in billions and tens of billions, men and women and children, kings and priests and beggars, all wearing the garments of their age and country. They came like an ocean-tide, and their floating hair was the foam on the tide, and their eyes gleamed like the first shimmer of dawn above the snows. They came for hours and days and years and centuries, they came eternally, and as they came every finger of that host, compared to which all the sands of all the seas were but as a handful, was pointed at her, and every mouth shaped the words:

"Is it I whom thou seekest?"

Million by million she scanned them all, but the face of Richard Darrien was not there.

Now the dead Zulus were marching by. Down the stream of Time they marched in their marshalled regiments. Chaka stood over her—she knew him by his likeness to Dingaan—and threatened her with a little, red-handled spear, asking her how she dared to sit upon the throne of the Spirit of his nation. She began to tell him her story, but as she spoke the wide receding walls of that grey hall fell apart and crumbled, and amidst a mighty laughter the great-eyed Shapes rebuilt them to the fashion of the cave in the mound beneath the tree of the dwarf-folk. The sound of the trumpets died away, the shrill, sweet music of the spheres grew far and faint.

Rachel opened her eyes. There in front of her sat Nya, crooning her low song, and there, on either side crouched the mutes tapping upon their little drums and gazing into their bowls of water, while against her leaned Noie, who stirred like one awaking from sleep. Ages and ages ago when she started on that dread journey, the dwarf to her left was stretching out her hand to steady the bowl at her feet, and now it had but just reached the bowl. A great moth had singed its wings in the lamp, and was fluttering to the ground—it was still in mid-air. Noie was placing her arm about her neck, and it had but begun to fall upon her shoulder!

## Chapter 22

# In the Sanctuary

Nya ceased her singing, and the dwarf women their beating on the drums.

"Hast thou been a journey, Maiden?" she asked, looking at Rachel curiously.

"Aye, Mother," she answered in a faint voice, "and a journey far and strange."

"And thou, Noie, my niece?"

"Aye, Mother," she answered, shivering as though with cold or fear, "but I went not with my Sister here, I went alone—for years and years."

"A far journey thou sayest, *Inkosazana*, and one that was for years and years, thou sayest, Noie, yet the eyes of both of you have been shut for so long only as it takes a burnt moth to fall from the lamp flame to the ground. I think that you slept and dreamed a moment, that is all."

"Mayhap, Mother," replied Rachel, "but if so mine was a most wondrous dream, such as has never visited me before, and as I pray, never may again. For I was borne beyond the stars into the glorious cities of the dead, and I saw all the dead, and those that I had known in life were brought to me by Shapes and Powers whereof I could only see the eyes."

"And didst thou find him whom thou soughtest most of all?"

"Nay," she answered, "him alone I did not find. I sought him, I prayed the Guardians of the dead to show him to me, and they called up all the dead, and I scanned them every one, and they summoned him by his name, but he was not of their number, and he came not. Only they spoke in my heart, bidding me to look for him in some other world."

"Ah!" exclaimed Nya starting a little, "they said that to thee, did they? Well, worlds are many, and such a search would be long." Then as though to turn the subject, she added, "And what sawest thou, Noie?"

"I, Mother? I went not beyond the stars, I climbed down endless ladders into the centre of the earth, my feet are still sore with them. I reached vast caves full of a blackness that shone, and there many dead folk were walking, going nowhere, and coming back from nowhere. They seemed strengthless but not unhappy, and they looked at me and asked me tidings of the upper world, but I could not answer them, for whenever I opened my lips to speak a cold hand was laid upon my mouth. I wandered among them for many moons, only there was no moon, nothing but the blackness that shone like polished coal, wandered from cave to cave. At length I came to a cave in which sat my father, Seyapi, and near to him my mother, and my other mothers, his wives, and my brothers and sisters, all of whom the Zulus killed, as the wild beast, Ibubesi, told them to do."

"I saw Ibubesi, and he prayed me for my pardon, and I granted it to him," broke in Rachel.

"I did not see him," went on Noie fiercely, "nor would I have pardoned him if I had. Nor do I think that my father and his family pardon him; I think that they wait to bear testimony against him before the Lord of the dead."

"Did Seyapi tell you so?" asked Rachel.

"Nay, he sat there beneath a black tree whereof I could not see the top, and gazed into a bowl of black water, and in that bowl he showed me many pictures of things that have been and things that are to come, but they are secret, I may say nothing of them."

"And what was the end of it, my niece?" asked Nya, bending forward eagerly.

"Mother, the end of it was that the black tree which was shaped like the tree of our tribe above us, took fire and went up in a fierce flame. Then the roofs of the caves fell in and all the people of the dwarfs flew through the roofs, singing and rejoicing, into a place of light; only," she added slowly, "it seemed to me that I was left alone amidst the ruins of the caves, I and the white ghost of the tree. Then a voice cried to me to make my heart bold, to bear all things with patience, since to those who dare much for love's sake, much will be forgiven. So I woke, but what those words mean I cannot guess, seeing that I love no man, and never shall," and she rested her chin upon her hand and sat there musing.

"No," replied Nya, "thou lovest no man, and therefore the riddle is hard," but as she spoke her eyes fell upon Rachel.

"Mother," said Rachel presently, "my heart is the hungrier for all that it has fed upon. Can thy magic send me back to that country of the dead that I may search for him again? If so, for his sake I will dare the journey."

"Not so," answered Nya shaking her head; "it is a road that very few have travelled, and none may travel twice and live."

Now Rachel began to weep.

"Weep not, Maiden, there are other roads and perchance tomorrow thou shall walk them. Now lie down and sleep, both of you, and fear no dreams."

So they laid themselves down and slept, but the old witch-wife, Nya, sat waiting and watched them.

"I think I understand," she murmured to herself, as She gazed at the slumbering Rachel, "for to her who is so pure and good, and who has suffered such cruel wrong, the Guardians would not lie. I think that I understand and that I can find a path. Sleep on, sweet maiden, sleep on in hope."

Then she looked at Noie and shook her grey head.

"I do not understand," she muttered. "The black tree shaped like the Tree of our Tribe, and Seyapi of the old blood seated beneath it. The tree that went up in fire, and the maid of the old blood left alone with the ghost of it, while the dwarf people fled into light and freedom. What does it mean? Ah! that picture in the bowl! Now I can guess. 'Those who dare much for love.' It did not say for love of man, and woman can love woman. But would she dare a deed that none of our race could even dream? Well, the Zulu blood is bold. Perhaps, perhaps. Oh! Eddo, thou black sorcerer, whither art thou leading the Children of the Tree? On thy head be it, Eddo, not on mine; on thy head for ever and for ever."

When Rachel awoke, refreshed, on the following day, she lay a while thinking. Every detail of her vision was perfectly clear in her mind, only now she was sure that it had been but a dream. Yet what a wonderful dream! How, even in her sleep, had she found the imagination to conceive circumstances so inconceivable? That magic rush beyond the stars; that mighty world set round with black cliffs against which rolled the waves of space; that changeful, wondrous world which unfolded itself petal by petal like a rose, every petal lovelier and different from the last; that grey hall roofed with tilted precipices; and then those dead, those multitudes of the dead!

What power had been born in her that she could imagine such things as these? Vision she had, like her mother, but not after this sort. Perhaps it was but an aftermath of her madness, for into the minds of the mad creep strange sights and sounds, and this place, and the people amongst whom she sojourned, the Ghost-people, the grey Dwarf-people, the Dealers in dreams, the Dwellers in the sombre forest, might well open new doors in such a soul as hers. Or perhaps she was still mad. She did not know, she did not greatly care. All she knew was that her poor heart ached with love for a man who was dead, and yet whom she could not find even among the dead. She had wished to die, but now she longed for death no more, fearing lest after all there should be something in that vision which the magic of Nya had summoned up, and that when she reached the further shore she might not find him who dwelt in a different world. Oh! if only she could find him, then she would be glad enough to go wherever it was that he had gone.

Now Noie was awake at her side, and they talked together.

"We must have dreamt dreams, Noie," she said. "Perhaps the Mother mingled some drug with our food."

"I do not know, Zoola," answered Noie; "but, if so, I want no more of those dreams which bode no good to me. Besides, who can tell what is dream and what is truth? Mayhap this world is the dream, and the truth is such things as we saw last night," and she would say no more on the matter.

Nothing happened within the Wall that day—that is, nothing out of the common. A certain number of the privileged, priestly caste of the dwarfs were carried or conducted into the holy place, and up to the Fence of Death that they might die there, and a certain number were brought out for burial. Some of those who came in were folk weary of life, or, in other words, suicides, and these walked; and some were sick of various diseases, and these were carried. But the end was the same, they always died, though whether this result was really brought about by some poison distilled from the tree, as Nya alleged, or whether it was the effect of a physical collapse induced by that inherited belief, Rachel never discovered.

At least they died, some almost at once, and some within a day or two of entering that deadly shade, and were borne away to burial by the mutes who spent their spare time in the digging of little graves which they must fill. Indeed, these mutes either knew, or pretended that they knew who would be the occupant of each grave. At least they intimated by signs that this was revealed to them in their bowls, and when the victims appeared within the Wall, took pleasure in leading them to the holes they had prepared, and showing to them with what care these had been dug to suit their stature. For this service they received a fee that such moribund persons brought with them, either of finely woven robes, or of mats, or of different sorts of food, or sometimes of gold and copper rings manufactured by the Umkulu or other subject savages, which they wore upon their wrists and ankles.

Certain of these doomed folk, however, went to their fate with no light hearts, which was not wonderful, as it seemed that these were neither ill nor sought a voluntary euthanasia. They were political victims sent thither by Eddo as an alternative to the terror of the Red Death, whereby according to their strange and ancient creed, they would have risked the spilling of their souls. For the most part the crime of these poor people was that they had been adherents and supporters of the old Mother of the Tree, Nya, over whom Eddo was at last triumphant. On their way up to the Fence such individuals would stop to exchange a last few, sad words with their dethroned priestess.

Then without any resistance they went on with the rest, but from them the mutes received scant offerings, or none at all, with the result that they were cast into the worst situated and most inconvenient graves, or even tumbled two or three together into some shapeless corner hole. But, after all, that mattered nothing to them so long as they received sepulchre within the Wall, which was their birth-or, rather, their death-right.

The priest-mutes themselves were a strange folk, and, oddly enough, Rachel observed, by comparison, quite cheerful in their demeanour, for when off duty they would smile and gibber at each other like monkeys, and carry on a kind of market between themselves. They lived in that part of the circumference of the Wall which was behind the hill whereon grew the sacred tree. Here no burials took place, and instead of graves appeared their tiny huts arranged in neat streets and squares. In these they and their forefathers had dwelt from time immemorial; indeed, each little hut with a few yards of fenced-in ground about it ornamented with dwarf trees, was a freehold that descended from father to son. For the mutes married, and were given in marriage, like other folk, though their children were few, a family of three being considered very large, while many of the couples had none at all. But those who were born to them were all deaf-mutes, although their other senses seemed to be singularly acute.

These mutes had their virtues; thus some of them were very kind to each other, and especially to those from the outer forest world who came hither to bid farewell to that world, and others, renouncing marriage and all earthly joys, devoted their lives, which appeared to be long, to the worship of the Spirit of the Tree. Also they had their vices, such as theft, and the seducing away of the betrothed of others, but the chief of them was jealousy, which sometimes led to murder by poisoning, an art whereof they were great masters.

When such a crime was discovered, and a case of it happened during the first days of Rachel's sojourn among them, the accused was put upon his trial before the chief of the mutes, evidence for and against him being given by signs which they all understood. Then if a case were established against him, he was forced to drink a bowl of medicine. If he did this with impunity he was acquitted, but if it disagreed with him his guilt was held to be established. Now came the strange part of the matter. All his life the evil-doer had been accustomed to go within the Fence about his business and take no harm, but after such condemnation he was conducted there with the usual ceremonies and very shortly perished like any other uninitiated person. Whether this issue was due to magic or to mental collapse, or to the previous administration of poison, no one seemed to know, not even Nya herself. So, at least, she declared to Rachel.

At each new moon these mutes celebrated what Rachel was informed they looked upon as a festival. That is, they climbed the Tree of the Tribe and scattered themselves among its enormous branches, where for several hours they mumbled and gibbered in the dark like a troop of baboons. Then they came down, and mounting the huge, surrounding wall, crept around its circumference. Occasionally this journey resulted in an accident, as one of them would fall from the wall and be dashed to pieces, although it was noticed that the unfortunate was generally a person who, although guilty of no actual crime, chanced to be out of favour with the other priests and priestesses. After the circuit of the wall had been accomplished, with or without accidents, the dwarfs feasted round a fire, drinking some spirit that threw them into a sleep in which wonderful visions appeared to them. Such was their only entertainment, if so it could be called, since doubtless the ceremony was of a religious character. For the rest they seldom if ever left the holy place, which was known as "Within the Wall," most of them never doing so in the course of a long life.

Beyond the burial of the dead they did no work, as their food was brought to them daily by outside people, who were called "the slaves of the Wall." Their only method of conversation was by signs, and they seemed to desire no other. Indeed, if, as occasionally happened, a child was born to any of them who could hear or speak like other human beings, it was either given over to the other dwarfs, or if the discovery was not made until it was old enough to observe, it was sacrificed by being bound to the trunk of the tribal tree "lest it should tell the secret of the Tree."

Such were the weird, half-human folk among whom Rachel was destined to dwell. The Zulus had been bad and bloodthirsty, but compared to these little wizards they seemed to her as angels. The Zulus at any rate had left her her thoughts, but these stunted wretches, she was sure, pried into them and read them with the help of their bowls, for often she caught sight of them signing to each other about her as she passed, and pointing with grins to pictures which they saw in the water.

********

It was night again, still, silent night made odorous with the heavy cedar scents of the huge tree upon the mound. Rachel and Noie sat before Nya in the cave beneath the burning lamp about which fluttered the big-winged, gilded moths.

"Thou didst not find him yonder among the Shades," said Nya suddenly, as though she were continuing a conversation. "Say now, Maiden, art thou satisfied, or wouldst thou seek for him again?"

"I would seek him through all the heavens and all the earths. Mother, my soul burns for a sight of him, and if I cannot find him, then I must die, and go perchance where he is not."

"Good," said Nya; "the effort wearies me, for I grow weak, yet for thy sake I will try to help thee, who saved me from the Red Death."

Then the dwarf-women came in and beat upon their drums, and, as before, the old Mother of the Trees began to sing, but Noie sat aside, for in this night's play she would take no part. Again Rachel sank into sleep, and again it seemed to her that she was swept from the earth into the region of the stars and there searched world after world.

She saw many strange and marvellous things, things so wonderful that her memory was buried beneath the mass of them, so that when she woke again she could not recall their details. Only of Richard she saw nothing. Yet as her life returned to her, it seemed to Rachel that for one brief moment she was near to Richard. She could not see him, and she could not hear him, yet certainly he was near her. Then her eyes opened, and Nya ceasing from her song, asked:

"What tidings, Wanderer?"

"Little," she answered feebly, for she was very tired, and in a faint voice she told her all.

"Good," said Nya, nodding her grey head. "This time he was not so far away. Tomorrow I will make thy spirit strong, and then perhaps he will come to thee. Now rest."

So next night Nya laid her charm upon Rachel as before, and again her spirit sought for Richard. This time it seemed to her that she did not leave the earth, but with infinite pain, with terrible struggling, wandered to and fro about it, bewildered by a multitude of faces, led astray by myriads of footsteps. Yet in the end she found him. She heard him not, she saw him not, she knew not where he was, but undoubtedly for a while she was with him, and awoke again, exhausted, but very happy.

Nya heard her story, weighing every word of it but saying nothing. Then she signed to the dwarfs to bring her a bowl of dew, and stared in it for a long while. The dwarf-women also stared into their bowls, and afterwards came to her, talking to her on their fingers, after which all three of them upset the dew upon a rock, "breaking the pictures."

"Hast thou seen aught?" asked Rachel eagerly.

"Yes, Maiden," answered the mother. "I and these wise women have seen something, the same thing, and therefore a true thing. But ask not what it was, for we may not tell thee, nor would it help thee if we did. Only be of a good courage, for this I say, there is hope for thee."

So Rachel went to sleep, pondering on these words, of which neither she nor Noie could guess the meaning. The next night when she prayed Nya to lay the spell upon her, the old Mother would not.

"Not so," she said. "Thrice have I rent thy soul from thy body and sent it afar, and this I may do no more and keep thee living, nor could I if I would, for I grow feeble. Neither is it necessary, seeing that although thou knowest it not, that spirit of thine, having found him, is with him wherever he may be, yes, at his side comforting him."

"Aye, but Where is he, Mother? Let me look in the bowl and see his face, as I believe that thou hast done."

"Look if thou wilt," and she motioned to one of the dwarf-women to place a bowl before her.

So Rachel looked long and earnestly, but saw nothing of Richard, only many fantastic pictures, most of which she knew again for scenes from her own past. At length, worn out, she thrust away the bowl, and asked in a bitter voice why they mocked her, and how it came about that she who had seen the coming of Richard in the pool in Zululand, and the fate of Dingaan the King in the bowl of Eddo, could now see nothing of any worth.

"As regards the vision of the pool I cannot say, Maiden," replied

Nya, "for that was born of thine own heart, and had nothing to do with our magic. As regards the visions in the bowl of Eddo, they were his visions, not thine, or rather my visions that I saw before he started hence. I passed them on to him, and he passed them on to thee, and thou didst pass them on to King Dingaan. Far-sighted and pure-souled as thou art, yet not having been instructed in their wizardry, thou wilt see nothing in the bowls of the dwarfs unless their blood is mingled with thy blood."

"'Their blood mingled with my blood?' What dost thou mean, Mother?"

"What I say, neither more nor less. If Eddo has his will, thou wilt rule after me here as Mother of the Trees. But first thy veins must be opened, and the veins of Eddo must be opened, and Eddo's blood must be poured into thee, and thy blood into him. Then thou wilt be able to read in the bowls as we can, and Eddo will be thy master, and thou must do his bidding while you both shall live."

"If so," answered Rachel, "I think that neither of us will live long."

That night Rachel felt too exhausted to sleep, though why this should be she could not guess, as she had done nothing all day save watch the mutes at their dreary tasks, and it was strange, therefore, that she should feel as though she had made a long journey upon her feet. About an hour before the dawn she saw Nya rise and glide past her towards the mouth of the cave, carrying in her hand a little drum, like those used by the mute women. Something impelled her to follow, and waking Noie at her side, she bade her come also.

Outside of the cave by the faint starlight they saw the little shape of Nya creeping down the mound, and thence across the open space towards the wall, and went after her, thinking that she intended to pass the wall. But this she did not do, for when she came to its foot Nya, notwithstanding her feebleness, began to climb the rough stones as actively as any cat, and though their ascent seemed perilous enough, reached the crest of the wall sixty feet above in safety, and there sat herself down. Next they heard her beating upon the drum she bore, single strokes always, but some of them slow, and some rapid, with a pause between every five or ten strokes, "as though she were spelling out words," thought Rachel.

After a while Nya ceased her beating, and in the utter silence of the night, which was broken only, as always, by the occasional crash of falling trees, for no breath of air stirred, and all the beasts of prey had sought their lairs before light came, both she and Noie seemed to hear, far, infinitely far away, the faint beat of an answering drum. It would appear that Nya heard it also, for she struck a single note upon hers as though in acknowledgement, after which the distant beating went on, paused as though for a reply from some other unheard drum, and again from time to time went on, perhaps repeating that reply.

For a long while this continued until the sky began to grow grey indeed, when Nya beat for several minutes and was answered by a single, far-off note. Then glancing at the heavens she prepared to descend the wall, while Rachel and Noie slipped back to the cave and feigned to be asleep. Soon she entered, and stood over them shaking her grey head and asking how it came about that they thought that she, the Mother of the Trees, should be so easily deceived.

"So thou sawest us," said Rachel, trying not to look ashamed.

"No; I saw you not with my eyes, either of you, but I felt both of you following me, and heard in my heart what you were whispering to each other. Well, *Inkosazana*, art thou the wiser for this journey?"

"No, Mother, but tell us if thou wilt what thou wast beating on that drum."

"Gladly," she answered. "I was sending certain orders to the slave peoples who still know me as Mother of the Trees, and obey my words. Perhaps thou dost not believe that while I sat upon yonder wall I talked across the desert to the chiefs of the marches upon the far border of the land of the Umkulu, and that by now at my bidding they have sent out men upon an errand of mine."

"What was the errand, Mother?" asked Rachel curiously.

"I said the errand was mine, not thine, Maiden. It is not pressing, but as I do not know how long my strength will last, I thought it well that it should be settled." Then without more words she coiled herself up on her mat and seemed to go to sleep.

It was after this incident of the drums that Rachel experienced the strangest days, or rather weeks of her life. Nya sent her into no more trances, and to all outward seeming nothing happened. Yet within her much did happen. Her madness had utterly left her and still she was not as other women are, or as she herself had been in health. Her mind seemed to wander and she knew not whither it wandered. Yet for long hours, although she was awake and, so Noie said, talking or eating or walking as usual, it was away from her, and afterwards she could remember nothing. Also this happened at night as well as during the day, and ever more and more often.

She could remember nothing, yet out of this nothingness there grew upon her a continual sense of the presence of Richard Darrien, a presence that seemed to come nearer and nearer, closer and closer to her heart. It was the assurance of this presence that made those long days so happy to her, though when she was herself, she felt that it could be naught but a dream. Yet why should a dream move her so strangely, and why should a dream weary her so much? Why, after sleeping all night, should she awake feeling as though she had journeyed all night? Why should her limbs ache and she grow thin like one who travels without cease? Why should she seem time after time to have passed great dangers, to have known cold, and heat and want and struggle against waters and the battling against storms? Why should her knowledge of this Richard, of the very heart and soul of Richard, grow ever deeper till it was as though they were not twain, but one?

She could not answer these questions, and Noie could not answer them, and when she asked Nya the old Mother shook her head and could not, or would not answer. Only the dwarf-mutes seemed to know the answer, for when she passed them they nudged each other, and grinned and thrust their little woolly heads together staring, several of them, into one bowl. But if Noie and Nya knew nothing of the cause of these things the effect of them stirred them both, for they saw that Rachel, the tall and strong, grew faint and weak and began to fade away as one fades upon whom deadly sickness has laid its hand.

Thus three weeks or so went by, until one day in some fashion of her own Nya caused to arise an the mind of Eddo a knowledge of her desire to speak with him. Early the next morning Eddo arrived at the Holy Place accompanied only by his familiar, Hana, and Nya met them alone in the mouth of the cave.

"I see that thou art very white and thin, but still alive, old woman," sneered Eddo, adding: "All the thousands of the people yonder thought that long ere this thou wouldst have passed within the Fence. May I take back that good tidings to them?"

The ancient Mother of the Trees looked at him sternly.

"It is true, thou evil mocker," she said, "that I am white and thin. It is true that I grow like to the skeleton of a rotted leaf, all ribs and netted veins without substance. It is true that my round eyes start from my head like to those of a bush plover, or the tree lizard, and that soon I must pass within the Fence, as thou hast so long desired that I should do that thou mayest reign alone over the thousands of the People of the Dwarfs and wield their wisdom to increase thy power, thou poison-bloated toad. All these things are true, Eddo, yet ere I go I have a word to say to thee to which thou wilt do well to listen."

"Speak on," said Eddo. "Without doubt thou hast wisdom of a sort; honey thou hast garnered during many years, and it is well that I should suck the store before it is too late."

"Eddo," said Nya, "I am not the only one in this Holy Place who grows white and thin. Look, there is another," and she nodded towards Rachel, who walked past them aimlessly with dreaming eyes, attended by Noie, upon whose arm she leant.

"I see," answered Eddo; "this haunted death-prison presses the life out of her, also I think that thou hast sent her Spirit travelling, as thou knowest how to do, and such journeys sap the strength of flesh and blood."

"Perhaps; but now before it is too late I would send her body travelling also; only thou, who hast the power for a while, dost bar the road."

"I know," said Eddo, nodding his bead and looking at his companion. "We all know, do we not, Hana? we who have heard certain beatings of drums in the night, and studied dew drops beneath the trees at dawn. Thou wouldst send her to meet another traveller."

"Yes, and if thou art wise thou wilt let her go."

"Why should I let her go," asked the priest passionately, "and with her all my greatness? She must reign here after thee, for at her feet thy Tree fell, and it is the will of the people, who weary of dwarf queens and desire one that is tall and beautiful and white. Moreover, when my blood has been poured into her, her wisdom will be great, greater than thine or that of any Mother that went before thee, for she is '*Wensi*' the Virgin, and her soul is purer than them all. I will not let her go. If she leaves this Holy Place where none may do her harm, she shall die, and then her Spirit may go to seek that other traveller."

"Thou art mad, Eddo, mad and blind with pride and folly. Let her be, and choose another Mother. Now, there is Noie."

"Thy great-niece, Nya, who thinks as thou thinkest, and hates those whom thou hatest. Nay, I will have none of that half-breed. Yonder white *Inkosazana* shall be our queen and no other."

"Then, Eddo," whispered Nya, leaning forward and looking into his eyes, "she shall be the last Mother of this people. Fool, there are those who fight for her against whom thou canst not prevail. Thou knowest them not, but I know them, and I tell thee that they make ready thy doom. Have thy way, Eddo; it was not for her that I pleaded with thee, but for the sake of the ancient People of the Ghosts, whose fate draws nigh to them. Fool, have thy way, spin thy web, and be caught in it thyself. I tell thee, Eddo, that thy death shall be redder than any thou hast ever dreamed, nor shall it fall on thee alone. Begone now, and trouble me no more till in another place all that is left of thee shall creep to my feet, praying me for a pardon thou shalt not find. Begone, for the last leaf withers on my Tree and tomorrow I pass within the Fence. Say to the people that their Mother against whom they rebelled is dead, and that she bids them prepare to meet the evil which, alive, she warded from their heads."

Now Eddo strove to answer, but could not, for there was something in the flaming eyes of Nya which frightened him. He looked at Hana, and Hana looked back at him, then taking each other's hand they slunk away towards the wall, staggering blindly through the sunshine towards the shade.

## Chapter 23

# The Dream in the North

Richard Darrien remembered drinking a bowl of milk in the hut in which he was imprisoned at Mafooti, and instantly feeling a cold chill run to his heart and brain, after which he remembered no more for many a day. At length, however, by slow degrees, and with sundry slips back into unconsciousness, life and some share of his reason and memory returned to him. He awoke to find himself lying in a hut roughly fashioned of branches, and attended by a Kaffir woman of middle age.

"Who are you?" he asked.

"I am named Mami," she answered.

"Mami, Mami! I know the name, and I know the voice. Say, were you one of the wives of Ibubesi, she who spoke with me through the fence?" and he strove to raise himself on his arm to look at her, but fell back from weakness.

"Yes, *Inkoos*, I was one of his wives."

"Was? Then where is Ibubesi now?"

"Dead, *Inkoos*. The fire has burned him up with his *kraal* Mafooti."

"With the *kraal* Mafooti! Where, then, is the *Inkosazana*? Answer, woman, and be swift," he cried in a hollow voice.

"Alas! *Inkoos*, alas! she is dead also, for she was in the *kraal* when the fire swept it, and was seen standing on the top of a hut where she had taken refuge, and after that she was seen no more."

"Then let me die and go to her," exclaimed Richard with a groan, as he fell back upon his bed, where he lay almost insensible for three more days.

Yet he did not die, for he was young and very strong, and Mami poured milk down his throat to keep the life in him. Indeed little by little something of his strength came back, so that at last he was able to think and talk with her again, and learned all the dreadful story.

He learned how the people of Mafooti, fearing the vengeance of Dingaan, had fled away from their *kraal*, carrying what they thought to be his body with them, lest it should remain in evidence against them, and taking all the cattle that they could gather. Every one of them had fled that could travel, only Ibubesi and a few sick, and certain folk who chanced to be outside the walls, remaining behind. It was from two of these, who escaped during the burning of the *kraal* by the Zulus, or by fire from the Heavens, they knew not which, that they had heard of the awful end of Ibubesi, and of his prisoner, the *Inkosazana*. As for themselves, they had travelled night and day, till they reached a certain secret and almost inaccessible place in the great Quathlamba Mountains, in which people had lived whom Chaka wiped out, and there hidden themselves. In this place they remained, hoping that Dingaan would not care to follow them so far, and purposing to make it their home, since here they found good mealie lands, and fortunately the most of their cattle remained alive. That was all the story, there was nothing more to tell.

A day or two later Richard was able to creep out of the hut and see the place. It was as Mami had said, very strong, a kind of tableland ringed round with precipices that could only be climbed through a single narrow *nek*, and overshadowed by the great Quathlamba range. The people, who were engaged in planting their corn, gathered round him, staring at him as though he were one risen from the dead, and greeted him with respectful words. He spoke to several of them, including the two men who had seen the burning of Mafooti, though from a little distance. But they could tell him no more than Mami had done, except that they were sure that the *Inkosazana* had perished in the flames, as had many of the Zulus, who broke into the town. Richard was sure of it also—who would not have been?—and crept back broken-hearted to his hut, he who had lost all, and longed that he might die.

But he did not die, he grew strong again, and when he was well and fit to travel, went to the headmen of the people, saying that now he desired to leave them and return to his own place in the Cape Colony. The headmen said No, he must not leave, for in their hearts they were sure that he would go, not to the Cape Colony, but to Zululand, there to discover all he could as to the death of the *Inkosazana*. So they told him that with them he must bide, for then if the Zulus tracked them out they would be able to produce him, who otherwise would be put to the spear, every man of them, as his murderers. The sin of Ibubesi who had been their chief, clung to them, and they knew well what Dingaan and Tamboosa had sworn should happen to those who harmed the white chief, Dario, who was under the mantle of their *Inkosazana.*

Richard reasoned with them, but it was of no use, they, would not let him go. Therefore in the end he appeared to fall in with their humour, and meanwhile began to plan escape. One dark night he tried it indeed, only to be seized in the mouth of the *nek*, and brought back to his hut. Next morning the headman spoke with him, telling him that he should only depart thence over their dead bodies, and that they watched him night and day; that the *nek*, moreover, was always guarded. Then they made an offer to him. He was a white man, they said, and cleverer than they were; let them come under his wing, let him be their chief, for he would know how to protect them from the Zulus and any other enemies. He could take over the wives of Ibubesi (at this proposition Richard shuddered), and they would obey him in all things, only he must not attempt to leave them—which he should never do alive.

Richard put the proposal by, but in the end, not because he wished it, but by the mere weight of his white man's blood, and for the lack of anything else to do, drifted into some such position. Only at the wives of Ibubesi, or any other wives, he would not so much as look, a slight that gave offence to those women, but made the others laugh.

So, for certain long weeks he sat in that secret nook in the mountains as the chief of a little Kaffir tribe, occupying himself with the planting of crops, the building of walls and huts, the drilling of men and the settling of quarrels. All day he worked thus, but after the day came the night when he did not work, and those nights he dreaded. For then the languor, not of body, but of mind, which the poison the old witch-doctoress had given to Ishmael had left behind it, would overcome him, bringing with it black despair, and his grief would get a hold of him, torturing his heart. For of the memory of Rachel he could never be rid for a single hour, and his love for her grew deeper day by day. And she was dead! Oh, she was dead, leaving him living.

One night he dreamed of Rachel, dreamed that she was searching for him and calling him. It was a very vivid dream, but he woke up and it passed away as such dreams do. Only all the day that followed he felt a strange throbbing in his head, and found himself turning ever towards the north. The next night he dreamed again of her, and heard her say, "The search has been far and long, but I have found you, Richard. Open your eyes now, and you will see my face." So he opened his eyes, and there, sure enough, in the darkness he perceived the outline of her sweet, remembered face, about which fell her golden hair. For one moment only he perceived it, then it was gone, and after that her presence never seemed to leave him. He could not see her, he could not touch her, and yet she was ever at his side. His brain ached with the thought of her, her breath seemed to fan his hands and hair. At night her face floated before him, and in his dreams her voice called him, saying: *"Come to me, come to me, Richard. I am in need of you. Come to me. I myself will be your guide."*

Then he would wake, and remembering that she was dead, grew sure and ever surer that the Spirit of Rachel was calling him down to death. It called him from the north, always from the north. Soon he could scarcely walk southwards, or east or west, for ere he had gone many yards his feet turned and set his face towards the north, that was to the narrow *nek* between the precipices which the Kaffirs guarded night and day.

One evening he went to his hut to sleep, if sleep would come to him. It came, and with it that face and voice, but the face seemed paler, and the voice more insistent.

"Will you not listen to me," it said, "you who were my love? For how long must I plead with you? Soon my power will leave me, the opportunity will be passed, and then how will you find me, Richard, my lover? Rise up, rise up and follow ere it be too late, for I myself will be your guide."

He awoke. He could bear it no more. Perhaps he was mad, and these were visions of his madness, mocking visions that led him to his death. Well, if so, he still would follow them. Perhaps her body was buried in the north. If so, he would be buried there also; perhaps her Soul dwelt in the north. If so, his soul would fly thither to join it. The Kaffirs would kill him in the pass. Well, if so, he would die with his face set northwards whither Rachel drew him.

He rose up and wrapped himself in a cloak of goatskins. He filled a hide bag with sun-dried flesh and parched corn, and hung it about his shoulders with a gourd of water, for after all he might live a little while and need food and drink. As he had no gun he took a staff and a knife and a broad-bladed spear, and leaving the hut, set his face northward and walked towards the mouth of the *nek*. At the first step which he took the torment in his head seemed to leave him, who fought no longer, who had seemed obedient to that mysterious summons. Quietness and confidence possessed him. He was going to his end, but what did it matter? The dream beckoned and he must follow. The moon shone bright, but he took no trouble to hide himself, it did not seem to be worth while.

Now he was in the *nek* and drawing near to the place where the guard was stationed, still he marched on, boldly, openly. As he thought, they were on the alert. They drew out from behind the rocks and barred his path.

"Whither goest thou, lord Dario?" asked their captain. "Thou knowest that here thou mayest not pass."

"I follow a Ghost to the north," he answered, "and living or dead, I pass."

"*Ow!*" said the captain. "He says that he follows a Ghost. Well, we have nothing to do with ghosts. Take him, unharmed if possible, but take him."

So, urged thereto by their own fears, since for their safety's sake they dared not let him go, the men sprang towards him. They sprang towards him where he stood waiting the end, for give back he would not, and of a sudden fell down upon their faces, hiding their heads among the stones. Richard did not know what had happened to them that they behaved thus strangely, nor did he care. Only seeing them fallen he walked on over them, and pursued his way along the *nek* and down it to the plains beyond.

All that night he walked, looking behind him from time to time to see if any followed, but none came. He was alone, quite alone, save for the dream that led him towards the north. At sunrise he rested and slept a while, then, awaking after midday, went on his road. He did not know the road, yet never was he in doubt for a moment. It was always clear to him whither he should go. That night he finished his food and again slept a while, going forward at the dawn. In the morning he met some Kaffirs, who questioned him, but he answered only that he was following a Dream to the north. They stared at him, seemed to grow frightened and ran away. But presently some of them came back and placed food in his path, which he took and left them.

He came to the *kraal* Mafooti. It was utterly deserted, and he wandered amidst its ashes. Here and there he found the bones of those who had perished in the fire, and turned them over with his staff wondering whether any of them had belonged to Rachel. In that place he slept a night thinking that perhaps his journey was ended, and that here he would die where he believed Rachel had died. But when he waked at the dawn, it was to find that something within him still drew him towards the north, more strongly indeed than ever before.

So he left what had been the town Mafooti. Walking along the edge of the cleft into which Ishmael had leapt on fire, he climbed the walls built with so much toil to keep out the Zulus, and at last came to the river which Rachel had swum. It was low now, and wading it he entered Zululand. Here the natives seemed to know of his approach, for they gathered in numbers watching him, and put food in his path. But they would not speak to him, and when he addressed them saying that he followed a Dream and asking if they had seen the Dream, they cried out that he was *tagali*, bewitched, and fled away.

He continued his journey, finding each night a hut prepared for him to sleep in, and food for him to eat, till at length one evening he reached the Great Place, Umgugundhlovu. Through its streets he marched with a set face, while thousands stared at him in silence. Then a captain pointed out a hut to him, and into it he entered, ate and slept. At dawn he rose, for he knew that here he must not tarry; the spirit face of Rachel still hung before him, the spirit voice still whispered—"*Forward, forward to the north. I myself will be your guide.*" In his path sat the King and his Councillors, and around them a regiment of men. He walked through them unheeding, till at length, when he was in front of the King, they barred his road, and he halted.

"Who art thou and what is thy business?" asked an old Councillor with a withered hand.

"I am Richard Darrien," he answered, "and here I have no business. I journey to the north. Stay me not."

"We know thee," said the Councillor, "thou art the lord Dario that didst dwell in the shadow of the *Inkosazana.* Thou art the white chief whom the wild beast, Ibubesi, slew at the *kraal* Mafooti. Why does thy ghost come hither to trouble us?"

"Living or dead, ghost or man, I travel to the north. Stay me not," he answered.

"What seekest thou in the north, thou lord Dario?"

"I seek a Dream; a Spirit leads me to find a Dream. Seest thou it not, Man with the withered hand?"

"Ah!" they repeated, "he seeks a Dream. A Spirit leads him to find a Dream in the north."

"What is this Dream like?" asked Mopo of the withered hand.

"Come, stand at my side and look. There, dost thou see it floating in the air before us, thou who hast eyes that can read a Dream?"

Mopo came and looked, then his knees trembled a little and he said: "Aye, lord Dario, I see and I know that face."

"Thou knowest the face, old fool," broke in Dingaan angrily. "Then whose is it?"

"O King," answered Mopo, dropping his eyes, "it is not lawful to speak the name, but the face is the face of one who sat where that wanderer stands, and showed thee certain pictures in a bowl of water."

Now Dingaan trembled, for the memory of those visions haunted him night and day; moreover he thought at times that they drew near to their fulfilment.

"The white man is mad," he said, "and thou, Mopo, art mad also. I have often thought it, and that it would be well if thou wentest on a long journey—for thy health. This Dario shall stay here a while. I will not suffer him to wander through my land crazing the people with his tales of dreams and visions. Take him and hold him; the Circle of the Doctors shall inquire into the matter."

So Dingaan spoke, who in his heart was afraid lest this wild-eyed Dario should learn that he had given the *Inkosazana* to the dwarf folk when she was mad, to appease them after they had prophesied evil to him. Also he remembered that it was because of the murders done by Ibubesi that the *Inkosazana* had gone mad, and did not understand if Dario had been killed at the *kraal* Mafooti how it could be that he now stood before him. Therefore he thought that he would keep him a prisoner until he found out all the truth of the matter, and whether he were still a man or a ghost or a wizard clothed in the shape of the dead.

At the bidding of the King, guards sprang forward to seize Richard, but the old Councillor, Mopo, shrunk away behind him hiding his eyes with his withered hand. They sprang forward, and yet they laid no finger on him, but fell oft to right and left, saying:

"Kill us, if thou wilt, Black One, we cannot!"

"The wizard has bewitched them," said Dingaan angrily. "Here, you Doctors, you whose trade it is to catch wizards, take this white fellow and bind him."

Unwillingly enough the Doctors, of whom there were eight or ten sitting apart, rose to do the King's bidding. They came on towards Richard, some of them singing songs, and some muttering charms, and as they came he laughed and said:

"Beware! you *Abangoma*, the Dream is looking at you very angrily." Then they too broke away to right and left, crying out that this was a wizard against whom they had no power.

Now Dingaan grew mad with wrath, and shouted to his soldiers to seize the white man, and if he resisted them to kill him with their sticks, for of witchcraft they had known enough in Zululand of late.

So thick as bees the regiment formed up in front of him, shouting and waving their *kerries*, for here in the King's Place they bore no spears.

"Make way there," said Richard, "I can stay no longer, I must to the north."

The soldiers did not stir, only a captain stepped out bidding him give up his spear and yield himself, or be killed. Richard walked forward and at a sign from the captain, men sprang at him, lifting their *kerries*, to dash out his brains. Then suddenly in front of Richard there appeared something faint and white, something that walked before him. The soldiers saw it, and the *kerries* fell from their hands. The regiment behind saw it, and turning, burst away like a scared herd of cattle. They did not wait to seek the gates, they burst through the fence of the enclosure, and were gone, leaving it flat behind them. The King and his Councillors saw it also, and more clearly than the rest.

"*The Inkosazana!*" they cried. "It is the *Inkosazana* who walks before him that she loved!" and they fell upon their faces. Only Dingaan remained seated on his stool.

"Go," he said hoarsely to Richard, "go, thou wizard, north or south or east or west, if only thou wilt take that Spirit with thee, for she bodes evil to my land."

So Richard, who had seen nothing, marched away from the *kraal* Umgugundhlovu, and once more set his face towards the north, the north that drew him as it draws the needle of a compass.

The road that Rachel and the dwarfs had travelled he travelled also. Although from day to day he knew not where his feet would lead him, still he travelled it step by step. Nor did any hurt come to him. In the country where men dwelt, being forewarned of his coming by messengers, they brought him food and guarded him, and when he passed out into the wilderness some other power guarded him. He had no fear at all. At night he would lie down without a fire, and the lions would roar about him, but they never harmed him. He would plunge into a swamp or a river and always pass it safely. When water failed he would find it without search; when there was no food, it would seem to be brought to him. Once an eagle dropped a bustard at his feet. Once he found a buck fresh slain by leopards. Once when he was very hungry he saw that he had laid down to sleep by a nest of ostrich eggs, and this food he cooked, making fire after the native fashion with sharp sticks, as he knew how to do.

At length all the swamps were passed and in the third week of his journeyings he reached the sloping uplands, on the edge of which he awoke one morning to find himself surrounded by a circle of great men, giants, who stood staring at him. He arose, thinking that at last his hour had come, as it seemed to him that they were about to kill him. But instead of killing him these huge men saluted him humbly, and offered him food upon their knees, and new hide shoes for his feet—for his own were worn out—and cloaks and garments of skin, which things he accepted thankfully, for by now he was almost naked. Then they brought a litter and wished him to enter it, but this he refused. Heeding them no more, as soon as he had eaten and filled his bag and water-bottle, he started on towards the north. Indeed, he could not have stayed if he had wished; his brain seemed to be full of one thought only, to travel till he reached his journey's end, whatever it might be, and before his eyes he saw one thing only, the spirit face of Rachel, that led him on towards that end. Sometimes it was there for hours, then for hours again it would be absent. When it was present he looked at it; when it was gone he dreamed of it, for him it was the same. But one thing was ever with him, that magnet in his heart which drew his feet towards the north, and from step to step showed him the road that he should travel.

A number of the giant men accompanied him. He noticed it, but took no heed. So long as they did not attempt to stay or turn him he was indifferent whether they came or went away. As a result he travelled in much more comfort, since now everything was made easy and ready for him. Thus he was fed with the best that the land provided, and at night shelters were built for him to sleep in. He discovered that a captain of the giants could understand a few words of some native language which he knew, and asked him why they helped him. The captain replied by order of "Mother of Trees." Who or what "Mother of Trees" might be Richard was unable to discover, so he gave up his attempts at talk and walked on.

They traversed the fertile uplands and reached the edge of the fearful desert. It did not frighten him; he plunged into it as he would have plunged into a sea, or a lake of fire, had it lain in his way. He was like a bird whose instinct at the approach of summer or of winter leads it without doubt or error to some far spot, beyond continents and oceans, some land that it has never seen, leads it in surety and peace to its appointed rest. A guard of the giant men came with him into the desert, also carriers who bore skins of water. In that burning heat the journey was dreadful, yet Richard accomplished it, wearing down all his escort, until at its further lip but one man was left. There even he sank exhausted and began to beat upon a little drum that he carried, which drum had been passed on to him by those who were left behind. But Richard was not exhausted. His strength seemed to be greater than it had ever been before, or that which drew him forward had acquired more power.

He wondered vaguely why a man should choose such a place and time to play upon a drum, and went on alone.

Before him, some miles away, he saw a forest of towering trees that stretched further than his eye could reach. As he approached that forest heading for a certain tall tree, why he knew not, the sunset dyed it red as though it had been on fire, and he thought that he discerned little shapes flitting to and fro amidst the boles of trees. Then he entered the forest, whereof the boughs arched above him like the endless roof of a cathedral borne upon innumerable pillars. There was deep gloom that grew presently to darkness wherein here and there glow-worms shone faintly like tapers dying before an altar, and winds sighed like echoes of evening prayers. He could see to walk no longer, sudden weariness overcame him, so according to his custom he laid himself down to sleep at the bole of a great tree.

A while had passed, he never knew how long, when Richard was awakened from deep slumber by feeling many hands fiercely at work upon him. These hands were small like those of children; this he could tell from the touch of them, although the darkness was so dense that he was able to see nothing. Two of them gripped him by the throat so as to prevent him from crying out; others passed cords about his wrists, ankles and middle until he could not stir a single limb. Then he was dragged back a few paces and lashed to the bole of a tree, as he guessed, that under which he had been sleeping. The hands let go of him, and his throat being free he called out for help. But those vast forest aisles seemed to swallow up his voice. It fell back on him from the canopy of huge boughs above, it was lost in the immense silence. Only from close at hand he heard little peals of thin and mocking laughter. So he too grew silent, for who was there to help him here? He struggled to loose himself, for the impalpable power which had guided him so far was now at work within him more strongly than ever before. It called to him to come, it drew him onward, it whispered to him that the goal was near. But the more he writhed and twisted the deeper did the cruel cords or creepers cut into his flesh. Yet he fought on till, utterly exhausted, his head fell forward, and he swooned away.

CHAPTER 24

# The End and the Beginning

On the day following that when she had summoned Eddo to speak with her, Nya sat at the mouth of the cave. It was late afternoon, and already the shadows gathered so quickly that save for her white hair, her little childlike shape, withered now almost to a skeleton, was scarcely visible against the black rock. Walking to and fro in her aimless fashion, as she would do for hours at a time, Rachel accompanied by Noie passed and re-passed her, till at length the old woman lifted her head and listened to something which was quite inaudible to their ears. Then she beckoned to Noie, who led Rachel to her.

"Maiden beloved," she said in a feeble voice, after they had sat down in front of her, "my hour has come, I have sent for thee to bid thee farewell till we meet again in a country where thou hast travelled for a little while. Before the sun sets I pass within the Fence."

At this tidings Rachel began to weep, for she had learned to love this old dwarf-woman who had been so kind to her in her misery, and she was now so weak that she could not restrain her fears.

"Mother," she said, "for thee it is joy to go. I know it, and therefore cannot wish that thou shouldst stay. Yet what shall I do when thou hast left me alone amidst all these cruel folk? Tell me, what shall I do?"

"Perchance thou wilt seek another helper. Maiden, and perchance thou shall find another to guard and comfort thee. Follow thy heart, obey thy heart, and remember the last words of Nya—that no harm shall come to thee. Nay—if I know it, I may tell thee no more, thou who couldst not hear what the drums said to me but now. Farewell," and turning round she made a sign to certain dwarf-mutes who were gathered behind her as though they awaited her commands.

"Hast thou no last word for me, Mother?" asked Noie.

"Aye, Child," she answered. "Thy heart is very bold, and thou also must follow it. Though thy sin should be great, perchance thy greater love may pay its price. At least thou art but an arrow set upon the string, and that which must be, will be. I think that we shall meet again ere long. Come hither and kneel at my side."

Noie obeyed, and for a little space Nya whispered in her ear, while as she listened Rachel saw strange lights shining in Noie's eyes, lights of terror and of pride, lights of hope and of despair.

"What did she say to you, Noie?" asked Rachel presently.

"I may not tell, Zoola," she answered. "Question me no more."

Now the mutes brought forward a slight litter woven of boughs on which the withered leaves still hung, boughs from Nya's fallen tree. In this litter they placed her, for she could no longer walk, and lifted it on to their shoulders. For one moment she bade them halt, and calling Rachel and Noie to her, kissed them upon the brow, holding up her thin child-like hands over them in blessing. Then followed by them both, the bearers went forward with their burden, taking the road that ran up the hill towards the sacred tree. As the sun set they passed within the Fence, and laying down the litter without a word by the bole of the tree, turned and departed.

The darkness fell, and through it Rachel and Noie heard Nya singing for a little while. The song ceased, and they descended the hill to the cave, for there they feared to stay lest the Tree should draw them also. They ate a little food whilst the two women mutes who had sat on each side of Nya when she showed her magic, stared, now at them, and now into the bowls of dew that were set before them, wherein they seemed to find something that interested them much. Noie prayed Rachel to sleep, and she tried to do so, and could not. For hour after hour she tossed and turned, and at length sat up, saying to Noie:

"I have fought against it, and I can stay here no longer. Noie, I am being drawn from this place out into the forest, and I must go."

"What draws thee, Sister?" asked Noie. "Is it Eddo?"

"No, I think not, nothing to do with Eddo. Oh! Noie, Noie, it is the spirit of Richard Darrien. He is dead, but for days and weeks his spirit has been with my spirit, and now it draws me into the forest to die and find him."

"Then that is an evil journey thou wouldst take, Zoola?"

"Not so, Noie, it is the best and happiest of journeys. The thought of it fills me with joy. What said Nya? Follow thy heart. So I follow it. Noie, farewell, for I must go away."

"Nay," answered Noie, "if thou goest I go, who also was bidden to follow my heart that is sister to thy heart."

Rachel reasoned with her, but she would not listen. The end of it was that the two of them rose and threw on their cloaks; also Rachel took the great Umkulu spear which she had used as a staff on her journey from the desert to the forest. All this while the dwarf-women watched her, but did nothing, only watched.

They left the cave and walked to the mouth of the zigzag slit in the great wall which was open.

"Perhaps the mutes will kill us in the heart of the wall," said Noie.

"If so the end will be soon and swift," answered Rachel.

Now they were in the cleft, following its slopes and windings. Above them they could hear the movements of the guardians of the wall who sat amongst the rough stones, but these did not try to stop them; indeed once or twice when they did not know which way to turn in the darkness, little hands took hold of Rachel's cloak and guided her. So they passed through the wall in safety. Outside of it Rachel paused a moment, looking this way and that. Then of a sudden she turned and walked swiftly towards the south.

It was dark, densely dark in the forest, yet she never seemed to lose her path. Holding Noie by the hand she wound in and out between the tree-trunks without stumbling or even striking her foot against a root. For an hour or more they walked on this, the strangest of strange journeys, till at length Rachel whispered;

"Something tells me to stay here," and she leaned against a tree and stayed, while Noie, who was tired, sat down between the jutting roots of the tree.

It was a dead tree, and the top of it had been torn off in some hurricane so that they could see the sky above them, and by the grey hue of it knew that it was drawing near to dawn.

The sun rose, and its arrows, that even at midday could never pass the canopy of foliage, shot straight and vivid between the tall bare trunks. Oh! Rachel knew the place. It was that place which she had dreamed of as a child in the island of the flooded river. Just so had the light of the rising sun fallen on the boles of the great trees, and on her white cloak and out-spread hair, fallen on her and on another. She strained her eyes into the gloom. Now those rays pierced it also, and now by them she saw the yellow-bearded, half-naked man of that long-dead dream leaning against the tree. His eyes were shut, without doubt he was dead, this was but a vision of him who had drawn her hither to share his death. It was the spirit of Richard Darrien!

She drew a little nearer, and the eyes opened, gazing at her. Also from that form of his was cast a long shadow—there it lay upon the dead leaves. How came it, she wondered, that a spirit could throw a shadow, and why was a spirit bound to a tree, as now she perceived he was? He saw her, and in those grey eyes of his there came a wonderful look. He spoke.

"You have drawn me from far, Rachel, but I have never seen all of you before, only your face floating in the air before me, although others saw you. Now I see you also, so I suppose that my time has come. It will soon be over. Wait a little there, where I can look at you, and presently we shall be together again. I am glad."

Rachel could not speak. A lump rose in her throat and choked her. Betwixt fear and hope her heart stood still. Only with the spear in her hand she pointed at her own shadow thrown by the level rays of the rising sun. He looked, and notwithstanding the straitness of his bonds she saw him start.

"If you are a ghost why have you a shadow?" he asked hoarsely. "And if you are not a ghost, how did you come into this haunted place?"

Still Rachel did not seem to be able to speak. Only she glided up to him and kissed him on the lips. Now at length he understood—they both understood that they were still living creatures beneath the sky, not the denizens of some dim world which lies beyond.

"Free me," he said in a faint voice, for his brain reeled. "I was bound here in my sleep. They will be back presently."

Her intelligence awoke. With a few swift cuts of the spear she held Rachel severed his bonds, then picked up his own *assegai* that lay at his feet she thrust it into his numbed hand. As he took it the forest about them seemed to become alive, and from behind the boles of the trees around appeared a number of dwarfs who ran towards them, headed by Eddo. Noie sprang forward also, and stood at their side. Rachel turned on Eddo swiftly as a startled deer. She seemed to tower over him, the spear in her hand.

"What does this mean, Priest?" she asked.

"*Inkosazana*," he answered humbly, "it means that I have found a way to tempt thee from within the Wall where none might break thy sanctuary. Thou drewest this man to thee from far with the strength that old Nya gave thee. We knew it all, we saw it all, and we waited. Day by day in our bowls of dew we watched him coming nearer to thee. We heard the messages of Nya on the drums, bidding the Umkulu meet and escort him; we heard the last answering message from the borders of the desert, telling her that he was nigh. Then while he followed his magic path through the darkness of the forest we seized and bound him, knowing well that if he could not come to thee, thou wouldst come to him. And thou hast come."

"I understand. What now, Eddo?"

"This, *Inkosazana*: Thou hast been named Mother of the Trees by the people of the Dwarfs; be pleased to come with us that we may install thee in thy great office."

"This lord here," said Rachel, "is my promised husband. What of him?"

Eddo bowed and smiled, a fearful smile, and answered:

"The Mother of the Trees has no husband. Wisdom is her husband. He has served his purpose, which was to draw thee from within the Wall, and for this reason only we permitted him to enter the holy forest living. Now he bides here to die, and since he has won thy love we will honour him with the White Death. Bind him to the tree again."

In an instant the spear that Rachel held was at Eddo's throat.

"Dwarf," she cried, "this is my man, and I am no Mother of Trees and no pale ghost, but a living woman. Let but one of these monkeys of thine lay a hand upon him, and thou diest, by the Red Death, Eddo, aye, by the Red Death. Stir a single inch, and this spear goes through thy heart, and thy spirit shall be spilled with thy blood."

The little priest sank to his knees trembling, glancing about him for a means of escape.

"If thou killest me, thou diest also," he hissed.

"What do I care if I die?" she answered. "If my man dies, I wish to die," then added in English: "Richard, take hold of him by one arm, and Noie, take the other. If he tries to escape kill him at once, or if you are afraid, I will."

So they seized him by his arms.

"Now," said Rachel, "let us go back to the Sanctuary, for there they dare not touch, us. We cannot try the desert without water; also they would follow and kill us with their poisoned arrows. Tell them, Noie, that if they do not attempt to harm us, we will set this priest of theirs free within the Wall. But if a hand is lifted against us, then he dies at once—by the Red Death,"

"Touch them not, touch them not," piped Eddo, "lest my ghost should be spilt with my blood. Touch them not, I command you."

The company of dwarfs chattered together like parrots at the dawn, and the march began. First went Eddo, dragged along between Richard and Noie, and after them, the raised spear in her hand, followed Rachel, while on either side, hiding themselves behind the boles of the trees, scrambled the people of the dwarfs. Back they went thus through the forest, Rachel telling them the road till at length the huge grey wall loomed up before them. They came to the slit in it, and Noie asked:

"What shall we do now? Kill this priest, take him in with us as a hostage, or let him go?"

"I said that he should be set free," answered Rachel, "and he would do us more harm dead than living; also his blood would be on our hands. Take him through the Wall, and loose him there."

So once more they passed the slopes and passages, while the mutes above watched them from their stones with marvelling eyes, till they reached the open space beyond, and there they loosed Eddo. The priest sprang back out of reach of the dreaded spears, and in a voice thick with rage, cried to them:

"Fools! You should have killed me while you could, for now you are in a trap, not I. You are strong and great, but you cannot live without food. We may not enter here to hurt you, but you shall starve, you shall starve until you creep out and beg my mercy."

Then making signs to the dwarfs who sat about above, he vanished between the stones.

"You should have killed him, Zoola," said Noie, "for now he will live to kill us."

"I think not, Sister," answered Rachel. "Nya said that I should follow my heart, and my heart bid me let him go. Our hands are clean of his blood, but if he had died, who can tell? Blood is a bad seed to sow."

Then, forgetting Eddo, she turned to Richard and began to ply him with questions.

But he seemed to be dazed and could answer little. It was as though some unnatural, supporting strength had been withdrawn, and now all the fatigues of his fearful journey were taking effect upon him. He could scarcely stand, but reeled to and fro like a man in drink, so that the two women were obliged to support him across the burial ground towards the cave. Advancing thus they entered into the shadow of the Holy Tree, and there at the edge of it met another procession descending from the mound. Eight mutes bore a litter of boughs, and on it lay Nya, dead, her long white hair hanging down on either side of the litter. With bowed heads they stood aside to let her pass to the grave made ready for her in a place of honour near the Wall where for a thousand years only the Mothers of the Trees had been laid to rest.

Then they went on, and entered the cave where the lamps burned before the great stalactite and the heap of offerings that were piled about it. Here sat the two women priests gazing into their bowls as they had left them. The death of Nya had not moved them, the advent of this white man did not seem to move them. Perhaps they expected him; at any rate food was made ready, and a bed of rugs prepared on which he could lie.

Richard ate some of the food, staring at Rachel all the while with vacant eyes as though she were still but a vision, the figment of a dream. Then he muttered something about being very tired, and sinking back upon the rugs fell into a deep sleep.

In that sleep he remained scarcely stirring for full four-and-twenty hours, while Rachel watched by his side, till at length her weariness overcame her, and she slept also. When she opened her eyes again they saw no other light than that which crept in from the mouth of the cave. The lamps which always burned there were out. Noie, who was seated near by, heard her stir, and spoke.

"If thou art rested, Zoola," she said, "I think that we had better carry the white lord from this place, for the two witch-women have gone, and I can find no more oil to fill the lamps."

So they felt their way to Richard, purposing to lift him between them, but at Rachel's touch he awoke, and with their help walked out of the cave. In the open space beyond they saw a strange sight, for across it were streaming all the dwarf-mutes carrying their aged and sick and infants, and bearing on their backs or piled up in litters their mats and cooking utensils. Evidently they were deserting the Sanctuary.

"Why are they going?" asked Rachel.

"I do not know," answered Noie, "but I think it is because no food has been brought to them as usual, and they are hungry. You remember that Eddo said we should starve. Only fear of death by hunger would make them leave a place where they and their forefathers have lived for generations."

Presently they were all gone. Not a living creature was left within the Wall except these three, nor were any more dwarfs brought in to die beneath the Holy Tree. Now, at length Richard seemed to awake, and taking Rachel by the hand began to ask questions of her in a low stammering voice, since words did not seem to come readily to him who had not spoken his own language for so long.

"Before you begin to talk, Sister," broke in Noie, "let us go and see if we can close the cleft in the Wall, for otherwise how shall we sleep in peace? Eddo and the dwarfs might creep in by night and murder us."

"I do not think they dare shed blood in their Holy Place," answered Rachel. "Still, let us see what we can do; it may be best."

So they went to the cleft, and as the stone door was open and they could not shut it, at one very narrow spot they rolled down rocks from the loose sides of the ancient wall above in such a fashion that it would be difficult to pass through or over them from without. This hard task took them many hours, moreover, it was labour wasted, since, as

Rachel had thought probable, the dwarfs never tried to pass the Wall, but waited till hunger forced them to surrender.

Towards evening they returned to the cave and collected what food they could find. It was but little, enough for two spare meals, no more; nor could they discover any in the town of the dwarfs behind the Tree. Only of water they had plenty from the stream that ran out of the cave.

They ate a few mouthfuls, then took their mats and cloaks and went to camp by the opening in the wall, so that they might guard against surprise. Now for the first time they found leisure to talk, and Rachel and Richard told each other a little of their wonderful stories. But they did not tell them all, for their minds seemed to be bewildered, and there was much that they were not able to explain. It was enough for them to know that they had been brought together again thus marvellously, by what power they knew not, and that still living, they who for long weeks had deemed the other dead, were able to hold each other's hands and gaze into each other's eyes. Moreover, now that this had been brought about they were tired, so tired that they could scarcely speak above a whisper. The end of it was that they fell asleep, all of them, and so slept till morning, when they awoke somewhat refreshed, and ate what remained of the food.

The second day was like the first, only hotter and more sultry. Noie climbed to the top of the wall to watch, while Richard and Rachel wandered about among the little, antheap-like graves, and through the dwarf village, talking and wondering, happy even in their wretchedness. But before the day was gone hunger began to get a hold of them; also the terrible, stifling heat oppressed them so that their words seemed to die between their lips, and they could only sit against the wall, looking at one another.

Towards evening Noie descended from the Wall and reported that large numbers of the dwarfs were keeping watch without, flitting to and fro between the trunks of the trees like shadows. The stifling night went by, and another day dawned. Having no food they went to the stream and drank water. Then they sat down in the shadow and waited through the long hot hours. Towards evening, when it grew a little cooler, they gathered up their strength and tried to find some way of escape before it was too late. Richard suggested that as flight was impossible they should give themselves up to the dwarfs, but Rachel answered No, for then Eddo would certainly kill him and Noie, and take her to fill the place of Mother of the Trees until she became useless to him, when she would be murdered also.

"Then there is nothing left for us but to die," said Richard.

"Nothing but to die," she answered, "to die together; and, dear, that should not be so hard, seeing that for so long we have thought each other dead apart."

"Yet it is hard," answered Richard, "after living through so much and being led so far to die at last and go whither we know not, before our time."

Rachel looked at Noie, who sat opposite to them, her head rested on her hand.

"Have you anything to say, Sister?" she asked.

"Yes, Zoola. Here is a little moss that I have found upon the stones," and she produced a small bundle. "Let us boil it and eat, it will keep us alive for another day."

"What is the use?" asked Rachel, "unless there is more."

"There is no more," said Noie, "for the leaves of yonder tree are deadly poison, and here grows no other living thing. Still, eat and live on, for I wait a message."

"A message from whom?" asked Rachel.

"A message from the dead, Sister. It was promised to me by Nya before she passed, and if it does not come, then it will be time to die."

So they made fire and boiled the moss till it was a horrible, sticky substance, which they swallowed as best they could, washing it down with gulps of water. Still it was food of a kind, and for a while stayed the gnawing, empty pains within them; only Noie ate but little, so that there might be more for the others.

That night was even hotter than those that had gone before, and during the day which followed the place became like a hell. They crept into the cave and lay there gasping, while from without came loud cracking sounds, caused, as they thought, by the trees of the forest splitting in the heat. About midday the sky suddenly became densely overcast, although no breath stirred; the air was thicker than ever, to breathe it was like breathing hot cream. In their restless despair they wandered out of the cave, and to their surprise saw a dwarf standing upon the top of the wall. It was Eddo, who called to them to come out and give themselves up.

"What are the terms?" asked Noie.

"That thou and the Wanderer shall die by the White Death, and that the *Inkosazana* shall be installed Mother of the Trees," was the answer.

"We refuse them," said Noie. "Let us go now and give us food and escort, and thou shall be spared. Refuse, and it is thou and thy people who will die by that Red Death which Nya promised thee."

"That we shall learn before tomorrow," said Eddo with a mocking laugh, and vanished down the wall.

As he went a hot gust of wind burst upon them, causing the forest without to rock and groan. Noie turned her face towards it and seemed to listen.

"What is it?" asked Rachel.

"I heard a voice in the wind, Sister," she answered. "The message I awaited has come to me."

"What message?" asked Richard listlessly.

"That I will tell you by and by, Chief," she answered. "Come to the cave, it is no longer safe here, the hurricane breaks."

So supporting each other they crept back to the cave, and there Noie made fire, feeding it with the idols and precious woods that had been brought thither as offerings. Richard and Rachel watched her wondering, for it seemed strange that she should make a fire in that heat where there was nothing to cook. Meanwhile gust succeeded gust, until a tempest of screaming wind swept over them, though no rain fell. Soon it was so fierce that the deep-rooted Tree of the Tribe rocked above them, and loose stones were blown from the crest of the great wall.

Then of a sudden Noie sprang up, and seized a flaming brand from the fire; it was the limb of a fetish, made of some resinous wood. She ran from the cave swiftly, before they could stop her, and vanished in the gathering gloom, to return again in a few moments weak and breathless. "Come out, now," she said, "and see a sight such as you shall never behold again," and there was something so strange in her voice that, notwithstanding their weakness, they rose and followed her.

Outside the cave they could not stand because of the might of the hurricane, but cast themselves upon the ground, and following Noie's outstretched arm, looked up towards the top of the mound. Then they saw that the Tree of the Tribe was *on fire*. Already its vast trunk and boughs were wrapped in flame, which burnt furiously because of the resin within them, while long flakes of blazing moss were being swept away to leeward, to fall among the forest that lay beyond the wall.

"Did you do this?" cried Rachel to Noie.

"Aye, Zoola, who else? That was the message which came to me. Now my office is fulfilled, but you two will live though I must die, I who have destroyed the People of the Dwarfs; I who was born that I should destroy them."

"Destroyed them!" exclaimed Rachel. "What do you mean?"

"I mean that when their Tree dies, they die, the whole race of them. Oh! Nya told me, Nya told me—they die as their Tree dies, by fire. To the Wall, to the Wall now, and look. Follow me."

Forgetting their hunger-bred weakness in the wild excitement of that moment, Rachel and Richard struggled hand in hand, after Noie's thin, ethereal form. Across the open space they struggled, through the furious bufferings of the gale, sometimes on their feet, sometimes on their hands and knees, till they came to the great wall where a stairway ran up it to an outlook tower. Up this stair they climbed slowly since at times the weight of the wind pinned them against the blocks of stone, till at length they reached its crest and crept into the shelter of the hollow tower. Hence, looking through the loopholes in the ancient masonry, they saw a fearful sight. The flakes of burning moss from the Tree of the Tribe had fallen among the tops of the forest, parched almost to tinder with drought and heat, and fired them here and there. Fanned by the screaming gale the flames spread rapidly, leaping from tree to tree, now in one direction, now in another, as the hurricane veered, which it did continually, till the whole green forest became a sheet of fire, an ever-widening sheet which spread east and west and north and south for miles and miles and tens of miles.

Earth and sky were one blaze of light given out by the torch-like resinous trees as they burned from the top downwards. By that intense light the three watchers could see hundreds of the People of the Dwarfs flitting about between the trunks. Waving their arms and gibbering, they rushed this way and that, to the north to be met by fire, to the south to be met by fire, till at length the blazing boughs and boles fell upon them and they disappeared in showers of red sparks, or, more fortunate, fled away, never to return, before the flame that leapt after them. One company of them ran towards the Sanctuary; they could see them threading their path between the trees, and growing ever fewer as the burning branches fell among them from above. They leapt, they ran, they battled, springing this way and that, but ever the great flaring boughs crashed down among them, crushing them, shrivelling them up, till at length of all their number but a single man staggered into the open belt between the edge of the forest and the wall. His white hair and his garments seemed to be smouldering. He gripped at them with his hands, then coming to a little bush—it was the top of Nya's tree which she had thrust into the ground to grow there—dragged it up and began to beat himself with it as though to extinguish the flames. In an instant it took fire also, burning him horribly, so that with a yell he threw it to the ground, and ran on towards the wall. As he came they saw his face. It was that of Eddo.

At this moment, seized by some sudden weakness, Noie sank down upon the stones. Richard bent over her to lift her to her feet again, but she thrust him away, saying slowly and in gasps:

"Let me be, the doom has hold of me, I am dying. I passed within the Fence to fire the Tree, and its poison is at work within me, and the curse of all my people has fallen on my head. Yet I have saved thee, my sister, I have saved thee and thy lover, for the Dwarfs are no more, the Grey People are grey ashes. For my love's sake I did the sin; let my love atone the sin if it may, or at the least think kindly of me through the long, happy years that are to come, and at the end of them then seek for lost Noie in the World of Ghosts if she may be found there."

As she spoke they heard a sound of something scrambling among the stones, and at one of the four entrances of the turret there appeared a hideous, fire-twisted face, and a little form about which hung charred and smouldering strips of raiment. It was Eddo, who had climbed the wall and found them out. There he sat glowering at them, or rather at Noie, who was crouched upon the floor.

"Come hither, daughter of Seyapi," he screamed in his hissing, snake-like voice, "come hither, and see thy work, thou who hast made an end of the ancient People of the Ghosts. Come hither and tell me why thou didst this thing, for I would learn the truth before I die, that I may make report of it to the Fathers of our race."

Noie heard, and crept towards him; to Rachel and Richard it seemed as though she could not disobey that summons. Now they sat face to face outside the turret, clinging to the stones, and her long hair flowed outwards on the gale.

"I did it, Eddo," she said, "to save one whom I love, and him whom she loves. I did it to avenge the death of Nya upon you all, as she bade me to do. I did it because the cup of thy wickedness is full, and because I was appointed to bring thy doom upon thee. Thus ends the greatness thou hast plotted so many years to win, Eddo."

"Aye," he answered, "thus it ends, for the magic of the White One there has overcome me, and thus with it ends the reign of the Ghost Kings, and the forest wherein they reigned, and thus too, thou endest, traitress, who hast murdered them and whose soul shall be spilt with their souls."

As the words left his lips suddenly Eddo sprang upon Noie and gripped her about the middle. Richard and Rachel leapt forward, but before ever they could lay a hand upon her to save her, the dwarf in his rage and agony had dragged her to the edge of the wall. For a moment they struggled there in the vivid light of the flaming forest. Then Eddo screamed aloud, one wild savage shriek, and still holding Noie in his arms hurled himself from the wall, to fall crushed upon its foundation stones sixty feet beneath.

Thus perished Noie, who, for love's sake, gave her life to save Rachel, as once Rachel had saved her.

********

It was morning, and after the tempest the sky was clear and cool, for heavy rain had fallen when the wind dropped, although far away the dense clouds of rolling smoke showed where the great fire still ate into the heart of the forest. Rachel and Richard, seated hand in hand in the little tower on the wall, looked at one another in that pure light, and saw signs in each other's face that could not be mistaken.

"What shall we do?" asked Richard. "Death is very near to us."

Rachel thought awhile, then answered:

"The dwarfs are gone, we have nothing more to fear from them. Yonder where the fire did not burn, dwell their slaves, whose villages are full of food, and beyond them live the Umkulu, who know and would befriend me. Let us go and seek food who desire to live on together, if we may."

So they climbed down the wall, and with difficulty, for they were very feeble, crawled over the stones which they had piled up in the passage to keep out the dwarfs, and thus passed to the open belt beyond. A strange scene met their eyes, all the wide lands that had been covered with giant trees were now piled over with white ashes amongst which, here and there, stood a black and smouldering trunk. The journey was terrible, but following a ridge of rock whereon no great trees had grown, hand in hand they passed through the outer edge of the burnt forest in safety, until they came to one of the towns of the slaves upon the fertile plain beyond, which led up to the desert. No human being could they see, since all had fled, but the *kraal* was full of sheep and cattle that had been penned there before the fire began, and in the huts were milk and food in plenty. They drank of the milk and, after a while, ate a little, then rested and drank more milk, till their strength began to return to them. Towards evening they went out of the town, and standing on a mound looked at the fire-wasted plain behind, and the green, grassy slopes in front.

They seemed quite alone in the world, those two, and yet their hearts were full of joy and thankfulness, for while they were left to each other they knew that they could never be alone.

"See, Rachel," said Richard, pointing to the smouldering wreck of the forest, "there lies our past, and here in front of us spreads the future clothed with flowers."

"Yes, Richard," she answered, "but Noie and all whom I love save you are buried in that past, and in front of us the desert is not far away."

"Life is ours, Rachel, and love is ours, and that which saved us through many a danger and brought me back to you, will surely keep us safe. Do you fear to pass the desert at my side?"

She looked at him with shining eyes, and answered:

"No, Richard, I fear no more, for now I seem to hear the voice of Noie speaking in my heart, telling me that trouble is behind us, and that we shall live out our lives together, as my mother foresaw that we should do."

And there on the mound, standing between that dead sea of ashes and the green slopes of flowering plain, Rachel stretched out her arms to the man to whom she was decreed.

# The Yellow Idol

## Chapter 1

# Sahara Limited

Sir Robert Aylward, Bart., M.P., sat in his office in the City of London. It was a very magnificent office, quite one of the finest that could be found within half a mile of the Mansion House. Its exterior was built of Aberdeen granite, a material calculated to impress the prospective investor with a comfortable sense of security. Other stucco, or even brick-built, offices might crumble and fall in an actual or a financial sense, but this rock-like edifice of granite, surmounted by a life-sized statue of Justice with her scales, admired from either corner by pleasing effigies of Commerce and of Industry, would surely endure any shock. Earthquake could scarcely shake its strong foundations; panic and disaster would as soon affect the Bank of England. That at least was the impression which it had been designed to convey, and not without success.

"There is so much in externals," Mr. Champers-Haswell, Sir Robert's partner, would say in his cheerful voice. "We are all of us influenced by them, however unconsciously. Impress the public, my dear Aylward. Let solemnity without suggest opulence within, and the bread, or rather the granite, which you throw upon the waters will come back to you after many days."

Mr. Aylward, for this conversation occurred before his merits or the depth of his purse had been rewarded by a baronetcy, looked at his partner in the impassive fashion for which he was famous, and answered:

"You mix your metaphors, Haswell, but if you mean that the public are fools who must be caught by advertisement, I agree with you. Only this particular advertisement is expensive and I do not want to wait many days for my reward. However, £20,000 one way or the other is a small matter, so tell that architect to do the thing in granite."

Sir Robert Aylward sat in his own quiet room at the back of this enduring building, a very splendid room that any Secretary of State might have envied, but arranged in excellent taste. Its walls were panelled with figured teak, a rich carpet made the footfall noiseless, an antique Venus stood upon a marble pedestal in the corner, and over the mantelpiece hung a fine portrait by Gainsborough, that of a certain Miss Aylward, a famous beauty in her day, with whom, be it added, its present owner could boast no connection whatsoever.

Sir Robert was seated at his ebony desk playing with a pencil, and the light from a cheerful fire fell upon his face.

In its own way it was a remarkable face, as he appeared then in his fourth and fortieth year; very pale but with a natural pallor, very well cut and on the whole impressive. His eyes were dark, matching his black hair and pointed beard, and his nose was straight and rather prominent. Perhaps the mouth was his weakest feature, for there was a certain shiftiness about it, also the lips were thick and slightly sensuous. Sir Robert knew this, and therefore he grew a moustache to veil them somewhat. To a careful observer the general impression given by this face was such as is left by the sudden sight of a waxen mask. "How strong! How lifelike!" he would have said, "but of course it isn't real. There may be a man behind, or there may be wood, but that's only a mask." Many people of perception had felt like this about Sir Robert Aylward, namely, that under the mask of his pale countenance dwelt a different being whom they did not know or appreciate.

If these had seen him at this moment of the opening of our story, they might have held that Wisdom was justified of her children. For now in the solitude of his splendid office, of a sudden Sir Robert's mask seemed to fall from him. His face broke up like ice beneath a thaw. He rose from his table and began to walk up and down the room. He talked to himself aloud.

"Great Heavens!" he muttered, "what a game to have played, and it will go through. I believe that it will go through."

He stopped at the table, switched on an electric light and made a rapid calculation on the back of a letter with a blue pencil.

"Yes," he said, "that's my share, a million and seventeen thousand pounds in cash, and two million in ordinary shares which can be worked off at a discount—let us say another seven hundred and fifty thousand, plus what I have got already—put that at only two hundred and fifty thousand net. Two millions in all, which of course may or may not be added to, probably not, unless the ordinaries boom, for I don't mean to speculate any more. That's the end of twenty years' work, Robert Aylward. And to think of it, eighteen months ago, although I seemed so rich, I was on the verge of bankruptcy—the very verge, not worth five thousand pounds. Now what did the trick? I wonder what did the trick?"

He walked down the room and stopped opposite the ancient marble, staring at it—

"Not Venus, I think," he said, with a laugh, "Venus never made any man rich." He turned and retraced his steps to the other end of the room, which was veiled in shadow. Here upon a second marble pedestal stood an object that gleamed dimly through the gloom. It was about ten inches or a foot high, but in that place nothing more could be seen of it, except that it was yellow and had the general appearance of a toad. For some reason it seemed to attract Sir Robert Aylward, for he halted to stare at it, then stretched out his hand and switched on another lamp, in the hard brilliance of which the thing upon the pedestal suddenly declared itself, leaping out of the darkness into light. It was a terrible object, a monstrosity of indeterminate sex and nature, but surmounted by a woman's head and face of extraordinary, if devilish loveliness, sunk back between high but grotesquely small shoulders, like to those of a lizard, so that it glared upwards. The workmanship of the thing was rude yet strangely powerful. Whatever there is cruel, whatever there is devilish, whatever there is inhuman in the dark places of the world, shone out of the jewelled eyes which were set in that yellow female face, yellow because its substance was of gold, a face which seemed not to belong to the embryonic legs beneath, for body there was none, but to float above them. A hollow, life-sized mask with two tiny frog-like legs, that was the fashion of it.

"You are an ugly brute," muttered Sir Robert, contemplating this effigy, "but although I believe in nothing in heaven above or earth below, except the abysmal folly of the British public, I am bothered if I don't believe in you. At any rate from the day when Vernon brought you into my office, my luck turned, and to judge from the smile on your sweet countenance, I don't think it is done with yet. I wonder what those stones are in your eyes. Opals, I suppose, from the way they change colour. They shine uncommonly today, I never remember them so bright. I——"

At this moment a knock came on the door. Sir Robert turned off the lamp and walked back to the fireplace.

"Come in," he said, and as he spoke once more his pale face grew impassive and expressionless.

The door opened and a clerk entered, an imposing-looking clerk with iron-grey hair, who wore an irreproachable frock coat and patent leather boots. Advancing to his master, he stood respectfully silent, waiting to be addressed. For quite a long while Sir Robert looked over his head as though he did not see him; it was a way of his. Then his eyes rested on the man dreamily and he remarked in his cold, clear voice:

"I don't think I rang, Jeffreys."

"No, Sir Robert," answered the clerk, bowing as though he spoke to Royalty, "but there is a little matter about that article in *The Cynic*."

"Press business," said Sir Robert, lifting his eyebrows; "you should know by this time that I do not attend to such details. See Mr. Champers-Haswell, or Major Vernon."

"They are both out at the moment, Sir Robert."

"Go on, then, Jeffreys," replied the head of the firm with a resigned sigh, "only be brief. I am thinking."

The clerk bowed again.

"The *Cynic* people have just telephoned through about that article we sent them. I think you saw it, sir, and you may remember it begins——" and he read from a typewritten copy in his hand which was headed "Sahara Limited":

"'We are now privileged to announce that this mighty scheme which will turn a desert into a rolling sea bearing the commerce of nations and cause the waste places of the earth to teem with population and to blossom like the rose, has been completed in its necessary if dull financial details and will within a few days be submitted to investors among whom it has already caused so much excitement. These details we will deal with fully in succeeding articles, and therefore now need only pause to say that the basis of capitalization strikes us as wonderfully advantageous to the fortunate public who are asked to participate in its vast prospective prosperity. Our present object is to speak of its national and imperial aspects——'"

Sir Robert lifted his eyes in remonstrance:

"How much more of that exceedingly dull and commonplace puff do you propose to read, Jeffreys?" he asked.

"No more, Sir Robert. We are paying *The Cynic* thirty guineas to insert this article, and the point is that they say that if they have to put in the 'national and imperial' business they must have twenty more."

"Indeed, Jeffreys? Why?"

"Because, Sir Robert—I will tell you, as you always like to hear the truth—their advertisement-editor is of opinion that Sahara Limited is a national and imperial swindle. He says that he won't drag the nation and the empire into it in an editorial under fifty guineas."

A faint smile flickered on Sir Robert's face.

"Does he, indeed?" he asked. "I wonder at his moderation. Had I been in his place I should have asked more, for really the style is a little flamboyant. Well, we don't want to quarrel with them just now—feed the sharks. But surely, Jeffreys, you didn't come to disturb me about such a trifle?"

"Not altogether, Sir Robert. There is something more important. *The Daily Judge* not only declines to put any article whatsoever, but refuses our advertisement, and states that it means to criticize the prospectus trenchantly."

"Ah!" said his master after a moment's thought, "that *is* rather serious, since people believe in the *Judge* even when it is wrong. Offer them the advertisement at treble rates."

"It has been done, sir, and they still refuse."

Sir Robert walked to the corner of the room where the yellow object squatted on its pedestal, and contemplated it a while, as a man often studies one thing when he is thinking of another. It seemed to give him an idea, for he looked over his shoulder and said:

"That will do, Jeffreys. When Major Vernon comes in, give him my compliments and say that I should be obliged by a word or two with him."

The clerk bowed and went as noiselessly as he had entered.

"Let's see," added Sir Robert to himself. "Old Jackson, the editor of *The Judge*, was a great friend of Vernon's father, the late Sir William Vernon, G.C.B. I believe that he was engaged to be married to his sister years ago, only she died or something. So the Major ought to be able to get round him if anybody can. Only the worst of it is I don't altogether trust that young gentleman. It suited us to give him a share in the business because he is an engineer who knows the country, and this Sahara scheme was his notion, a very good one in a way, and for other reasons. Now he shows signs of kicking over the traces, wants to know too much, is developing a conscience, and so forth. As though the promoters of speculative companies had any business with consciences. Ah! here he comes."

Sir Robert seated himself at his desk and resumed his calculations upon a half-sheet of note-paper, and that moment a clear, hearty voice was heard speaking to the clerks in the outer office. Then came the sound of a strong, firm footstep, the door opened and Major Alan Vernon appeared.

He was still quite a young man, not more than thirty-two or three years of age, though he lacked the ultra robust and rubicund appearance which is typical of so many Englishmen of his class at this period of life. A heavy bout of blackwater fever acquired on service in West Africa, which would have killed anyone of weaker constitution, had robbed his face of its bloom and left it much sallower, if more interesting than once it had been. For in a way there was interest about the face; also a certain charm. It was a good and honest face with a rather eager, rather puzzled look, that of a man who has imagination and ideas and who searches for the truth but fails to find it. As for the charm, it lay for the most part in the pleasant, open smile and in the frank but rather round brown eyes overhung by a somewhat massive forehead which projected a little, or perhaps the severe illness already alluded to had caused the rest of the face to sink. Though thin, the man was bigly built, with broad shoulders and well-developed limbs, measuring a trifle under six feet in height.

Such was the outward appearance of Alan Vernon. As for his mind, it was able enough in certain fashions, for instance those of engineering, and the soldier-like faculties to which it had been trained; frank and kindly also, but in other respects not quick, perhaps from its unsuspiciousness. Alan Vernon was a man slow to discover ill and slower still to believe in it even when it seemed to be discovered, a weakness that may have gone far to account for his presence in the office of those eminent and brilliant financiers, Messrs. Aylward & Champers-Haswell. Just now he looked a little worried, like a fish out of water, or rather a fish which has begun to suspect the quality of the water, something in its smell or taste.

"Jeffreys tells me that you want to see me, Sir Robert," he said in his low and pleasant voice, looking at the baronet rather anxiously.

"Yes, my dear Vernon, I wish to ask you to do something, if you kindly will, although it is not quite in your line. Old Jackson, the editor of *The Judge*, is a friend of yours, isn't he?"

"He was a friend of my father's, and I used to know him slightly."

"Well, that's near enough. As I daresay you have heard, he is an unreasonable old beggar, and has taken a dislike to our Sahara scheme. Someone has set him against it and he refuses to receive advertisements, threatens criticisms, etc. Now the opposition of *The Judge* or any other paper won't kill us, and if necessary we can fight, but at the same time it is always wise to agree with your enemy while he is in the way, and in short—would you mind going down and explaining his mistake to him?"

Before answering Major Vernon walked to the window leisurely and looked out.

"I don't like asking favours from family friends," he replied at length, "and, as you said, I think it isn't quite my line. Though of course if it has anything to do with the engineering possibilities, I shall be most happy to see him," he added, brightening.

"I don't know what it has to do with; that is what I shall be obliged if you will find out," answered Sir Robert with some asperity. "One can't divide a matter of this sort into watertight compartments. It is true that in so important a concern each of us has charge of his own division, but the fact remains that we are jointly and severally responsible for the whole. I am not sure that you bear this sufficiently in mind, my dear Vernon," he added with slow emphasis.

His partner moved quickly; it might almost have been said that he shivered, though whether the movement, or the shiver, was produced by the argument of joint and several liability or by the familiarity of the "my dear Vernon," remains uncertain. Perhaps it was the latter, since although the elder man was a baronet and the younger only a retired Major of Engineers, the gulf between them, as any one of discernment could see, was wide. They were born, lived, and moved in different spheres unbridged by any common element or impulse.

"I think that I do bear it in mind, especially of late, Sir Robert," answered Alan Vernon slowly.

His partner threw a searching glance on him, for he felt that there was meaning in the words, but only said:

"That's all right. My motor is outside and will take you to Fleet Street in no time. Meanwhile you might tell them to telephone that you are coming, and perhaps you will just look in when you get back. I haven't got to go to the House tonight, so shall be here till dinner time, and so, I think, will your cousin Haswell. Muzzle that old bulldog, Jackson, somehow. No doubt he has his price like the rest of them, in meal or malt, and you needn't stick at the figure. We don't want him hanging on our throat for the next week or two."

Ten minutes later the splendid, two-thousand guinea motor brougham drew up at the offices of the *Judge* and the obsequious motor-footman bowed Major Vernon through its rather grimy doorway. Within, a small boy in a kind of box asked his business, and when he heard his name, said that the "Guvnor" had sent down word that he was go up at once—third floor, first to the right and second to the left. So up he went, and when he reached the indicated locality was taken possession of by a worried-looking clerk who had evidently been waiting for him, and almost thrust through a door to find himself in a big, worn, untidy room. At a huge desk in this room sat an elderly man, also big, worn, and untidy-looking, who waved a long slip of galley-proof in his hand, and was engaged in scolding a sub-editor.

"Who is that?" he said, wheeling round. "I'm busy, can't see anyone."

"I beg your pardon," answered the Major with humility, "your people told me to come up. My name is Alan Vernon."

"Oh! I remember. Sit down for a moment, will you, and—Mr. Thomas, oblige me by taking away this rot and rewriting it entirely in the sense I have outlined."

Mr. Thomas snatched his rejected copy and vanished through another door, whereon his chief remarked in an audible voice:

"That man is a perfect fool. Lucky I thought to look at his stuff. Well, he is no worse than the rest, in this weary world," and he burst into a hearty laugh and swung his chair round, adding, "Now then, Alan, what is it? I have a quarter of an hour at your service. Why, bless me! I was forgetting that it's more than a dozen years since we met; you were still a boy then, and now you have left the army with a D.S.O. and gratuity, and turned financier, which I think wouldn't have pleased your old father. Come, sit down here and let us talk."

"I didn't leave the army, Mr. Jackson," answered his visitor; "it left me; I was invalided out. They said I should never get my health back after that last go of fever, but I did."

"Ah! bad luck, very bad luck, just at the beginning of what should have been a big career, for I know they thought highly of you at the War Office, that is, if they can think. Well, you have grown into a fine-looking fellow, like your father, very, and someone else too," and he sighed, running his fingers through his grizzled hair. "But you don't remember her; she was before your time. Now let us get to business; there's no time for reminiscences in this office. What is it, Alan, for like other people I suppose that you want something?"

"It is about that Sahara flotation, Mr. Jackson," he began rather doubtfully.

The old editor's face darkened. "The Sahara flotation! That accursed——" and he ceased abruptly. "What have you, of all people in the world, got to do with it? Oh! I remember. Someone told me that you had gone into partnership with Aylward the company promoter, and that little beast, Champers-Haswell, who really is the clever one. Well, set it out, set it out."

"It seems, Mr. Jackson, that *The Judge* has refused not only our article, but also the advertisement of the company. I don't know much about this side of the affair myself, but Sir Robert asked me if I would come round and see if things couldn't be arranged."

"You mean that the man sent you to try and work on me because he knew that I used to be intimate with your family. Well, it is a poor errand and will have a poor end. You can't—no one on earth can, while I sit in this chair, not even my proprietors."

There was silence broken at last by Alan, who remarked awkwardly:

"If that is so, I must not take up your time any longer."

"I said that I would give you a quarter of an hour, and you have only been here four minutes. Now, Alan Vernon, tell me as your father's old friend, why you have gone to herd with these gilded swine?"

There was something so earnest about the man's question that it did not even occur to his visitor to resent its roughness.

"Of course it is not original," he answered, "but I had this idea about flooding the Desert; I spent a furlough up there a few years ago and employed my time in making some rough surveys. Then I was obliged to leave the Service and went down to Yarleys after my father's death—it's mine now, you know, but worth nothing except a shooting rent, which just pays for the repairs. There I met Champers-Haswell, who lives near and is a kind of distant cousin of mine—my mother was a Champers—and happened to mention the thing to him. He took it up at once and introduced me to Aylward, and the end of it was, that they offered me a partnership with a small share in the business, because they said I was just the man they wanted."

"Just the man they wanted," repeated the editor after him. "Yes, the last of the Vernons, an engineer with an old name in his county, a clean record and plenty of ability. Yes, you would be just the man they wanted. And you accepted?"

"Yes. I was on my beam ends with nothing to do; I wanted to make some money. You see Yarleys has been in the family for over five hundred years, and it seemed hard to have to sell it. Also—also——" and he paused.

"Ever meet Barbara Champers?" asked Mr. Jackson inconsequently. "I did once. Wonderfully nice girl, and very good-looking too. But of course you know her, and she is her uncle's ward, and their place isn't far off Yarleys, you say. Must be a connection of yours also."

Major Vernon started a little at the name and his face seemed to redden.

"Yes," he said, "I have met her and she is a connection."

"Will be a big heiress one day, I think," went on Mr. Jackson, "unless old Haswell makes off with her money. I think Aylward knows that; at any rate he was hanging about when I saw her."

Vernon started again, this time very perceptibly.

"Very natural—your going into the business, I mean, under all the circumstances," went on Mr. Jackson. "But now, if you will take my advice, you'll go out of it as soon as you can."

"Why?"

"Because, Alan Vernon, I am sure you don't want to see your name dragged in the dirt, any more than I do." He fumbled in a drawer and produced a typewritten document. "Take that," he said, "and study it at your leisure. It's a sketch of the financial career of Messrs. Aylward and Champers-Haswell, also of the companies which they have promoted and been connected with, and what has happened to them and to those who invested in them. A man got it out for me yesterday and I'm going to use it. As regards this Sahara business, you think it all right, and so it may be from an engineering point of view, but you will never live to sail upon that sea which the British public is going to be asked to find so many millions to make. Look here. We have only three minutes more, so I will come to the point at once. It's Turkish territory, isn't it, and putting aside everything else, the security for the whole thing is a Firman from the Sultan?"

"Yes, Sir Robert Aylward and Haswell procured it in Constantinople. I have seen the document."

"Indeed, and are you well acquainted with the Sultan's signature? I know when they were there last autumn that potentate was very ill——"

"You mean——" said Major Vernon, looking up.

"I mean, Alan, that I like not the security. I won't say any more, as there is a law of libel in this land. But *The Judge* has certain sources of information. It may be that no protest will be made at once, for baksheesh can stop it for a while, but sooner or later the protest or repudiation will come, and perhaps some international bother; also much scandal. As to the scheme itself, it is shamelessly over-capitalized for the benefit of the promoters—of whom, remember, Alan, you will appear as one. Now time's up. Perhaps you will take my advice, and perhaps you won't, but there it is for what it's worth as that of a man of the world and an old friend of your family. As for your puff article and your prospectus, I wouldn't put them in *The Judge* if you paid me a thousand pounds, which I daresay your friend, Aylward, would be quite ready to do. Goodbye. Come and see me again sometime, and tell me what has happened—and, I say"—this last was shouted through the closing door,—"give my kind regards to Miss Barbara, for wherever she happens to live, she is an honest woman."

## Chapter 2

# The Yellow God

Alan Vernon walked thoughtfully down the lead-covered stairs, hustled by eager gentlemen hurrying up to see the great editor, whose bell was already ringing furiously, and was duly ushered by the obsequious assistant-chauffeur back into the luxurious motor. There was an electric lamp in this motor, and by the light of it, his mind being perplexed, he began to read the typewritten document given to him by Mr. Jackson, which he still held in his hand.

As it chanced they were blocked for a quarter of an hour near the Mansion House, so that he found time, if not to master it, at least to gather enough of its contents to make him open his brown eyes very wide before the motor pulled up at the granite doorway of his office. Alan descended from the machine, which departed silently, and stood for a moment wondering what he should do. His impulse was to jump into a bus and go straight to his rooms or his club, to which Sir Robert did not belong, but being no coward, he dismissed it from his mind.

His fate hung in the balance, of that he was well aware. Either he must disregard Mr. Jackson's warning, confirmed as it was by many secret fears and instincts of his own, and say nothing except that he had failed in his mission, or he must take the bull by the horns and break with the firm. To do the latter meant not only a good deal of moral courage, but practical ruin, whereas if he chose the former course, probably within a fortnight he would find himself a rich man. Whatever Jackson and a few others might say in its depreciation, he was certain that the Sahara flotation would go through, for it was underwritten, of course upon terms, by responsible people, moreover the unissued preferred shares had already been dealt in at a heavy premium. Now to say nothing of the allotment to which he was entitled upon his holding in the parent Syndicate, the proportion of cash due to him as a partner, would amount to quite a hundred thousand pounds. In other words, he, who had so many reasons for desiring money, would be wealthy. After working so hard and undergoing so much that he felt to be humiliating and even degrading, why should he not take his reward and clear out afterwards?

This he remembered he could do, since probably by some oversight of Aylward's, who left such matters to his lawyers, his deed of partnership did not bind him to a fixed term. It could be broken at any moment. To this argument there was only one possible answer, that of his conscience. If once he were convinced that things were not right, it would be dishonest to participate in their profits. And he was convinced. Mr. Jackson's arguments and his damning document had thrown a flood of light upon many matters which he had suspected but never quite understood. He was the partner of, well, adventurers, and the money which he received would in fact be filched from the pockets of unsuspecting persons. He would vouch for that of which he was doubtful and receive the price of sharp practice. In other words he, Alan Vernon, who had never uttered a wilful untruth or taken a halfpenny that was not his own, would before the tribunal of his own mind, stand convicted as a liar and a thief. The thing was not to be borne. At whatever cost it must be ended. If he were fated to be a beggar, at least he would be an honest beggar.

With a firm step and a high head he walked straight into Sir Robert's room, without even going through the formality of knocking, to find Mr. Champers-Haswell seated at the ebony desk by his partner's side examining some document through a reading-glass, which on his appearance, was folded over and presently thrust away into a drawer. It seemed, Alan noticed, to be of an unusual shape and written in some strange character.

Mr. Haswell, a stout, jovial-looking, little man with a florid complexion and white hair, rose at once to greet him.

"How do you do, Alan," he said in a cheerful voice, for as a cousin by marriage he called him by his Christian name. "I am just this minute back from Paris, and you will be glad to learn that they are going to support us very well there; in fact I may say that the Government has taken up the scheme, of course under the rose. You know the French have possessions all along that coast and they won't be sorry to find an opportunity of stretching out their hand a little further. Our difficulties as to capital are at an end, for a full third of it is guaranteed in Paris, and I expect that small investors and speculators for the rise will gobble a lot more. We shall plant £10,000,000 worth of Sahara scrip in sunny France, my boy, and foggy England has underwritten the rest. It will be a case of 'letters of Allotment and regret,' *and* regret, Alan, financially the most successful issue of the last dozen years. What do you say to that?" and in his elation the little man puffed out his chest and pursing up his lips, blew through them, making a sound like that of wind among wires.

"I don't know, Mr. Haswell. If we are all alive I would prefer to answer the question twelve months hence, or later, when we see whether the company is going to be a practical success as well, or not."

Again Mr. Haswell made the sound of wind among wires, only this time there was a shriller note in it; its mellowness was gone, it was as though the air had suddenly been filled with frost.

"A practical success!" he repeated after him. "That is scarcely our affair, is it? Promoters should not bother themselves with long views, Alan. These may be left to the investing public, the speculative parson and the maiden lady who likes a flutter—those props of modern enterprise. But what do you mean? You originated this idea and always said that the profits should be great."

"Yes, Mr. Haswell, on a moderate capitalization and provided that we are sure of the co-operation of the Porte."

Mr. Haswell looked at him very searchingly and Sir Robert, who had been listening, said in his cold voice:

"I think that we thrashed out these points long ago, and to tell you the truth I am rather tired of them, especially as it is too late to change anything. How did you get on with Jackson, Vernon?"

"I did not get on at all, Sir Robert. He will not touch the thing on any terms, and indeed means to oppose it tooth and nail."

"Then he will find himself in a minority when the articles come out tomorrow. Of course it is a bore, but we are strong enough to snap our fingers at him. You see they don't read *The Judge* in France, and no one has ever heard of it in Constantinople. Therefore we have nothing to fear—so long as we stick together," he added meaningly.

Alan felt that the crisis had come. He must speak now or for ever hold his peace; indeed Aylward was already looking round for his hat.

"Sir Robert and Mr. Haswell," he broke in rather nervously, "I have something to say to you, something unpleasant," and he paused.

"Then please say it at once, Vernon. I want to dress for dinner, I am going to the theatre tonight and must dine early," replied Aylward in a voice of the utmost unconcern.

"It is, Sir Robert," went on Alan with a rush, "that I do not like the lines upon which this business is being worked, and I wish to give up my interest in it and retire from the firm, as I have a right to do under our deed of partnership."

"Have you?" said Aylward. "Really, I forget. But, my dear fellow, do not think that we should wish to keep you for one moment against your will. Only, might I ask, has that old puritan, Jackson, hypnotized you, or is it a case of sudden madness after influenza?"

"Neither," answered Alan sternly, for although he might be diffident on matters that he did not thoroughly understand, he was not a man to brook trifling or impertinence. "It is what I have said, no more nor less. I am not satisfied either as to the capitalization or as to the guarantee that the enterprise can be really carried out. Further"—and he paused,—"Further, I should like what I have never yet been able to obtain, more information as to that Firman under which the concession is granted."

For one moment a sort of tremor passed over Sir Robert's impassive countenance, while Mr. Haswell uttered his windy whistle, this time in a tone of plaintive remonstrance.

"As you have formally resigned your membership of the firm, I do not see that any useful purpose can be served by discussing such matters. The fullest explanations, of course, we should have been willing to give——"

"My dear Alan," broke in Mr. Champers-Haswell, who was quite upset, "I do implore you to reflect for one moment, for your own sake. In a single week you would have been a wealthy man; do you really mean to throw away everything for a whim?"

"Perhaps Vernon remembers that he holds over 1700 of the Syndicate shares which we have worked up to £18, and thinks it wiser to capture the profit in sight, generally speaking a very sound principle," interrupted Aylward sarcastically.

"You are mistaken, Sir Robert," replied Alan, flushing. "The way that those shares have been artificially put up is one of the things to which I most object. I shall only ask for mine the face value which I paid for them."

Now notwithstanding their experience, both of the senior partners did for a moment look rather scared. Such folly, or such honesty, was absolutely incredible to them. They felt that there must be much behind. Sir Robert, however, recovered instantly.

"Very well," he said; "it is not for us to dictate to you; you must make your own bed and lie on it. To argue or remonstrate would only be rude." He put out his hand and pushed the button of an electric bell, adding as he did so, "Of course we understand one thing, Vernon, namely, that as a gentleman and a man of honour you will make no public use of the information which you have acquired during your stay in this office, either to our detriment, personal or financial, or to your own advantage."

"Certainly you may understand that," replied Vernon. "Unless my character is attacked and it becomes necessary for me to defend myself, my lips are sealed."

"That will never happen—why should it?" said Sir Robert with a polite bow.

The door opened and the head clerk, Jeffreys, appeared.

"Mr. Jeffreys," said Sir Robert, "please find us the deed of partnership between Major Vernon and ourselves, and bring it here. One moment. Please make out also a transfer of Major Vernon's parcel of Sahara Syndicate shares to Mr. Champers-Haswell and myself at par value, and fill in a cheque for the amount. Please remove also Major Vernon's name wherever it appears in the proof prospectus, and—yes—one thing more. Telephone to Specton—the Right Honourable the Earl of Specton, I mean, and say that after all I have been able to arrange that he shall have a seat on the Board and a block of shares at a very moderate figure, and that if he will wire his assent, his name shall be put into the prospectus. You approve, don't you, Haswell?—yes—then that is all, I think, Jeffreys, only please be as quick as you can, for I want to get away."

Jeffreys, the immaculate and the impassive, bowed, and casting one swift glance at Vernon out of the corner of his eye, departed.

What is called an awkward pause ensued; in fact it was a very awkward pause. The die was cast, the matter ended, and what were the principals to do until the ratifications had been exchanged or, a better simile perhaps, the *decree nisi* pronounced absolute. Mr. Champers-Haswell remarked that the weather was very cold for April, and Alan agreed with him, while Sir Robert found his hat and brushed it with his sleeve. Then Mr. Haswell, in desperation, for in minor matters he was a kindly sort of man who disliked scenes and unpleasantness, muttered something as to seeing him—Alan—at his house, The Court, in Hertfordshire, from Saturday to Monday.

"That was the arrangement," answered Alan bluntly, "but possibly after what has happened you will not wish that it should be kept."

"Oh! why not, why not?" said Mr. Haswell. "Sunday is a day of rest when we make it a rule not to talk business, and if we did, perhaps we might all change our minds about these matters. Sir Robert is coming, and I am sure that your cousin Barbara will be very disappointed if you do not turn up, for she understands nothing about these city things which are Greek to her."

At the mention of the name of Barbara Sir Robert Aylward looked up from the papers which he affected to be tidying, and Alan thought that there was a kind of challenge in his eyes. A moment before he had made up his mind that no power on earth would induce him to spend a Sunday with his late partners at The Court. Now, acting upon some instinct or impulse, he reversed his opinion.

"Thanks," he said, "if that is understood, I shall be happy to come. I will drive over from Yarleys in time for dinner tomorrow. Perhaps you will say so to Barbara."

"She will be glad, I am sure," answered Mr. Haswell, "for she told me the other day that she wants to consult you about some outdoor theatricals that she means to get up in July."

"In July!" answered Alan with a little laugh. "I wonder where I shall be in July."

Then came another pause, which seemed to affect even Sir Robert's nerves, for abandoning the papers, he walked down the room till he came to the golden object that has been described, and for the second time that day stood there contemplating it.

"This thing is yours, Vernon," he said, "and now that our relations are at an end, I suppose that you will want to take it away. What is its history? You never told me."

"Oh! that's a long story," answered Alan in an absent voice. "My uncle, who was a missionary, brought it from West Africa. I rather forget the facts, but Jeekie, my negro servant, knows them all, for as a lad my uncle saved him from sacrifice, or something, in a place where they worship these things, and he has been with us ever since. It is a fetish with magical powers and all the rest of it. I believe they call it the Swimming Head and other names. If you look at it, you will see that it seems to swim between the shoulders, doesn't it?"

"Yes," said Sir Robert, "and I admire the beautiful beast. She is cruel and artistic, like—like finance. Look here, Vernon, we have quarrelled, and of course henceforth are enemies, for it is no use mincing matters, only fools do that. But in a way you are being hardly treated. You could get £10 apiece today for those shares of yours in a block on the market, and I am paying you £1. I understand your scruples, but there is no reason why we should not square things. This fetish of yours has brought me luck, so let's do a deal. Leave it here, and instead of a check for £1700, I will make you one out for £17,000."

"That's a very liberal offer," said Vernon. "Give me a moment to think it over."

Then he also walked into the corner of the room and contemplated the golden mask that seemed to float between the frog-like shoulders. The shimmering eyes drew his eyes, though what he saw in them does not matter. Indeed he could never remember. Only when he straightened himself again there was left on his mind a determination that not for seventeen or for seventy thousand pounds would he part with his ownership in this very unique fetish.

"No, thank you," he said presently. "I don't think I will sell the Yellow God, as Jeekie calls it. Perhaps you will kindly keep her here for a week or so, until I make up my mind where to stow her."

Again Mr. Champers-Haswell uttered his windy whistle. That a man should refuse £17,000 for a bit of African gold worth £100 or so, struck him as miraculous. But Sir Robert did not seem in the least surprised, only very disappointed.

"I quite understand your dislike to selling," he said. "Thank you for leaving it here for the present to see us through the flotation," and he laughed.

At that moment Jeffreys entered the room with the documents. Sir Robert handed the deed of partnership to Alan, and when he had identified it, took it from him again and threw it on the fire, saying that of course the formal letter of release would be posted and the dissolution notified in the *Gazette*. Then the transfer was signed and the cheque delivered.

"Well, goodbye till Saturday," said Alan when he had received the latter, and nodding to them both, he turned and left the room.

The passage ran past the little room in which Mr. Jeffreys, the head clerk, sat alone. Catching sight of him through the open door, Alan entered, shutting it behind him. Finding his key ring he removed from it the keys of his desk and of the office strongroom, and handed them to the clerk who, methodical in everything, proceeded to write a formal receipt.

"You are leaving us, Major Vernon?" he said interrogatively as he signed the paper.

"Yes, Jeffreys," answered Alan, then prompted by some impulse, added, "Are you sorry?"

Mr. Jeffreys looked up and there were traces of unwonted emotion upon his hard, regulated face.

"For myself, yes, Major—for you, on the whole, no."

"What do you mean, Jeffreys? I do not quite understand."

"I mean, Major, that I am sorry because you have never tried to shuffle off any shady business on to my back and leave me to bear the brunt of it; also because you have always treated me as a gentleman should, not as a machine to be used until a better can be found, and kicked aside when it goes out of order."

"It is very kind of you to say so, Jeffreys, but I can't remember having done anything particular."

"No, Major, you can't remember what comes natural to you. But I and the others remember, and that's why I am sorry. But for yourself I am glad, since although Aylward and Haswell have put a big thing through and are going to make a pot of money, this is no place for the likes of you, and now that you are going I will make bold to tell you that I always wondered what you were doing here. By and by, Major, the row will come, as it has come more than once in the past, before your time."

"And then?" said Alan, for he was anxious to get to the bottom of this man's mind, which hitherto he had always found so secret.

"And then, Major, it won't matter much to Messrs. Aylward and Champers-Haswell, who are used to that kind of thing and will probably dissolve partnership and lie quiet for a bit, and still less to folk like myself, who are only servants. But if you were still here it would have mattered a great deal to you, for it would blacken your name and break your heart, and then what's the good of the money? I tell you, Major," the clerk went on with quiet intensity, "though I am nobody and nothing, if I could afford it I would follow your example. But I can't, for I have a sick wife and a family of delicate children who have to live half the year on the south coast, to say nothing of my old mother, and—I was fool enough to be taken in and back Sir Robert's last little venture, which cost me all I had saved. So you see I must make a bit before the machine is scrapped, Major. But I tell you this, that if I can get £5000 together, as I hope to do out of Saharas before I am a month older, for they had to give me a look-in, as I knew too much, I am off to the country, where I was born, to take a farm there. No more of Messrs. Aylward and Haswell for Thomas Jeffreys. That's my bell. Goodbye, Major, I'll take the liberty to write you a line sometimes, for I know you won't give me away. Goodbye and God bless you, as I am sure He will in the long run," and stretching out his hand, he took that of the astonished Alan and wrung it warmly.

When he was gone Alan went also, noticing that the clerks, whom some rumour of these events seemed to have reached, eyed him curiously through the glass screens behind which they sat at their desks, as he thought not without regret and a kind of admiration. Even the magnificent be-medalled porter at the door emerged from the carved teak box where he dwelt and touching his cap asked if he should call a cab.

"No, thank you, Sergeant," answered Alan, "I will take a bus, and, Sergeant, I think I forgot to give you a present last Xmas. Will you accept this?—I wish I could make it more," and he presented him with ten shillings.

The Sergeant drew himself up and saluted.

"Thank you kindly, Major," he said. "I'd rather take that from you than £10 from the other gentlemen. But, Major, I wish we were out on the West Coast again together. It's a stinking, barbarous hole, but not so bad as this 'ere city."

For once these two had served as comrades, and it was through Alan that the sergeant obtained his present lucrative but somewhat uncongenial post.

He was outside at last. The massive granite portal vanished behind him in the evening mists, much as a nightmare vanishes. He, Alan Vernon, who for a year or more had been in bondage, was a free man again. All his dreams of wealth had departed; indeed if anything, save in experience, he was poorer than when first the shadow of yonder doorway fell upon him. But at least he was safe, safe. The deed of partnership which had been as a chain about his neck, was now white ashes; his name was erased from that fearful prospectus of Sahara Limited, wherein millions which someone would provide were spoken of like silver in the days of Solomon, as things of no account. The bitterest critic could not say that he had made a halfpenny out of the venture, in fact, if trouble came, his voluntary abandonment of the profits due to him must go to his credit. He had plunged into the icy waters of renunciation and come up clean if naked. Never since he was a boy could Alan remember feeling so utterly light-hearted and free from anxiety. Not for a million pounds would he have returned to gather gold in that mausoleum of reputations. As for the future, he did not in the least care what happened. There was no one dependent on him, and in this way or in that he could always earn a crust, a nice, honest crust.

He ran down the street and danced for joy like a child, yes, and presented a crossing-sweeper against whom he butted with a whole sixpence in compensation. Thus he reached the Mansion House, not unsuspected of inebriety by the police, and clambered to the top of a bus crowded with weary and anxious-looking City clerks returning home after a long day's labour at starvation wage. In that cold company and a chilling atmosphere some of his enthusiasm evaporated. He remembered that this step of his meant that sooner or later, within a year or two at most, Yarleys, where his family had dwelt for centuries, must go to the hammer. Why had he not accepted Aylward's offer and sold that old fetish to him for £17,000? There was no question of share-dealing there, and if a very wealthy man chose to give a fancy price for a curiosity, he could take it without doubt or shame. At least it would have sufficed to save Yarleys, which after all was only mortgaged for £20,000. For the life of him he could not tell. He had acted on impulse, a very curious impulse, and there was an end of it perhaps; it might be because his uncle had told him as a boy that the thing was unique, or perhaps because old Jeekie, his negro servant, venerated it so much and swore that it was "lucky." At any rate he had declined and there was an end.

But another and a graver matter remained. He had desired wealth to save Yarleys, but he desired it still more for a different purpose. Above everything on earth he loved Barbara, his distant cousin and the niece of Mr. Champers-Haswell, who until an hour ago had been his partner. Now she was a great heiress, and without fortune he could not marry her, even if she would marry him, which remained in doubt. For one thing her uncle and guardian Haswell, under her father's will, had absolute discretion in this matter until she reached the age of twenty-five, and for another he was too proud. Therefore it would seem that in abandoning his business, he had abandoned his chance of Barbara also, which was a truly dreadful thought.

Well, it was in order that he might see her, that he had agreed to visit The Court on the morrow, even though it meant a meeting with his late partners, who were the last people with whom he desired to foregather again so soon. Then and there he made up his mind that before he bade Barbara farewell, he would tell her the whole story, so that she might not misjudge him. After that he would go off somewhere—to Africa perhaps. Meanwhile he was quite tired out, as tired as though he had lain a week in the grip of fever. He must eat some food and get to bed. Sufficient unto the day was the evil thereof, yet on the whole he blessed the name of Jackson, editor of *The Judge* and his father's old friend.

********

When Alan had left the office Sir Robert turned to Mr. Champers-Haswell and asked him abruptly, "What the devil does this mean?"

Mr. Haswell looked up at the ceiling and whistled in his own peculiar fashion, then answered:

"I cannot say for certain, but our young friend's strange conduct seems to suggest that he has smelt a rat, possibly even that Jackson, the old beast, has shown him a rat—of a large Turkish breed."

Sir Robert nodded.

"Vernon is a fellow who doesn't like rats; they seem to haunt his sleep," he said; "but do you think that having seen it, he will keep it in the bag?"

"Oh! certainly, certainly," answered Mr. Haswell with cheerfulness; "the man is the soul of honour; he will never give us away. Look how he behaved about those shares. Still, I think that perhaps we are well rid of him. Too much honour, like too much zeal, is a very dangerous quality in any business."

"I don't know that I agree with you," answered Sir Robert. "I am not sure that in the long run we should not do better for a little more of the article. For my part, although it will not hurt us publicly, for the thing will never be noticed, I am sorry that we have lost Vernon, very sorry indeed. I don't think him a fool, and awkward as they may be, I respect his qualities."

"So do I, so do I," answered Mr. Haswell, "and of course we have acted against his advice throughout, which must have been annoying to him. The scheme as he suggested it was a fair business proposition that might have paid ten per cent. on a small capital, but what is the good of ten per cent. to you and me? We want millions and we are going to get them. Well, he is coming to The Court tomorrow, and perhaps after all we shall be able to arrange matters. I'll give Barbara a hint; she has great influence with him, and you might do the same, Aylward."

"Miss Champers has great influence with everyone who is fortunate enough to know her," answered Sir Robert courteously. "But even if she chooses to use it, I doubt if it will avail in this case. Vernon has been making up his mind for a long while. I have watched him and am sure of that. Tonight he determined to take the plunge and I do not think that we shall see any more of him in this office. Haswell," he added with sudden energy, "I tell you that of late our luck has been too good to last. The boom, the real boom, came in with Vernon, and with Vernon I think that it will go."

"At any rate it must leave something pretty substantial behind it this time, Aylward, my friend. Whatever happens, within a week we shall be rich, really rich for life."

"For life, Haswell, yes, for life. But what is life? A bubble that any pin may prick. Oh! I know that you do not like the subject, but it is as well to look it in the face sometimes. I'm no church-goer, but if I remember right we were taught to pray the good Lord to deliver us especially 'in all times of our wealth,' which is followed by something about tribulation and sudden death, for when they wrote that prayer the wheel of human fortune went round just as it does today. There, let's get out of this before I grow superstitious, as men who believe in nothing sometimes do, because after all they must believe in something, I suppose. Got your hat and coat? So have I, come on," and he switched off the light, so that the room was left in darkness except for the faint glimmering of the fire.

His partner grumbled audibly, for in turning he had knocked his hand against the desk.

"Leave me my only economy, Haswell," he answered with a hard little laugh. "Electricity is strength and I hate to see strength burning to waste. Why do you mind?" he went on as he stepped towards the door. "Is it the contrast? In all times of our wealth, in all times of our tribulation, from sickness and from sudden death——"

"Good Lord deliver us," chimed in Mr. Haswell in a shaking voice behind him. "What the devil's that?"

Sir Robert looked round and saw, or thought that he saw, something very strange. From the pillar on which it stood the golden fetish with a woman's face, appeared to have floated. The firelight showed it gliding towards them across, but a few inches above the floor of the great room. It came very slowly, but it came. Now it reached them and paused, and now it rose into the air until it attained the height of Mr. Champers-Haswell and stayed there, staring into his face and not a hand's breadth away, just as though it were a real woman glaring at him.

He uttered a sound, half whistle and half groan, and fell back, as it chanced on to a morocco-covered seat behind him. For a moment or two the gleaming, golden mask floated in the air. Then it turned very deliberately, rose a little way, and moving sidelong to where Sir Robert stood, hung in front of *his* face.

Presently Aylward staggered to the mantelpiece and began to fumble for the switch; in the silence his nails scratching at the panelling made a sound like to that of a gnawing mouse. He found it at last, and next instant the office broke into a blaze of light, showing Mr. Haswell, his rubicund face quite pale, his hat and umbrella on the floor, gasping like a dying man upon the couch, and Sir Robert himself clinging to the mantel-shelf as a person might do who had received a mortal wound, while the golden fetish reposed calmly on its pillar, to all appearance as immovable and undisturbed as the antique Venus which matched it at the other end of the room. For a while there was silence. Then Sir Robert, recovering himself, asked:

"Did you notice anything unusual just now, Haswell?"

"Yes," whispered his partner. "I thought that hideous African thing which Vernon brought here, came sliding across the floor and stared into my face with its glittering eyes, and in the eyes——"

"Well, what was in the eyes?"

"I can't remember. It was a kind of picture and the meaning of it was Sudden Death—oh Lord! Sudden Death. Tell me it was a fancy bred of that ill-omened talk of yours?"

"I can't tell you anything of the sort," answered Aylward in a hollow voice, "for I saw something also."

"What?" asked his partner.

"Death that wasn't sudden, and other things."

Again the silence fell till it was broken by Aylward.

"Come," he said, "we have been over-working—too much strain, and now the reaction. Keep this rubbish to yourself, or they will lock you up in an asylum."

"Certainly, Aylward, certainly. But can't you get rid of that beastly image?"

"Not on any account, Haswell, even if it haunts us all day. Here it shall stop until the Saharas are floated on Monday, if I have to lock it in the strongroom and throw the keys into the Thames. Afterwards Vernon can take it, as he has a right to do, and I am sure that with it will go our luck."

"Then the sooner our luck goes, the better," replied Haswell, with a mere ghost of his former whistle. "Life is better than luck, and—Aylward, that Yellow God you are so fond of means to murder us. We are being fatted for the sacrifice, that is all. I remember now, that was one of the things I saw written in its eyes!"

## Chapter 3

# Jeekie Tells a Tale

The Court, Mr. Champers-Haswell's place, was a very fine house indeed, of a sort. That is, it contained twenty-nine bedrooms, each of them with a bathroom attached, a large number of sitting-rooms, ample garages, stables, and offices, the whole surrounded by several acres of newly-planted gardens. Incidentally it may be mentioned that it was built in the most atrocious taste and looked like a suburban villa seen through a magnifying glass.

It was in this matter of taste that it differed from Sir Robert Aylward's home, Old Hall, a few miles away. Not that this was old either, for the original house had fallen down or been burnt a hundred years before. But Sir Robert, being gifted with artistic perception, had reared up in place of it a smaller but really beautiful dwelling of soft grey stone, long and low, and built in the Tudor style with many gables.

This house, charming as it was, could not of course compare with Yarleys, the ancient seat of the Vernons in the same neighbourhood. Yarleys was pure Elizabethan, although it contained an oak-roofed hall which was said to date back to the time of King John, a remnant of a former house. There was no electric light or other modern convenience at Yarleys, yet it was a place that everyone went to see because of its exceeding beauty and its historical associations. The moat by which it was surrounded, the grass court within, for it was built on three sides of a square, the mullioned windows, the towered gateway of red brick, the low-panelled rooms hung with the portraits of departed Vernons, the sloping park and the splendid oaks that stood about, singly or in groups, were all of them perfect in their way. It was one of the most lovely of English homes, and oddly enough its neglected gardens and the air of decay that pervaded it, added to rather than decreased its charm.

But it is with The Court that we have to do at present, not with Yarleys. Mr. Champers-Haswell had a week-end party. There were ten guests, all men, and with the exception of Alan, who it will be remembered was one of them, all rich and in business. They included two French bankers and three Jews, everyone a prop of the original Sahara Syndicate and deeply interested in the forthcoming flotation. To describe them is unnecessary, for they have no part in our story, being only financiers of a certain class, remarkable for the riches they had acquired by means that for the most part would not bear examination. The riches were evident enough. Ever since the morning the owners of this wealth had arrived by ones or twos in their costly motorcars, attended by smart chauffeurs and valets. Their fur coats, their jewelled studs and rings, something in their very faces suggested money, which indeed was the bond that brought and held them together.

Alan did not come until it was time to dress for dinner, for he knew that Barbara would not appear before that meal, and it was her society he sought, not that of his host or fellow guests. Accompanied by his negro servant, Jeekie, for in a house like this it was necessary to have someone to wait upon him, he drove over from Yarleys, a distance of ten miles, arriving about eight o'clock.

"Mr. Haswell as gone up to dress, Major, and so have the other gentlemen," said the head butler, Mr. Smith, "but Miss Champers told me to give you this note and to say that dinner is at half-past eight."

Alan took the note and asked to be shown to his room. Once there, although he had only five and twenty minutes, he opened it eagerly, while Jeekie unpacked his bag. It ran:

*Dear Alan*
Don't be late for dinner, or I may not be able to keep a place next to me. Of course Sir Robert takes me in. They are a worse lot than usual this time, odious—odious!—and I can't stand one on the left hand as well as on the right.
Yours
*B*
P.S. What *have* you been doing? Our distinguished guests, to say nothing of my uncle, seem to be in a great fuss about you. I overheard them talking when I was pretending to arrange some flowers. One of them called you a sanctimonious prig and an obstinate donkey, and another answered—I think it was Sir Robert —'No doubt, but obstinate donkeys can kick and have been known to upset other people's applecarts ere now.' Is the Sahara Syndicate the applecart? If so, I'll forgive you.
P.P.S. Remember that we will walk to church together tomor-

row, but come down to breakfast in knickerbockers or something to put them off, and I'll do the same—I mean I'll dress as if I were going to golf. We can turn into Christians later. If we don't—dress like that, I mean—they'll guess and all want to come to church, except the Jews, which would bring the judgment of Heaven on us.

P.P.P.S. Don't be careless and leave this note lying about, for the under-footman who waits upon you reads all the letters. He steams them over a kettle. Smith the butler is the only respectable man in this house.

Alan laughed outright as he finished this peculiar and outspoken epistle, which somehow revived his spirits, that since the previous day had been low enough. It refreshed him. It was like a breath of frosty air from an open window blowing clean and cold into a scented, overheated room. He would have liked to keep it, but remembering Barbara's injunctions and the under-footman, threw it onto the fire and watched it burn. Jeekie coughed to intimate that it was time for his master to dress, and Alan turned and looked at him in an absent-minded fashion.

He was worth looking at, was Jeekie. Let the reader imagine a very tall and powerfully-built negro with a skin as black as a well-polished boot, woolly hair as white as snow, a little tufted beard also white, a hand like a leg of mutton, but with long delicate fingers and pink, filbert-shaped nails, an immovable countenance, but set in it beneath a massive brow, two extraordinary humorous and eloquent black eyes which expressed every emotion passing through the brain behind them, that is when their owner chose to allow them to do so. Such was Jeekie.

"Shall I unlace your boots, Major?" he said in his full, melodious voice and speaking the most perfect English. "I expect that the gong will sound in nine and a half minutes."

"Then let it sound and be hanged to it," answered Alan; "no, I forgot—I must hurry. Jeekie, put that fire out and open all the windows as soon as I go down. This room is like a hot-house."

"Yes, Major, the fire shall be extinguished and the sleeping-chamber ventilated. The other boot, if you please, Major."

"Jeekie," said Alan, "who is stopping in this place? Have you heard?"

"I collected some names on my way upstairs, Major. Three of the gentlemen you have never met before, but," he added suddenly breaking away from his high-flown book-learned English, as was his custom when in earnest, "Jeekie think they just black niggers like the rest, thief people. There ain't a white man in this house, except you and Miss Barbara and me, Major. Jeekie learnt all that in servant's hall palaver. No, not now, other time. Everyone tell everything to Jeekie, poor old African fool, and he look up an answer, 'O law! you don't say so?' but keep his eyes and ears open all the same."

"I'll be bound you do, Jeekie," replied Alan, laughing again. "Well, go on keeping them open, and give me those trousers."

"Yes, Major," answered Jeekie, reassuming his grand manner, "I shall continue to collect information which may prove to your advantage, but personally I wish that you were clear of the whole caboodle, except Miss Barbara."

"Hear, hear," ejaculated Alan, "there goes the gong. Mind you come in and help to wait," and hurrying into his coat he departed downstairs.

The guests were gathered in the hall drinking sherry and bitters, a proceeding that to Alan's mind set a stamp upon the house. His host, Mr. Champers-Haswell, came forward and greeted him with much affectionate enthusiasm, and Alan noticed that he looked very pale, also that his thoughts seemed to be wandering, for he introduced a French banker to him as a noted Jew, and the noted Jew as the French banker, although the distinction between them was obvious and the gentlemen concerned evidently resented the mistake. Sir Robert Aylward, catching sight of him, came across the hall in his usual, direct fashion, and shook him by the hand.

"Glad to see you, Vernon," he said, fixing his piercing eyes upon Alan as though he were trying to read his thoughts. "Pleasant change this from the City and all that eternal business, isn't it? Ah! you are thinking that one is not quite clear of business after all," and he glanced round at the company. "That's one of your cousin Haswell's faults; he can never shake himself free of the thing, never get any real recreation. I'd bet you a sovereign that he has a stenographer waiting by a telephone in the next room, just in case any opportunity should arise in the course of conversation. That is magnificent, but it is not wise. His heart can't stand it; it will wear him out before his time. Listen, they are all talking about the Sahara. I wish I were there; it must be quiet at any rate. The sands beneath, the eternal stars above. Yes, I wish I were there," he repeated with a sigh, and Alan noted that although his face could not be more pallid than its natural colour, it looked quite worn and old.

"So do I," he answered with enthusiasm.

Then a French gentleman on his left, having discovered that he was the engineer who had formulated the great flooding scheme, began to address him as *"Cher maitre,"* speaking so rapidly his own language that Alan, whose French was none of the best, struggled after him in vain. Whilst he was trying to answer a question which he did not understand, the door at the end of the hall opened, and through it appeared Barbara Champers.

It was a large hall and she was a long way off, which caused her to look small, who indeed was only of middle height. Yet even at that distance it was impossible to mistake the dignity of her appearance. A slim woman with brown hair, cheerful brown eyes, a well-modelled face, a rounded figure and an excellent complexion, such was Barbara. Ten thousand young ladies could be found as good, or even better looking, yet something about her differentiated her from the majority of her sex. There was determination in her step, and overflowing health and vigour in her every movement. Her eyes had a trick of looking straight into any other eyes they met, not boldly, but with a kind of virginal fearlessness and enterprise that people often found embarrassing. Indeed she was extremely virginal and devoid of the usual fringe of feminine airs and graces, a nymph of the woods and waters, who although she was three and twenty, as yet recked little of men save as companions whom she liked or disliked according to her instincts. For the rest she was sweetly dressed in a white robe with silver on it, and wore no ornaments save a row of small pearls about her throat and some lilies of the valley at her breast.

Barbara came straight onwards, looking neither to the right or to the left, till she reached her uncle, to whom she nodded. Then she walked to Alan and, offering him her hand, said:

"How do you do! Why did you not come over at lunch time? I wanted to play a round of golf with you this afternoon."

Alan answered something about being busy at Yarleys.

"Yarleys!" she replied. "I thought that you lived in the City now, making money out of speculations, like everyone else that I know."

"Why, Miss Champers," broke in Sir Robert reproachfully, "I asked you to play a round of golf before tea and you would not."

"No," she answered, "because I was waiting for my cousin. We are better matched, Sir Robert."

There was something in her voice, usually so soft and pleasant, as she spoke these words, something of steeliness and defiance that caused Alan to feel at once happy and uncomfortable. Apparently also it caused Aylward to feel angry, for he flashed a glance at Alan over her head of which the purport could not be mistaken, though his pale face remained as immovable as ever. "We are enemies. I hate you," said that glance. Probably Barbara saw it; at any rate before either of them could speak again, she said:

"Thank goodness, there is dinner at last. Sir Robert, will you take me in, and, Alan, will you sit on the other side of me? My uncle will show the rest their places."

The meal was long and magnificent; the price of each dish of it would have kept a poor family for a month, and on the cost of the exquisite wines they might have lived for a year or two. Also the last were well patronized by everyone except Barbara, who drank water, and Alan, who since his severe fever took nothing but weak whiskey and soda and a little claret. Even Aylward, a temperate person, absorbed a good deal of champagne. As a consequence the conversation grew animated, and under cover of it, while Sir Robert was arguing with his neighbour on the left, Barbara asked in a low voice:

"What is the row, Alan? Tell me, I can't wait any longer."

"I have quarrelled with them," he answered, staring at his mutton as though he were criticizing it. "I mean, I have left the firm and have nothing more to do with the business."

Barbara's eyes lit up as she whispered back:

"Glad of it. Best news I have heard for many a day. But then, may I ask why you are here?"

"I came to see you," he replied humbly—"thought perhaps you wouldn't mind," and in his confusion he let his knife fall into the mutton, whence it rebounded, staining his shirt front.

Barbara laughed, that happy, delightful little laugh of hers, presumably at the accident with the knife. Whether or no she "minded" did not appear, only she handed her handkerchief, a costly, last-fringed trifle, to Alan to wipe the gravy off his shirt, which he took thinking it was a napkin, and as she did so, touched his hand with a little caressing movement of her fingers. Whether this was done by chance or on purpose did not appear either. At least it made Alan feel extremely happy. Also when he discovered what it was, he kept that gravy-stained handkerchief, nor did she ever ask for it back again. Only once in after days when she happened to come across it stuffed away in the corner of a despatch-box, she blushed all over, and said that she had no idea that any man could be so foolish out of a book.

"Now that *you* are really clear of it, I am going for them," she said presently when the wiping process was finished. "I have only restrained myself for your sake," and leaning back in her chair she stared at the ceiling, lost in meditation.

Presently there came one of those silences which will fall upon dinner-parties at times, however excellent and plentiful the champagne.

"Sir Robert Aylward," said Barbara in that clear, carrying voice of hers, "will you, as an expert, instruct a very ignorant person? I want a little information."

"Miss Champers," he answered, "am I not always at your service?" and all listened to hear upon what point their hostess desired to be enlightened.

"Sir Robert," she went on calmly, "everyone here is, I believe, what is called a financier, that is except myself and Major Vernon, who only tries to be and will, I am sure, fail, since Nature made him something else, a soldier and—what else did Nature make you, Alan?"

As he vouchsafed no answer to question, although Sir Robert muttered an uncomplimentary one between his lips which Barbara heard, or read, she continued: "And you are all very rich and successful, are you not, and are going to be much richer and much more successful—next week. Now what I want to ask you is—how is it done?"

"Accepting the premises for the sake of argument, Miss Champers," replied Sir Robert, who felt that he could not refuse the challenge, "the answer is that it is done by finance."

"I am still in the dark," she said. "Finance, as I have heard of it, means floating companies, and companies are floated to earn money for those who invest in them. Now this afternoon as I was dull, I got hold of a book called the Directory of Directors, and looked up all your names in it, except those of the gentlemen from Paris, and the companies that you direct—I found out about those in another book. Well, I could not make out that any of these companies have ever earned any money, a dividend, don't you call it? Therefore how do you all grow so rich, and why do people invest in them?"

Now Sir Robert frowned, Alan coloured, two or three of the company laughed outright, and one of the French gentlemen who understood English and had already drunk as much as was good for him, remarked loudly to his neighbour, "Ah! she is charming. She do touch the spot, like that ointment you give me today. How do we grow rich and why do the people invest? *Mon Dieu!* why do they invest? That is the great mystery. I say that *cette belle demoiselle, votre nièce, est ravissante. Elle a d'esprit, mon ami Haswell.*"

Apparently her uncle did not share these sentiments, for he turned as red as any turkey-cock, and said across the great round table:

"My dear Barbara, I wish that you would leave matters which you do not understand alone. We are here to dine, not to talk about finance."

"Certainly, Uncle," she answered sweetly. "I stand, or rather sit, reproved. I suppose that I have put my foot into it as usual, and the worst of it is," she added, turning to Sir Robert, "that I am just as ignorant as I was before."

"If you want to master these matters, Miss Champers," said Aylward with a rather forced laugh, "you must go into training and worship at the shrine of"—he meant to say Mammon, then thinking that the word sounded unpleasant, substituted—"the Yellow God as we do."

At these words Alan, who had been studying his plate, looked up quickly, and her uncle's face turned from red to white. But the irrepressible Barbara seized upon them.

"The Yellow God," she repeated. "Do you mean money or that fetish thing of Major Vernon's with the terrible woman's face that I saw at the office in the City. Well, to change the subject, tell us, Alan, what is that yellow god of yours and where did it come from?"

"My uncle Austin, who was my mother's brother and a missionary, brought it from West Africa a great many years ago. He was the first to visit the tribe who worship it; in fact I do not think that anyone has ever visited them since. But really I do not know all the story. Jeekie can tell you about it if you want to know, for he is one of that people and escaped with my uncle."

Now Jeekie having left the room, some of the guests wished to send for him, but Mr. Champers-Haswell objected. The end of it was that a compromise was effected, Alan undertaking to produce his retainer afterwards when they went to play billiards or cards.

********

Dinner was over at length and the diners, who had dined well, were gathered in the billiard room to smoke and amuse themselves as they wished. It was a very large room, sixty feet long indeed, with a wide space in the centre between the two tables, which was furnished as a lounge. When the gentlemen entered it they found Barbara standing by the great fireplace in this central space, a little shape of white and silver in its emptiness.

"Forgive me for intruding on you," she said, "and please do not stop smoking, for I like the smell. I have sat up expressly to hear Jeekie's story of the Yellow God. Alan, produce Jeekie, or I shall go to bed at once."

Her uncle made a movement as though to interfere, but Sir Robert said something to him which appeared to cause him to change his mind, while the rest in some way or another signified an enthusiastic assent. All of them were anxious to see this Jeekie and hear his tale, if he had one to tell. So Jeekie was sent for and presently arrived clad in the dress clothes which are common to all classes in England and America. There he stood before them white-headed, ebony-faced, gigantic, imperturbable. There is no doubt that his appearance produced an effect, for it was unusual and indeed striking.

"You sent for me, Major?" he said, addressing his master, to whom he gave a military salute, for he had been Alan's servant when he was in the Army.

"Yes, Jeekie. Miss Barbara here and these gentlemen, wish you to tell them all that you know about the Yellow God."

The negro started and rolled his round eyes upwards till the whites of them showed, then began in his school-book English:

"That is a private subject, Major, upon which I should prefer not to discourse before this very public company."

A chorus of remonstrance arose and one of the Jewish gentlemen approaching Jeekie, slipped a couple of sovereigns into his great hand, which he promptly transferred to his pocket without seeming to notice them.

"Jeekie," said Barbara, "don't disappoint me."

"Very well, miss, I fall in with your wishes. The Yellow God that all these gentlemen worship, quite another god to that of which you desire that I should tell you. You know all about him. My god is of female sex."

At this statement his audience burst into laughter while Jeekie rolled his eyes again and waited till they had finished. "My god," he went on presently, "I mean, gentlemen, the god I used to pray to, for I am a good Christian now, has so much gold that she does not care for any more," and he paused.

"Then what does she care for?" asked someone.

"Blood," answered Jeekie. "She is god of Death. Her name is Little Bonsa or Small Swimming Head; she is wife of Big Bonsa or Great Swimming Head."

Again there was laughter, though less general—for instance, neither Sir Robert nor Mr. Champers-Haswell laughed. This merriment seemed to excite Jeekie. At any rate it caused him to cease his stilted talk and relapse into the strange vernacular that is common to all negroes, tinctured with a racy slang that was all his own.

"You want to hear Yellow God palaver?" he said rapidly. "Very well, I tell you, you cocksure white men who think you know everything, but know nothing at all. My people, people of the Asiki, that mean people of Spirits, what you call ghosts and say you no believe in, but always look for behind door, they worship Yellow God, Bonsa Big and Bonsa Little, worship both and call them one; only Little Bonsa on trip to this country just now and sit and think in City office. Yellow God live long way up a great river, then turn to the left and walk six days through big forest where dwarf people shoot you with poisoned arrow. Then turn to the right, walk up stream where many wild beasts. Then turn to the left again and go in canoe through swamp where you die of fever, and across lake. Then walk over grassland and mountains. Then in kloof of the mountains where big black trees make a roof and river fall like thunder, find Asiki and gold house of the Yellow God. All that mountain gold, full of gold and beneath gold house Yellow God afloat in water. She what you call Queen, priestess, live there also, always there, very beautiful woman called Asika with face like Yellow God, cruel, cruel. She take a husband every year, and every year he die because she always hunt for right man but never find him."

"Does she kill him then?" asked Barbara.

"Oh! no, she no kill him, Miss, he kill himself at end of year, glad to get away from Asika and go to spirits. While he live he have a very good time, plenty to eat, plenty wives, fine house, much gold as he like, only nothing to spend it on, pretty necklace, nice paint for face. But Asika, little bit by little bit she eat up his spirit. He see too many ghosts. The house where he sleep with dead men who once have his billet, full of ghosts and every night there come more and sit with him, sit all round him, look at him with great eyes, just like you look at me, till at last when Asika finish eating up his spirit, he go crazy, he howl like man in hell, he throw away all the gold they give him, and then, sometimes after one week, sometimes after one month, sometimes after one year if he be strong but never more, he run out at night and jump into canal where Yellow God float and god get him, while Asika sit on the bank and laugh, 'cause she hungry for new man to eat up his spirit too."

Jeekie's big voice died away to a whisper and ceased. There was a silence in the room, for even in the shine of the electric light and through the fumes of champagne, in more than one imagination there rose a vision of that haunted water in which floated the great Yellow God, and of some mad being casting himself to his death beneath the moon, while his beautiful witch wife who was "hungry for more spirits" sat upon its edge and laughed. Although his language was now commonplace enough, even ludicrous at times, the negro had undoubtedly the art of narration. His auditors felt that he spoke of what he knew, or had seen, that the very recollection of it frightened him, therefore he frightened them.

Again Barbara broke the silence which she felt to be awkward.

"Why do more ghosts come very night to sit with the queen's husband, Jeekie?" she asked. "Where do they come from?"

"Out of the dead, miss, dead husbands of Asika from beginning of the world; what they call *Munganas*. Also always they make sacrifice to Yellow God. From far, far away them poor niggers send people to be sacrifice that their house or tribe get luck. Sometimes they send kings, sometimes great men, sometimes doctors, sometimes women what have twin babies. Also the Asiki bring people what is witches, or have drunk poison stuff which blacks call *muavi* and have not been sick, or perhaps son they love best to take curse off their roof. All these come to Yellow God. Then Asiki doctor, they have Death-palaver. On night of full moon they beat drum, and drum go *Wow! Wow! Wow!* and doctors pick out those to die that month. Once they pick out Jeekie, oh! good Lord, they pick out *me*," and as he said the words he gasped and with his great hand wiped off the sweat that started from his brow. "But Yellow God no take Jeekie that time, no want him and I escape."

"How?" asked Sir Robert.

"With my master, Major's uncle, Reverend Austin, he who come try to make Asiki Christian. He snap his fingers, put on small mask of Yellow God which he prig, Little Bonsa herself, that same face which sit in your office now," and he pointed to Sir Robert, "like one toad upon a stone. Priests think that god make herself into man, want holiday, take me out into forest to kill me and eat my life. So they let us go by and we go just as though devil kick us—fast, fast, and never see the Asiki any more. But Little Bonsa I bring with me for luck, tell truth I no dare leave her behind, she not stand that; and now she sit in your office and think and think and make magic there. That why you grow rich, because she know you worship her."

"That's a nice way for a baptized Christian to talk," said Barbara, adding, "But Jeekie, what do you mean when you say that the god did not take you?"

"I mean this, miss; when victim offered to Big Yellow God, priest-men bring him to edge of canal where the great god float. Then if Yellow God want him, it turn and swim across water."

"Swim across water! I thought you said it was only a mask of gold?"

"I don't know, miss, perhaps man inside the mask, perhaps spirit. I say it swim across water in the night, always in the night, and lift itself up and look in victim's face. Then priest take him and kill him, sometimes one way—sometimes another. Or if he escape and they not kill him, all same for that Johnnie, he die in about one year, always die, no one ever live long if Yellow God swim to him in dark and rise up and smile in his face. No matter if it Big Bonsa or Little Bonsa, for they man and wife joined in holy matrimony and either do trick."

As these words left Jeekie's lips Alan became aware of some unusual movement on his left and looking round, saw that Mr. Champers-Haswell, who stood by him, had dropped the cigar which he held and, white as a sheet, was swaying to and fro. Indeed in another instant he would have fallen had not Alan caught him in his arms and supported him till others came to his assistance, when between them they carried him to a sofa. On their way they passed a table where spirits and soda water were set out, and to his astonishment Alan noticed that Sir Robert Aylward, looking little if at all better than his partner, had helped himself to half a tumbler of cognac, which he was swallowing in great gulps. Then there was confusion and someone went to telephone the doctor, while the deep voice of Jeekie was heard exclaiming:

"That Yellow God at work—oh yes, Little Bonsa on the job. Jeekie Christian man but no doubt she very powerful fetish and can do anything she like to them that worship her, and you see, she sit in office of these gentlemen. 'Spect she make Reverend Austin and me bring her to England because she got eye on firm of Messrs. Aylward & Haswell, London, E.C. Oh, shouldn't wonder at all, for Bonsa know everything."

"Oh, confound you and your fetish! Be off, you old donkey," almost shouted Alan.

"Major," replied the offended Jeekie, assuming his grand manner and language, "it was not I who wished to narrate this history of blood-stained superstitions of poor African. Mustn't blame old Jeekie if they make Christian gents sick as Channel steamer."

"Be off," repeated Alan, stamping his foot.

So Jeekie went, but outside the door, as it chanced, he encountered one of the Jew gentlemen who also appeared to be a little "sick." An idea striking him, he touched his white hair with his finger and said:

"You like Jeekie's pretty story, sir? Well, Jeekie think that if you make little present to him, like your brother in there, it please Yellow God very much, and bring you plenty luck."

Then acting upon some unaccustomed impulse, that Jew became exceedingly generous. In his pocket was a handful of sovereigns which he had been prepared to stake at bridge. He grasped them all and thrust them into Jeekie's outstretched palm, where they seemed to melt.

"Thank you, sir," said Jeekie. "Now I sure you have plenty luck, just like your grandpa Jacob in Book when he do his brudder in eye."

## Chapter 4

# Alan and Barbara

There was no bridge or billiards at the Court that night, where ordinarily the play ran high enough. After Mr. Haswell had been carried to his room, some of the guests, among them Sir Robert Aylward, went to bed, remarking that they could do no good by sitting up, while others, more concerned, waited to hear the verdict of the doctor, who must drive from six miles away. He came, and half an hour later Barbara entered the billiard room and told Alan, who was sitting there smoking, that her uncle had recovered from his faint, and that the doctor, who was to stay all night, said that he was in no danger, only suffering from a heart attack brought on apparently by overwork or excitement.

When Alan woke next morning the first thing that he heard through his open window was the sound of the doctor's departing dogcart. Then Jeekie appeared and told him that Mr. Haswell was all right again, but that all night he had shaken "like one jelly." Alan asked what had been the matter with him, but Jeekie only shrugged his shoulders and said that he did not know—"perhaps Yellow God touch him up."

At breakfast, as in her note she had said she would, Barbara appeared wearing a short skirt. Sir Robert, who was there, also looked extremely pale even for him and with black rims round his eyes, asked her if she were going to golf, to which she answered that she would think it over. It was a somewhat melancholy meal, and as though by common consent no mention was made of Jeekie's tale of the Yellow God, and beyond the usual polite inquiries, very little of their host's seizure.

As Barbara went out she whispered to Alan, who opened the door for her, "Meet me at half-past ten in the kitchen garden."

Accordingly, having changed his clothes surreptitiously, Alan, avoiding the others, made his way by a circuitous route to this kitchen garden, which after the fashion of modern places was hidden behind a belt of trees nearly a quarter of a mile from the house. Here he wandered about till presently he heard Barbara's pleasant voice behind him saying:

"Don't dawdle so, we shall be late for church."

So they started, somewhat furtively like runaway children. As they went Alan asked how her uncle was.

"All right now," she answered, "but he has had a bad shake. It was that Yellow God story which did it. I know, for I was there when he was coming to, with Sir Robert. He kept talking about it in a confused manner, saying that it was swimming to him across the floor, till at last Sir Robert bent over him and told him to be quiet quite sternly. Do you know, Alan, I believe that your pet fetish has been manifesting itself in some unpleasant fashion up there in the office?"

"Indeed. If so, it must be since I left, for I never heard of anything of the sort, nor are Aylward and your uncle likely people to see ghosts. In fact Sir Robert wished to give me about £17,000 for the thing only the day before yesterday, which doesn't look as though it had been frightening him."

"Well, he won't repeat the offer, Alan, for I heard him promise my uncle only this morning that it should be sent back to Yarleys at once. But why did he want to buy it for such a lot of money? Tell me quickly, Alan, I am dying to hear the whole story."

So he began and told her, omitting nothing, while she listened eagerly to every word, hardly interrupting him at all. As he finished his tale they reached the door of the quaint old village church just as the clock was striking eleven.

"Come in, Alan," she said gently, "and thank Heaven for all its mercies, for you should be a grateful man today."

Then without giving him time to answer she entered the church and they took their places in the great square pew that for generations had been occupied by the owners of the ancient house which Mr. Haswell pulled down when he built The Court. There were their monuments upon the wall and their gravestones in the chancel floor. But now no one except Barbara ever sat in their pew; even the benches set aside for the servants were empty, for those who frequented The Court were not church-goers and "like master, like man." Indeed the gentle-faced old clergyman looked quite pleased and surprised when he saw two inhabitants of that palatial residence amongst his congregation, although it is true that Barbara was his friend and helper.

The simple service went on; the first lesson was read. It cried woe upon them that joined house to house and field to field, that draw iniquity with cords of vanity and sin as it were with a cart rope; that call evil good and good evil, that put darkness for light and light for darkness, that justify the wicked for reward; that feast full but regard not the work of the Lord, neither consider the operation of His hand, for of such it prophesied that their houses great and fair should be without inhabitant and desolate.

It was very well read, and Alan, listening, thought that the denunciations of the old seer of thousands of years ago were not inappropriate to the dwellers in some houses great and fair of his own day, who, whatever they did or left undone, regarded not the work of the Lord, neither considered the operation of His hand. Perhaps Barbara thought so too; at any rate a rather sad little smile appeared once or twice upon her sweet, firm face as the immortal poem echoed down the aisle.

The peace that passeth understanding was invoked upon their heads, and rising with the rest of the scanty congregation they went away.

"Shall we walk home by the woods, Alan?" asked Barbara. "It is three miles round, but we don't lunch till two."

He nodded, and presently they were alone in those woods, the beautiful woods through which the breath of spring was breathing, treading upon carpets of bluebells, violet and primrose; quite alone, unaccompanied save by the wild things that stole across their path, undisturbed save by the sound of the singing birds and of the wind among the trees.

"What did you mean, Barbara, when you said that I should be a grateful man today?" asked Alan presently.

Barbara looked him in the eyes in that open, virginal fashion of hers and answered in the words of the lesson, "'Woe unto them that draw iniquity with the cords of vanity and sin as it were with a cart-rope, that lay house to house,'" and through an opening in the woods she pointed to the roof of The Court standing on one hill, and to the roof of Old Hall standing upon another—"'and field to field,'" and with a sweep of her hand she indicated all the country round, "'for many houses great and fair that have music in their feasts shall be left desolate.'" Then turning she said:

"Do you understand now, Alan?"

"I think so," he answered. "You mean that I have been in bad company."

"Very bad, Alan. One of them is my own uncle, but the truth remains the truth. Alan, they are no better than thieves; all this wealth is stolen, and I thank God that you have found it out in time before you became one of them in heart as well as in name."

"If you refer to the Sahara Syndicate," he said, "the idea is sound enough; indeed, I am responsible for it. The thing can be done, great benefits would result, too long to go into."

"Yes, yes, Alan, but you know that they never mean to do it, they only mean to get the millions from the public. I have lived with my uncle for ten years, ever since my poor father died, and I know the backstairs of the business. There have been half a dozen schemes like this, and although they have had their bad times, very bad times, he and Sir Robert have grown richer and richer. But what has happened to those who have invested in them? Oh! let us drop the subject, it is unpleasant. For myself it doesn't matter, because although it isn't under my control, I have money of my own. You know we are a plebeian lot on the male side, my grandfather was a draper in a large way of business, my father was a coal-merchant who made a great fortune. His brother, my uncle, in whom my father always believed implicitly, took to what is called Finance, and when my father died he left me, his only child, in his guardianship. Until I am five and twenty I cannot even marry or touch a halfpenny without his consent; in fact if I should marry against his will the most of my money goes to him."

"I expect that he has got it already," said Alan.

"No, I think not. I found out that, although it is not mine, it is not his. He can't draw it without my signature, and I steadily refuse to sign anything. Again and again they have brought me documents, and I have always said that I would consider them at five and twenty, when I came of age under my father's will. I went on the sly to a lawyer in Kingswell and paid him a guinea for his advice, and he put me up to that. 'Sign nothing,' he said, and I have signed nothing, so, except by forgery nothing can have gone. Still for all that it may have gone. For anything I know I am not worth more than the clothes I stand in, although my father was a very rich man."

"If so, we are about in the same boat, Barbara," Alan answered with a laugh, "for my present possessions are Yarleys, which brings in about £100 a year less than the interest on its mortgages and cost of upkeep, and the £1700 that Aylward paid me back on Friday for my shares. If I had stuck to them I understand that in a week or two I should have been worth £100,000, and now you see, here I am, over thirty years of age without a profession, invalided out of the army and having failed in finance, a mere bit of driftwood without hope and without a trade."

Barbara's brown eyes grew soft with sympathy, or was it tears?

"You are a curious creature, Alan," she said. "Why didn't you take the £17,000 for that fetish of yours? It would have been a fair deal and have set you on your legs."

"I don't know," he answered dejectedly. "It went against the grain, so what is the use of talking about it? I think my old uncle Austin told me it wasn't to be parted with—no, perhaps it was Jeekie. Bother the Yellow God! it is always cropping up."

"Yes," replied Barbara, "the Yellow God is always cropping up, especially in this neighbourhood."

They walked on a while in silence, till suddenly Barbara sat down upon a bole of felled oak and began to cry.

"What is the matter with you?" asked Alan.

"I don't know," she answered. "Everything goes wrong. I live in a kind of gilded hell. I don't like my uncle and I loath the men he brings about the place. I have no friends, I scarcely know a woman intimately, I have troubles I can't tell you and—I am wretched. You are the only creature I have left to talk to, and I suppose that after this row you must go away too to make your living."

Alan looked at her there weeping on the log and his heart swelled within him, for he had loved this girl for years.

"Barbara," he gasped, "please don't cry, it upsets me. You know you are a great heiress——"

"That remains to be proved," she answered. "But anyway, what has it to do with the case?"

"It has everything to do with it, at least so far as I am concerned. If it hadn't been for that I should have asked you to marry me a long while ago, because I love you, as I would now, but of course it is impossible."

Barbara ceased her weeping, wiped her eyes with the back of her hand, and looked up at him.

"Alan," she said, "I think that you are the biggest fool I ever knew—not but that a fool is rather refreshing when one lives among knaves."

"I know I am a fool," he answered. "If I wasn't I should not have mentioned my misfortune to you, but sometimes things are too much for one. Forget it and forgive me."

"Oh! yes," she said; "I forgive you; a woman can generally forgive a man for being fond of her. Whatever she may be, she is ready to take a lenient view of his human weakness. But as to forgetting, that is a different matter. I don't exactly see why I should be so anxious to forget, who haven't many people to care about me," and she looked at him in quite a new fashion, one indeed which gave him something of a shock, for he had not thought the nymph-like Barbara capable of such a look as that. She and any sort of passion had always seemed so far apart.

Now after all Alan was very much a man, if a modest one, with all a man's instincts, and therefore there are appearances of the female face which even such as he could not entirely misinterpret.

"You—don't—mean," he said doubtfully, "you don't really mean——" and he stood hesitating before her.

"If you would put your question a little more clearly, Alan, I might be able to give you an answer," she replied, that quaint little smile of hers creeping to the corners of her mouth like sunshine through a mist of rain.

"You don't really mean," he went on, "that you care anything about me, like, like I have cared for you for years?"

"Oh! Alan," she said, laughing outright, "why in the name of goodness shouldn't I care about you? I didn't say that I do, mind, but why shouldn't I? What is the gulf between us?"

"The old one," he answered, "that between Dives and Lazarus—that between the rich and the poor."

"Alan," said Barbara, looking down, "I don't know what has come over me, but for some unexplained and inexplicable reason I am inclined to give Lazarus a lead—across that gulf, the first one, I mean, not the second!"

Like the glance which preceded it, this was a saying that even Alan could not misunderstand. He sat himself on the log beside her, while she, still looking down, watched him out of the corners of her eyes. He went red, he went white, his heart beat very violently. Then he stretched out his big brown hand and took her small white one, and as this familiarity produced no remonstrance, let it fall, and passing his arm about her, drew her to him and embraced her, not once, but often, with such vigour that a squirrel which had been watching these proceedings from a neighbouring tree, bolted round it scandalized and was seen no more.

"I love you, I love you," he said huskily.

"So I gather," she answered in a feeble voice.

"Do you care for me?" he asked.

"It would seem that I must, Alan, otherwise I should scarcely—oh! you foolish Alan," and heedless of her Sunday hat, which never recovered from this encounter, but was kept as a holy relic, she let her head fall upon his shoulder and began to cry again, this time for very happiness.

He kissed her tears away, then as he could think of nothing else to say, asked her if she would marry him.

"It is the general sequel to this kind of thing, I believe," she answered; "or at any rate it ought to be. But if you want a direct answer—yes, I will, if my uncle will let me, which he won't, as you have quarrelled with him, or at any rate two years hence, when I am five and twenty and my own mistress; that is if we have anything to marry on, for one must eat. At present our worldly possessions seem to consist chiefly of a large store of mutual affection, a good stock of clothes and one Yellow God, which after what happened last night, I do not think you will get another chance of turning into cash."

"I must make money somehow," he said.

"Yes, Alan, but I am afraid it is not easy to do—honestly. Nobody wants people without capital whose only stock in trade is a brief but distinguished military career, and a large experience of African fever."

Alan groaned at this veracious but discouraging remark, and she went on quickly:

"I mean to spend another guinea upon my friend the lawyer at Kingswell. Perhaps he can raise the wind, by a post-obit, or something," she added vaguely, "I mean a post-uncle-obit."

"If he does, Barbara, I can't live on your money alone, it isn't right."

"Oh! don't you trouble about that, Alan. If once I can get hold of those dim thousands you will soon be able to make more, for unto him that hath shall be given. But at present they are very dim, and for all I know may be represented by stock in deceased companies. In short, the financial position is extraordinarily depressed, as they say in the Market Intelligence in *The Times*. But that's no reason why we should be depressed also."

"No, Barbara, for at any rate we have got each other."

"Yes," she answered, springing up, "we have got each other, dear, until Death do us part, and somehow I don't think he'll do that yet awhile; it comes into my heart that he won't do that, Alan, that you and I are going to live out our days. So what does the rest matter? In two years I shall be a free woman. In fact, if the worst comes to the worst, I'll defy them all," and she set her little mouth like a rock, "and marry you straight away, as being over age, I can do, even if it costs me every halfpenny that I've got."

"No, no," he said, "it would be wrong, wrong to yourself and wrong to your descendants."

"Very well, Alan, then, we will wait, or perhaps luck will come our way—why shouldn't it? At any rate for my part I never felt so happy in my life; for, dear Alan, we have found what we were born to find, found it once and for always, and the rest is mere etceteras. What would be the use of all the gold of the Asiki people that Jeekie was talking about last night, to either of us, if we had not each other? We can get on without the wealth, but we couldn't get on apart, or at least I couldn't and I don't mind saying so."

"No, my darling, no," he answered, turning white at the very thought, "we couldn't get on apart—now. In fact I don't know how I have done so so long already, except that I was always hoping that a time would come when we shouldn't be apart. That is why I went into that infernal business, to make enough money to be able to ask you to marry me. And now I have gone out of the business and asked you just when I shouldn't."

"Yes, so you see you might as well have done it a year or two ago when perhaps things would have been simpler. Well, it is a fine example of the vanity of human plans, and, Alan, we must be going home to lunch. If we don't, Sir Robert will be organizing a search party to look for us; in fact, I shouldn't wonder if he is doing that already, in the wrong direction."

The mention of Sir Robert Aylward's name fell on them both like a blast of cold wind in summer, and for a while they walked in silence.

"You are afraid of that man, Barbara," said Alan presently, guessing her thoughts.

"A little," she answered, "so far as I can be afraid of anything any more. And you?"

"A little also. I think that he will give us trouble. He can be very malevolent and resourceful."

"Resourceful, Alan; well, so can I. I'll back my wits against his any day. He shan't separate us by anything short of murder, which he won't go in for. Men like that don't like to break the law; they have too much to lose. But no doubt he will make things uncomfortable for you, if he can, for several reasons."

Again they walked on lost in reflections, when Barbara suddenly saw her lover's face brighten. "What is it, Alan?" she asked.

"Something that is rare enough with me, Barbara—an idea. You remember speaking about that Asiki gold just now. Well, why shouldn't I go and get it?"

She stared at him.

"It sounds a little speculative," she said; "something like one of my uncle's companies."

"Not half so speculative as you think. I have no doubt it is there and Jeekie knows the way. Also I seem to remember that there is a map and an account of the whole thing in Uncle Austin's diaries, though to tell you the truth the old fellow wrote such a fearful hand, that I have never taken the trouble to read it. You see," he went on with enthusiasm, "it is the kind of business that I can do. I am thoroughly salted to fever, I know the West Coast, where I spent three years on that Boundary Commission, I have studied the natives and can talk several of their dialects. Of course there would be a risk, but there are risks in everything, and like you I am not afraid about that, for I believe that we have got our lives before us."

"Read up those diaries, Alan, and we will talk the thing over again. I'll pump Jeekie, who will tell me anything by coaxing, and try to get at the truth. Meanwhile what are you going to do about my uncle?"

"Speak to him, of course, and have the row over."

"Yes," she answered, "that is the best and the most honest. Of course he can turn you out, but he can't prevent my seeing you. If he does, go home to Yarleys and I'll come over and call. Here we are, let us go in by the back door," and she pointed to her crushed hat, and laughed.

## Chapter 5

# Barbara Makes a Speech

While Alan and Barbara, on the most momentous occasion of their lives, were seated upon the fallen oak in the woods that thrilled with the breath of spring, another interview was taking place in Mr. Champers-Haswell's private suite at The Court, the decorations of which, as he was wont to inform his visitors, had cost nearly £2000. Sir Robert, whose taste at any rate was good, thought them so appalling that while waiting for his host and partner, whom he had come to see, he took a seat in the bow window of the sitting-room and studied the view that nobody had been able to spoil. Presently Mr. Haswell emerged from his bedroom, wrapped in a dressing gown and looking very pale and shaky.

"Delighted to see you all right again," said Sir Robert as he wheeled up a chair into which Mr. Haswell sank.

"I am not all right, Aylward," he answered; "I am not all right at all. Never had such an upset in my life; thought I was going to die when that accursed savage told his beastly tale. Aylward, you are a man of the world, tell me, what is the meaning of the thing? You remember what we thought we saw in the office, and then—that story."

"I don't know," he answered; "frankly I don't know. I am a man who has never believed in anything I cannot see and test, one who utterly lacks faith. In my leisure I have examined into the various religious systems and found them to be rubbish. I am convinced that we are but highly-developed mammals born by chance, and when our day is done, departing into the black nothingness out of which we came. Everything else, that is, what is called the higher and spiritual part, I attribute to the superstitions incident to the terror of the hideous position in which we find ourselves, that of gods of a sort hemmed in by a few years of fearful and tormented life. But you know the old arguments, so why should I enter on them? And now I am confronted with an experience which I cannot explain. I certainly thought that in the office on Friday evening I saw that gold mask to which I had taken so strange a fancy that I offered to give Vernon £17,000 for it because I thought that it brought us luck, swim across the floor of our room and look first into your face and then into mine. Well, the next night that negro tells his story. What am I to make of it?"

"Can't tell you," answered Mr. Champers-Haswell with a groan. "All I know is that it nearly made a corpse of me. I am not like you, Aylward, I was brought up as an Evangelical, and although I haven't given much thought to these matters of late years—well, we don't shake them off in a hurry. I daresay there is something somewhere, and when the black man was speaking, that something seemed uncommonly near. It got up and gripped me by the throat, shaking the mortal breath out of me, and upon my word, Aylward, I have been wishing all the morning that I had led a different kind of life, as my old parents and my brother John, Barbara's father, who was a very religious kind of man, did before me."

"It is rather late to think of all that now, Haswell," said Sir Robert, shrugging his shoulders. "One takes one's line and there's an end. Personally I believe that we are overstrained with the fearful and anxious work of this flotation, and have been the victims of an hallucination and a coincidence. Although I confess that I came to look upon the thing as a kind of mascot, I put no trust in any fetish. How can a bit of gold move, and how can it know the future? Well, I have written to them to clear it out of the office tomorrow, so it won't trouble us any more. And now I have come to speak to you on another matter."

"Not business," said Mr. Haswell with a sigh. "We have that all the week and there will be enough of it on Monday."

"No," he answered, "something more important. About your niece Barbara."

Mr. Haswell glanced at him with those little eyes of his which were so sharp that they seemed to bore like gimlets.

"Barbara?" he said. "What of Barbara?"

"Can't you guess, Haswell? You are pretty good at it, generally. Well, it is no use beating about the bush; I want to marry her."

At this sudden announcement his partner became exceedingly interested. Leaning back in the chair he stared at the decorated ceiling, and uttered his favourite wind-in-the-wires whistle.

"Indeed," he said. "I never knew that matrimony was in your line, Aylward, any more than it has been in mine, especially as you are always preaching against it. Well, has the young lady given her consent?"

"No, I have not spoken to her. I meant to do so this morning, but she has slipped off somewhere, with Vernon, I suppose."

Mr. Haswell whistled again, but on a new note.

"Pray do stop that noise," said Sir Robert; "it gets upon my nerves, which are shaky this morning. Listen: It is a curious thing, one less to be understood even than the coincidence of the Yellow God, but at my present age of forty-four, for the first time in my life I have committed the folly of what is called falling in love. It is not the case of a successful, middle-aged man wishing to *ranger* himself and settle down with a desirable *partie*, but of sheer, stark infatuation. I adore Barbara; the worse she treats me the more I adore her. I had rather that the Sahara flotation should fail than that she should refuse me. I would rather lose three-quarters of my fortune than lose her. Do you understand?"

His partner looked at him, pursed up his lips to whistle, then remembered and shook his head instead.

"No," he answered. "Barbara is a nice girl, but I should not have imagined her capable of inspiring such sentiments in a man almost old enough to be her father. I think that you are the victim of a kind of mania, which I have heard of but never experienced. Venus—or is it Cupid?—has netted you, my dear Aylward."

"Oh! pray leave gods and goddesses out of it, we have had enough of them already," he answered, exasperated. "That is my case at any rate, and what I want to know now is if I have your support in my suit. Remember, I have something to offer, Haswell, for instance, a large fortune of which I will settle half—it is a good thing to do in our business,—and a baronetcy that will be a peerage before long."

"A peerage! Have you squared that?"

"I think so. There will be a General Election within the next three months, and on such occasions a couple of hundred thousand in cool cash come in useful to a Party that is short of ready money. I think I may say that it is settled. She will be the Lady Aylward, or any other name she may fancy, and one of the richest women in England. Now have I your support?"

"Yes, my dear friend, why not, though Barbara does not want money, for she has plenty of her own, in first-class securities that I could never persuade her to vary, for she is shrewd in that way and steadily refuses to sign anything. Also she will probably be my heiress—and, Aylward," here a sickly look of alarm spread itself over his face, "I don't know how long I have to live. That infernal doctor examined my heart this morning and told me that it was weak. Weak was his word, but from the tone in which he said it, I believe that he meant more. Aylward, I gather that I may die any day."

"Nonsense, Haswell, so may we all," he replied, with an affectation of cheerfulness which failed to carry conviction.

Presently Mr. Haswell, who had hidden his face in his hand, looked up with a sigh and said:

"Oh! yes, of course you have my support, for after all she is my only relation and I should be glad to see her safely married. Also, as it happens, she can't marry anyone without my consent, at any rate until she is five and twenty, for if she does, under her father's will all her property goes away, most of it to charities, except a beggarly £200 a year. You see my brother John had a great horror of imprudent marriages and a still greater belief in me, which as it chances, is a good thing for you."

"Had he?" said Sir Robert. "And pray why is it a good thing for me?"

"Because, my dear Aylward, unless my observation is at fault, there is another Richard in the field, our late partner, Vernon, of whom, by the way, Barbara is extremely fond, though it may only be in a friendly fashion. At any rate she pays more attention to his wishes and opinions than to mine and yours put together."

At the mention of Alan's name Aylward started violently.

"I feared it," he said, "and he is more than ten years my junior and a soldier, not a man of business. Also there is no use disguising the truth, although I am a baronet and shall be a peer and he is nothing but a beggarly country gentleman with a D.S.O. tacked on to his name, he belongs to a different class to us, as she does too on her mother's side. Well, I can smash him up, for you remember I took over that mortgage on Yarleys, and I'll do it if necessary. Practically our friend has not a shilling that he can call his own. Therefore, Haswell, unless you play me false, which I don't think you will, for I can be a nasty enemy," he added with a threat in his voice, "Alan Vernon hasn't much chance in that direction."

"I don't know, Aylward, I don't know," replied Haswell, shaking his white head. "Barbara is a strong-willed woman and she might choose to take the man and let the money go, and then—who can stop her? Also I don't like your idea of smashing Vernon. It isn't right, and it may come back on our own heads, especially yours. I am sorry that he has left us, as you were on Friday night, for somehow he was a good, honest stick to lean on, and we want such a stick. But I am tired now, I really can't talk any more. The doctor warned me against excitement.

Get the girl's consent, Aylward, and we'll see. Ah! here comes my soup. Goodbye for the present."

When Sir Robert came down to luncheon he found Barbara looking particularly radiant and charming, already presiding at that meal and conversing in her best French to the foreign gentlemen, who were paying her compliments.

"Forgive me for being late," he said; "first of all I have been talking to your uncle, and afterwards skimming through the articles in yesterday's papers on our little venture which comes out tomorrow. A cheerful occupation on the whole, for with one or two exceptions they are all favourable."

*"Mon Dieu,"* said the French gentlemen on the right, "seeing what they did cost, that is not strange. Your English papers they are so expensive; in Paris we have done it for half the money."

Barbara and some of the guests laughed outright, finding this frankness charming.

"But where have you been, Miss Champers? I thought that we were going to have a round of golf together. The caddies were there, I was there, the greens had been specially rolled this morning, but there was no You."

"No," she answered, "because Major Vernon and I walked to church and heard a very good sermon upon the observance of the Sabbath."

"You are severe," he said. "Do you think it wrong for men who work hard all the week to play a harmless game on Sunday?"

"Not at all, Sir Robert." Then she looked at him and, coming to a sudden decision, added, "If you like I will play you nine holes this afternoon and give you a stroke a hole, or would you prefer a foursome?"

"No, let us fight alone and let the best player win."

"Very well, Sir Robert; but you mustn't forget that I am handicapped."

"Don't look angry," she whispered to Alan as they strolled out into the garden after lunch, "I must clear things up and know what we have to face. I'll be back by tea-time, and we will have it out with my uncle."

********

The nine holes had been played, and by a single stroke Barbara had won the match, which pleased her very much, for she had done her best, and with such heavy odds in his favour Sir Robert, who had also done his best, was no mean opponent, even for a player of her skill. Indeed the fight had been quite earnest, for each party knew that it was but a prelude to another and more serious fight, and looked upon the result as in some sense an omen.

"I am conquered," he said in a voice in which vexation struggled with a laugh, "and by a woman over whom I had an advantage. It is humiliating, for I confess I do not like being beaten."

"Don't you think that women generally win if they mean to?" asked Barbara. "I believe that when they fail, which is often enough, it is because they don't care, or can't make up their minds. A woman in earnest is a dangerous antagonist."

"Yes," he answered, "or the best of allies." Then he gave the clubs and half-a-crown to the caddies, and when they were out of hearing, added, "Miss Champers, I have been wondering for some time whether it is possible that you would become such an ally to me."

"I know nothing of business, Sir Robert; my tastes do not lie that way."

"You know well that I was not speaking of business, Miss Champers. I was speaking of another kind of partnership, that which Nature has ordained between men and women—marriage. Will you accept me as a husband?"

She opened her lips to speak, but he lifted his hand and went on. "Listen before you give that ready answer which it is so hard to recall, or smooth away. I know all my disadvantages, my years, which to you may seem many; my modest origin; my trade, which, not altogether without reason, you despise and dislike. Well, the first two cannot be changed except for the worse; the second can be, and already is, buried beneath the gold and ermine of wealth and titles. What does it matter if I am the son of a City clerk who never earned more than £2 a week and was born in a tenement at Battersea, when I am one of the rich men of this rich land and shall die a peer in a palace, leaving millions and honours to my children? As for the third, my occupation, I am prepared to give it up. It has served my turn, and after next week I shall have earned the amount that years ago I determined to earn. Thenceforth, set above the accidents of fortune, I propose to devote myself to higher aims, those of legitimate ambition. So far as my time would allow I have already taken some share in politics as a worker; I intend to continue in them as a ruler which I still have the health and ability to do. I mean to be one of the first men in this Empire, to ride to power over the heads of all the nonentities whose only claim upon the confidence of their countrymen is that they were born in a certain class, with money in their pockets and without the need to spend the best of their manhood in work.

With you at my side I can do all these things and more, and such is the future that I have to offer you."

Again she would have broken in upon his speech and again he stopped her, reading the unspoken answer on her lips.

"Listen: I have not told you all. Perhaps I have put first what should have come last. I have not told you that I love you earnestly and sincerely, with the settled, unalterable love that sometimes comes to men in middle-age who have never turned their thought that way before. I will not attempt the rhapsodies of passion which at my time of life might sound foolish or out of place; yet it is true that I am filled with this passion which has descended on me and taken possession of me. I who often have laughed at such things in other men, adore you. You are a joy to my eyes. If you are not in the room, for me it is empty. I admire the uprightness of your character, and even your prejudices, and to your standard I desire to approximate my own. I think that no man can ever love you quite so well as I do, Barbara Champers. Now speak. I am ready to meet the best or the worst."

After her fashion Barbara looked him straight in the face with her steady eyes, and answered gently enough, for the man's method of presenting his case, elaborate and prepared though it evidently was, had touched her.

"I fear it is the worst, Sir Robert. There are hundreds of women superior to myself in every way who would be glad to give you the help and companionship you ask, with their hearts thrown in. Choose one of them, for I cannot do so."

He heard and for the first time his face broke, as it were. All this while it had remained masklike and immovable, even when he spoke of his love, but now it broke as ice breaks at the pressure of a sudden flood beneath, and she saw the depths and eddies of his nature and understood their strength. Not that he revealed them in speech, angry or pleading, for that remained calm and measured enough. She did not hear, she saw, and even then it was marvellous to her that a mere change in a man's expression could explain so much.

"Those are very cruel words," he said. "Are they unalterable?"

"Quite. I do not play in such matters, it would be wicked."

"May I ask you one question, for if the answer is in the negative, I shall still continue to hope? Do you care for any other man?"

Again she looked at him with her fearless eyes and answered:

"Yes, I am engaged to another man."

"To Alan Vernon?"

She nodded.

"When did that happen? Some years ago?"

"No, this morning."

"Great Heavens!" he muttered in a hoarse voice turning his head away, "this morning. Then last night it might not have been too late, and last night I should have spoken to you, I had arranged it all. Yes, if it had not been for the story of that accursed fetish and your uncle's illness, I should have spoken to you, and perhaps succeeded."

"I think not," she said.

He turned upon her and notwithstanding the tears in his eyes they burned like fire.

"You think—you think," he gasped, "but I know. Of course after this morning it was impossible. But, Barbara, I say that I will win you yet. I have never failed in any object that I set before myself, and do not suppose that I shall fail in this. Although in a way I liked and respected him, I have always felt that Vernon was my enemy, one destined to bring grief and loss upon me, even if he did not intend to do so. Now I understand why, and he shall learn that I am stronger than he. God help him! I say."

"I think He will," Barbara answered, calmly. "You are speaking wildly, and I understand the reason and hope that you will forget your words, but whether you forget or remember, do not suppose that you frighten me. You men who have made money," she went on with swelling indignation, "who have made money somehow, and have bought honours with the moneys somehow, think yourselves great, and in your little day, your little, little day that will end with three lines in small type in *The Times*, you are great in this vulgar land. You can buy what you want and people creep round you and ask you for doles and favours, and railway porters call you 'my Lord' at every other step. But you forget your limitations in this world, and that which lives above you. You say you will do this and that. You should study a book which few of you ever read, where it tells you that you do not know what you will be on the morrow; that your life is even as a vapour appearing for a little time and then vanishing away. You think that you can crush the man to whom I have given my heart because he is honest and you are dishonest, because you are rich and he is poor, and because he chances to have succeeded where you have not. Well, for myself and for him I defy you. Do your worst and fail, and when you have failed, in the hour of your extremity remember my words today. If I have given you pain by refusing you it is not my fault and I am sorry, but when you threaten the man who has honoured me with his love and whom I honour above every creature upon the earth, then I threaten back, and may the Power that made us all judge between you and me, as judge it will," and bursting into tears she turned and left him.

Sir Robert watched her go.

"What a woman!" he said meditatively, "what a woman—to have lost. Well she has set the stakes and we will play out the game. The cards all seem to be in my hands, but it would not in the least surprise me if she won the rubber, for the element that I call Chance and she would call something else, may come in. Still, I never refused a challenge yet and we will play the game out without pity to the loser."

********

That night the first trick was played. When he got back to The Court Sir Robert ordered his motorcar and departed on urgent business, either to his own place, Old Hall, or to London, saying only that he had been summoned away by telegram. As the 70-horse-power Mercedes glided out of the gates a pencilled note was put into Mr. Haswell's hand. It ran:

> I have tried and failed—for the present. By ill-luck A.V. had been before me, only this morning. If I had not missed my chance last night owing to your illness, it would have been different. I do not, however, in the least abandon my plan, in which of course I rely on and expect your support. Keep V. in the office or let him go as you like. Perhaps it would be better if you could prevail upon him to stop there until after the flotation. But whatever you say at the moment, I trust to you to absolutely veto any engagement between him and your niece, and to that end to use all your powers and authority as her guardian. Burn this note.
>
> *R.A.*

## Chapter 6

# Mr. Haswell Loses His Temper

Alan and Barbara sat in Mr. Champers-Haswell's private sitting-room with the awful decorations, and before them by the fire Mr. Champers-Haswell reclined upon his couch. Alan in a few, brief, soldier-like words had just informed him of his engagement to Barbara. During the recital of this interesting fact Barbara said nothing, but Mr. Haswell had whistled several times. Now at length he spoke, in that tone of forced geniality which he generally adopted towards his cousin.

"You are asking for the hand of a considerable heiress, Alan my boy," he said, "but you have neglected to inform me of your own position."

"Where is the use of telling you what you know already, Mr. Haswell? I have left the firm, therefore I have practically nothing."

"You have practically nothing, and yet——Well, in my young days men were more delicate, they did not like being called fortune-hunters, but of course times have changed."

Alan bit his lip and Barbara sat up quite straight in her chair, observing which indications, Mr. Haswell went on hurriedly:

"Now if you had stopped in the firm and earned the very handsome competence in a small way which would have become due to you this week, instead of throwing us over at the last moment for some quixotic reasons of your own, it might have been a different matter. I do not say it would have been, I say it might have been, and you may remember a proverb about winks and nods and blind horses. So I ask you whether you are inclined to withdraw that resignation of yours and bring up this question again let us say, next Sunday?"

Alan thought a while before he answered. As he understood Mr. Haswell practically was promising to assent to the engagement upon these terms. The temptation was enormously great, the fiercest that he had ever been called upon to face. He looked at Barbara. She had closed her eyes and made absolutely no sign. For some reason of her own she had elected that he should determine this vital point without the slightest assistance from her. And it must be determined at once; procrastination was impossible. For a moment he hesitated. On the one side was Barbara, on the other his conscience. After long doubts he had come to a certain conclusion which he quite understood to be inconvenient to his partners. Should he throw it over now? Should he even try to make a sure and certain bargain as the price of his surrender? Probably he would not suffer if he did. The flotation was underwritten and bound to go through; the scandal would come afterwards, months or years hence, long before which he might get out, as most of the others meant to do. No, he could not. His conscience was too much for him.

"I do not see any use in reconsidering that question, Mr. Haswell," he said quietly; "we settled it on Friday night."

Barbara reopened her brown eyes and stared amiably at the painted ceiling, and Mr. Haswell whistled.

"Then I am afraid," he said, "that I do not see any use in discussing your kind proposal for my niece's hand. Listen—I will be quite open with you. I have other views for Barbara, and as it happens I have the power to enforce them, or at any rate to prevent their frustration by you. If Barbara marries against my will before she is five and twenty, that is within the next two years, her entire fortune, with the exception of a pittance, goes elsewhere. This I am sure is a fact that will influence you, who have nothing and even if it did not, I presume that you are scarcely so selfish as to wish to beggar her."

"No," answered Alan, "you need not fear that, for it would be wrong. I understand that you absolutely refuse to sanction my suit on the ground of my poverty, which under the circumstances is perhaps not wonderful. Well, the only thing to do is to wait for two years, a long time, but not endless, and meanwhile I can try to better my position."

"Do what you will, Alan," said Mr. Haswell harshly, for now all his *faux bonhomie* manner had gone, leaving him revealed in his true character of an unscrupulous tradesman with dark ends of his own to serve. "Do what you will, but understand that I forbid all communication between you and my niece, and that the sooner you cease to trespass upon a hospitality which you have abused, the better I shall be pleased."

"I will go at once," said Alan, rising, "before my temper gets the better of me and I tell you some truths that I might regret, for after all you are Barbara's uncle. But on your part I ask you to understand that I refuse to cut off from my cousin, who is of full age and has promised to be my wife," and he turned to go.

"Stop a minute, Alan," said Barbara, who all this while had sat silent. "I have something to say which I wish you to hear. You told us just now, uncle, that you have other views for me, by which you meant that you wish me to marry Sir Robert Aylward, whom, as you are probably aware, I refused definitely this afternoon. Now I wish to make it clear at once that no earthly power will induce me to take as a husband a man whom I dislike, and whose wealth, of which you think so much, has in my opinion been dishonestly acquired."

"What are you saying?" broke in her uncle furiously. "He has been my partner for years, you are reflecting upon me."

"I am sorry, uncle, but I withdraw nothing. Even if Alan here were dead, I would not marry that man, and perhaps you will make him understand this," she added with emphasis. "Indeed I had sooner die myself. You told us also that if I marry against your will, you can take away all the property that my father left to me. Uncle, I shall not give you that satisfaction. I shall wait until I am twenty-five and do what I please with myself and my fortune. Lastly, you said that you forbade us to see each other or to correspond. I answer that I shall both write to and see Alan as often as I like. If you attempt to prevent me from doing so, I shall go to the Court of Chancery, lay all the facts before it, as I have been advised that I can do—not by Alan—please remember, *all* the facts, and ask for its protection and for a separate maintenance out of my estate until I am twenty-five. I am sure that the Court would grant me this and would declare that considering his distinguished family and record Alan is a perfectly proper person to be my affianced husband. I think that is all I have to say."

"All you have to say!" gasped Mr. Haswell, "all you have to say, you impertinent and ungrateful minx!" Then he fell into a furious fit of rage and in language that need not be repeated, poured a stream of threats and abuse upon Alan and herself. Barbara waited until he ceased from exhaustion.

"Uncle," she said, "you should remember that your heart is weak and you must not overexcite yourself, also when you are calmer, that if you speak to me like that again, I shall go to the Court at once, for I will not be sworn at by you or by any other man. I apologize to you, Alan; I am afraid I have brought you into strange company. Come, my dear, we will go and order your dogcart," and putting her arm affectionately through his, she went with him from the room.

"I wonder who put her up to all this?" gasped Haswell, as the door closed behind them. "Some infernal lawyer, I'll be bound. Well, she has got the whip hand of me, and I can't face an investigation in Chancery, especially as the only thing against Vernon is that the value of his land has fallen. But I swear that she shall never marry him while I live," he ended in a kind of shout and the domed and painted ceiling echoed back his words—"*while I live*" after which the room was silent, save for the heavy thumping of his heart.

********

When Alan reached home that night after his ten-mile drive he sent Jeekie to tell the housekeeper to find him some food. In his mysterious African fashion the negro had already collected much intelligence as to the events of the day, mostly in the servants' hall, and more particularly from the two golf-caddies, sons of one of the gardeners, who it seemed instead of retiring with the clubs, had taken shelter in some tall *whins* and thence followed the interview between Barbara and Sir Robert with the intensest interest. Reflecting that this was not the time to satisfy his burning curiosity, Jeekie went and in due course returned with some cold mutton and a bottle of claret. Then came his chance, for Alan could scarcely touch the mutton and demanded toast and butter.

"Very inferior chop"—that was his West African word for food—"for a gentleman, Major," he said, shaking his white head sympathetically and pointing to the mutton,—"specially when he has unexpectedly departed from magnificent eating of The Court. Why did you not wait till after dinner, Major, before retiring?"

Alan laughed at the man's inflated English, and answered in a more nervous and colloquial style:

"Because I was kicked out, Jeekie."

"Ah! I gathered that kicking was in the wind, Major. Sir Robert Aylward, Bart., he also was kicked out, but by smaller toe."

Again Alan laughed and, as it was a relief to talk even to Jeekie, asked him:

"How do you know that?"

"I gathered it out of atmosphere, Major; from Sir Robert's gentleman, from two youths who watch Sir Robert and Miss Barbara talking upon golf green No. 9, from the machine driver of Sir Robert whose eyes he damn in public, and last but not least from his own noble countenance."

"I see that you are observant, Jeekie."

"Observation, Major, it is art of life. I see Miss Barbara's eyes red like morning sky and I deduct. I see you shot out and gloomy like evening cloud, and I deduct. I listen at door of Mr. Haswell's room, I hear him curse and swear like holy saint in Book, and you and Miss Barbara answer him not like saint, though what you speak I cannot hear, and I deduct. Jeekie deduct this—that you make love to Miss Barbara in proper gentlemanlike, 'nogamous, Christian fashion such as your late Reverend Uncle approve, and Miss Barbara, she make love to you with ten per cent. compound interest, but old gent with whistle, he *not* approve; he say, 'Where corresponding cash!' He say 'Noble Sir Robert have much cash and interested in identical business. I prefer Sir Robert. Get out, you Cashless.' Often I see this same thing when boy in West Africa, very common wherever sun shine. I note all these matters and I deduct—that Jeekie's way and Jeekie seldom wrong."

Alan laughed for the third time, until the tears ran down his face indeed.

"Jeekie," he said, "you are a great rascal——"

"Yes, yes," interrupted Jeekie, "great rascal. Best thing to be in this world, Major. Honourable Sir Robert, Bart., M.P., and Mr. Champers-Haswell, D.L., J.P., they find that out long ago and sit on top of tree of opulent renown. Jeekie great rascal and therefore have Savings Bank account—go on, Major."

"Well, Jeekie, because if you are a rascal you are kind-hearted and because I believe that you care for me——"

"Oh! Major," broke in Jeekie again, "that most 'utterably true. Honour bright I love you, Major, better than anyone on earth, except my late old woman, now happily dead, gone and forgotten in best oak coffin, £4-10s without fittings but polished, and perhaps your holy uncle, Reverend Mr. Austin, also coffined and departed, who saved me from early extinction in a dark place. Major, I no like graves, I see too much of them, and can't tell what lie on other side. Though everyone say they know, Jeekie not quite sure. May be all light and crowns of glory, may be damp black hole and no way out. But this at least true, that I love you better, yes, better than Miss Barbara, for love of woman very poor, uncertain thing, quick come, quick go. Jeekie find that out—often. Yes, if need be, though death most nasty, if need be I say I die for you, which great unpleasant sacrifice," and Jeekie in the genuine enthusiasm of his warm heart, throwing himself upon his knees after the African fashion, seized his master's hand and kissed it.

"Thanks, Jeekie," said Alan, "very kind of you, I am sure. But we haven't come to that yet, though no one knows what may happen later on. Now sit upon that chair and take a little whisky—not too much—for I am going to ask your advice."

"Major," said Jeekie, "I obey," and seizing the whisky bottle in a casual manner, he poured out half a tumbler full, for Jeekie was fond of whisky. Indeed before now this taste had brought him into conflict with the local magistrates.

"Put back three parts of that," said Alan, and Jeekie did so. "Now," he went on, "listen: this is the case, Miss Barbara and I are——" and he hesitated.

"Oh! I know; like me and Mrs. Jeekie once," said Jeekie, gulping down some of the neat whisky. "Go on, Major."

"And Sir Robert Aylward is——"

"Same thing, Major. Continue."

"And Mr. Haswell has——"

"Those facts all ascertained, Major," said Jeekie, contemplating his glass with a mournful eye. "Now come to the point, Major."

"Well, the point is, Jeekie, that I am what you called just now cashless, and therefore——"

"Therefore," interrupted Jeekie again, "stick fast in honourable intention towards Miss Barbara owing to obstinate opposition of Mr. Haswell, legal uncle with control of property fomented by noble Sir Robert who desire same girl."

"Quite right, Jeekie, but if you would talk a little less and let me talk a little more, we might get on better."

"I henceforth silent, Major," and lifting his empty tumbler Jeekie looked through it as if it were a telescope, a hint that Alan ignored.

"Jeekie, you infernal old fool, I want money."

"Yes, Major, I understand, Major. Forgive me for breaking conspiracy of silence, but if £500 in Savings Bank any use, very much at your service, Major; also £20 more extracted last night from terror of wealthy Jew who fear fetish."

"Jeekie, you old donkey, I don't want your £500; I want a great deal more, £50,000 or £500,000. Tell me how to get it."

"City best place, Major. But you chuck City, too much honest man, great mistake to be honest in this terrestrial sphere. Often notice that in West Africa."

"Perhaps, Jeekie, but I have done with the City. As you would say, for me it is 'wipe out, finish.'"

"Yes, Major, too much pickpocket, too much dirt. Bottom always drop out of bucket shop at last. I understand, end in police court and severe magistrate, or perhaps even 'Gentlemen of Jury'; *etcetera*."

"Well, Jeekie, then what remains? Now last night when you told us that amazing yarn of yours, you said something about a mountain full of gold, and houses full of gold, among your people. Jeekie, do you think——" and he paused, looking at him.

Jeekie rolled his black eyes round the room and in a fit of absent-mindedness helped himself to some more whisky.

"Do I think, Major, that this useless lucre could be converted into coin of gracious King Edward? Not at all, Major, by no one, Major, by no one whatsoever, except possibly by Major Alan Vernon, D.S.O., and by one, Jeekie, Christian surname Smith."

"Proceed, Jeekie," said Alan, removing the whisky bottle, "proceed and explain."

"Major, thus: The Asiki tribe care nothing about all that gold, it no good to them. Dead people who live long, long ago, no one know when, dig it up and store it there and make the great fetish which they call Bonsa to keep away enemy who want to steal. Also old custom when any one in country round find big nugget, or pretty stone, like ladies wear on bosom, to bring it as offering to Bonsa, so that there now great plenty of all this stuff. But no one use it for anything except to set on walls of house of Asiki, or to make basin, stool, table and pot to cook with. Once Arab come there and I see the priests give him weight in gold for iron hoe, though afterwards they murder him, not for the gold, but lest he go away and tell their secret."

"One might trade with them then, Jeekie?"

He shook his white head doubtfully.

"Yes, perhaps, if you can find anything they want buy and can carry it there. But I think there only one thing they want, and you got that, Major."

"I, Jeekie! What have I got?"

The negro leant forward and tapped his master on the knee, saying in a portentous whisper:

"You got Little Bonsa, which much more holy than anything, even than Big Bonsa her husband, I mean greater, more powerful devil. That Little Bonsa sit in front room Asika's house, and when she want see things, she put it in big basin of gold, but I no tell you what it float in. Also once or twice every year they take out Little Bonsa; Asika wear it on head as mask, and whoever they meet they kill as offering to Little Bonsa, so that spirit come back to world to be priest of Bonsa. I tell you, Major, that Yellow God see many thousand of people die."

"Indeed," said Alan. "A pleasing fetish truly. I should think that the Asiki must be glad it is gone."

"No, not glad, very sorry. No luck for them when Little Bonsa go away, but plenty luck for those who got her. That why firm Aylward & Haswell make so much money when you join them and bring her to office. She drop green in eye of public so they no smell rat. That why you so lucky, not die of blackwater fever when you should; get safe out of den of thieves in City with good name; win love of sweet maiden, Miss Barbara. Little Bonsa do all those things for you, and by and by do plenty more, as Little Bonsa bring my old master, your holy uncle, safe out of that country because all the Asiki run away when they see him wear her on head, for they think she come sacrifice them after she eat up my life."

"I don't wonder that they ran," said Alan, laughing, for the vision of a missionary with Little Bonsa on his head caught his fancy. "But come to the point, you old heathen. What do you mean that I should do?"

"Jeekie not heathen now, Major, but plenty other things true in this world, besides Christian religion. I no want you do anything, but I say this—you go back to Asiki wearing Little Bonsa on head and dressed like Reverend uncle whom you very like, for he just your age then thirty years ago, and they give you all the gold you want, if you give them back Little Bonsa whom they love and worship for ever and ever, for Little Bonsa very, very old."

Alan sat up in his chair and stared at Jeekie, while Jeekie nodded his head at him.

"There is something in it," he said slowly, speaking more to himself than to the negro, "and perhaps that is why I would not sell the fetish, for as you say, there are plenty of true things in the world besides those which we believe. But, Jeekie, how should I find the way?"

"No trouble, Major, Little Bonsa find way, want to get back home, very hungry by now, much need sacrifice. Think it good thing kill pig to Little Bonsa—or even lamb. She know you do your best, since human being not to be come at in Christian land, and say 'thank you for life of pig.'"

"Stop that rubbish," said Alan. "I want a guide; if I go, will you come with me?"

At this suggestion the negro looked exceedingly uncomfortable.

"Not like to, not like to at all," he said, rolling his eyes. "Asiki-land very funny place for native-born. But," he added sadly, "if you go Jeekie must, for I servant of Little Bonsa and if I stay behind, she angry and kill me because I not attend her where she walk. But perhaps if I go and take her to Gold House again, she pleased and let me off. Also I able help you there. Yes, if you and Little Bonsa go, think I go too."

After this announcement Jeekie rose and walked down the room, carrying the cold mutton in his hand. Then he returned, replaced it on the table and standing in front of Alan, said earnestly: "Major, I tell you all truth, just this once. Jeekie believe he *got* go with you to Asiki-land. Jeekie have plenty bad dream lately, Little Bonsa come in middle of the night and sit on his stomach and scratch his face with her gold leg, and say, 'Jeekie, Jeekie, you son of Bonsa, you get up quick and take me back Bonsa Town, for I darned tired of City fog and finished all I come here to do. Now I want jolly good sacrifice and got plenty business attend to there at home, things you not understand just yet. You take me back sharp, or I make you sit up, Jeekie, my boy;'" and he paused.

"Indeed," said Alan; "and did she tell you anything else in her midnight visitations?"

"Yes, Major. She say, 'You take that white master of yours along also, for I want come back Asiki-land on his head, and someone wish see him there, old pal, what he forget but what not forget him. You tell him Little Bonsa got score she wants settle with that party and wish use him to square account. You tell him too that she pay him well for trip; he lose nothing if he play her game 'cause she got no score against him. But if he not go, that another matter, then he look out, for Little Bonsa very nasty customer if she riled, as his late partners find out one day.'"

"Oh! shut up, Jeekie. What's the use of wasting time telling me your nightmares?"

"Very well, Major, just as you like, Major. But I got other reasons why I willing go. Jeekie want see his ma."

"Your ma? I never heard you had a ma. Besides she must be dead long ago."

"No, Major, 'cause she turn up in dream too, very much alive, swear at me 'cause I bag her blanket. Also she tough old woman, take lot kill her."

"Perhaps you have a pa too," suggested Alan.

"Think not, Major, my ma always say she forget him. What she mean, she not like talk about him, he such a swell. Why Jeekie so strong, so clever and with such beautiful face? No doubt because he is son of very great man. All this true reason why he want to go with you, Major. Still, p'raps poor old Jeekie make mistake, p'raps he dream 'cause he eat too much supper, p'raps his ma dead, after all. If so, p'raps better stay at home—not know."

"No," answered Alan, "not know. What between Little Bonsa and one thing and another my head is swimming—like Little Bonsa in the water."

"Big Bonsa swim in water," interrupted Jeekie. "Little Bonsa swim in gold tub."

"Well, Big Bonsa, or Little Bonsa, I don't care which. I'm going to bed and you had better clear away these things and do the same. But, Jeekie, if you say a word of our talk to anyone, I shall be very angry. Do you understand?"

"Yes, Major, I understand. I understand that if I tell secrets of Little Bonsa to anyone except you with whom she live in strange land far away from home, Little Bonsa come at me like one lion, and cut my throat. No fear Jeekie split on Little Bonsa, oh! no fear at all," and still shaking his head solemnly, for the second time he seized the cold mutton and vanished from the room.

"A farrago of superstitious nonsense," thought Alan to himself when he had gone. "But still there may be something to be made out of it. Evidently there is lots of gold in this Asiki country, if only one can persuade the people to deal."

Then weary of Jeekie and his tribal gods, Alan lit his pipe and sat a while thinking of Barbara and all the events of that tumultuous day. Notwithstanding his rebuff at the hands of Mr. Haswell and the difficulties and dangers which threatened, he felt even then that it had been a happy and a fortunate day. For had he not discovered that Barbara loved him with all her heart and soul as he loved Barbara? And as this was so, he did not care a—Little Bonsa about anything else. The future must look to itself, sufficient to the day was the abiding joy thereof.

So he went to bed and for a while to sleep, but he did not sleep very long, for presently he fell to dreaming, something about Big Bonsa and Little Bonsa which sat, or rather floated on either side of his couch and held an interminable conversation over him, while Jeekie and Sir Robert Aylward, perched respectively at its head and its foot, like the symbols of the good and evil genii on a Mahomedan tomb, acted as a kind of insane chorus. He struck his repeater, it was only one o'clock, so he tried to go to sleep again, but failed utterly. Never had he been more painfully awake.

For an hour or more Alan persevered, then at last in despair he jumped out of bed wondering what he could do to occupy his mind. Suddenly he remembered the diary of his uncle, the Rev. Mr. Austin, which he had inherited with the Yellow God and a few other possessions, but never examined. They had been put away in a box in the library about fifteen years before, just at the time he entered the army, and there doubtless they remained. Well, as he could not sleep, why should he not examine them now, and thus get through some of this weary night?

He lit a candle and went down to the library, an ancient and beautiful apartment with black oak panelling between the bookcases, set there in the time of Elizabeth. In this panelling there were cupboards, and in one of the cupboards was the box he sought, made of teak wood. On its lid was painted, "The Reverend Henry Austin. Passenger to Acra," showing that it had once been his uncle's cabin box. The key hung from the handle, and having lit more candles, Alan drew it out and unlocked it, to be greeted by a smell of musty documents done up in great bundles. One by one he placed them on the floor. It was a dreary occupation alone there in that great, silent room at the dead of night, one indeed with which he was soon satisfied, for somehow it reminded him of rifling coffins in a vault. Before him so carefully put away lay the records of a good if not a distinguished life, and until this moment he had never found the energy even to look through them.

At length he came to the end of the bundles and saw that beneath lay a number of manuscript books packed closely with their backs upwards, marked—*Journal*—and with the year and sometimes the place of the author's residence. As he glanced at them in dismay, for they were many, his eye caught the title of one inscribed—as were several others—*West Africa*, and written in brackets beneath—*This vol. contains all that is left of the notes of my escape with Jeekie from the Asiki Devil-worshippers.*

Alan drew it out, and having refilled and closed the box, bore it off to his room, where he proceeded to read it in bed. As a matter of fact he found that there was not very much to read, for the reason that most of the closely-written volume had been so damaged by water, that the pencilled writing had run and become utterly illegible. The centre pages, however, not having been soaked, could still be deciphered, at any rate in part, also there was a large manuscript map, executed in ink, apparently at a later date, on the back of which was written:

> I purpose, D.V., to re-write at some convenient time all the history of my visit to the unknown Asiki people, as my original notes were practically destroyed when the canoe overset in the rapids and most of our few possessions were lost, except this book and the gold fetish mask which is called Little Bonsa or Small Swimming Head. This I think I can do with the aid of Jeekie from memory, but as the matter has only a personal and no religious interest, seeing that I was not able even to preach the Word among those benighted and blood-thirsty savages in

whose country, as I verily believe, the Devil has one of his principal habitations, it must stand over till a convenient season, such as the time of old age or sickness. *H.A.*

P.S. I ought to add with gratitude that even out of this hell fire I was enabled to snatch one brand from the burning, namely, the negro lad, Jeekie, to whose extraordinary resource and faithfulness I owe my escape. After a long hesitation I have been able to baptize him, although I fear that the taint of heathenism still clings to him. Thus not six months ago I caught him sacrificing a white cock to the image, Little Bonsa, in gratitude, as to my horror he explained, for my having been appointed an Honorary Canon of the Cathedral. I have told him to take that ugly mask which has been so often soaked in human blood, and melt it down over the kitchen stove, after picking out the gems in the eyes, that the proceeds may be given to the poor.

*Note.* I had better see to this myself, as where Little Bonsa is concerned, Jeekie is not to be trusted. He says (with some excuse) that it has magic, and that if he melts it down, he will melt down too, and so shall I. How dark and ridiculous are the superstitions of the heathen! Perhaps, however, instead of destroying the thing, which is certainly unique, I might sell it to a museum, and thus spare the feelings of that weak vessel, Jeekie, who otherwise would very likely take it into his head to waste away and die, as these Africans do when their nerves are affected by terror of their fetish.

## Chapter 7

# The Diary

Reflecting that time evidently had made little change in Jeekie, Alan studied this route map with care, and found that it started from Old Calabar, in the Bight of Biafra, on the west coast of Africa, whence it ran up to the Great Qua River, which it followed for a long way. Then it struck across country marked "dense forest," northwards, and came to a river called Katsena, along the banks of which the route went eastwards. Thence it turned northward again through swamps, and ended in mountains called Shaku. In the middle of these mountains was written "Asiki People live here on Raaba River."

The map was roughly drawn to scale, and Alan, who was an engineer accustomed to such things, easily calculated that the distance of this Raaba River from Old Calabar was about 350 miles as the crow flies, though probably the actual route to be travelled was nearer five hundred miles.

Having mastered the map, he opened the water-soaked diary. Turning page after page, only here and there could he make out a sentence, such as "so I defied that beautiful but terrific woman. I, a Christian minister, the husband of a heathen priestess! Perish the thought. Sooner would I be sacrificed to Bonsa."

Then came more illegible pages and again a paragraph that could be read—"They gave me 'The Bean' in a gold cup, and knowing its deadly nature I prepared myself for death. But happily for me my stomach, always delicate, rejected it at once, though I felt queer for days afterwards. Whereon they clapped their hands and said I was evidently innocent and a great medicine man."

And again, further on—"never did I see so much gold whether in dust, nuggets, or worked articles. I imagine it must be worth millions, but at that time gold was the last thing with which I wished to trouble myself."

After this entry many pages were utterly effaced.

The last legible passage ran as follows—"So guided by the lad Jeekie, and wearing the gold mask, Little Bonsa, on my head, I ran through them all, holding him by the hand as though I were dragging him away. A strange spectacle I must have been with my old black clergyman's coat buttoned about me, my naked legs and the gold mask, as pretending to be a devil such as they worship, I rushed through them in the moonlight, blowing the whistle in the mask and bellowing like a bull. . . . Such was the beginning of my dreadful six months' journey to the coast. Setting aside the mercy of Providence that preserved me for its own purposes, I could never have lived to reach it had it not been for Little Bonsa, since curiously enough I found this fetish known and dreaded for hundreds of miles, and that by people who had never seen it, yes, even by the wild cannibals. Whenever it was produced food, bearers, canoes, or whatever else I might want were forthcoming as though by magic. Great is the fame of Big and Little Bonsa in all that part of West Africa, although, strange as it may seem, the outlying tribes seldom mention them by name. If they must speak of either of these images which are supposed to be man and wife, they call it the 'Yellow-God-who-lives-yonder.'"

Not another word of all this strange history could Alan decipher, so with aching eyes he shut up the stained and tattered volume, and at last, just as the day was breaking, fell asleep.

At eleven o'clock on that same morning, for he had slept late, Alan rose from his breakfast and went to smoke his pipe at the open door of the beautiful old hall in Yarleys that was clad with brown Elizabethan oak for which any dealer would have given hundreds of pounds. It was a charming morning, one of those that comes to us sometimes in an English April when the air is soft like that of Italy and the smell of the earth rises like that of incense, and little clouds float idly across a sky of tender blue. Standing thus he looked out upon the park where the elms already showed a tinge of green and the ash-buds were coal black. Only the walnuts and the great oaks, some of them pollards of a thousand years of age, remained stark and stern in their winter dress.

Alan was in a reflective mood and involuntarily began to wonder how many of his forefathers had stood in that same spot upon such April mornings and looked out upon those identical trees wakening in the breath of spring. Only the trees and the landscape knew, those trees which had seen every one of them borne to baptism, to bridal and to burial. The men and women themselves were forgotten.

Their portraits, each in the garb of his or her generation, hung here and there upon the walls of the ancient house which once they had owned or inhabited, but who remembered anything of them today? In many cases their names even were lost, for believing that they, so important in their time, could never sink into oblivion, they had not thought it necessary to record them upon their pictures.

And now the thing was coming to an end. Unless in this way or in that he could save it, what remained of the old place, for the outlying lands had long since been sold, must go to the hammer and become the property of some pushing and successful person who desired to found a family, and perhaps in days to be would claim these very pictures that hung upon the walls as those of his own ancestors, declaring that he had brought in the estate because he was a relative of the ancient and ruined race.

Well, it was the way of the world, and perhaps it must be so, but the thought of it made Alan Vernon sad. If he could have continued that business, it might have been otherwise. By this hour his late partners, Sir Robert Aylward and Mr. Champers-Haswell, were doubtless sitting in their granite office in the City, probably in consultation with Lord Specton, who had taken his place upon the Board of the great Company which was being subscribed that day. No doubt applications for shares were pouring in by the early posts and by telegram, and from time to time Mr. Jeffreys respectfully reported their number and amount, while Sir Robert looked unconcerned and Mr. Haswell rubbed his hands and whistled cheerfully. Almost he could envy them, these men who were realizing great fortunes amidst the bustle and excitement of that fierce financial life, whilst he stood penniless and stared at the trees and the ewes which wandered among them with their lambs, he who, after all his work, was but a failure. With a sigh he turned away to fetch his cap and go out walking—there was a tenant whom he must see, a shifty, new-fangled kind of man who was always clamouring for fresh buildings and reductions in his rent. How was he to pay for more buildings? He must put him off, or let him go.

Just then a sharp sound caught his ear, that of an electric bell. It came from the telephone which, since he had been a member of a City firm, he had caused to be put into Yarleys at considerable expense in order that he might be able to communicate with the office in London. "Were they calling him up from force of habit?" he wondered. He went to the instrument which was fixed in a little room he used as a study, and took down the receiver.

"Who is it?" he asked. "I am Yarleys. Alan Vernon."

"And I am Barbara," came the answer. "How are you, dear? Did you sleep well?"

"No, very badly."

"Nerves—Alan, you have got nerves. Now although I had a worse day than you did, I went to bed at nine, and protected by a perfect conscience, slumbered till nine this morning, exactly twelve hours. Isn't it clever of me to think of this telephone, which is more than you would ever have done? My uncle has departed to London vowing that no letter from you shall enter this house, but he forgot that there is a telephone in every room, and in fact at this moment I am speaking round by his office within a yard or two of his head. However, he can't hear, so that doesn't matter. My blessing be on the man who invented telephones, which hitherto I have always thought an awful nuisance. Are you feeling cheerful, Alan?"

"Very much the reverse," he answered; "never was more gloomy in my life, not even when I thought I had to die within six hours of blackwater fever. Also I have lots that I want to talk to you about and I can't do it at the end of this confounded wire that your uncle may be tapping."

"I thought it might be so," answered Barbara, "so I just rang you up to wish you good-morning and to say that I am coming over in the motor to lunch with my maid Snell as chaperone. All right, don't remonstrate, I *am coming* over to lunch—I can't hear you—never mind what people will say. I am coming over to lunch at one o'clock, mind you are in. Goodbye, I don't want much to eat, but have something for Snell and the chauffeur. Goodbye."

Then the wire went dead, nor could all Alan's "Hello's" and "Are you there's?" extract another syllable.

Having ordered the best luncheon that his old housekeeper could provide Alan went off for his walk in much better spirits, which were further improved by his success in persuading the tenant to do without the new buildings for another year. In a year, he reflected, anything might happen. Then he returned by the wood where a number of new-felled oaks lay ready for barking. This was not a cheerful sight; it seemed so cruel to kill the great trees just as they were pushing their buds for another summer of life. But he consoled himself by recalling that they had been too crowded and that the timber was really needed on the estate. As he reached the house again carrying a bunch of white violets which he had plucked in a sheltered place for Barbara, he perceived a motor travelling at much more than the legal speed up the walnut avenue which was the pride of the place. In it sat that young lady herself, and her maid, Snell, a middle-aged woman with whom, as it chanced, he was on very good terms, as once, at some trouble to himself, he had been able to do her a kindness.

The motor pulled up at the front door and out of it sprang Barbara, laughing pleasantly and looking fresh and charming as the spring itself.

"There will be a row over this, dear," said Alan, shaking his head doubtfully when at last they were alone together in the hall.

"Of course, there'll be a row," she answered. "I mean that there should be a row. I mean to have a row every day if necessary, until they leave me alone to follow my own road, and if they won't, as I said, to go to the Court of Chancery for protection. Oh! by the way, I have brought you a copy of *The Judge*. There's a most awful article in it about that Sahara flotation, and among other things it announces that you have left the firm and congratulates you upon having done so."

"They'll think I have put it in," groaned Alan as he glanced at the head lines, which were almost libellous in their vigour, and the summaries of the financial careers of Sir Robert Aylward and Mr. Champers-Haswell. "It will make them hate me more than ever, and I say, Barbara, we can't live in an atmosphere of perpetual warfare for the next two years."

"I can, if need be," answered that determined young woman. "But I admit that it would be trying for you, if you stay here."

"That's just the point, Barbara. I must not stay here, I must go away, the further the better, until you are your own mistress."

"Where to, Alan?"

"To West Africa, I think."

"To West Africa?" repeated Barbara, her voice trembling a little. "After that treasure, Alan?"

"Yes, Barbara. But first come and have your lunch, then we will talk. I have got lots to tell and show you."

So they lunched, speaking of indifferent things, for the servant was there waiting on them. Just as they were finishing their meal Jeekie entered the room carrying a box and a large envelope addressed to his master, which he said had been sent by special messenger from the office in London.

"What's in the box?" asked Alan, looking somewhat nervously at the envelope, which was addressed in a writing that he knew.

"Don't know for certain, Major," answered Jeekie, "but think Little Bonsa; think I smell her through wood."

"Well, look and see," replied Alan, while he broke the seal of the envelope and drew out its contents. They proved to be sundry documents sent by the firm's lawyers, among which were a notice of the formal dissolution of partnership to be approved by him before it appeared in the *Gazette*, a second notice calling in a mortgage for fifteen thousand and odd pounds on Yarleys, which as a matter of business had been taken over by the firm while he was a partner; a cash account showing a small balance against him, and finally a receipt for him to sign acknowledging the return of the gold image that was his property.

"You see," said Alan with a sigh, pushing over the papers to Barbara, who read them carefully one by one.

"I see," she answered presently. "It is war to the knife. Alan, I hate the idea of it, but perhaps you had better go away. While you are here they will harass the life out of you."

Meanwhile with the aid of a big jack-knife and the dining-room poker, Jeekie had prized off the lid of the box. Chancing to look round Barbara saw him on his knees muttering something in a strange tongue, and bowing his white head until it touched an object that lay within the box.

"What are you doing, Jeekie?" she asked.

"Make bow to Little Bonsa, Miss Barbara, tell her how glad I am see her come back from town. She like feel welcome. Now you come bow too, Little Bonsa take that as compliment."

"I won't bow, but I will look, Jeekie, for although I have heard so much about it I have never really examined this Yellow God."

"Very good, you come look, miss," and Jeekie propped up the case upon the end of the dining-room table. As from its height and position she could not see its contents very well whilst standing above it, Barbara knelt down to get a better view of it.

"My goodness!" she exclaimed, "what a terrible face, beautiful too in its way."

Hardly had the words left her lips when for some reason unexplained that probably had to do with the shifting of the centre of gravity, Little Bonsa appeared to glide or fall out of her box with a startling suddenness, and project herself straight at Barbara, who, with a faint scream, fearing lest the precious thing should be injured, caught it in her arms and for a moment hugged it to her breast.

"Saved!" she exclaimed, recovering herself and placing it on the table, whereon Jeekie, to their astonishment, began to execute a kind of war dance.

"Oh! yes," he said, "saved, very much saved. All saved, most magnificent omen. Lady kneel to Little Bonsa and Little Bonsa nip out of box, make bow and jump in lady's arms. That splendid, first-class luck, for miss and everybody. When Little Bonsa do that need fear nothing no more. All come right as rain."

"Nonsense," said Barbara, laughing. Then from a cautious distance she continued her examination of the fetish.

"See," said Jeekie, pointing to the misshapen little gold legs which were yet so designed that it could be stood up upon them, "when anyone wear Little Bonsa, tie her on head behind by these legs; look, here same old leather string. Now I put her on, for she like to be worn again," and with a quick movement he clapped the mask on to his face, manipulated the greasy black leather thongs and made them fast. Thus adorned the great negro looked no less than terrific.

"I see you, miss," he said, turning the fixed eyes of opal-like stone, bloodshot with little rubites, upon Barbara, "I see you, though you no see me, for these eyes made very cunning. But listen, you hear me," and suddenly from the mask, produced by some contrivance set within it, there proceeded an awful, howling sound that made her shiver.

"Take that thing off, Jeekie," said Alan, "we don't want any banshees here."

"Banshees? Not know him, he poor English fetish p'raps," said Jeekie, as he removed the mask. "This real African god, howl banshee and all that sort into middle of next week. This Little Bonsa and no mistake, ten thousand years old and more, eat up lives, so many that no one can count them, and go on eating for ever, yes unto the third and fourth generation, as Ten Commandments lay it down for benefit of Christian man, like me. Look at her again, Miss Barbara."

Miss Barbara took the hateful, ancient thing in her hands and studied it. No one could doubt its antiquity, for the gold plate of which it was made was literally worn away wherever it had touched the foreheads of the high priests or priestesses who donned it upon festive occasions or days of sacrifice, showing that hundreds and hundreds of them must have used it thus in succession. So was the vocal apparatus within the mouth, and so were the little toad-like feet upon which it was stood up. Also the substance of the gold itself as here and there pitted as though with acid or salts, though what those salts were she did not inquire. And yet, so consummate was the art with which it had originally been fashioned, that the battered beautiful face of Little Bonsa still peered at them with the same devilish smile that it had worn when it left the hands of its maker, perhaps before Mohammed preached his holy war, or even earlier.

"What is all that writing on the back of it?" asked Barbara, pointing to the long lines of rune-like characters which were inscribed within it.

"Not know, miss, think they dead tongue cut in the beginning when black men could write. But Asiki priests swear they remember every one of them, and that why no one can copy Little Bonsa, for they look inside and see if marks all right. They say they names of those who died for Little Bonsa, and when they all done, Little Bonsa begin again, for Little Bonsa never die. But p'raps priests lie."

"I daresay," said Barbara, "but take Little Bonsa away, for however lucky she may be, she makes me feel sick."

"Where I put her, Major?" asked Jeekie of Alan. "In box in library where she used to live, or in plate-safe with spoons? Or under your bed where she always keep eye on you?"

"Oh! put her with the spoons," said Alan angrily, and Jeekie departed with his treasure.

"I think, dear," remarked Barbara as the door closed behind him, "that if I come to lunch here any more, I shall bring my own christening present with me, for I can't eat off silver that has been shut up with that thing. Now let us get to business—show me the diary and the map."

"Dearest Alan," wrote Barbara from The Court two days later, "I have been thinking everything over, and since you are so set upon it, I suppose that you had better go. To me the whole adventure seems perfectly mad, but at the same time I believe in our luck, or rather in the Providence which watches over us, and I don't believe that you, or I either, will come to any harm. If you stop here, you will only eat your heart out and communication between us must become increasingly difficult. My uncle is furious with you, and since he discovered that we were talking over the telephone, to his own great inconvenience he has had the wires cut outside the house. That horrid letter of his to you saying that you had 'compromised' me in pursuance of a 'mercenary scheme' is all part and parcel of the same thing. How are you to stop here and submit to such insults? I went to see my friend the lawyer, and he tells me that of course we can marry if we like, but in that case my father's will, which he has consulted at Somerset House, is absolutely definite, and if I do so in opposition to my uncle's wishes, I must lose everything except £200 a year. Now I am no money-grubber, but I will not give my uncle the satisfaction of robbing me of my fortune, which may be useful to both of us by and by. The lawyer says also that he does not think that the Court of Chancery would interfere, having no power to do so as far as the will is concerned, and not being able to make a ward of a person like myself who is over age and has the protection of the common law of the country. So it seems to me that the only thing to do is to be patient, and wait until time unties the knot.

"Meanwhile, if you can make some money in Africa, so much the better. So go, Alan, go as soon as you like, for I do not wish to prolong this agony, or to see you exposed daily to all you have to bear. Whenever you return you will find me waiting for you, and if you do not return, still I shall wait, as you in like circumstances will wait for me. But I think you will return."

Then followed much that need not be written, and at the end a postscript which ran:

"I am glad to hear that you have succeeded in shifting the mortgage on Yarleys, although the interest is so high. Write to me whenever you get a chance, to the care of the lawyer, for then the letters will reach me, but never to this house, or they may be stopped. I will do the same to you to the address you give. Goodbye, dearest Alan, my true and only lover. I wonder where and when we shall meet again. God be with us both and enable us to bear our trial.

"P.P.S. I hear that the Sahara flotation was *really* a success, notwithstanding the *Judge* attacks. Sir Robert and my uncle have made millions. I wonder how long they will keep them."

A week after he received this letter Alan was on the seas heading for the shores of Western Africa.

## Chapter 8
# The Dwarf Folk

It was dawn at last. All night it had rained as it can rain in West Africa, falling on the wide river with a hissing splash, sullen and continuous. Now, towards morning, the rain had ceased and everywhere rose a soft and pearly mist that clung to the face of the waters and seemed to entangle itself like strands of wool among the branches of the bordering trees. On the bank of the river at a spot that had been cleared of bush, stood a tent, and out of this tent emerged a white man wearing a sun helmet and grey flannel shirt and trousers. It was Alan Vernon, who in these surroundings looked larger and more commanding than he had done at the London office, or even in his own house of Yarleys. Perhaps the moustache and short brown beard which he had grown, or his skin, already altered and tanned by the tropics, had changed his appearance for the better. At any rate it was changed. So were his manner and bearing, whereof all the diffidence had gone. Now they were those of a man accustomed to command who found himself in his right place.

"Jeekie," he called, "wake up those fellows and come and light the oil-stove. I want my coffee."

Thereon a deep voice was heard speaking in some native tongue and saying:

"Cease your snoring, you black dogs, and arouse yourselves, for your lord calls you," an invocation that was followed by the sound of kicks, thumps, and muttered curses.

A minute or two later Jeekie himself appeared, and he also was much changed in appearance, for now instead of his smart, European clothes, he wore a white robe and sandals that gave him an air at once dignified and patriarchal.

"Good-morning, Major," he said cheerfully. "I hope you sleep well, Major, in this low-lying and accursed situation, which is more than we do in boat that half full of water, to say nothing of smell of black man and prevalent mosquito. But the rain it over and gone, and presently the sun shine out, so might be much worse, no cause at all complain."

"I don't know," answered Alan, with a shiver. "I believe that I am fever proof, but otherwise I should have caught it last night, and—just give me the quinine, I will take five grains for luck."

"Yes, yes, for luck," answered Jeekie as he opened the medicine chest and found the quinine, at the same time glancing anxiously out of the corner of his eye at his master's face, for he knew that the spot where they had slept was deadly to white men at this season of the year. "You not catch fever, Little Bonsa," here he dropped his voice and looked down at the box which had served Alan for a pillow, "see to that. But quinine give you appetite for breakfast. Very good chop this morning. Which you like best? Cold ven'son, or fish, or one of them ducks you shoot yesterday?"

"Oh! some of the cold meat, I think. Give the ducks to the boatmen, I don't fancy them in this hot place. By the way, Jeekie, we leave the Qua River here, don't we?"

"Yes, yes, Major, just here. I 'member spot well, for your uncle he pray on it one whole hour; I pretend pray too, but in heart give thanks to Little Bonsa, for heathen in those days, quite different now. This morning we begin walk through forest where it rather dark and cool and comfortable, that is if we no see dwarf people from whom good Lord deliver us," and he bowed towards the box containing Little Bonsa.

"Will those four porters come with us through the forest, Jeekie, as they promised?"

"Yes, yes, they come. Last night they say they not come, too much afraid of dwarf. But I settle their hash. I tell them I save up bits of their hair and toe nails when they no thinking, and I mix it with medicine, and if they not come, they die every one before they get home. They think me great doctor and they believe. Perhaps they die if they go on. If so, I tell them that because they want show white feather, and they think me greater doctor still. Oh! they come, they come, no fear, or else Jeekie know reason why. Now, here coffee, Major. Drink him hot before you go take tub, but keep in shallow water, because crocodile he very early riser."

Alan laughed, and departed to "take tub." Notwithstanding the mosquitoes that buzzed round him in clouds, the water was cool and pleasant by comparison with the hot, sticky air, and the feel of it seemed to rid him of the languor resulting from his disturbed night.

A month had passed since he had left Old Calabar, and owing to the incessant rains the journeying had been hard. Indeed the white men there thought that he was mad to attempt to go up the river at this season. Of course he had said nothing to them of the objects of his expedition, hinting only that he wished to explore and shoot, and perhaps prospect for mines. But knowing as they did, that he was an Engineer officer with a good record and much African experience, they soon made up their minds that he had been sent by Government upon some secret mission that for reasons of his own he preferred to keep to himself. This conclusion, which Jeekie zealously fostered behind his back, in fact did Alan a good turn, since owing to it he obtained boatmen and servants at a season when, had he been supposed to be but a private person, these would scarcely have been forthcoming at any price. Hitherto his journey had been one long record of mud, mosquitoes, and misery, but otherwise devoid of incident, except the eating of one of his boatmen by a crocodile which was a particularly "early riser," for it had pulled the poor fellow out of the canoe in which he lay asleep at night. Now, however, the real dangers were about to begin, since at this spot he left the great river and started forward through the forest on foot with Jeekie and the four bearers whom he had paid highly to accompany him.

He could not conceal from himself that the undertaking seemed somewhat desperate. But of this he said nothing in the long letter he had written to Barbara on the previous night, sighing as he sealed it, at the thought that it might well be the last which would ever reach her from him, even if the boatmen got safely back to Calabar and remembered to put it in the post. The enterprise had been begun and must be carried through, until it ended in success—or death.

An hour later they started. First walked Alan as leader of the expedition, carrying a double-barrelled gun that could be used either for ball or shot, about fifty cartridges with brass cases to protect them from the damp, a revolver, a hunting-knife, a cloth mackintosh, and lastly, strapped upon his back like a knapsack, a tin box containing the fetish, Little Bonsa, which was too precious to be trusted to anyone else. It was quite a sufficient load for any white man in that climate, but being very wiry, Alan did not feel its weight, at any rate at first.

After him in single file came the four porters, laden with a small tent, some tinned provisions and brandy, ammunition, a box containing beads, watches, etc. for presents, blankets, spare clothing and so forth. These were stalwart fellows enough, who knew the forest, but their dejected air showed that now they had come face to face with its dangers, they heartily wished themselves anywhere else. Indeed, notwithstanding their terror of Jeekie's medicine, at the last moment they threw down their loads intending to make a wild rush for the departing boat, only to be met by Jeekie himself who, anticipating some such move, was waiting for them on the bank with a shotgun. Here he remained until the canoe was too far out in the stream for them to reach it by swimming. Then he asked them if they wished to sit and starve there with the devils he would leave them for company, of if they would carry out their bargain like honest men?

The end of it was they took up their loads again and marched, while behind them walked the terrible and gigantic Jeekie, the barrels of the shotgun which he carried at full cock and occasionally used to prod them, pointing directly at their backs. A strange object he looked truly, for in addition to the weapons with which he bristled, several cooking-pots were slung about him, to say nothing of a cork mattress and a mackintosh sheet tied in a flat bundle to his shoulders, a box containing medicines and food which he carried on his head, and fastened to the top of it with string like a helmet on a coffin, an enormous solar-tope stuffed full of mosquito netting, of which the ends fell about him like a green veil. When Alan remonstrated with him as to the cork mattress, suggesting that it should be thrown away as too hot to wear, Jeekie replied that he had been cold for thirty years, and wished to get warm again. Guessing that his real reason for declining to part with the article, was that his master should have something to lie on, other than the damp ground, Alan said no more at the time, which, as will be seen, was fortunate enough for Jeekie.

For a mile or more their road ran through fantastic-looking mangrove trees rooted in the mud, that in the mist resembled, Alan thought, many-legged arboreal octopi feeling for their food, and tall reeds on the tops of which sat crowds of chattering finches. Then just as the sun broke out, strongly, cheering them with its warmth and sucking up the vapours, they entered sparse bush with palms and great cotton trees growing here and there, and so at length came to the borders of the mighty forest.

Oh! dark, dark was that forest; he who entered it from the cheerful sunshine felt as though suddenly and without preparation he had wandered out of the light we know into some dim Hades such as the old Greek fancy painted, where strengthless ghosts flit aimlessly, mourning the lost light. Everywhere the giant boles of trees shooting the height of a church tower into the air without a branch; great rib-rooted trees, and beneath them a fierce and hungry growth of creepers. Where a tree had fallen within the last century or so, these creepers ramped upwards in luxuriance, their stems thick as the body of a man, drinking the shaft of light that pierced downwards, drinking it with eagerness ere the boughs above met again and starved them. Where no tree had fallen the creepers were thin and weak; from year to year they lived on feebly, biding their time, but still they lived, knowing that some day it would come. And always it was coming to those expectant parasites, since from minute to minute, somewhere in the vast depths, miles and miles away perhaps, a great crash echoed in the stillness, the crash of a tree that, sown when the Saxons ruled in England, or perhaps before Cleopatra bewitched Anthony, came to its end at last.

On the second day of their march in the forest Alan chanced to see such a tree fall, and the sight was one that he never could forget. As it happened, owing to the vast spread of its branches which had killed out all rivals beneath, for in its day it had been a very successful tree imbued with an excellent constitution by its parent, it stood somewhat alone, so that from several hundred yards away as these six human beings crept towards it like ants towards a sapling in a cornfield, its mighty girth and bulk set upon a little mound and the luxuriant greenness of its far-reaching boughs made a kind of landmark. Then in the hot noon when no breath of wind stirred, suddenly the end came. Suddenly that mighty bole seemed to crumble; suddenly those far-reaching arms were thrown together as their support failed, gripping at each other like living things, flogging the air, screaming in their last agony, and with an awful wailing groan sinking, a tumbled ruin, to the earth.

Silence again, and in the midst of the silence Jeekie's cheerful voice.

"Old tree go flop! Glad he no flop on us, thanks be to Little Bonsa. Get on, you lazy nigger dog. Who pay you stand there and snivel? Get on or I blow out your stupid skull," and he brought the muzzle of the full-cocked, double-barrelled gun into sharp contact with that part of the terrified porter's anatomy.

Such was the forest. Of their march through it for the first four days, there is nothing to tell. Its depths seemed to be devoid of life, although occasionally they heard the screaming of parrots in the treetops a couple of hundred feet above, or caught sight of the dim shapes of monkeys swinging themselves from bough to bough. That was in the daytime, when, although they could not see it, they knew that the sun was shining somewhere. But at night they heard nothing, since beasts of prey do not come where there is no food. What puzzled Alan was that all through these impenetrable recesses there ran a distinct road which they followed. To the right and left rose a wall of creepers, but between them ran this road, an ancient road, for nothing grew on it, and it only turned aside to avoid the biggest of the trees which must have stood there from time immemorial, such a tree as that which he had seen fall; indeed it was one of those round which the road ran.

He asked Jeekie who made the road.

"People who come out Noah's Ark," answered Jeekie, "I think they run up here to get out of way of water, and sent them two elephants ahead to make path. Or perhaps dwarf people make it. Or perhaps those who go up to Asiki-land to do sacrifice like old Jews."

"You mean you don't know," said Alan.

"No, of course don't know. Who know about forest path made before beginning of world. You ask question, Major, I answer. More lively answer than to shake head and roll eyes like them silly fool porters."

It was on the fourth night that the trouble began. As usual they had lit a huge fire made of the fallen boughs and rotting tree trunks that lay about in plenty. There was no reason why the fire should be so large, since they had little to cook and the air was hot, but they made it so for the same reason that Jeekie answered questions, for the sake of cheerfulness. At least it gave light in the darkness, leaping up in red tongues of flame twenty or thirty feet high, and its roar and crackle were welcome in the primeval silence.

Alan lay upon the cork mattress in the open, for here there was no need to pitch the tent; if any rain fell above, the canopy of leaves absorbed it. He was amusing himself while he smoked his pipe with watching the reflection of the fire-light against a patch of darkness caused probably by some bush about twenty yards away, and by picturing in his own mind the face of Barbara, that strong, pleasant English face, as it might appear on such a background. Suddenly there, on the identical spot he did see a face, though one of a very different character. It was round and small and hideous, resembling in its general outline that of a bloated child. At this distance he could not distinguish the features, except the lips, which were large and pendulous, and between them the flash of white teeth.

"Look here," he whispered to Jeekie in English, and Jeekie looked, then without saying a word, lifted the shotgun that lay at his side and fired straight at the bush. Instantly there arose a squeaking noise, such as might be made by a wounded animal, and the four porters sprang up in alarm.

"Sit down," said Jeekie to them in their own tongue, "a leopard was stalking us and I fired to frighten it away. Don't go near the place, as it may be wounded and angry, but drag up some boughs and make a fence round the fire, for fear of others."

The men who dreaded leopards, looking on these animals, indeed, with superstitious reverence, obeyed readily enough, and as there was plenty of wood lying within a few yards, soon constructed a *boma* fence that, rough as it was, would serve for protection.

"Jeekie," said Alan presently as they laboured at the fence, "that was not a leopard, it was a man."

"No, no, Major, not man, little dwarf devil, him that have poisoned arrow. I shoot at once to make him sit up. Think he no come back tonight, too much afraid of shot fetish. But tomorrow, can't say. Not tell those fellows anything," and he nodded towards the porters, "or perhaps they bolt."

"I think you would have done better to leave the dwarf alone," said Alan, "and they might have left us alone. Now they will have a blood feud against us."

"Not agree, Major, only chance for us put him in blue funk. If I not shoot, presently he shoot," and he made a sound that resembled the whistling of an arrow, then added, "Now you go sleep. I not tired, I watch, my eyes see in dark better than yours. Only two more days of this damn forest, then open land with tree here and there, where dwarf no come because he afraid of lion and cannibal man, who like eat him."

As there was nothing else to be done Alan took Jeekie's advice and in time fell fast asleep, nor did he wake again till the faint light which for the want of a better name they called dawn, was filtering down to them through the canopy of boughs.

"Been to look," said Jeekie as he handed him his coffee. "Hit that dwarf man, see his blood, but think others carry him away. Jeekie very good shot, stone, spear, arrow, or gun, all same to him. Now get off as quick as we can before porters smell a rat. You eat chop, Major, I pack."

Presently they started on their trudge through those endless trees, with Fear for a companion. Even the porters, who had been told nothing, seemed more afraid than usual, though whether this was because they "smell rat," as Jeekie called it, or owing to the progressive breakdown of their nervous systems, Alan did not know. About midday they stopped to eat because the men were too tired to walk further without rest. For an hour or more they had been looking for a comparatively open place, but as it chanced could find none, so were obliged to halt in dense forest. Just as they had finished their meal and were preparing to proceed, that which they had feared, happened, since from somewhere behind the tree boles came a volley of reed arrows. One struck a porter in the neck, one fixed itself in Alan's helmet without touching him, and no less than three hit Jeekie on the back and stuck there, providentially enough in the substance of the cork mattress that he still carried on his shoulders, which the feeble shafts had not the strength to pierce.

Everybody sprang up and with a curious fascination instead of attempting to do anything, watched the porter who had been hit in the neck somewhere in the region of the jugular vein. The poor man rose to his feet with great deliberation, reminding Alan in some grotesque way of a speaker who has suddenly been called on to address a meeting and seeks to gain time for the gathering of his thoughts. Then he turned towards that vast audience of the trees, stretched out his hand with a declamatory gesture, said something in a composed voice, and fell upon his face stone dead! The swift poison had reached his heart and done its work.

His three companions looked at him for a moment and the next with a yell of terror, rushed off into the forest, hurling down their loads as they ran. What became of them Alan never learned, for he saw them no more, and the dwarf people keep their secrets. At the time indeed he scarcely noticed their departure, for he was otherwise engaged.

One of their hideous little assailants, made bold by success, ventured to run across an open space between two trees, showing himself for a moment. Alan had a gun in his hand, and mad with rage at what had happened, he raised it and swung on him as he would upon a rabbit. He was a quick and practised shot and his skill did not fail him now, for just as the dwarf was vanishing behind a tree, the bullet caught him and next instant he was seen rolling over and over upon its further side.

"That very nice," said Jeekie reflectively, "very nice indeed, but I think we best move out of this."

"Aren't you hurt?" gasped Alan. "Your back is full of arrows."

"Don't feel nothing, Major," he answered, "best cork mattress, 25/3 at Stores, very good for poisoned arrow, but leave him behind now, because perhaps points work through as I run, one scratch do trick," and as he spoke Jeekie untied a string or several strings, letting the little mattress fall to the ground.

"Great pity leave all those goods," said Jeekie, surveying the loads that the porters had cast away, "but what says Book? Life more than raiment. Also take no thought for morrow. Dwarf people do that for us. Come, Major, make tracks," and dashing at a bag of cartridges which he cast about his neck, a trifling addition to his other impedimenta, and a small case of potted meats that he hitched under his arm, he poked his master in the back with the muzzle of his full-cocked gun as a signal that it was time to start.

"Keep that cursed thing off me," said Alan furiously. "How often have I told you never to carry firearms at full cock?"

"About one thousand times, Major," answered Jeekie imperturbably, "but on such occasion forget discreetness. My ma just same, it run in family, but story too long tell you now. Cut, Major, cut like hell. Them dwarfs be back soon, but," he puffed, "I think, I think Little Bonsa come square with them one day."

So Alan "cut" and the huge Jeekie blundered along after him, the paraphernalia with which he was hung about rattling like the hoofs of a galloping giraffe. Nor for all his load did he ever turn a hair. Whether it were fear within or a desire to save his master, or a belief in the virtues of Little Bonsa, or that his foot was, as it were, once more upon his native heath, the fact remained that notwithstanding the fifty years, almost, that had whitened his wool, Jeekie was absolutely inexhaustible. At least at the end of that fearful chase, which lasted all the day, and through the night also, for they dared not camp, he appeared to be nearly as fresh as when he started from Old Calabar, nor did his spirits fail him for one moment.

When the light came on the following morning, however, they perceived by many signs and tokens that the dwarf people were all about them. Some arrows were shot even, but these fell short.

"Pooh!" said Jeekie, "all right now, they much afraid. Still, no time for coffee, we best get on."

So they got on as they could, till towards midday the forest began to thin out. Now as the light grew stronger they could see the dwarfs, of whom there appeared to be several hundred, keeping a parallel course to their own on either side of them at what they thought to be a safe distance.

"Try one shot, I think," said Jeekie, kneeling down and letting fly at a clump of the little men, which scattered like a covey of partridges, leaving one of its number kicking on the ground. "Ah! my boy," shouted Jeekie in derision, "how you like bullet in tummy? You not know Paradox guaranteed flat trajectory 250 yard. You remember that next time, sonny." Then off they went again up a long rise.

"River other side of that rise," said Jeekie. "Think those tree-monkeys no follow us there."

But the "monkeys" appeared to be angry and determined. They

would not come any more within the range of the Paradox, but they still marched on either side of the two fugitives, knowing well that at last their strength must fail and they would be able to creep up and murder them. So the chase went on till Alan began to wonder whether it would not be better to face the end at once.

"No, no, if say die, can't change mind tomorrow morning," gasped Jeekie in a hoarse voice. "Here top rise, much nearer than I thought. Oh, my aunt! who those?" and he pointed to a large number of big men armed with spears who were marching up the further side of the hill from the river that ran below.

At the same moment these savages, who were not more than two hundred yards away, caught sight of them and of their pursuers, who just then appeared on the ridge to the right and left. The dwarfs, on perceiving these strangers, uttered a shrill yell of terror, and wheeled about to fly to their fastnesses in the forest, which evidently they regretted ever having left. It was too late. With an answering shout the spearsmen, who were extended in a long line, apparently hunting for game, charged after them at full speed. They were fresh and their legs were long. Therefore very soon they overtook the dwarfs and even got in front of them, heading them off from the forest. The end may be guessed,—save a few whom they reserved alive, they killed them mercilessly, and almost without loss to themselves, since the little forest folk were too terrified and exhausted to shoot at them with their poisoned arrows, and they had no other weapons.

In fact, as Alan discovered afterwards, for generations there had been war between them, since all the other tribes hate the dwarfs, whom they look upon as dangerous human monkeys, and never before had the big men found such a chance of squaring their account.

When Jeekie saw this fearful-looking company, for the first time his spirits seemed to fail him.

"Ogula!" he exclaimed with a groan and sat himself upon a flat rock, pulling Alan down beside him. "Ogula! Know them by hair and spears," he repeated. "Up gum tree now, say good-night."

"Why? Who are they?" gasped Alan.

"Great cannibal, Major, eat man, eat us tonight, or perhaps tomorrow morning when we nice and cool. Say prayers, Major, quick no time waste."

"I think I will shoot an Ogula or two first," said Alan grimly, as he stood up and lifted his gun.

"No, not shoot, no good. Pretend not be afraid, best chance. Let Jeekie think, let Jeekie think," and he slapped his forehead with his large hand.

Apparently the action brought inspiration, for next instant he grabbed his master by the arm and dragged him back behind the shelter of a big boulder which they had just passed. Then with really marvellous swiftness he cut the straps of the tin box that Alan wore upon his back, and since there was no time to find the key and unlock it, seized the little padlock with which it was fastened between his finger and thumb, and putting out his great strength, with a single wrench twisted it off.

"What are you——" began Alan.

"Hold tongue," he answered savagely, "make you god, I priest. Ogula know Little Bonsa. Quick, quick!"

In a minute it was done, the golden mask was clapped on to Alan's head, and the leather thongs were fastened. Moreover, Jeekie himself was arrayed in the solar-tope to which all this while he had clung, allowing streams of green mosquito netting to hang down over his white robe.

"Come out now, Major," he said, "and play god. You whistle, I do palaver."

Then hand in hand they walked from behind the rock. By this time the particular company of the cannibals that was opposite to them, which happened to include their chief, had climbed the steep slope of the hill and arrived within a distance of twenty yards. Having seen the two men and guessed that they had taken refuge behind the rock, their spears were lifted to kill them, since when he beholds anything strange, the first impulse of a savage is to bring it to its death. They looked; they saw. Of a sudden down went the raised spears.

Some of those who held them fell upon their faces, while others turned to fly, appalled by the vision of this strangely clad man with the head of gold. Only their chief, a great yellow-toothed fellow who wore a necklace of baboon claws, remained erect, staring at them with open mouth.

Alan blew the whistle that was set between the lips of the mask, and they shivered. Then Jeekie spoke to them in some tongue which they understood, saying:

"Do you, O Ogula, dare to offer violence to Little Bonsa and her priests? Say now, why should we not strike you dead with the magic of the god which she has borrowed from the white man?" and he tapped the gun he held.

"This is witchcraft," answered the chief. "We saw two men running, hunted by the dwarfs, not three minutes ago, and now we see—what we see," and he put his hand before his eyes, then after a pause went on—"As for Little Bonsa, she left this country in my father's day. He gave her passage upon the head of a white man and the Asiki wizards have mourned her ever since, or so I hear."

"Fool," answered Jeekie, "as she went, so she returns, on the head of a white man. Yonder I see an elder with grey hair who doubtless knew of Little Bonsa in his youth. Let him come up and look and say whether or no this is the god."

"Yes, yes," exclaimed the chief, "go up, old man, go up," and he jabbed at him with his spear until, unwillingly enough, he went.

The elder arrived, making obeisance, and when he was near, Alan blew the whistle in his face, whereon he fell to his knees.

"It is Little Bonsa," he said in a trembling voice, "Little Bonsa without a doubt. I should know, as my father and my elder brother were sacrificed to her, and I only escaped because she rejected me. Down on your face, Chief, and do honour to the Yellow God before she slay you."

Instantly every man within hearing prostrated himself and lay still. Then Jeekie strode up and down among them shouting out:

"Little Bonsa has come back and brought to you, Man-eaters, a fat offering, an offering of the dwarf-people whom you hate, of the treacherous dwarf-people who when you walk the ancient forest path, murder you with their poisoned arrows. Praise Little Bonsa who delivers you from your foes, and hearken to her bidding. Send on messengers to the Asiki saying that Little Bonsa comes home again from across the Black Water bringing the White Preacher, whom she led away in the day of their fathers. Say to them that the Asiki must send out a company that Little Bonsa and the Magician with whom she ran away, may be escorted back to her house with the state which has been hers from the beginning of time. Say to them also that they must prepare a great offering of pure gold out of their store, as much gold as fifty strong men can carry, not one handful less, to be given to the White Magician who brings back Small Swimming Head, for if they withhold such an offering, he and Little Bonsa will vanish never to be seen again, and curses and desolation will fall upon their land. Rise and obey, Chief of the Ogula."

Then the man scrambled to his feet and answered:

"It shall be done, O Priest of the Yellow God. Tomorrow at the dawn swift messengers will start for the Gold House of the Asiki. Tonight they cannot leave, as we are all very hungry and must eat."

"What must you eat?" asked Jeekie suspiciously.

"O Priest," answered the chief with a deprecatory gesture, "when first we saw you we hoped that it would be the white man and yourself, for we have never tasted white man. But now we fear that you will not consent to this, and as you are holy and the guardian of the god, we cannot eat you without your own consent. Therefore fat dwarf must be our food, of which, however, there will be plenty for you as well as us."

"You dog!" exclaimed Jeekie in a voice of furious indignation. "Do you think that white men and their high-born companions, such as myself, were made to fill your vile stomachs? I tell you that a meal of the deadly Bean would agree better with you, for if you dare so much as to look on us, or on any of the white race with hunger, agony shall seize your vitals and you and all your tribe shall die as though by poison. Moreover, we do not touch the flesh of men, nor will we see it eaten. It is our '*orunda*,' it is consecrate to us, it must not pass our lips, nor may our eyes behold it. Therefore we will camp apart from you further up the stream and find our own food. But tomorrow at the dawn the messengers must leave as we have commanded. Also you shall provide strong men and a large canoe to bear Little Bonsa forward towards her own home until she finds her people coming out to greet her.

"It shall be done," answered the chief humbly, "Everything shall be done according to the will of Little Bonsa spoken by her priest, that she may leave a blessing and not a curse upon the heads of the tribe of the Ogula. Say where you wish to camp and men shall run to build a house of reeds for the god to dwell in."

## Chapter 9
# The Dawn

Jeekie looked up and down the river and saw that in the centre of it about half a mile away, there was an island on which grew some trees.

"Little Bonsa will camp yonder," he said. "Go, make her house ready, light fire and bring canoe to paddle us across. Now leave us, all of you, for if you look too long upon the face of the Yellow God she will ask a sacrifice, and it is not lawful that you should see where she hides herself away."

At this saying the cannibals departed as one man, and at top speed, some of the canoes and others to warn their fellows who were engaged in the congenial work of hunting and killing the dwarfs, not to dare to approach the white man and his companion. A third party ran to the bank of the river that was opposite to the island to make ready as they had been bidden, so that presently Alan and Jeekie were left quite alone.

"Ah!" said Jeekie, with a gasp of satisfaction, "*that* all right, everything arranged quite comfortable. Thought Little Bonsa come out top somehow and score off dirty dwarf monkeys. *They* never get home to tea anyway—stay and dine with Ogula."

"Stop chattering, Jeekie, and untie this infernal mask, I am almost choked," broke in Alan in a hollow voice.

"Not say 'infernal mask,' Major, say 'face of angel.' Little Bonsa woman and like it better, also true, if on this occasion only, for she save our skins," said Jeekie as he unknotted the thongs and reverently replaced the fetish in its tin box. "My!" he added, contemplating his master's perspiring countenance, "you blush like garden carrot; well, gold hot wear in afternoon sun beneath Tropic of Cancer. Now we walk on quietly and I tell you all I arrange for night's lodging and future progress of joint expedition."

So gathering together what remained of their few possessions, they started leisurely down the slope towards the island, and as they went Jeekie explained all that had happened, since Ogula was not one of the African languages with which Alan was acquainted and he had only been able to understand a word here and there.

"Look," said Jeekie when he had finished, and turning, he pointed to the cannibals who were driving the few survivors of the dwarfs before them to the spot where their canoes were beached. "Those dwarfs done for; capital business, forest road quite safe to travel home by; Ogula best friends in world; very remarkable escape from delicate situation."

"Very remarkable indeed," said Alan; "I shall soon begin to believe in the luck of Little Bonsa."

"Yes, Major, you see she anxious to get home and make path clear. But," he added gloomily, "how she behave when she reach there, can't say."

"Nor can I, Jeekie, but meanwhile I hope she will provide us with some dinner, for I am faint for want of food and all the tinned meat is lost."

"Food," repeated Jeekie. "Yes, necessity for human stomach, which unhappily built that way, so Ogula find out, and so dwarfs find out presently." Then he looked about him and in a kind of aimless manner lifted his gun and fired. "There we are," he said, "Little Bonsa understand bodily needs," and he pointed to a fat buck of the sort that in South Africa is called Duiker, which his keen eyes had discovered in its form against a stone where it now lay shot through the head and dying. "No further trouble on score of grub for next three day," he added. "Come on to camp, Major. I send one savage skin and bring that buck."

So on they went to the river bank, Alan so tired now that the excitement was over, that he was not sorry to lean upon Jeekie's arm. Reaching the stream they drank deep of its water, and finding that it was shallow at this spot, waded through it to the island without waiting for a canoe to ferry them over. Here they found a party of the cannibals already at work clearing reeds with their large, curved knives, in order to make a site for the hut. Another party under the command of their chief himself had gone to the top end of the island, to cut the stems of a willow-like shrub to serve as uprights. These people stared at Alan, which was not strange, as they had never before seen the face of a white man and were wondering, doubtless, what had become of the ancient and terrible fetish that he had worn. Without entering into explanations Jeekie in a great voice ordered two of them to fetch the buck, which the white man, whom he described as "husband of the goddess," had "slain by thunder." When these had departed upon their errand, leaving Jeekie to superintend the building operations, Alan sat down upon a fallen tree, watching one of the savages making fire with a pointed stick and some tinder.

Just then from the head of the island where the willows were being cut, rose the sound of loud roarings and of men crying out in affright. Seizing his gun Alan ran towards the spot whence the noise came. Forcing his way through a brake of reeds, he saw a curious sight. The Ogula in cutting the willows which grew about some tumbled rocks, had disturbed a lioness that had her lair there, and being fearless savages, had tried to kill her with their spears. The brute, rendered desperate by wounds, and the impossibility of escape, for here the surrounding water was deep, had charged them boldly, and as it chanced, felled to the ground their chief, that yellow-toothed man to whom Jeekie gave his orders. Now she was standing over him looking round her royally, her great paw upon his breast, which it seemed almost to cover, while the Ogula ran round and round shouting, for they feared that if they tried to attack her, she would kill the chief. This indeed she seemed about to do, for just as Alan arrived she dropped her head as though to tear out the man's throat. Instantly he fired. It was a snap shot, but as it chanced a good one, for the bullet struck the lioness in the back of the neck just forward of and between the shoulders, severing the spine so that without a sound or any further movement she sank stone dead upon the prostrate cannibal. For a while his followers stood astonished. They might have heard of guns from the coast people, but living as they did in the interior where white folk did not dare to travel, they had never seen their terrible effects.

"Magic!" they cried. "Magic!"

"Of course," exclaimed Jeekie, who by now had arrived upon the scene. "What else did you expect from the husband of Little Bonsa? Magic, the greatest of magic. Go, roll that beast away before your chief is crushed to death."

They obeyed, and the man sat up, a fearful spectacle, for he was smothered with the blood of the lion and somewhat cut by her claws, though otherwise unhurt. Then feeling that the life was still whole in him, he crept on his hands and knees to where Alan stood, and kissed his feet.

"Aha!" said Jeekie, "Little Bonsa score again. Cannibal tribe our slave henceforth for evermore. Yes, till kingdom come. Come on, Major, and cook supper in perfect peace."

The supper was cooked and eaten with gratitude, for seldom had two men needed a square meal more, and never did venison taste better. By the time that it was finished darkness had fallen, and before they turned in to sleep in the neat reed hut that the Ogula had built, Alan and Jeekie walked up the island to see if the lioness had been skinned, as they directed. This they found was done; even the carcase itself had been removed to serve as meat for these foul-feeding people. They climbed on to the pile of rocks in which the beast had made her lair, and looked down the river to where, two hundred yards away, the Ogula were encamped. From this camp there rose a sound of revelry, and by the light of the great fires that burned there, they perceived that the hungry savages were busy feasting, for some of them sat in circles, whilst others, their naked forms looking at that distance like those of imps in the infernal regions, flitted to and fro against the glowing background of the fires, bearing strange-looking joints on prongs of wood.

"I suppose they are eating the lioness," said Alan doubtfully.

"No, no, Major, not lioness; eat dwarf by dozen—just like oysters at seaside. But for Little Bonsa *we* sit on those forks now and look uncommon small."

"Beasts!" said Alan in disgust; "they make me feel uncommon sick. Let us go to bed. I suppose they won't murder us in our sleep, will they?"

"Not they, Major, too much afraid. Also we their blood-brothers now, because we bring them first-class dinner and save chief from lion's fury. No blame them too much, Major, good fellows really with gentle heart, but grub like that from generation to generation. Every mother's son of them have many men inside, that why they so big and strong. Ogula people cover great multitude like Charity in Book. No doubt sent by Providence to keep down extra pop'lation. Not right to think too hard of poor fellows who, as I say, very kind and gentle at heart and most loving in family relation, except to old women whom they eat also, so that they no get bored with too long life."

Weary and disgusted by this abominable sight though he was, Alan burst out laughing at his retainer's apology for the sweet-natured Ogula, who struck him as the most repulsive blackguards that he had ever met or heard of in all his experience of African savages. Then wishing to see and hear no more of them that night, he retreated rapidly to the hut and was soon fast asleep with his head pillowed on the box that hid the charms of Little Bonsa. When he awoke it was broad daylight. Rising he went down to the river to wash, and never had a bath been more welcome, for during all their journey through the forest no such thing was obtainable. On his return he found his garments well brushed with dry reeds and set upon a rock in the hot sun to air, while Jeekie in a cheerful mood, was engaged cooking breakfast in the frying-pan, to which he had clung through all the vicissitudes of their flight.

"No coffee, Major," he said regretfully, "that stop in forest. But never mind, hot water better for nerve. Ogula messengers gone in little canoe to Asiki at break of day. Travel slow till they work off dwarf, but afterwards go quick. I send lion skin with them as present from you to great high-priestess Asika, also claws for necklace. No lions there and she think much of that. Also it make her love mighty man who can kill fierce lion like Samson in Book. Love of head woman very valuable ally among beastly savage peoples."

"I am sure I hope it won't," said Alan with earnestness, "but no doubt it is as well to keep on the soft side of the good lady if we can. What time do we start?"

"In one hour, Major. I been to camp already, chosen best canoe and finest men for rowers. Chief—he called Fanny—so grateful that he come with them himself."

"Indeed. That is very kind of him, but I say, Jeekie, what are these fellows going to live on? I can't stand what you call their 'favourite chop.'"

"No, no, Major, that all right. I tell them that when they travel with Little Bonsa, they must keep Lent like pious Roman Catholic family that live near Yarleys. They catch plenty fish in river, and perhaps we shoot game, or rich 'potamus, which they like 'cause he fat."

Evidently the Ogula chief, Fahni by name, not Fanny, as Jeekie called him, was a man of his word, for before the hour was up he appeared at the island in command of a large canoe manned by twelve splendid-looking savages. Springing to land, he prostrated himself before Alan, kissing his feet as he had done on the previous night, and making a long speech.

"That very good spirit," exclaimed Jeekie. "Like to see heathen in his darkness lick white gentleman's boot. He say you his lord and great magician who save his life, and know all Little Bonsa's secrets, which many and unrepeatable. He say he die for you twice a day if need be, and go on dying tomorrow and all next year. He say he take you safe till you meet Asiki and for your sake, though he hungry, eat no man for one whole month, or perhaps longer. Now we start at once."

So they started up the river that was called Katsena, Alan and Jeekie seated in a lordly fashion near the stern of the canoe beneath an awning made out of some sticks and a grass mat. In truth after their severe toil and adventures in the forest, this method of journeying proved quite luxurious. Except for a rapid here and there over or round which the canoe must be dragged, the river was broad and the scenery on its banks park-like and beautiful. Moreover the country, perhaps owing to the appetites of the Ogula, appeared to be practically uninhabited except by vast herds of every sort of game.

All day they sat in the canoe which the stalwart rowers propelled, in silence for the most part, since they were terribly afraid of the white man, and still more so of the renowned fetish which they knew he carried with him. Then when evening came they moored their craft to the bank and camped till the following morning. Nor did they lack for food, since game being so plentiful, it was only necessary for Alan to walk a few hundred yards and shoot a fat eland, or hartebeest, or other buck which in its ignorance of guns would allow him to approach quite close. Elephants, rhinoceros, and buffalo were also common, while great herds of giraffe might be seen wandering between the scattered trees, but as they were not upon a hunting trip and their ammunition was very limited, with these they did not interfere.

Having their daily fill of meat which their souls loved, the Ogula oarsmen remained in an excellent mood, indeed the chief, Fahni, informed Alan that if only they had such magic tubes wherewith to slaughter game, he and his tribe would gladly give up cannibalism—except on feast days. He added sadly that soon they would be obliged to do so, or die, since in those parts there were now few people left to eat, and they hated vegetables. Moreover, they kept no cattle, it was not the custom of that tribe, except a very few for milk. Alan advised them to increase their herds, since, as he pointed out to them, "dog should not eat dog" or the human being his own kind.

The chief answered that there was a great deal in what he said, which on his return he would lay before his head men. Indeed Alan, to his astonishment, discovered that Jeekie had been quite right when he alleged that these people, so terrible in their mode of life, were yet "kind and gentle at heart." They preyed upon mankind because for centuries it had been their custom so to do, but if anyone had been there to show them a better way, he grew sure that they would follow it gladly. At least they were brave and loyal and even after their first fear of the white man had worn off, fulfilled their promises without a murmur. Once, indeed, when he chanced to have gone for a walk unarmed and to be charged by a bull elephant, these Ogula ran at the brute with their spears and drove it away, a rescue in which one of them lost his life, for the "rogue" caught and killed him.

So the days went on while they paddled leisurely up the river, Alan employing the time by taking lessons in the Asiki tongue from Jeekie, a language which he had been studying ever since he left England. The task was not easy, as he had no books and Jeekie himself after some thirty years of absence, was doubtful as to many of its details. Still being a linguist by nature and education and finding in the tongue similarities to other African dialects which he knew, he was now able to speak it a little, in a halting fashion.

On the fifth day of their ascent of the river, they came to a tributary that flowed into it from the north, up which the Ogula said they must proceed to reach Asiki-land. The stream was narrow and sluggish, widening out here and there into great swamps through which it was not easy to find a channel. Also the district was so unhealthy that even several of the Ogula contracted fever, of which Alan cured them by heavy doses of quinine, for fortunately his travelling medicine chest remained to him. These cures were effected after their chief suggested that they should be thrown overboard, or left to die in the swamp as useless, with the result that the white man's magical powers were thenceforth established beyond doubt or cavil. Indeed the poor Ogula now looked on him as a god superior even to Little Bonsa, whose familiar he was supposed to be.

The journey through that swamp was very trying, since in this wet season often they could find no place on which to sleep at night, but must stay in the canoe tormented by mosquitoes, and in constant danger of being upset by the hippopotami that lived there. Moreover, as no game was now available, they were obliged to live on these beasts, fish when they could catch them, and wildfowl, which sometimes they were unable to cook for lack of fuel. This did not trouble the Ogula, who ate them raw, as did Jeekie when he was hungry. But Alan was obliged to starve until they could make a fire. This it was only possible to do when they found drift or other wood, since at that season the rank vegetation was in full growth. Also the fearful thunderstorms which broke continually and in a few minutes half filled their canoe with water, made the reeds and the soil on which they grew, sodden with wet. As Jeekie said:

"This time of year only fit for duck and crocodile. Human should remember uncontrollable forces of nature and wait till winter come in due course, when quagmire bear sole of his foot."

This elaborate remark he made to Alan during the progress of a particularly fearful tempest. The lightning blazed in the black sky and seemed to strike all about them like stabbing swords of fire, the thunder crashed and bellowed as it may be supposed that it will do on that day when the great earth, worn out at last, shall reel and stagger to its doom. The rain fell in a straight and solid sheet; the tall reeds waved confusedly like millions of dim arms and while they waved, uttered a vast and groaning noise; the scared wildfowl in their terror, with screams and the sough of wings, rushed past them in flocks a thousand strong, now seen and now lost in the vapours. To keep their canoe afloat the poor, naked Ogula oarsmen, shivering with cold and fear, baled furiously with their hands, or bowls of hollowed wood, and called back to Alan to save them as though he were the master of the elements. Even Jeekie was depressed and appeared to be offering up petitions, though whether these were directed to Little Bonsa or elsewhere it was impossible to know.

As for Alan, the heart was out of him. It is true that so far he had escaped fever or other sickness, which in itself was wonderful, but he was chilled through and through and practically had eaten nothing for two days, and very little for a week, since his stomach turned from half-cooked hippopotamus fat and wildfowl. Moreover, they had lost the channel and seemed to be wandering aimlessly through a wilderness of reeds broken here and there by lines of deeper water.

According the Ogula they should have reached the confines of the great lake several days before and landed on healthful rising ground that was part of the Asiki territory. But this had not happened, and now he doubted whether it ever would happen. It was more likely that they would come to their deaths, there in the marsh, especially as the few ball and shot cartridges which they had saved in their flight were now exhausted. Not one was left; nothing was left except their revolvers with some charges, which of course were quite useless for the killing of game. Therefore they were in a fair way to die of hunger, for here if fish existed, they refused to be caught and nought remained for them to fill themselves with except water slugs, and snails which the boatmen were already gathering and crunching up in their great teeth. Or, perhaps the Ogula, forgetting friendship under the pressure of necessity, would murder them as they slept and—revert to their usual diet.

Jeekie was right, he should have remembered the "uncontrollable forces of Nature." Only a madman would have undertaken such an expedition in the rains. No wonder that the Asiki remained a secret and hidden people when their frontier was protected by such a marsh as this upon the one side and, as he understood, by impassable mountains upon the other.

There came a lull in the tempest and the boatmen began to get the better of the water, which now was up to their knees. Alan asked Jeekie if he thought it was over, but that worthy shook his white head mournfully, causing the spray to fly as from a twirling mop, and replied:

"Can't say, cats and dogs not tumble so many for present, only pups and kitties left, so to speak, but think there plenty more up there," and he nodded at the portentous fire-laced cloud which seemed to be spreading over them, its black edges visible even through the gloom.

"Bad business, I am afraid, Jeekie. Shouldn't have brought you here, or those poor beggars either," and he looked at the scared, frozen Ogula. "I begin to wonder——"

"Never wonder, Major," broke in Jeekie in alarm. "If wonder, not live, if wonder, not be born, too much wonder about everywhere. Can't understand nothing, so give it up. Say, 'Right-O and devil hindermost!' Very good motto for biped in tight place. Better drown here than in City bucket shop. But no drown. Should be dead long ago, but Little Bonsa play the game, she not want to sink in stinking swamp when so near her happy home. Come out all right somehow, as from dwarf. Every cloud have silver lining, Major, even that black chap up there. Oh! my golly!"

This last exclamation was wrung from Jeekie's lips by a sudden development of "forces of Nature" which astonished even him. Instead of a silver lining the "black chap" exhibited one of gold. In an instant it seemed to turn to acres of flame; it was as though the heavens had taken fire. A flash or a thunderbolt struck the water within ten yards of their canoe, causing the boatmen to throw themselves upon their faces through shock or terror. Then came the hurricane, which fortunately was so strong that it permitted no more rain to fall. The tall reeds were beaten flat beneath its breath; the canoe was seized in its grip and whirled round and round, then driven forward like an arrow. Only the weight of the men and the water in it prevented it from oversetting. Dense darkness fell upon them and although they could see no star, they knew that it must be night. On they rushed, driven by that shrieking gale, and all about and around them this wall of darkness. No one spoke, for hope was abandoned, and if they had, their voices could not have been heard. The last thing that Alan remembered was feeling Jeekie dragging a grass mat over him to protect him a little if he could. Then his senses wavered, as does a dying lamp. He thought that he was back in what Jeekie had rudely called "City bucket shop," bargaining across the telephone wire, upon which came all the sounds of the infernal regions, with a financial paper for an article on a Little Bonsa Syndicate that he proposed to float. He thought he was in The Court woods with Barbara, only the birds in the trees sang so unnaturally loud that he could not hear her voice, and she wore Little Bonsa on her head as a bonnet. Then she departed in flame, leaving him and Death alone.

********

Alan awoke. Above the sun shone hotly, warming him back to life, but in front was a thick wall of mist and rising beyond it in the distance he saw the rugged swelling forms of mountains. Doubtless these had been visible before, but the tall reeds through which they travelled had hid the sight of them. He looked behind him and there in a heap lay the Ogula around their chief, insensible or sleeping. He counted them and found that two were gone, lost in the tempest, how or where no man ever learned. He looked forward and saw a peculiar sight, for in the prow of the drifting canoe stood Jeekie clad in the remains of his white robe and wearing on his head the battered helmet and about his shoulders the torn fragments of green mosquito net. While Alan was wondering strangely why he had adopted this ceremonial garb, from out of the mist there came a sound of singing, of wild and solemn singing. Jeekie seemed to listen to it; then he lifted up his great musical voice and sang as though in answer. What he sang Alan could not understand, but he recognized that the language which he used was that of the Asiki people.

A pause and a confused murmuring, and now again the wild song rose and again Jeekie answered.

"What the deuce are you doing? Where are we?" asked Alan faintly.

Jeekie turned and beamed upon him; although his teeth were chattering and his face was hollow, still he beamed.

"You awake, Major?" he said. "Thought good old sun do trick. Feel your heart now and find it beat. Pulse, too, strong, though temp'rature not normal. Well, good news this morning. Little Bonsa come out top as usual. Asiki priests on bank there. Can't see them, but know their song and answer. Same old game as thirty years ago. Asiki never change, which good business when you been away long while."

"Hang the Asiki," said Alan feebly, "I think all these poor beggars are dead, and he pointed to the rowers.

"Look like it, Major, but what that matter now since you and I alive? Plenty more where they come from. Not dead though, think only sleep, no like cold, like dormouse. But never mind cannibal pig. They serve our turn, if they live, live; if they die, die and God have mercy on souls, if cannibal have soul. Ah! here we are," and from beneath six inches of water he dragged up the tin box containing Little Bonsa, from which he extracted the fetish, wet but uninjured.

"Put her on now, Major. Put her on at once and come sit in prow of canoe. Must reach Asiki-land in proper style. Priests think it your reverend uncle come back again, just as he leave. Make very good impression."

"I can't," said Alan feebly. "I am played out, Jeekie."

"Oh! buck up, Major, buck up!" he replied imploringly. "One kick more and you win race, mustn't spoil ship for ha'porth of tar. You just wear fetish, whistle once on land, and then go to sleep for whole week if you like. I do rest, say it all magic, and so forth—that you been dead and just come out of grave, or anything you like. No matter if you turn up as announced on bill and God bless hurricane that blow us here when we expect die. Come, Major, quick, quick! mist melt and soon they see you." Then without waiting for an answer Jeekie clapped the wet mask on his master's head, tied the thongs and led Alan to the prow of the canoe, where he set him down on a little cross bench, stood behind supporting him and again began to sing in a great triumphant voice.

The mist cleared away, rolling up like a curtain and revealing on the shore a number of men and women clad in white robes, who were martialled in ranks there, chanting and staring out at the dim waters of the lagoon. Yonder upon the waters, driven forward by the gentle breeze, floated a canoe and lo! in the prow of that canoe sat a white man and on his head the god which they had lost a whole generation gone. On the head of a white man it had departed; on the head of a white man it returned. They saw and fell upon their knees.

"Blow, Major, blow!" whispered Jeekie, and Alan blew a feeble note through the whistle in the mouth of the mask. It was enough, they knew it. They sprang into the water and dragged the canoe to land. They set Alan on the shore and worshipped him. They haled up a lad as though for sacrifice, for a priest flourished a great knife above his head, but Jeekie said something that caused them to let him go. Alan thought it was to the effect that Little Bonsa had changed her habits across the Black Water, and wanted no blood, only food. Then he remembered no more; again the darkness fell upon him.

## Chapter 10

# Bonsa Town

When consciousness returned to Alan, the first thing of which he became dimly aware was the slow, swaying motion of a litter. He raised himself, for he was lying at full length, and in so doing felt that there was something over his face.

"That confounded Little Bonsa," he thought. "Am I expected to spend the rest of my life with it on my head like the man in the iron mask?"

Then he put up his hand and felt the thing, to find that it was not Little Bonsa, but something made apparently of thin, fine linen, fitted to the shape of his face, for there was a nose on it, and eyeholes through which he could see, yes, and a mouth whereof the lips by some ingenious contrivance could be moved up and down.

"Little Bonsa's undress uniform, I expect," he muttered, and tried to drag it off. This, however, proved to be impossible, for it was fitted tightly to his head and laced or fastened at the back of his neck so securely that he could not undo it. Being still weak, soon he gave up the attempt and began to look about him.

He was in a litter, a very fine litter hung round with beautifully woven and coloured grass mats, inside of which were a kind of couch and cushions of soft wool or hair, so arranged that he could either sit up or lie down. He peeped between two of these mats and saw that they were travelling in a mountainous country over a well-beaten road or trail, and that his litter was borne upon the shoulders of a double line of white-robed men, while all around him marched numbers of other men. They seemed to be soldiers, for they were arranged in companies and carried large spears and shields. Also some of them wore torques and bracelets of yellow metal that might be either brass or gold. Turning himself about he found an eyehole in the back of the litter so contrived that its occupant could see without being seen, and perceived that his escort amounted to a veritable army of splendid-looking, but sombre-faced savages of a somewhat Semitic cast of countenance. Indeed many of them had aquiline features and hair that, although crisped, was long and carefully arranged in something like the old Egyptian fashion. Also he saw that about thirty yards behind and separated from him by a bodyguard, was borne a second litter. By means of a similar aperture in front he discovered yet more soldiers, and beyond them, at the head of the procession, was what appeared to be a body of white-robed men and women bearing strange emblems and banners. These he took to be priests and priestesses.

Having examined everything that was within reach of his eye, Alan sank back upon his cushions and began to realize that he was very faint and hungry. It was just then that the sound of a familiar voice reached his ears. It was the voice of Jeekie, and he did not speak, he chanted in English to a melody which Alan at once recognized as a Gregorian tone, apparently from the second litter.

"Oh, Major," he sang, "have you yet awoke from refre-e-eshing sleep? If so, please answer me in same tone of voice, for remember that you de-e-evil of a swell, Lord of the Little Bonsa, and must not speak like co-o-ommon cad."

Feeble as he was Alan nearly burst out laughing, then remembering that probably he was expected not to laugh, chanted his answer as directed, which having a good tenor voice, he did with some effect, to the evident awe and delight of all the escort within hearing.

"I am awake, most excellent Jee-e-ekie, and feel the need of food, if you have such a thing abou-ou-out you and it is lawful for the Lord of Little Bonsa to take nu-tri-ment."

Instantly Jeekie's deep voice rose in reply.

"That good tidings upon the mountain tops, Ma-ajor. Can't come out to bring you chop because too i-i-infra dig, for now I also biggish bug, the little bird what sit upon the rose, as poet sa-a-ays. I tell these Johnnies bring you grub, which you eat without qualm, for Asiki Al coo-o-ook."

Then followed loud orders issued by Jeekie to his immediate entourage, and some confusion.

As a result presently Alan's litter was halted, the curtains were opened and kneeling women thrust through them platters of wood upon which, wrapped up in leaves, were the dismembered limbs of a bird which he took to be chicken or guinea-fowl, and a gold cup containing water pleasantly flavoured with some essence. This cup interested him very much both on account of its shape and workmanship, which if rude, was striking in design, resembling those drinking vessels that have been found in Mycenaean graves. Also it proved to him that Jeekie's stories of the abundance of the precious metal among the Asiki had not been exaggerated. If it were not very plentiful, they would scarcely, he thought, make their travelling cups of gold. Evidently there was wealth in the land.

After the food had been handed to him the litter went on again, and seated upon his cushions, he ate and drank heartily enough, for now that the worst of his fatigue had passed away, his hunger was great. In some absurd fashion this meal reminded him of that which a traveller makes out of a luncheon basket upon a railway line in Europe or America. Only there the cups are not of gold and among the Asiki were no paper napkins, no salt and mustard, and no three and sixpence or dollar to pay. Further, until he got used to it, luncheon in a linen mask with a moveable mouth was not easy. This difficulty he overcame at last by propping the imitation lips apart with a piece of bone, after which things were easier.

When he had finished he threw the platter and the remains out of the litter, retaining the cup for further examination, and recommenced his intoned and poetical converse with Jeekie.

To set it out at length would be wearisome, but in the course of an hour or so he collected a good deal of information. Thus he learned that they were due to arrive at the Asiki city, which was called Bonsa Town, by nightfall, or a little after. Also he was informed that the mask he wore was, as he had guessed, a kind of undress uniform without which he must never appear, since for anyone except the Asika herself to look upon the naked countenance of an individual so mysteriously mixed up with Little Bonsa, was sacrilege of the worst sort. Indeed Jeekie assured him that the priests who had put on the headdress when he was insensible were first blindfolded.

This news depressed Alan very much, since the prospect of living in a linen mask for an indefinite period was not cheerful. Recovering, he chanted a query as to the fate of the Ogula crew and their chief Fahni.

"Not de-ad," intoned Jeekie in reply, "and not gone back. A-all alive-O, somewhere behind there. Fanny very sick about it, for he think Asiki bring them along for sacrifice, poo-or beg-gars."

Finally he inquired where Little Bonsa was and was answered that he himself as its lawful guardian, was sitting on the fetish in its tin box, tidings that he was able to verify by groping beneath the cushions.

After this his voice gave out, though Jeekie continued to sing items of interesting news from time to time. Indeed there were other things that absorbed Alan's attention. Looking through the peepholes and cracks in the curtains, he saw that at last they had reached the crest of a ridge up which they had been climbing for hours. Before them lay a vast and fertile valley, much of which seemed to be under cultivation, and down it flowed a broad and placid river. Opposite to him and facing west a great tongue of land ran up to a wall of mountains with stark precipices of black rock that seemed to be hundreds, or even thousands, of feet high, and at the tip of this tongue a mighty waterfall rushed over the precipice, looking at that distance like a cascade of smoke. This torrent, which he remembered was called Raaba, fell into a great pool and there divided itself into two rushing branches that enclosed an ellipse of ground, surrounded on all sides by water, for on its westernmost extremity the branches met again and after flowing a while as one river, divided once more and wound away quietly to north and south further than the eye could reach. On the island thus formed, which may have been three miles long by two in breadth, stood thousands of straw-roofed, square-built huts with verandas, neatly arranged in blocks and lines and having between them streets that were edged with palms.

On the hither side of the pool was what looked like a park, for here grew great, black trees, which from their flat shape Alan took to be some variety of cedar, and standing alone in the midst of this park where no other habitations could be discovered, was a large, low building with dark-coloured walls and gabled roofs that flashed like fire.

"The Gold House!" said Alan to himself with a gasp. "So it is not a dream or a lie."

The details at that distance he could not discover, nor did he try to do so, for the general glory of the scene held him in its grip. At this evening hour, for a little while, the level rays of the setting sun poured straight up the huge, water-hollowed *kloof*. They struck upon the face of the fall, staining it and the clouds of mist that hung above, to a hundred glorious hues; indeed the substance of the foaming water seemed to be interlaced with rainbows whereof the arch reached their crest and the feet were lost in the sullen blackness of the pool beneath. Beautiful too was the valley, glowing in the quiet light of evening, and even the native town thus gilded and glorified, looked like some happy home of peace.

The sun was sinking rapidly, and before the litter reached the foot of the hill and began to cross the rich valley, all the glory had departed and only the cataract showed white and ghost-like through the gloom. But still the light, which seemed to gather to itself, gleamed upon that golden roof amid the cedar trees; then the moon rose and the gold was turned to silver. Alan lay back upon his cushions full of wonder, almost of awe. It was a marvellous thing that he should have lived to reach this secret place hidden in the heart of Africa and defended by swamps, mountains and savages to which, so far as he knew, only one white man had ever penetrated. And to think of it! That white man, his own uncle, had never even held it worth while to make public any account of its wonders, which apparently had seemed to him of no importance. Or perhaps he thought that if he did he would not be believed. Well, there they were before and about him, and now the question was, what would be his fate in this Gold House where the great fetish dwelt with its priestess?

Ah! that priestess! Somehow he shivered a little when he thought of her; it was as though her influence were over him already. Next moment he forgot her for a while, for they had come to the river brink and the litter was being carried on to a barge or ferry, about which were gathered many armed men. Evidently the Gold House was well defended both by Nature and otherwise. The ferry was pulled or rowed across the river, he could not see which, and they passed through a gateway into the town and up a broad street where hundreds of people watched his advent. They did not seem to speak, or if they spoke their voices were lost in the sound of the thunder of the great cataract which dominated the place with its sullen, continuous roar. It took Alan days to become accustomed to that roar, but by the inhabitants of Asiki-land apparently it was not noticed; their ears and voices were attuned to overcome its volume which their fathers had known from the beginning.

Presently they were through the town and a wooden gate in an inner wall which surrounded the park where the cedars grew. At this spot Alan noted that everybody left them except the bearers and a few men whom he took to be priests. On they stole like ghosts beneath the mighty trees, from whose limbs hung long festoons of moss. It was very dark there, only in places where a bough was broken the moonlight lay in white gules upon the ground. Another wall and another gate, and suddenly the litter was set down. Its curtains opened, torches flashed, women appeared clad in white robes, veiled and mysterious, who bowed before him, then half led and half lifted him from his litter. He could feel their eyes on him through their veils, but he could not see their faces. He could see nothing except their naked, copper-coloured arms and long thin hands stretched out to assist him.

Alan descended from the litter as slowly as he could, for somehow he shrank from the quaint, carved portal which he saw before him. He did not wish to pass it; its aspect filled him with reluctance. The women drew him on, their hands pulled at his arms, their shoulders pressed him from behind. Still he hung back, looking about him, till to his delight he saw the other litter arrive and out of it emerge Jeekie, still wearing his sun-helmet with its fringe of tattered mosquito curtain.

"Here we are, Major," he said in his cheerful voice, "turned up all right like a bad ha'penny, but in odd situation."

"Very odd," echoed Alan. "Could you persuade these ladies to let go of me?"

"Don't know," answered Jeekie. "'Spect they doubtfully your wives; 'spect you have lots of wives here; don't get white man every day, so make most of him. Best thing you do, kick out and teach them place. Rub nose in dirt at once and make them good, that first-class plan with female. I no like interfere in such delicate matter."

Terrified by this information, Alan put out his strength and shook the women off him, whereon without seeming to take any offence they drew back to a little distance and began to bow, like automata. Then Jeekie addressed them in their own language, asking them what they meant by defiling this mighty lord, born of the Heavens, with the touch of their hands, whereat they went on bowing more humbly than before. Next he threw aside the cushions of the litter and finding the tin box containing Little Bonsa, held it before him in both hands and bade the women lead on.

The march began, a bewildering march. It was like a nightmare. Veiled women with torches before and behind, Jeekie stalking ahead carrying the battered tin box, long passages lined with gold, a vision of black water edged with a wide promenade, and finally a large lamp-lit room whereof the roof was supported by gilded columns, and in the room couches of cushions, wooden stools inlaid with ivory, vessels of water, great basins made of some black, hard wood, and in the centre a block of stone that looked like an altar.

Jeekie set down the tin box upon the altar-like stone, then he turned to the crowd of women and said, "Bring food." Instantly they departed, closing the door of the room behind them.

"Now for a wash," said Alan, "unlace this confounded mask, Jeekie."

"Mustn't, Major, mustn't. Priests tell me that. If those girls see you without mask, perhaps they kill them. Wait till they gone after supper, then take it off. No one allowed see you without mask except Asika herself."

Alan stepped to one of the wooden bowls full of water which

stood under a lamp, and gazed at his own reflection. The mask was gilded; the sham lips were painted red and round the eye-holes were black lines.

"Why, it is horrible," he exclaimed, starting back. "I look like a devil crossed with Guy Fawkes. Do you mean to tell me that I have got to live in this thing?"

"Afraid so, Major, upon all public occasion. At least they say that. You holy, not lawful see your sacred face."

"Who do the Asiki think I am, then, Jeekie?"

"They think you your reverend uncle come back after many, many year. You see, Major, they not believe uncle run away with Little Bonsa; they believe Little Bonsa run away with uncle just for change of air and so on, and that now, when she tired of strange land, she bring him back again. That why you so holy, favourite of Little Bonsa who live with you all this time and keep you just same age, bloom of youth."

"In Heaven's name," asked Alan, exasperated, "what is Little Bonsa, beyond an ancient and ugly gold fetish?"

"Hush," said Jeekie, "mustn't call her names here in her own house. Little Bonsa much more than fetish, Little Bonsa alive, or so," he added doubtfully, "these silly niggers say. She wife of Big Bonsa, you see, to-morrow p'raps. But their story this, that she get dead sick of Big Bonsa and bolt with white Medicine man, who dare preach she nothing but heathen idol. She want show him whether or no she only idol. That the yarn, priests tell it me today. They always watch for her there by the edge of the lake. They always sure Little Bonsa come back. Not at all surprised, but as she love you once, you stop holy; and I holy also, thank goodness, because she take me too as servant. Therefore we sleep in peace, for they not cut out throats, at any rate at present, though I think," he added mournfully, "they not let us go either."

Alan sat down on a stool and groaned at the appalling prospect suggested by this information.

"Cheer up, Major," said Jeekie sympathetically. "Perhaps manage hook it somehow, and meanwhile make best of bad business and have high old time. You see you want to come Asiki-land, though I tell you it rum place, and," he added with certitude and a circular sweep of his hand, "by Jingo! you here now and I daresay they give you all the gold you want."

"What's the good of gold unless one can get away with it? What's the good of anything if we are prisoners among these devils?"

"Perhaps time show, Major. Hush! here come dinner. You sit still on stool and look holy."

The door opened and through it appeared four of the women bearing dishes and cups full of drink, fashioned of gold like that which had been given to Alan in the litter. He noticed at once that they had removed their veils and outer garments, if indeed they were the same women, and now, like many other Africans, were but lightly clad in linen capes open in front that hung over their shoulders, short petticoats or skirts about their middles, and sandals. Such was their attire which, scanty as it might be, was yet becoming enough and extremely rich. Thus the cape was fastened with a brooch of worked gold, so were the sandal straps, while the petticoat was adorned with beads of gold that jingled as they walked, and amongst them strings of other beads of various and beautiful colours, that might be glass or might be precious stones. Moreover, these women were young and handsome, having splendid figures and well-cut features, soft, dark eyes and rather long hair worn in the formal and attractive fashion that has been described.

Advancing to Alan two of them knelt before him, holding out the trays upon which was the food. So they remained while he ate, like bronze statues, nor would they consent to change their posture even when he told them in their language to be pleased to go away. On hearing themselves addressed in the Asiki language, they seemed surprised, for their faces changed a little, but go they would not. The result was that Alan grew extremely nervous and ate and drank so rapidly that he scarcely noted what he was putting into his mouth. Then before Jeekie, to whom the women did not kneel, had half finished his dinner, Alan rose and walked away, whereon two of the women gathered up everything, including the dishes that had been given to Jeekie, and in spite of his remonstrances carried them out of the room.

"I say, Major," said Jeekie, "if you gobble chop so fast you go ill inside. Poor nigger like me can't keep up with you and sleep hungry tonight."

"I am sorry, Jeekie," said Alan with a little laugh, "but I can't eat off living tables, especially when they stare at one like that. You tell them that tomorrow we will breakfast alone."

"Oh, yes, I tell them, Major, but I don't know if they listen. They mean it great compliment and only think you not like those girls and send others."

"Look here, Jeekie," exclaimed Alan, turning his masked face towards the two who remained, "let us come to an understanding at once. Clear them out. Tell them I am so holy that Little Bonsa is enough for me. Say I can't bear the sight of females, and that if they stop here I will sacrifice them. Say anything you like, only get rid of them and lock the door."

Thus adjured, Jeekie began to reason with the women, and as they treated his remarks with lofty disdain, at last seized first one and then the other by the elbows and literally ran them out of the room.

"There," he said, "baggage gone since you make such fuss about it, though I 'spect they try to give me Bean for this job" (here he spoke not in figurative English slang, but of the Calabar bean, which is a favourite native poison). "Well, dinner gone and girls gone, and we tired, so best go to bed. Think we all private here now, though in Gold House never can be sure," and he looked round him suspiciously, adding, "rummy place, Gold House, full of all sort of holes made by old fellows thousand year ago, which no one know but Bonsa priests. Still, best risk it and take off your face so that you have decent wash," and he began to unlace the mask on his master's head.

Never has a City clerk dressed up for a fancy ball in the armour of a Norman knight, been more glad to get rid of his costume than was Alan of that hateful head-dress. At length it was gone with his other garments and the much-needed wash accomplished, after which he clothed himself in a kind of linen gown which apparently had been provided for him, and lay down on one of the couches, placing his revolver by his side.

"Will those lamps burn all night, Jeekie?" he asked.

"Hope so, Major, as we haven't got no match. Not fond of dark in Gold House," answered Jeekie sleepily. Then he began to snore.

Alan fell asleep, but was too excited and tired to rest very soundly. All sorts of dreams came to him, one of which he remembered on awakening, perhaps because it was the last. He dreamed that he heard some noise and opened his eyes, to see that they were no longer alone in the room. The oil lamps had burned quite low, indeed some of them were out, but by the light of those that remained he saw a tall figure which seemed to appear at the edge of the surrounding blackness, a woman's figure. It walked forward to the altar-like stone upon which lay the tin box containing Little Bonsa, and after several rather awkward attempts, succeeded in opening it, thereby making a noise which, in his dream, finally awoke Alan. For a while the figure gazed at the fetish. Then it shut the box, glided to his bed and bent down as though to study him. Out of the corners of his eyes he peered up at it, pretending all the while to be fast asleep.

It was that of a woman wonderfully clad in gold-spangled, veil-like garments with round bosses shaped to the breast, covered with thin plates of gold fashioned like the scales of a fish which showed off the extraordinary elegance of her lithe form. The low lamp-light shone upon her face and the coronet of gold set upon her dark hair. What a face it was! Never in all his days had he seen its like for evil loveliness. The great, languid, oblong eyes, the rich red lips bent like a bow, the cruel smile of the mouth, the broad forehead on which the hair grew low, the delicately arched eyebrows and the long curving lashes of the heavy lids beneath them, the rounded cheeks, smooth as a ripe fruit, the firm, shapely chin, the snake-like poise of the head, the long bending neck, and the feline smile; all of these combined made such a dream-vision as he had never seen before, and to tell the truth, notwithstanding its beauty, for that could not be doubted, never wished to see again. Somehow he felt that if Satan should happen to have a copper-coloured wife, the exact picture of that lady had projected itself upon his sleeping senses.

She seemed to study him very earnestly, with a kind of passionate eagerness, indeed, moving a little now and again to let the light fall upon some part that was in shadow. Once even she stretched out her rounded arm and just lifted the edge of the blanket so as to expose his hand, the left. As it chanced on the little finger of this hand Alan wore a plain gold ring which Barbara had given him; once it had been her grandfather's signet. This ring, which had a coat of arms cut upon its bezel seemed to interest her very much as she examined it for a long while. Then she drew off from her own finger another ring of gold fashioned of two snakes curiously intertwined, and gently, so gently that in his sleep he scarcely felt it, slipped it on to his finger above Barbara's ring.

After this she seemed to vanish away, and Alan slept soundly until the morning, when he awoke to find the light of the sun pouring into the room through the high-set latticed window places.

## Chapter 11
# The Hall of the Dead

Alan rose and stretched himself, and hearing him, Jeekie, who had a dog's faculty of instantly awaking from what seemed to be the deepest sleep, sat up also.

"You rest well, Major? No dream, eh?" he asked curiously.

"Not very," answered Alan, "and I had a dream, of a woman who stood over me and vanished away, as dreams do."

"Ah!" said Jeekie. "But where you find that new ring on finger, Major?"

Alan stared at his hand and started, for there set on it above that of Barbara, was the little circlet formed of twisted snakes which he had seen in his sleep.

"Then it must have been true," he said in a low and rather frightened voice. "But how did she come and go?"

"Funny place, Gold House. I tell you that yesterday, Major. People come up through hole, like rat. Never quite sure you alone in Gold House. But what this lady like?"

Alan described his visitor to the best of his ability.

"Ah!" said Jeekie, "pretty girl. Big eyes, gold crown, gold stays which fit tight in front, very nice and decent; sort of night-shirt with little gold stars all over—by Jingo! I think that Asika herself. If so—great compliment."

"Confound the compliment, I think it great cheek," answered Alan angrily. "What does she mean by poking about here at night and putting rings on my finger?"

"Don't know, Major, but p'raps she wish make you understand that she like cut of your jib. Find out by and by. Meanwhile you wear ring, for while that on finger no one do you any harm."

"You told me that this Asika is a married woman, did you not?" remarked Alan gloomily.

"Oh, yes, Major, always married; one down, other come on, you see. But she not always like her husband, and then she make him sit up, poor devil, and he die double quick. Great honour to be Asika's husband, but soon all finished. P'raps——"

Then he checked himself and suggested that Alan should have a bath while he cleaned his clothes, an attention that they needed.

Scarcely had Alan finished his toilet, donned the Arab-looking linen robe over his own fragmentary flannels, and above it the hateful mask which Jeekie insisted he must wear, when there came a knocking on the door. Motioning to Alan to take his seat upon a stool, Jeekie undid the bars, and as before women appeared with food and waited while they ate, which this time, having overcome his nervousness, Alan did more leisurely.

Their meal done, one of the women asked Jeekie, for to his master they did not seem to dare to speak, whether the white lord did not wish to walk in the garden. Without waiting for an answer she led him to the end of the large room and, unbarring another door that they had not noticed, revealed a passage, beyond which appeared trees and flowers. Then she and her companions went away with the fragments of the meal.

"Come on," said Alan, taking up the box containing Little Bonsa, which he did not dare to leave behind, "and let us get into the air."

So they went down the passage and at the end of it through gates of copper or gold, they knew not which, that had evidently been left open for them, into the garden. It was a large place, a good many acres in extent indeed, and kept with some care, for there were paths in it and flowers that seemed to have been planted. Also here grew certain of the mighty cedar trees that they had seen from far off, beneath those spreading boughs twilight reigned, while beyond, not more than half a mile away, the splendid river-fall thundered down the precipice. For the rest they could find no exit to that garden which on one side was enclosed by a sheer cliff of living rock, and on the others with steep stone walls beyond which ran a torrent, and by the buildings of the Gold House itself.

For a while they walked up and down the rough paths, till at last Jeekie, wearying of this occupation, remarked:

"Melancholy hole this, Major. Remind me of Westminster Abbey in London fog, where your uncle of blessed mem'ry often take me pray and look at fusty tomb of king. S'pose we go back Gold House and see what happen. Anything better than stand about under cursed old cedar tree."

"All right," said Alan, who through the eyeholes of his mask had been studying the walls to seek a spot in them that could be climbed if necessary, and found none.

So they returned to the room, which had been swept and garnished in their absence. No sooner had they entered it than the door opened and through it came long lines of Asiki priests, each of whom staggered beneath the weight of a hide bag that he bore upon his shoulder, which bags they piled up about the stone altar. Then, as though at some signal, each priest opened the mouth of his bag and Alan saw that they wee filled with gold, gold in dust, gold in nuggets, gold in vessels perfect or broken; more gold than Alan had ever seen before.

"Why do they bring all this stuff here?" he asked, and Jeekie translated his question.

"It is an offering to the lord of Little Bonsa," answered the head priest, bowing, "a gift from the Asika. The heaven-born white man sent word by his Ogula messengers that he desired gold. Here is the gold that he desired."

Alan stared at the treasure, which after all was what he had come to seek. If only he had it safe in England, he would be a rich man and his troubles ended. But how could he get it to England? Here it was worthless as mud.

"I thank the Asika," he said. "I ask for porters to bear her gift back to my own country, since it is too heavy for me and my servant to carry alone."

At these words the priest smiled a little, then said that the Asika desired to see the white lord and to receive from him Little Bonsa in return for the gold, and that he could proffer his request to her.

"Good," replied Alan, "lead me to the Asika."

Then they started, Alan bearing the box containing Little Bonsa, and Jeekie following after him. They went down passages and through sundry doors till at length they came to a long and narrow hall that seemed to be lined with plates of gold. At the end of this hall was a large chair of black wood and ivory placed upon a dais, and sitting in this chair with the light pouring on her from some opening above, was the woman of Alan's dream, beautiful to look on in her crown and glittering garments. Upon a stool at the foot of the dais sat a man, a handsome and melancholy man. His hair was tied behind his head in a pigtail and gilded, his face was painted red, white and yellow; he wore ropes of bright-coloured stones about his neck, middle, arms and ankles, and held a kind of sceptre in his hand.

"Who is that creature?" asked Alan over his shoulder to Jeekie. "The Court fool?"

"That husband of Asika, Major. He not fool, very big gun, but look a little low now because his time soon up. Come on, Major, Asika beckon us. Get on stomach and crawl; that custom here," he added, going down on to his hands and knees, as did all the priests who followed them.

"I'll see her hanged first," answered Alan in English.

Then accompanied by the creeping Jeekie and the train of prostrate priests, he marched up the long hall to the edge of the dais and there stood still and bowed to the woman in the chair.

"Greeting, white man," she said in a low voice when she had studied him for a while. "Do you understand my tongue?"

"A little," he answered in Asiki, "moreover, my servant here knows it well and can translate."

"I am glad," she said. "Tell me then, in your country do not people go on to their knees before their queen, and if not, how do they greet her?"

"No," answered Alan with the help of Jeekie. "They greet her by raising their head-dress or kissing her hand."

"Ah!" she said. "Well, you have no head-dress, so kiss *my* hand," and she stretched it out towards him, at the same time prodding the man whom Jackie had said was her husband, in the back with her foot, apparently to make him get out of the way.

Not knowing what to do, Alan stepped on to the dais, the painted man scowling at him as he passed. Then he halted and said:

"How can I kiss your hand through this mask, Asika?"

"True," she answered, then considered a little and added, "White man, you have brought back Little Bonsa, have you not, Little Bonsa who ran away with you a great many years ago?"

"I have," he said, ignoring the rest of the question.

"Your messengers said that you required a present of gold in return for Little Bonsa. I have sent you one, is it sufficient? If not, you can have more."

"I cannot say, O Asika, I have not examined it. But I thank you for the present and desire porters to enable me to carry it away."

"You desire porters," she repeated meditatively. "We will talk of that when you have rested here a moon or two. Meanwhile, give me Little Bonsa that she may be restored to her own place."

Alan opened the tin box and lifting out the fetish, gave it to the priestess, who took it and with a serpentine movement of extraordinary grace glided from her chair on to her knees, holding the mask above her head in both hands, then thrice covered her face with it. This done, she called to the priests, bidding them take Little Bonsa to her own place and give notice throughout the land that she was back again. She added that the ancient Feast of Little Bonsa would be held on the night of the full moon within three days, and that all preparations must be made for it as she had commanded.

Then the head medicine-man, raising himself upon his knees, crept on to the dais, took the fetish from her hands, and breaking into a wild song of triumph, he and his companions crawled down the hall and vanished through the door, leaving them alone save for the Asika's husband.

When they had gone the Asika looked at this man in a reflective way, and Alan looked at him also through the eyeholes of his mask, finding him well worth studying. As has been said, notwithstanding his paint and grotesque decorations, he was very good-looking for a native, with well-cut features of an Arab type. Also he was tall and muscular and not more than thirty years of age. What struck Alan most, however, was none of these things, nor his jewelled chains, nor even his gilded pigtail, but his eyes, which were full of terrors. Seeing them, Alan remembered Jeekie's story, which he had told to Mr. Haswell's guests at The Court, of how the husband of the Asika was driven mad by ghosts.

Just then she spoke to the man, addressing him by name and saying: "Leave us alone, Mungana, I wish to speak with this white lord."

He did not seem to hear her words, but continued to stare at Alan.

"Hearken!" she exclaimed in a voice of ice. "Do my bidding and begone, or you shall sleep alone tonight in a certain chamber that you know of."

Then Mungana rose, looked at her as a dog sometimes does at a cruel master who is about to beat it, yes, with just that same expression, put his hands before his eyes for a little while, and turning, left the hall by a side door which closed behind him. The Asika watched him go, laughed musically and said:

"It is a very dull thing to be married,—but how are you named, white man?"

"Vernon," he answered.

"Vernoon, Vernoon," she repeated, for she could not pronounce the O was we do. "Are you married, Vernoon?"

He shook his head.

"Have you been married?"

"No," he answered, "never, but I am going to be."

"Yes," she repeated, "you are going to be. You remember that you were near to it many years ago, when Little Bonsa got jealous and ran away with you. Well, she won't do that again, for doubtless she is tired of you now, and besides," she added with a flash of ferocity, "I'd melt her with fire first and set her spirit free."

While Jeekie was trying to explain this mysterious speech to Alan, the Asika broke in, asking:

"Do you always want to wear that mask?"

He answered, "Certainly not," whereon she bade Jeekie take it off, which he did.

"Understand me," she said, fixing her great languid eyes upon his in a fashion that made him exceedingly uncomfortable, "understand, Vernoon, that if you go out anywhere, it must be in your mask, which you can only put off when you are alone with me?"

"Why?"

"Because, Vernoon, I do not choose that any other woman should see your face. If a woman looks upon your uncovered face, remember that she dies—not nicely."

Alan stared at her blankly, being unable to find appropriate Asiki words in which to reply to this threat. But the Asika only leaned back in her chair and laughed at his evident confusion and dismay, till a new thought struck her.

"Your lips are free now," she said; "kiss my hand after the fashion of your own country," and she stretched it out to Alan, leaving him no choice but to obey her.

"Why," she went on mischievously, taking his hand and in turn touching it with her red lips, "why, are you a thief, Vernoon? That ring was mine and you have stolen it. How did you steal that ring?"

"I don't know," he answered, through Jeekie, "I found it on my finger. I cannot understand how it came there. I understand nothing of all this talk."

"Well, well, keep it, Vernoon, only give me that other ring of yours in exchange."

"I cannot," he replied, colouring. "I promised to wear it always."

"Whom did you promise?" she asked with a flash of rage. "Was it a woman? Nay, I see, it is a man's ring, and that is well, for otherwise I would bring a curse on her, however far off she may be dwelling. Say no more and forgive my anger. A vow is a vow—keep your ring. But where is that one you used to wear in bygone days? I recall that it had a cross upon it, not this star and figure of an eagle."

Now Alan remembered that his uncle owned such a ring with a cross upon it, and was frightened, for how did this woman know these things?

"Jeekie," he said, "ask the Asika if I am mad, or if she is. How can she know what I used to wear, seeing that I was never in this place till yesterday, and certainly I have not met her anywhere else."

"She mean when you your reverend uncle," said Jeekie, wagging his great head, "she think you identical man."

"What troubles you, Vernoon," the Asika asked softly, then added anything but softly to Jeekie, "Translate, you dog, and be swift."

So Jeekie translated in a great hurry, telling her what Alan had said, and adding on his own account that he, silly white man that he was, could not understand how, as she was quite a young woman, she could have seen him before she was born. If that were so, she would be old and ugly now, not beautiful as she was.

"I never saw you before, and you never saw me, Lady, yet you talk as though we had been friends," broke in Alan in his halting Asiki.

"So we were in the spirit, Vernoon. It was she who went before me who loved that white man whose face was as your face is, but her ghost lives on in me and tells me the tale. There have been many Asikas, for thousands of years they have ruled in this land, yet but one spirit belongs to them all; it is the string upon which the beads of their lives are threaded. White man, I, whom you think young, know everything back to the beginning of the world, back to the time when I was a monkey woman sitting in those cedar trees, and if you wish, I can tell it you."

"I should like to hear it very much indeed," answered Alan, when he had mastered her meaning, "though it is strange that none of the rest of us remember such things. Meanwhile, O Asika, I will tell you that I desire to return to my own land, taking with me that gift of gold that you have given me. When will it please you to allow me to return?"

"Not yet a while, I think," she said, smiling at him weirdly, for no other word will describe that smile. "My spirit remembers that it was always thus. Those wanderers who came hither always wished to return again to their own country, like the birds in spring. Once there was a white man among them, that was more than twenty hundred years ago; he was a native of a country called Roma, and wore a helmet. He wished to return, but my mother of that day, she kept him and by and by I will show him to you if you like. Before that there was a brown man who came from a land where a great river overflows its banks every year. He was a prince of his own country, who had fled from his king and the desert folk made a slave of him, and so he drifted hither. He wished to return also, for my mother of that day, or my spirit that dwelt in her, showed to him that if he could but be there they would make him king in his own land. But my mother of that day, she would not let him go, and by and by I will show him to you, if you wish."

Bewildered, amazed, Alan listened to her. Evidently the woman was mad, or else she played some mystical part for reasons of her own.

"When will you let me go, O Asika?" he repeated.

"Not yet a while, I think," she said again. "You are too comely and I like you," and she smiled at him. There was nothing coarse in the smile, indeed it had a certain spiritual quality which thrilled him. "I like you," she went on in her dreamy voice, "I would keep you with me until your spirit is drawn up into my spirit, making it strong and rich as all the spirits that went before have done, those spirits that my mothers loved from the beginning, which dwell in me today."

Now Alan grew alarmed, desperate even.

"Queen," he said, "but just now your husband sat here, is it right then that you should talk to me thus?"

"My husband," she answered, laughing. "Why, that man is but a slave who plays the part of husband to satisfy an ancient law. Never has he so much as kissed my finger tips; my women—those who waited on you last night—are his wives, not I,—or may be, if he will. Soon he will die of love for me, and then when he is dead, though not before, I may take another husband, any husband that I choose, and I think that no black man shall be my lord, who have other, purer blood in me. Vernoon, five centuries have gone by since an Asika was really wed to a foreign man who wore a green turban and called himself a son of the Prophet, a man with a hooked nose and flashing eyes, who reviled our gods until they slew him, even though he was the beloved of their priestess. She who went before me also would have married that white man whose face was like your face, but he fled with Little Bonsa, or rather Little Bonsa fled with him. So she passed away unwed, and in her place I came."

"How did you come, if she whom you call your mother was not your mother?" asked Alan.

"What is that to you, white man?" she replied haughtily. "I am here, as my spirit has been here from the first. Oh! I see you think I lie to you, come then, come, and I will show you those who from the beginning have been the husbands of the Asika," and rising from her chair she took him by the hand.

They went through doors and by long, half-lit passages till they came to great gates guarded by old priests armed with spears. As they drew near to these priests the Asika loosed a scarf that she wore over her breast-plate of gold fish scales, and threw the star-spangled thing over Alan's head, that even these priests should not see his face. Then she spoke a word to them and they opened the gates. Here Jeekie evinced a disposition to remain, remarking to his master that he thought that place, into which he had never entered, "much too holy for poor nigger like him."

The Asika asked him what he had said and he explained his sense of unworthiness in her own tongue.

"Come, fellow," she exclaimed, "to translate my words and to bear witness that no trick is played upon your lord."

Still Jeekie lingered bashfully, whereon at a sign from her one of the priests pricked him behind with his great spear, and uttering a low howl he sprang forward.

The Asika led the way down a passage, which they saw ended in a big hall lit with lamps. Now they were in it and Alan became aware that they had entered the treasure house of the Asiki, since here were piled up great heaps of gold, gold in ingots, gold in nuggets, in stone jars filled with dust, in vessels plain or embossed with monstrous shapes in fetishes and in little squares and discs that looked as though they had served as coins. Never had he seen so much gold before.

"You are rich here, Lady," he said, gazing at the piles astonished.

She shrugged her shoulders. "Yes, as I have heard that some people count wealth. These are the offerings brought to our gods from the beginning; also all the gold found in the mountains belongs to the gods, and there is much of it there. The gift I sent to you was taken from this heap, but in truth it is but a poor gift, seeing that although this stuff is bright and serves for cups and other things, it has no use at all and is only offered to the gods because it is harder to come by than other metals. Look, these are prettier than the gold," and from a stone table she picked up at hazard a long necklace of large, uncut stones, red and white in colour and set alternatively, that Alan judged to be crystals and spinels.

"Take it," she said, "and examine it at your leisure. It is very old. For hundreds of years no more of these necklaces have been made," and with a careless movement she threw the chain over his head so that it hung upon his shoulders.

Alan thanked her, then remembered that the man called Mungana, who was the husband, real or official, of this priestess, had been somewhat similarly adorned, and shivered a little as though at a presage of advancing fate. Still he did not return the thing, fearing lest he should give offence.

At this moment his attention was taken from the treasure by the sound of a groan behind him. Turning round he perceived Jeekie, his great eyes rolling as though in an extremity of fear.

"Oh my golly! Major," he ejaculated, pointing to the wall, "look there."

Alan looked, but at first in that dim light could only discover long rows of gleaming objects which reached from the floor to the roof.

"Come and see," said the Asika, and taking a lamp from that table on which lay the gems, she led him past the piles of gold to one side of the vault or hall. Then he saw, and although he did not show it, like Jeekie he was afraid.

For there, each in his own niche and standing one above the other, were what looked like hundreds of golden men with gleaming eyes. At first until the utter stillness undeceived him, he thought that they *must* be men. Then he understood that this was what they had been; now they were corpses wrapped in sheets of thin gold and wearing golden masks with eyes of crystal, each mask being beaten out to a hideous representation of the man in life.

"All these are the husbands of my spirit," said the priestess, waving the lamp in front of the lowest row of them, "*Munganas* who were married to the Asikas in the past. Look, here is he who said that he ought to be king of that rich land where year after year the river overflows its banks," and going to one of the first of the figures in the bottom row, she drew out a fastening and suffered the gold mask to fall forward on a hinge, exposing the face within.

Although it had evidently been treated with some preservative, this head now was little more than a skull still covered with dark hair, but set upon its brow appeared an object that Alan recognized at once, a simple band of plain gold, and rising from it the head of an asp. Without doubt it was the *uraeus*, that symbol which only the royalties of Old Egypt dared to wear. Without doubt also either this man had brought it with him from the Nile, or in memory of his rank and home he had fashioned it of the gold that was so plentiful in the place of his captivity. So this woman's story was true, an ancient Egyptian had once been husband to the Asika of his day.

Meanwhile his guide had passed a long way down the line and halting in front of another gold-wrapped figure, opened its mask.

"This is that man," she said, "who told us he came from a land called Roma. Look, the helmet still rests upon his head, though time has eaten into it, and that ring upon your hand was taken from his finger. I have a head-dress made upon the model of that helmet which I wear sometimes in memory of this man who, my soul remembers, was brave and pleasant and a gallant lover."

"Indeed," answered Alan, looking at the sunken face above which a rim of curls appeared beneath the rusting helmet. "Well, he doesn't look very gallant now, does he?" Then he peered down between the body and its gold casing and saw that in his body hand the man still held a short Roman sword, lifted as though in salute. So she had not lied in this matter either.

Meanwhile the Asika had glided on to the end of the hall behind the heaps of treasure.

"There is one more white man," she said, "though we know little of him, for he was fierce and barbarous and died without learning our tongue, after killing a great number of the priests of that day because they would not let him go; yes, died cutting them down with a battle-axe and singing some wild song of his own country. Come hither, slave, and bend yourself so, resting your hands upon the ground."

Jeekie obeyed, and actively as a cat the priestess leaped on to his back, and reaching up opened the mask of a corpse in the second row and held her lamp before its face.

It was better preserved than the others, so that its features remained comparatively perfect, and about them hung a tangle of golden hair. Moreover, a broad battle-axe appeared resting on the shoulder.

"A Viking," thought Alan. "I wonder how *he* came here."

When he had looked the Asika leaped from Jeekie's back to the ground and waving her arm around her, began to talk so rapidly that Alan could understand nothing of her words, and asked Jeekie to translate them.

"She say," explained Jeekie between his chattering teeth, "that all rest these Johnnies very poor crew, natives and that lot except one who worship false Prophet and cut throat of Asika of that time, because she infidel and he teach her better; also eat his dinner out of Little Bonsa and chuck her into water. Very wild man, that Arab, but priests catch him at last and fill him with hot gold before Little Bonsa because he no care a damn for ghosts. So he die saying Hip, hip, hurrah! for *houri* and green field of Prophet and to hell with Asika and Bonsa, Big and Little! Now he sit up there and at night time worst ghost of all the crowd, always come to finish off Mungana. That all she say, and quite enough too. Come on quick, she want you and no like wait."

By now the Asika had passed almost round the hall, and was standing opposite to an empty niche beyond and above which there were perhaps a score of bodies gold-plated in the usual fashion.

"That is your place, Vernoon," she said gently, contemplating him with her soft and heavy eyes, "for it was prepared for the white man with whom Little Bonsa fled away, and since then, as you see, there have been many *Munganas*, some of whom belong to me; indeed, that one," and she touched a corpse on which the gold looked very fresh, "only left me last year. But we always knew that Little Bonsa would bring you back again, and so you see, we have kept your place empty."

"Indeed," remarked Alan, "that is very kind of you," and feeling that he would faint if he stayed longer in this horrible and haunted vault, he pushed past her with little ceremony and walked out through the gates into the passage beyond.

## Chapter 12
# The Gold House

"How you like Asiki-land, Major?" asked Jeekie, who had followed him and was now leaning against a wall fanning himself feebly with his great hand. "Funny place, isn't it, Major? I tell you so before you come, but you no believe me."

"Very funny," answered Alan, "so funny that I want to get out."

"Ah! Major, that what eel say in trap where he go after lob-worm, but he only get out into frying pan after cook skin him alive-o. Ah! here come cook—I mean Asika. She only stop shut up those stiff 'uns, who all love lob-worm one day. Very pretty woman, Asika, but thank God she not set cap at me, who like to be buried in open like Christian man."

"If you don't stop it, Jeekie," replied Alan in a concentrated rage, "I'll see that you are buried just where you are."

"No offence, Major, no offence, my heart full and bubble up. I wonder what Miss Barbara say if she see you mooing and cooing with dark-eyed girl in gold snake skin?"

Just then the Asika arrived and by way of excuse for his flight, Alan remarked to her that the treasure-hall was hot.

"I did not notice it," she answered, "but he who is called my husband, Mungana, says the same. The Mungana is guardian of the dead," she explained, "and when he is required so to do, he sleeps in the Place of the Treasure and gathers wisdom from the spirits of those *Munganas* who were before him."

"Indeed. And does he like that bed-chamber?"

"The Mungana likes what I like, not what he likes," she replied haughtily. "Where I send him to sleep, there he sleeps. But come, Vernoon, and I will show you the Holy Water where Big Bonsa dwells; also the house in which I have my home, where you shall visit me when you please."

"Who built this place?" asked Alan as she led him through more dark and tortuous passages. "It is very great."

"My spirit does not remember when it was built, Vernoon, so old is it, but I think that the Asiki were once a big and famous people who traded to the water upon the west, and even to the water on the east, and that was how those white men became their slaves and the *Munganas* of their queens. Now they are small and live only by the might and fame of Big and Little Bonsa, not half filling the rich land which is theirs. But," she added reflectively and looking at him, "I think also that this is because in the past fools have been thrust upon my spirit as *Munganas*. What it needs is the wisdom of the white man, such wisdom as yours, Vernoon. If that were added to my magic, then the Asiki would grow great again, seeing that they have in such plenty the gold which you have shown me the white man loves. Yes, they would grow great and from coast to coast the people should bow at the name of Bonsa and send him their sons for sacrifice. Perhaps you will live to see that day, Vernoon. Slave," she added, addressing Jeekie, "set the mask upon your lord's head, for we come where women are."

Alan objected, but she stamped her foot and said it must be so, having once worn Little Bonsa, as her people told her he had done, his naked face might not be seen. So Alan submitted to the hideous head-dress and they entered the Asika's house by some back entrance.

It was a place with many rooms in it, but they were all remarkable for extreme simplicity. With a single exception no gilding or gold was to be seen, although the food vessels were made of this material here as everywhere. The chambers, including those in which the Asika lived and slept, were panelled, or rather boarded with cedar wood that was almost black with age, and their scanty furniture was mostly made of ebony. They were very insufficiently lighted, like his own room, by means of barred openings set high in the wall. Indeed gloom and mystery were the keynotes of this place, amongst the shadows of which handsome, half-naked servants or priestesses flitted to and fro at their tasks, or peered at them out of dark corners. The atmosphere seemed heavy with secret sin; Alan felt that in those rooms unnameable crimes and cruelties had been committed for hundreds or perhaps thousands of years, and that the place was yet haunted by the ghosts of them. At any rate it struck a chill to his healthy blood, more even than had that Hall of the Dead and of heaped-up golden treasure.

"Does my house please you?" the Asika asked of him.

"Not altogether," he answered, "I think it is dark."

"From the beginning my spirit has ever loved the dark, Vernoon. I think that it was shaped in some black midnight."

They passed through the chief entrance of the house which had pillars of woodwork grotesquely carved, down some steps into a walled and roofed-in yard where the shadows were even more dense than in the house they had left. Only at one spot was there light flowing down through a hole in the roof, as it did apparently in that hall where Alan had found the Asika sitting in state. The light fell on to a pedestal or column made of gold which was placed behind an object like a large Saxon font, also made of gold. The shape of this column reminded Alan of something, namely of a very similar column, although fashioned of a different material which stood in the granite-built office of Messrs. Aylward & Haswell in the City of London. Nor did this seem wonderful to him, since on top of it, squatting on its dwarf legs, stood a horrid but familiar thing, namely Little Bonsa herself come home at last. There she sat smiling cruelly, as she had smiled from the beginning, forgetful doubtless of her wanderings in strange lands, while round her stood a band of priests armed with spears.

Followed by the Asika and Jeekie, Alan walked up and looked her in the face and to his excited imagination she appeared to grin at him in answer. Then while the priests prostrated themselves, he examined the golden basin or laver, and saw that at the further side of it was a little platform approached by steps. On the top of these golden steps were two depressions such as might have been worn out in the course of ages by persons kneeling there. Also the flat edge of the basin which stood about thirty inches above the level of the topmost step, was scored as though by hundreds of sword cuts which had made deep lines in the pure metal. The basin itself was empty.

Seeing that these things interested him, the Asika volunteered the information through Jeekie, that this was a divining-bowl, and that if those who went before her had wished to learn the future, they caused Little Bonsa to float in it and found out all they wanted to know by her movements. She, however, she added, had other and better methods of learning things that were predestined.

"Where does the water come from?" asked Alan thoughtlessly searching the bowl for some tap or inlet.

"Out of the hearts of men," she answered with a low and dreadful laugh. "These marks are those of swords and every one of them means a life." Then seeing that he looked incredulous she added, "Stay, I will show you. Little Bonsa must be thirsty who has fasted so long, also there are matters that I desire to know. Come hither—you, and you," and she pointed at hazard to the two priests who knelt nearest to her, "and do you bid the executioner bring his axe," she went on to a third.

The dark faces of the men turned ashen, but they made no effort to escape their doom. One of them crept up the steps and laid his neck upon the edge of gold, while the other, uttering no word, threw himself on his face at the foot of them, waiting his turn. Then a door opened and there appeared a great and brutal-looking fellow, naked except for a loin cloth, who bore in his hand a huge weapon, half knife and half axe.

First he looked at the Asika, who nodded almost imperceptibly, then sprang on to a prolongation of the golden steps, bowed to Little Bonsa on her column behind and heaved up his knife.

Now for the first time Alan really understood what was about to happen, and that what he had imagined a stage rehearsal, was to become a hideous murder.

"Stop!" he shouted in English, being unable to remember the native word.

The executioner paused with his axe poised in mid-air; the victim turned his head and looked, as though surprised; the second victim and the priests their companions looked also. Jeekie fell on to his knees and burst into fervent prayer addressed apparently to Little Bonsa. The Asika smiled and did nothing.

Again the weapon was lifted and as he felt that words were no longer of any use, even if he could find them, Alan took refuge in action. Springing on to the other side of the little platform, he hit out with all his strength across the kneeling man. Catching the executioner on the point of the chin, he knocked him straight backwards in such fashion that his head struck upon the floor before any other portion of his body, so that he lay there either dead or stunned. Alan never learned which, since the matter was not thought of sufficient importance to be mentioned.

At this sight the Asika burst into a low laugh, then asked Alan why he had felled the executioner. He answered because he would not stand by and see two innocent men butchered.

"Why not," she said in an astonished voice; "if Little Bonsa, whose priests they are, needs them, and I, who am the Mouth of the gods declare that they should die? Still, she has been in your keeping for a long while and you may know her will, so if you wish it, let them live. Or perhaps you require other victims," and she fixed her eyes upon Jeekie with a glance of suggestive hope.

"Oh my golly!" gasped Jeekie in English, "tell her not for Joe, Major, tell her most improper. Say Yellow God my dearest friend and go mad as hatter if my throat cut——"

Alan stopped his protestations with a secret kick.

"I choose no victims," he broke in, "nor will I see man's blood shed—to me it is *orunda*—unholy; I may not look on human blood, and if you cause me to do so, Asika, I shall hate you because you make me break my oath."

The Asika reflected for a moment, while Jeekie behind muttered between his chattering teeth:

"Good missionary talk that, Major. Keep up word in season, Major. If she make Christian martyr of Jeekie, who get you out of this confounded hole?"

Then the Asika spoke.

"Be it as you will, for I desire neither that you should hate me, nor that you should look on that which is unlawful for your eyes to see. The feasts and ceremonies you must attend, but if I can help it, no victim shall be slain in your presence, not even that whimpering hound, your servant," she added with a contemptuous glance at Jeekie, "who it seems, fears to give his life for the glory of the god, but who because he is yours, is safe now and always."

"That *very* satisfactory," said Jeekie, rising from his knees, his face wreathed in smiles, for he knew well that a decree of the Asika could not be broken. Then he began to explain to the priestess that it was not fear of losing his own life that had moved him, but the certainty that this occurrence would disagree morally with Little Bonsa, whose entire confidence he possessed.

Taking no notice of his words, with a slight reverence to the fetish, she passed on, beckoning to Alan. As he went by the two prostrate priests whose lives he had saved, lifted their heads a little and looked at him with heartfelt gratitude in their eyes; indeed one of them kissed the place where his foot had trodden. Jeekie, following, gave him a kick to intimate that he was taking a liberty, but at the same time stooped down and asked the man his name. It occurred to him that these rescued priests might some day be useful.

Alan followed her through a kind of swing door which opened into another of the endless halls, but when he looked for her there she was nowhere to be seen. A priest who was waiting beyond the door bowed and informed him that the Asika had gone to her own place, and would see him that evening. Then bowing again he led them back by various passages to the room where they had slept.

"Jeekie," said Alan after their food had been brought to them, this time, he observed, by men, for it was now past midday, "you were born in Asiki-land; tell me the truth of this business. What does that woman mean when she talks about her spirit having been here from the beginning."

"She mean, Major, that every time she die her soul go into someone else, whom priests find out by marks. Also Asika always die young, they never let her become old woman, but how she die and where they bury her, no one know 'cept priests. Sometimes she have girl child who become Asika after her, but if they have boy child, they kill him. I think this Asika daughter of her who make love to your reverend uncle. All that story 'bout her mother not being married, lies, and all her story lies too, she often marry."

"But how about the spirit coming back, Jeekie?"

"'Spect that lie too, Major, though she think it solemn fact. Priests teach her all those old things. Still," he added doubtfully, "Asika great medicine-woman and know a lot we don't know, can't say how. Very awkward customer, Major."

"Quite so, Jeekie, I agree with you. But to come to the point, what is her game with me?"

"Oh! Major," he answered with a grin, "*that* simple enough. She tired of black man, want change, mean to marry you according to law, that is when Mungana dies, and he die jolly quick now. She mustn't kill him, but polish him off all the same, stick him to sleep with those dead uns, till he go like drunk man and see things and drown himself. Then she marry you. But till he dead, you all right, she only talk and make eyes, 'cause of Asiki law, not 'cause she want to stop there."

"Indeed, Jeekie, and how long do you think that Mungana will last?"

"Perhaps three months, Major, and perhaps two. Think not more than two. Strong man, but he look devilish dicky this morning. Think he begin see snakes."

"Very well, Jeekie. Now listen to me—you've got to get us out of Asiki-land by this day two months. If you don't, that lady will do anything to oblige me and no doubt there are more executioners left."

"Oh! Major, don't talk like silly fool. Jeekie always hate fools and suffer them badly—like holy first missionary bishop. You know very well this no place for ultra-Christian man like Jeekie, who only come here to please you. Both in same bag, Major, if I die, you die and leave Miss Barbara up gum tree. I get you out if I can. But this stuff the trouble," and he pointed to the bags of gold. "Not want to leave all that behind after such arduous walk. No, no, I try get you out, meanwhile you play game."

"The game! What game, Jeekie?"

"What game? Why, Asika-game of course. If she sigh, you sigh; if she look at you, you look at her; if she squeeze hand, you squeeze hand; if she kiss, you kiss."

"I am hanged if I do, Jeekie."

"Must, Major; must or never get out of Asiki-land. What all that matter?" he added confidentially. "Miss Barbara never know. Jeekie doesn't split, also quite necessary in situation, and you can't be married till that Mungana dead. All matter business, Major; make time pass pleasant as well. Asika jolly enough if you stroke her fur right way, but if you put her back up—oh Lor! No trouble, sit and smile and say, 'Oh, ducky, how beautiful you are!' that not hurt anybody."

In spite of himself Alan burst out laughing.

"But how about the Mungana?" he asked.

"Mungana, he got take that with rest. Also I try make friends with that poor devil. Tell him it all my eye. Perhaps he believe me—not sure. If he me, I no believe *him*. Mungana," he added oracularly, "Mungana take his chance. What matter? In two months' time he nothing but gold figure, No. 2403; just like one mummy in museum. Now I try catch my ma. I hear she alive somewhere. They tell me she used keep lodging house for Bonsa pilgrim, but steal grub, say it cat, all that sort of thing, and get run in as thief. Afraid my ma come down very much in world, not society lady now, shut up long way off in suburb. Still p'raps she useful so best send her message by p'liceman, say how much I love her; say her dear little Jeekie turn up again just to see her sweet face. Only don't know if she swallow that or if they let her out prison unless I pay for all she prig."

## Chapter 13

# The Feast of Little Bonsa

It was the night of full moon and of the great feast of the return of Little Bonsa. Alan sat in his chamber waiting to be summoned to take part in this ceremony and listening the while to that *Wow! Wow! Wow!* of the death drums, whereof Jeekie had once spoken in England, which could be clearly heard even above the perpetual boom of the cataract tumbling down its cliff behind the town. By now he had recovered from the fatigue of his journey and his health was good, but the same could not be said of his spirits, for never in his life had he felt more downhearted, not even when he was sickening for blackwater fever, or lay in bondage in the City, expecting every morning to wake up and find his reputation blasted. He was a prisoner in this dreadful, gloomy place where he must live like a second Man in the Iron Mask, without recreation or exercise other than he could find in the walled garden where grew the black cedar trees, and, so far as he could see, a prisoner without hope of escape.

Moreover, he could no longer disguise from himself the truth; Jeekie was right. The Asika had fallen in love with him, or at any rate made up her mind that he should be her next husband. He hated the sight of the woman and her sinuous, evil beauty, but to be free of her was impossible, and to offend her, death. All day long she kept him about her, and from his sleep he would wake up and as on the night of his arrival, distinguish her leaning over him studying his face by the light of the faintly-burning lamps, as a snake studies the bird it is about to strike. He dared not stir or give the slightest sign that he saw her. Nor indeed did he always see her, for he kept his eyes closely shut. But even in his heaviest slumber some warning sense told him of her presence, and then above Jeekie's snores (for on these occasions Jeekie always snored his loudest) he would hear a soft footfall, as cat-like, she crept towards him, or the sweep of her spangled robe, or the tinkling of the scales of her golden breastplate. For a long while she would stand there, examining him greedily and even the few little belongings that remained to him, and then with a hungry sigh glide away and vanish in the shadows. How she came or how she vanished Alan could not discover. Clearly she did not use the door, and he could find no other entrance to the room. Indeed at times he thought he must be suffering from delusion, but Jeekie shook his great head and did not agree with him.

"She there right enough," he said. "She walk over me as though I log and I smell stuff she put on hair, but I think she come and go by magic. Asika do that if she please."

"Then I wish she would teach me the secret, Jeekie. I should soon be out of Asiki-land, I can tell you."

All that day Alan had been in her company, answering her endless questions about his past, the lands that he had visited, and especially the women that he had known. He had the tact to tell her that none of these were half so beautiful as she was, which was true in a sense and pleased her very much, for in whatever respects she differed from them, in common with the rest of her sex she loved a compliment. Emboldened by her good humour, he had ventured to suggest that being rested and having restored Little Bonsa, he would be glad to return with her gifts to his own country. Next instant he was sorry, for as soon as she understood his meaning she grew almost white with rage.

"What!" she said; "you desire to leave me? Know, Vernoon, that I will see you dead first and myself also, for then we shall be born again together and can never more be separated."

Nor was this all, for she burst into weeping, threw her arms about him, drew him to her, kissed him on the forehead, and then thrust him away, saying:

"Curses on the priests' law that makes us wait so long, and curses on that Mungana who will not die and may not be killed. Well, he shall pay for it and within two months, Vernoon, oh! within two months——" and she stretched out her arms with a gesture of infinite passion, then turned and left him.

"My!" said Jeekie afterwards, for he had watched all this scene open-mouthed, "my! but she mean business. Mrs. Jeekie never kiss me like that, nor any other female either. She dead nuts on you, Major. Very great compliment! 'Spect when you Mungana, she keep you alive a long time, four or five years perhaps, if no other white man come this way. Pity you can't take it on a bit, Major," he added insidiously, "because then she grow careless and make you chief and we get chance scoop out that gold house and bolt with bally lot. Miss Barbara sensible woman, when she see all that cash she not mind, she say 'Bravo, old boy, quite right spoil Lady Potiphar in land of bondage, but Jeekie must have ten per cent. because he show you how do it.'"

Alan was so depressed, and indeed terrified by this demonstration on the part of his fearful hostess, that he could neither laugh at Jeekie, nor swear at him. He only sat still and groaned, feeling that bad as things were they were bound to become worse.

********

Above the perpetual booming of the death drums rose a sound of wild music. The door burst open, and through it came a number of priests, their nearly naked bodies hideously painted and on their heads the most devilish-looking masks. Some of them clashed cymbals, some blew horns and some beat little drums all to time which was given to them by a bandmaster with a golden rod. In front of them with painted face and decked in his gorgeous apparel, walked the Mungana himself.

"They come to take us to Bonsa worship," explained Jeekie. "Cheer up, Major, very exciting business, no go to sleep there, as in English church. See the god all time and no sermon."

Alan, who wore a linen robe over the remains of his European garments, and whose mask was already on his head, rose listlessly and bowed to the gorgeous Mungana who, poor man, answered him with a stare of hate, knowing that this wanderer was destined to fill his place. Then they started, Jeekie accompanying them, and walked a long way through various halls and passages, bearing first to the left and then to the right again, till suddenly through some side door they emerged upon a marvellous scene. The first impressions that reached Alan's mind were those of a long stretch of water, very black and still and not more than eighty feet in width. On the hither edge of this canal, seated upon a raised dais in the midst of a great open space of polished rock, was the Asika, or so he gathered from her gold breastplate and sparkling garments, for her fierce and beautiful features were hid beneath an object familiar enough to him, the yellow, crystal-eyed mask of Little Bonsa. Arranged in companies about and behind her were hundreds of people, male and female, clad in hideous costumes to resemble demons, with masks to match. Some of these masks were semi-human and some of them bore a likeness to the heads of animals and had horns on them, while their wearers were adorned with skins and tails. To describe them in their infinite variety would be impossible; indeed the recollection that Alan carried away was one of a medieval hell as it is occasionally to be found portrayed upon "Doom pictures" in old churches.

On the further side of the water the entire Asiki people seemed to be gathered, at least there were thousands of them seated upon a rising rocky slope as in an amphitheatre, clad only in the ordinary costume of the Western African native, and in some instances in linen cloaks. This great amphitheatre was surrounded by a high wall with gates, but in the moonlight he found it difficult to discern its exact limits.

Jeekie nudged Alan and pointed to the centre of the canal or pool. He looked and saw floating there a huge and hideous golden head, twenty times as large as life perhaps, with great prominent eyes that glared up to the sky. Its appearance was quite unlike anything else in the world, more loathsome, more horrible, man, fish and animal, all seemed to have their part in it, human mouth and teeth, fish-like eyes and snout, bestial expression.

"Big Bonsa," whispered Jeekie. "Just the same as when I sweet little boy.—He live here for thousand of years."

Preceded by the Mungana and followed by Jeekie and the priests, the band bringing up the rear, Alan was marched down a lane left open for him till he came to some steps leading to the dais, upon which in addition to that occupied by the Asika, stood two empty chairs. These steps the Mungana motioned him to mount, but when Jeekie tried to follow him he turned and struck him contemptuously in the face. At once the Asika, who was watching Vernon's approach through the eye-holes in the Little Bonsa mask, said fiercely:

"Who bade you strike the servant of my guest, O Mungana? Let him come also that he may stand behind us and interpret."

Her wretched husband, who knew that this public slight was put upon him purposely, but did not dare to protest against it, bowed his head. Then all three of them climbed to the dais, the priests and the musicians remaining below.

"Welcome, Vernoon," said the Asika through the lips of the mask, which to Alan, notwithstanding the dreadful cruelty of its expression, looked less hateful than the lovely, tigerish face it hid. "Welcome and be seated here on my left hand, since on my right you may not sit—as yet."

He bowed and took the chair to which she pointed, while her husband placed himself in the other chair upon her right, and Jeekie stood behind, his great shape towering above them all.

"This is a festival of my people, Vernoon," she went on, "such a festival as has not been seen for years, celebrated because Little Bonsa has come back to them."

"What is to happen?" he asked uneasily. "I have told you, Lady, that blood is *orunda* to me. I must not witness it."

"I know, be not afraid," she answered. "Sacrifice there must be, since it is the custom and we may not defraud the gods, but you shall not see the deed. Judge from this, Vernoon, how greatly I desire to please you."

Now Alan, looking about him, saw that immediately beneath the dais and between them and the edge of the water, were gathered his cannibal friends, the Ogula, and Fahni their chief who had rowed him to Asiki-land, and with them the messengers whom they had sent on ahead. Also he saw that their arms were tied behind them and that they were guarded by men dressed like devils and armed with spears.

"Ask Fahni why he and his people are bound, Jeekie," said Alan, "and why have they not returned to their own country."

Jeekie obeyed, putting the question in the Ogula language, whereon the poor men turned and began to implore Alan to save their lives, Fahni adding that he had been told they were to be killed that night.

"Why are these men to be slain?" asked Alan of the Asika.

"Because I have learned that they attacked you in their own country, Vernoon," she answered, "and would have killed you had it not been for Little Bonsa. It is therefore right that they should die as an offering to you."

"I refuse the offering since afterwards they dealt well with me. Set them free and let them return to their own land, Asika."

"That cannot be," she replied coldly. "Here they are and here they remain. Still, their lives are yours to take or to spare, so keep them as your servants if you will," and bending down she issued a command which was instantly obeyed, for the men dressed like devils cut the bonds of the Ogula and brought them round to the back of the dais, where they stood blessing Alan loudly in their own tongue.

Then the ceremonies began with a kind of infernal ballet. On the smooth space between them and the water's edge appeared male and female bands of dancers who emerged from the shadows. For the most part they were dressed up like animals and imitated the cries of the beasts that they represented, although some of them wore little or no clothing. To the sound of wild music of horns and drums these creatures danced a kind of insane quadrille which seemed to suggest everything that is cruel and vile upon the earth. They danced and danced in the moonlight till the madness spread from them to the thousands who were gathered upon the farther side of the water, for presently all of these began to dance also. Nor did it stop there, since at length the Asika rose from her chair upon the dais and joined in the performance with the Mungana her husband. Even Jeekie began to prance and shout behind, so that at last Alan and the Ogula alone remained still and silent in the midst of a scene and a noise which might have been that of hell let loose.

Leaving go of her husband, the Asika bounded up to Alan and tried to drag him from his chair, thrusting her gold mask against his mask. He refused to move and after a while she left him and returned to Mungana. Louder and louder brayed the music and beat the drums, wilder and wilder grew the shrieks. Individuals fell exhausted and were thrown into the water where they sank or floated away on the slow moving stream, as part of some inexplicable play that was being enacted.

Then suddenly the Asika stood still and threw up her arms and they fell upon their faces and lay as though they were dead. A third time she threw up her arms and they rose and remained so silent that the only sound to be heard was that of their thick breathing. Then she spoke, or rather screamed, saying:

"Little Bonsa has come back again, bringing with her the white man whom she led away," and all the audience answered, "Little Bonsa has come back again. Once more we see her on the head of the Asika as our fathers did. Give her a sacrifice. Give her the white man."

"Nay," she screamed back, "the white man is mine. I name him as the next Mungana."

"Oho!" roared the audience, "Oho! she names him as the next Mungana. Goodbye, old Mungana! Greeting, new Mungana! When will be the marriage feast?"

"Tell us, Mungana, tell us," cried the Asika, patting her wretched husband on the cheek. "Tell us when you mean to die, as you are bound to do."

"On the night of the second full moon from now," he answered with a terrible groan that seemed to be wrung out of his heavy heart; "on that night my soul will be eaten up and my day done. But till then I am lord of the Asika, and if she forgets it, death shall be her portion, according to the ancient law."

"Yes, yes," shouted the multitude, "death shall be her portion, and her lover we will sacrifice. Die in honour, Mungana, as all those died that went before you."

"Thank Heaven!" muttered Alan to himself, "I am safe from that witch for the next two months," and through the eye-holes of his mask he contemplated her with loathing and alarm.

At the moment, indeed, she was not a pleasing spectacle, for in the heat and excitement of her mad dance she had cast off her gold breast-plate or stomacher, leaving herself naked except for her kirtle and the thin, gold-spangled robe upon her shoulders over which streamed her black, disordered hair. Contrasting strangely in the silver moonlight with her glistening, copper-coloured body, the mask of Little Bonsa on her head glared round with its fixed crystal eyes and fiendish smile as she turned her long neck from side to side. Seen thus she scarcely looked human, and Alan's heart was filled with pity for the poor bedizened wretch she named her husband, who had just been forced to announce the date of his own suicide.

Soon, however, he forgot it, for a new act in the drama had begun. Two priests clad in horns and tails leapt on to the dais and at a signal unlaced the mask of Little Bonsa. Now the Asika lifted it from her streaming face and held it on high, then she lowered it to the level of her breast, and holding it in both hands, walked to the edge of the dais, whereon priests, disguised as fiends, began to leap at it, striving to reach it with their fingers and snatch it from her grasp. One by one they leapt with the most desperate energy, each man being allowed to make three attempts, and Alan noted that this novel jumping competition was watched with the deepest interest by all the audience, at the time he knew not why.

The first two were evidently elderly men who failed to come anywhere near the mark. Their failure was received with shouts of derision. They sank exhausted to the ground and from the motion of his body Alan could see that one of them was weeping, while the other remained sullenly silent. Then a younger man advanced and at the third try almost grasped the fetish. Indeed he would have grasped it had he not met with foul play, for the Asika, seeing that he was about to succeed, lifted it an inch or two, so that he also missed and with a groan joined the band of the defeated. Next appeared a fourth priest, even more horribly arrayed than those before him, but Alan noticed that his mask was of the lightest, and that his garments consisted chiefly of paint, the main idea of his make-up being that of a skeleton. He was a thin active fellow, and all the watching thousands greeted him with a shout. For a few seconds he stood back gazing at the mask as a wolf might at an unapproachable bone. Then suddenly he ran forward and sprang into the air. Such an amazing jump Alan had never seen before. So high was it indeed that his head came level with that of the fetish, which he snatched with both hands tearing it from Asika's grasp. Coming to the ground again with a thud, he began to caper to and fro, kissing the mask, while the audience shouted:

"Little Bonsa has chosen. What fate for the fallen? Ask her, priest?"

The man stopped his capering and held the mouth of Little Bonsa to his ear, nodding from time to time as though she were speaking to him and he heard what she said. Then he passed round the dais where Alan could not see him, and presently reappeared holding Little Bonsa in his right hand and in his left a great gold cup. A silence fell upon the place. He advanced to the first man who had jumped and offered him the cup. He turned his head away, but a thousand voices thundered "Drink!" Then he took it and drank, passing it to a companion in misfortune, who in turn drank also and gave it to the third priest, he who would have snatched the mask had not the Asika lifted it out of his reach.

This man drained it to the dregs, and with an exclamation of rage dashed the empty vessel into the face of the chosen priest with such fury that the man rolled upon the ground and for a while lay there stunned. Now he who had drunk first began to spring about in a ludicrous fashion, and presently was joined in his dance by the other two. So absurd were their motions and tumblings and clownlike grimaces, for they had dragged off their masks, that roars of brutal laughter rose from the audience, in which the Asika joined.

At first Alan thought that the thing was a joke, and that the men had merely been made mad drunk, till catching sight of their eyes in the moonlight, he perceived that they were in great pain and turned indignantly to remonstrate with the Asika.

"Be silent, Vernoon," she said savagely, "blood is your *orunda* and I respect it. Therefore by decree of the god these die of poison," and again she fell to laughing at the contortions of the victims.

Alan shut his eyes, and when at length, drawn by some fearful fascination, he opened them once more, it was to see that the three poor creatures had thrown themselves into the water, where they rolled over and over like wounded porpoises, till presently they sank and vanished there.

This farce, for so they considered it, being ended and the stage, so to speak, cleared, the audience having laughed itself hoarse, set itself to watch the proceedings of the newly chosen high-priest of Little Bonsa, who by now had recovered from the blow dealt to him by one of the murdered men. With the help of some other priests he was engaged in binding the fetish on to a little raft of reeds. This done he laid himself flat upon a broad plank which had been made ready for him at the edge of the water, placing the mask in front of him and with a few strokes of his feet that hung over the sides of the plank, paddled himself out to the centre of the canal where the god called Big Bonsa floated, or was anchored. Having reached it he pushed the little raft off the plank into the water, and in some way that Alan could not see, made it fast to Big Bonsa, so that now the two of them floated one behind the other. Then while the people cheered, shouting out that husband and wife had come together again at last, he paddled his plank back to the water's edge, sat down and waited.

Meanwhile, at a sign from the Asika, all the scores of priests and priestesses who were dressed as devils had filed off to right and left, and vanished, presumably to cross the water by bridges or boats that were out of sight. At any rate now they began to appear upon its further side and to wind their way singly among the thousands of the Asiki people who were gathered upon the rocky slope beyond in order to witness this fearsome entertainment. Alan observed that the spectators did not appear to appreciate the arrival amongst them of these priests, from whom they seemed to edge away. Indeed many of them rose and tried to depart altogether, only to be driven back to their places by a double line of soldiers armed with spears, who now for the first time became visible, ringing in the audience. Also other soldiers and with them bodies of men who looked like executioners, showed themselves upon the further brink of the water and then marched off, disappearing to left and right.

"What's the matter now?" Alan asked of Jeekie over his shoulder.

"All in blue funk," whispered Jeekie back, "joke done. Get to business now. Silly fools forget that when they laugh so much. Both Bonsas very hungry and Asika want wipe out old scores. Presently you see."

Presently Alan did see, for at some preconcerted signal the devil priests, each of them, jumped with a yell at a person near to them, gripping him or her by the hair, whereon assistants rushed in and dragged them down to the bank of the canal. Here to the number of a hundred or more, a wailing, struggling mass, they were confined in a pen like sheep. Then a bar was lifted and one of them allowed to escape, only to find himself in a kind of gangway which ran down into shallow water. Being forced along this he came to an open space of water exactly opposite to the floating fetishes, and there was kept a while by men armed with spears. As nothing happened they lifted their spears and the man bolted up an incline and was lost among the thousands of spectators.

The next one, evidently a person of rank, was not so fortunate. Jumping into the pool off the gangway, he stood there like a sheep about to be washed, the water reaching up to his middle. Then Alan saw a terrifying thing, for suddenly the horrid, golden head of Big Bonsa, towing Little Bonsa behind it, began to swim with a deliberate motion across the stream until, reaching the man, it seemed to rear itself up and poke him with its snout in the chest as a turtle might do. Then it sank again into the water and slowly floated back to its station, directed by some agency or power that Alan could not discover.

At the touch of the fetish the man screamed like a horse in pain or terror, and soldiers leaping on him with a savage shout, dragged him up another gangway opposite to that by which he had descended, whereon, to all appearances more dead than alive, he departed into the shadows. The horns and drums set up a bray of triumph, the Asika clapped her hands approvingly, the spectators cheered, and another victim was bundled down the gangway and submitted to the judgment of the Bonsas, which came at him like a hungry pike at a frog. Then followed more and more, some being chosen and some let go, till at last, growing weary, the priests directed the soldiers to drive the prisoners down in batches until the pen in the water was full as though with huddled sheep. If the horrible golden masks swam at them and touched one of their number, they were all dragged away; if these remained quiescent they were let go.

So the thing went on until at length Alan could bear no more of it.

"Lady," he said to the Asika when she paused for a moment from her hand-clapping, "I am weary, I would sleep."

"What!" she exclaimed, "do you wish to sleep on such a glorious night when so many evil doers are coming to their just doom? Well, well, go if you will, for then my promise is off me and I can hasten this business and deal with the wicked before the people according to our custom. Good-night to you, Vernoon, tomorrow we will meet," and she called to some priests to lead him away, and with him the Ogula cannibals whom she had given to him as servants.

Alan went thankfully enough. As he plunged into one of the passages the sound of frightful yelling reached his ears, followed by loud, triumphant shouts.

"Now you gone they kill those who Bonsa smell out," said Jeekie. "Why you no wait and see? Very interesting sight."

"Hold your tongue," answered Alan savagely. "Did you think so years ago when you were put into that pen to be butchered?"

"No, Major," replied the unabashed Jeekie, "not think at all then, too far gone. But see other people in there and know it not *you*, quite different matter."

They reached their room. At the door of it Fahni and his followers were led off to some quarters near by, blessing Alan as they went because he had saved their lives.

"Jeekie," he said when they were alone, "tell me, what makes that hellish idol swim about in the water picking out some people and leaving others alone?"

"Major, I not know, no one know except top priest and Asika. Perhaps there man underneath, perhaps they pull string, or perhaps fetish alive and he do what he like. Please don't call him names, Major, or he remember and come after us one time, and that bad job," and Jeekie shivered visibly.

"Bosh!" answered Alan, but all the same he shivered also. "Jeekie," he asked again, "what happens to those people whom the Bonsas smell out?"

"Case of goodbye, Major. Sometimes they chop off nut, sometimes they spiflicate in gold tub, sometimes priest-man make hole in what white doctor call *diagram*—and shake hands with heart.—All matter of taste, Major, just as Asika please. If she like victim or they old friends, chop off head; if she not like him—do worse things."

More than satisfied with his information Alan went to bed. For hour after hour that night he lay tossing and turning, haunted by the recollections of the dreadful sights that he had seen and of the horrible Asika, horrible and half-naked, glaring at him amorously through the crystal eyes of Little Bonsa. When at last he fell asleep it was to dream that he was alone in the water with the god which pursued him as a shark pursues a shipwrecked sailor. Never did he experience a nightmare that was half so awful. Only one thing could be more awful, the reality itself.

## Chapter 14
# The Mother of Jeekie

"Jeekie," said Alan next morning, "I tell you again that I have had enough of this place, I want to get out."

"Yes, Major, that just what mouse say when he finish cheese in trap, but missus come along, call him 'Pretty, pretty,' and drown him all the same," and he nodded in the direction of the Asika's house.

"Jeekie, it has got to be done—do you hear me? I had rather die trying to get away than stop here till the next two months are up. If I am here on the night of the next full moon but one, I shall shoot that Asika and then shoot myself, and you must take your chance. Do you understand?"

"Understand that foolish game and poor lookout for Jeekie, Major, but can't think of any plan." Then he rubbed his big nose reflectively and added, "Fahni and his people your slaves now, 'spose we have talk with him. I tell priests to bring him along when they come with breakfast. Leave it to me, Major."

Alan did leave it to him, with the result that after long argument the priests consented or obtained permission to produce Fahni and his followers, and a little while after the great men arrived looking very dejected, and saluted Alan humbly. Bidding the rest of them be seated, he called Fahni to the end of the room and asked him through Jeekie if he and his men did not wish to return home.

"Indeed we do, white lord," answered the old chief, "but how can we? The Asika has a grudge against our tribe and but for you would have killed every one of us last night. We are snared and must stop here till we die."

"Would not your people help you if they knew, Fahni?"

"Yes, lord, I think so. But how can I tell them who doubtless believe us dead? Nor can I send a messenger, for this place is guarded and he would be killed at once. We came here for your sake because you had Little Bonsa, a god that is known in the east and the west, in the north and the south, and because you saved me from the lion, and here, alas! we must perish."

"Jeekie," said Alan, "can you not find a messenger? Have you, who were born of this people, no friend among them at all?"

Jeekie shook his white head and rolled his eyes. Then suddenly an idea struck him.

"Yes," he said, "I think one, p'raps. I mean my ma."

"Your ma!" said Alan. "Oh! I remember. Have you heard anything more about her?"

"Yes, Major. Very old girl now, but strong on leg, so they say. Believe she glad go anywhere, because she public nuisance; they tired of her in prison and there no workhouse here, so they want turn her out starve, which of course break my heart. Perhaps she take message. Some use that way. Only think she afraid go Ogula-land because they nasty cannibal and eat old woman."

When all this was translated to Fahni he assured Jeekie with earnestness that nothing would induce the Ogula people to eat his mother; moreover, that for her sake they would never look carnivorously on another old woman, fat or thin.

"Well," said Jeekie, "I try again to get hold of old lady and we see. I pray priests, whom you save other day, let her out of chokey as I sick to fall upon bosom, which quite true, only so much to think of that no time to attend to domestic relation till now."

That very afternoon, on returning to his room from walking in the dismal cedar garden, Alan's ears were greeted by a sound of shrill quarrelling. Looking up he saw an extraordinary sight. A tall, gaunt, withered female who might have been of any age between sixty and a hundred, had got Jeekie's ear in one hand, and with the other was slapping him in the face while she exclaimed:

"O thief, whom by the curse of Bonsa I brought into the world, what have you done with my blanket? Was it not enough that you, my only son, should leave me to earn my own living? Must you also take my best blanket with you, for which reason I have been cold ever since. Where is it, thief, where is it?"

"Worn out, my mother, worn out," he answered, trying to free himself. "You forget, honourable mother, that I grow old and you should have been dead years ago. How can you expect a blanket to last so long? Leave go of my ear, beloved mother, and I will give you another. I have travelled across the world to find you and I want to hear news of your husband."

"My husband, thief, which husband? Do you mean your father, the one with the broken nose, who was sacrificed because you ran away with the white man whom Bonsa loved? Well, you look out for him when you get into the world of ghosts, for he said that he was going to wait for you there with the biggest stick that he could find. Why I haven't thought of him for years, but then I have had three other husbands since his time, bad enough, but better than he was, so who would? And now Bonsa has got the lot, and I have no children alive, and they say I am to be driven out of the prison to starve next week as they won't feed me any longer, I who can still work against any one of them, and—you've got my blanket, you ugly old rascal," and collapsing beneath the weight of her recited woes, the hag burst into a melancholy howl.

"Peace, my mother," said Jeekie, patting her on the head. "Do what I tell you and you shall have more blankets than you can wear and, as you are still so handsome, another husband too if you like, and a garden and slaves to work for you and plenty to eat."

"How shall I get all these things, my son?" asked the old woman, looking up. "Will you take me to your home and support me, or will that white lord marry me? They told me that the Asika had named him as the Mungana, and she is very jealous, the most jealous Asika that I have ever known."

"No, mother, he would like to, but he dare not, and I cannot support you as I should wish, as here I have no house or property. You will get all this by taking a walk and holding your tongue. You see this man here, he is Fahni, king of a great tribe, the Ogula. He wants you to carry a message for him, and by and by he will marry you, won't you, Fahni?"

"Oh! yes, yes," said Fahni; "I will do anything she likes. No one shall be so rich and honoured in my country, and for her sake we will never eat another old woman, whereas if she stays here she will be driven to the mountains to starve in a week."

"Set out the matter," said the mother of Jeekie, who was by no means so foolish as she seemed.

So they told her what she must do, namely, travel down to the Ogula and tell them of the plight of their chief, bidding them muster all their fighting men and when the swamps were dry enough, advance as near as they dared to the Asiki country and, if they could not attack it, wait till they had further news.

The end of it was that the mother of Jeekie, who knew her case to be desperate at home, where she was in no good repute, promised to attempt the journey in consideration of advantages to be received. Since she was to be turned adrift to meet her fate with as much food as she could carry, this she could do without exciting any suspicion, for who would trouble about the movements of a useless old thief? Meanwhile Jeekie gave her one of the robes which the Asika had provided for Alan, also various articles which she desired and, having learned Fahni's message by heart and announced that she considered herself his affianced bride, the gaunt old creature departed happy enough after exchanging embraces with her long lost son.

"She will tell somebody all about it and we shall only get our throats cut," said Alan wearily, for the whole thing seemed to him a foolish farce.

"No, no, Major. I make her swear not split on ghosts of all her husbands and by Big Bonsa hisself. She sit tight as wax, because she think they haunt her if she don't and I too by and by when I dead. P'raps she get to Ogula country and p'raps not. If she don't, can't help it and no harm done. Break my heart, but only one old woman less. Anyhow she hold tongue, that main point, and I really very glad find my ma, who never hoped to see again. Heaven very kind to Jeekie, give him back to family bosom," he added, unctuously.

That day there were no excitements, and to Alan's intense relief he saw nothing of the Asika. After its orgy of witchcraft and bloodshed on the previous night, weariness and silence seemed to have fallen upon the town. At any rate no sound came from it that could be heard above the low, constant thunder of the great waterfall rushing down its precipice, and in the cedar-shadowed garden where Alan walked till he was weary, attended by Jeekie and the Ogula savages, not a soul was to be seen.

On the following morning, when he was sitting moodily in his room, two priests came to conduct him to the Asika. Having no choice, followed by Jeekie, he accompanied them to her house, masked as usual, for without this hateful disguise he was not allowed to stir. He found her lying upon a pile of cushions in a small room that he had never seen before, which was better lighted than most in that melancholy abode, and seemed to serve as her private chamber. In front of her lay the skin of the lion that he had sent as a present, and about her throat hung a necklace made of its claws, heavily set in gold, with which she was playing idly.

At the opening of the door she looked up with a swift smile that turned to a frown when she saw that he was followed by Jeekie.

"Say, Vernoon," she asked in her languorous voice, "can you not stir a yard without that ugly black dog at your heels? Do you bring him to protect your back? If so, what is the need? Have I not sworn that you are safe in my land?"

Alan made Jeekie interpret this speech, then answered that the reason was that he knew but little of her tongue.

"Can I not teach it to you alone, then, without this low fellow hearing all my words? Well, it will not be for long," and she looked at Jeekie in a way that made him feel very uncomfortable. "Get behind us, dog, and you, Vernoon, come sit on these cushions at my side. Nay, not there, I said upon the cushions—so. Now I will take off that ugly mask of yours, for I would look into your eyes. I find them pleasant, Vernoon," and without waiting for his permission, she sat up and did so. "Ah!" she went on, "we shall be happy when we are married, shall we not? Do not be afraid, Vernoon, I will not eat out your heart as I have those of the men that went before you. We will live together until we are old, and die together at last, and together be born again, and so on and on till the end which even I cannot foresee. Why do you not smile, Vernoon, and say that you are pleased, and that you will be happy with me who loved you from the moment that my eyes fell upon you in sleep? Speak, Vernoon, lest I should grow angry with you."

"I don't know what to say," answered Alan despairingly through Jeekie, "the honour is too great for me, who am but a wandering trader who came here to barter Little Bonsa against the gold I need"—to support my wife and family, he was about to add, then remembering that this statement might not be well received, substituted, "to support my old parents and eight brothers and sisters who are dependent upon me, and remain hungry until I return to them."

"Then I think they will remain hungry a long time, Vernoon, for while I live you shall never return. Much as I love you I would kill you first," and her eyes glittered as she said the words. "Still," she added, noting the fall in his face, "if it is gold that they need, you shall send it them. Yes, my people shall take all that I gave you down to the coast, and there it can be put in a big canoe and carried across the water. See to the packing of the stuff, you black dog," she said to Jeekie over her shoulder, "and when it is ready I will send it hence."

Alan began to thank her, though he thought it more than probable that even if she kept her word, this bullion would never get to Old Calabar, and much less to England. But she waived the matter aside as one in which she was not interested.

"Tell me," she asked; "would you have me other than I am? First, do you think me beautiful?"

"Yes," answered Alan honestly, "very beautiful when you are quiet as now, not when you are dancing as you did the other night without your robes."

When she understood what he meant the Asika actually blushed a little.

"I am sorry," she answered in a voice that for her was quite humble. "I forget that it might seem strange in your eyes. It has always been the custom for the Asika to do as I did at feasts and sacrifices, but perhaps that is not the fashion among your women; perhaps they always remain veiled, as I have heard the worshippers of the Prophet do, and therefore you thought me immodest. I am very, very sorry, Vernoon. I pray you to forgive me who am ignorant and only do what I have been taught."

"Yes, they always remain veiled," stammered Alan, though he was not referring to their faces, and as the words passed his lips he wondered what the Asika would think if she could see a ballet at a London music-hall.

"Is there anything else wrong?" she went on gently. "If so, tell me that I may set it right."

"I do not like cruelty or sacrifices, O Asika. I have told you that bloodshed is *orunda* to me, and at the feast those men were poisoned and you mocked them in their pain; also many others were taken away to be killed for no crime."

She opened her beautiful eyes and stared at him, answering:

"But, Vernoon, all this is not my fault; they were sacrifices to the gods, and if I did not sacrifice, I should be sacrificed by the priests and wizards who live to sacrifice. Yes, myself I should be made to drink the poison and be mocked at while I died like a snake with a broken back. Or even if I escaped the vengeance of the people, the gods themselves would kill me and raise up another in my place. Do they not sacrifice in your country, Vernoon?"

"No, Asika, they fight if necessary and kill those who commit murder. But they have no fetish that asks for blood, and the law they have from heaven is a law of mercy."

She stared at him again.

"All this is strange to me," she said. "I was taught otherwise. Gods are devils and must be appeased, lest they bring misfortune on us; men must be ruled by terror, or they would rebel and pull down the great House; doctors must learn magic, or how could they avert spells? wizards must be killed, or the people would perish in their net. May not we who live in a hell, strive to beat back its flame with the wisdom our forefathers have handed on to us? Tell me, Vernoon, for I would know."

"You make your own hell," answered Alan when with the help of Jeekie he understood her talk.

She pondered over his words for a while, then said:

"I must think. The thing is big. I wander in blackness; I will speak with you again. Say now, what else is wrong with me?"

Now Alan thought that he saw opportunity for a word in season and made a great mistake.

"I think that you treat your husband, that man whom you call Mungana, very badly. Why should you drive him to his death?"

At these words the Asika leapt up in a rage, and seeking something to vent her temper on, violently boxed Jeekie's ears and kicked him with her sandaled foot.

"The Mungana!" she exclaimed, "that beast! What have I to do with him? I hate him, as I hated the others. The priests thrust him on me. He has had his day, let him go. In your country do they make women live with men whom they loathe? I love *you*, Bonsa himself knows why? Perhaps because you have a white skin and white thoughts. But I hate that man. What is the use of being Asika if I cannot take what I love and reject what I hate? Go away, Vernoon, go away, you have angered me, and if it were not for what you have said about that new law of mercy, I think that I would cut your throat," and again she boxed Jeekie's ears and kicked him in the shins.

Alan rose and bowed himself towards the door while she stood with her back towards him, sobbing. As he was about to pass it she wheeled round, wiping the tears from her eyes with her hand, and said:

"I forgot, I sent for you to thank you for your presents; that," and she pointed to the lion skin, "which they tell me you killed with some kind of thunder to save the life of that old cannibal, and this," and she pulled off the necklace of claws, then added, "as I am too bad to wear it, you had better take it back again," and she threw it with all her strength straight into Jeekie's face.

Fearing worse things, the much maltreated Jeekie uttered a howl and bolted through the door, while Alan, picking up the necklace, returned it to her with a bow. She took it.

"Stop," she said. "You are leaving the room without your mask and my women are outside. Come here," and she tied the thing upon his head, setting it all awry, then pushed him from the place.

"Very poor joke, Major, very poor indeed," said Jeekie when they had reached their own apartment. "Lady make love to *you*; *you* play prig and lecture lady about holy customs of her country and she box *my* ear till head sing, also kick me all over and throw sharp claws in face. Please you do it no more. The next time, who knows? she stick knife in *my* gizzard, then kiss *you* afterward and say she so sorry and hope she no hurt *you*. But how that help poor departed Jeekie who get all kicks, while you have ha'pence?"

"Oh! be quiet," said Alan; "you are welcome to the halfpence if you would only leave me the kicks. The question is, how am I to get out of this mess? While she was a beautiful savage devil, one could deal with the thing, but if she is going to become human it is another matter."

Jeekie looked at him with pity in his eyes.

"Always thought white man mad at bottom," he said, shaking his big head. "To benighted black nigger thing so very simple. All you got to do, make love and cut when you get chance. Then she pleased as Punch, everything go smooth and Jeekie get no more kicks. Christian religion business very good, but won't wash in Asiki-land. Your reverend uncle find out that."

Not wishing to pursue the argument, Alan changed the subject by asking his indignant retainer if he thought that the Asika had meant what she said when she offered to send the gold down to the coast.

"Why not, Major? That good lady always mean what she say, and what she do too," and he dabbed wrathfully at the scratches made by the lion's claws on his face, then added, "She know her own mind, not like shilly-shally, see-saw white woman, who get up one thing and go to bed another. If she love she love, if she hate she hate. If she say she send gold, she send it, though pity to part with all that cash, because 'spect someone bag it."

Alan reflected a while.

"Don't you see, Jeekie, that here is a chance, if a very small one, of getting a message to the coast. Also it is quite clear that if we are ever able to escape, it will be impossible for us to carry this heavy stuff, whereas if we send it on ahead, perhaps some of it might get through. We will pack it up, Jeekie, at any rate it will be something to do. Go now and send a message to the Asika, and ask her to let us have some carpenters, and a lot of well-seasoned wood."

The message was sent and an hour later a dozen of the native craftsmen arrived with their rude tools and a supply of planks cut from a kind of iron-wood or ebony tree. They prostrated themselves to Alan, then the master of them rising, instantly began to measure Jeekie with a marked reed. That worthy sprang back and asked what in the name of Bonsa, Big and Little, they were doing, whereon the man explained with humility that the Asika had said that she thought the white lord wanted the wood to make a box to bury his servant in, as he, the said servant, had offended her that morning, and doubtless the white lord wished to kill him on that account, or perhaps to put him away under ground alive.

"Oh, my golly!" said Jeekie, shaking till his great knees knocked together, "oh! my golly! here pretty go. She think you want bury me all alive. That mean she want to be rid of Jeekie, because he got sit there and play gooseberry when she wish talk alone with you. Oh, yes! I see her little game."

"Well, Jeekie," said Alan, bursting into such a roar of laughter that he nearly shook off his mask, "you had better be careful, for you just told me that the Asika is not like a see-saw white woman and never changes her mind. Say to this man that he must tell the Asika there is a mistake, and that however much I should like to oblige her, I can't bury you because it has been prophesied to me that on the day you are buried, I shall be buried also, and that therefore you must be kept alive."

"Capital notion that, Major," said Jeekie, much relieved. "She not want bury you just at present; next year perhaps, but not now. I tell him." And he did with much vigour.

This slight misconception having been disposed of, they explained to the carpenters what was wanted. First, all the gold was emptied out of the sacks in which it remained as the priests had brought it, and divided into heaps, each of which weighed about forty pounds, a weight that with its box Alan considered would be a good load for a porter. Of these heaps there proved to be fifty-three, their total value, Alan reckoned, amounting to about £100,000 sterling. Then the carpenters were set to work to make a model box, which they did quickly enough and with great ingenuity, cutting the wood with their native saws, dovetailing it as a civilized craftsman would do, and finally securing it everywhere with ebony pegs, driven into holes which they bored with a hot iron. The result was a box that would stand any amount of rough usage and when finally pegged down, one that could only be opened with a hammer and a cold chisel.

This box-making went on for two whole days. As each of them was filled and pegged down, the gold within being packed in sawdust to keep it from rattling, Alan amused himself in adding an address with a feather brush and a supply of red paint such as the Asiki priests used to decorate their bodies. At first he was puzzled to know what address to put, but finally decided upon the following: *Major A. Vernon, care of Miss Champers, The Court, near Kingswell, England.* Adding in the corner, *From A. V., Asiki Land, Africa.*

It was all childish enough, he knew, yet when it was done he regarded his handiwork with a sort of satisfaction. For, reflected Alan, if but one of those boxes should chance to get through to England, it would tell Barbara a great deal, and if it were addressed to himself, her uncle could scarcely dare to take possession of it.

Then he bethought him of sending a letter, but was obliged to abandon the idea, as he had neither pen, pencil, ink, nor paper left to him. Whatever arts remained to them, that of any form of writing was now totally unknown to the Asiki, although marks that might be writing, it will be remembered, did appear on the inner side of the Little Bonsa mask, an evidence of its great antiquity. Even in the days when they had wrapped up the Egyptian, the Roman, and other early *Munganas* in sheets of gold and set them in their treasure-house, apparently they had no knowledge of it, for not even an hieroglyph or a rune appeared upon the imperishable metal shrouds. Since that time they had evidently decreased, not advanced, in learning till at the present day, except for these relics and some dim and meaningless survival of rites that once had been religious and were still offered to the same ancient idols, there was little to distinguish them from other tribes of Central African savages. Still Alan did something, for obtaining a piece of white wood, which he smoothed as well as he was able with a knife, he painted on it this message:

> Messrs. Aston
> Old Calabar.
> Please forward accompanying fifty-three packages, or as many as arrive, and cable as follows (all costs will be remitted): Miss Champers, Kingswell, England. Prisoner among Asiki. No present prospect of escape, but hope for best. Jeekie and I well. Allowed send this, but perhaps no future message possible. Goodbye.
> Alan.

As it happened just as Alan was finishing this scrawl with a sad heart, he heard a movement and glancing up, perceived standing at his side the Asika, of whom he had seen nothing since the interview when she had beaten Jeekie:

"What are those marks that you make upon the board, Vernoon?" she asked suspiciously.

With the assistance of Jeekie, who kept at a respectful distance, he informed her that they were a message in writing to tell the white men at the coast to forward the gold to his starving family.

"Oh!" she said, "I never heard of writing. You shall teach it me. It will serve to pass the time till we are married, though it will not be of much use afterwards, as we shall never be separated any more and words are better than marks upon a board. But," she added cheerfully, "I can send away this black dog of yours," and she looked at Jeekie, "and he can write to us. No, I cannot, for an accident might happen to him, and they tell me you say that if he dies, you die also, so he must stop here always. What have you in those little boxes?"

"The gold you gave me, Asika, packed in loads."

"A small gift enough," she answered contemptuously; "would you not like more, since you value that stuff? Well, another time you shall send all you want. Meanwhile the porters are waiting, fifty men and three, as you sent me word, and ten spare ones to take the place of any who die. But how they will find their way, I know not, since none of them have ever been to the coast."

An idea occurred to Alan, who had small faith in Jeekie's "ma" as a messenger.

"The Ogula prisoners could show them," he said; "at any rate as far as the forest, and after that they could find out. May they not go, Asika?"

"If you will," she answered carelessly. "Let them be ready to start tomorrow at the dawn, all except their chief, Fahni, who must stop here as a hostage. I do not trust those Ogula, who more than once have threatened to make war upon us," she added, then turned and bade the priests bring in the bearers to receive their instructions.

Presently they came, picked men all of them, under the command of an Asiki captain, and with them the Ogula, whom she summoned also.

"Go where the white lord sends you," she said in an indifferent voice, "carrying with you these packages. I do not know where it is, but these man-eaters will show you some of the way, and if you fail in the business but live to come back again, you shall be sacrificed to Bonsa at the next feast; if you run away then your wives and children will be sacrificed. Food shall be given you for your journey, and gold to buy more when it is gone. Now, Vernoon, tell them what they have to do."

So Alan, or rather Jeekie, told them, and these directions were so long and minute, that before they were finished the Asika grew tired of listening and went away, saying as she passed the captain of the company:

"Remember my words, man, succeed or die, but of your land and its secrets say nothing."

"I hear," answered the captain, prostrating himself.

That night Alan summoned the Ogula and spoke to them through Jeekie in their own language. At first they declared that they would not leave their chief, preferring to stay and die with him.

"Not so," said Fahni; "go, my children, that I may live. Go and gather the tribe, all the thousands of them who are men and can fight, and bring them up to attack Asiki-land, to rescue me if I still live, or to avenge me if I am dead. As for these bearers, do them no harm, but send them on to the coast with the white man's goods."

So in the end the Ogula said that they would go, and when Alan woke up on the following morning, he was informed that they and the Asiki porters had already departed upon their journey. Then he dismissed the matter from his mind, for to tell the truth he never expected to hear of them any more.

## Chapter 15

# Alan Falls Ill

After the departure of the messengers a deep melancholy fell upon Alan, who was sure that he had now no further hope of communicating with the outside world. Bitterly did he reproach himself for his folly in having ever journeyed to this hateful place in order to secure—what? About £100,000 worth of gold which of course he never could secure, as it would certainly vanish or be stolen on its way to the coast. For this gold he had become involved in a dreadful complication which must cost him much misery, and sooner or later life itself, since he could not marry that beautiful savage Asika, and if he refused her she would certainly kill him in her outraged pride and fury.

Day by day she sent for him, and when he came, assumed a new character, that of a woman humbled by a sense of her own ignorance, which she was anxious to amend. So he must play the role of tutor to her, telling her of civilized peoples, their laws, customs and religions, and instructing her how to write and read. She listened and learned submissively enough, but all the while Alan felt as one might who is called upon to teach tricks to a drugged panther. The drug in this case was her passion for him, which appeared to be very genuine. But when it passed off, or when he was obliged to refuse her, what, he wondered, would happen then?

Anxiety and confinement told on him far more than all the hardships of his journey. His health ran down, he began to fall ill. Then as bad luck would have it, walking in that damp, unwholesome cedar garden, out of which he might not stray, he contracted the germ of some kind of fever which in autumn was very common in this poisonous climate. Three days later he became delirious, and for a week after that hung between life and death. Well was it for him that his medicine-chest still remained intact, and that recognizing his own symptoms before his head gave way, he was able to instruct Jeekie what drugs to give him at the different stages of the disease.

For the rest his memories of that dreadful illness always remained very vague. He had visions of Jeekie and of a robed woman whom he knew to be the Asika, bending over him continually. Also it seemed to him that from time to time he was talking with Barbara, which even then he knew must be absurd, for how could they talk across thousands of miles of land and sea.

At length his mind cleared suddenly, and he awoke as from a nightmare to find himself lying in the hall or room where he had always been, feeling quite cool and without pain, but so weak that it was an effort to him to lift his hand. He stared about him and was astonished to see the white head of Jeekie rolling uneasily to and fro upon the cushions of another bed near by.

"Jeekie," he said, "are you ill too, Jeekie?"

At the sound of that voice his retainer started up violently.

"What, Major, you awake?" he said. "Thanks be to all gods, white and black, yes, and yellow too, for I thought your goose cooked. No, no, Major, I not ill, only Asika say so. You go to bed, so she make me go to bed. You get worse, she treat me cruel; you seem better, she stuff me with food till I burst. All because you tell her that you and I die same day. Oh, Lord! poor Jeekie think his end very near just now, for he know quite well that she not let him breathe ten minutes after you peg out. Jeekie never pray so hard for anyone before as he pray this week for you, and by Jingo! I think he do the trick, he and that medicine stuff which make him feel very bad in stomach," and he groaned under the weight of his many miseries.

Weak as he was Alan began to laugh, and that laugh seemed to do him more good than anything that he could remember, for after it he was sure that he would recover.

Just then an agonized whisper reached him from Jeekie.

"Look out!" it said, "here come Asika. Go sleep and seem better, Major, please, or I catch it hot."

So Alan almost shut his eyes and lay still. In another moment she was standing over him and he noticed that her hair was dishevelled and her eyes were red as though with weeping. She scanned him intently for a little while, then passed round to where Jeekie lay and appeared to pinch his ear so hard that he wriggled and uttered a stifled groan.

"How is your lord, dog?" she whispered.

"Better, O Asika, I think that last medicine do us good, though it make me very sick inside. Just now he spoke to me and said that he hoped that your heart was not sad because of him and that all this time in his dreams he had seen and thought of nobody but you, O Asika."

"Did he?" asked that lady, becoming intensely interested. "Then tell me, dog, why is he ever calling upon one Bar-bar-a? Surely that is a woman's name?"

"Yes, O Asika, that is the name of his mother, also of one of his sisters, whom, after you, he loves best of anyone in the whole world. When you are here he talks of them, but when you are not here he talks of no one but you. Although he is so sick he remembers white man's custom, which tells him that it is very wrong to say sweet things to lady's face till he is quite married to her. After that they say them always."

She looked at him suspiciously and muttering, "Here it is otherwise. For your own sake, man, I trust that you do not lie," left him, and drawing a stool up beside Alan's bed, sat herself down and examined him carefully, touching his face and hands with her long thin fingers. Then noting how white and wasted he was, of a sudden she began to weep, saying between her sobs:

"Oh! if you should die, Vernoon, I will die also and be born again not as Asika, as I have been for so many generations, but as a white woman that I may be with you. Only first," she added, setting her teeth, "I will sacrifice every wizard in this land, for they have brought the sickness on you by their magic, and I will burn Bonsa-town and cast its gods to melt in the flames, and the Mungana with them. And then amid their ashes I will let out my life," and again she began to weep very piteously and to call him by endearing names and pray him that he would not die.

Now Alan thought it time to wake up. He opened his eyes, stared at her vacantly, and asked if it were raining, which indeed it might have been, for her big tears were falling on his face. She uttered a gasp of joy.

"No, no," she answered, "the weather is very fine. It is I—I who have rained because I thought you die." She wiped his forehead with the soft linen of her robe, then went on, "But you will not die; say that you will live, say that you will live for me, Vernoon."

He looked at her, and feeble though he was, the awfulness of the situation sank into his soul.

"I hope that I shall live," he answered. "I am hungry, please give me some food."

Next instant there was a tumult near by, and when Alan looked up again it was to see Jeekie, very lightly clad, flying through the door.

"It will be here presently," she said. "Oh! if you knew what I have suffered, if you only knew. Now you will recover whom I thought dead, for this fever passes quickly and there shall be such a sacrifice—no, I forgot, you hate sacrifices—there shall be no sacrifice, there shall be a thanksgiving, and every woman in the land shall break her bonds to husband or to lover and take him whom she desires without reproach or loss. I will do as I would be done by, that is the law you taught me, is it not?"

This novel interpretation of a sacred doctrine, worthy of Jeekie himself, so paralyzed Alan's enfeebled brain that he could make no answer, nor do anything except wonder what would happen in Asiki-land when the decree of its priestess took effect. Then Jeekie arrived with something to drink which he swallowed with the eagerness of the convalescent and almost immediately went to sleep in good earnest.

Alan's recovery was rapid, since as the Asika had told him, if a patient lives through it, the kind of fever that he had taken did not last long enough to exhaust his vital forces. When she asked him if he needed anything to make him well, he answered:

"Yes, air and exercise."

She replied that he should have both, and next morning his hated mask was put upon his face and he was supported by priests to a door where a litter, or rather litters were waiting, one for himself and another for Jeekie who, although in robust health, was still supposed to be officially ill and not allowed to walk upon his own legs. They entered these litters and were borne off till presently they met a third litter of particularly gorgeous design carried by masked bearers, wherein was the Asika herself, wearing her coronet and a splendid robe.

Into this litter, which was fitted with a second seat, Alan was transferred, the Mungana, for whom it was designed, being placed in that vacated by Alan, which either by accident or otherwise, was no more seen that day. They went up the mountain side and to the edge of the great fall and watched the waters thunder down, though the crest of them they could not reach. Next they wandered off into the huge forests that clothed the slopes of the hills and there halted and ate. Then as the sun sank they returned to the gloomy Bonsa-Town beneath them.

For Alan, notwithstanding his weakness and anxieties, it was a heavenly day. The Asika was passive, some new mood being on her, and scarcely troubled him at all except to call his attention to a tree, a flower, or a prospect of the scenery. Here on the mountain side, too, the air was sweet, and for the rest—well, he who had been so near to death, was escaped for an hour from that gloomy home of bloodshed and superstition, and saw God's sky again.

This journey was the first of many. Every day the litters were waiting and they visited some new place, although into the town itself they never went. Moreover, if they passed through outlying villages, though Alan was forced to wear his mask, their inhabitants had been warned to absent themselves, so that they saw no one. The crops were left untended and the cattle and sheep lowed hungrily in their kraals. On certain days, at Alan's request, they were taken to the spots where the gold was found in the gravel bed of an almost dry stream that during the rains was a torrent.

He descended from the litter and with the help of the Asika and Jeekie, dug a little in this gravel, not without reward, for in it they found several nuggets. Above, too, where they went afterwards, was a huge quartz reef denuded by water, which evidently had been worked in past ages and was still so rich that in it they saw plenty of visible gold. Looking at it Alan bethought him of his City days and of the hundreds of thousands of pounds capital with which this unique proposition might have been floated. Afterwards they were carried to the places where the gems were found, stuck about in the clay, like plums in a pudding, though none ever sought them now. But all these things interested the Asika not at all.

"What is the good of gold," she asked of Alan, "except to make things of, or the bright stones except to play with? What is the good of anything except food to eat and power and wisdom that can open the secret doors of knowledge, of things seen and things unseen, and love that brings the lover joy and forgetfulness of self and takes away the awful loneliness of the soul, if only for a little while?"

Not wishing to drift into discussion on the matter of love, Alan asked the priestess to define her "soul," whence it came and whither she believed it to be going.

"My soul is I, Vernoon," she answered, "and already very, very old. Thus it has ruled amongst this people for thousands of years."

"How is that?" he asked, "seeing that the Asika dies?"

"Oh! no, Vernoon, she does not die; she only changes. The old body dies, the spirit enters into another body which is waiting. Thus until I was fourteen I was but a common girl, the daughter of a headman of that village yonder, at least so they tell me, for of this time I have no memory. Then the Asika died and as I had the secret marks and the beauty that is hers the priests burnt her body before Big

Bonsa and suffocated me, the child, in the smoke of the burning. But I awoke again and when I awoke the past was gone and the soul of the Asika filled me, bringing with it its awful memories, its gathered wisdom, its passion of love and hate, and its power to look backward and before."

"Do you ever do these things?" asked Alan.

"Backward, yes, before very little; since you came, not at all, because my heart is a coward and I fear what I might see. Oh! Vernoon, Vernoon, I know you and your thoughts. You think me a beautiful beast who loves like a beast, who loves you because you are white and different from our men. Well, what there is of the beast in me the gods of my people gave, for they are devils and I am their servant. But there is more than that, there is good also which I have won for myself. I knew you would come even before I had seen your face, I knew you would come," she went on passionately, "and that is why I was yours already. But what would befall after you came, that I neither knew, nor know, because I will not seek, who could learn it all."

He looked at her and she saw the doubt in his eyes.

"You do not believe me, Vernoon. Very well, this night you shall see, you and that black dog of yours, that you may know I do not trick you, and he shall tell me what you see, for he being but a low-born pig will speak the truth, not minding if it hurts me, whereas you are gentle and might spare, and myself I have sworn not to search the future by an oath that I may not break."

"What of the past?" asked Alan.

"We will not waste time on it, for I know it all. Vernoon, have you no memories of Asiki-land? Do you think you never visited it before?"

"Never," said Alan; "it was my uncle who came and ran away with Little Bonsa on his head."

"That is news indeed," she replied mockingly. "Did you then think that I believed it to be you, though it is true that she who went before, or my spirit that was in her, fell into error for an hour, and thought that fool-uncle of yours was *the Man*. When she found her mistake she let him go, and bade the god go with him that it might bring back the appointed Man, as it has done; yes, that Little Bonsa, who knew him of old, might search him out from among all the millions of men, born or unborn, and bring him back to me. Therefore also she chose a young black dog who would live for many years, and bade the god to take him with her, and told him of the wealth of our people that it might be a bait upon the hook. Do you see, Vernoon, that yellow dirt was the bait, that I—I am the hook? Well, you have felt it before, so it should not gall you overmuch."

Now Alan was more frightened than he had been since he set foot in Asiki-land, for of a sudden this woman became terrible to him. He felt that she knew things which were hidden from him. For the first time he believed in her, believed, that she was more than a mere passionate savage set by chance to rule over a bloodthirsty tribe; that she was one who had a part in his destiny.

"Felt the hook?" he muttered. "I do not understand."

"You are very forgetful," she answered. "Vernoon, we have lived and loved before, who were twin souls from the first. That man now, whom I told you lived once on the great river called the Nile, have you no memory of him? Well, well, let it be, I will tell you afterwards. Here we are at the Gold House again, tonight when I am ready I will send for you, and this I promise, you shall leave me wiser than you were."

When they were alone in their room Alan told Jeekie of the expected entertainment of crystal gazing, or whatever it might be, and the part that he was to play in it.

"You say that again, Major," said Jeekie.

Alan repeated the information, giving every detail that he could remember.

"Oh!" said Jeekie, "I see Asika show us things, 'cause she afraid to look at them herself, or take oath, or can't, or something. She no ask you tell her what she see, because you too kind hurt her feeling, if happen to be something beastly. But Jeekie just tell her because he so truthful and not care curse about her feeling. Well, that all right, Jeekie tell her sure enough. Only, Major, don't you interrupt. Quite possible these magic things, I see one show, you see another. So don't you go say, 'Jeekie, that a lie,' and give me away to Asika just because you think you see different, 'cause if so you put me into dirty hole, and of course I catch it afterwards. You promise, Major?"

"Oh! yes, I promise. But, Jeekie, do you really think we are going to see anything?"

"Can't say, Major," and he shook his head gloomily. "P'raps all put up job. But lots of rum things in world, Major, specially among beastly African savage who very curious and always ready pay blood to bad Spirit. Hope Asika not get this into her head, because no one know what happen. P'raps we see too much and scared all our lives; but p'raps all tommy rot."

"That's it—tommy rot," answered Alan, who was not superstitious.

"Well, I suppose that we must go through with it. But oh! Jeekie, I wish you would tell me how to get out of this."

"Don't know, Major, p'raps never get out; p'raps learn how tonight. Have to do something soon if want to go. Mungana's time nearly up, and then—oh my eye!"

********

It was night, about ten o'clock indeed, the hour at which Alan generally went to bed. No message had come and he began to hope that the Asika had forgotten, or changed her mind, and was just going to say so to Jeekie when a light coming from behind him attracted his attention and he turned to see her standing in a corner of the great room, holding a lamp in her hand and looking towards him. Her gold breastplate and crown were gone, with every other ornament, and she was clad, or rather muffled in robes of pure white fitted with a kind of nun's hood which lay back upon her shoulders. Also on her arm she carried a shawl or veil. Standing thus, all undecked, with her long hair fastened in a simple knot, she still looked very beautiful, more so than she had ever been, thought Alan, for the cruelty of her face had faded and was replaced by a mystery very strange to see. She did not seem quite like a natural woman, and that was the reason, perhaps, that Alan for the first time felt attracted by her. Hitherto she had always repelled him, but this night it was otherwise.

"How did you come here?" he asked in a more gentle voice than he generally used towards her.

Noting the change in his tone, she smiled shyly and even coloured a little, then answered:

"This house has many secrets, Vernoon. When you are lord of it you shall learn them all, till then I may not tell them to you. But, come, there are other secrets which I hope you shall see tonight, and, Jeekie, come you also, for you shall be the mouth of your lord, so that you may tell me what perhaps he would hide."

"I will tell you everything, everything, O Asika," answered Jeekie, stretching out his hands and bowing almost to the ground.

Then they started and following many long passages as before, although whether they were the same or others Alan could not tell, came at last to a door which he recognized, that of the Treasure House. As they approached this door it opened and through it, like a hunted thing, ran the bedizened Mungana, husband of the Asika, terror, or madness, shining in his eyes. Catching sight of his wife, who bore the lamp, he threw himself upon his knees and snatching at her robe, addressed some petition to her, speaking so rapidly that Alan could not follow his words.

For a moment she listened, then dragged her dress from his hand and spurned him with her foot. There was something so cruel in the gesture and the action, so full of deadly hate and loathing, that Alan, who witnessed it, experienced a new revulsion of feeling towards the Asika. What kind of a woman must she be, he wondered, who could treat a discarded lover thus in the presence of his successor?

With a groan or a sob, it was difficult to say which, the poor man rose and perceived Alan, whose face he now beheld for the first time, since the Asika had told him not to mask himself as they would meet no one. The sight of it seemed to fill him with jealous fury; at any rate he leapt at his rival, intending, apparently, to catch him by the throat. Alan, who was watching him, stepped aside, so that he came into violet contact with the wall of the passage and, half-stunned by the shock, reeled onwards into the darkness.

"The hog!" said the Asika, or rather she hissed it, "the hog, who dared to touch me and to strike at you. Well, his time is short—would that I could make it shorter! Did you hear what he sought of me?"

Alan, who wished for no confidences, replied by asking what the Mungana was doing in the Treasure House, to which she answered that the spirits who dwelt there were eating up his soul, and when they had devoured it all he would go quite mad and kill himself.

"Does this happen to all *Munganas*?" inquired Alan.

"Yes, Vernoon, if the Asika hates them, but if she loves them it is otherwise. Come, let us forget the wretch, who would kill you if he could," and she led the way into the hall and up it, passing between the heaps of gold.

On the table where lay the necklaces of gems she set down her lamp, whereof the light, all there was in that great place, flickered feebly upon the mask of Little Bonsa, which had been moved here apparently for some ceremonial purpose, and still more feebly upon the hideous, golden countenances and winding sheets of the ancient, yellow dead who stood around in scores placed one above the other, each in his appointed niche. It was an awesome scene and one that oppressed Jeekie very much, for he murmured to Alan:

"Oh my! Major, family vault child's play to this hole, just like——" here his comparison came to an end, for the Asika cut it short with a single glance.

"Sit here in front of me," she said to Alan, "and you, Jeekie, sit at your lord's side, and be silent till I bid you speak."

Then she crouched down in a heap behind them, threw the cloth or veil she carried over her head, and in some way that they did not see, suddenly extinguished the lamp.

Now they were in deep darkness, the darkness of death, and in utter silence, the silence of the dead. No glimmer of light, and yet to Alan it seemed as though he could feel the flash of the crystal eyes of Little Bonsa, and of all the other eyes set in the masks of those departed men who once had been the husbands of the bloodstained priestess of the Asiki, till one by one, as she wearied of them, they were bewitched to madness and to doom. In that utter quiet he thought even that he could hear them stir within their winding sheets, or it may have been that the Asika had risen and moved among them on some errand of her own. Far away something fell to the floor, a very light object, such as flake of rock or a scale of gold. Yet the noise of it struck his nerves loud as a clap of thunder, and those of Jeekie also, for he felt him start at his side and heard the sudden hammerlike beat of his heart.

What was the woman doing in this dreadful place, he wondered. Well, it was easy to guess. Doubtless she had brought them here to scare and impress them. Presently a voice, that of some hidden priest, would speak to them, and they would be asked to believe it a message from the spirit world, or a spirit itself might be arranged—what could be easier in their mood and these surroundings?

Now the Asika was speaking behind them in a muffled voice. From the tone of it she appeared to be engaged in argument or supplication in some strange tongue. At any rate Alan could not understand a word of what she said. The argument, or prayer, went on for a long while, with pauses as though for answers. Then suddenly it ceased and once more they were plunged into that unfathomable silence.

## Chapter 16

# What the Asika Showed Alan

It seemed to Alan that he went to sleep and dreamed.

He dreamed that it was late autumn in England. Leaves drifted down from the trees beneath the breath of a strong, damp wind, and ran or floated along the road till they vanished into a ditch, or caught against a pile of stones that had been laid ready for its repair. He knew the road well enough; he even knew the elm tree beneath which he seemed to stand on the crest of a hill. It was that which ran from Mr. Champers-Haswell's splendid house, The Court, to the church; he could see them both, the house to the right, the church to the left, and his eyesight seemed to have improved, since he was able to observe that at either place there was bustle and preparation as though for some big ceremony.

Now the big gates of The Court opened and through them came a funeral. It advanced toward him with unnatural swiftness, as though it floated upon air, the whole melancholy procession of it. In a few seconds it had come and gone and yet during those seconds he suffered agony, for there arose in his mind a horrible terror that this was Barbara's burying. He could not have endured it for another moment; he would have cried out or died, only now the mourners passed him following the coffin, and in the first carriage he saw Barbara seated, looking sad and somewhat troubled, but well. A little further down the line came another carriage, and in it was Sir Robert Aylward, staring before him with cold, impassive face.

In his dream Alan thought to himself that he must have borrowed this carriage, which would not be strange, as he generally used motors, for there was a peer's coronet upon the panels and the silver-mounted harness.

The funeral passed and suddenly vanished into the churchyard gates, leaving Alan wondering why his cousin Haswell was not seated at Barbara's side. Then it occurred to him that it might be because he was in the coffin, and at that moment in his dream he heard the Asika asking Jeekie what he saw; heard Jeekie answering also, "A burying in the country called England."

"Of whom, Jeekie?" Then after some hesitation, the answer:

"Of a lady whom my lord loves very much. They bury her."

"What was her name, Jeekie?"

"Her name was Barbara."

"Bar-bara, why that you told me was the name of his mother and his sister. Which of them is buried?"

"Neither, O Asika. It was another lady who loved him very much and wanted to marry him, and that was why he ran away to Africa. But now she is dead and buried."

"Are all women in England called Barbara, Jeekie?"

"Yes, O Asika, Barbara means woman."

"If your lord loved this Barbara, why then did he run away from her? Well, it matters not since she is dead and buried, for whatever their spirits may feel, no man cares for a woman that is dead until she clothes herself in flesh again. That was a good vision and I will reward you for it."

"I have earned nothing, O Asika," answered Jeekie modestly, "who only tell you what I see as I must. Yet, O Asika," he added with a note of anxiety in his voice, "why do you not read these magic writings for yourself?"

"Because I dare not, or rather because I can not," she answered fiercely. "Be silent, slave, for now the power of the good broods upon my soul."

The dream went on. A great forest appeared, such a forest as they had passed before they met the cannibals, and set beneath one of the trees, a tent and in that tent Barbara, Barbara weeping. Someone began to lift the flap of the tent. She sprang up, snatching at a pistol that lay beside her, turning its muzzle towards her breast. A man entered the tent. Alan saw his face, it was his own. Barbara let fall the pistol and fell backwards as though a bullet from it had pierced her heart. He leapt towards her, but before he came to where she lay everything had vanished and he heard Jeekie droning out his lies to the Asika, telling her that the vision he had seen was one of her and his master seated with their arms about each other in a chamber of the Golden House.

A third time the dream descended on Alan like a cloud. It seemed to him that he was borne beyond the flaming borders of the world. Everything around was new and unfamiliar, vast, changing, lovely, terrible. He stood alone upon a pearly plain and the sky above him was lit with red moons, many and many of them that hung there like lamps. Spirits began to pass him. He could catch something of their splendour as they sped by with incredible swiftness; he could hear the music of their laughter. One rose up at his side. It was the Asika, only a thousand times more splendid; clothed in all the glory of hell. Majestically she bent towards him, her glowing eyes held his, the deadly perfume of her breath beat upon his brow and made him drunken.

She spoke to him and her voice sounded like distant bells.

"Through many a life, through many a life," she said, "bought with much blood, paid for with a million tears, but mine at last, the soul that I have won to comfort my soul in the eternal day. Come to the place I have made ready for you, the hell that shall turn to heaven at your step, come, you by whom I am redeemed, and drive away those gods that torture me because I was their servant that I might win you."

So she spoke, and though all his soul revolted, yet the fearful strength that was in her seemed to draw him onward whither she would go. Then a light shone and that light was the face of Barbara and with a suddenness that was almost awful, the wild dream came to an end.

********

Alan was in his own room again, though how he got there he did not recollect.

"Jeekie," he said, "what has happened? I seem to have had a very curious dream, there in the Treasure-place, and to have heard you telling the Asika a string of incredible falsehoods."

"Oh! no, Major, Jeekie can't lie, too good Christian; he tell her what *he* see, or what he think she see if she look, 'cause though p'raps he see nothing, she never believe that. And," he added with a burst of confidence, "what the dickens it matter what he tell her, so long as she swallow same and keep quiet? Nasty things always make women like Asika quite outrageous. Give them sweet to suck, say Jeekie, and if they ill afterwards, that no fault of his. They had sweet."

"Quite so, Jeekie, quite so, only I should advise you not to play too many tricks upon the Asika, lest she should happen to find you out. How did I get back here?"

"Like man that walk in his sleep, Major. She go first, you follow, just as little lamb after Mary in hymn."

"Jeekie, did you really see anything at all?"

"No, Major, nothing partic'lar, except ghost of Mrs. Jeekie and of your reverend uncle, both of them very angry. That magic all stuff,

Major. Asika put something in your grub make you drunk, so that you think her very wise. Don't think of it no more, Major, or you go off your chump. If Jeekie see nothing, depend on it there nothing to see."

"Perhaps so, Jeekie, but I wish I could be sure you had seen nothing. Listen to me; we must get out of this place somehow, or as you say, I shall go off my chump. It's haunted, Jeekie, its haunted, and I think that Asika is a devil, not a woman."

"That what priests say, Major, very old devil—part of Bonsa," he answered, looking at his master anxiously. "Well, don't you fret, Jeekie not afraid of devils, Jeekie get you out in good time. Go to bed and leave it all to Jeekie."

********

Fifteen more days had gone by, and it was the eve of the night of the second full moon when Alan was destined to become the husband of the Asika. She had sent for him that morning and he found her radiant with happiness. Whether or no she believed Jeekie's interpretation of the visions she had called up, it seemed quite certain that her mind was void of fears and doubts. She was sure that Alan was about to become her husband, and had summoned all the people of the Asiki to be present at the ceremony of their marriage, and incidentally of the death of the Mungana who, poor wretch, was to be forced to kill himself upon that occasion.

Before they parted she had spoken to Alan sweetly enough.

"Vernoon," she said, "I know that you do not love me as I love you, but the love will come, since for your sake I will change myself. I will grow gentle; I will shed no more blood; that of the Mungana shall be the last, and even him I would spare if I could, only while he lives I may not marry you; it is the one law that is stronger than I am, and if I broke it I and you would die at once. You shall even teach me your faith, if you will, for what is good to you is henceforth good to me. Ask what you wish of me, and as an earnest I will do it if I can."

Now Alan looked at her. There was one thing that he wished above all others—that she would let him go. But this he did not dare to ask; moreover, it would have been utterly useless. After all, if the Asika's love was terrible, what would be the appearance of her outraged hate? What could he ask? More gold? He hated the very name of the stuff, for it had brought him here. He remembered the old cannibal chief, Fahni, who, like himself, languished a prisoner, daily expecting death. Only that morning he had implored him to obtain his liberty.

"I thank you, Asika," he said. "Now, if your words are true, set Fahni free and let him return to his own country, for if he stays here he will die."

"Surely, Vernoon, that is a small thing," she answered, smiling, "though it is true that when he gets there he will probably make war upon us. Well, let him, let him." Then she clapped her hands and summoned priests, whom she bade go at once and conduct Fahni out of Bonsa-Town. Also she bade them loose certain slaves who were of the Ogula tribe, that they might accompany him laden with provisions, and send on orders to the outposts that Fahni and his party should pass unmolested from the land.

This done, she began to talk to Alan about many matters, however little he might answer her. Indeed it seemed almost as though she feared to let him leave her side; as though some presentiment of loss oppressed her.

At length, to Alan's great relief, the time came when they must part, since it was necessary for her to attend a secret ceremony of preparation or purification that was called "Putting-off-the-Past." Although she had been thrice summoned, still she would not let him go.

"They call you, Asika," said Alan.

"Yes, yes, they call me," she replied, springing up. "Leave me, Vernoon, till we meet tomorrow to part no more. Oh! why is my heart so heavy in me? That black dog of yours read the visions that I summoned but might not look on, and they were good visions. They showed that the woman who loved you is dead; they showed us wedded, and other deeper things. Surely he would not dare to lie to me, knowing that if he did I would flay him living and throw him to the vultures. Why, then, is my heart so heavy in me? Would you escape me, Vernoon? Nay, you are not so cruel, nor could you do it except by death. Moreover, man, know that even in death you cannot escape me, for there be sure I shall follow you and claim you, to whose side my spirit has toiled for ages, and what is there so strong that it can snatch you from my hand?"

She looked at him a moment, and seizing his hand burst into a flood of tears, and seizing his hand threw herself upon her knees and kissed it again and again.

"Go now," she said, "go, and let my love go with you, through lives and deaths, and all the dreams beyond, oh! let my love go with you, as it shall, Vernoon."

So he went, leaving her weeping on her knees.

********

During the dark hours that followed Alan and madness were not far apart. What could he do? Escape was utterly impossible. For weeks he and Jeekie had considered it in vain. Even if they could win out of the Gold House fortress, what hope had they of making their way through the crowded, tortuous town where, after the African fashion, peopled walked about all night, every one of whom would recognize the white man, whether he were masked or no? Besides, beyond the town were the river and the guarded walls and gates and beyond them open country where they would be cut off or run down. No, to attempt escape was suicide. Suicide! That gave him an idea, why should he not kill himself? It would be easy enough, for he still had his revolver and a few cartridges, and surely it was better than to enter on such a life as awaited him as the plaything of a priestess of a tribe of fetish-worshipping savages.

But if he killed himself, how about Barbara and how about poor old Jeekie, who would certainly be killed also? Besides, it was not the right thing to do, and while there is life there is always hope.

Alan paused in his walk up and down the room and looked at Jeekie, who sat upon the floor with his back resting against the stone altar, reflectively pulling down his thick under-lip and letting it fly back, negro-fashion.

"Jeekie," he said, "time's up. What am I to do?"

"Do, Major?" he replied with affected cheerfulness. "Oh! that quite simple. Jeekie arrange everything. You marry Asika and by and by, when you master here and tired of her, you give her slip. Very interesting experience; no white man ever have such luck before. Asika not half bad, *if* she fond of you; she like little girl in song, when she good, she very, very good. At any rate, nothing else to do. Marry Asika or spiflicate, which mean, Major, that Jeekie spiflicate too, and," he added, shaking his white head sadly, "he no like *that*. One or two little things on his mind that no get time to square up yet. Daren't pray like Christian here, 'cause afraid of Bonsas, and Bonsas come even with him by and by, 'cause he been Christian, so poor Jeekie fall down bump between two stools. 'Postles kick him out of heaven and Bonsas kick him out of hell, and where Jeekie go to then?"

"Don't know, I am sure," answered Alan, smiling a little in spite of his sorrow, "but I think the Bonsas might find a corner for you somewhere. Look here, Jeekie, you old scamp, I am sorry for you, for you have been a good friend to me and we are fond of each other. But just understand this, I am not going to marry that woman if I can help it. It's against my principles. So I shall wait till tomorrow and then I shall walk out of this place. If the guards try to stop me I shall shoot them while I have any cartridges. Then I shall go on until they kill me."

"Oh! But Major, they not kill you—never; they chuck blanket over your head and take you back to Asika. It Jeekie they kill, skin him alive-o, and all the rest of it."

"Hope not, Jeekie, because they think we shall die the same day. But if so, I can't help it. Tomorrow morning I shall walk out, and now that's settled. I am tired and going to sleep," and he threw himself down upon the bed and, being worn out with weariness and anxiety, soon fell fast asleep.

But Jeekie did not sleep, although he too lay down upon his bed. On the contrary, he remained wide awake and reflected, more deeply perhaps than he had ever done before, being sure the superstition as to the dependence of Alan's life upon his own was now worn very thin, and that his hour was at hand. He thought of making Alan's wild attempt to depart impossible by the simple method of warning the Asika, but, notwithstanding his native selfishness, was too loyal to let that idea take root in his mind. No, there was nothing to be done; if the Major wished to start, the Major must start, and he, Jeekie, must pay the price. Well, he deserved it, who had been fool enough to listen to the secret promptings of Little Bonsa and conduct him to Asiki-land.

Thus he passed several hours, for the most part in melancholy speculations as to the exact fashion of his end, until at length weariness overcame him also and, shutting his eyes, Jeekie began to doze. Suddenly he grew aware of the presence of some other person in the room, but thinking that it was only the Asika prowling about in her uncanny fashion, or perhaps her spirit, for how her body entered the place he could not guess, he did not stir, but lay breathing heavily and watching out of the corner of his eye.

Presently a figure emerged from the shadows into the faint light thrown by the single lamp that burned above, and though it was wrapped in a dark cloak, Jeekie knew at once that it was not the Asika. Very stealthily the figure crept towards him, as a leopard might creep, and bent down to examine him. The movement caused the cloak to slip a little, and for an instant Jeekie caught sight of the wasted, half-crazed face of the Mungana, and of a long, curved knife that glittered in his hand. Paralyzed with fear, he lay quite still, knowing that should he show the slightest sign of consciousness that knife would pierce his heart.

The Mungana watched him a while, then satisfied that he slept, turned round and, bending himself almost double, glided with infinite precautions towards Alan's bed, which stood some twelve or fourteen feet away. Silently as a snake that uncoils itself, Jeekie slipped from between his blankets and crept after him, his naked feet making no noise upon the mat-strewn floor. So intent was the Mungana upon the deed which he had come to do that he never looked back, and thus it happened that the two of them reached the bed one immediately behind the other.

Alan was lying on his back with his throat exposed, a very easy victim. For a moment the Mungana stared. Then he erected himself like a snake about to strike, and lifted the great curved knife, taking aim at Alan's naked breast. Jeekie erected himself also, and even as the knife began to fall, with one hand he caught the arm that drove it and with the other the murderer's throat. The Mungana fought like a wild-cat, but Jeekie was too strong for him. His fingers held the man's windpipe like a vice. He choked and weakened; the knife fell from his hand. He sank to the ground and lay there helpless, whereon Jeekie knelt upon his chest and, possessing himself of the knife, held it within an inch of his heart.

It was at this juncture that Alan woke up and asked sleepily what was the matter.

"Nothing, Major," answered Jeekie in low and cheerful tones. "Snake just going to bite you and I catch him, that all," and he gave an extra squeeze to the Mungana's throat, who turned black in the face and rolled his eyes.

"Be careful, Jeekie, or you will kill the man," exclaimed Alan, recognizing the Mungana and taking in the situation.

"Why not, Major? He want kill you, and me too afterwards. Good riddance of bad rubbish, as Book say."

"I am not so sure, Jeekie. Give him air and let me think. Tell him that if he makes any noise, he dies."

Jeekie obeyed, and the Mungana's darkening eyes grew bright again as he drew his breath in great sobs.

"Now, friend," said Alan in Asiki, "why did you wish to stab me?"

"Because I hate you," answered the man, "who tomorrow will take my place and the wife I love."

"As a year or two ago you took someone else's place, eh? Well, suppose now that I don't want either your place or your wife."

"What would that matter even it if were true, white man, since she wants you?"

"I am thinking, friend, that there is someone else she will want when she hears of this. How do you suppose that you will die tomorrow? Not so easily as you hope, perhaps."

The Mungana's eyes seemed to sink into his head, and his face to sicken with terror. That shaft had gone home.

"Suppose I make a bargain with you," went on Alan slowly. "Supposing I say: 'Mungana, show me the way out of this place, as you can, now at once. Or if you prefer it, refuse and be given up to the Asika?' Come, you are not too mad to understand. Answer—and quickly."

"Would you kill me afterwards?" he asked.

"Not I. Why should I wish to kill you? You can come with us and go where you will. Or you can stay here and die as the Asika directs."

"I cannot believe you, white man. It is not possible that you should wish to run away from so much love and glory, or to spare one who would have slain you. Also it would be difficult to get you out of Bonsa-town."

"Jeekie," said Alan, "this fellow is mad after all, I think you had better go to the door and shout for the priests."

"No, no, lord," begged the wretched creature, "I will trust you; I will try, though it is you who must be mad."

"Very good. Stand over him, Jeekie, while I put on my things and, yes, give me that mask. If he stirs, kill him at once."

So Alan made himself ready. Then he mounted guard over the Mungana, as did Jeekie, although he shook his head over their prospect of escape.

"No go," he muttered, "no go! If we get past priests, Asika catch us with her magic. When I bolt with your reverend uncle last time, Little Bonsa arrange business because she go abroad fetch you. Now likely as not she bowl you out, and then goodbye Jeekie."

Alan sternly bade him be quiet and stop behind if he did not wish to come.

"No, no, Major," he answered, "I come all right. Asika very prejudiced beggar, and if she find me here alone—oh my! Better die double after all, Two's company, Major. Now, all ready, *March!*" and he gave the unfortunate Mungana a fearful kick as a hint to proceed.

So utterly crushed was the poor wretch that even this insult did not stir him to resentment.

"Follow me, white man," he said, "and if you desire to live, be silent. Throw your cloaks about your heads."

They did so, and holding their revolvers in their right hands, glided after the Mungana. In the corner of the big room they came to a little stair. How it opened in that place where no stair had been, they could not see or even guess, for it was too dark, only now they knew the means by which the Asika had been able to visit them at night.

The Mungana went first down the stair. Jeekie followed, grasping him by the arm with one hand, while in the other he kept his own knife ready to stab him at the first sign of treachery. Alan brought up the rear, keeping hold of Jeekie's cloak. They passed down twelve steps of stair, then turned to the right along a tunnel, then to the left, then to the right again. In the pitch darkness it was an awful journey, since they knew not whither they were being led, and expected that every moment would be their last. At length, quite of a sudden, they emerged into moonlight.

Alan looked about him and knew the place. It was where the feast had been held two months before, when the priests were poisoned and the Bonsas chose the victims for sacrifice. Already it was prepared for the great festival of tomorrow, when the Mungana should drown himself and Alan be married to the Asika. There on the dais were the gold chairs in which they were to sit, and green branches of trees mixed with curious flags decked the vast amphitheatre beyond. Moreover, there was the broad canal, and floating in the midst of it the hideous gold fetish, Big Bonsa. The moon shone on its glaring, deathly eyes, its fish-like snout and its huge, pale teeth. Alan looked at it and shivered, for the thing was horrid and uncanny, and the utter loneliness in which it lay staring up at the moon, seemed to accentuate the horror.

The Mungana noticed his fear and whispered:

"We must swim the water. If you have a god, white man, pray him to protect you from Bonsa."

"Lead on," answered Alan, "I do not dread a foul fetish, only the look of it. But is there no way round?"

The Mungana shook his head and began to enter the canal. Jeekie, whose teeth were chattering, hung back, but Alan pushed him from behind, so sharply that he stumbled and made a splash. Then Alan followed, and as the cold, black water rose to his chest, looked again at Big Bonsa.

It seemed to him that the thing had turned round and was staring at them. Surely a few seconds ago its snout pointed the other way. No, that must be fancy. He was swimming now, they were all swimming, Alan and Jeekie holding their pistols and little stock of cartridges above their heads to keep them dry. The gold head of Big Bonsa appeared to be lifting itself up in the water, as a reptile might, in order to get a better view of these proceedings, but doubtless it was the ripples that they caused which gave it this appearance. Only why did the ripples make it come towards them, quite gently, like an investigating fish?

It was about ten yards off and they were in the middle of the canal. The Mungana had passed it. It was in a line with Alan's head. Oh Heavens! a sudden smother of foam, a rush like that of a torpedo, and set low down between two curving waves, a flash of gold. Then a gurgling, inhuman laugh and a weight upon his back. Down went Alan, down and down!

## CHAPTER 17

# The End of the Mungana

The moonlight above vanished. Alan was alone in the depths with this devil, or whatever it might be. He could feel hands and feet gripping and treading on him, but they did not seem to be human, for there were too many of them. Also they were very cold. He gave himself up for dead and thought of Barbara.

Then something flashed into his mind. In his hand he still held the revolver. He pressed it upwards against the thing that was smothering him, and pulled the trigger. Again he pulled it, and again, for it was a self-cocking weapon, and even there deep down in the water he heard the thud of the explosion of the damp-proof copper cartridges. His lungs were bursting, his senses reeled, only enough of them remained to tell him that he was free of that strangling grip and floating upwards. His head rose above the surface, and through the mouth of his mask he drew in the sweet air with quick gasps. Down below him in the clear water he saw the yellow head of Big Bonsa rocking and quivering like a great reflected moon, saw too that it was beginning to rise. Yet he could not swim away from it, the fetish seemed to have hypnotized him. He heard Jeekie calling to him from the shallow water near the further bank, but still he floated there like a log and stared down at Big Bonsa wallowing beneath.

Jeekie plunged back into the canal and with a few strong strokes reached him, gripped him by the arm and began to tow him to the shore. Before they came there Big Bonsa rose like a huge fish and tried to follow them, but could not, or so it seemed. At any rate it only whirled round and round upon the surface, while from it poured a white fluid that turned the black water to the hue of milk. Then it began to scream, making a thin and dreadful sound more like that of an infant in pain than anything they had ever heard, a very sickening sound that Alan never could forget. He staggered to the bank and stood staring at it where it bled, rolled and shrieked, but because of the milky foam could make nothing out in that light.

"What is it, Jeekie?" he said with an idiotic laugh. "What is it?"

"Oh! don't know. Devil and all, perhaps. Come on, Major, before it catch us."

"I don't think it will catch anyone just at present. Devil or not hollow-nosed bullets don't agree with it. Shall I give it another, Jeekie?" and he lifted the pistol.

"No, no, Major, don't play tomfool," and Jeekie grabbed him by the arm and dragged him away.

A few paces further on stood the Mungana like a man transfixed, and even then Alan noticed that he regarded him with something akin to awe.

"Stronger than the god," he muttered, "stronger than the god," and bounded forward.

Following the path that ran beside the canal, they plunged into a tunnel, holding each other as before. In a few minutes they were through it and in a place full of cedar trees outside the wall of the Gold House, under which evidently the tunnel passed, for there it rose behind them. Beneath these cedar trees they flitted like ghosts, now in the moonlight and now in the shadow.

The great fall to the back of the town was on their left, and in front of them lay one of the arms of the river, at this spot a raging torrent not much more than a hundred feet in width, spanned by a narrow suspension bridge which seemed to be supported by two fibre ropes. On the hither side of this bridge stood a guard hut, and to their dismay out of this hut ran three men armed with spears, evidently to cut them off. One of these men sped across the bridge and took his stand at the further end, while the other two posted themselves in their path at the entrance to it.

The Mungana slacked his speed and said one word—"Finished!" and Jeekie also hesitated, then turned and pointed behind them.

Alan looked back and flitting in and out between the cedar trees, saw the white robes of the priests of Bonsa. Then despair seized them all, and they rushed at the bridge. Jeekie reached it first and dodging beneath the spears of the two guards, plunged his knife into the breast of one of them, and butted the other with his great head, so that he fell over the side of the bridge on to the rocks below.

"Cut, Major, cut!" he said to Alan, who pushed past him. "All right now."

They were on the narrow swaying bridge—it was but a single

plank—Alan first, then the Mungana, then Jeekie. When they were half way across Alan looked before him and saw a sight he could never forget.

The third guard at the further side was sawing through one of the fibre ropes with his spear. There they were on the middle of the bridge with the torrent raving fifty feet beneath them, and the man had nearly severed the rope! To get over before it parted was impossible; behind were the priests; beneath the roaring river. All three of them stopped as though paralyzed, for all three had seen. Something struck against Alan's leg, it was his pistol that still remained fastened to his wrist by its leather thong. He cocked and lifted it, took aim and fired. The shot missed, which was not wonderful considering the light and the platform on which the shooter stood. It missed, but the man, astonished, for he had never seen or heard such a thing before, stopped his sawing for a moment, and stared at them. Then as he began again Alan fired once more, and this time by good fortune the bullet struck the man somewhere in the body. He fell, and as he fell grasped the nearly separated rope and hung to it.

"Get hold of the other rope and come on," yelled Alan, and once more they bounded forward.

"My God! it's going," he yelled again. "Hold fast, Jeekie, hold fast!"

Next instant the rope parted and the man vanished. The bridge tipped over, and supported by the remaining rope, hung edgeways up. To this rope the three of them clung desperately, resting their feet upon the edge of the swaying plank. For a few seconds they remained thus, afraid to stir, then Jeekie called out:

"Climb on, Major, climb on like one monkey. Look bad, but quite safe really."

As there was nothing else to be done Alan began to climb, shifting his feet along the plank edge and his hands along the rope, which creaked and stretched beneath their threefold weight.

It was a horrible journey, and in his imagination took at least an hour. Yet they accomplished it, for at last they found themselves huddled together but safe upon the further bank. The sweat pouring down from his head almost blinded Alan; a deadly nausea worked within him, sickly tremors shot up and down his spine; his brain swam. Yet he could hear Jeekie, in whom excitement always took the form of speech, saying loudly:

"Think that man no liar what say our great papas was monkeys. Never look down on monkey no more. Wake up, Major, those priests monkey-men too, for we all brothers, you know. Wait a bit, I stop their little game," and springing up with three or four cuts of the big curved knife, he severed the remaining rope just as their pursuers reached the further side of the chasm.

They shouted with rage as the long bridge swung back against the rock, the cut end of it falling into the torrent, and waved their spears threateningly. To this demonstration Jeekie replied with gestures of contempt such as are known to street Arabs. Then he looked at the Mungana, who lay upon the ground a melancholy and dilapidated spectacle, for the perspiration had washed lines of paint off his face and patches of dye from his hair, also his gorgeous robes were water-stained and his gem necklaces broken. Having studied him a while Jeekie kicked him meditatively till he got up, then asked him to set out the exact situation. The Mungana answered that they were safe for a while, since that torrent could only be crossed by the broken bridge and was too rapid to swim. The Asiki, he added, must go a long journey round through the city in order to come at them, though doubtless they would hunt them down in time.

Here Jeekie cut him short, since he knew all that country well and only wished to learn whether any more bridges had been built across the torrent since he was a boy.

"Now, Major," he said, "you get up and follow me, for I know every inch of ground, also by and by good short cut over mountains. You see Jeekie very clever boy, and when he herd sheep and goat he made note of everything and never forget nothing. He pull you out of this hole, never fear."

"Glad to hear it, I am sure," answered Alan as he rose. "But what's to become of the Mungana?"

"Don't know and don't care," said Jeekie; "no more good to us. Can go and see how Big Bonsa feel, if he like," and stretching out his big hand as though in a moment of abstraction, he removed the costly necklaces from their guide's neck and thrust them into the pouch he wore. Also he picked up the gilded linen mask which Alan had removed from his head and placed it in the same receptacle, remarking, that he "always taught that it wicked to waste anything when so many poor in the world."

Then they started, the Mungana following them. Jeekie paused and waved him off, but the poor wretch still came on, whereon Jeekie produced the big, crooked knife, Mungana's own knife.

"What are you going to do," said Alan, awaking to the situation.

"Cut off head of that cocktail man, Major, and so save him lot of trouble. Also we got no grub, and if we find any he want eat a lot.

Chop what do for two p'raps, make very short commons for three. Also he might play dirty trick, so much best dead."

"Nonsense," said Alan sternly; "let the poor devil come along if he likes. One good turn deserves another."

"Just so, Major; that hello-swello want cut our throats, so I want cut his—one good turn deserve another, as wise king say in Book, when he give half baby to woman what wouldn't have it. Well, so be, Major, specially as it no matter, for he not stop with us long."

"You mean that he will run away, Jeekie?"

"Oh! no, he not run away, he in too blue funk for that. But something run away with him, because he ought die tomorrow night. Oh! yes, you see, you see, and Jeekie hope that something not run away with you too, Major, because you ought be married at same time."

"Hope not, I am sure," answered Alan, and bethinking him of Big Bonsa wallowing and screaming on the water and bleeding out white blood, he shivered a little.

By this time, advancing at a trot, the Mungana running after them like a dog, they had entered the bush pierced with a few wandering paths. Along these paths they sped for hour after hour, Jeekie leading them without a moment's hesitation. They met no man and heard nothing, except occasional weird sounds which Alan put down to wild beasts, but Jeekie and the Mungana said were produced by ghosts. Indeed it appeared that all this jungle was supposed to be haunted, and no Asiki would enter it at night, or unless he were very bold and protected by many charms, by day either. Therefore it was an excellent place for fugitives who sorely needed a good start.

At length the day began to dawn just as they reached the main road where it crossed the hills, whence on his journey thither Alan had his first view of Bonsa Town. Peering from the edge of the bush, they perceived a fire burning near the road and round it five or six men, who seemed to be asleep. Their first thought was to avoid them, but the Mungana, creeping up to Alan, for Jeekie he would not approach, whispered:

"Not Asiki, Ogula chief and slaves who left Bonsa Town yesterday."

They crept nearer the fire and saw that this was so. Then rejoicing exceedingly, they awoke the old chief, Fahni, who at first thought they must be spirits. But when he recognized Alan, he flung himself on his knees and kissed his hand, because to him he owed his liberty.

"No time for all that, Fahni," said Alan. "Give us food."

Now of this as it chanced there was plenty, since by the Asika's orders the slaves had been laden with as much as they could carry.

They ate of it ravenously, and while they ate, told Fahni something of the story of their escape. The old chief listened amazed, but like Jeekie asked Alan why he had not killed the Mungana, who would have killed him.

Alan, who was in no mood for long explanations, answered that he had kept him with them because he might be useful.

"Yes, yes, friend, I see," exclaimed the old cannibal, "although he is so thin he will always make a meal or two at a pinch. Truly white men are wise and provident. Like the ants, you take thought for the morrow."

As soon as they had swallowed their food they started all together, for although Alan pointed out to Fahni that he might be safer apart, the old chief who had a real affection for him, would not be persuaded to leave him.

"Let us live or die together," he said.

Now Jeekie, abandoning the main road, led them up a stream, walking in the water so that their footsteps might leave no trace, and thus away into the barren mountains which rose between them and the great swamp. On the crest of these mountains Alan turned and looked back towards Bonsa Town. There far across the fertile valley was the hateful, river-encircled place. There fell the great cataract in the roar of which he had lived for so many weeks. There were the black cedars and there gleamed the roofs of the Gold House, his prison where dwelt the Asika and the dreadful fetishes of which she was the priestess. To him it was like the vision of a nightmare, he could scarcely think it real. And yet by this time doubtless they sought him far and wide. What mood, he wondered, would the Asika be in when she learned of his escape and the fashion of it, and how would she greet him if he were recaptured and taken back to her? Well, he would not be recaptured. He had still some cartridges and he would fight till they killed him, or failing that, save the last of them for himself. Never, never could he endure to be dragged back to Bonsa Town there to live and die.

They went on across the mountains, till in the afternoon once more they saw the road running beneath them like a ribbon, and at the end of it the lagoon. Now they rested a while and held a consultation while they ate. Across that lagoon they could not escape without a canoe.

"Lord," said the Mungana presently, "yesterday when these cannibals were let go a swift runner was sent forward commanding that a good boat should be provisioned and made ready for them, and by now doubtless this has been done. Let them descend to the road, walk on to the bay and ask for the boat. Look, yonder, far away a tongue of land covered with trees juts out into the lake. We will make our way thither and after nightfall this chief can row back to it and take us into the canoe."

Alan said that the plan was good, but Jeekie shook his head, asking what would happen if Fahni, finding himself safe upon the water, thought it wisest not to come to fetch them.

Alan translated his words to the old chief, whereon Fahni wanted to fight Jeekie because of the slur that he had cast upon his honour. This challenge Jeekie resolutely declined, saying that already there were plenty of ways to die in Asiki-land without adding another to them. Then Fahni swore by his tribal god and by the spirit of every man he had ever eaten, that he would come to that promontory after dark, if he were still alive.

So they separated, Fahni and his men slipping down to the road, which they did without being seen by anyone, while Alan, Jeekie and the Mungana bore away to the right towards the promontory. The road was long and rough and, though by good fortune they met no one, since the few who dwelt in these wild parts had gone up to Bonsa Town to be present at the great feast, the sun was sinking before ever they reached the place. Moreover, this promontory proved to be covered with dense thorn scrub, through which they must force a way in the gathering darkness, not without hurt and difficulty. Still they accomplished it and at length, quite exhausted, crept to the very point, where they hid themselves between some stones at the water's edge.

Here they waited for three long hours, but no boat came.

"All up a gum-tree now, Major," said Jeekie. "Old blackguard, Fanny, bolt and leave us here, and tomorrow morning Asika nobble us. Better have gone down to bay, steal his boat and leave him behind, because Asika no want *him*."

Alan made no answer. He was too tired, and although he trusted Fahni, it seemed likely enough that Jeekie was right, or perhaps the cannibals had not been able to get the boat. Well, he had done his best, and if Fate overtook them it was no fault of his. He began to doze, for even their imminent peril could not keep his eyes open, then presently awoke with a start, for in his sleep he thought he heard the sounds of paddles beating the quiet water. Yes, there dimly seen through the mist, was a canoe, and seated in the stern of it Fahni. So that danger had gone by also.

He woke his companions, who slept at his side, and very silently they rose, stepping from rock to rock till they reached the canoe and entered it. It was not a large craft, barely big enough to hold them all indeed, but they found room, and then at a sign from Fahni the oarsmen gave way so heartily that within half an hour they had lost sight of the accursed shores of Asiki-land, although presently its mountains showed up clearly beneath the moon.

Meanwhile Fahni had told his tale. It appeared that when he reached the bay he found the Asiki headman who dwelt there, and those under him, in a state of considerable excitement.

Rumours had reached them that someone had escaped from Bonsa Town; they thought it was the Mungana. Fahni asked who had brought the rumour, whereon the headman answered that it came "in a dream," and would say no more. Then he demanded the canoe which had been promised to him and his people, and the headman admitted that it was ready in accordance with orders received from the Asika, but demurred to letting him have it. A long argument followed, in the midst of which Fahni and his men got into the canoe, the headman apparently not daring to use force to prevent him. Just as they were pushing off a messenger arrived from Bonsa Town, reeling with exhaustion and his tongue hanging from his jaws, who called out that it was the white man who had escaped with his servant and the Mungana, and that although they were believed to be still hidden in the holy woods near Bonsa Town, none were to be allowed to leave the bay. So the headman shouted to Fahni to return, but he pretended not to hear and rowed away, nor did anyone attempt to follow him. Still it was only after nightfall that he dared to put the boat about and return to the headland to pick up Alan and the others as he had promised. That was all he had to say.

Alan thanked him heartily for his faithfulness and they paddled on steadily, putting mile after mile of water between them and Asiki-land. He wondered whether he had seen the last of that country and its inhabitants. Something within him answered No. He was sure that the Asika would not allow him to depart in peace without making some desperate effort to recapture him. Far as he was away, it seemed to him that he could feel her fury hanging over him like a cloud, a cloud that would burst in a rain of blood. Doubtless it would have burst already had it not been for the accident that he and his companions were still supposed to be hiding in the woods. But that error must be discovered, and then would come the pursuit.

He looked at the full moon shining upon him and reflected that at this very hour he should have been seated upon the chair of state, wedding, or rather being wedded by the Asika in the presence of Big and Little Bonsa and all the people. His eye fell upon the Mungana, who had also been destined to play a prominent part in that ceremony. At once he saw that there was something wrong with the man. A curious change had come over his emaciated face. It was working like that of a maniac. Foam appeared upon his dyed lips, his haunted eyes rolled, his thin hands gripped the side of the canoe and he began to sing, or rather howl like a dog baying at the stars. Jeekie hit him on the head and bade him be silent, but he took no notice, even when he hit him again more heavily. Presently came the climax. The man sprang up in the canoe, causing it to rock from side to side. He pointed to the full moon above and howled more loudly than before; he pointed to something that he seemed to see in the air near by and gibbered as though in terror. Then his eyes fixed themselves upon the water at which he stared.

Harder and harder he stared, his head sinking lower every moment, till at length without another sound, very quietly and unexpectedly he went over the side of the boat. For a few seconds they saw his bright-coloured garments sinking to the depths, then he vanished.

They waited a while, expecting that he would rise again. But he never rose. A shot-weighted corpse could not have disappeared more finally and completely. The thing was very awful, and for a while there was silence, which as usual was broken by Jeekie.

"That gay dog gone," he said in a reflective voice. "All those old ghosts come to fetch him at proper time. No good run away from ghosts; they travel too quick; one jump, and pop up where you no expect. Well, more place for Jeekie now," and he spread himself out comfortably in the empty seat, adding, "like hello-swello's room much better than company, he go in scent-bath every day and stink too much, all that water never wash *him* clean."

Thus died the Mungana, and such was the poor wretch's requiem. With a shiver Alan reflected that had it not been for him and his insane jealousy, he too might have been expected to go into that same scent-bath and have his face painted like a chorus girl. Only would he escape the spell that had destroyed his predecessor in the affections of the priestess of the Bonsas? Or would some dim power such as had drawn Mungana to the death drag him back to the arms of the Asika or to the torture pit of "Great Swimming Head." He remembered his dream in the Treasure Hall and shuddered at the very thought of it, for all he had undergone and seen made him superstitious; then bade the men paddle faster, ever faster.

All that night they rowed on, taking turns to rest, except Alan and Jeekie, who slept a good deal and as a consequence awoke at dawn much refreshed. When the sun rose they found themselves across the lagoon, over thirty miles from the borders of Asiki-land, almost at the spot where the river up which they had travelled some months before, flowed out of the lake. Whether by chance or skill Fahni had steered a wonderfully straight course. Now, however, they were face to face with a new trouble, for scarcely had they begun to descend the river when they discovered that at this dry season of the year it was in many places too shallow to allow the canoe to pass over the sand and mud banks. Evidently there was but one thing to be done—abandon it and walk.

So they landed, ate from their store of food and began a terrible and toilsome journey. On either side of the river lay desiccated swamp covered with dead reeds ten or twelve feet high. Doubtless beyond the swamp there was high land, but in order to reach this, if it existed, they would be obliged to force a path through miles of reeds. Therefore they thought it safer to follow the river bank. Their progress was very slow, since continually they must make detours to avoid a quicksand or a creek, also the stones and scrubby growth delayed them so that fifteen or at most twenty miles was a good day's march.

Still they went on steadily, seeing no man, and when their food was exhausted, living on the fish which they caught in plenty in the shallows, and on young flapper ducks that haunted the reeds. So at length they came to the main river into which this tributary flowed, and camped there thankfully, believing that if any pursuit of them had been undertaken, it was abandoned. At least Alan and the rest believed this, but Jeekie did not.

On the following morning, shortly after dawn, Jeekie awoke his master.

"Come here, Major," he said in a solemn voice, "I got something pretty show you," and he led him to the foot of an old willow tree, adding, "now up you go, Major, and look."

So Alan went up and from the topmost fork of that tree saw a sight at which his blood turned cold. For there, not five miles behind them, on either side of the river bank, the light gleaming on their spears, marched two endless columns of men, who from their head-dresses he took to be Asiki. For a minute he looked, then descended the tree and approaching the others, asked what was to be done.

"Hook, scoot, bolt, leg it!" exclaimed Jeekie emphatically; then he licked his finger, held it up to the wind and added, "but first fire reeds and make it hot for Bonsa crowd."

This was a good suggestion and one on which they acted without delay. Taking red embers, they blew them into a flame and lit torches, which they applied to the reeds over a width of several hundred yards. The strong northward wind soon did the rest; indeed with a quarter of an hour a vast sheet of flame twenty or thirty feet in height was rushing towards the Asiki columns. Then they began their advance along the river bank, running at a steady trot, for here the ground was open.

All that day they ran, pausing at intervals to get their breath, and at night rested because they must. When the light came upon the following morning they looked back from a little hill and saw the outposts of the Asiki advancing not a mile behind. Doubtless some of the army had been burned, but the rest, guessing their route, had forced a way through the reeds and cut across country. So they began to run again harder than before, and kept their lead during the morning. But when afternoon came the Asika gained on them. Now they were breasting a long rise, the river running in the cleft beneath, and Jeekie, who seemed to be absolutely untiring, held Alan by the hand, Fahni following close behind. Two of their men had fallen down and been abandoned, and the rest straggled.

"No go, Jeekie," gasped Alan, "they will catch us at the top of the hill."

"Never say die, Major, never say die," puffed Jeekie, "they get blown too and who know what other side of hill?"

Somehow they struggled to the crest and behold! there beneath them was a great army of men.

"Ogula!" yelled Jeekie, "Ogula! Just what I tell you, Major, who know what other side of *any* hill."

## Chapter 18

# A Meeting in the Forest

In five minutes more Alan and Jeekie were among the Ogula, who, having recognized their chief while he was yet some way off, greeted him with rapturous cheers and the clapping of hands. Then as there was no time for explanation, they retreated across a little stream which ran down the valley, four thousand or more of them, and prepared for battle. That evening, however, there was no fighting, for when the first of the Asiki reached the top of the rise and saw that the fugitives had escaped to the enemy, who were in strength, they halted and finally retired.

Now Alan, and Fahni also, hoped that the pursuit was abandoned, but again Jeekie shook his big head, saying:

"Not at all, Major, I know Asiki and their little ways. While one of them alive, not dare go back to Asika without *you*, Major."

"Perhaps she is with them herself," suggested Alan, "and we might treat with her."

"No, Major, Asika never leave Bonsa Town, that against law, and if she do so, priests make another Asika and kill her when they catch her."

After this a council of war was held, and it was decided to camp there that night, since the position was good to meet an attack if one should be made, and the Ogula were afraid of being caught on the march with their backs towards the enemy. Alan was glad enough to hear this decision, for he was quite worn out and ready to take any risk for a few hours' rest. At this council he learned also that the Asiki bearers carrying his gold with their Ogula guides had arrived safely among the Ogula, who had mustered in answer to their chief's call and were advancing towards Asiki-land, though the business was one that did not please them. As for these Asiki bearers, it seemed that they had gone on into the forest with the gold, and nothing more had been heard of them.

As they were leaving the council Alan asked Jeekie if he had any tidings of his mother, who had been their first messenger.

"No, Major," he answered gloomily, "can't learn nothing of my ma, don't know where she is. Ogula camp no place for old girl if they short of chop and hungry. But p'raps she never get there; I nose round and find out."

Apparently Jeekie did "nose round" to some purpose, for just as Alan was dropping off to sleep in his bough shelter a most fearful din arose without, through which he recognized the vociferations of Jeekie. Running out of the shelter he discovered his retainer and a great Ogula whom he knew again as the headman who had been imprisoned with him and freed by the Asika to guide the bearers, rolling over and over on the ground, watched by a curious crowd. Just as he arrived Jeekie, who notwithstanding his years was a man of enormous strength, got the better of the Ogula and kneeling on his stomach, was proceeding to throttle him. Rushing at him, Alan dragged him off and asked what was the matter.

"Matter, Major!" yelled the indignant Jeekie. "My ma inside this black villain, *that* the matter. Dirty cannibal got digestion of one ostrich and eat her up with all his mates, all except one who not like her taste and tell me. They catch poor old lady asleep by road so stop and lunch at once when Asiki bearers not looking. Let me get at him, Major, let me get at him. If I can't bury my ma, as all good son ought to do, I bury him, which next best thing."

"Jeekie, Jeekie," said Alan, "exercise a Christian spirit and let bygones be bygones. If you don't, you will make a quarrel between us and the Ogula, and they will give us up to the Asiki. Perhaps the man did not eat your mother; I understand that he denies it, and when you remember what she was like, it seems incredible. At any rate he has a right to a trial, and I will speak to Fahni about it tomorrow."

So they were separated, but as it chanced that case never came on, for next morning this Ogula was killed in the fighting together with two of his companions, while the others involved in the charge kept themselves out of sight. Whether Jeekie's "ma" was or was not eaten by the Ogula no one ever learned for certain. At least she was never heard of any more.

Alan was sleeping heavily when a sound of rushing feet and of strange, thrilling battle-cries awoke him. He sprang up, snatching at a spear and shield which Jeekie had provided for him, and ran out to find from the position of the moon that dawn was near.

"Come on, Major," said Jeekie, "Asiki make night attack; they always like do everything at night who love darkness, because their eye evil. Come on quick, Major," and he began to drag him off toward the rear.

"But that's the wrong way," said Alan presently. "They are attacking over there."

"Do you think Jeekie fool, Major, that he don't know that? He take you where they *not* attacking. Plenty Ogula to be killed, but not *many* white men like you, and in all world only *one* Jeekie!"

"You cold-blooded old scoundrel!" ejaculated Alan as he turned and bolted back towards the noise of fighting, followed by his reluctant servant.

By the time that he reached the first ranks, which were some way off, the worst of the attack was over. It had been short and sharp, for the Asiki had hoped to find the Ogula unprepared and to take their camp with a rush. But the Ogula, who knew their habits, were waiting for them, so that presently they withdrew, carrying off their wounded and leaving about fifty dead upon the ground. As soon as he was quite sure that the enemy were all gone, Jeekie, armed with a large battle-axe, went off to inspect these fallen soldiers. Alan, who was helping the Ogula wounded, wondered why he took so much interest in them. Half an hour later his curiosity was satisfied, for Jeekie returned with over twenty heavy gold rings, torques, and bracelets slung over his shoulder.

"Where did you get those, Jeekie?" he asked.

"Off poor chaps that peg out just now, Major. Remember Asiki soldiers nearly always wear these things and that they no more use to them. But if ever he get out of this Jeekie want spend his old age in respectable peace. So he fetch them. Hard work, though, for rings all in one bit and Asiki very tough to chop. Don't look cross, Major; you remember what 'postle say, that he who no provide for his own self worse than cannibal."

Just then Fahni came up and announced that the Asiki general had sent a messenger into the camp proposing terms of peace.

"What terms?" asked Alan.

"These, white man: that we should surrender you and your servant and go our way unharmed."

"Indeed, Fahni, and what did you answer?"

"White man, I refused; but I tell you," he added warningly, "that my captains wished to accept. They said that I had come back to them safe and that they fear the Asiki, who are devils, not men, and who will bring the curse of Bonsa on us if we go on fighting with them. Still I refused, saying that if they gave you up I would go with you, who saved my life from the lion and afterwards from the priests of Bonsa. So the messenger went back and, white man, we march at once, and I pray you always to keep close to me that I may watch over you."

Then began that long tramp down the river, which Alan always thought afterwards tried him more than any of the terrible events of his escape. For although there was but little fighting, only rearguard actions indeed, every day the Asiki sent messengers renewing their offers of peace on the sole condition of the surrender of himself and Jeekie. At last one evening they came to that place where Alan first met the Ogula, and once more he camped upon the island on which he had shot the lion. At nightfall, after he had eaten, Fahni visited him here and Alan boded evil from his face.

"White man," he said, "I can protect you no longer. The Asiki messengers have been with us again and they say that unless we give you up tomorrow at the dawn, their army will push on ahead of us and destroy my town, which is two days' march down the river, and all the women and children in it, and that afterwards they will fight a great battle with us. Therefore my people say that I must give you up, or that if I do not they will elect another chief and do so themselves."

"Then you will give up a dead man, Fahni."

"Friend," said the old chief in a low voice, "the night is dark and the forest not so far away. Moreover, I have set no guards on that side of the river, and Jeekie here does not forget a road that he has travelled. Lastly, I have heard it said that there are some other white people with soldiers camped in the edge of the forest. Now, if you were not here in the morning, how could I give you up?"

"I understand, Fahni. You have done your best for me, and now, good-night. Jeekie and I are going to take a walk. Sometimes you will think of the months we spent together in Bonsa-Town, will you not?"

"Yes, and of you also, white man, for so long as I shall live. Walk fast and far, for the Asiki are clever at following a spoor. Good-night, Friend, and to you, Jeekie the cunning, good-night also. I go to tell my captains that I will surrender you at dawn," and without more words he vanished out of their sight and out of their lives.

Meanwhile Jeekie, foreseeing the issue of this talk, was already engaged in doing up their few belongings, including the gold rings, some food, and a native cooking pot, in a bundle surrounded by a couple of bark blankets.

"Come on, Major," he said, handing Alan one spear and taking another himself. "Old cannibal quite right, very nice night for a walk. Come on, Major, river shallow just here. I think this happen and try it before dark. You just follow Jeekie, that all you got to do."

So leaving the fire burning in front of their bough shelter, they waded the stream and started up the opposing slope, meeting no man. Dark as it was, Jeekie seemed to have no difficulty in finding the way, for as Fahni said, a native does not forget the path he has once travelled. All night long they walked rapidly, and when dawn broke found themselves at the edge of the forest.

"Jeekie," said Alan, "what did Fahni mean by that tale about white people?"

"Don't know, Major, think perhaps he lie to let you down easy. My golly! what that?"

As he spoke a distant echo reached their ears, the echo of a rifle shot. "Think Fanny not lie after all," went on Jeekie; "that white man's gun, sharp crack, smokeless powder, but wonder how he come in this place. Well, we soon find out. Come on, Major."

Tired as they were they broke into a run; the prospect of seeing a white face again was too much for them. Half a mile or so further on they caught sight of a figure evidently engaged in stalking game among the trees, or so they judged from his cautious movements.

"White man!" said Jeekie, and Alan nodded.

They crept forward silently and with care, for who knew what this white man might be after, keeping a great tree between them and the man, till at length, passing round its bole, they found themselves face to face with him and not five yards away. Notwithstanding his unaccustomed tropical dress and his face burnt copper colour by the sun, Alan knew the man at once.

"Aylward!" he gasped; "Aylward! You here?"

He started. He stared at Alan. Then his countenance changed. Its habitual calm broke up as it was wont to do in moments of deep emotion. It became very evil, as though some demon of hate and jealousy were at work behind it. The thin lips quivered, the eyes glared, and without spoken word or warning, he lifted the rifle and fired straight at Alan. The bullet missed him, for the aim was high. Passing over Alan's head, it cut a neat groove through the hair of the taller Jeekie who was immediately behind him.

Next instant, with a spring like that of a tiger Jeekie was on Aylward. The weight of his charge knocked him backwards to the ground, and there he lay, pinned fast.

"What for you do that?" exclaimed the indignant Jeekie. "What for you shoot through wool of respectable nigger, Sir Robert Aylward, Bart.? Now I throttle you, you dirty hog-swine. No Magistrates' Court here in Dwarf Forest," and he began to suit the action to the word.

"Let him go, Jeekie. Take his rifle and let him go," exclaimed Alan, who all this while had stood amazed. "There must be some mistake, he cannot have meant to murder me."

"Don't know what he mean, but know his bullet go through my hair, Major, and give me new parting," grumbled Jeekie as he obeyed.

"Of course it was a mistake, Vernon, for I suppose it is Vernon," said Aylward, as he rose. "I do not wonder that your servant is angry, but the truth is that your sudden appearance frightened me out of my wits and I fired automatically. We have been living in some danger here and my nerves are not as strong as they used to be."

"Indeed," answered Alan. "No, Jeekie will carry the rifle for you; yes, and I think that pistol also, every ounce makes a difference walking in a hot climate, and I remember that you always were dangerous with firearms. There, you will be more comfortable so. And now, who do you mean by 'we'?"

"I mean Barbara and myself," he answered slowly.

Alan's jaw dropped, he shook upon his feet.

"Barbara and yourself!" he said. "Do I understand——"

"Don't you understand nothing, Major," broke in Jeekie. "Don't you believe one word what this pig dog say. If Miss Barbara marry him he no want shoot you; he ask you to tea to see the Missus and how much she love him, ducky! We just go on and call on Miss Barbara and hear the news. Walk up, Sir Robert Aylward, Bart., and show us which way."

"I do not choose to receive you and your impertinent servant at my camp," said Aylward, grinding his teeth.

"We quite understand that, Sir Robert Aylward——"

"Lord Aylward, if you please, Major Vernon."

"I beg your pardon—Lord Aylward. I was aware of the contemplated purchase of that title, I did not know that it had been completed. I was about to add that all the same we mean to go to that camp, and that if any violence towards us is attempted as we approach it, you will remember that you are in our hands."

"Yes, my Lord," added Jeekie, bowing, "and that monkeys don't tell no tales, my Lord, and that here there ain't no twelve Good-Trues to sit on noble corpse unhappily deceased, my Lord, and to bring in Crowner's verdict of done to death lawful or unlawful, according as evidence may show when got, my Lord. So march on, for we no breakfast yet. No, not that way, round here to left, where I think I hear kettle sing."

So having no choice, Aylward came, marching between the other two and saying nothing. When they had gone a couple of hundred yards Alan also heard something, and to him it sounded like a man crying out in pain. Then suddenly they passed round some great trees and reached a glade in the forest where there was a spring of water which Alan remembered. In this glade the camp had been built, surrounded by a "*boma*" or palisade of rough wood, within which stood two tents and some native shelters made of tall grass and boughs. Outside of this camp a curious and unpleasant scene was in progress.

To a small tree that grew there was tied a man, whom from the fashion of his hair Alan knew to belong to the Coast negroes, while two great fellows, evidently of another tribe, flogged him unmercifully with hide whips.

"Ah!" exclaimed Jeekie, "that the kettle I hear sing. Think you better taken him off the fire, my Lord, or he boil over. Also his brothers no seem to like that music," and he pointed to a number of other men who were standing round watching the scene with sullen dissatisfaction.

"A matter of camp discipline," muttered Aylward. "This man has disobeyed orders."

By now Jeekie was shouting something to the natives in an unknown tongue, which they seemed to understand well enough. At any rate the flogging ceased, the two fellows who were inflicting it slunk away, and the other men ran towards them, shouting back as they came.

"All right, Major. You please stop here one minute with my Lord, late Bart. of Bloody Hand. Some of these chaps friends of mine, I meet them Old Calabar while we get ready to march last rains. Now I have little talk with them and find out thing or two."

Aylward began to bluster about interference with his servants and so forth. Jeekie turned on him with a very ugly grin, and showing his white teeth, as was his fashion when he grew fierce.

"Beg pardon, Right Honourable Lord," he said, or rather snarled, "you do what I tell you just to please Jeekie. Jeekie no one in England, but Jeekie damn big Lord too out here, great medicine man, pal of Little Bonsa. You remember Little Bonsa, eh! These chaps think it great honour to meet Jeekie, so, Major, if he stir, please shoot him through head; Jeekie 'sponsible, not you. Or if you not like do it, I come back and see to job myself and don't think those fellows cry very much."

There was something about Jeekie's manner that frightened Aylward, who understood for the first time that beneath all the negro's grotesque talk lay some dreadful, iron purpose, as courage lay under his affected cowardice and under his veneer of selfishness, fidelity. At any rate he halted with Alan, who stood beside him, the revolver of which Aylward had been relieved by Jeekie, in his hand. Meanwhile Jeekie, who held the rifle which he had reloaded, went on and met the natives about twenty yards away.

"We always disliked each other, Vernon, but I must say that I never thought a day would come when you proposed to murder me in my own camp," said Aylward.

"Odd thing," answered Alan, "but a very similar idea was in my mind. I never thought, Lord Aylward, that however unscrupulous you might be—financially—a day would come when you would attempt to shoot down an unarmed man in an African forest. Oh! don't waste breath in lying; I saw you recognize me, aim, and fire, after which Jeekie would have had the other barrel, and who then would have remained to tell the story, Lord Aylward?"

Aylward made no answer, but Alan felt that if wishes could kill him he would not live long. His eye fell upon a long, unmistakable mound of fresh earth, beneath a tree. He calculated its length, and with a thrill of terror noticed that it was too small for a negro.

"Who is buried there?" he asked.

"Find out for yourself," was the sneering answer.

"Don't be afraid, Lord Aylward; I shall find out everything in time."

The conversation between Jeekie and the natives proceeded, their heads were close together; it grew animated. They seemed to be coming to some decision. Presently one of them ran and cut the lashings of the man who had been bound to the tree, and he staggered towards them and joined in the talk, pointing to his wounds. Then the two fellows who had been engaged in flogging him, accompanied by eight companions of the same type—they appeared to be soldiers, for they carried guns—swaggered towards the group who were being addressed by Jeekie, of whom Alan counted twenty-three. As they approached Jeekie made some suggestion which, after one hesitating moment, the others seemed to accept, for they nodded their heads and separated out a little.

Jeekie stepped forward and asked a question of the guards, to which they replied with a derisive shout. Then without a word of warning he lifted Aylward's express rifle which he carried, and fired first one barrel and then the other, shooting the two leading soldiers dead. Their companions halted amazed, but before they could lift their guns, Jeekie and those with him rushed at them and began stabbing them with spears and striking them with sticks. In three minutes it was over without another shot being fired. Most of them were despatched, and the others, throwing down their guns, had fled wounded into the forest.

Now, shouting in jubilation, some of the men began to drag away the dead bodies, while others collected the rifles and the remainder, headed by Jeekie, advanced towards Alan and Aylward, waving their red spears. Alan stood staring, for he did not in the least understand the meaning of what had happened, but Aylward, who had turned very pale, addressed Jeekie, saying:

"I suppose that you have come to murder me also, you black villain."

"No, no, my Lord," answered Jeekie politely, "not at present. Also that wrong word, execute, not murder, just what you do to some of these poor devils," and he pointed to the mob of porters. "Besides, mustn't kill holy white man, poor black chap don't matter, plenty more where he come from. Think we all go see Miss Barbara now. You come too, my Lord Bart., but p'raps best tie your hands behind you first; if you want scratch head, I do it for you. That only fair, you scratch mine this morning."

Then at a word from Jeekie some of the natives sprang on Aylward and tied his hands behind his back.

"Is Miss Barbara alive?" said Alan to Jeekie in an agonized whisper, at the same time nodding towards the grave that was so ominously short.

"Hope so, think so, these cards say so, but God He know alone," answered Jeekie. "Go and look, that best way to find out."

So they advanced into the camp through a narrow gateway made of a V-shaped piece of wood, to where the two tents were placed in its inner division. Of these tents, the first, was open, whereas the second was closed. As the open tent was obviously empty, they went to the second, whereof Jeekie began to loosen the lashings of the flap. It was a long business, for they seemed to have been carefully knotted inside; indeed at last, growing impatient, Jeekie cut the cord, using the curved knife with which the Mungana had tried to kill Alan.

Meanwhile Alan was suffering torments, being convinced that Barbara was dead and buried in that new-made grave beneath the trees. He could not speak, he could scarcely stand, and yet a picture began to form in his numb mind. He saw himself seated in the dark in the Treasure-house at Bonsa-Town; he saw a vision in the air before him.

Lo! the tent door opened and that vision reappeared.

There was the pale Barbara seated, weeping. There again, as he entered she sprang up and snatching the pistol that lay beside her, turned it to her breast. Then she perceived him and the pistol sank downwards till from her relaxed hand it dropped to the ground. She threw up her arms and without a sound fell backwards, or would have fallen, had he not caught her.

## Chapter 19

# The Last of the Asiki

Barbara had recovered. She sat upon her bed in the tent and by her sat Alan, holding her hand, while before them stood Aylward like a prisoner in the dock, and behind him the armed Jeekie.

"Tell me the story, Barbara," said Alan, "and tell it briefly, for I cannot bear much more of this."

She looked at him and began in a slow, even voice:

"After you had gone, dear, things went on as usual for a month or two. Then came the great Sahara Company trouble. First there were rumours and the shares began to go down. My uncle bought them in by tens and hundreds of thousands, to hold up the market, because he was being threatened, but of course he did not know then that Lord Aylward—for I forgot to tell you, he had become a lord somehow—was secretly one of the principal sellers, let him deny it if he can. At last the Ottoman Government, through the English ambassador, published its repudiation of the concession, which it seems was a forgery, actually executed or obtained in Constantinople by my uncle. Well, there was a fearful smash. Writs were taken out against my uncle, but before they could be served, he died suddenly of heart disease. I was with him at the time and he kept saying he saw that gold mask which Jeekie calls Bonsa, the thing you took back to Africa. He had a fine funeral, for what he had done was not publicly known, and when his will was opened I found that he had left me his fortune, but made Lord Aylward there my trustee until I came to the full age of twenty-five under my father's will. Alan, don't force me to tell you what sort of a guardian he was to me; also there was no fortune, it had all gone; also I had very, very little left, for almost all my own money had gone too. In his despair he had forged papers to get it in order to support those Sahara Syndicate shares. Still I managed to borrow about £2000 from that little lawyer out of the

£5000 that remain to me, an independent sum which he was unable to touch, and, Alan, with it I came to find you.

"Alan, Lord Aylward followed me; although everybody else was ruined, he remained rich, very very rich, they say, and his fancy was to marry me, also I think it was not comfortable for him in England. It is a long tale, but I got up here with about five-and-twenty servants, and Snell, my maid, whom you remember. Then we were both taken ill with some dreadful fever and had it not been for those good black people, I should have died, for I have been very sick, Alan. But they nursed me and I recovered; it was poor Snell who died, they buried her a few days ago. I thought that she would live, but she had a relapse. Next Lord Aylward appeared with twelve soldiers and some porters who, I believe, have run away now,—oh! you can guess, you can guess. He wanted my people to carry me away somewhere, to the coast, I suppose, but they were faithful to me and would not. Then he set his soldiers on to maltreat them. They shot several of them and flogged them on every opportunity; they were flogging one of them just now, I heard them. Well, the poor men made me understand that they could bear it no longer and must do what he told them.

"And so, Alan, as I was quite hopeless and helpless, I made up my mind to kill myself, hoping that God would forgive me and that I should find you somewhere, perhaps after sleeping a while, for it was better to die than to be given into the power—of that man. I thought that he was coming for me just now and I was about to do it, but it was you instead, Alan, *you*, and only just in time. That is all the story, and I hope you will not think that I have acted very foolishly, but I did it for the best. If you only knew what I have suffered, Alan, what I have gone through in one way and another, I am sure that you would not judge me harshly; also I kept dreaming that you were in trouble and wanted me to come to you, and of course I knew where you were gone and had that map. Send him away, Alan, for I am still so weak and I cannot bear the sight of his face. If you knew everything, you would understand."

Alan turned on Aylward and in a cold, quiet voice asked him what he had to say to this story.

"I have to say, Major Vernon, that it is a clever mixture of truth and falsehood. It is true that your cousin, Champers-Haswell, has been proved guilty of some very shameful conduct. For instance it appears that he did forge, or rather cause to be forged that Firman from the Sultan, although I knew nothing of this until it was publicly repudiated. It is also true that fearing exposure he entirely lost his head and spent not only his own great fortune but that of Miss Champers also, in trying to support Sahara shares. I admit also that I sold many hundreds of thousands of those shares in the ordinary way, having made up my mind to retire from business when I was raised to the peerage. I admit further, what you knew before, that I was attached to Miss Champers and wished to marry her. Why should I not, especially as I had a good deal to offer to a lady who has been proved to be almost without fortune?

"For the rest she set out secretly on this mad journey to Africa, whither both my duty as her trustee and my affection prompted me to follow her. I found her here recovering from an illness, and since she has dwelt upon the point, in self-defence I must tell you that whatever has taken place between us, has been with her full consent and encouragement. Of course I allude only to those affectionate amenities which are common between people who purpose to marry as soon as opportunity may offer."

At this declaration poor Barbara gasped and leaned back against her pillow. Alan stood silent, though his lips turned white, while Jeekie thrust his big head through the tent opening and stared upwards.

"What are you looking at, Jeekie?" asked Alan irritably.

"Seem to want air, Major, also look to see if clouds tumble. Believe partickler big lie do that sometimes. Please go on, O good Lord, for Jeekie want his breakfast."

"As regards the execution of two of Miss Champers' bearers and the flogging of some others, these punishments were inflicted for mutiny," went on Aylward. "It was obviously necessary that she should be moved back to the coast, but I found out that they were trying to desert her in a body and to tamper with my own servants, and so was obliged to take strong measures."

"Sure those clouds come down now," soliloquized Jeekie, "or least something rummy happen."

"I have only to add, Major Vernon, that unless you make away with me first, as I daresay you will, as soon as we reach civilization again I shall proceed against you and this fellow for the cold-blooded murder of my men, in punishment of which I hope yet to live to see you hanged. Meanwhile, I have much pleasure in releasing Miss Champers from her engagement to me which, whatever she may have said to you in England, she was glad enough to enter on here in Africa, a country of which I have been told the climate frequently deteriorates the moral character."

"Hear, hear!" ejaculated Jeekie, "he say something true at last; by accident, I think, like pig what find pearl in muck-heap."

"Hold your tongue, Jeekie," said Alan. "I do not intend to kill you, Lord Aylward, or to do you any harm——"

"Nor I neither," broke in Jeekie, "all I do to my Lord just for my Lord's good; who Jeekie that he wish to hurt noble British 'ristocrat?"

"But I do intend that it shall be impossible that Miss Champers should be forced to listen to more of your insults," went on Alan, "and to make sure that your gun does not go off again as it did this morning. So, Lord Aylward, until we have settled what we are going to do, I must keep you under arrest. Take him to his tent, Jeekie, and put a guard over him."

"Yes, Major, certainly, Major. Right turn, march! my Lord, and quick, please, since poor, common Jeekie not want dirty his black finger touching you."

Aylward obeyed, but at the door of the tent swung round and favoured Alan with a very evil look.

"Luck is with you for the moment, Major Vernon," he said, "but if you are wise you will remember that you never have been and never will be my match. It will turn again, I have no doubt, and then you may look to yourself, for I warn you I am a bad enemy."

Alan did not answer, but for the first time Barbara sprang to her feet and spoke.

"You mean that you are a bad man, Lord Aylward, and a coward too, or otherwise you would not have tortured me as you have done. Well, when it seemed impossible that I should escape from you except in one way, I was saved by another way of which I never dreamed. Now I tell you that I do not fear you any more. But I think," she added slowly, "that you would do well to fear for yourself. I don't know why, but it comes into my mind that though neither Alan nor I shall lift a finger against you, you have a great deal of which to be afraid. Remember what I said to you months ago when you were angry because I would not marry you. I believe it is all coming true, Lord Aylward."

Then Barbara turned her back upon him, and that was the last time that either she or Alan ever saw his face.

He was gone, and Barbara, her head upon her lover's shoulder and her sweet eyes filled with tears of joy and gratitude, was beginning to tell him everything that had befallen her when suddenly they heard a loud cough outside the tent.

"It's that confounded Jeekie," said Alan, and he called to him to come in.

"What's the matter now?" he asked crossly.

"Breakfast, Major. His lordship got plenty good stores, borrow some from him and give him chit. Coming in one minute—hot coffee, kipper herring, rasher bacon, also butter (best Danish), and Bath Oliver biscuit."

"Very well," said Alan, but Jeekie did not move.

"Very well," repeated Alan.

"No, Major, not very well, very ill. Thought those lies bring down clouds."

"What do you mean, Jeekie?"

"Mean, Major, that Asiki smelling about this camp. Porter-man what go to fetch water see them. Also believe they catch rest of those soldier chaps and polish them, for porter-man hear the row."

Alan sprang up with an exclamation; in his new-found joy he had forgotten all about the Asiki.

"Keep hair on, Major," said Jeekie cheerfully; "don't think they attack yet, plenty of time for breakfast first. When they come we make it very hot for them, lots of rifle and cartridge now."

"Can't we run away?" asked Barbara.

"No, Missy, can't run; must stop here and do best. Camp well built, open all round, don't think they take it. You leave everything to Jeekie, he see you through, but p'raps you like come breakfast outside, where you know all that go on."

Barbara did like, but as it happened they were allowed to consume their meal in peace, since no Asiki appeared. As soon as it was swallowed she returned to her tent, while Alan and Jeekie set to work to strengthen the defences of the little camp as well as they were able, and to make ready and serve out the arms and ammunition.

About midday a man whom they had posted in a tree that grew inside the camp announced that he saw the enemy, and next moment a company of them rushed towards them across the open and were greeted by a volley which killed and wounded several men. At this exhibition of miraculous power, for none of these soldiers had ever heard the report of firearms or seen their effect, they retreated rapidly, uttering shouts of dismay and carrying their dead and wounded with them.

"Do you suppose they have gone, Jeekie?" asked Alan anxiously.

He shook his head.

"Think not, Major, think they frightened, by big bullet magic, and go consult priest. Also only a few of them here, rest of army come later and try rush us tomorrow morning before dawn. That Asiki custom."

"Then what shall we do, Jeekie? Run for it or stop here?"

"Think must stop here, Major. If we bolt, carrying Miss Barbara, who can't walk much, they follow on spoor and catch us. Best stick inside this fence and see what happen. Also once outside p'raps porters desert and leave us."

So as there was nothing else to do they stayed, labouring all day at the strengthening of their fortifications till at length the *boma* or fence of boughs, supported by earth, was so high and thick that while any were left to fire through the loopholes, it would be very difficult to storm by men armed with spears.

It was a dreadful and arduous day for Alan, who now had Barbara's safety to think of, Barbara with whom as yet he had scarcely found time to exchange a word. By sunset indeed he was so worn out with toil and anxiety that he could scarcely stand upon his feet. Jeekie, who all that afternoon had been strangely quiet and reflective, surveyed him critically, then said:

"You have good drink and go sleep a bit, Major. Very good little shelter there by Miss Barbara's tent, and you hold her hand if you like underneath the canvas, which comforting and all correct. Jeekie never get tired, he keep good lookout and let you know if anything happen, and then you jump up quite fresh and fight like tom-cat in corner."

At first Alan refused to listen, but when Barbara added her entreaties to those of Jeekie he gave way, and ten minutes later was as soundly asleep as he had ever been in his life.

"Keep eye on him, Miss Barbara, and call me if he wake. Now I go give noble lord his supper and see that he quite comfortable. Jeekie seem very busy tonight, just like when Major have dinner-party at Yarleys and old cook get drunk in kitchen."

If Barbara could have followed Jeekie's movements for the next few hours, she would probably have agreed that he was busy. First he went to Aylward's tent, and as he had said he would, gave him his supper, and with it half a bottle of whisky from the stores which he had been carrying about with him for some time, as he said, to prevent the porters from getting at it. Aylward would little, though as his arms were tied to the tent-pole, Jeekie sat beside him and fed him like a baby, conversing pleasantly with him all the while, informing him amongst other things that he had better say "big prayer," because the Asiki would probably cut his throat before morning.

Aylward, who was in a state of sullen fury, scarcely replied to this talk, except to say that if so, there was one comfort, they would cut his and his master's also.

"Yes, my Lord," answered Jeekie, "that quite true, so drink to next meeting, though I think you go different place to me, and when you got tail and I wing, you horn and I crown of glory, of course we not talk much together," and he held a mug of whisky and water—a great deal of whisky and a very little water—to his prisoner's mouth.

Aylward drained it, feeling a need for stimulant.

"There," said Jeekie, holding it upside down, "you drink every drop and not offer one to poor old Jeekie. Well, he turned teetotaller, so no matter. Good-night, my Lord, I call you if Asiki come."

"Who are the Asiki?" asked Aylward drowsily.

"Oh! you want to know? I tell you," and he began a long, rambling story.

Before he ever came to the end of it Aylward had fallen on his side and was fast asleep.

"Dear me!" said Jeekie, contemplating him, "that whisky very strong, though bottle say same as they drink in House of Common. That whisky so strong I think I pour away rest of it," and he did to the last drop, even taking the trouble to wash out the bottle with water. "Now you no tempt anyone," he said, addressing the said bottle with a very peculiar smile, "or if you tempt, at least do no harm—like kiss down telephone!" Then he laid down the bottle on its side and left the tent.

Outside of it three of the head porters, who appeared to be friends of his, were waiting for him, and with these men he engaged in low and earnest conversation. Next, after they had arrived at some agreement, which they seemed to ratify by a curious oath that involved their crossing and clasping hands in an odd fashion, and other symbols known to West African secret societies, Jeekie went the round of the camp to see that everyone was at his post. Then he did what most people would have thought a very curious and strange thing, namely climbed the fence and vanished into the forest, where presently a sound was heard as of an owl hooting.

A little while later and another owl began to hoot in the distance, whereat the three head porters nudged each other. Perhaps they had heard such owls hoot before at night, and perhaps they knew that Jeekie, who had "passed Bonsa," could only be harmed by the direct command of Bonsa speaking through the mouth of the Asika herself. Still they might have been interested in the nocturnal conversation of those two owls, which, as is common with such magical fowl in West Africa, had transformed themselves into human shapes, the shape of Jeekie and the shape of an Asiki priest, who was, as it happened, a blood relation of Jeekie.

"Very good, Brother," said Owl No. 1; "all you want is this white man whom the Asika desires for a husband. Well, I have done my best for him, but I must think of myself and others, and he goes to great happiness. I have given him something to make him sleep; do you come presently with eight men, no more, or we shall kill you, to the fence of the camp, and we will hand over the white man, Vernoon, to you to take back to the Asika, who will give you a wonderful reward, such a reward as you have never imagined. Now let me hear your word."

Then Owl No. 2 answered:

"Brother, I make the bargain on behalf of the army, and swear to it by the double Swimming Head of Bonsa. We will come and take the white man, Vernoon, who is to be Mungana, and carry him away. In return we promise not to follow or molest you, or any others in your camp. Indeed, why should we, who do not desire to be killed by the dreadful magic that you have, a magic that makes a noise and pierces through our bodies from afar? What were the words of the Asika? 'Bring back Vernoon, or perish. I care for nothing else, bring back Vernoon to be my husband.'"

"Good," said Owl No. 1, "within the half of an hour Vernoon shall be ready for you."

"Good," answered Owl No. 2, "within half an hour eight of us will be without the east face of your camp to receive him."

"Silently?"

"Silently, my brother in Bonsa. If he cries out we will gag him. Fear not, none shall know your part in this matter."

"Good, my brother in Bonsa. By the way, how is Big Bonsa? I fear that the white man, Vernoon, hurt him very much, and that is why I give him up—because of his sacrilege."

"When I left the god was very sick and all the people mourned, but doubtless he is immortal."

"Doubtless he is immortal, my brother, a little hard magic in his stomach—if he has one—cannot hurt *him*. Farewell, dear brother in Bonsa, I wish that I were you to get the great reward that the Asika will give to you. Farewell, farewell."

Then the two owls flitted apart again, hooting as they went, till they came to their respective camps.

********

Jeekie was in the tent performing a strange toilet upon the sleeping Aylward by the light of a single candle. From his pouch he produced the mask of linen painted with gold that Alan used to be forced to wear, and tied it securely over Aylward's face, murmuring:

"You always love gold, my Lord Aylward, and Jeekie promise you see plenty of it now."

Then he proceeded to remove his coat, his waistcoat, his socks, and his boots and to replace these articles of European attire by his own worn Asiki sandals and his own dirty Asiki robe.

"There," he said, "think that do," and he studied him by the light of the candle. "Same height, same colour hair, same dirty clothes, and as Asiki never see Major's face because he always wear mask in public, like as two peas on shovel. *Oh my!* Jeekie clever chap, Jeekie devilish clever chap. But when Asika pull off that mask to give him true lover kiss, *Oh my!* wonder that happen then? Think whole of Bonsa-Town bust up; think big waterfall run backwards; think she not quite pleased; think my good Lord find himself in false position; think Jeekie glad to be on coast; think he not go back to Bonsa-Town no more. *Oh my aunt!* no, he stop in England and go church twice on Sunday," and pressing his big hands on the pit of his stomach he rocked and rolled in fierce, silent laughter.

Then an owl hooted again immediately beneath the fence and Jeekie, blowing out the candle, opened the flap of the tent and tapped the head porter, who stood outside, on the shoulder. He crept in and between them they lifted the senseless Aylward and bore him to the V-shaped entrance of the *boma* which was immediately opposite to the tent and, oddly enough, half open. Here the two other porters with whom Jeekie had performed some ceremony, chanced to be on guard, the rest of their company being stationed at a distance. Jeekie and the head porter went through the gap like men carrying a corpse to midnight burial, and presently in the darkness without two owls began to hoot.

Now Aylward was laid upon a litter that had been prepared, and eight white-robed Asiki bearers stared at his gold mask in the faint starlight.

"I suppose he is not dead, brother," said Owl No. 2 doubtfully.

"Nay, brother," said Owl No. 1, "feel his heart and his pulse. Not dead, only drunk. He will wake up by daylight, by which time you should be far upon your way. Be good and gentle to the white man Vernoon, who has been my master. Be careful, too, that he does not escape you, brother, for as you know he is very strong and cunning. Say to the Asika that Jeekie her servant makes his reverence to her, and hopes that she will have many, many happy years with the husband that he sends her; also that she will remember him whom she called 'Black Dog,' in her prayers to the gods and spirits of our people."

"It shall be done, brother, but why do you not return with us?"

"Because, brother, I have ties across the Black Water—dear children, almost white—whom I love so much that I cannot leave them. Farewell, brethren, the blessings of the Bonsas be on you, and may you grow fat and prosper in the love and favour of our lady the Asika."

"Farewell," they murmured in answer. "Good fortune be your bedfellow."

Another minute and they had lifted up the litter and vanished at a swinging trot into the shadow of the trees. Jeekie returned to the camp and ordered the three men to re-stop the gateway with thorns, muttering in their ears:

"Remember, brethren, one word of this and you die, all of you, as those die who break the oath."

"Have we not sworn?" they whispered, as they went back to their posts.

Jeekie stood a while in front of the empty tent and if any had been there to note him, they might have seen a shadow as of compunction creep over his powerful black face.

"When he wake up he won't know where he are," he reflected, "and when he get to Bonsa-Town he'll wonder where he is, and when he meet Asika! Well, he very big blackguard; try to murder Major, whom Jeekie nurse as baby, the only thing that Jeekie care for—except—Jeekie; try to make love to Miss Barbara against will when he catch her alone in forest, which not playing game. Jeekie self not such big blackguard as that dirt-born noble Lord; Jeekie never murder no one—not quite; Jeekie never make love to girl what not want him—no need, so many what do that he have to shove them off, like good Christian man. Mrs. Jeekie see to that while she live. Also better that mean white man go call on Bonsas than Major and Missy Barbara and all porters, and Jeekie—specially Jeekie—get throat cut. No, no, Jeekie nothing to be ashamed of, Jeekie do good day's work, though Jeekie keep it tight as wax since white folk such silly people, and when Major in a rage, he very nasty customer and see everything upside down. Now, Jeekie quite tired, so say his prayers and have nap. No, think not in tent, though very comfortable. Major might wake up, poke his nose in there, and if he see black face instead of white one, ask ugly question, which if Jeekie half asleep he no able to answer nice and neat. Still he just arrange things a little so they look all right."

## Chapter 20

# The Asika's Message

Dawn began to break in the forest and Alan woke in his shelter and stretched himself. He had slept soundly all the night, so soundly that the innocent Jeekie wondered much whether by any chance he also had taken a tot out of that particular whisky bottle, as indeed he had recommended him to do. People who drink whisky after long abstinence from spirits are apt to sleep long, he reflected.

Alan crept out of the shelter and gazed affectionately at the tent in which Barbara slumbered. Thank Heaven she was safe so far, as for some unknown reason, evidently the Asiki had postponed their attack. Just then a clamour arose in the air, and he perceived Jeekie striding towards him waving one arm in an excited fashion, while with the other he dragged along the captain of the porters, who appeared to be praying for mercy.

"Here pretty go, Major," he shouted, "devil and all to pay! That my Lord, he gone and bolted. This silly fool say that three hours ago he hear something break through fence and think it only hyena what come to steal, so take no notice. Well, that hyena, you guess who he is. You come look, Major, you come look, and then we tie this fellow up and flog him."

Alan ran to Aylward's tent to find it empty.

"Look," said Jeekie, who had followed, "see how he do business, that jolly clever hyena," and he pointed to a broken whisky bottle and some severed cords. "You see he manage break bottle and rub rope against cut glass till it come in two. Then he do hyena dodge and hook it."

Alan inspected the articles, nor did any shadow of doubt enter his mind.

"Certainly he managed very well," he said, "especially for a London-bred man, but, Jeekie, what can have been his object?"

"Oh! who know, Major? Mind of man very strange and various

thing; p'raps he no bear to see you and Miss Barbara together; p'raps he bolt coast, get ear of local magistrate before you; p'raps he sit up tree to shoot you; p'raps nasty temper make him mad. But he gone any way, and I hope he no meet Asiki, poor fellow, 'cause if so, who know? P'raps they knock him on head, or if they think him you, they make him prisoner and keep him quite long while before they let him go again."

"Well," said Alan, "he has gone of his own free will, so we have no responsibility in the matter, and I can't pretend that I am sorry to see the last of him, at any rate for the present. Let that poor beggar loose, there seems to have been enough flogging in this place, and after all he isn't much to blame."

Jeekie obeyed, apparently with much reluctance, and just then they saw one of their own people running towards the camp.

"'Fraid he going to tell us Asiki come attack," said Jeekie, shaking his head. "Hope they give us time breakfast first."

"No doubt," answered Alan nervously, for he feared the result of that attack.

Then the man arrived breathless and began to gasp out his news, which filled Alan with delight and caused a look of utter amazement to appear upon the broad face of Jeekie. It was to the effect that he had climbed a high tree as he had been bidden to do, and from the top of that tree by the light of the first rays of the rising sun, miles away on the plain beyond the forest, he had seen the Asiki army in full retreat.

"Thank God!" exclaimed Alan.

"Yes, Major, but that very rum story. Jeekie can't swallow it all at once. Must send out see none of them left behind. P'raps they play trick, but if they really gone, 'spose it 'cause guns frightens them so much. Always think powder very great 'vention, especially when enemy hain't got none, and quite sure of it now. Jeekie very, very seldom wrong. Soon believe," he added with a burst of confidence, "that Jeekie never wrong at all. He look for truth so long that at last he find it *always*."

********

Something more than a month had gone by and Major and Mrs. Vernon, the latter fully restored to health and the most sweet and beautiful of brides, stood upon the steamship *Benin*, and as the sun sank, looked their last upon the coast of Western Africa.

"Yes, dear," Alan was saying to his wife, "from first to last it has been a very queer story, but I really think that our getting that Asiki gold after all was one of the queerest parts of it; also uncommonly convenient, as things have turned out."

"Namely that you have got a little pauper for a wife instead of a great heiress, Alan. But tell me again about the gold. I have had so much to think of during the last few days," and she blushed, "that I never quite took it all in."

"Well, love, there isn't much to tell. When that forwarding agent, Mr. Aston, knew that we were in the town, he came to me and said that he had about fifty cases full of something heavy, as he supposed samples of ore, addressed to me to your care in England which he was proposing to ship on by the *Benin*. I answered 'Yes, that was all right,' and did not undeceive him about their contents. Then I asked how they had arrived, and if he had not received a letter with them. He replied that one morning before the warehouse was open, some natives had brought them down in a canoe, and dumped them at the door, telling the watchman that they had been paid to deliver them there by some other natives whom they met a long way up the river. Then they went away without leaving any letter or message. Well, I thanked Aston and paid his charges and there's an end of the matter. Those fifty-three cases are now in the hold invoiced as ore samples and, as I inspected them myself and am sure that they have not been tampered with, besides the value of the necklace the Asika gave me we've got £100,000 to begin our married life upon with something over for old Jeekie, and I daresay we shall do very well on that."

"Yes, Alan, very well indeed." Then she reflected a while, for the mention of Jeekie's name seemed to have made her thoughtful, and added, "Alan, what *do* you think became of Lord Aylward?"

"I am sure I don't know. Jeekie and I and some of the porters went to see the Old Calabar officials and made affidavits as to the circumstances of his disappearance. We couldn't do any more, could we?"

"No, Alan. But do you think that Jeekie quite understands the meaning of an oath? I mean it seems so strange that we should never have found the slightest trace of him, and, Alan, I don't know if you noticed it, but why did Jeekie appear that morning wearing Lord Aylward's socks and boots?"

"He ought to know all about oaths, he has heard enough of them in Magistrates' Courts, but as regards the boots, I am sure I can't say, dear," answered Alan uneasily. "Here he comes, we will ask him," and he did.

"Sock and boot," replied Jeekie, with a surprised air, "why, Mrs. Major, if that good lord go mad and cut off into forest leaving them behind, of course I put them on, as they no more use to him, and I just burn my dirty old Asiki dress and sandal and got nothing to keep jigger out of toe. Don't you sit up here in this damp, cold, Mrs. Major, else you get more fever. You go down and dress dinner, which at half-past six tonight. I just come tell you that."

So Barbara went, leaving the other two talking about various matters, for they were alone together on the deck, all the passengers, of whom there were but few, having gone below.

The short African twilight had come, a kind of soft blue haze that made the ship look mysterious and unnatural. By degrees their conversation died away. They lapsed into a silence, which Alan was the first to break.

"What are you thinking of, Jeekie?" he asked nervously.

"Thinking of Asika, Major," he answered in a scared whisper. "Seem to me that she about somewhere, just as she use pop up in room in Gold House; seem to me I feel her all down my back, likewise in head wool, which stand up."

"It's very odd, Jeekie," replied Alan, "but so do I."

"Well, Major, 'spect she thinking of us, specially of you, and just throw what she think at us, like boy throw stones at bird what fly away out of cage. Asika do all that, you know, she not quite human, full of plenty Bonsa devil, from gen'ration to gen'rations, amen! P'raps she just find out something what make her mad."

"What could she find out after all this time, Jeekie?"

"Oh, don't know. How I know? Jeekie can't guess. Find out you marry Miss Barbara, p'raps. Very sick that she lose you for this time, p'raps. Kill herself that she keep near you, p'raps, while she wait till you come round again, p'raps. Asika can do all these things if she like, Major."

"Stuff and rubbish," answered Alan uneasily, for Jeekie's suggestions were most uncomfortable, "I believe in none of your West Coast superstitions."

"Quite right, Major, nor don't I. Only you 'member, Major, what she show us there in Treasure-place—Mr. Haswell being buried, eh? Miss Barbara in tent, eh? t'other job what hasn't come off yet, eh? Oh! my golly! Major, just you look behind you and say you see nothing, please," and the eyes of Jeekie grew large as Maltese oranges, while with chattering teeth he pointed over the bulwark of the vessel.

Alan turned and saw.

This was what he saw or seemed to see: The figure of the Asika in her robes and breastplate of gold, standing upon the air, just beyond the ship, as though on it she might set no foot. Her waving black hair hung about her shoulders, but the sharp wind did not seem to stir it nor did her white dress flutter, and on her beautiful face was stamped a look of awful rage and agony, the rage of betrayal, the agony of loss. In her right hand she held a knife, and from a wound in her breast the red blood ran down her golden corselet. She pointed to Jeekie with the knife, she opened her arms to Alan as though in unutterable longing, then slowly raised them upwards towards the fading glory of the sky above—and was gone.

********

Jeekie sat down upon the deck, mopping his brow with a red handkerchief, while Alan, who felt faint, clung to the bulwarks.

"Tell you, Major, that Asika can do all that kind of thing. Never know where you find her next. 'Spect she come to live with us in England and just call in now and again when it dark. Tell you, she very awkward customer, think p'raps you done better stop there and marry her. Well, she gone now, thank Heaven! seem to drop in sea and hope she stay there."

"Jeekie," said Alan, recovering himself, "listen to me; this is all infernal nonsense; we have gone through a great deal and the nerves of both of us are overstrained. We think we saw what we did not see, and if you dare to say a single word of it to your mistress, I'll break your neck. Do you understand?"

"Yes, Major, think so. All 'fernal nonsense, nerves strained, didn't see what we see, and say nothing of what did see to Mrs. Major, if either do say anything, t'other one break his neck. That all right, quite understand. Anything else, Major?"

"Yes, Jeekie. We have had some wonderful adventures, but they are past and done with and the less we talk or even think about them the better, for there is a lot that would be rather difficult to explain, and that if explained would scarcely be believed."

"Yes, Major, for instance, very difficult explain Mrs. Barbara how Asika so fond of you if you only tell her, 'Go away, go away!' all the time, like old saint-gentleman to pretty girl in picture. P'raps she smell rat."

"Stop your ribald talk," said Alan in a stern voice. "It would be better if instead of making jokes you gave thanks to Providence for bringing both of us alive and well out of very dreadful dangers. Now I am going to dress for dinner," and with an anxious glance seaward into the gathering darkness, he turned and went.

********

Jeekie stood alone upon the empty deck, wagging his great white head to and fro and soliloquizing thus: "Wonder if Major see what under lady Asika's feet when she stand out there over nasty deep. Think not or he say something. That noble lord not look nice. No, private view for Jeekie only, free ticket and nothing to pay and me hope it no come back when I go to bed. Major know nothing about it, so he not see, but Jeekie know a lot. Hope that Aylward not write any letters home, or if he write, hope no one post them. Ghost bad enough, but murder, oh my!"

He paused a while, then went on:

"Jeekie do big sacrifice to Bonsa when he reach Yarleys, get lamb in back kitchen at night, or if ghost come any more, calf in wood outside. Not steal it, pay for it himself. Then think Jeekie turn Cath'lic; confess his sins, they say them priest chaps not split, and after they got his sins, they tackle Asika and Bonsas too," and he uttered a series of penitent groans, turning slowly round and round to be sure that nothing was behind him.

Just then the full moon appeared out of a bank of clouds, and as it rose higher, flooding the world with light, Jeekie's spirits rose also.

"Asika never come in moonshine," he said, "that not the game, against rule, and after all, what Jeekie done bad? He very good fellow really. Aylward great villain, serve him jolly well right if Asika spiflicate him, that not Jeekie's fault. What Jeekie do, he do to save master and missus who he love. Care nothing for his self, ready to die any day. Keep it dark to save them too, 'cause they no like the story. If once they know, it always leave taste in mouth, same as bad oyster. Also Jeekie manage very well, take Major safe Asiki-land ('cause Little Bonsa make him), give him very interesting time there, get him plenty gold, nurse him when he sick, nobble Mungana, bring him out again, find Miss Barbara, catch hated rival and bamboozle all Asiki army, bring happy pair to coast and marry them, arrange first-class honeymoon on ship—Jeekie do all these things, and lots more he could tell, if he vain and not poor humble nigger."

Once more he paused a while, lost in the contemplation of his own modesty and virtues, then continued:

"This very ungrateful world. Major there, he not say, 'Thank you, Jeekie, Jeekie, you great, wonderful man. Brave Jeekie, artful Jeekie. Jeekie smart as paint who make all world believe just what he like, and one too many for Asika herself.' No, no, he say nothing like that. He say 'thank Prov'dence,' not 'Jeekie,' as though Prov'dence do all them things. White folk think they clever, but great fools, really, don't know nothing. Prov'dence all very well in his way—p'raps, but Prov'dence not a patch on Jeekie.

"Hullo! moon get behind cloud and there second bell; think Jeekie go down and wait dinner; lonely up here and sure Asika never stand 'lectric light."

# ALSO FROM LEONAUR

## AVAILABLE IN SOFTCOVER OR HARDCOVER WITH DUST JACKET

**TROS OF SAMOTHRACE 1: WOLVES OF THE TIBER** *by Talbot Mundy*—When his ship is taken and his crew slaughtered Tros of Samothrace is captured by Imperial Rome.

**TROS OF SAMOTHRACE 2: DRAGONS OF THE NORTH** *by Talbot Mundy*—Tros of Samothrace burns for vengeance and has declared himself the implacable enemy of Rome.

**TROS OF SAMOTHRACE 3: SERPENT OF THE WAVES** *by Talbot Mundy*—Tros, his allies and the forces of Rome have drawn apart to prepare for the conflict to come.

**TROS OF SAMOTHRACE 4: CITY OF THE EAGLES** *by Talbot Mundy*—As Tros of Samothrace continues in his attempts to confound Caesar's plans for the invasion of Britain, he journeys to the Eternal City to seek the aid of its great leaders—and Caesar's opponents—Cato, Pompey and the Vestal Virgins themselves!

**TROS OF SAMOTHRACE 5: CLEOPATRA** *by Talbot Mundy*—Cleopatra—Queen of Egypt—is a formidable character ever ready to play the game of intrigue, betrayal and shifting loyalties to suit her own objectives. Blood will surely be spilt and once again Tros finds himself inexorably caught up in monumental events that threaten his life and those he loves.

**TROS OF SAMOTHRACE 6: THE PURPLE PIRATE** *by Talbot Mundy*—The epic saga of the ancient world—Tros of Samothrace—draws to a conclusion in this sixth—and final—volume. Julius Caesar has been assassinated and Queen Cleopatra of Egypt finds herself in a perilous position and desperate for allies to secure her power.

**THE ILLUSTRATED & COMPLETE BRIGADIER GERARD** *by Sir Arthur Conan Doyle*—These are the adventures of Conan Doyle's incomparable French hero-the finest swordsman in the Light Cavalry-Etienne Gerard. Arranged for the first time in historical chronological order, his many enthusiasts can now properly appreciate his colourful career as he fights, loves and blunders his way through the Napoleonic epoch-from his earliest adventure as a young blade determined to reach his lady love despite the unwelcome attention of her fathers bull-through many campaigns and special missions-to the bloody field of Waterloo, the downfall of his beloved Emperor and beyond. This is the complete collection of these classic stories. What makes this edition exceptional is the inclusion of nearly 140 illustrations-mostly by the famed military artist William Barnes Wollen-which accurately portray the spirit of the stories and the uniforms and scenes of the events they portray.

www.ingramcontent.com/pod-product-compliance
Lightning Source LLC
LaVergne TN
LVHW050911080826
845145LV00001B/51

* 9 7 8 1 8 4 6 7 7 7 9 9 8 *